Also by Mark Billingham

MARK BILLINGHAM

A TOM THORNE THRILLER

Lifeless

Sphere
An imprint of
Little, Brown Book Group
50 Victoria Embankment
London EC4Y 0DZ

An Hachette UK Company
www.hachette.co.uk

SPHERE

First published in Great Britain in 2005 by Little, Brown
Paperback published in 2006 by Times Warner Paperbacks
This reissue published by Sphere in 2020

3 5 7 9 10 8 6 4 2

A CIP catalogue record for this book
is available from the British Library.

ISBN 978-0-7515-4881-5

Typeset in Plantin by M Rules
Printed and bound in Great Britain by
Clays Ltd, Elcograf S.p.A.

Papers used by Sphere are from well-managed forests
and other responsible sources.

MIX
Paper from
responsible sources
FSC
www.fsc.org   FSC® C104740

I won't waste any time
know, and I don't muc
about me, plus you'd h
that things have been le
have to be stupid (which
out what I want.

I don't think I'm better
guessing you're a bit bet
I'm asking. I just need a
aside from unpleasant m
concrete reminder, of cours
each of us still has.

I can't afford to care how
having to come to you li
steamroller across self-resp
hate me more than I hate m
there. For dredging it all up
hundred quid.

That's all I need . . .

You'll notice a lack of add
ious; I just don't really have o
wearing out the welcomes of w
I've got left.

I'll write again to fix up the
arrange a time and place to me
Anonymity is all very well
Bond, but unless you've been

Hell is a ... much like London.

No one

For Mike Gunn.

And his son, William Roan Gunn.

us, I can't see why you should have a bloody clue who I am. Which _one_, I mean. You'll find out soon enough, obviously, but it can't hurt to keep the suspense going for a bit, can it?

Could be any one of four, right? Any member of the crew. I'd be amazed if a single one of us is particularly well off.

So . . . for now,

Happy New Year

PART ONE

BREAKFAST AND BEFORE

The first kick wakes him and shatters his skull at the same time.

He begins to drift back towards unconsciousness almost immediately, but is aware of the intervals between each subsequent kick – though actually no more than a second or two – warping and stretching. It gives his brain, which is itself already beginning to swell, the time for one final, random series of thoughts and instructions.

Counting the kicks. Counting each smash of boot into flesh and bone. Counting the strange and, oh God, the glorious spaces in between.

Two . . .

Cold, in the early hours of the morning and damp. And the attempt to cry out is agonising as the message from the brain dances between the fragments of bone in what had once been his jaw.

Three . . .

Warm, the face of the baby in his hands. His baby. The face of the child before it grew and learned to despise him. Reaching in vain for the letter, dog-eared and greasy, in the inside pocket of his coat. The last link to the life he had before. Groping for it, his flappy fingers useless at the end of a broken arm.

Four . . .

Turning his head, trying to turn it away from the pain towards the wall. His face moving against the floor, the stubble-rasp like the breaking of far-away waves. Feeling the blood, warm and sticky between his cheek and the cold cardboard beneath. Thinking that the shadow he'd glimpsed, where the *face of his attacker should have been, looked blacker than black. Slick, like tarmac after a shower. Thinking that it was probably a trick of the light.*

Five ...

Seeming to feel the tip of the boot as it breaks through the delicate network of ribs. Aware of it in there, stamping around, distorting his organs. Kidneys – are they his kidneys? – squeezed out of shape like water-filled balloons.

Sinking fast through six, seven and eight, their impact like crashes at a distant front door, vibrating through his shoulder and his back and the tops of his legs. The grunts and growls of the man standing above him, of the man who is kicking him to death, growing quieter and further away.

And, Christ, what a jumble, such a scramble of words. Riot of colours and sounds. All slipping away from him now. Fuzzing and darkening ...

Thinking. Thinking that this was a terrible and desperate kind of thinking, if it could still be called such a thing. Sensing that the shadow had finally turned away from him. Luxuriating then, in the bliss as the space grew, as the knowing grew that, sweet Jesus, the kicking had finally stopped.

Everything so strange now, and shapeless and bleeding away into the gutter.

He lies quite still. He knows there's little point in trying to move. He holds on tight to his name and to the name of his only child. Wraps what's left of his mind around these two names, and around the name of the Lord.

Prays that he might cling on to the shape of these few, precious words until death comes.

ONE

He woke up in a doorway opposite Planet Hollywood, with a puddle of piss at his feet that was not his own and the sickening realisation that this was real, that there was no soft mattress beneath him. He exchanged a few words with the police officer whose heavy hand had shaken him roughly awake. Began to gather up his things.

He raised his face slowly skywards as he started to walk, hoped that the weather would stay fine. He decided that the emptiness at the centre of him, which might have been simple fear, was probably even simpler hunger.

He wondered whether Paddy Hayes was dead yet. Had the young man charged with making the decision pulled the plug?

Moving through the West End as it shook away the sleep and slowly came to life was always a revelation. Each day he saw something he had never seen before.

Piccadilly Circus was glorious. Leicester Square was better than it looked. Oxford Street was even shittier than he'd thought it was.

There were still plenty of people about, of course. Plenty of traffic. Even at this time the streets were busier than most others in the country would be during the rush hour. He remembered a film he'd seen on DVD, set in London after most of the population had been turned into crazed zombies by some plague. There were bizarre scenes where the whole city appeared to be utterly deserted, and to this day he didn't really know how they'd managed to do it. Computer tricks, like as not. This – the hour or so when the capital showered, shaved and shat – was about as close as it ever came. Far from deserted, but quite a few zombies shuffling about.

Most of the shops would be shut for another hour or two yet. Very few opened their doors before ten these days. The caffs and sandwich bars were already up and running, though. Hoping to pull in passing trade for tea and a bacon sandwich, for coffee and croissants, in much the same way that the burger vans and kebab shops had tempted those weaving their way home only a few hours earlier.

Tea and a sandwich. Normally he'd have spent the previous night gathering enough together to get himself something to eat, but today someone would be buying him breakfast.

Halfway along Glasshouse Street, a man in a dark green suit stepped out of a doorway in front of him and tried to pass. They moved the same way across the pavement, and back again. Smiled at each other, embarrassed.

'Nice morning for a dance . . . '

The sudden knowledge that he'd clearly encountered a nutcase caused the smile to slide off the man's face. He turned sideways and dropped his head. Shuffled quickly past muttering, 'Sorry' and, 'I can't . . . '

He hoisted his backpack higher on to his shoulder and carried on walking, wondering just what it was that the man in the suit couldn't do.

Return a simple greeting? Spare any change? Give a toss?

He walked up Regent Street, then took a right, cutting through the side streets of Soho towards Tottenham Court Road. A strange yet familiar figure, stepping in unison alongside him, caught his eye. He slowed, then stopped, watching the stranger do the same thing.

He took a step forward and stared into the plate glass at the reflection of the man he'd become in such a short time. His hair seemed to be growing faster than usual, the grey more pronounced against the black. The neat-ish goatee he'd been cultivating had been subsumed under the scrubby growth that sprouted from his cheeks and spilled down his throat. His red nylon backpack, though already stained and grubby, was the only flash of real colour to be seen in the picture staring back at him from the shop window. The grease-grey coat and dark jeans were as blank, as *anonymous*, as the face that floated above them. He leaned towards the glass and contorted his features;

pulling back his lips, raising his eyebrows, puffing out his cheeks. The eyes, though – and it was the man's eyes that told you *everything* – stayed flat and uninvolved.

A vagrant. With the emphasis on vague ...

He turned from the window to see someone he recognised on the other side of the road. A young man – a boy – arms around his knees, back pressed against a dirty white wall, sleeping bag wrapped around his shoulders. He'd spoken to the boy a couple of nights before. Somewhere near the Hippodrome, he thought. Maybe outside one of the big cinemas in Leicester Square. He couldn't be certain. He did remember that the boy had spoken with a thick, north-east accent: Newcastle or Sunderland. Most of what the boy had said was indecipherable, rattled through chattering teeth at machine-gun speed. Head turning this way and that. Fingers grasping at his collar as he gabbled. So completely ripped on Ecstasy that it looked as though he was trying to bite off his own face.

He waited for a taxi to pass, then stepped into the road. The boy looked up as he approached and drew his knees just a little closer to his chest.

'All right?'

The boy turned his head to the side and gathered the sleeping bag tighter around his shoulders. The moisture along one side of the bag caught the light, and grey filling spilled from a ragged tear near the zip.

'Don't think there's any rain about ...'

'Good,' the boy said. It was as much a grunt as anything.

'Staying dry, I reckon.'

'What are you, a fucking weatherman?'

He shrugged. 'Just saying . . .'

'I've seen you, haven't I?' the boy asked.

'The other night.'

'Was you with Spike? Spike and One-Day Caroline, maybe?'

'Yeah, they were around, I think . . .'

'You're new.' The boy nodded to himself. He seemed pleased that it was coming back to him. 'I remember you were asking some fucking stupid questions . . .'

'Been knocking about a couple of weeks. Picked a fucking stupid time, didn't I? You know, with everything that's going on?'

The boy stared at him for a while. He narrowed his eyes, then let his head drop.

He stood where he was, kicking the toe of one shoe against the heel of the other until he was certain that the boy had nothing further to say. He thought about chucking in another crack about the weather, making a joke of it. Instead, he turned back towards the road. 'Be lucky,' he said. He moved away, his parting words getting nothing in return.

As he walked north, it struck him that the encounter with the boy had not been a whole lot friendlier than the one earlier with the man in the green suit who'd been so keen to avoid him. The boy's reaction had been no more than he'd come to expect in the short time he'd spent living as he was now. Why should it have been? A wariness – a suspicion, even – was the natural reaction of *most* Londoners, whatever their circumstances. Those who lived and slept on the city's streets were naturally that bit more cautious when it came to strangers. It went without saying that anyone who wasn't abusing or avoiding them was to be viewed with a healthy degree of mistrust until they'd proved themselves. One way or another . . .

It was a lot like prison. Like the way a life was defined behind bars. And he knew a fair bit about how *that* worked.

Those who slept rough in the centre of London had a lot in common, he decided, with those sleeping in white-washed cells at Her Majesty's pleasure. Both were communities with their own rules, their own hierarchies and an understandable suspicion of outsiders. If you were going to survive in prison, you had to fit in; do what was necessary. You'd try not to eat shit, of course you would, but if that's what it took to get by, you'd tuck right in. What he'd seen of life since he began sleeping rough told him that things were pretty much the same on the streets.

The café was a greasy spoon with ideas above its station. The sort of place that thought a few cheap sandwich fillings in Tupperware containers made it a delicatessen. The reaction, within a minute or two of him shambling in, sitting down and showing no obvious intention of buying anything, was predictable.

'Hey!'

He said nothing.

'You going to order something?'

He reached across for a magazine that had been left on an adjacent table and began to read.

'This is not a dosshouse, you know.'

He smiled.

'You think I'm joking . . . ?'

He nodded towards a familiar figure outside the window as the fat, red-faced proprietor came around the counter towards him. With impeccable timing, the man he'd been smiling at pushed through the door, just as the café owner was leaning in menacingly.

'It's OK, he's with me . . .'

The threatening expression on the proprietor's face softened, but only marginally, when he turned from the tramp's table and looked at the Metropolitan Police warrant card that was being thrust at him.

Detective Sergeant Dave Holland pocketed his ID, reached across and dragged back a chair. 'We'll have two teas,' he said.

The man sitting at the table spoke in earnest. '*Mugs* of tea.'

The owner shuffled back towards the counter, somehow managing to sigh and clear his throat at the same time.

'My hero,' the tramp said.

Holland put his briefcase on the floor and sat down. He glanced round at the two other customers: a smartly dressed woman and a middle-aged man in a postal uniform. Back behind his counter, the owner of the place glared at him as he took a pair of white mugs from a shelf.

'He looked like he was ready to chuck you out if I hadn't

come in just then. I was tempted to stand there and watch. See what happened.'

'You'd have seen me deck the fat fucker.'

'Right. Then I'd've had to arrest you.'

'That would have been interesting ...'

Holland shrugged and pushed dirty blond hair back from his forehead. 'Paddy Hayes died just after eleven-thirty last night,' he said.

'How's the son doing?'

'He was pretty upset beforehand. Wrestling with it, you know? Once he'd decided, once they turned off the machines, he seemed a lot calmer.'

'Probably only *seemed*.'

'Probably ...'

'When's he going home?'

'He's getting a train back up north this morning,' Holland said. 'He'll be getting home around the time they start the PM on his old man.'

'Won't be too many surprises there.'

They both leaned back in their chairs as the tea arrived with very little ceremony. The fat man plonked down two sets of cutlery, wrapped in paper serviettes. He pointedly nudged a laminated menu towards each of them before turning to empty the ashtray on the adjoining table.

'You hungry?' Holland asked.

The man opposite glanced up from the menu he was already studying. 'Not really. I had a huge plate of smoked salmon and scrambled eggs first thing.' His eyes went back to the menu. 'Of *course* I'm fucking hungry.'

16

'All right . . .'

'I hope you've brought your chequebook. This could get expensive.'

Holland picked up his tea. He cradled the mug against his chin and let the heat drift up to his face. He stared through the narrow curtain of steam at the dishevelled figure sitting across from him. 'I still can't get used to this,' he said.

'What?'

'This. You.'

'*You* can't get used to it? Jesus!'

'You know what I mean. I just never imagined you anything like this. You were the last person . . . You *are* the last person . . .'

Tom Thorne dropped his menu and crossed stained fingers above it. The decision made. He stared hard across the table.

'Things change,' he said.

TWO

Lots of things had changed . . .

What everything was bloody-well called for a start. When he'd returned to work, it had seemed to Thorne that in the short time he'd been away they'd decided to change the name of just about everything. The Serious Crime Group, in which Thorne had been a detective inspector on one of the nine Major Investigation Teams in Murder Command (West), was now part of what had laughably been christened the Specialist Crime Directorate. *Directorate*, for crying out loud. Did the people who pushed pens around and decided these things really think that changing something's name made a scrap of difference to what it actually *did*?

Directorate, group, pool, squad, team, unit . . . posse, gang, shower, whatever.

Just a bunch of people, of mixed ability, scrabbling

around in various degrees of desperation, trying to catch those that had killed. That were still killing.

Or, if they were really lucky, those that were planning to kill.

The Specialist Crime Directorate. Thorne remembered a vacancy advertised by a well-known supermarket in something called 'ambient replenishment'. The job had turned out to be stacking shelves.

Naturally, the structure Thorne came back to had changed as well. Each MIT on the Murder Squad was now composed of three detective inspectors, each at the head of a smaller, core team and each with that much more paperwork, that much more administrative responsibility and that much more time spent behind a desk. Each with another few hours of their working life spent ensuring that staff morale was high while levels of sick leave stayed low, and that actions were carried out within those very necessary constraints of bloody time and sodding budget, and so fucking on and so fucking forth ...

'I know this stuff has all got to be done, and I know it's got to be done properly, but there have to be priorities. Don't there? For Christ's sake, I've got two Asian kids with bullets in their heads and some nutcase who seems to take great delight in sticking a sharpened bicycle spoke into people's spines, but I'm being prevented from getting out and doing anything about it.'

'Listen ...'

'Every time I so much as set foot outside the office, one

19

or other of my so-called colleagues starts bitching about having to do my share of the fucking paperwork and it's getting stupid. I just want to do the job, you know? Especially now. You can understand that, can't you? I'm just a copper, that's all. It's not complicated. I'm not a resource, or a facilitator, or a fucking homicidal-perpetration-prevention operative ...'

'Tom ...'

'Do you think whoever shot those two kids is sitting at home doing his paperwork? Is this lunatic I'm trying to catch filling in forms? Making a careful note, no, making *several copies* of a careful note about how many different bicycle spokes he's used, and how much they cost him and exactly how long it took him to get them just sharp enough to paralyse somebody? I don't think so. I don't fucking think so ...'

The man sitting in the armchair wore his usual black hooded top and combats. There was a selection of rings and studs in both ears, and the spike below his bottom lip shifted as he moved his tongue around in his mouth. Dr Phil Hendricks was a pathologist who worked closely with Thorne's team. He was also the nearest thing Tom Thorne had to a best friend. Violent death and its charged aftermath had forged a strong bond between them. He'd caught a taxi to the flat in Kentish Town as soon as Thorne had called.

Hendricks waited just long enough to be sure that Thorne had run out of steam, without giving him the time to get up another head. 'How are you sleeping?' he asked.

Thorne had stopped pacing, had sat down heavily on the arm of the sofa. 'Do I sound tired to you?'

'You sound ... hyper. It's understandable.'

Thorne jumped up again, marched across to the fireplace. 'Don't start that lowering-your-voice shit, Phil. Like I'm not well. I'm right about this.'

'Look, I'm sure you're right. I'm not there enough to see it.'

'*Everything's* different.'

'Maybe it's you that's different ... '

'Trust me, mate, this job's going tits up. It's like working in a bank in there sometimes. Like working in the fucking City!'

'What happened when you saw Jesmond?'

Thorne took a deep breath, placed the flat of his hand against his chest, watched it jump. Once, twice, three times ...

'I got a lecture,' he said. 'Apparently, these days, there's a lot less tolerance for dead wood.'

Lots of things had changed ...

Hendricks shifted in the armchair, opened his mouth to speak ...

'Dead wood,' Thorne said, repeating the words as if they were from a foreign language. 'How fucked is that from *him*? Pointless, tight-arsed tosser!'

'OK, look, he's all those things, we know that, but ... maybe the caseload *is* getting on top of you a bit. Don't you think? Come on, you're not really dealing with the work properly, with *any* of it.'

'Right, and why's that, d'you reckon? What have I just been telling you?'

'You haven't been telling me anything; you've been shouting at me. And what you've *actually* been doing is making excuses. I'm on your side, Tom, but you need to face a few facts. You're either completely out of it or you're ranting like an idiot, and either way people are getting pissed off with you. Getting *more* pissed off with you . . .'

'Which people?'

Then, despite what Thorne had said a few moments earlier, Hendricks lowered his voice: 'You weren't ready to start work again.'

'That's bollocks.'

'You came back too soon . . .'

It was not much more than eight weeks since Thorne's father had died in a house fire. Jim Thorne had been suffering from advanced Alzheimer's at the time of his death, and the blaze had almost certainly been no more than an accident. A misfired synapse. A piece of tragic forgetfulness.

There were other possibilities, though. Thorne had been working on a case involving a number of powerful organised-crime figures. It was possible that one of them – that one man in particular – had decided to strike at Thorne via those closest to him. To inflict pain that would stay with him far longer than anything of which a simple blade or bullet was capable.

Other possibilities . . .

Thorne was still coming to terms with a lot of things.

Among them, the fact that he might never know for sure whether his father had been murdered. Either way, Thorne knew he was to blame.

'I would have come back earlier if I could,' Thorne said. 'I'd've come back the day I buried him. What else am I going to do?'

Hendricks pushed himself out of the chair. 'Do you want some tea?'

Thorne nodded and turned towards the fireplace. He leaned against the stripped-pine mantelpiece, staring at himself in the mirror above as he spat out the words. 'Detective Chief Superintendent Jesmond is thinking about a few weeks' "gardening leave".'

Standing in front of Trevor Jesmond's desk that afternoon, Thorne had felt like he'd been punched in the stomach. He'd dug down deep for something like a smile. Deeper still for the flippant comeback. '*I've only got a window-box . . .*'

Now the anger rose up again, but quickly gave way to a perverse amusement at yet another ridiculous euphemism. '"Gardening leave",' he said. 'How nice. How fucking cosy.'

It made sense, he supposed. You could hardly call it what it was: some pointless, hastily invented desk job designed to get shot of anyone who was causing a problem. Anyone embarrassing, but not quite sackable. *Gardening* sounded so much better than *burned out* or *fucked up*. So much more pleasant than *drunk, traumatised* or *mental*.

Hendricks walked slowly towards the kitchen. 'I think you should take it,' he said.

The next day, Thorne had discovered how the odds against him were stacking up.

'I'm in a corner here, aren't I?'

Russell Brigstocke had looked down at his desktop. Straightened his blotter. 'We'll find you something that won't drive you too barmy,' he said.

Thorne pointed across the desk at his DCI. A jokey threat. 'You'd better.'

It was a close call as to which of them had been more embarrassed when the tears had suddenly appeared. Had sprung up in corners. Thorne had pressed the heel of his hand quickly against each eye, and wiped, and kicked the metal wastepaper basket halfway across Russell Brigstocke's office.

'Fuck ...'

Scotland Yard.

Perhaps the single most famous location in the history of detection. A place synonymous with the finest brains and with cutting-edge, crime-fighting technology. Where mysteries were solved and the complexities of the world's most twisted criminal minds were examined.

Where for three weeks, Thorne had been forced to sit in a room no bigger than an airing cupboard, going quietly insane, and trying to work out how many ways a man could kill himself using only standard office equipment.

He had thought, understandably, that the *Demographics of Recruitment* could not possibly be as boring as it sounded. He had been wrong. Although, the first few days hadn't been so bad. He'd been taught how the software program – with which he was supposed to turn hundreds of pages of research into a presentation document, complete with block graphs and pie-charts – worked. His computer instructor was about as interesting as Thorne had expected him to be. But he was, at least, someone to talk to.

Then, left to his own devices, Thorne had quickly discovered the most enjoyable way to pass the time. He was just as quickly rumbled. It didn't take someone long to work out that most of those websites being visited via one particular terminal had very little to do with the recruitment of ethnic minorities, or why more dog-handlers seemed to come from the south-west. Overnight, and without warning, internet access was denied and, from then on, outside the job itself, there was little for Thorne to do but eke out the daily paper and think about methods of topping himself.

He was considering death from a thousand papercuts when a face appeared around the door. It looked a little thinner than usual, and the smile was nervous. It had been four weeks since Thorne had seen the man who was at least partly responsible for putting him where he was, and Russell Brigstocke had every right to be apprehensive.

He held up a hand, and spoke before Thorne had a chance to say anything. 'I'm sorry. I'll buy you lunch.'

Thorne pretended to consider it. 'Does it include beer?'

Brigstocke winced. 'I'm on a bloody diet, but for you, yes.'

'Why are we still here?'

Thorne hadn't even clocked the name of the place as they'd gone in. They'd come out of the Yard, turned up towards Parliament Square and walked into the first pub they'd come to. The food was bog-standard – chilli con carne that was welded to the dish in places and tepid in others – but they had decent crisps and Stella on draught.

A waitress was clearing away the crockery as Brigstocke came back from the bar with more drinks.

'What's all this in aid of, anyway?' Thorne asked.

Brigstocke sat and leaned towards his glass. Took a sip of mineral water. 'Why's it have to be in aid of anything? Just friends having a drink.'

'You weren't much of a friend a few weeks ago, in your office.'

Brigstocke made eye contact, held it for as long as was comfortable. 'I *was*, Tom.'

The slightly awkward silence that followed was broken by murmured 'sorry's and 'excuse me's as a big man who'd been wedged into the corner next to Thorne stood and squeezed out. Thorne pulled his battered, brown leather jacket from the back of a chair and folded it on to the bench next to him. Relaxed into the space. The pub was busy, but now they had something approaching a bit of privacy.

'Either you want to have a good moan about something,' Thorne said, 'or you want to talk about a case that's pissing you off.'

Brigstocke swallowed, nudged at his glasses with a knuckle. 'Bit of both.'

'Mid-life crisis?' Thorne asked.

'Come again?'

Thorne gestured with his glass. 'Trendy new specs. Diet. You got a bit on the side, Russell?'

Brigstocke reddened slightly, pushed fingers through his thick, black hair. 'Might just as well have, the amount of time I'm spending at home.'

'The rough-sleeper killings, right?' Thorne grinned, enjoying the look of surprise on Brigstocke's face. 'It's not like I've been in Timbuktu, Russ. I spoke to Dave Holland on the phone a few nights ago. Saw a bit in the paper before that. A couple of bodies, isn't it?'

'It *was* a couple ...'

'Shit ...'

'"Shit" is bang on. Deep shit is what we're in.'

'There's been a lid on this, right? It literally was a "bit" I saw in the paper.'

'That was the way it was being played until last night. There's going to be a press conference tomorrow afternoon.'

'Tell me ...'

Brigstocke leaned across the table and spoke, his voice just loud enough for Thorne to hear above Dido, who was whining from the speakers above the bar.

Three victims so far.

The first body had been found almost exactly a month earlier. A homeless man somewhere in his forties, murdered in an alleyway off Golden Square. Four weeks on, and his identity remained unknown.

'We've spoken to other rough sleepers in the area and can't get so much as a nickname. They reckon he was new and he certainly hadn't made any contact with local care services. Some of these people like to matey up and some just want to be left alone. Same as anybody else, I suppose.'

'DSS?'

'We're still checking missed appointments, but I'm not holding my breath. They don't all sign on anyway. Some of them are on the street because they don't want to be found.'

'Everyone's got some official stuff *somewhere*, though. Haven't they? A birth certificate. Something.'

'Maybe he had,' Brigstocke said. 'He might have left it somewhere for safe keeping, in which case that's where it's going to stay. We also have to consider the possibility that he kept it on him, and whoever killed him took it.'

'Either way, you've got sod all.'

'There's a tattoo, that's about it. It's pretty distinctive. It's the only thing we've got to work on at the moment . . .'

There was less of a problem putting a name to the second rough sleeper, killed a couple of streets away a fortnight later. Raymond Mannion was a known drug abuser with a criminal record. He had been convicted a few years earlier of violent assault and, though there was no ID found on the body, his DNA was on record.

Both men had been kicked to death. They were of similar ages and had been killed in the early hours of the morning. Both Mannion's body and that of the anonymous first victim had been found with twenty-pound notes pinned to their chests.

Thorne took a mouthful of beer and swallowed. 'A series?'

'Looks likely.'

'And now there's been another one?'

'Night before last. Same area, same sort of age, but there are differences. There was no money left on the body.'

'Unless it was taken.'

'That's possible, obviously. No money was *found* on the body.'

'You said differences. What else?'

'He's still breathing,' Brigstocke said. Thorne raised his eyebrows. 'Not that the poor bugger knows a great deal about it. Name's Paddy Hayes. He's on life support at the Middlesex ...'

Thorne felt a shudder, like cold fingers brushing against the soft hairs at the nape of his neck. He remembered a girl he'd known a few years earlier: attacked and left a fraction from death by a man who'd murdered three before her. Helpless, kept alive by machines. When they'd found her, the police thought that the man they were after had made his first mistake. It was Thorne who had worked out that this killer wasn't actually *trying* to kill anyone. That what he'd done to this girl was what he'd been attempting with the rest of his victims. It was one of those ice-cold/white-hot moments when Thorne had realised the truly monstrous nature of what he was up against.

There'd been far too many since.

'So you think Hayes is part of the pattern or not?'

'It's a bloody coincidence if he isn't.'

'How did you get his ID?'

'Again, nothing official on him, but we found a letter jammed down inside a pocket. Someone from the day centre where he hung out took a look at him and confirmed the name. They had to take a damn good look, though. His head looked like a sack of rotten fruit.'

'What sort of letter?'

'From his son. Telling his father just how much of a useless, drunken bastard he was. How he couldn't give a toss if he never set eyes on him again.' With a finger, Brigstocke pushed what was left of an ice cube around his glass. 'Now the son's the one who's got to decide whether or not to pull the plug ...'

Thorne grimaced. 'So I take it you're not exactly on the verge of making an arrest?'

'It was always going to be a pig,' Brigstocke said. 'When the first one wasn't sorted within a week it started to look very dodgy, and as soon as the second body turned up they were passing the case around like a turd. That's when *we* ran out of luck and picked the bloody thing up. Just after you went gardening, as it happens.'

'Maybe God was punishing you.'

'Somebody's fucking punishing me. I've had officers on fourteen-hour tours for three weeks and we're precisely nowhere.'

'Grief from above?'

'Grief from *everywhere*. The Commissioner's on our backs because he's getting it in the neck from every homeless charity and pressure group out there. They seem to think because we aren't making any obvious progress that we must be dragging our feet. That, basically, we don't care.'

'Do we?'

Brigstocke ignored him. 'So now it's a *political* issue, and we're fucked because the homeless community itself has bought into this idea that we're not trying very hard. So they've more or less stopped talking to us.'

'You can hardly blame them, though.'

'I'm not *blaming* them. They've got every right to be suspicious.'

'They've got every right to be *scared*, if there's a killer out there. These are people who can't lock the door, remember.'

They said nothing for a few moments. Dido had given way to Norah Jones. Thorne wondered if there was an album titled *Now That's What I Call Scampi in a Basket*.

'There's another reason they're not talking to us,' Brigstocke said. Thorne looked up from the beer mat. 'There was a statement taken early on from a kid sleeping rough. He reckoned that a police officer had been asking questions.'

Thorne jammed a fist under his chin. 'Sorry, I'm probably being a bit bloody thick, but ...'

'It was *before* the first murder. He claimed that a police officer had been asking questions the day before the first body was found. Showing a picture. Like he was looking for someone.'

'Looking for who, exactly? I mean, this is the victim you still haven't identified, right?' Brigstocke nodded. 'So didn't this person who was supposedly looking for him mention his name?'

'We could check if we had such a thing as a name and address for the kid who gave the statement. Honestly, nothing about this is simple, Tom.'

Thorne watched Brigstocke take a drink. Took one himself. 'A copper?'

'We've had to tread a bit bloody carefully.'

'Keep it out of the press, you mean?'

Brigstocke raised his voice, irritated. 'Come on, you know damn well that's not the only reason we don't want it plastered all over the papers ...'

'"It is considered good practice to deliberately withhold details of the MO used by the offender."' Thorne yawned theatrically as he quoted from the most recent edition of the *Murder Investigation Manual*, the detective's bible.

'Right, like the money left on the bodies. So we know the other killings weren't copycats.'

'You can't be sure about Paddy Hayes,' Thorne said.

'No ...'

Thorne knew that there were certainly sound procedural

grounds for keeping things quiet. But he also knew that even the *possible* involvement of a police officer in a case such as this would make the Job's top brass extremely jumpy.

Thorne could see that the next day's press conference made sense. The third body had undoubtedly forced a swift and radical change in media strategy. Now, the public had to be told – but only up to a point – what was going on. It was all spelled out in the *Murder Investigation Manual*: the public had to be reassured, advised, appealed to.

The Met, of course, was also doing the smart thing by covering its arse. God forbid any more bodies should turn up and they had forgotten that the public also needed to be *warned*.

'So, what do you think?' Brigstocke asked. 'Any bright ideas?'

'I think you need to forget about mineral water and go and get yourself a proper drink. A beer gut's the least of your worries.'

'Seriously ...'

'*Seriously*?' Thorne swilled what little beer there was left around the bottom of his glass. 'You should have tried picking my brains before you bought me three pints of Stella, mate.' He puffed out his cheeks, let the air out slowly. 'My afternoon of recruitment demographics is shot to shit as it is.'

THREE

It was a forty-minute tube ride home from St James's Park. As soon as he walked through his front door that evening he took the CD from his Walkman and transferred it into his main deck. It was part of a boxed set of out-takes and demos from the *American Recordings* sessions, released a few months after Johnny Cash had died in 2003. Thorne cued up 'Redemption Song' – a cover of the Bob Marley classic that Cash had recorded with Joe Strummer. Neither of them had lived to see its release.

Thorne moved around the kitchen, making tea, wondering at how Marley and Strummer could both have gone so young, while Mick Hucknall and Phil Collins were still walking around.

Though he'd been joking with Brigstocke, Thorne hadn't actually got a whole lot done that afternoon. He'd stared at columns of figures, had stabbed perfunctorily at his keyboard, but all the time he'd been thinking about Paddy Hayes and the machines that were keeping him alive. Thinking about the letter the man had carried in his pocket. About the *damn good look* those who knew him had needed before they were able to confirm his identity.

Thorne carried his tea through to the sitting room. He sat and considered everything that Brigstocke had told him, and why. Now that those who were seemingly being targeted had stopped talking to the police, the investigation would stutter and stall very bloody quickly. In all probability, it would grind spectacularly to a halt.

Russell Brigstocke had to have been pretty desperate to come to him for advice in the first place. From what Thorne had heard about the case, that desperation was well founded.

So, what do you think?

In the silence between the tracks, Thorne could hear the distant hum of traffic from the Kentish Town Road, the rumble of a train on the overground line that ran to Camden Town or Gospel Oak. He felt suddenly nostalgic for those few months earlier in the year when he'd shared the flat with Phil Hendricks, whose own place was being treated for damp. It had been cramped and chaotic, with Hendricks dossing down on the sofa bed, and there'd been a good deal of arguing. He remembered the two of them drunkenly rowing about football the day before Hendricks had moved out. That would have been a couple of weeks before the fire . . .

Before the fire. Not 'before my father died'.

That was the way his mind tended to go: the comforting way, towards the absolute. There *was* a fire. The fire was a fact. So was his father's death, of course, but even to form the phrase in his head was to invite in the doubt and the torment to fuck with him for a time. To crack open the carapace of everyday nonsense and force that fissure wider, until it gaped. Until Thorne could do nothing but shut himself down and wait for the churning in his guts and the pounding in his head to stop.

He guessed that Hendricks had done the post-mortems on Mannion and the first victim. That he'd also do the PM on Paddy Hayes when the time came. Hendricks hadn't mentioned the case when they'd spoken, but then Holland had been a bit cagey about it, too. Thorne knew that they were trying to protect him. They believed he was better off where he was. Uninvolved.

Grief and work, so everybody seemed to think, were mutually exclusive. Each got in the way of the other.

Any bright ideas?

Perhaps, though he wasn't sure how bright it was.

Moving to the window, Thorne could feel the draught creeping beneath the sash. Not so long ago the country had been at a standstill for a week as temperatures climbed towards three figures. Now, three weeks into August, and the summer was on its last legs. He thought about how those that lived on the streets were at the mercy of the seasons. How that first hint of autumn would change everything. For those that slept outdoors, that had no other options, a harsh winter could be far more serious than any amount of burst pipes or shunts on black ice.

Not so long ago ...

Thorne blinked and remembered the feel of the pew beneath him. The smell of himself, sweating in a black suit. No more than three rows filled and most of them there to support him. Feeling a bead of perspiration roll behind his ear and creep down inside the tight, white collar. Knowing he would soon have to stand up and say something ...

He couldn't carry on with what he was doing now. He wasn't ready to go back to what he'd done before. He could work through grief, or he could grieve at work, but guilt choked the life out of everything.

He moved quickly to the phone and dialled.

'You should think about sending an officer in undercover. Among the rough sleepers.' Thorne wasn't sure if Brigstocke was thinking about his suggestion or had just been stunned into silence. 'It makes sense,' he continued. 'Nobody's talking to you. I can't see there are many other options.'

'It'll take too long to set up.'

'I don't see why; it isn't complicated. You're sending one officer on to the streets, into that community. All we need to set up is a simple line of communication with him.'

'I'll talk to Jesmond, see what he thinks. See if he can *find* anybody. Thanks for the call, Tom ...'

'Give it some thought.'

A shorter silence this time and then a snort. 'How much more have you had to drink since lunchtime?'

'I can do this, Russell. I did the course ...'

'Don't be so bloody stupid. An Undercover Two course?'

'Right ...'

'And how many years ago was that?'

Thorne tuned Brigstocke out momentarily. Elvis was rubbing herself against his shins. He wondered who would feed her if he was away for a while. The woman upstairs would do it if he asked her nicely. She had a couple of her own cats ...

'I'm hardly going deep inside an organised-crime firm, am I?' Thorne said. 'I can't see how this can be high risk. We're talking about gathering information, that's all.'

'*That's all?*'

'Yes.'

'So you haven't really thought about this bloke who's going round kicking people to death?'

'I want to help catch the fucker, yes.'

'What, you think you can ... draw him out or something?'

'I don't see how I could ...'

'Some crap like that?'

'No ...'

'How does putting yourself in danger help anyone, Tom? How does it help *you*?'

'I'm just going to sleep rough, for Christ's sake,' Thorne said. 'Presuming for a second that this killer *is* still around, how can it be dangerous if he doesn't know I'm there?'

He heard the click of a lighter on the other end of the phone. There was a pause and then the noisy exhalation of smoke.

'The mouse doesn't know there's cheese on the trap,' Brigstocke said. 'But we still call it bait . . .'

FOUR

If a man jumped out in front of him with a severed head in one hand and a blood-spattered axe in the other, gibbering about how the voices in his head had made him do it, Detective Superintendent Trevor Jesmond would be a little out of his depth. He was not, however, a man who thought the *Murder Investigation Manual* was boring, and when it came to 'Communications Strategy' – Chapter Seven, Section Seven, Sub-section Two (Managing the Media) – there was nobody to touch him.

'Let me stress again that the victim of this despicable crime is among the most vulnerable members of our society. His attacker is someone whom we believe has killed twice already. Make no mistake, we will do whatever it takes to apprehend this man before he has a chance to kill again.'

They were gathered in the Press Room at Colindale

40

Police Station; five minutes away from the Peel Centre, where the Murder Squad was based in Becke House. Thorne watched from the back. Staring across the heads of several dozen assembled hacks. Leaning one way and then another to get a clear view of the stage between an assortment of camera tripods.

'Is this latest victim expected to live?'

'Mr Hayes is in a critical condition. He is presently on life support at Middlesex Hospital. Without talking further to those doctors caring for him, I'm not in a position to give any more information than that.'

There can't have been too many people in the room who couldn't work out that Paddy Hayes was fucked.

'You've suggested that the attempted murder of Mr Hayes is connected to the two other murders of rough sleepers. That this latest attack is part of a series . . .'

Jesmond held up a hand, nodded. He was acknowledging that the journalist was right, but only up to a point. He was also stopping him before he ventured too far down that avenue of questioning. Of course, they'd had to come out and admit that the murders were connected. When the tabloids were putting two and two together, the Met could not afford to appear dim by looking as if they hadn't.

'We must assume there's a connection, yes,' Jesmond said.

'So we're talking about motiveless killings, then? Random attacks?'

A grim half smile. 'DCI Brigstocke and his team believe

41

that they are hunting a killer who has struck before. The investigation is proceeding, vigorously, along those lines.'

He was playing it very nicely. Striking that essential balance between reassurance and warning. It was, of course, crucial not to alarm the public.

Thorne knew, as Jesmond must have known, that, irrespective of what was said, the papers would print stories about a serial killer. It would shift copies quicker than Posh and Becks, and Fleet Street editors didn't have any qualms about alarming anybody.

It was a phrase Thorne hated. He had caught, and *not caught*, a number of those who had murdered strangers, and none had borne the slightest resemblance to the creature conjured up by the words 'serial killer'. All the men and women he'd known who had taken more than one life had done so with what they believed to be good reason. None had thought themselves superhuman, or hunted their victims when the moon was full. They had motives for what they did that had nothing to do with being locked in a cellar when they were children, or made to dress up in their mother's clothes ...

'As always, we are seeking the co-operation of the public in helping to put an end to these appalling attacks.'

The appeal was textbook stuff. Jesmond gave out the salient facts, insisted that anyone with information, anyone who was in the vicinity, had a duty to come forward. It would, more than likely, prove useless. There can't have been many people hanging around in dark alleyways in the dead of night, and if there had been, it was unlikely, for one reason or another, that any of them would want to come forward. Still, it had to be done, and it had to be specific: dates and times and localities. The last thing they needed was a bland, generalised plea that gave out the wrong message.

We haven't got the first idea who's doing this, but somebody out there must know something. Please help us ...

'We *will* catch this man,' Jesmond said, winding up. Public confidence was important but so was his own, and he made a point of showing it. Hearts and minds were not won by being mealy-mouthed. His body language and the expression on his face were determined and dynamic. Thorne could easily picture him learning how to project the image, on a weekend course at a country-house hotel. It was as though he were inviting those present to take a bloody careful note of the message, written in foot-high letters across the smart, blue Metropolitan Police backdrop: '*WORKING FOR A SAFER LONDON*'.

Thorne knew that it was smoke and mirrors.

The press conference was there as much as anything to project an image of confidence and efficiency, but Thorne knew that the investigation was in trouble. He knew it was easy enough to marshal resources, to gather significant numbers of officers and be gung-ho about catching a killer when it was only for forty-five minutes in front of the media.

Thorne wondered how anybody was ever fooled.

*

He hung around in the car park, waiting for Jesmond. Trying to work out the best way of making the approach.

At the sound of the door, Thorne looked up to see two men coming out of the station. Recognising one of them, he tried immediately to turn away without being seen, but he was a fraction too late. He had little choice but to smile and give a small nod. The man he'd been trying to avoid nodded back and Thorne was horrified to see him start to walk over, bringing with him the other man, whose face was vaguely familiar.

Steve Norman was a Senior Force Press Officer, a civilian. He was small and wiry, with a helmet of dark hair and an overinflated sense of his own importance. He and Thorne had crossed swords on a case a couple of years earlier.

'Tom ...' Still six feet away from him, Norman extended a hand.

Thorne took it, remembering an ill-tempered meeting when Norman had jabbed a finger into his chest. Remembering that he'd threatened to break it ...

'I hadn't expected to see you,' Norman continued.

So, the gardening leave had become common knowledge. Thorne nodded back towards the main building. 'Conference went well, I thought.' Norman had been heavily involved, of course. Thorne had seen him, lurking at the side of the stage looking pleased with himself. He'd stepped up at one point and whispered something to Russell Brigstocke.

Norman put a hand on his friend's arm and looked towards Thorne. 'Do you two ... ?'

Thorne leaned across. 'Sorry, Tom Thorne ...'

The man stepped smartly forward and they shook hands. He was mid-fortyish, taller than Thorne and Norman by six inches or more, and thickset.

'This is Alan Ward, from Sky,' Norman said. Thorne could see how much he relished making the introduction.

'Good to meet you,' Ward said. He had large, wire-framed glasses beneath a tangle of dark, curly hair that was three-quarters grey. He put his hand back into the pocket of what Thorne would have described as a denim blazer.

'You too ...'

Several typically English moments of social awkwardness followed. Thorne would have left, but for the fact that he didn't want to seem rude and had nowhere to go. Norman and Ward, who had clearly been in mid-conversation, were also too polite to excuse themselves immediately. They stood and carried on talking, while Thorne hovered and listened, as though the three of them were old friends.

'I can't remember you at one of these before, Alan,' Norman said.

'It's news, so we're covering it.'

'Bit below your weight though, isn't it?'

Ward stared over Norman's head as he spoke, looking around as if he were taking in a breathtaking view. 'We aren't bombing the shit out of anybody at the moment, thank God, so I'm just here giving the lads on the crew a bit of moral support. Keeping an eye on one or two of the newer guys.'

There was a bit of chuckling, then a pause. Thorne felt like he should say something to justify his presence. 'What is it you do then, Alan?'

Norman took great pride in answering for Ward. 'Alan's a TV reporter. He's normally working in places a little more dangerous than Colindale.'

'Tottenham?' Thorne asked.

Ward laughed and started to speak, but again Norman was in there first. 'Bosnia, Afghanistan, Northern Ireland.' Norman listed the names with great pride, and Thorne realised that he was showing off, like a kid with a new bike. That, however close a friend Ward actually was, Norman got off on knowing him.

Thorne looked at Ward and could see that he was embarrassed, that he and Norman were not really close friends at all. The glance Thorne got back, the momentary discreet roll of the eyes, told him Ward thought Norman was every bit as much of a tit as he did. Thorne took an enormous liking to Alan Ward immediately.

Suddenly it was Thorne's turn to feel embarrassed. 'I thought you looked familiar,' he said. 'I've just realised. I've seen you on the box, haven't I?'

Norman looked like he would wet himself with excitement.

'Have you got Sky, then?' Ward asked.

'I tend to use it for the football mostly I'm ashamed to say.'

'Who are you, Arsenal?'

'God, no!'

At that moment, over Norman's shoulder, Thorne saw Trevor Jesmond emerge. Jesmond looked across, froze, then quickly tried – as Thorne himself had done a few minutes earlier – to spin away without being spotted. Thorne raised a hand, horrified that he and Jesmond shared anything at all in common.

'Well then . . .' Norman said.

To the press officer's obvious delight, Thorne said hasty goodbyes. Ward shook his hand again, and gave him a business card. As Thorne walked away, the reporter said something he didn't altogether catch about getting free tickets for matches.

He caught up with Jesmond just as the Detective Superintendent reached his car.

'Shouldn't you be at Scotland Yard?'

'I was wondering if DCI Brigstocke had said anything to you, sir.'

Jesmond pressed a button on his key to unlock the car. He opened the Rover's door and tossed his cap and briefcase on to the passenger seat.

'My sympathies for recent events are a matter of record . . .'

'Sir . . .'

'But if they have left you in an emotionally charged state, where you are not presently fit to work as a member of my team, what on earth makes you think you'd be able to function efficiently as an undercover officer?'

'I don't think what I'm suggesting is ... complicated,' Thorne said. 'I think I'm perfectly able—'

Jesmond cut him off. 'Or perhaps that's it.' He blinked slowly. His lashes were sandy, all but lost against his dry skin. He might have been trying to appear knowing and thoughtful, but Thorne watched the thin lips set themselves into what looked to him like a smirk. 'Perhaps your emotional state is precisely *why* you think you should be doing this. Perhaps it's why you consider yourself suitable; why you consider this job suitable for *you*. Have I hit it on the head, Tom? Are you going to be dossing down in a hair shirt?'

Thorne could say nothing. He flicked his eyes away and watched the light slide off the chromed edge of the car's indicators, catching the buttons of Jesmond's immaculate uniform.

'Look, I'm not saying it's a *completely* stupid idea,' Jesmond said. 'You've certainly had stupider.'

Thorne smiled at the line, seeing the glimmer of possibility. 'This one's not even in the top ten,' he said.

'On the plus side, even if you screw it up, I can't see that we have a great deal to lose.'

'I can't see there's *anything* to lose.'

'Give me a day or two, yes?' Jesmond stepped between Thorne and the car door. 'It won't be solely my decision anyway. I'll have to talk to SO10.'

'I really think we can get something out of this,' Thorne said.

'Like I said, a day or two.'

'We can get it quickly as well. There's no need for a long lead-up time. We just do it.' He stared at Jesmond, trying hard to look relaxed even as his stomach jumped and knotted. 'Come on, you've seen some of these down and outs. Staggering around, ranting at the world with a can of cheap lager in their hand. You know me well enough. How hard can that possibly be?'

FIVE

The mood of the café owner had obviously not improved as he cleared away the plates. Holland had eaten toast before he'd left home, but had done his best with a bacon sandwich. Thorne had made short work of the fullest of full English breakfasts.

'The eggs were hard,' Thorne said.

'So? You ate them, didn't you? If you don't like the place, you can fuck off.'

'We'll have two more mugs of tea.'

The owner trudged back behind his counter. The place was a lot busier now, and he had more to do, so it was difficult to tell whether he had any intention of ever bringing the tea as requested.

'Can you find something to arrest him for?' Thorne said. 'Being fat and miserable in a built-up area, maybe?'

'I'm not sure who he hates more, coppers or tramps. We're obviously not doing much for his ambience.'

Thorne stared hard across the room. 'Fuck him. It's hardly the Ritz, is it?'

'I picked up a couple of papers on my way here,' Holland said. He reached down for his bag, dug out a stack of newspapers and dropped them on the table. 'Our picture of Victim One's on virtually every front page today.'

Thorne pulled a couple of the papers towards him. 'TV?'

Holland nodded. 'All the national TV news broadcasts as well. Both ends of *London Tonight*. It's pretty comprehensive ...'

Thorne stared down at the *Mirror*, at the *Independent*, into a pair of eyes that had been generated by a software program, but nonetheless had the power to find his own, and hold them. Victim One was long-haired and bearded. His flat, black and white features were fine, the line of jaw and cheekbones perhaps a little extreme to be lifelike. But the eyes, like the heavy bags beneath them, looked real enough. Dark, narrow, and demanding to be recognised. It was a face that said, *Know me.*

'What do you think?' Holland asked.

Thorne looked at the text that accompanied the pictures. The crucial facts rehashed: a brutal reminder of just how much was known about this man's death when nothing at all was known about the life that had been stolen from him.

Then, the reproduction of the tattoo. The vital collection of letters found on the victim's shoulder. It had been hoped early on – as Brigstocke had told Thorne in the pub – that this might help identify the body, but that hope had proved as temporary as the tattoo itself was permanent.

AB-
S.O.F.A.

The decision not to print a photograph of the tattoo had been taken on grounds of taste. A similar decision with regard to the victim's face had not been necessary: they'd had no choice but to computer-generate, and not just because the face itself was unrecognisable. It was unrecognisable *as a face*: every feature had been all but kicked or stamped clean off the victim's head. The unmarked face that was confronting thousands of people, that very minute over their cornflakes, had been fashioned by a microchip from little more than bone and bruise.

'It's like King's Cross,' Thorne said. 'It's what they did with the victim they couldn't put a name to.'

The fire at King's Cross Underground station in November 1987 had killed thirty-one people, but only thirty bodies were ever claimed. One victim had remained anonymous – in spite of numerous appeals to those who might have known who he was. Thorne remembered that face, too: the sketch on the poster in a hundred tube stations; the clay reconstruction of the head that was lovingly fashioned and paraded in front of the television cameras. Ironically, the dead man, known for years only as Victim 115, had finally been identified just the year before, nearly twenty years after his death, and had turned out to have been a rough sleeper. Many commentators in the press claimed to have been unsurprised. It was obvious he was homeless, or else someone would surely have come forward much earlier, wouldn't they? Thorne wasn't so sure. He doubted that material belongings had a great deal to do with being missed. He thought it was perfectly possible to have a roof over your head, a decent car and two nice holidays a year, yet still go unacknowledged and unclaimed if you had the misfortune to find yourself trapped on a burning escalator.

Thorne reckoned it was less to do with being unknown than with being un*loved*.

'I think we're in with more of a chance though,' Holland said, looking at the picture. 'The quality of this is far higher. It's got to ring a bell with somebody.'

'Let's hope somebody loved him enough.'

Thorne handed the *Independent* back across the table and turned the *Mirror* over to the sports page. He wondered how many footballers had been accused of rape since the last time he'd read a newspaper.

SIX

Thorne leaned in close and stared at himself in the small, square mirror. A week without razor, soap or shampoo didn't seem to have made a great deal of difference. Seven days during which he'd tried to start looking the part, while a pair of stroppy sorts from SO10 – the unit that ran undercover operations – had done their best to put him through a refresher course.

It had all been fairly straightforward. As Thorne had been keen to stress to Brigstocke, the job would be purely about intelligence gathering. There would be no real need to fabricate a detailed back-story – to create what those who worked in this area called a 'deep legend'. When necessary, tax details, Land Registry records and electoral rolls would be doctored, but there would be no need for any such elaborate preparations in this case. Whatever the reason for them being there, those who ended up on the street tended to reinvent themselves anyway; to keep their pasts to themselves. They were starting again.

Thorne took one last look, slammed the locker-door shut and hoisted the rucksack on to his shoulder.

'Once you've been out there a couple of weeks you'll see the difference. Black snot and a proper layer of London grime that won't wash off easily ...'

Thorne turned to look across at the man standing by the door. 'Who am I fucking kidding, Bren?'

Brendan Maxwell was to be the only person connected with the homeless community who would know what Thorne was doing. What he really was. Maxwell worked as a Senior Outreach Officer for London Lift, an organisation providing counselling and practical help for the city's homeless, in particular those more entrenched rough sleepers who were over twenty-five.

He was also Phil Hendricks' boyfriend. Thorne had been privy to the ups and downs of their often stormy relationship for the last few years and had come to know the tall, skinny Irishman pretty well. Aside from Hendricks himself, and those few officers on the investigation who had been briefed, Maxwell would be – for however long the operation lasted – the only real connection Thorne had between his two lives.

'Don't lose the key,' Maxwell said. 'There aren't any spares.'

Thorne put the key into the front pocket of his rucksack. The locker, where he would leave spare clothes, was one of fifty or so provided for the use of clients at the Lift's mixed-age day centre off St Martin's Lane. The organisation's offices were on the top floor, with the lockers in the basement, along with washing and laundry facilities. On the ground floor were the advice counter, a seating area and a no-frills café serving hot drinks and heavily subsidised meals.

Maxwell walked over. He had short blond hair and wore a brown corduroy shirt tucked into jeans. He cast an amused eye over Thorne's outfit, which he'd already referred to sarcastically as his 'dosser costume'. The sweater and shoes had come from Oxfam and the black jeans were an old pair of Thorne's own.

The grey coat had belonged to his father.

'There's all sorts out there,' Maxwell said. His accent was heavy and the disgust was audible beneath the arch, jokey tone. 'There isn't really a *look*, you know? You could be wearing a three-piece suit and spats, but if you've got a can of Tennent's Extra or a needle in your arm, you'll fit right in.'

'I'll bear that in mind.'

There was a scarred, metal rubbish bin mounted to the wall. Maxwell moved across and took out the stuffed, white bin-liner. Began tying a knot in the top of it. 'This is very bizarre . . .'

'What?'

'First thing I do, with a lot of the younger ones anyway, is give them a reality check. You know? They're straight off the coach or they've hitched here from wherever and some of these kids really do think the place is paved with gold. I swear to God. It's my job, very gently you understand, to point out to them how very wrong, how completely fucking stupid they are. It's usually a waste of time, but even if they tell me to piss off, they find out themselves quickly enough.' He pointed towards a high, dirty window behind a mesh of black metal. 'It's dogshit and fucking despair holding the pavements together out there. A reality check?' He looked across at Thorne. 'Not much point with *you*, is there?'

'Not really.'

Maxwell dropped the bin-bag on to the floor. He reached into his back pocket for a new roll, tore one off. 'Phil thinks you're mental, by the way.'

'I know.'

'I can't say I disagree with him. Why all this De Niro shite?'

'All this what?'

'You know what I mean ...'

'What are you on about?' Thorne said. 'I've got a mobile phone in my pocket and I'm wearing thermal underwear.'

Maxwell smiled. 'Fair play. You could still go a bit easier though, spend the first couple of nights in a hostel.'

'The men who were killed were all sleeping rough. They died outdoors.' Thorne caught the smell of hot food drifting down from the café. 'Besides, if I'm going to do this, I might as well bloody *do* it.'

Maxwell picked up the full bin-bag and walked to the door. 'Listen, I'm not having a go, Tom, and I'll be around if you need any help, but don't make any mistake about it. However much you *think* you're doing this, you can always walk away.' He opened the door, then turned back into the room. 'You can dirty yourself up and spend a bit of time kipping on cardboard, but you've got the option to cut and run any bloody time you feel like it. Any time you like. Jump in a taxi back to your flat and your cowboy music.'

Thorne was getting irritated, but had to smile. *Cowboy music*. That was one of Hendricks'. 'I'll see you upstairs,' he said. 'I'd better grab some food before I make a move.'

Maxwell nodded and stepped out into the corridor. 'Stew's good . . . '

It had seemed like as good a spot as any.

Three steps up from pavement level and fairly sheltered. Odd as it was to sleep surrounded by giant black-and-white photographs of actors and extravagant quotes testifying to their skill and comic timing, Thorne figured that a theatre doorway was a safe bet. As long as he waited until the show had finished and the place had shut its doors for the night, he probably wouldn't be bothered. Plus, of course, theatres – unlike shops – tended not to open first thing in the morning.

Two days shy of September, it was a relatively mild night, but within half an hour of lying down, his arse was dead and it felt as though a corpse's feet had been pressed against his neck.

Thorne hitched up the sleeping bag and leaned back

against the doors. He'd felt ready to drop only an hour before. Having walked around since the day centre had closed its doors at four o'clock, he'd been stone-cold dead on his feet by the time he'd staked his claim to the theatre doorway. Now, suddenly, he was horribly awake. He thought about getting his gear together again and walking some more, but he didn't want to run the risk of losing his pitch. He'd seen one or two characters earlier in the surrounding streets, mooching around, looking like they were searching for a good spot to spend the night. For a second he decided that reading a book might help him sleep, and then he remembered where he was and what he was doing. It struck him that the first few days would be about similar moments of desire and realisation. About feeling spoiled and stupid every few minutes.

Remembering, and perhaps forgetting, the thousand everyday things that he would be going without.

Music, TV, decent food. But it wasn't even so much about these obvious things themselves. He would eat. There was a television in the day centre if he had a desperate desire to watch *Richard and Judy*. It was getting used to such things not being available whenever he felt like them. It was a question of choice, and space. Somewhere to lie down, to feel comfortable, to have a piss ...

He started to make a list in his head of all these things and it didn't take him long to work out exactly what it was that he needed. He couldn't believe that he'd been so stupid as not to get it organised. Christ, he'd have had a beer at home, wouldn't he? He decided that tomorrow night he'd make sure he stashed a couple of cans in his rucksack. Maybe something even stronger.

He sat, bored and scared, letting his head drop back against the polished wooden doors and staring at the photographs all around him. Listening to people shouting and to cars accelerating away. Smelling the aftershave on his father's coat.

It was, he guessed, not even one o'clock yet. People still walked past his doorway every few minutes or so. Thorne wondered how long it would be before he no longer bothered looking up at them.

*

In retrospect, his one regret about killing the Driver was that he hadn't given the pathetic twat time to get a proper look at him. He'd have liked to have seen the shock register, just for a second, before the first kick had ...

Mind you, there was no point dwelling on it. Most of them had been so out of it, so away with the fairies, that they hadn't registered much of *anything*. The Driver was in such a state, he wouldn't have recognised him anyway, likely as not. He could smell the beer on the poor sod, alongside that stink they all had. That tangy, tramp stink. Sharp and musty at the same time, like cats had been pissing in a charity shop.

He turned off the bathroom light and moved into the darkness of the bedroom. He thought about checking to see if there was any metal on MTV, maybe working out for twenty minutes. He decided against it and began to undress; it was easy enough to do a bit more in the morning. He'd eaten late and the food hadn't had a chance to go down.

Things in London had been fairly straightforward up to now, so it annoyed him that this last one, Hayes, had survived. It sounded, from what they'd said on the news and in the paper, that he wouldn't survive for very long, but still, it rankled with him. It made him swear at the mirror and kick out at stuff. You did a good job and you took a pride in it. That mattered. It was important that you did what was required.

He flicked on the TV. The light from the small screen danced across his clothes as he folded them carefully on to the chair at the foot of his bed.

He'd already made up his mind to do another one. This one would be just for him, would go some way towards making up for botching the last one. It wasn't strictly necessary, but it couldn't do much harm. It would cost him another note, of course, but twenty quid a pop wasn't a lot for reinforcement *that* bloody good.

He climbed beneath the blanket in his vest and pants and began jabbing at the remote. Having looked at what was showing on all the stations a few times, it was obvious that there was nothing he fancied, but he carried on regardless. Moving methodically through the channels with the sound down.

*

When he'd finished, Thorne tucked himself in and turned from the wall to find himself being studied.

'You want to be careful, mate. There's one or two coppers round here'll do you for that. Take great delight in doing it, an' all . . . '

He stood directly opposite Thorne on the other side of the road, with a grey blanket wrapped around his shoulders. Early twenties was Thorne's best estimate. He had delicate features set below spikes of blond hair and his cheeks hollowed dramatically as he dragged hard on a cigarette.

'I can show you a place thirty seconds from here which is a bit more private, like, and a lot bloody safer. Of course, there's always McDonald's if you want to go before midnight, though there *is* one down towards Trafalgar Square that sometimes stays open a bit longer. With a piss, like, there's always *somewhere*, but there's nothing quite like seeing them golden arches when you're bursting for a shit.' He reached up a hand from beneath the blanket to take the cigarette from his mouth.

Thorne said nothing for a few seconds. The boy seemed friendly enough, but still, Thorne sensed that caution would be best. It would certainly *look* best. 'Right,' he said. His voice was flat, with just a hint of aggression in the delivery.

The boy looked to his right. 'You're in the theatre doorway, yeah? Just round the corner there?'

Thorne nodded, began to walk slowly towards it.

'Just so as you know, that's Terry T's spot.' He began to

move in the same direction as Thorne, walking parallel to him on the other side of the narrow street.

'So, where is he?'

'He's gone visiting, so you'll be all right for the time being. He'll be back at some point, though, so just as long as you know, yeah? As long as you know that's Terry T's spot.'

'Well, I know now. Thanks.'

The boy crossed the road, moving over to Thorne in a couple of strides and walking alongside him. 'It's a good spot, like. Sheltered ...'

'That's why I took it,' Thorne said. 'I think I'll move around a bit anyway, see how it pans out.'

'Only Terry can be a right psycho, like. Goes a bit mental sometimes and, you know, with him being so enormous and that ...'

'Mental *how* exactly?'

The boy chucked his cigarette into the road and hissed out a laugh. 'I'm winding you up. I'm kidding, like. Terry's all right, plus he's my mate, so I'll square things if he does get a bit funny with you.'

Thorne had seen the joke coming, but had let the boy have his moment. 'Thanks,' he said.

They rounded the corner and Thorne was relieved to see that his sleeping bag and rucksack were still there. He'd decided to risk leaving them for a minute or two while he'd gone to answer the call of nature. The relief must have been clear to see on his face.

'Don't worry, mate, people only tend to nick what they

can sell. Nothing valuable in your bag, is there?' Thorne shook his head. 'Don't worry about your sleeping bag though, you can pick one of them up anywhere. Salvation Army's got thousands of the bloody things, or you'll just see 'em lying around, so you can help yourself. You want to watch out for scabies, though, that is *not* fucking pleasant.'

'Cheers ... ?'

'Best not to cart that much around at all if you can help it. Leave your stuff somewhere else, you know, one of the day centres or whatever. Trust me, even a plastic bag with some old papers and a pair of socks in it gets dead heavy if you're carrying it around all the time, like.'

Thorne climbed the marble steps and sat down in the doorway. 'How come you're such a font of all fucking knowledge? You're only twelve.'

The boy laughed again, nodding his head and spitting out the laugh between his teeth. 'Right, mate, you're right, but it's like dog years on the streets, so I'm a lot older than you where it counts, you know?'

'If you say so.'

'How long you been around, then? I've not seen you ... '

'First night,' Thorne said.

'Fuck.' The boy pulled the blanket tighter around his shoulders. He repeated himself, drawing out the word, respectfully.

'So, what? You're the welcoming committee, are you?'

'Nearest thing to it, yeah, if you like.'

Thorne watched the boy rummage beneath the blanket

and emerge with another cigarette. He could see that the boy was much taller than he'd first appeared.

He'd walked with hunched shoulders, eyes down, as though he could tell exactly which way he were going by looking at the cracks in the stone slabs, by studying the pattern of discarded chewing gum on the pavement.

'You look like the Man With No Name,' Thorne said.

The boy finished lighting up, blew out a thin stream of smoke. 'You what?'

Thorne pointed towards the blanket around the boy's shoulders. 'With that. Like Clint Eastwood in the movie, you know? *The Good, The Bad and The Ugly.*'

The boy shrugged and thought for a minute. He shifted his weight from foot to foot, rocking from side to side. 'He the one did those films with the monkey?'

'Doesn't matter.' Thorne shoved his feet down inside the sleeping bag. 'Good time for your mate Terry to go visiting.'

'Why's that, then?'

'One less for this nutter to go after. This loony that's killing rough sleepers.'

The boy's cheeks sank into shadow again as he took a deep drag. He held in the smoke until he needed to take a breath. 'I suppose. He's still got plenty to choose from.' His mood had changed suddenly: fear, suspicion or perhaps a bit of both. It was hard for Thorne to work out which.

'Did you know any of them?' Thorne asked the question casually, through a yawn. 'Any of the blokes who were . . . ?'

65

'I knew Paddy a bit, yeah. Mad as a snake, like, but totally harmless. Paddy was happy with God and a bottle.'

'So you don't reckon he could have fallen out with somebody? Nobody had a reason to give him a kicking?'

The boy looked straight at Thorne but it was as though he'd heard a totally different question. He nodded once, twice, quickly. Repeated what he'd just said: 'God and a bottle ...'

'Right.'

'What's your name?' Another, equally sudden, change of mood and tone.

'Tom.'

'I'll see you around, Tom ...'

'What about you? You might look like the Man With No Name, but you must have one.'

'Spike. Because of the hair, you know? Like the vampire in *Buffy*.'

Now it was Thorne's turn to be the one on whom a reference was lost. 'OK, but what's your real name?'

The boy cocked his head, looked at Thorne as though he too were a harmless old nutcase. 'Just Spike.'

Then he turned, hoiked up his blanket and began walking north towards Soho.

SEVEN

The mobile phone Thorne had been issued with was permanently set to vibrate, and had been shoved deep inside the pocket of his overcoat. It had been agreed that Thorne and Holland would talk twice every day, morning and evening. Contact either way could, of course, be made at other times if necessary, and a face-to-face meeting, with either Holland or Brigstocke, would take place, all being well, once a week.

Thorne had already spoken to Holland by the time he walked into the London Lift day centre, just after the place opened at nine o'clock. He found himself in a small holding area between the front entrance and a larger glass door. The young Asian man on duty at the reception desk eyed him through the glass for ten, maybe fifteen seconds, before pressing the button that allowed him through the second set of doors.

'All right?' Thorne stepped up and leaned against the counter.

'I'm good, mate. You?'

Thorne shrugged and scribbled his name in the register that had been passed across to him. The receptionist, who wore an ID badge that said *RAJ*, tapped a couple of keys on his computer and Thorne was buzzed through the steel door into the café area.

A fair number of the grey or orange plastic chairs – scattered around tables or lined against the walls – were already taken. Most people sat alone, nursing hot drinks and rolls, and though a few had gathered in groups, the sound of a knife scraping across a plate rose easily above the muted level of conversation. Considering how busy it was, the place was oddly still and quiet. Thorne knew that half as many people would be making twice as much noise in the Starbucks across the road.

He moved to the end of a short queue, studied the price list on the blackboard behind the counter. He saw a familiar figure rise from a table across the room and nod. Spike walked across, moving a little slower than he had done the night before.

'Found this place quick enough, then?'

'I saw an outreach worker,' Thorne said. 'Came along last night after you left, told me if I got down here first thing, I could get a decent breakfast.' The second lie of the day came easily. He'd told the first on the phone half an hour earlier, when Dave Holland had asked him how his night had been.

Thorne looked around. It was a big room, and bright.

One wall was dominated by a vast, glossy mural; notice-boards ran the length of another.

'You signing on?' Spike asked.

Thorne nodded. He wouldn't be going to the dole office, but he'd taken the decision early to live on the equivalent of state benefit. He would exist on the princely sum of forty-six pounds a week, and if he wanted any more he was going to have to find his own way to come up with it, same as anybody else sleeping on the street.

He took a step closer to the counter, remembering what Brendan had said about *De Niro shite*.

'The rolls aren't bad,' Spike said. 'Bacon could be crispier.'

'I just want tea.'

Thorne's instinct at that moment was to put his hand a little deeper into his pocket and offer to buy tea for Spike, too, but he stamped on the natural impulse to be generous. The idea was to fit in, and he knew damn well that, where he was, nobody would make that kind of gesture.

They reached the front of the queue and Spike stepped in front of him. 'I'll get the teas in.'

Thorne watched Spike hand over forty pence for two cups of tea and realised that there was precious little he could take for granted.

They walked over to a table, Thorne a step or two behind Spike, thinking, *He must want something*. Then, *Fuck, I'm doing it again*.

'You get much sleep?' Thorne asked.

Spike grinned. 'Haven't been to bed yet, like. Busy night. I'll crash for a couple of hours later on.'

'Where d'you bed down?'

Spike seemed distracted, nodding to himself. Thorne repeated the question.

'The subway under Marble Arch. I only come into the West End during the day, like, to make some money.' The grin again, spreading slowly. 'I commute.'

Thorne laughed, slurped at his tea.

'It's not bad this place,' Spike said. He leaned down low across the table and dropped his voice. Thorne could just make out the last gasp of an accent. Somewhere in the south-west he reckoned. 'There's not many centres around like this, where under twenty-fives and over twenty-fives can hang around together. Most of 'em are one or the other. They prefer it if we don't mix.'

Thorne shook his head. 'Why?'

'Stands to reason, when you think about it. The older ones've picked up every bad habit going, haven't they? You take somebody fresh on the streets. After a couple of weeks knocking about with someone who's been around a while, he'll be a pisshead or he'll be selling his arse or whatever.'

It made sense, Thorne thought, but only up to a point. 'Yeah, but look at us two. I've got twenty-odd years on you and you're the one that's been around.'

Spike laughed. Thorne listened to the breath rattling out of him and looked into the pinprick of light at the centre of his shrunken pupils, and thought:

You're the one that's picked up the bad habit . . .

Thorne had seen it the previous night: the glow from a

70

streetlamp catching a sheen of sweat across Spike's forehead, heightening the waxy pallor of his skin. This morning, it was obvious that he'd not long got his fix. Thorne knew that without it he'd have no chance of getting any sleep.

'Can you not get a hostel place?'

'Not really bothered at the moment. When I wake up covered in frost, like, I'll be well up for it, no question, but I'm all right where I am just now. Been in plenty of hostels, but I'm not really cut out for 'em. I'm too ... chaotic, and that's a technical term. "Chaotic". I'm fine for a few days or a week, and then I fuck up, and end up back on the street, so ...'

Spike's speech had slowed dramatically, and his gaze had become fixed on a spot above Thorne and to the right of him. Slowly, he lowered his head and turned, and it was as though the eyes followed reluctantly, a second later. 'I think ... it's bedtime,' he said.

Thorne shrugged. A junkie's hours.

Spike slid his chair slowly away from the table, though he showed no sign of getting up from it. On the other side of the room voices were raised briefly, but by the time Thorne looked across, whatever had kicked off seemed to have died down again.

'Maybe see you back here lunchtime.'

'Maybe,' Thorne said.

'Had enough yet?' Brendan Maxwell asked.

Thorne ignored the sarcasm. 'Tell me about Spike,' he said.

As soon as the breakfast rush had started to die down, Thorne had wandered out. Holland had told him earlier that Phil Hendricks would be coming in, and Thorne was keen to see him. He'd headed surreptitiously towards the offices. The admin area was on the far side of the top floor, and Maxwell had given him the four-digit staff code to get through each of the doors. There were coded locks on every door in the place.

With the open-plan arrangement of offices offering little privacy, Thorne, Maxwell and Hendricks had gathered in a small meeting room at the back of the building. If anyone wandered in, it would look like a case-worker–client conference of some sort, but Thorne wasn't planning to hang around very long, anyway. It was just a quick catch-up.

Maxwell was perched on the edge of a table next to Hendricks. 'He's not quite twenty-five, so Spike's not one of mine yet, but I couldn't tell you anything even if he was.'

Hendricks looked sideways at his boyfriend. To Thorne, it seemed like a look that was asking Maxwell to lighten up a little. To bend the rules.

'Come on, Phil,' Maxwell said. 'You know how it works.' He turned back to Thorne. 'Look, I had a long chat with your boss about this. There are major confidentiality issues that have to be considered.'

'Fair enough,' Thorne said. Brigstocke had made the position very clear to him. Unless he had good reason to think it would directly aid the investigation, Thorne would be given no personal information about other rough sleepers.

'It's just the way we do things. I've had Samaritans on the phone trying to trace someone on behalf of parents. People who just want to know if their kid's alive or dead. The person they're looking for might be downstairs drinking tea, but I can't say anything. I can't tell them because maybe they're the reason why the kid's on the street in the first place, you know?'

'Just talk to this kid if you're interested,' Hendricks said.

Maxwell nodded his agreement, leaned gently against his partner. 'Spike's not shy, I can tell you that much. You'll get his life story if he's in the mood to tell you.'

For a few moments nobody said anything. Hendricks and Maxwell were usually a demonstrative couple physically, but Thorne sensed that, at that moment, Hendricks was a little uncomfortable with Maxwell's arm resting on his shoulder.

There had been periods in the past when the relationship between the three of them had become somewhat complex. Thorne thought that Maxwell could, on occasion, be jealous of the platonic relationship he shared with Hendricks. At other times, after a beer or three, Thorne was not beyond wondering if it were he himself who was the jealous one. Right that minute, he was too tired to think much about anything at all. He took a moment. He knew that if he was going to last the course, this was a level of tiredness he was going to have to get used to pretty bloody quickly.

'So, what's happening?' he asked Hendricks. Having spoken to Holland, he was practically up to speed, but

Hendricks' take on things, as the civilian member of the team, was always worth getting. 'Anything I should know?'

Hendricks looked thoughtful, then began listing the headlines. 'Brigstocke's talking to a profiler. They're re-canvassing the area where Paddy Hayes was attacked. Everyone's waiting around for the next body to show up, to be honest. Oh, and Spurs lost three–one at Aston Villa last night.'

'Cheers . . . '

There was a knock and a man stepped smartly into the room. He was somewhere in his late forties with neatly combed brown hair and glasses. He wore jeans that were a fraction too tight and a blue blazer over a checked shirt.

The man took in the scene quickly, then addressed himself to Maxwell. 'Sorry, Brendan. Can I have a word when you've got a minute?'

Maxwell pushed himself away from the table, but before he could say anything the man was already on his way out.

'Bollocks,' Maxwell muttered.

Hendricks leaned towards Thorne, spoke in a theatrical whisper. 'Brendan's new boss.'

Maxwell looked none too pleased. 'He's not my boss. He's just the arsehole who controls our budget.' He walked to the door, stopped and turned back to Thorne. 'I was wrong about it taking a couple of weeks, by the way. You look pretty rough already.'

Thorne watched him leave. There'd been a smile on Maxwell's face, but it hadn't taken all the edge off the comment.

'Don't worry about it.' Hendricks rubbed his palm rapidly back and forth across his shaved head. 'He's just in a shitty mood because he isn't getting on with . . . ' He pointed at the door.

Thorne nodded. 'The arsehole. He sounded pretty posh.'

'Horribly posh. There's a big consortium running all the outreach stuff now, and they want people with more of a business background. Brendan and a few of the others can't even fill in a claim form for their expenses, so this bloke's been shaking things up. There's a bit of tension.' Hendricks was clearly struck by something hugely funny. 'It's like Brendan's you, and this new bloke's Trevor Jesmond.'

Thorne scowled. 'Then Brendan has my deepest sympathy.'

'Actually, this new bloke's not *quite* as bad as Jesmond.'

'That would be going some . . . '

'Stupid bugger had some high-powered banking job before this. Jetting all round the world for multinationals, oil companies, whatever, and he chucks it all in. Takes a massive pay cut to come and work for the care services.'

'Bloody do-gooder.'

'Mind you, you could be a *paperboy* and you'd still be taking a pay-cut . . . '

Thorne stretched, yawned noisily. 'I'd better get back out there. I'm sure you must have things that need cutting up.'

'I'll find something.'

'Brendan told me you think I'm mad,' Thorne said.

'Only moderately.'

'I didn't see what else we could do. Still don't.'

Hendricks opened the door. 'I'm not worried about the *investigation* ... '

They both turned at the sound of rain blowing against the window, exchanged the comically world-weary look of a practised double act.

'Brendan really doesn't approve of this,' Thorne said. The silence told him that this was something Hendricks didn't need to be told; that this was an issue he and Brendan had probably argued about. 'Listen, I know how seriously Brendan takes his job, and I know that all he cares about is getting his clients off the streets. So tell him this when you two kiss and make up later on ... '

'Before or after?'

'I'm serious, Phil. Remind him why we're doing this again, will you? Tell him that there's someone else out there who wants to get rough sleepers off the street, and this fucker's got his own way of doing it ... '

By lunchtime, the London Lift's café area was busy again. The tables had been pushed closer together and some-where between thirty and forty people sat eating, or queuing for food at the counter.

Thorne carried a plate of stew across to a table and got stuck in.

Around him were a few faces he recognised. He exchanged nods with one or two people he'd run into during the course of the day so far: an old man he'd walked the length of the Strand with; a Glaswegian with a woolly Chelsea hat and no teeth; a scowling, stick-thin Welshman who'd become aggressive when he'd thought Thorne was stealing his begging pitch, and had then turned scarily affectionate once Thorne had explained that he was doing no such thing. On the opposite side of the room, Thorne saw Spike, sitting with his back to him with his arm around the shoulders of an equally skinny girl.

Again, it was quieter than it might have been. By far the loudest noise came from a big, white-haired man at the other end of the table from Thorne. The man beamed and frowned – pushing a spoon distractedly through his food – far more intent on the two-way conversation he was having with himself on an invisible radio. Every half a minute or so he would hiss, imitating the sound of static, before delivering his message. Then, a few seconds later, he would move his hand, switch the 'radio' to the other ear, and give himself an answer.

'This is London calling the President,' he said.

Spike went to the counter to collect his pudding. On the way back to his table he saw Thorne and shouted a hello. Thorne briefly waved a spoon, then carried on eating. The stew was thick with pearl barley and the gravy was tasteless, but at £1.25 for two courses, he had little cause for complaint.

Once he'd finished eating, Spike walked over, hand in hand with the girl, to where Thorne was sitting.

'This is Caroline,' he said. 'Caz.'

'Nice to meet you. I'm Tom . . .'

The girl had red-rimmed eyes and hair like sticky strands of dark toffee. She wore a faded rugby shirt under a zip-up top, and nervously spun multi-coloured beads and thin leather bracelets around her wrists.

'Spike and me are engaged,' she said.

Spike and his girlfriend sat and talked to Thorne while he finished his lunch. They told him about the time when they were asleep and they'd been sprayed with graffiti, and how another time they'd been pissed on by a gang of teenage boys. About how Caroline had once been propositioned by a woman off the telly and told her to go and fuck herself. About the flat they were planning to move into together once they had a bit of luck.

'It's well fucking overdue, you know?'

'I do know,' Thorne said.

Spike did most of the talking. Thorne figured that this was about as close to normal as the boy ever got: a few hours of balance, of *numbness* between being wasted and needy. It was a window of opportunity that Thorne knew would get smaller and smaller as time went on.

'Everyone deserves a bit of luck, don't they?'

When Caroline did speak, it was in a low mumble. Her voice had the flat vowels and slightly nasal tone of the West Midlands, but Thorne could hear a stronger influence.

Smack had an accent of its own.

There was a sudden, loud hiss from the other end of the table. The big man was receiving another message. Thorne stared at his red face and fat, flapping hands.

'That's Radio Bob,' Spike said. He leaned in and shouted, 'Oi, Bob. Say hello, you cunt ...'

A pair of small dark eyes blinked and swivelled and settled on Thorne. 'Houston, we have a problem,' Radio Bob said.

Spike sniffed and pointed to a man sitting on an adjacent table. 'And that's Moony,' he said. 'He knew Paddy as well.'

'Did he?'

Spike shouted, beckoned over a skinny character with a sparse, gingery beard. His straw-coloured thatch hid the clumps of dandruff far better than the vast lapels of his dirty brown sports jacket.

'This is Tom,' Spike said.

Moony fiddled with the top of what looked like the plastic Coke bottle he had jammed into his pocket. Cooking-sherry was Thorne's best guess. It was certainly a long time since the bottle had seen anything as benign as Coca-Cola.

'Give me a minute or two,' Moony said, sitting. The voice was high and light; effete, even. 'Just one minute, and I'll tell you what you do. I'll tell you what you *did*, I should really say. In your previous life. I'm never wrong, never. I've got a knack for it ...'

Thorne spooned stew into his mouth, grunted a marginal interest.

Spike hauled Caroline to her feet and moved towards the counter. 'I'm going to get some tea.' He screwed up his face, put on a posh voice and brayed. 'Perhaps a crumpet, if they have such a thing.'

Moony watched them go, expressionless, stroking the neck of his bottle.

Thorne wondered if Moony was a surname or a nick-name, but knew better than to ask. If the latter, then its origin was not obvious. Haggard and pockmarked, he certainly didn't have a moonface. Maybe he was partial to showing people his arse when he'd had a few too many. If so, a sighting might well be on the cards, judging by the state of him. By the stink of him.

'You knew this poor bastard that was half kicked to death, then?' Thorne spoke without looking up from his dish. 'Haynes, was it?'

'Hayes, right. Paddy Hayes. I knew Paddy well enough, certainly. On a life-support machine, according to the television, but we all know that means "vegetable", don't we?'

'Right.' Thorne had spoken to Holland about Paddy Hayes first thing that morning. There was no change. None was expected.

'Not that he can think anything now, of course, but if he could, I wonder if he'd still think that everything happened for a reason. I wonder if he'd still be on good terms with Him upstairs. I wonder if he'd be all *forgiving*.' He scoffed, pointed a finger heavenwards. 'Mysterious ways, my arse.'

Thorne folded a slice of tacky white bread in half and began to mop up the last of his stew.

'I knew the second victim too, you know.'

Raymond Mannion. Found fourteen days after the first

victim. Killed three streets away. Thorne looked up, but just for a second, doing his best not to appear overly interested.

'Ray and I talked a great deal,' Moony said. 'A great deal.'

Thorne pushed a dollop of soggy bread into his mouth and wondered who it was that Moony reminded him of. He realised that it was Steve Norman, the press officer: Moony had that same self-importance that Norman had been full of when he'd introduced Thorne to his friend from Sky. He was enjoying himself.

'What did you talk about?' Thorne asked.

'When you've got as much time to talk as *we* had, you tend to cover the entire spectrum. He was drug-fucked, so there were occasions when he couldn't string a sentence together, but we discussed most things at one time or another.'

'Did you talk to him on the night he was killed?'

'*Hours* before he was killed, mate. Just hours before.'

'Christ.'

Moony lowered his voice. 'Which is how I know he was scared.'

'Scared of what?'

'Like I said, he was a junkie, so I thought it was just that at first, you know? Then I could see that something had really put the wind up him. Or some*one* had . . . '

There was certainly an element of grandstanding to the way Moony was telling it, but Thorne thought he could smell truth as well as bullshit.

'He'd said something before about someone asking him

questions. It was just after that first bloke was killed he told me this, the one they can't identify.'

'Did you know *him*?'

Moony shook his head.

'So who was asking your friend these questions, then?'

A flash of gold in his mouth, and a snigger that carried the smell of booze right across the table. 'Well, this is the thing, isn't it? Ray reckoned it was a copper, reckoned that he was looking for the bloke that turned up stiff a couple of days later.'

Thorne let a look that said *I'm impressed* pass slowly across his face, while his mind raced. Mannion was a druggie. What he told Moony, if he told him anything at all, could easily have been down to a dose of everyday delusional paranoia. But what if this wasn't a story cooked up in a dirty spoon? Was it at least possible that Raymond Mannion was terrified because he knew something, because he'd seen something? Did he think that someone he'd spoken to had kicked one rough sleeper to death and might fancy coming back for him?

'So this is what he tells me,' Moony said. 'And every time I run into him after that, he looks like he can't decide whether to leg it or shit himself and, lo and behold, suddenly it's Ray who's the one with his brains kicked all over the shop and a twenty-quid note pinned to his fucking chest.' He leaned back, pleased with himself. 'You've got to admit, it's bloody strange.'

Thorne grunted. He did think it was strange, but he was already thinking about something else, something

Moony had just said. There was only one thing it could possibly mean . . .

He became aware of Moony talking again and looked up. 'What?'

'She's pretty fit,' Moony said. He nodded across to where Spike and his girlfriend were talking to one of the care-workers. The three of them were laughing, drinking tea. '*Her*. One-Day Caroline.'

Thorne's mind was still in several places at once, but one part of it was curious enough. 'Why d'you call her that?'

Moony looked pleased with himself again, like this was something else he was going to relish passing on. 'Because she's always bleating on about how she's going to get herself clean "*one day*". Then, when she tries to give up, *one day* is usually as long as she lasts . . .'

Thorne looked over, watched Caroline absently trailing her fingers down Spike's arm as she listened to the care-worker, nodding intently.

He pushed his chair away from the table. 'So, come on then,' he said. 'You've had more than a couple of minutes. What did I do before this?'

Moony looked suddenly serious, as if he were getting in touch with something significant, something profound, deep down in his pickled innards. 'It's business, definitely business,' he said. 'Some sort of financial thing. Accountancy or stocks and shares. I reckon you were loaded and then you lost the fucking lot. I'm right, aren't I? I'm never fucking wrong.'

'Bang on, mate.' Thorne raised his hands. 'You are

absolutely bang on. That's seriously spooky.' He stood and walked away, leaving Moony nodding slowly, gently patting the bottle in his pocket as though it were his pet. Or his muse.

Out near the reception desk, Thorne all but bumped straight into the man who'd walked in when he'd been talking to Maxwell and Hendricks that morning. Maxwell's new boss . . .

'Oh, hi, I'm Lawrence Healey.'

The tone was not one Thorne had been on the receiving end of for a few days. It was brisk but friendly; respectful, even. Healey proffered a hand and Thorne shook it, wondering for just a second or two if the man knew he was really a police officer.

'Brendan tells me you're new.'

'New-ish,' Thorne said.

'Well, I know how you feel. I'm a new boy myself. If there's anything you need, anything you want to talk about, you mustn't be shy about it. Yes? You know where we are . . .'

Thorne said that he did, and that he certainly wouldn't be.

As he moved towards the exit he could still make out the hiss and blather of Radio Bob's broadcasts, coming from the café, on the other side of the door behind him.

'Are you receiving me? Are you receiving me . . . ?'

EIGHT

London stank of desperation.

This time of night, of course, it smelled of all sorts of things: fags and fast food; piss and petrol. Still, in spite of all the money that was clearly being spent – the wealth on display in the rows of Mercs, Jags and Beamers, and in the ranks of overpriced restaurants – you could catch the whiff of desperation almost everywhere. Pungent and unmistakable. Classless and clinging, and far stronger than anything being rubbed on to wrists, or rolled across armpits, or sprayed over shoppers by those grotesquely made-up hags in Harrods and Selfridges.

Where he was walking, the desperation was of the common or garden variety. A need for warmth, food or a fix. A need for comfort. But some of the rarer blends of that distinctive scent were around as well, drifting through the West End, there if you could nose them out beneath the everyday stink of chicken and vomit and beer.

From Oxford Street and Tottenham Court Road, it floated south – the stale desperation for a smarter phone and a younger partner mingling with those more basic, bodily needs, reeking in Soho and the Circus – before moving along Piccadilly, where the drive to be better dressed, better off and better *than* gave off the sharpest stench of all. It was a world away from the gutters and the shitty cut-throughs, of course – from the alleyways that were presently his own area of operation – but he knew that the desperation was of an even headier kind in Old Bond Street and the Burlington Arcade . . .

It was already clear to him that things had changed since he'd killed the Driver. Walking around within that rough square bordered by Oxford Street, Regent Street, Shaftesbury Avenue and Charing Cross Road, he'd noticed that more of them were settling down in pairs. Looking out for each other: one asleep and the other keeping at least one eye open.

It was understandable. More than that, it was commendable.

Word would probably have spread faster than head lice anyway after the Driver had been killed. After the second one, for certain. But now the television and the newspapers were all banging on about the danger to what they'd all taken to calling the city's 'most vulnerable citizens'. It was tricky to see it clearly in a community as shifting – as *tidal*, they said – as this one was, but panic was starting to set in.

Now, *that* was another smell he knew far better than most people.

He also knew very well that panic wouldn't save anyone. Panic was what you saw in the eyes of dead men and what stained the floor beneath them.

Moving past Charing Cross Station for the second time that evening and on towards Waterloo Bridge, he peered up every likely-looking side street and into every pool of shadow, humming a song from the mid-eighties. Something about panic on the streets of London. He couldn't remember who the song was by.

It wasn't as if he was going to have any problem finding someone alone and fucked-up and begging for a good kicking. The very nature of these people would work against them in the end. If they were cut out to stick together, to bond with others, you'd hardly see them curling up in puddles and sleeping in their own shit, would you?

Singling one of them out would be easy enough.

They were the leavings; the ones who had failed at everything and would ultimately fuck up at the most basic task of staying alive. Failure was their strong suit, and, at the end of the day, helping one more of them do what they were obviously good at wasn't going to cost him a great deal of sleep.

How could you take someone's life when they didn't really have one in the first place?

*

Moony was two bottles dead to the world, but he still woke up the second the boot was placed across his neck.

'Jesus!'

The sole was wiped slowly across a cheek, then lifted. 'I thought it was your mate Paddy who was the religious one.'

As Moony turned to look up, Thorne bent and grabbed hold of the conveniently wide lapels. He dragged him fast across the narrow street, leaving sheets of cardboard and blankets trailing in his wake. Moony yelped like a throttled dog.

'Hey!' A figure took two tentative steps towards them from the end of the street.

'Fuck off,' Thorne said, and the figure did as he'd been told.

Thorne slammed Moony into a wall plastered with posters for boy bands and nightclubs, pushed him hard on to his arse and squatted down close to him.

'Oh my Christ,' Moony said, breathless.

'There you go again,' Thorne said. 'Strange how people turn to Him when they think their number's up.' He pressed a palm against Moony's heart. 'That's going ten to the dozen, that is.'

'What do you ...' – three gulps of air – '... fucking expect?'

'You thought I was the man who killed Ray, didn't you? The man who kicked Paddy's brains into the middle of next week.' Thorne took a handful of the loose flesh around Moony's chest and dug in his fingers. 'You thought you were about to get some dosh pinned on to you, right?'

Moony squealed and grabbed at Thorne's fist but Thorne calmly raised his other hand and slapped him twice, a little harder than he might have slapped someone who was unconscious. Moony's hands flew to his face and he stopped struggling.

'Only it's the money that's bothering me,' Thorne said. 'Well, not the money itself so much as the fact that you knew about it. Do you see what I'm saying?'

Moony shook his head.

'There's been nothing on the news about any money being pinned to the victims' chests. Nothing in the papers either, as far as I can remember.'

'I don't understand . . . '

'My guess is it's one of those things they're keeping back, you know? They do that sometimes, the police. They keep certain facts out of the press so they can weed out the cranks and the copycats.'

'I must have read about it somewhere.'

'No. You didn't. Not unless it was written on the side of a beer can. There are only two reasons why you'd know about money being pinned to the chests of the victims, and as I don't think you're the murderer . . . You're *not*, are you?'

Moony was starting to snivel.

'I thought not. Which means that you must be the kind of snot-gobbling tosspot that steals money from the body of a dying man.'

'No ...'

Thorne grabbed an ear, and twisted. 'Tell me.'

'I thought Paddy was just pissed, that's all.' Moony spluttered out his confession between sniffs and yelps. 'I didn't know he was hurt.'

'You lying little turd. There was blood everywhere.' Thorne knew that now he was revealing a knowledge of the facts few would be privy to, but he also knew that Moony was too far gone, and too terrified, to take it in or realise its significance.

'I didn't know he was that bad ...'

'You didn't *care* how bad he was. You just wanted the money.'

'I needed it ...'

'Did you take anything else?'

Moony tried to turn away but Thorne yanked on his ear again, turned his face back around. 'There was a watch.'

Long since sold, Thorne knew, and the money – a fraction of whatever the watch might have been worth – spent on cider or sweet sherry.

'Taking the money and the watch is bad enough,' Thorne said. 'The fact that you robbed a man who was supposed to be your friend, whose life was bleeding away into the gutter, makes me sick, but it doesn't surprise me. What I *really* can't understand is why you didn't call the police. Why you didn't tell anybody ...'

'I told you, I didn't think he was—'

Thorne could feel the cartilage buckle beneath his

fingers as he closed his fist hard around Moony's ear. 'If you tell me that again, I'll rip this off.'

Moony gurgled his understanding.

'See, I'm guessing that if you'd called an ambulance, if they could have got to Paddy a little earlier than they did, he might not be hooked up to a machine right now. I'm not a doctor or anything, but there's got to be a chance.'

'No ...'

'No, you're probably right. Chances are he was already brain dead by the time you started going through his pockets. But you couldn't possibly have known that, could you? You just thought he was ... what, exactly? Moderately badly injured? Serious but hopefully not critical? So you took what you wanted and left him there to die because, basically, at the end of the day, you didn't give a fuck. Simple as that.'

The recognisable rumble of a diesel engine grew louder as a black cab drove slowly past the end of the street and stopped. Thorne heard a door slam, the exchange of voices before the cab moved off again.

'Leave me alone,' Moony said.

'I will, but what if I was to hurt you first?'

'Please ...'

'What if I was to injure you in some way? I don't know what exactly, something serious but hopefully not critical.' Thorne watched Moony's eyelids flutter and close. He caught the sudden, sharp smell of urine that drifted up from his crotch. 'If I was to do that and then leave you alone, do you think anyone would help *you*? What d'you reckon?' Thorne leaned in close to Moony's face. 'Would anyone give a fuck?'

Because the average rough sleeper wasn't usually to be seen blathering into a state-of-the-art mobile phone, Thorne had been finding discreet locations from which to check in with Holland. Tonight, he couldn't be bothered, and besides, the phone was small enough to fit easily into his palm. So, sitting in his theatre doorway with it pressed close to his ear, he figured he looked no stranger than Radio Bob, muttering happily into an invisible handset . . .

'So Hayes was definitely a victim of the same killer,' Holland said. 'If he had the money on him.'

Thorne swallowed a mouthful of lager. 'Looks that way,' he said.

'More than "looks", I would have thought.'

'Whatever . . . '

'We've got two murders, *three*, if you count Paddy Hayes, and I think we can—'

'I'm not arguing.'

'You've still got a problem with the whole serial-killer angle, though?'

'Look, Raymond Mannion was terrified. I've got a witness.'

'Of course he was scared—'

'Not in the general way you mean, because there was a killer around. He was scared of *someone*. I think he was killed because of what he knew or what he'd seen.'

'It's a leap.'

'Which means that the killing of the first victim takes on a greater significance. Don't you think?'

'Maybe . . .'

'Come on, Dave. While everyone's looking for all the usual perverse, serial-killer motives, it's worth considering that there might just be something a bit more basic going on here.'

'That's just it, though. Everyone here *is* looking for the perverse serial-killer motives. That's our major line of inquiry at the moment.'

'Right.'

'Well, it has to be until we've got something better to go on, doesn't it?'

'So what's Brigstocke's profiler come up with?'

'Not a lot at the moment.'

'What? Not even the "white, male, started fires as a child and tortured small furry animals" cobblers?'

'What do you want us to do about Moony?'

'Nick him.'

'For what?'

'I don't care. Being a reprehensible shitbag. Think of something . . .'

'It'll be hard to make a theft charge stick when all we've got is what he told you. There's no material evidence. How *did* you get him to tell you, by the way, or don't I want to know that?'

'Look, there's always a chance Moony might sober up and start asking awkward questions, so let's just get him off the street. Give him a nice, warm cell and a bottle of Strongbow and he won't complain.'

'Fair enough . . . '

They chatted for another few minutes, but Thorne spent most of the conversation thinking about what Holland had just said. About the question he'd asked, only half-jokingly.

Don't I want to know that . . . ?

As the last major case Thorne had been working on before his leave had moved towards its resolution, he'd been involved in things, he'd *done* things, far worse than slapping a few answers out of someone.

Holland talked and Thorne talked back, but he was thinking about the smell of flesh beneath the weight of a hot steam-iron. Thinking about what Jesmond had said about wearing a hair shirt. Thinking about how good the beer tasted . . .

He woke violently, knowing for certain that he was being watched.

The room he'd been standing in began to go fuzzy around the edges and then to disappear. Of the men in there, one had been his father; near enough, but not quite as he'd been before the Alzheimer's. There'd been no violent mood swings, no inappropriate language. Instead, there'd been only a priceless look on his old man's face: a bemused half smile at knowing that he'd said something funny without having the first idea why. So the three of them – his father, his father's friend Victor and Thorne himself – had begun to laugh, until the laughter had become all that mattered. So that even the first, delicate wisps of smoke creeping underneath the door had seemed completely hysterical.

Thorne sat bolt upright, breathing heavily.

His tongue was thick and vile against the roof of his mouth. He couldn't tell New York from New Year, let alone the difference between concern and contempt on the faces of the young couple staring at him. So he shouted at them, calling them cunts and telling them to fuck off, before dropping back hard against the door behind him and then down.

For a while, he stared out at the street through a curtain of drizzle. Then, he closed his eyes. Hoping there might be some way back into that room filled with laughter and smoke.

NINE

For Robert Asker, it had begun with the simple, over-powering conviction that there were people living beneath the shower tray ...

He'd heard them, their voices muffled at first by the rush of the water and then a little clearer, but still indistinct, once he'd turned off the shower. He'd stood stock-still and dripping wet above the plughole and stared down. He'd seen the faintest orange glow, a light of some sort, way down in the pipes. He knew what it meant: they had to be living in the pipework, which meant that they could travel quickly and talk to him from almost anywhere in the house.

It wasn't long before they were using the network of major drains and sewer pipes to follow him when he was outside, when he was away from home. Then he began to hear the voices at work and in his car. It was like several voices at once, each cancelling out the others so that he could only make out one word in ten and could never really get the gist of what they were saying. What they were trying to tell him.

Of course, it *really* began when he told his wife about the voices. That's when he lost control of everything. It all began to fall apart from that moment onwards …

It wasn't long after he told her, that he got laid off. From then on it was hard to know whether her attitude stemmed from anger at his getting himself sacked or frustration at his ramblings, at his insistence on what he was hearing. Either way, he was damn sure that she was withdrawing from him and that she was taking his daughter with her. He noticed that she was keeping the girl with her more and more, that she would always take her along, even if she was popping out for just a few minutes.

She was afraid for their daughter to be left alone in the house with a madman.

He wasn't sleeping. They spoke loudest of all at night, and he paced the house with his hands over his ears and with the music turned up so loud that people several houses away would phone the police at regular intervals.

She made him talk to people, to half a dozen different doctors, but nothing they gave him made any difference, except for making him moody, which meant that he started to shout. He shouted because he was sick of not being listened to and he shouted to make himself heard above the constant chatter of the voices. Once he'd started shouting, it was only a matter of time before she left.

It all happened quickly enough. Job, wife, child, house ...

There was hospital for a while after that, several of them, but the drugs only made him unresponsive, almost catatonic, and the voices were still there, growing in number and urgency. Barracking as he plummeted towards the tender mercies of the community. Towards the net he was destined to slip through.

It wasn't until he was on the street that he discovered the radio. Left to himself he found out how to tune in the voices to make their messages clearer. He also learned how to turn down the volume of the voices when he needed a break, and most importantly of all, he found out how *he* could talk to *them*. He never actually turned the radio off; he couldn't do it, even if he'd wanted to. The best he could manage was to tune it out for a few minutes at a time, but he was loath to do that in case he missed those transmissions he was always hoping to hear: the message offering him his job back; the message from his wife saying that she understood now, and that she was coming back; a message from his daughter ...

Robert moved slowly past the design stores and clothes shops on Long Acre. Listening, then talking. Laughing every now and then.

He felt all right now, despite everything. It was shitty and he got ill with his guts, and with leg ulcers sometimes, but he was on the air. Radio Bob was as happy as he'd been at any time since he'd first seen that small circle of light, liquid and winking in the belly of a waste pipe.

'There are three basic types of begging,' Spike said. 'There's a couple of other odd ones, there's the specialised varieties, like, but at the end of the day you've got your three main types. I'm not talking about getting cash – there's loads of ways to do that. I'm talking about just *asking* people for it, right?

'There's your simple hungry-and-homeless style, which is what I do most often, which is what we're doing now. It's the best if you're a bit out of it 'cause you can just nod off sat there, and people will still chuck a few coins down if you look pathetic enough. That's the pity approach, like.

'Then there's the hassle approach, which involves a bit more spiel. You can chase after people on the street, which they're trying to clamp down on 'cause it's antisocial or what have you. Or you can do what Caroline does sometimes, which is to blag a tube ticket and wander through the carriages making a bit of a speech and holding a cup out. You're appealing to the punter's better nature with that one, or else they might just give you the cash to make you fuck off, but either way that can be a good earner.

'Or you can just go for the straight-up, in-your-face way of doing things. None of this "I need some money to get into a shelter" or "Please help me get a hot meal" or shit like that. You just look someone in the eye and ask them for a bit of change because the truth is that you're fucking gagging for a can of Special Brew. Some people prefer that . . . '

Thorne thought about it and decided that, as the person being asked to hand over the cash, it was definitely *his* favourite approach. Like most people, though, his normal reaction, however he was being asked for money, was to look away and mutter nonsense, or pretend that he hadn't heard. He'd certainly ignored his fair share of beggars on the tube.

'Right, thanks,' Thorne said. 'I'll bear all that in mind.'

They were sitting against the wall just inside the entrance to Tottenham Court Road tube station. The sign scrawled on a strip of cardboard in front of them said, 'PLEASE HELP' and the small plastic bowl in front of that contained a handful of coins. One-, two- and five-pence pieces.

'Tell me about some of these other ways,' Thorne said. 'Loads of ways to get cash, you said . . . '

Spike leaned his head back. A poster for a new Brad Pitt movie was backlit behind him. 'Yeah, well, there's a few. Busking, *Big Issue*, whatever . . . '

Busking was out of the question, but Thorne had wondered about selling the *Big Issue*. He wasn't sure how many of those who made money selling the magazine slept rough.

'Don't you have to register or something to do that? Get a badge?'

Spike shook his head and leaned forward. He straightened the cardboard sign that was already sodden around the edges. It was chucking it down outside and the floor around them was becoming increasingly wet as rush-hour travellers brought the rain in on their way down from the street to the ticket hall.

'Look, there's selling the *Big Issue* and selling the *Big Issue*, like. Some people just get hold of one copy and sell it over and over again. You tell people it's your last one and most punters won't have the heart to take it. It's a good scam.'

'I might give that a go.' Thorne looked up at a young, black woman coming down the steps towards them. She looked quickly away and stayed close to the far wall as she moved past them and on down the next set of stairs.

'Or there's poncing used travelcards and selling them on. I used to do a fair bit of that. That's a good one an' all, but they're starting to clamp down a bit.'

'Right . . .'

'Oh, shit.'

Thorne followed Spike's gaze and watched a dumpy, dark-haired man walking down the steps in their direction. He was dressed in a grey hooded top and black combats, but it was the way he *wore* the clothes more than anything that identified him as a copper quicker than any warrant card could have done.

'All right, Spike?' the man asked.

'I *was*.'

'Be fair.' The police officer held out his hands. 'There's two of you, so you're actually causing an obstruction. Someone could get hurt.'

'Whatever,' Spike said.

'Where's your girlfriend today?'

Spike ignored the question. He pointed down the corridor towards the platforms, from where the less-than-melodic sound of voice and guitar had been echoing for the previous hour or more. 'Why don't you do something useful and go and hassle the arsehole who's murdering "Wonderwall" at the bottom of the escalators?'

'I'll see what I can do.' He turned, looked down, squatted on his haunches next to Thorne. 'I'm Sergeant Dan Britton from the Homeless Unit at Charing Cross. You're new, yeah?'

There was no sign of any ID being produced. Maybe this was one of those coppers who didn't think that everyone merited an official introduction. This and the counsellor-meets-children's-TV-presenter voice were not facets of a winning personality, but it didn't really matter. In that utterly irrational yet completely straightforward way that Thorne had – that he was convinced most people had if they were honest – he'd marked Britton down as a tosser before he'd so much as opened his mouth.

'New-ish,' Thorne said.

'Well, if you have any problems, just come down to the station and ask for someone from the Homeless Unit.'

Thorne remembered what Lawrence Healey had said to him. There seemed to be no shortage of people offering their help.

'Can you do anything about the price of heroin?' Spike said. 'It's fucking extortionate . . .'

Britton ignored him, carried on talking to Thorne. 'Any problems, yeah?'

'Right,' Thorne said.

Staring at the floor in front of him, Spike raised a hand, slowly, like a sullen schoolboy with a question. 'Actually, there *is* something that's a bit of a bloody nuisance . . .'

Thorne could hear the mischief in Spike's drawl, but Britton took the bait.

'What?'

'It's this bloke. He appears to be going round killing people like me and I was wondering, you know, if you might be able to help with that. Sorry to be a bother, like . . .'

Britton made a poor job of hiding what, to Thorne, looked a lot like embarrassment. He stood up and gave Spike's outstretched leg a nudge with his scuffed training shoe. 'Come on then, off you go. It's getting busy down here and people'll be tripping over you.'

Spike climbed slowly to his feet and Thorne did the same.

'Don't worry,' Thorne said. 'For some reason, people are careful to keep as far away from us as they can.'

They'd taken half an hour or so, wandering slowly along a darkening Oxford Street, saying very little. They'd seen a couple of familiar faces, waved at Radio Bob talking animatedly to himself outside a sandwich bar. They were loitering just inside the entrance to Borders when Spike suddenly began talking as if the earlier conversation had never ended. As if no time had passed at all.

'Begging's getting bloody tricky now . . .'

Thorne had seen the same thing with his father when the Alzheimer's had begun to take hold. He knew that naturally occurring chemicals could be every bit as potent as the ones that people stole, and killed, and sold themselves for.

'Is it?'

'If you just sit there with your hand out, you get moved on, and if you're too pushy, you run the risk of getting an ASBO, like.'

Thorne knew what Spike was talking about. The Anti-Social Behaviour Act, launched in a blaze of Blairite glory, was supposed to curb the activities of nuisance neighbours, of tearaway teenagers and of others who blighted the lives of the majority living in the inner cities. Overly aggressive begging certainly came within the remit of the legislation, but it had become clear pretty quickly that certain councils were using their own interpretation of 'aggressive' in an effort to eradicate beggars of any description. Westminster Council, in particular, was chucking Anti-Social Behaviour Orders around like they were parking tickets – making a sustained effort to criminalise begging, the consumption of alcohol on the street, and any other activity liable to offend. God forbid they should upset those honest, upright citizens who might be

104

confronted by such indecent behaviour on their way home to beat their children and drink themselves into a stupor indoors ...

'Plus, there's the asylum seekers,' Spike said. 'A lot of them use their kids, or borrow other people's, and if punters are going to give their change to beggars, like as not they'll give it to them. So, you know, you need a bit of extra dosh, you have to be clever. You have to get a bit naughty now and again.'

'*Naughty?*'

'Yeah, naughty. Now, I mean, there's degrees of naughtiness, like ...'

Thorne nodded. He'd seen just about every sort.

'Some of the ones with a real bad habit can get a bit desperate, you know? There was this one bloke used to put on a crash helmet and run into the chemist's with a claw hammer. I seen him one time running out carrying the dangerous-drugs cabinet on his back. Lugging this dirty great metal box up the fucking street. Another mate of mine used to go into shops just before they closed and hide, like. Then, after they shut up he'd rob the place, then break *out*.'

'Breaking and exiting ...'

Spike cackled, enjoying Thorne's joke, repeating it a couple of times. 'I'm just talking about a bit of nicking, yeah? A spot of light shoplifting. Marks & Spencer is the best. You used to be able to nick stuff, take it back and they'd give you the money for it. These days they just give you vouchers, but you can sell them easily enough. Say you sell twenty quid's worth of vouchers to some punter for fifteen? You're sorted, and they get an extra fiver's worth of pants and socks, right? Caz is ace at all that stuff . . . '

Thorne was fairly sure he'd need to supplement his forty-six pounds a week somehow, but wasn't convinced that shoplifting was the best way to do it. It wasn't any sort of ethical problem: minor offences would be countenanced as part of his undercover role. It was more about avoiding the hassle of getting caught. He hadn't nicked anything since he was thirteen or fourteen, and that had been a short-lived shoplifting career. He could still remember the look on his old man's face after he'd been marched back from the local branch of WH Smith by a beat bobby.

'You all right?' Spike asked.

'I'm fine.'

He could still remember the look . . .

'I got done for nicking an Elton John album from Smith's when I was a kid.' Thorne hadn't intended to say anything at all, but once it had started coming out of his mouth he felt good sharing the memory. 'They didn't actually prosecute me in the end, but it put the shits up me, I can tell you. My dad went fucking mental.'

'Did he belt you?'

'No, my mum did.' Thorne remembered his mum's largely unsuccessful efforts to instil a bit of discipline. She'd used her hand on the back of his leg, or sometimes a spiky blue hairbrush, but her heart had never really been in it. 'The look on my dad's face was far worse, though.'

'Were you scared of him?'

Thorne was about to make some crack about his father being afraid of *him*, but stopped himself. He thought about how, towards the end, his father had spent most of his time afraid. Thorne hated the idea that this might be the way he remembered him.

'Fucking hell,' Spike said. '*Elton John?*'

Thorne stared blankly back at the security guard who was eyeing them from a corner. 'He was better then . . .'

They stepped back out on to the street and stood for a minute, unsure exactly what to do next. Suddenly Spike raised his arm and pointed back in the direction they'd come. 'My sister works there.' He flapped his hand towards Tottenham Court Road and beyond. 'In the City. Working with stocks and bonds or something. She's got a posh flat in Docklands.'

Thorne was surprised, more at what Spike had said than the fact that he was following Thorne's lead, and talking about his family. Thorne had clearly been wrong in assuming that people who lived like Spike couldn't possibly have any close relatives near by.

'Do you see her?'

'I've seen her a couple of times since I started living on the street. Both times she got a bit upset.' He began to step from foot to foot, rocking, as Thorne had seen him do on the night he'd first met him. 'I've not seen her for a while, like.'

Thorne wanted to know more, but before he could say anything Spike began moving away quickly.

'Let's have something to eat . . .'

Thorne hadn't eaten for eight hours. He hurried to catch up.

Spike pointed ahead again. 'There's a McDonald's back up here on the right. Shall we go mad?'

'I knew there was more to this place than just somewhere to have a shit.' Thorne shoved the last of the cheeseburger into his mouth and chewed enthusiastically. The food tasted fantastic.

Spike was on his third Crunchie Macflurry. Chocolate and ice-cream. Standard smackhead fare.

'The H-Plan diet,' Spike said, grinning. The ice-cream coated his teeth, making them far whiter than they were normally.

'What about that copper Britton, then?' Thorne asked. 'What's he like?'

'He's all right.'

'*All right?*'

'Yeah, well, he's about the same as the rest of 'em, isn't he? None of that lot down Charing Cross can make their minds up what bloody side they're on, like.' Spike was talking faster, running one word into the next. His face was suddenly grey and Thorne could see the goose pimples standing out across the backs of his hands. 'Can't decide if they're there to help us or sweep us off the street.'

'Where is Caroline, anyway?' Thorne asked.

Spike grunted. '*What?*'

'That copper was asking, wasn't he? I haven't seen her all day. You two fallen out?'

'She had to go and meet her case-worker. He keeps trying to encourage her to get a hostel place, but she's even less keen on 'em than I am.'

'She's "chaotic" too, right?'

'Not really. She's just got a problem with institutions. Spent a lot of time in care when she was a kid and stuff. In homes. It was things that happened to her in institutions that put her on the street in the first place, d'you know what I mean?'

Thorne thought that he probably did.

There were few women visible among the community of rough sleepers. So far, Thorne had seen no more than a handful. He'd asked Brendan Maxwell about it, who had explained how a great number of women ended up among the vast population of the city's 'hidden' homeless.

Spike used language that was a little more basic.

'See, a lot of girls *can* get a bed for the night, but they have to share it with some fat, sweaty cunt whose wife doesn't understand him. Selling their arses, them and a few young boys, right? That's what these case-workers are worried about. Don't have to worry about Caroline, though. She'd rather starve.'

'It's not food that's the problem though, is it?' Thorne said.

Spike took another mouthful of ice-cream, and was off on another tangent. He and Thorne began to speculate on just how shitty you'd have to look to be refused entry to various London restaurants. Dressed as they were now, Spike decided that there'd be little or no problem in any KFC or Pizza Hut. Thorne thought they'd have no chance whatsoever of making it past the doormen at The Ivy or Quaglino's, but still had a fair way to go yet before they were considered too shitty to be allowed into a Garfunkel's.

'McDonald's is a one-off, though,' Spike said. 'I reckon you could order a burger in here stark-bollock naked with your underpants on your head and a turd in each hand and they'd still ask you if you wanted fries with it.'

It was genuinely funny, but even as Thorne laughed he was watching Spike press his hands hard into the sides of his face. The boy pushed the skin back towards his ears. He pinched up pieces of sweaty skin and tugged at them, as if the flesh on his face no longer fitted.

Bob knew the image of himself that came across.

He was well aware what others thought, but it didn't really bother him. In fact, he played up to it, muttering a bit more than he otherwise would, putting on a bit of a show by giving them all that 'Come in, come in, this is Radio Bob calling the mother ship' rubbish. He'd seen a film set in a prison once, and while everyone else was getting brutalised, they tended to leave the loonies alone. Most people were a little bit scared of them. So he let them all think it was harmless and that he was communicating with aliens, or receiving transmissions from God, or whatever.

Nobody could even begin to guess at what he actually heard. They couldn't possibly know that the voices rising above the constant hiss in his head had real things to say: news and rumours and secret theories; politics, history and religion spoken of in strong accents and strange languages. Profound, frightening things that would cause him to giggle or weep, or fill his pants where he stood.

He never passed on any of this information, of course. If he did, everyone would *know* he was a nutcase.

He was just drifting off when the man appeared above him. Losing himself in the soporific hiss, with only the faintest of voices breaking in occasionally from far away, the words no more than a distant rhythm.

If the man spoke to him before he struck, Bob didn't hear anything.

When it began, the shadow like a bludgeon, it was as if he could feel each part of it in isolation: the laces and the metal eyelets tearing the skin around his mouth and nose; the flesh of lips and nose flattening; the force that drove his head back against the wall shattering bones on both sides of his skull.

Then, finally, those messages he had waited so long to hear began to come through.

Something had been booted loose or realigned and suddenly the wave of pain became a frequency he had never received before. He couldn't make out all of his wife's words, but the tone of her voice told him everything he needed to know. The lilt of sorrow was unmistakable.

He tried to shut out everything else – *every other*

sound – and listen harder. The voices were still so familiar. There was something wet in his ear, something warm
and sticky on his handset. His daughter's voice was
deeper than he remembered, and that made sense
because she would be older now. As it began to break up,
only one word in three, and then in five, was clear, but it
was more than enough. It had faded away, though,
before he could try to answer. Before he could send out
any message of his own.

Then, it was only the swing of his attacker's leg.
Imagined, as he'd already ceased being able to see anything
at all. The swing and the stamp and the desperate breath
kicked out of him.

Aware, in those final few seconds before everything
went dark. Aware, for the first time in as long as he could
remember, that no one was talking to him.

TEN

The fat café owner had managed an even more miserable expression when he'd sloped across to deliver Holland's change.

Holland watched him walk back and begin stabbing at the buttons on his till. 'What are your plans for today?'

'No plans,' Thorne said. 'I'll just carry on drifting around, see who I run into.'

'So, much like you'd be doing if you were in the office, then?'

'The lack of any formal structure to the day is quite appealing, as a matter of fact. If it wasn't for the cold, and the hunger, and the fact that you haven't actually got anywhere to sleep, this homeless lark wouldn't be too bad.'

'Some people'll do anything to avoid paperwork.'

'That's definitely a bonus.'

'When this is all over, you *will* have to write up a report,' Holland said. 'You do know that, don't you?'

Thorne's arm snaked across the plastic tablecloth and he tipped the change from the plate into his hand.

Holland watched him pocket the cash. 'That's cheating. It'd take you a couple of hours' begging to make that.'

'I'm only doing it to piss him off.' Thorne nodded towards the proprietor. 'You think that's bad?' he said. 'He'll have a face like a smacked arse when he doesn't get a fucking tip ...'

Outside, they stood on the pavement and stared across at a newsagent's on the other side of the road. A blown-up front page from *The Sun* was stuck in the front window: HOMELESS MURDERS: THE FACE OF THE FIRST VICTIM.

'He's the key to this, you know?' Thorne said.

'Let's hope there *is* a key.'

'Well, it won't be found by any profiler. I'm telling you, it's all about the first victim. The killer was looking for him.'

'Speculation, based on highly unreliable hearsay.'

'Unreliable or not, it also suggests that the second victim wasn't selected randomly, either. Mannion was killed because he'd seen something, because he knew something.'

They moved a couple of steps apart to let a woman in a smart business suit through and into the café behind them.

'Look, it's understandable,' Holland said. 'I see why you're fixing on the unidentified victim—'

'I'm not *fixing*—'

'But three more people have been killed since then. Raymond Mannion, Paddy Hayes, Robert Asker. I know you don't want to hear this, but whoever's responsible *is* a serial killer, whether you like it or not. By definition, if nothing else.'

'There *is* nothing else,' Thorne said.

'There's the money he leaves on the bodies. Like it's all he thinks the victims are worth. It's a signature.'

'If I was Ross Kemp and this was a two-part thriller on ITV, then maybe I'd agree with you. Come on, Dave, we've both been after people like this before and you know bloody well that the only signature most of them ever leave is a body. This is somebody saying, "Look at me! I'm a serial killer."' Holland went to say something himself, but Thorne cut across him. 'Yes, I know, he *is*.'

'Even if you're right and the first victim *was* killed for a specific reason, that's not what it's about now, is it?' Holland got no response, pressed on. 'Say he killed Mannion to cover up, and Hayes to make it look like something random. What about Asker, and whoever's next? He's obviously started to enjoy himself now, hasn't he?'

'Maybe . . .'

They looked over at the picture in the newsagent's window; at the face staring back at them from across the road. This was a face that had been generated by a computer, and yet it had something of the same expression Thorne had seen many times already in the previous couple of weeks. The post-mortem had confirmed that this man was not a drug addict, and yet there was the same look

Thorne had seen on Spike's face, and on Caroline's, and on a handful of others. It was a look that was difficult to describe. That he could best place at a tipping point, somewhere directly between terrified and dangerous. Thorne knew he was projecting, yet he was sure he saw something around the mouth, and in the eyes, of course, that demanded a reckoning. Or perhaps it was a plea to be reckoned *with* . . .

'Where are you sleeping tonight?' Holland asked.

'Don't know yet.' Thorne had spent the last week moving around, bedding down in a series of different locations, but in terms of shelter and security, his original choice had certainly been the best. 'I might go back to the doorway at the theatre.'

'That's the closest you've been to culture for a while.'

'There's an Andrew Lloyd-Webber musical on. It's as close as I ever want to get . . . '

As he watched Thorne go, Holland had to remind himself that the scruffy figure walking slowly back towards the West End was, theoretically at any rate, still his boss. There'd never been a great deal of 'yes sir, no sir' flying about between them, except when Thorne was in a really bad mood. He was not normally the type to demand, or to dish out that type of deference. Even so, Holland was aware that over the last couple of weeks he'd begun speaking to Thorne differently and that it had nothing to do with his own recent promotion to sergeant.

It shamed him, but if Holland was being honest, his

attitude had far more to do with what Thorne had become, with the part he was playing, than with anything that might have happened to *him*.

He watched Thorne pull the dirty red rucksack up on to his shoulder before turning the corner. It had never been easy to read the man, but physically at least he was pretty bloody close to being unrecognisable. Holland knew that it had only been a fortnight, and that it was probably his imagination, but had he seen a stoop there, and something genuinely shambling in the gait?

It worried him more than a little, because Tom Thorne might well be sleeping in a theatre doorway, but he was no actor.

Peter Hayes sat on the train back to Carlisle, thinking of little but how desperate he was to get home and to kiss his son. He decided that this was because he'd watched his father die a few hours earlier, having just turned off the machine that had been keeping him alive.

For the umpteenth time since he'd been given it, he smoothed down the pages of the handwritten letter and read. The words he'd scrawled in such an adolescent fury a dozen years before seemed rather clumsy now, their intention no more or less than to wound.

He looked up from the page and out of the window.

To wound. It was hard to imagine that they had done otherwise. So why the hell had the stupid, drunken fucker held on to the bloody thing?

You left us like a snake, like we were shit, so you could

crawl into a bottle and forget we were there at all. You fucking coward. Crawling, beery snake ...

He read the passage over again, each faded loop and slash of his handwriting like a decaying tooth to probe. Like a mouth-ulcer to gnaw at.

The buffet trolley was coming down the aisle towards him and he decided that he'd have tea, and perhaps a sandwich. He'd wait and see what they had.

He'd wait and see just how hard the questions would be to answer, and how many times he'd ask them of himself. Questions about his judgement back then. About whether he'd pushed his father away until there'd been nobody for the poor old bugger to turn to except God.

He put the letter away.

He ordered tea and a chicken sandwich. He watched the scenery change as the train carried him further north, and counted the minutes until he could hold his son again.

PART TWO

BLOOD AND PETROL

1991

There are two groups of men, four in each group.

The differences between the two groups are striking, though the greatest differences are not the most immediate.

Four men are sitting and four standing. The men on the floor are spaced out on the ground, each several feet from the next. Not within touching distance. They are all wearing drab, olive-coloured clothing, though they're not dressed identically: two have boots on their feet and two are wearing sandals; one has a hat but the other three are bare-headed. The black hair plastered to their skulls is all that can be seen of the men for the most part, until one of them raises his head and takes a bite from what looks like a chocolate bar. He chews mechanically.

The rain and the darkness make everything appear slightly blurred and hard to make out clearly.

In contrast to the first group, the men who are standing are dressed identically. Nothing of these men's faces can be seen beneath the goggles and the multi-coloured kerchiefs or *shamags* that cover their mouths. Two are standing together, one of them flicking through a sheaf of papers which flaps noisily in the wind. The other pair are placed like bookends: one at either end of the row of men on the floor.

Each is pointing a pistol.

The man who is holding the papers waves them in the air, and shouts something across to the men on the floor. It is hard to make out all the words above the noise of the rain: '. . . are keeping . . . Do you understand?'

The man on the floor who is chewing looks up at him, then back to the men who are sitting next to him. They all look up, their faces wet. Two of the others are also eating, but none of them says anything.

The rain is fat, and black. Sputtering and hissing as it drops on to heads and hands and bodies. The man with the papers shouts louder: 'We are keeping these. Do you understand?' And the man who is chewing nods quickly, twice.

Nothing else is said for a while, and some time passes, though it is impossible to say how much. It is suddenly raining more heavily, and the dark hair and the olive clothes of the men on the ground are slick with it.

The men who are standing use their sleeves to wipe the water from their guns.

The light is even poorer than before, but the dull circle

in the sky is most certainly the sun rather than the moon. It is dimmest, shittiest daytime, and now all the men with goggles are carrying pistols and pointing them.

It's virtually impossible to tell the four men who are standing apart from one another. Their faces are hidden, but even if they weren't, the light would make it hard to read their expressions clearly. Yet, despite all this, the difference between them and the group of men on the floor is suddenly blindingly obvious.

The men with guns are much more afraid.

ELEVEN

'That isn't Christopher.'

'Are you sure? It's understandable if you're not, what with the face being so—'

'No, I'm sorry. I'm sorry that I can't help you, I mean . . . But that's not him. That's not my brother's body . . . '

Susan Jago turned away as the sheet was lifted and placed back across the dead man's face. Even though Phil Hendricks tried to be as gentle as he could, the noise of the drawer clanging shut seemed to hang in the air, as awkward as the pause that followed it.

DI Yvonne Kitson put a hand on the woman's arm. 'Dr Hendricks will show you out,' she said. 'Phil . . . ?'

Hendricks led Jago to the door and through it. Unlike the heavy steel drawer that had been built to take the weight of the dead, the door closed behind them with a soft snick.

'Fuck,' Kitson said.

Holland groaned. 'She sounded so positive on the phone. And I thought we were in, you know, when she first saw his face.'

Jago's hand had flown to her mouth a second after the breath she'd sucked into it. She'd shaken her head and gasped, 'Oh, Christ.'

'That could just have been shock at seeing the body,' said Kitson. 'Or most likely relief.'

'I suppose.'

'It's a natural reaction.'

'It feels terrible, though, doesn't it?' Holland walked slowly over to the wall of steel drawers. 'Wanting it to be him so much. Is *that* a natural reaction?'

There had certainly been a mood of celebration when Jago had called two days before. She'd seen the picture in the papers and on the TV and was fairly positive that she could identify the man who'd been murdered two months earlier. She was confident that the first victim of the rough-sleeper killings was her missing elder brother. Brigstocke had said it sounded as much like a decent break as any he'd ever heard, and the case certainly needed it. The powers that be were thrilled. More than a pint or two had been downed in the Royal Oak that evening.

Holland stuck a thumb inside his sleeve, rubbed at a smear on the metal. 'Wanting the body to be her brother's. It feels selfish . . . '

Kitson shrugged and walked across to where her coat and handbag were hung in the corner of the mortuary suite. There was a small red sofa and a low table, a box of tissues on a pine shelf. 'It's going to feel a damn sight worse telling Russell Brigstocke that we didn't get a result. I'd as good as promised him a name.'

Having made pretty much the same promise, Holland would be the one to break the bad news to Tom Thorne. Kitson didn't know about Thorne working undercover. As far as Holland was aware, below the level of the DCI, he was the only person who *did* know.

He wondered why that was.

Maybe he'd been included because of what was perceived as some kind of special relationship between himself and Thorne. Maybe they just thought that dogsbody and go-between were his special areas of expertise ...

'I'm sure the DCI will take it in his stride. He must be getting used to disappointment by now.'

Kitson turned sharply. 'Sorry?'

'On this case, I mean.' Holland could see that Kitson was annoyed, that she'd misunderstood him somehow. He tried to back-pedal: 'It's been a bastard from the off, hasn't it?'

'I don't care what it *has* been. Christ, what sort of attitude is that?'

'I wasn't implying anything, Guv ... '

Kitson shoved her arm through the straps of her bag, lifted it up on to her shoulder. 'Sorry, Dave. I'm just cheesed off and a bit snappy.'

She walked towards the door and Holland followed.

'Is everything all right?' Even as he asked, he guessed it

was a pointless question. Kitson rarely revealed anything of her private life any more.

'My eldest got sent home from school yesterday for punching another kid. Some little toe-rag who was picking on his younger brother.' She looked at Holland, unable to keep the grin at bay. 'Of course, secretly I'm *hugely* proud of him ...'

Holland smiled and opened the door for her.

Kitson had really got herself back together of late. A couple of years earlier she'd been seen as very much the role model for high-achieving female officers: on the fastest of fast-tracks with job and family seemingly balanced perfectly. Then the news got out that her old man had caught her screwing a senior officer and had walked out, taking their three children with him. Though she'd got her kids back soon enough, everything else had unravelled very bloody quickly. It wasn't the affair itself as much as the fact that it had become common knowledge that made things so tough, but she'd eventually come through it.

She'd proved how bloody-minded she was, if nothing else.

In the last few months she'd started to return to her old self. Progress through the ranks would not be quite as mercurial from now on, but she didn't seem overly concerned. She'd even begun seeing someone new; someone who most certainly was not a copper. 'He wouldn't know the Criminal Justice Act from the hole in his arse,' she'd announced gleefully.

Thorne had raised his head wearily from a copy of *Police*. 'Neither would a lot of coppers ...'

It was odd, but Kitson's life had taken a turn for the better at around the same time that Thorne's had begun its free fall. Now, with Thorne not around, Kitson was more or less running the show day to day; reporting to Brigstocke, who, as nominal Senior Investigating Officer, was kept busy enough dealing with the press and the pressure from above.

Stepping out of the mortuary suite, Holland could see Hendricks and Jago on a bench at the other end of the narrow corridor. Jago was sobbing and shaking her head. Hendricks had his arm around her shoulder.

Holland and Kitson walked towards them, talking quietly to each other as they went.

'Like I said, relief.'

'If she's crying like that *now* ...'

Kitson looked sideways at him. 'She won't have any tears left if her brother ever *does* turn up dead.'

'I got the impression she's expecting him to.'

They arrived in front of the green plastic bench. Jago looked up at them. Managed to blurt out a broken 'sorry' between sobs.

'Don't be silly, Susan,' said Holland.

'I know you're desperate to get out of here,' Kitson said. 'I just wanted to be certain about a few things.' She gave Hendricks a look. He moved to the end of the bench and Kitson slid in next to Jago. 'The thing is, I don't quite understand why you thought the picture was your brother in the first place. I know it's not a real photo, but you sounded so certain when you called us.'

Jago took a few seconds, brought the crying under control. 'It does look like Chris ...' The accent was marked. 'Look' rhyming with 'spook'. She'd come down on the train that morning from Stoke-on-Trent.

She nodded back towards the mortuary suite. 'That poor sod probably *did* look a lot like Chris. It's hard to tell, you know? I haven't seen him in so long now that I've no idea what he might look like any more, if he's lost weight or grown a beard or whatever ...'

'I can see that, but even so ...'

'It's definitely not him, 'cause there's no scar.' She rubbed her right arm, just above the elbow. 'Chris caught his arm on some barbed wire, there, when he was a kid. Trying to get a ball back.'

'Right ...'

'And the tattoo was wrong. I was so sure it was the same, you know? Then, when I saw it, I could tell it was different. Maybe it was the position of it. It might have been a bit lower down Chris's arm than it was on ... that bloke.'

'How exactly was it different?'

Jago started crying again, snatching breaths between the sobs. She raised her eyes to the ceiling and chewed her bottom lip.

Holland looked down at her. He'd thought she was somewhere in her early thirties, but seeing her now he wondered if she might be younger. The mascara that was smeared all over her face made it difficult to tell one way or the other. She had very dark hair and extremely pale skin. Similar colouring to the dead man lying in a drawer along the corridor.

'How was the tattoo different?' Kitson asked again. 'Different letters? Colour? Was it laid out differently?'

Hendricks drew Jago a little closer, nodded his encouragement.

Between sobs: 'I don't . . . know.'

'You're certain it *is* different, though?'

'Yes . . . I think so.'

Kitson glanced up at Holland, raised an eyebrow. When she spoke again, her voice was still low and soothing, but Holland could hear the determination.

'Look, we know the man in the mortuary isn't Chris, which is great.' Holland caught Hendricks' eye and had to look away for a second, embarrassed by the lie. 'But I have to ask you if you recognised him at all. Had you ever seen him before?'

The shake of the head was as definite as it could be.

'I'm only asking you because of the tattoo. It's such a unique design. Do you understand, Susan? Why would someone have a tattoo so similar?'

Again she brought the crying under control, pressing a sodden tissue hard into both eyes.

'There was a time, years ago, when Chris and his mates all went out one night and got one. They got pissed up and got their tattoos at the same time. They got the same sort of thing done. I don't know why. I don't know what it means.'

Excitement flashed across Kitson's face. 'Chris and his mates? Is the man in the mortuary one of your brother's mates, do you think? Is that possible?'

Jago shook her head. 'I told you, no. I've never seen him before ...'

The excitement had gone by the time Kitson had stood up. She nodded to Holland. 'We'd better be getting back.' To Jago: 'Do you want us to arrange a cab for you?'

Hendricks moved his arm from her shoulder and took hold of her hand. 'Why don't I give you a lift?'

'Could you?'

'Yeah, no problem. I'll run you to Euston ...'

She looked up at Holland and Kitson. 'I'll have to sort out my ticket when I get there. I'm not sure what train I'm allowed to get, because I got an open return.' Her eyes were red beneath a film of tears, but Holland thought he could see real happiness in them for the first time. 'I thought it was Christopher, you see? I didn't think I'd be going straight back.'

Thorne raised his hands, backing away. Though he could make out precious little of what the man was saying, the words 'fuck', 'off' and 'bastard' were clear enough, so he picked up the gist of it.

'Calm down, pal,' Spike said.

The man hurled another torrent of incoherent abuse at them and wheeled away, just managing to avoid walking straight into the wall behind him.

Spike hawked into the gutter and picked up his pace.

'Fucking old tosser has a right go at me every time I walk past.'

Thorne caught him up. They were walking north up Greek Street, towards Soho Square. The two of them had hooked up in a greasy spoon for breakfast and been mooching around fairly aimlessly ever since. Now, it was raining and they were keen to get indoors; Spike had said he knew somewhere warm where they could get a cup of tea.

'Why?' Thorne said. 'What's he got against you, then?'

'He's a boozer, so he doesn't want anything to do with the likes of me, does he? With a junkie.'

It was a word Thorne was used to hearing spoken with distaste. Spike said it casually, as if it were just another word to describe himself, like 'blond'.

In a little under three weeks, Thorne had seen enough to know exactly what Spike was talking about. The homeless community had its divisions like any other; its imagined hierarchies. There were, by and large, three main groups: drug addicts, drinkers and those with mental-health problems. As might be expected, there were one or two who could claim membership of all three groups, but on the whole they stayed separate. And those with mental-health problems tended to keep themselves to themselves, so any antagonism festered mainly between the drinkers and the addicts.

'It's mad,' Thorne said. 'The boozers can't stand the junkies; the junkies hate the boozers; nobody much likes the nutters ...'

'And we all hate the asylum seekers!' Spike cackled, loving his own joke, flicking his fingers together like a young black man. 'It's a right old mix, though. I fucking love it, like. You've got your immigrants, you've got blokes who used to be in the army, you've got blokes who've been inside. There's all sorts on the street, mate. All sorts.'

Thorne wasn't going to argue.

They'd reached Oxford Street, where they waited for a gap in the traffic and started to cross. 'You're right, though, it *is* a bit mental that we don't all get on.' Spike spun round, pointed back towards where they'd had their altercation. 'Mind you, you saw what that boozer was like. They're a mad, smelly bunch of fuckers. No offence, like . . .'

'Eh?'

'See, that's another reason why the two of us wouldn't normally get on, apart from the age difference thing. A junkie and a boozer. You *are* a boozer, right?'

For as long as he could remember, people had liked to imagine that Thorne drank a lot more than was actually the case. It was something expected of people who did what he did, saw the things he'd seen. The truth was that he liked expensive wine and cheap beer, and though he and Phil Hendricks could put a few away in front of the football, he didn't have anything like a drink problem . . . not really.

Yes, he'd drunk a little more than normal of late for obvious reasons, and he *was* drinking on the street, but only because the undercover role demanded it. As it was, he'd taken to buying piss-weak lager and pouring it into empty cans of Tennent's Extra and Special Brew. No self-respecting alcoholic would be seen dead with a can of Carling or Sainsbury's own-brand first thing in the morning.

'I mean, it's not like you're *always* drinking,' Spike said. 'But I've smelled it on you.'

Thorne ran a hand through his hair and shook away the water. He winked at Spike. 'I like a drink ... '

They walked on past the Wheatsheaf and the Black Horse. Past the Marquess of Granby on Rathbone Street. This pub was a favourite of Thorne's, as it had once been of Dylan Thomas. The Welsh poet had been a regular visitor and enjoyed trying to provoke guardsmen, who had popped in to pick on, or pick up, homosexuals.

Spike suddenly cut left, and within a minute or two they were in one of the quiet side streets behind the Middlesex Hospital, where Paddy Hayes had finally died almost a week earlier.

'It's like it is in prison,' Thorne said. 'The way the groups don't get on. Everyone thinking they're better than everyone else. The white-collar brigade, the dodgy businessmen and the conmen think they should be kept separate from the "real" criminals. The honest-to-goodness armed robbers think they're better than the murderers. *Everyone* hates the sex-offenders ... '

Spike stepped ahead and turned round, talked to Thorne as he was half skipping backwards, away from him. He looked like an excited, adolescent boy. 'So, were you inside, then?'

In retrospect, it hadn't been the cleverest thing in the world he could have said, but Spike's presumption wouldn't do him any harm. He decided to just say nothing.

'Listen, I'm sorry,' Spike said. 'I didn't mean to pry, like, and you don't have to say nothing if you don't want to.'

He stopped suddenly, stood still for a second or two before heading up a narrow alleyway. Thorne followed.

It was the sort of crooked cut-through that London was riddled with; that hadn't changed in hundreds of years. The windowless buildings seemed to press in on either side, closer to each other at the top than they were at street level. The black bricks were greasy, and the floor was rutted and puddled.

A figure stepped into view at the other end of the alleyway and Thorne froze.

'S'all right,' Spike said. He walked towards the man who had clearly been waiting for him, while Thorne stayed where he was, and watched.

It happened quickly enough: hands emerging from pockets, taking, handing over and put swiftly back again.

While Thorne waited for Spike to finish his shopping, he thought about those different groups within the community of rough sleepers. The junkies, the drinkers, the nutcases. He realised that as far as the dead men who had been identified went, there was one from each group: Mannion was a drug user, Hayes was never seen without a bottle and Radio Bob had certainly had mental problems. Was this a coincidence? Or could it be part of the way the killer selected his victims?

Thanks to that woman who'd called to say the dead man might be her brother, they could well have a name for the first victim by now. Did he fit into this pattern at all? The post-mortem had not told them much. There'd certainly been no evidence of drug use or excessive drinking . . .

Thorne turned and walked slowly back towards the street. He wondered what *his* own internal organs, furred and fucked up as they probably were, might one day tell an eager pathologist. What they might have to say for themselves.

He remembered a slight judder; the squeak of the belt as his father's coffin had slid forward, a second before the organist had picked up her cue.

Stopping and leaning against a wall, he hoped that when the time came, his innards would be there undisturbed and intact. Melting nicely. Burning along with the rest of him, having said fuck-all of any consequence to anyone.

'Why did you never report your brother missing?' Hendricks asked.

'I just kept expecting him to pop up again. He always has done before.' Susan Jago had a red vinyl overnight bag on her knees. She twisted the handles around each other as she spoke. 'Chris has been doing this on and off for years. He'll go a bit funny and vanish off the face of the earth for a while, then come waltzing back like there's no problem.'

There were a variety of routes from Westminster Hospital to Euston Station, and Hendricks had mentally tossed a coin. He was driving along Victoria Street towards Parliament Square and from there he'd head north up Whitehall and keep going.

'Was he on any medication?'

'Blimey, he's been on everything at one time or another. You name it ... '

'Got a loyalty card at the chemist's, has he?'

She laughed and let her head drop back. 'He's a complete mess, Christopher is. Has been for ages.'

Hendricks steered the Ford Focus skilfully through the traffic, though the wet streets weren't making him slow down overmuch. He'd already apologised once when he'd jumped a light and the woman in the passenger seat had sucked in a noisy, nervous breath. Now, he raced to overtake a bus that was pulling out, and she did it again.

'Sorry ... '

'It's OK.'

'Just trying to get you there a bit quicker. If you miss the next one, you'll have a bit of a wait.'

'Like I said, no one's expecting me back. The kids are at a friend's.'

Despite the weather, Parliament Square was thick with people, and cars were taking an age to get around it. Hendricks had definitely chosen the tourist route.

'Did he never have a job?'

'He had all sorts of jobs, but they were all shit. Couldn't even hold on to *them*. He'd get into a fight at work or just stop turning up. Then he'd be off on one of his walk-abouts.' She shrugged, stared out of the window at the crowds under umbrellas outside Westminster Abbey.

'Was there any kind of trigger for Chris's illness? You said he'd been like it for ages . . . '

'I wouldn't call it an illness, exactly. He just gets depressed, you know?'

'It's an illness.'

'OK,' she said.

'I just wondered if there'd been a single event that might have sparked him off? A break-up with someone. A death in the family . . . '

'I don't think so.'

'Nothing you can think of?'

'All of them things happen to everybody, don't they?'

'Yes, but we all have a different brain chemistry.'

'He's always had mates and girlfriends and all that, and a lot of the time he's as happy as anyone is, but for ages now he's just been liable to go off on one. I don't know why. I don't know what causes it. I just want to find him and keep a better eye on him this time. I want to get him some help.'

She was starting to get worked up again, and Hendricks could hear in her voice that tears weren't far away. He thought it was odd, considering how much she clearly cared for her brother, that she seemed to know so little about what was wrong with him. She was vague about the whats and the whens, but then denial tended to do that. He sensed that she blamed herself, that she somehow felt guilty for what had happened, for what *might* have happened, to her brother. He wished that there was something he could do to help her. He thought about the tattoo, about what Kitson had said back at the hospital. If Chris Jago *was* dead – and his sister had obviously thought that was possible – Hendricks thought there might be something he could do to help find him. But first he needed to go home, or back to his office at the hospital . . .

She was staring at him. 'Can I ask you, are you gay?' she said.

Hendricks was stunned at her directness. He took a second, then barked out a laugh. 'Yes, I am.' He was struck by a possibility. 'Was Chris?'

'God, no,' she said. 'I've got a mate at work who is, and you're a lot like him. It doesn't bother me, though.'

They drove on, making small talk until the traffic began to thin out at the top end of the Tottenham Court Road. Hendricks checked the clock on the dash. 'It'll be close, but I think we'll make it,' he said.

Next to him, Susan Jago clutched the handles of her bag a little bit tighter.

Chloe Holland took half a dozen unsteady steps towards her father, and banged her head against the top of his leg. 'Dada . . .'

Holland picked up his daughter and carried her over to the sofa in the corner of the living room.

'Come on then, chicken. A quick cuddle before bed ... '

His girlfriend, Sophie Wagstaffe, stood in the doorway. 'Don't get her too excited, Dave.'

He thought about saying something about how *any* excitement round the place would be welcome, but he bit his tongue. Its absence was almost certainly down to him. Yes, they were both tired at the end of the day, and fractious, but he was also bringing the frustration of the case home with him. His mood flung a coarse, heavy blanket across everything. He couldn't blame Sophie for being thoroughly fed up.

The little girl pointed to her favourite video, lying on the carpet in front of the VCR. 'Arnee,' she said.

'Barney, yes. Good girl ... '

His daughter would be a year old in a couple of days.

Chloe had been conceived just in time to stop his relationship with Sophie from falling apart completely. Pregnancy changed the emphasis of everything. The stupid affair he'd had became a weapon that was wielded only rarely, and most of the conversations that took place in raised voices became about the Job. Did he not think that perhaps now he should find something a bit safer? Something that paid a bit more, maybe, before he became completely institutionalised?

Once Chloe had been around for a while, once they'd got over the heart-stopping, joyous shellshock of it, they discussed their future again, though now nobody had the energy to do a lot of shouting. Or to do a lot of anything else. The flat they'd shared for years in Elephant and

Castle was far too small, no question, so they talked about moving; about getting out of London altogether. They'd decided that Holland should sit the sergeant's exam, but the increase in pay had been more than cancelled out by a greater caseload. With Sophie back teaching again, and childcare to be paid for, they were no better off. Any move in the short term was out of the question.

'Come on, Dave.'

'All right . . .'

'I need to change her and get her down.'

'Just give me a minute . . .'

The tiredness never seemed to ease up. Just as Chloe had started to sleep that bit longer, he'd been required to do longer tours of duty. His new seniority, together with the seriousness of this particular case, meant that sixteen- and eighteen-hour shifts were becoming increasingly common. He wanted nothing more at that moment than to hug his baby girl tight to his chest, close his eyes and stay where he was until the morning.

'Dave, please.'

That was what was really going on, he thought, when couples stayed together because of the children. The truth was that they were just too exhausted to leave.

It wasn't that bad, of course. He knew that actually he could count himself lucky that Sophie hadn't walked out on *him*. It was amazing that she hadn't packed a bag and done a bunk with someone. Some teacher maybe, same as Tom Thorne's missus. Creative-writing lecturer that had been, years back. Jesus . . .

Holland opened his eyes as he felt Chloe being lifted from him.

'Right, OK then. I need to make a call anyway.'

He watched as Sophie gathered stuff up: the necessary books and an armful of soft toys. He waved his daughter goodnight as Sophie carried her through into the bedroom. If only they could get away, he thought. Just the two of them. Leave the baby with grandparents, then head off somewhere to laze around and fuck each other's brains out in the sunshine. He'd see what he could manage when the case had cooled down a little.

Holland crossed to the door and pushed it shut. He took out his mobile, scrolled through for the number and dialled. He needed peace and quiet to make this call, but he also needed the privacy. He couldn't tell Sophie anything about Thorne working undercover.

Though she'd only met him a couple of times, Sophie had never been a fan of Tom Thorne. She'd decided early on that his would be a bad influence on Holland and had tried, without much success, to make as much obvious to Holland himself. She was not, though, the type to kick anyone too hard when they were down, and had hardly mentioned Thorne's name since she'd heard about the death of his father, and the problems he'd had since. As far as she knew, Thorne had been taken off the squad and given something a little less taxing to do.

Holland waited for an answer, smiling at a memory of Sophie badgering him one night when he'd been cooking dinner. It had been just before the second part of his

sergeant's exam, when candidates were faced with hypo-
thetical problems to solve. 'Let the bugger *really* help you
for a change,' she'd said. 'If you get stuck, just think about
what Tom Thorne would do, then make sure you do the
exact opposite ... '

'Sir?'

There was a grunt at the other end of the line.

'Can you talk?'

Another grunt, but definitely in the affirmative.

Holland told Thorne about Susan Jago having failed to
identify the body of the first victim. The reaction had been
predictably blunt and blasphemous. Holland guessed that
if Thorne, wherever he was, was being watched at that
moment by passers-by, his pissed-up dosser act would be
highly convincing.

Thorne began to sound a little more upbeat as he spoke
about a possible pattern to the killings. He was talking
about the different groups of rough sleepers, and a possibility that the killer was carefully selecting victims from
among each one.

Holland reached for a pen and a scrap of paper. He
began to scribble it down.

'Are you getting this down?' Thorne said.

He'd write it out properly later, pass as full a version as
possible on to Brigstocke in the morning. For now he
jotted down the bare essentials: 'Killer's basis for choosing.
Junkie/Alcoholic/Mental Case ... '

From next door he could hear Sophie softly singing the
'I Love You' song from *Barney*.

TWELVE

Thorne remembered what Brendan had said about real London grime as he watched it darkening the water. Running to his shins in inky trails and spinning away down the waste in a grey-black gurgle. A knock on the door told him that somebody else was waiting, so he tried to get a move on. It wasn't easy. The flow from the shower head was little more than a trickle, and he had to slam his palm repeatedly into a steel button on the tiled wall to keep the water coming.

As he scrubbed himself, he sang an old Patsy Cline song, quietly enough to go unheard by whoever was outside the door. He didn't know what had put the tune into his head, but it was appropriate enough; he'd certainly been doing a fair amount of walking after midnight. Sometimes he thought that sitting and walking were virtually all that any rough sleeper did when they weren't actually sleeping. Come to think of it, weren't they all that anybody did? Sitting behind a desk or at a till or in a doorway. Walking to work or to the pub or to wherever you could get what you needed to help you through the next few hours. Everyone was sitting and walking and scoring something . . .

There was another knock, louder this time. Something was shouted through the door.

For a final few seconds he stood letting the warm water run across his face and thought about what he'd said to Holland the previous night. Maybe what looked like a pattern was in reality no more than simple chance. Was it likely that the killer would be selecting his victims so carefully when, as Thorne still believed, they were only there to cover up something rather more down to earth? It was perfectly possible, of course, that both theories were true. Even if the later victims *were* there purely as dressing, selecting them in this way would hardly take a great deal of time and effort. The junkies and the drinkers were easy enough to spot as they tended to hang out in their own groups, and you could hardly miss the likes of Radio Bob.

Things had been made nice and easy for him. All the killer had to do was wait, and watch for the people that the rest of the world avoided.

Brendan Maxwell came into the locker room as Thorne was changing back into his dirty clothes.

'Why don't you put clean ones on?' he said.

Thorne shoved a plastic bag containing soap and shampoo into the top of his locker. He turned to a mirror on the wall and stared at himself. 'I'm OK with these.'

'Everyone else uses the washing machines ...'

'These are fine.'

Maxwell moved so that Thorne could see him in the mirror. He stuck out his bottom lip, shrugged his shoulders and struck a pose. 'You talking to me? You talking to *me*?'

Thorne laughed, stepped right to obscure the Irishman's reflection. 'Fuck off.'

Though he'd been into the café at the London Lift a couple of times, this was the first time Thorne had seen Brendan Maxwell in over a week. The first time since Radio Bob Asker's funeral.

'How was it?' Thorne asked.

'Even grimmer than you'd expect. We took a few of Bob's mates up in a minibus, you know? A couple of the older guys he used to knock around with.' He began to gesture with his hands. 'So, it's us and all of them on the right and his ex-wife and kid plus a couple of cousins or whatever on the left.'

Thorne was thinking there were probably more people there than at the last funeral he'd attended ...

'It was fucking weird,' Maxwell said. 'Like you've got this poor old fella's two lives right there, one on either side of the church. No prizes for guessing which side was having the most fun, either. There was a bottle of something in a pocket or two, right, and all his mates were going on about what a laugh Bob had been, you know? How they should have been playing appropriate songs in the church like "Radio Ga-Ga", and how bloody funny Bob would have thought that was.'

He smiled wryly and Thorne reciprocated.

Maxwell's smile became a snort. 'That *would* have been funny, right?'

Thorne had wanted to have something meaningful played at his dad's funeral, but he hadn't been able to think of a particular song or piece of music. He'd never had a chance to ask. They'd settled for some dirge of a hymn that his father would have hated.

Maxwell leaned back against a locker. 'No chance of any laughter, though. No fucking way. No chance of any *joy*. Bob's ex-wife sat there like the whole thing was keeping her from something important like a manicure, and the daughter just cried and cried. All the way through.' He kicked his heel against the metal door behind him. 'They're burying Paddy Hayes day after tomorrow. I'm getting plenty of wear out of the black suit.'

'We're doing our best, Bren.'

Maxwell raised his eyebrows as if to ask exactly what constituted Thorne's or anybody else's best? Thorne was well aware that, although Maxwell was privy to his role within the investigation, he couldn't say too much about how it was progressing.

'We need to find out who the first bloke was,' he said. 'The first victim.'

Maxwell said nothing for ten, maybe fifteen, seconds,

then pushed himself away from the locker. 'Good luck with that. Because I want to put the fucking suit away for a while.' He put on the De Niro voice to lighten the mood a little: 'Do you know what I'm saying here?' He stopped at the door. 'Phil's coming in later, by the way, for the fortnightly surgery. I think he wants a word.'

'Fair enough.' Hendricks had been providing an ad hoc medical service to some of the Lift's clients for the last couple of years. Doling out bandages, plasters and, best of all, the odd prescription. He had some cracking stories about the absurd lengths people had gone to to get him to prescribe something. To get him to prescribe *anything* . . .

'He's got a bee in his bonnet about something or other,' Maxwell said.

'About the case?'

'God knows. He wouldn't tell me if it was.'

'Right.'

Thorne looked at him and wondered if that were true. He knew very well that where partners were concerned, the rules about not discussing certain aspects of a case *could* become distinctly bendable. When it came down to it, Thorne really didn't give a monkey's, but he reckoned he knew his friend pretty well: Phil Hendricks would sell state secrets for a blow job or a Thierry Henry hat-trick.

The morning briefing was becoming more like morning assembly all the time.

Brigstocke stopped in mid-sentence, waited for the

murmuring at the back of the room to die down. 'What's so fucking important?' he said.

'Sorry, sir. We were just talking about the horse.' The last word was more spluttered than spoken, and the rest of the room immediately broke up.

'Right.' Brigstocke sighed. 'Anyone *not* heard the horse story?'

A few hands were raised among the forty or so in the room. One or two blank faces.

The area car had, by all accounts, been called out in the early hours after reports of a horse running along the A1. Having caught the animal, the two officers were then faced with the problem of getting it anywhere, and hit on the bright idea of *towing* the horse. They wrapped a length of POLICE – DO NOT CROSS tape around the animal's neck and while one officer drove, his mate crouched in the open boot of the car and pulled the horse along. This worked fine for a while, with the car gradually speeding up and the horse cantering along quite nicely. *Unfortunately,* what they had fashioned was less of a tow-rope and more of a noose, so that without warning the horse had suddenly collapsed in a heap on the road and begun to shake dramatically. Certain that he'd killed it, the officer climbed out of the boot and walked over to the stricken beast, just in time for the horse to leap to its feet and charge through the nearest hedge, dragging the stunned copper behind him.

Brigstocke wound up by explaining that the officer concerned was recovering in Chase Farm Hospital, while the horse, who was still at large, had last been sighted galloping gaily along a B-road near the gloriously named Trotter's Bottom.

Then he finished his briefing.

'That sort of thing's good for morale,' Brigstocke said. 'Pretty welcome round here at the moment.'

Holland piped up. 'It can't hurt to remind ourselves every so often that it isn't all murder and mayhem.'

'Right, and you told it very well,' Kitson said.

Russell Brigstocke seemed pleased with the compliment as he walked around his desk and sat down in the chair behind. His office was one of three on a corridor that snaked alongside the large, open-plan Incident Room. Holland and DC Andy Stone were based in one of the other two; and, while the man she usually shared it with was on gardening leave, Yvonne Kitson was the sole ccupant of the third. These officers – together with office manager DS Samir Karim – had followed Brigstocke into his office. As the everyday core of Team 3, it was their practice to gather here after the formalities of the morning and catch up. To brainstorm and to bitch a little. It was off the record, and what was said was usually nearer the mark than much of the official briefing that preceded it.

'It's not . . . hugely exciting, is it?' Brigstocke said.

Holland and Stone were leaning against the wall near the door. Kitson and Karim had commandeered the available chairs.

Holland replied for all of them: 'We nearly got lucky with Susan Jago. We'll get lucky next time.'

'Right,' Kitson said. 'There's still plenty of calls coming in.'

'Plenty of 'em from fruitcakes.' Brigstocke straightened the picture of his wife and kids that sat on his desk in a scarred, metal frame. This sole attempt at personalising his office had made it far more attractive than most of the other airless, magnolia boxes that honeycombed Becke House. 'Why *do* these morons ring up?'

'I've got three officers on the phones full time,' Karim said.

Stone shrugged. 'It's got to be our best bet, though.'

Brigstocke was not one of them, but there were plenty of senior officers who spoke, who *thought*, only in clichés. As the case stood, they'd have been spoiled for choice. Every available drawing board had been located and gone back to. The book by which things were done was being pawed until its spine cracked. 'Our *only* bet,' Brigstocke said.

There'd been a flurry of activity in the days following Robert Asker's murder, but now, in reality, there was little to be done but donkey-work. The response to appeal posters, press updates and the continuing profile being appended to the picture of the first victim meant dozens of calls to be chased up daily. There were the obvious cranks to be eliminated; those who turned out to be cranks and were then eliminated; and those, like Susan Jago, who were genuine, but proved to be ultimately worthless. The team's dedicated Intelligence Unit, meanwhile, was sifting through endless hours of CCTV footage taken in and around the relevant area. Aside from the predictable brawls and drug deals, and the occasional bout of drunken coupling in a doorway, there was nothing much to merit pressing freeze-frame. It was hard when nobody really knew what they were looking for.

Suspicious behaviour in London's glittering West End? There was plenty of that. Dodgy-looking characters? More than you could shake a shitty stick at ...

What few officers were left had gone back out on to the streets, but with even less luck than before. If there was any information out there to be gathered, people were keeping it to themselves. The latest death had only led those who might still be at risk to close ranks even further.

There were tighter lips and still greater suspicion.

'Trevor Jesmond was less than thrilled with last night's *Standard*,' Brigstocke said.

Kitson groaned. 'It was silliness, Guv, that's all ... '

'It just got blown up,' Karim said.

Close enough to the same responses Brigstocke had heard when he'd raised the subject at the main briefing. But it was still embarrassing ...

The day before, an officer had been trying to question a group of older rough sleepers by the Embankment. When they'd become what he deemed to be over-aggressive, he'd panicked and handcuffed one of them to some railings. The old man's case-worker had contacted the team at Charing Cross, and although the mess had eventually been sorted out, some bright spark had called the *Evening Standard* and the old man had cheerfully recreated the incident for a photographer.

Russell Brigstocke had spent an hour on the phone the night before, having his ear chewed. He looked up at the four in front of him. 'This is not how we deal with this community. Especially not now.'

'It was a one-off,' Holland said. 'I know it looked bad . . .'

Brigstocke shook his head, unimpressed, and looked over at Kitson. 'Spread the word, will you, Yvonne? These people were vulnerable enough before some nutter started killing them. We're starting to look like fucking idiots.'

He leaned back in his chair, exhausted at a little after ten in the morning. Hendon and beyond were the colour of oatmeal outside his window.

Thorne had spent most of the morning begging. Sitting against a wall at the top end of Regent Street, with a blanket across his legs and his rucksack laid out in front to catch the coins. He'd picked a spot nice and close to a cashpoint, and while he wasn't expecting too many banknotes to come his way, people *did* already have their wallets out, so he'd done fairly well.

He had also turned down a fairly lucrative offer of work . . .

A man in Timberland boots and designer casuals had squatted down and asked if Thorne would be interested in making some real money. It was messy work, as it turned out, but certainly paid better than begging. All Thorne had to do was catch a tube up to Camden or Hampstead – a travelcard would be supplied – and spend a few hours going through the bins at the back of one or two big houses. Thorne could guess how it worked. He'd be paid a few quid an hour and then anything useful he dug up and handed over – credit-card slips, bank statements, whatever – would be sold on for a very healthy profit. You could get fifty notes for someone's credit-card details; passport documents and the like were worth even more. The homeless were perfect for the job, of course. They were smelly and shitty already, so why would they object to rooting through someone's garbage?

Thorne had told the man that he'd think about it and the man had given him the name of a pub where he could be contacted. Someone would certainly be making contact with him once Thorne had passed the details on ...

When a five-pound note fluttered down on to his rucksack, Thorne looked up and saw Hendricks looming above him.

'A cup of tea's bloody extortionate these days,' Hendricks said. 'And coffee's just ridiculous. You won't see a lot of change out of that if you go to Starbucks ...'

'I'll try not to.'

'So, how's it going?'

Hendricks squatted down next to him, much as the bin-man had done earlier. They spoke in low voices, but Thorne was relaxed enough. If any rough sleeper were to see them talking, it would not look out of the ordinary.

Most of them knew Hendricks from the surgery work he did at the Lift.

'If anyone comes by, I'll have to start examining you,' Hendricks said.

'Did you actually *want* something?'

'I just wanted to run this idea by you ... Well, I've done it anyway, but I wanted to let you know.'

'Is this the bee in your bonnet that Brendan was on about?'

Hendricks rolled his eyes. 'He's a wanker sometimes ...'

'Are you two not getting on?'

Hendricks was about to say something, but stopped himself. He took a moment and the irritation seemed to disappear. 'He's very down about what's happening, which is understandable. A lot of his clients are obviously upset, so things are tense all round.'

Thorne knew that Maxwell was right to be worried. For anyone left behind after a murder, life was changed, was blighted for ever. The others sleeping rough on the streets were the closest thing these murder victims had to friends and family. Even if the man responsible was caught, readjustment would not be easy. Maxwell and others like him would be the ones who had to deal with the fallout ...

'So, run it by me,' Thorne said.

'It's this tattoo thing. We know that the tattoo on the first victim isn't unique any more, right? Susan Jago thinks the one her brother's got is a *bit* different, but it's got to be fairly close to identical or she wouldn't have thought it was him. So we can look for it. We can try and find another one. I mean, all this is dependent on her brother being dead, so it might be a waste of time, but ... '

'Have you talked to Brigstocke about this?'

'It's probably a stupid idea. I was just thinking about how I could do something to help Susan Jago.'

Thorne pulled up his knees, hugged them to his chest. 'Let's hear it, then.'

'It's not complicated. I just went to a few websites. The Pathological Society of Great Britain, the Association of Clinical Pathologists, the Royal College of Pathologists ... '

'How many bloody pathologists *are* there?'

'I went on to the message boards and described the tattoo. Asked anyone who'd come across anything similar to get in touch. The RCP's got an online database which I can access because I'm a member, so I basically sent out a mass email to pretty much every pathologist in the country. If Chris Jago *is* dead, this might be a way to trace him. Like I said, probably a waste of time ... '

'Worth a try, though,' Thorne said.

'Actually, it wasn't a *complete* waste of time. I managed to sign up for a course on stem-cell differentiation and I applied for a credit card.'

'There you go, then.'

They looked up and watched as a gaggle of jabbering American teenagers hurried past in a frenzy of clean hair and perfect teeth. When the group had cleared, Thorne found himself staring across the pavement, exchanging blank looks with a man wearing a sandwich board. Thorne had earned enough in the morning to treat himself to the £4.95 all-you-can-eat Chinese buffet being advertised ...

'Why didn't you go home to have a shower?' Hendricks said.

'You and Brendan really *do* tell each other everything.'

'Seriously, though ...'

Thorne looked at him as if he were losing his mind. 'I'm supposed to be working undercover, Phil. I can hardly just pop home when I'm feeling a bit grubby.'

'That's crap. This is a transient community, you know it is. People come and go all the time. No one's keeping tabs on you, are they? Nobody's going to bat an eyelid if you disappear for an afternoon. You could jump on a tube and go home for a few hours. Recharge your batteries. You could watch a game and get a decent bloody *curry* if you felt like it.'

'I've got a job to do.'

'It's mental ...'

'Have you finished?' Thorne leaned forward, began to scoop up the coins from his flattened rucksack. A ten-pence piece fell to the pavement and rolled towards the man with the sandwich board. 'Haven't you got any bodies waiting for you?'

The young Trainee Detective Constable would have found conversation on just about *any* topic more interesting than the work he was supposed to be doing, but the salacious detail *was* coming thick and fast.

'I swear, I'm knackered, mate,' Stone said. 'She wants a

good seeing to every lunchtime. I've hardly got time to squeeze in a sandwich.'

Karim leered. 'What? She's kinky about *food* as well?'

Stone, Karim and Holland were gathered around an L-shaped arrangement of desks in the Incident Room. The TDC, whose name was Mackillop, sat at a computer, his mouth hanging slightly open.

'You can keep your eighteen-year-olds,' Stone said. 'This woman's divorced, in her forties ...'

Karim lifted his backside on to the desk, slapped out a complex rhythm on his thighs. 'Single and up for it.'

'She's fit, she knows what she's doing ...'

'She's *obviously* desperate,' Holland said.

Stone nodded, laughing. 'She's fucking *grateful*, is what she is. And she goes like a bat in a biscuit tin.'

The reaction from the other three was predictably noisy. The laughter began to die down quickly when Kitson was spotted coming across. Mackillop was tapping at his keyboard again by the time she arrived at the desk.

'What am I missing?' she said.

Stone didn't miss a beat. 'Not a lot, Guv. Just talking about that pair of plonkers with the horse ...'

'Right.' She didn't buy it for a minute.

Holland saw her flush slightly as she picked up a piece of paper from the desk and pretended to read it. He knew very well that Kitson had once been used to this. That the sudden descent of awkward silences on to groups of her colleagues had been an everyday occurrence for her. He

158

felt bad, but there was little he could do. She was one of the boys only up to a point, and even if they *were* happy to tell her what they'd been talking about, the lie had already made it impossible. What could he possibly say, anyway: 'It's OK, Guv, we were talking about Stoney's sex life, not yours?'

After a minute or two of stilted shop-talk, Kitson drifted away. Soon afterwards, Holland did the same.

The coffee machine had been on the blink for months now, and had been replaced by a cheap kettle, mugs from home and catering-sized packs of tea and coffee from the cash and carry. With Sam Karim in the office, only the foolish or the desperate brought in biscuits.

While Holland waited for the kettle to boil, he considered the way he reacted these days to the racy tales of Stone's love-life. He was generally hugely disapproving or insanely jealous; either way, his reaction was more extreme than it would have been before the baby. He'd decided that, although Andy Stone liked himself a little too much, he was basically all right. He could be flash and lazy and prone to getting only half the job done, but he was a lot better than some.

It was hard to work with someone for a while and then watch them promoted above you, but Holland had been impressed by the generosity of Stone's reaction when he'd made sergeant. Much to his own surprise, Holland had been hungry – at first, anyway – for the 'sirs' and the 'Guvs'. For the deference to rank. Though it didn't kick in properly until you made inspector, Holland made sure he got it where he could. But with Stone he was never really bothered one way or another. Perhaps it was similar to the working relationship he normally had with Tom Thorne: the lack of emphasis placed on seniority, which Holland hoped said something pretty decent about both of them . . .

'Make one for me, would you, Dave?'

He turned to see Brigstocke beside him. Everyone pulled rank when they wanted a cup of tea made.

Holland tossed a tea-bag into his own mug and another into one with 'World's Greatest Dad' emblazoned on the side.

'How was DI Thorne when you spoke to him last night?' Brigstocke asked. 'I know he must have been pissed off when you told him about Susan Jago.'

'*Very* pissed off.'

'Apart from that, though?'

'OK, I suppose . . .'

'I passed that stuff about the different groups on to Paul Cochrane, by the way.'

Holland nodded. Cochrane was the profiler Brigstocke had brought in via the National Crime Faculty. 'Good.'

'He was already taking it into account, in fact.'

'Right . . .' Holland unscrewed the top off the milk. He raised the plastic bottle to his nose and took a sniff.

'I should have had a coffee,' Brigstocke said. 'I'm half asleep.'

Holland poured hot water into the mugs, then the two

of them stood for a minute, prodding at their tea-bags with stained teaspoons.

'So, how d'you *really* think Thorne's getting on?'

Holland thought about it, but not for long. 'Not brilliantly,' he said.

They might have been talking about the case, about Thorne's undercover role. But neither of them was.

The lights from the South Bank lay as ragged blades of colour on the water, while the river breathed, black beneath them. Thorne stared out across the Thames from the wide, concrete platform above Temple Gardens. The place had once been popular with prostitutes, but was frequented these days by those with nothing worth selling. At the other end of the bench, Spike and Caroline sat cuddled up.

It was somewhere near midnight, and chilly.

Thorne cradled a beer: the 2 per cent stuff in a Special Brew can. Spike and Caroline were swigging from cans of Fanta. They were both in their early twenties, but when he glanced at them, Thorne thought they looked like they had barely made their teens. They hadn't spoken for a few minutes and suddenly Thorne became aware that Caroline was crying softly. Spike had put his head against hers, begun to murmur and shush.

When Thorne asked what was wrong, Caroline turned and demanded to know why anyone could be sick and cruel enough to hurt the likes of them. People who wouldn't, who *couldn't*, hurt anyone themselves. She spat, and wiped snot from her nose with her palm, and Spike explained to Thorne – as he'd done the day after they'd found the body – that she had been fond of Radio Bob. That he'd made her laugh and stuck up for her sometimes. Caroline kept asking why, and shouted for a time, while for Thorne, there was little to do but wait for it to stop.

Then, all he could tell her was that the man who was doing these things would be caught. That he would be stopped and punished. He said it slowly, then repeated it until he almost believed it himself.

Later, after Spike and Caroline had left, Thorne sat and finished his beer, and thought about what Phil Hendricks had said.

He knew bloody well that Hendricks had been as unconvinced by that 'work to do' crap as he had been himself. To the right and left of him, cars carried people out of the city centre across Waterloo and Blackfriars bridges. Thorne watched them go, wondering how long it would be before he could consider going home himself. Wondering how long before he no longer felt the dread, squatting in his belly.

Since the loss of his father, he'd increasingly begun to think of *home* as the house where he'd grown up: the big old place in Holloway where his parents had lived until his mum had died six years earlier. Suddenly, his own flat felt like no more than a space in which to store things. A furnished turning-circle he could change in before heading out of the door as someone else. A locker room with Ikea furniture.

Maybe, when this was all over, he should move.

Now there was some money . . .

Down below him a large pleasure boat yawed and creaked against Temple Pier. Thorne watched a group of people in suits and evening gowns leave, stepping off the boat and moving carefully along the walkway. A necklace of bulbs had been strung between the grey funnels of the boat. When Thorne closed his eyes it swung and shifted; bright for a moment behind his lids, as the beads of light had been against the darkness of the river, before starting to fade.

1991

It's dark still, like the smoke from burning rubber, and now there are only three men sitting on the floor.

The fourth is standing between two of the men with guns and goggles. While one points a pistol, the other drags back the dark-haired man's arms and walks around behind him. He takes out a length of clear, thin plastic and ties the man at the wrists. While this is going on the three men on the floor, whose wrists are already bound, look up and watch. One of them spits and shouts something, and the two other men with guns appear on either side of him. A pistol is jammed, hard, against the man's head, and one of the men wearing goggles and kerchiefs leans down to say something. Then he steps back, raises a boot to the seated man's chest and pushes. The man topples backwards on to the sand, which is saturated now, and solid.

All the men, sitting and standing, are soaked through. The men with goggles raise gloved hands to clear their lenses, while those who are tied can do little but shake their heads like wet dogs.

The dark-haired man, who was last to be tied, is pushed down on to his knees by the two men. A gun is put to the back of his head and he closes his eyes. Nobody moves for a long time until the men who have the guns start to laugh and the barrel of the pistol is raised. The man on his knees slumps towards the floor, moaning, but is hauled back up again. He is kicked between the legs, then allowed to fall.

Some time passes before one of the men with guns begins to wave a plastic bag around. He starts to take things out of it. Dark strips . . .

The man on his knees sees what is happening and his eyes widen. His friends on the floor start to protest, try to move, but guns are smartly raised and levelled. The kneeling man is jerked hard backwards by an arm around his neck.

Then voices are raised to be heard above the noise of the rain. Words are nevertheless lost.

'. . . d'you get it?'

'Say again?'

'Where d'you get it?'

'Brought it with me.'

'. . . reminds me . . . could *kill* a fry-up . . . '

'That stuff fucking stinks, Ian . . . '

Then a few muffled words. Something muttered from

close by, the voice somehow far louder than the others but deep and distorted; impossible to make out clearly.

The one holding the plastic bag stretches out an arm. There is something flopping at the end of it. He pushes it towards the man on his knees, who tries to turn his head, but his hair is seized and tightened until he cannot look away.

Then they are placed on his face; laid across his mouth, nose and forehead as he screams.

Rashers of bacon.

THIRTEEN

A few years before, a major inquiry had been launched as to why the murderer of two young girls had been allowed to work as a school caretaker, having been investigated for serious sexual offences on a number of previous occasions. This inquiry revealed a nationwide system that was both unwieldy and seriously flawed. The country's police forces were supposed to be able to cross-reference, check and liaise with one another and with external bodies, yet the inquiry found that effective communication was thwarted at nearly every turn.

This was hard to believe, three decades on from the hunt for the Yorkshire Ripper – a man who had been questioned several times, eliminated on each occasion, and then caught by accident. Mistakes of this nature were understandable, back in those dark days of card indexes and case-notes exploding from mountains of overstuffed files, but *now*?

However many officers were sent on IT courses, and despite the many millions that were spent on tailor-made software and state-of-the-art networking, people still fucked up. Sometimes it wasn't ineptitude so much as incompatibility. Not only were some police computing systems not able to communicate with those of associated services, but often they could not even talk to each other. There were firewalls and brick walls; there were untraceable programs and intractable machines. While a perfectly diligent and proficient detective could store the complete works of Shakespeare on a keyring and send naked pictures of his girlfriend round the world with the click of a mouse, he might easily find himself unable to access intelligence on another floor of the same building.

Computers had become smaller of course, and lighter, but there were still plenty of police officers who didn't trust them as far as they could throw them. In this brave new world, the Met got through as much paper as ever ...

Hendricks didn't know if there was a name for the electronic equivalent of red tape. He did know it was a reality of British policing, and that it was easy to get caught up in. To get *lost* in. This had been at the back of his mind when he'd decided to do some detection on his own: to switch on a single, steam-powered PC and go looking for tattoos. Much to his own amazement, less than twenty-four hours after his testy conversation with Tom Thorne, he'd got lucky. He'd accessed the site postings and email from his office at Westminster Hospital. There were several dozen new responses. A couple looked like they might be worth following up, most were at least trying to be helpful and a couple were downright weird.

And Graham Hipkiss, FRCP, had left a phone number.

Hendricks reached across his desk for the phone. 'This is Phil Hendricks. I saw your note on the RCP message board ...'

'Right. I think I've a tattoo that might interest you.'

Dr Hipkiss was a consultant pathologist at a hospital in Nottingham. He described the tattoo, one of several he'd seen on a hit-and-run victim found on the outskirts of the city six months earlier. Though the man – who appeared to have been sleeping rough – had been found alive, he'd died from multiple injuries on the way to hospital. Neither the driver nor the car had been traced, and the police had fared little better in putting a name to the victim. Appeals had been made on *Midlands Today* and in the Nottingham *Evening Post*, but no one had come forward to claim the body. Six weeks after he'd been found in the road, the John Doe was given a simple, Social Services funeral.

Hendricks was certainly interested. He pushed aside a sheaf of student papers and began scribbling down the letters in his notebook, arranging them as Hipkiss read from his original post-mortem notes. They chatted for a few minutes more before Hendricks requested a copy of the post-mortem and thanked Hipkiss for his time.

Then he looked down at the tattoo:

B+
S.O.F.A.

The top row was different from that found on the body of the unknown man in the mortuary downstairs. Hendricks laid out the original tattoo underneath:

AB-
S.O.F.A.

Seeing them together, it became obvious. He flicked quickly through the Rolodex, furious with himself, until he found Russell Brigstocke's direct line.

Thorne pressed his mouth close to the handset, spoke quietly. 'Don't let Hendricks get big-headed about this,' he said. 'It's good news, but it only leaves us with another question. And we still don't know what the rest of it means.'

'Maybe the bottom bit's a club of some sort,' Holland said. 'Maybe the A is for Association. Something Something Football Association?'

'We'll figure it out.'

'We need someone who does crosswords, like Inspector Morse.'

'Inspector Morse never slept in a doorway or got thrashed at table-tennis by a heroin addict.'

'Sorry?'

'I've got to go,' Thorne said. 'Listen, I wanted to wish Chloe a happy birthday. I couldn't get her anything, obviously.'

'How the hell did you remember *that*?'

It was a very good question. Thorne pushed open the cubicle door and stepped out. 'I've absolutely no idea . . . '

When Thorne returned from the toilet, Spike was sitting on the edge of the pool table, his legs dangling.

'I've not moved any of the balls, honest,' he said.

Thorne didn't think for a minute that he had. There was no more need for Spike to cheat at pool than there had been on the table-tennis table half an hour earlier: he'd already been four balls ahead when Thorne had felt the phone vibrate in his pocket and excused himself.

'My shot, right?' Thorne lined up a yellow ball. Missed it by six inches.

There were several people watching. Each duff shot was greeted with a certain amount of half-hearted jeering and a less than flattering commentary.

'No mercy,' Spike said. He put away the remaining red balls, then slammed in the black, acknowledging the apathy of the onlookers by raising the cue above his head and cheering himself.

'Jammy fucker,' Thorne said.

'You need to take me on later in the day, mate. When I'm a bit shakier . . . '

Two men who might have been anywhere between twenty and forty stepped forward to play. Spike asked if they fancied a game of doubles and was impolitely refused.

'The facilities are pretty good in here,' Thorne said.

They walked away up a short flight of whitewashed steps, heading back towards the cafeteria.

'Yeah, not bad.'

'Not bad?' They walked past the TV room, then another that had been converted into a chiropodist's surgery. A woman stepped out, asked if either of them needed anything doing. They kept going up towards the ground floor, the walls of the winding staircase covered with Aids-awareness and drug-counselling posters.

'Junkies don't want a fucking chiropodist,' Spike said. 'There's nothing worth nicking in there, for a start. How much gear d'you think you can get for a box of corn plasters and some verruca ointment?'

'It doesn't mean no one wants to use it, though, does it?'

Spike shrugged. 'Nah, I suppose not. Maybe some of the old boys, like ...'

The centre would soon be closing for the afternoon and there were only a handful of people left in the cafeteria. Thorne and Spike stopped at a large noticeboard, stared at the jumble of printouts, leaflets and handwritten messages.

'You ever hear of rough sleepers tattooing their blood groups on themselves?' Thorne asked.

'Eh?'

'Their blood groups. You know, AB negative, O positive, whatever. As a tattoo.'

Spike stuck out his bottom lip, thought for a few seconds, then shook his head. 'I've seen most things, like, but ...'

'It doesn't matter ...'

Spike pointed at the noticeboard. 'You're right about this place, though, about the facilities. Look at all this stuff.'

172

There were notices about computer-training sessions, film showings and book groups. There were adverts for the latest performances by an opera company called Street-voice, a homeless theatre group and a free course of DJ workshops.

'Pretty impressive,' Thorne said.

Spike pulled out a small bottle of water from his pocket, unscrewed it and took a swig. 'There's a place in Maryle-bone that's even better, but it's a bit further out, isn't it? They do some strange shit there, like. They were giving people free acupuncture last week, which is a bit over the top, if you ask me. I mean, I like needles, don't get me wrong ... ' He cackled, offered Thorne the water.

Thorne took a drink then handed it back. 'Don't some people get a bit pissed off though? Like it's all *too* good.'

'Oh yeah.' Spike spread his arms. 'They reckon laying all this on is encouraging the likes of me to stay on the street. Like there's no incentive for us to get off our arses ... '

These were the same people, Thorne guessed, who thought life was too cushy in prison. That it was a soft option for many of those inside. He knew that when it had come to *certain* prisoners, he'd been one of those people himself.

'Most places are fuck all like this, though,' Spike said. 'You wait 'til you've been inside a few of the other centres. Some of them are well rough. You been in any of the wet places yet?'

'I don't think so ... '

'*Wet.* Means you can take booze in with you. Good from

that point of view, like, but they're shit-holes, most of them.'

Spike crushed the empty water bottle in his hand. They moved away from the noticeboard and walked slowly towards the exit.

'They can get a bit naughty as well, so you need to be careful. You look like you can take care of yourself, though ...'

A few months ago, Thorne might have agreed with him. Right now he felt weak and incapable. Then he remembered the anger that had boiled up as he'd dragged Moony from one side of the street to the other ...

Near the door that led from the café into the reception area, a trophy cabinet was mounted on the wall. There were a number of highly polished cups and shields, and a note taped to the glass showing the position of the centre's five-a-side team in the Street League.

Spike turned to Thorne as though divine inspiration had struck. 'I knew some football fans who had 'em. What you were asking about before. A couple of Chelsea boys who had tattoos with their blood group or what have you. They had blue dotted lines an' all, tattooed around their wrists and necks, saying "cut here" ...'

Thorne thought about what Holland had been saying on the phone: *Something Something Football Association.* He found it hard to believe that either of the men with the mysterious tattoos was a football hooligan, but it might still be worth considering.

*

It wasn't as if she hadn't *thought* her brother might be dead ...

While he was talking to Susan Jago, Stone told himself that it could have been an awful lot worse. It wasn't a bolt from the blue. They were the ones nobody wanted.

I'm sorry to have to tell you that your son/daughter/husband/wife ... I'm afraid there's been an accident ... I think perhaps you might want to sit down.

Every copper he knew had their own way of handling those awkward moments, his or her own style. The death message was usually delivered in person, of course, but as this was more of a confirmation than anything, it was decided that a phone call would not be improper. Even so, he'd been annoyed when Holland had palmed the job off on him, but, all in all, it hadn't gone too badly. He'd told Susan Jago about the hit-and-run; about the scar on the dead man's arm that had been detailed in the post-mortem report, and led them to believe that the victim had been her brother ...

'I don't understand why they couldn't get hold of any of us when they found him.'

'Your brother had no identification, Miss Jago. There was no way to—'

'How bloody hard did they try?'

'I couldn't possibly say, I'm afraid.'

Sam Karim walked past Stone's desk and raised his eyebrows. Stone shook his head, puffed out his cheeks.

'It's just the thought that nobody was with him,' she said. 'You know?'

'Of course. We understand, and we're all very sorry for your loss.' It was a phrase he'd picked up from American cop shows.

'Couldn't they have put something in the press and on TV? Like they did with the man I *thought* was Chris?'

'They did. Locally . . . '

Susan Jago repeated the word on an exasperated breath. There was a pause and Stone waited, expecting there to be tears. They didn't come.

'Right, well, I'm sorry to be . . . you know, the bearer—'

'It's all right. It's a relief in a funny sort of way.'

'I forgot to say, about the tattoos. We know now that some of the letters are a blood group. Your brother had his blood group tattooed on his arm. We wondered if you had any idea why.'

'I'm afraid I don't.'

Stone began to doodle in the corner of his notebook. 'So you don't know what it means?'

'I have to go now. I've got to try and find out where they've buried my brother.'

'Right. I'm sorry . . . '

There was another pause. Then: 'Will you remember to thank Dr Hendricks for me?'

Brigstocke was clearly still on his diet.

'You need to get a few pork pies down you, Russell. You're starting to look gaunt.'

'I can't say that you're looking too good yourself.'

Thorne and Brigstocke had arranged to meet up in

Chelsea, a good distance south of the West End. They stood together outside the Royal Hospital, lingering awkwardly for a few minutes like spies who've forgotten their code words, before they started to walk.

'I was going to ask,' Thorne said. 'That fascinating report I did so much work on at Scotland Yard. I do hope someone's polishing it up.'

'I think they binned it,' Brigstocke said.

'Excellent . . . '

They walked through the grounds of the hospital – still an almshouse for more than four hundred red-coated Chelsea Pensioners – past the National Army Museum and down towards Albert Bridge.

'I bet Phil Hendricks is pleased with himself,' Thorne said.

'Actually, he's pissed off because he didn't see it before. AB negative is the rarest blood group of the lot, and even though he typed those letters out himself several times on the post-mortem report, he never made the connection with the tattoo.'

'Tell him well done from me, but that he shouldn't make a habit of it. If he carries on playing detective, I might have to start slicing up corpses.'

Brigstocke laughed. 'Quite right too. God forbid he should make us look like we don't know what we're doing . . . '

'Did you see the PM report on Jago?'

'It was faxed over this morning, and I managed to get hold of the original SIO in Nottingham.'

'And?'

'It was a hit and run. As to whether it was a *deliberate* hit and run ...'

'We've got two rough sleepers,' Thorne said. 'Both with practically identical tattoos, and both dying violent deaths. What are the odds of there *not* being a connection?'

'I think we're working on the presumption that they're connected.'

'It's just a question of finding the link between Christopher Jago and our friend in Westminster Morgue ...'

It was a few minutes before seven o'clock and the bridge was already illuminated; the lamps swooping and arcing above the dusty-pink metalwork.

'It blows this serial-killer shit out of the water, anyway,' Thorne said.

Brigstocke looked genuinely curious. 'I really don't see why.'

'The MO, for a kick-off. He runs one over in Nottingham, then six months later he comes down to London and kicks another one to death.'

'More than another *one*.'

'It's the first victim that counts. It's about him and Jago. The others are nothing to do with it.'

'I'm not sure their nearest and dearest would agree, Tom ...'

Thorne hadn't meant it to come out that way. All the same, he knew he was in danger of focusing too hard on the first victim, and of forgetting those still mourning the other men who had died. He thought about Paddy Hayes' son pulling the plug; about Caroline and the others trying to smile through Radio Bob's funeral.

'So what about this blood-group business?' Brigstocke asked.

On the left of them, Battersea Park lay spread out to the east. Thorne could make out a few joggers and cyclists moving along the avenues. There was some sort of event taking place by the Peace Pagoda.

'I can't see that it's medical,' Thorne said. 'The first victim didn't have any condition that would make it necessary. What about Jago?'

'No, nothing.'

'Right . . .'

'A bracelet's a damn sight easier anyway.'

'What about the football angle?'

Brigstocke had already heard Holland's thoughts on what the initials might stand for, and Thorne had told him what Spike had said about hooligans. 'It's possible, I suppose. We certainly can't discount it.'

'What's your profiler make of all this?'

'Well, it's a bit early. Cochrane's feeding the new information into his report and we should get something in the next day or two. He's been considering the idea that the killer might be someone who used to be homeless himself.'

'And he's basing that on what?' Thorne asked.

'The killer obviously has a knowledge of that community.'

'Because he found a few rough sleepers? They're hardly invisible, Russell.'

'If he *had* lived in that world himself, feeling powerless and marginalised, and escaped it somehow, it's possible that he's trying to wipe out that part of his life. He's showing that *he*'s got the power now. The money's a symbol of that. How he's worth so much more than they are.'

Thorne looked sideways at him, held the look until eventually Brigstocke gave in and smiled; like he wasn't exactly convinced by any of it himself.

'And they binned *my* report?' Thorne said.

They turned into the park and walked down towards the all-weather football pitches. There was a game being played under floodlights and they stopped to watch.

'I'm not a hundred per cent sure the undercover thing's working out,' Brigstocke said.

Thorne, who had arbitrarily picked the team playing in red and begun rooting for them, winced at a particularly high tackle. 'That must have hurt ... '

'Tom?'

Thorne had heard him well enough. 'I don't know what you mean by "working out".'

'Are you really getting any more out of people than we were before?'

'What about the information I got out of that fucker Moony?'

'It's not hard to threaten somebody, is it?'

As if on cue, words were exchanged and a couple of

players squared up in the centre circle, every breath visible in the air as they spat curses at each another. Thorne and Brigstocke watched until they were sure no punches would be thrown.

'All I'm saying is that we should maybe take a view on it,' Brigstocke said. 'It's been three weeks . . . '

'Give me a bloody chance.'

'I'm getting pushed on this . . . '

Thorne turned from the game to look at Brigstocke. 'I don't know if anybody knows anything,' he said. 'And I'm not expecting them to just spill the beans over a can of strong lager if they do. I still believe we need a presence, though, and by being part of that community I'm learning stuff that I think's going to help. I mean, Christ, if you're willing to put faith in your *profiler* . . . '

'A limited amount.'

'You never know, if he's right, by living as a rough sleeper I might be able to get some idea of how the killer thinks. Ask him. I bet he'll tell you it's a good idea.'

Brigstocke couldn't help but look impressed by the cheek of it. 'You've always got an answer, haven't you? Always got some angle.'

'Whatever it takes.'

Thorne turned around and they watched for another few minutes, during which the team in red conceded two soft goals.

'I need to get back,' Brigstocke said. 'I'm in the shit for missing a parent–teacher conference.'

Thorne stayed on, the solitary spectator for a while.

At half-time, the red team's dumpy left-back trotted slowly across to the touchline. His face was scarlet, running with sweat, and the fat on his chest and belly strained against the nylon of his shirt. Thorne watched through the chain-link fence as he wheezed and hawked, bent to take hold of his knees, then threw up on to the AstroTurf.

It seemed as good a time as any to head back to the West End. Thorne turned and walked away, thinking, I know how you feel, mate.

FOURTEEN

There were a surprising number of places that gave out free food if you knew where to go and when.

Spike had given him the low-down early on, and Thorne had thought that it was quite an achievement to keep all those different names, places and times in your head. On any one day in the very centre of London alone, you could get a free breakfast, lunch or dinner in one of a dozen different churches, hostels and ad hoc street cafés. Some operated a ticketing system and with others it was first-come, first-served; some provided full meals while others offered tea, coffee and biscuits, or maybe sandwiches on certain days. With all these possibilities open to those in the know, and with a three-course meal available for little more than a pound at the London Lift, Thorne could not understand why so many were still willing to hang about in all weathers for a bowl of free soup on the street.

Caroline had spoken like someone who knew what she was talking about. 'Some people just don't like going *into* places. You know? They're not happy in buildings, for whatever reason. Centres like the Lift aren't for everyone ...'

'And cheap's not the same as free, is it?' Spike had added. 'When you've got fuck all and there's free stuff on offer, you take everything that's going.'

The three of them were walking quickly, from the Trafalgar Square end of the Strand, heading for the nine o'clock soup run behind Temple underground station. The street was gaudy with lights: the multicoloured neon from the Vaudeville and Adelphi theatres; the huge yellow lamps across the front of the Strand Palace Hotel; the pulsing red or bright white of the cars, crawling in both directions.

The night was cold again, but as yet mercifully dry.

'You get whatever you can, whenever you can, 'cause there's not a lot to go round,' Spike said. 'Yeah?'

Caroline had slowed to light a cigarette, and was just catching up with Spike and Thorne again. 'Except at fucking Christmas,' she said.

Thorne told them about something he'd read once: a quote from one of those pointless 'It' girls with too many names and too little to do. She'd said something about how dreadful it was to be without shelter at Christmas, and suggested that all homeless people should move to the Caribbean during the winter, and live on fresh fish.

Caroline's laughter quickly turned into a coughing fit.

'Dozy posh cunt,' Spike said.

December was still a few months away, but plenty of shops had already put out the decorations. Thorne had no idea where he'd be when it came. His father's sister Eileen had offered, as had Hendricks. Everyone said that the first one was the most difficult ...

'It's supposed to be the worst time to be on the street, right?' he said. 'There's always documentaries on the telly. Women in green wellies taking a tramp home for Christmas.'

Spike shrugged. 'It's the same as the rest of the year, just a bit colder. It's every *other* punter that changes.' He put on his best Islington trendy accent: 'It's when people really start to care ...'

They told Thorne about the cold-weather shelters that Crisis and other organisations would open. About the donations that poured in from members of the public, and from some of the more forward-thinking companies. Big-name stores playing Santa and clearing out old stock.

'You can pop along Christmas Day, get yourself turkey and all the trimmings, and as many Gap sweatshirts as you can carry.'

'It's hysterical,' Caroline said. 'You get these poor bastards walking into day centres and hostels all through January with nothing except major drug habits and enormous bags of brand-new toiletries.'

Spike took Caroline's cigarette from her mouth, used it to light one of his own. 'The new clothes thing is ace, though. People who give stuff to Oxfam or whatever seem to think we're all desperate to dress like some old grandad. Fucking cardigans and pyjamas that somebody died in.'

'Nothing wrong with a decent cardy,' Thorne said.

Caroline took hold of his arm. 'Yeah, but you *are* an old grandad, aren't you?'

They drifted across the pavement towards a gift shop and stationer's, whose window was already well stocked with tinsel and tat. They stared for a few seconds.

'Too bloody soon,' Thorne said. There was a Dixon's next door and he turned his attention to the television screens still flickering in the window. A soap-opera, *The Bill*, Sky News. He watched a journalist talking to camera and tried, without the benefit of sound, to work out what he might be talking about. He remembered Alan Ward, the reporter he'd met outside Colindale Station when he'd run into Steve Norman. Thorne decided that if Spurs were at home over the Christmas period – if *he* were at home – he'd take the man up on his offer of football tickets. He thought about the pies and the hot-dogs and the scalding tea at half-time; more attractive, at that moment, than the prospect of watching the game itself . . .

Spike leaned his face against the glass, steaming it up as he spoke. 'I think I might go to my sister's this year. She's got a fantastic flat in Docklands . . . '

Thorne nodded. Spike was constantly telling him things that he'd told him once or twice already.

'I don't care, as long as I'm indoors,' Caroline said. 'This year more than any.'

Thorne knew that she was talking about the murders.

For the families, wherever they were, and for those still sleeping on the same streets as their dead friends, this would be that first, difficult Christmas.

'Killing people, or scaring them into leaving,' Caroline said. 'One way and another, he's clearing a lot of us off the street.'

Spike leaned back, drew a face on the window with his finger. 'Maybe he's working for the council.'

As with those places that dispensed more substantial meals, there were soup runs happening across the West End at different times during the evening. There was one at ten o'clock, just around the corner on the Strand, where, with irony far thicker than the soup itself, the homeless were fed within spitting distance – within *sniffing* distance – of the Savoy. Again, it was all about knowing when and where. There were some, with appetites all but destroyed by drugs, who would go all day without eating and get by on two or three bowls of soup; trudging between the various locations with the weary resignation of those for whom eating has long ceased being a pleasure.

There were a dozen or more people already waiting by the time they arrived, including a good few that Thorne had come across before. He recognised faces he'd seen at the Lift, from the streets around the theatre where he bedded down for the night. He met – but only briefly – the disturbing gaze of the man who'd come close to attacking him and Spike a couple of days earlier.

Thorne, Spike and Caroline joined those who were milling around outside a building which was – according to a discreet but highly polished nameplate – the headquarters of British and American Tobacco. Some lurked as close as possible to where they were expecting the van to stop, while others hung back, preferring to wait across the road. They gathered in small groups, talking or staring into space: the pale-faced kids in dirty anoraks, and the entrenched, long-haired and bearded, in dark clothes that seemed smeared across their bulky frames in grease. One group looked like backpackers who'd run out of money. Thorne caught a word or two in an Australian accent and decided that's exactly what they were.

Standing alone on the other side of the road near the tube station was one of the few black men Thorne had seen in his time on the streets. Maxwell had told him early on that there were so few black and Asian rough sleepers because those communities were closer-knit; that they believed in the extended family. Basically, he'd said, it came down to how much people gave a shit. It made sense to Thorne, who knew that were he even able to *find* any of his cousins – first, second or whatever – none of them would be inclined to take him in if he found himself in real trouble. He also knew, of course, that he'd be equally reluctant were he the one being asked to help. He'd seen enough blood to know that it was certainly thicker than water. But he'd also seen enough of it spilled within families to know that the phrase meant less than bugger all.

Spike saw Thorne looking around. 'Told you. There's all sorts ... '

'Must be great soup,' Thorne said.

188

It arrived, and it wasn't. Ladled into styrofoam bowls from a huge metal saucepan in the back of a Volvo estate. But it was hot, dished out with a smile and, crucially, with no questions asked. This was another reason why the soup run remained popular, and why teenage backpackers could stand in line with those who'd been sleeping rough for decades.

Caroline crossed the road to a bench and lit up, as a very tall man, six feet five or more and cradling his bowl of soup, sauntered up to where Spike and Thorne were finishing theirs. Thorne put his empty bowl on to the window sill behind him, watched as Spike tossed his into the gutter. Thorne had to fight the urge to march over and pick it up.

The tall man and Spike greeted each other warmly and Spike made the introductions.

'This is Holy Joe.'

The man looked down at Thorne and gave a small nod. He was wearing a Queen's Park Rangers bobble hat and trainers, and what looked like a long brown robe beneath a tightly buttoned donkey-jacket.

'Who was it this time?' Spike asked.

'Nuns,' the man said. 'They're the fucking worst.'

Spike explained that Joe spent most of his time falling upon the tender mercies of a variety of different church organisations: the Jesus Army; the Salvation Army; the Quakers; the Young Jewish Volunteer Corps; the Sisters and Brothers of Just About Anybody. A few weeks at a time of free food and accommodation for the price of a daily Bible class or prayer meeting.

'I've got a hundred and seven crosses in a plastic bag,' Joe said. He took a slurp of soup. 'Wooden ones, plastic ones. There's dozens of Bibles ...'

'I bet you knew Paddy Hayes,' Thorne said. 'Spike's mate. The one who was killed. He was a God-botherer, wasn't he?'

Joe took a step back into the road, scraped the sole of his training shoe against the kerb as though he were trying to remove dog-shit. 'Yeah, but Paddy was a bit of a light-weight.'

Thorne was still convinced that Jago and the first victim would provide the answer as to why these murders had happened. Why they were *still* happening. But how the killer selected the subsequent victims, if it was anything other than random, might give the police their best chance of catching him quickly. The idea that he was choosing victims from among distinct groups was definitely a strong possibility, but Thorne suddenly wondered if there might be a church connection.

'You can ask this man anything,' Spike said. 'He could do religion and all that shit on *Mastermind*. Your specialist subject, innit, Joe?'

Hadn't Robert Asker thought that he could talk to God on his radio? Maybe he'd been to a meeting or two. Thorne made a mental note to ask Caroline when he got the chance.

Spike was getting excited, shifting from foot to foot. 'Go on, ask him something. He knows the Bible fucking backwards.'

Joe nodded solemnly. 'And the Talmud. And the Koran. I'm not fussy.'

'I can't think of anything,' Thorne said.

'Ask him all the books in the Bible. Ask him to do them in order . . .'

'Too easy,' Joe said.

Thorne thought about his father, who would have loved a game like this. The old man wouldn't have slept until he'd found out the right answer and written it down somewhere. In his last few years he'd taken to ringing Thorne up in the early hours of the morning, demanding lists of answers to all manner of bizarre trivia questions.

'Ask him,' Spike said.

Give me a dozen big cats . . . The three fastest ball-games in the world . . . All the kings and queens of England. Go on, I'll give you the first couple to start . . .

'Go on, anything you like.'

'OK,' Thorne said. He pointed to the bowl in Joe's hands. 'Could Jesus have turned that into soup?'

There was the swish of a revolving door behind them and a man walked quickly from the B & A Tobacco building and hurried across the road. He wore a tailored overcoat and carried a metal briefcase, and his free hand struggled to tuck in one end of a bright red scarf that had caught in the wind.

Holy Joe turned and shouted cheerily after him. 'Oi, mate, got any ciggies for me?'

The man didn't even bother to look up. 'Piss off,' he said.

*

Back on the Strand, they walked east towards Fleet Street. They passed the 'ghost' Aldwych underground station, half of its boarded-up entrance now home to a Photo-Me booth, and Thorne gave Spike and Caroline a potted history. He told them how the station, originally called Strand, had fallen into disuse a number of times in the century since it had been opened; how a man had been eaten on one of the escalators in *An American Werewolf in London*; and how, during the Second World War, it had been home to the British Museum's collection of mummies.

As they crossed towards St Clement Danes, serene on its traffic island, Thorne pointed towards the spikes and spires of the Royal Courts of Justice, brutal against the night sky beyond the church. As a civil court, it was not a place Thorne knew well, but he *did* know that the man who built its clock was strangled to death when his tie got caught in the mechanism.

'Bloody hell,' Spike said. 'You know some seriously weird shit.'

Thorne thought about everything he'd learned, from Spike more than anyone, in the past few weeks. He thought about the things he'd been shown and the people he'd met. He thought about the knowledge that had been passed on to him.

'*I* know some weird shit ...?'

Around the back of the church, a number of those who had been at the soup run had gathered to stand around and drink. To kill time until the next one. Caroline and

Spike drifted away to talk to a couple of junkies whose conversation, by the look of them, would not be sparkling.

'Gotabeer?'

Thorne turned to see an older man with a shock of white hair and a nose like an overripe strawberry standing far too close to him.

'Gotabeer, mate?'

The words weren't slurred exactly, but ran easily into one as though they belonged together. It sounded both casual and aggressive, the last word fading into a breath like hot fat spitting. Thorne wasn't sure if the man had simply not got him down as a fellow rough sleeper, or was just so far gone that he didn't care who he asked. Either way, the answer was going to be the same.

'Sorry.' Thorne patted the can in his pocket. 'Just got the one and that's mine.'

'You're not drinking it.'

Thorne took the can of Special Brew from his pocket. He was going to fill it with weak stuff later, but what the hell. He yanked back the ring pull. 'Yes I am.'

As Thorne brought the can to his mouth, the man stepped even closer. 'Give us a fucking swig then.'

The man was leaning into him from the side. Thorne could feel the material of the man's filthy bodywarmer against his father's coat.

'Just the one swig . . . '

'Fuck off,' Thorne said.

The man moved back sharply as though he'd been pushed. He squinted at Thorne for ten or fifteen seconds, his feet planted firmly enough, but the top half of his body swaying gently. Then he cocked his head. 'You're a copper,' he said.

Thorne grunted and laughed. Took a mouthful of beer. It tasted vile.

'You're Old Bill. Course you are.' He was starting to raise his voice. 'I *know* you are.'

'Listen, mate ...'

'I know a piggy ...'

Thorne thrust the can towards him. 'Here, you can take it ...'

'Oink! Oink!' He smacked a fat hand against the side of his leg over and over as he shouted: 'You're a *copper*, you're a *rozzer*, you're a rotten, filthy *fucker* ...'

Thorne was on the verge of driving the base of the can against the old man's head when Spike appeared next to him.

'All right?'

As Thorne turned his head, the man reached out and grabbed the beer.

Spike took hold of his arm. 'Give us that back, you twat ...'

'Let him have it,' said Thorne.

When Spike let go, the man took a couple of steps back, pulling the can of beer close to his chest. 'He's a copper. I swear he's a fucking copper.'

Spike spoke like he was humouring a mental patient. 'Course he is.' He cupped his hands around his mouth, shouted after the old man, although he was no more than a few feet away. 'You don't know how fucking wrong you are, pal.'

They watched as the man walked to the railings at the edge of the kerb and started to drink.

Spike looked at Thorne. 'You didn't *used* to be a copper, did you?'

Thorne turned and walked away, heading around the narrow strip of pavement that circled the church.

The old man was clearly a headcase, yet Thorne was still unnerved by the confrontation. Was there a chance he *had* been recognised? Could the old man have been someone Thorne had put away years before? It didn't really matter; from what Spike had shouted, it was clear that *he* still believed Thorne had spent time in prison.

He thought back to the case he'd been working on just before his father had died. The case that might have been the *reason* his father had died. He thought about a line he'd drawn, and then stepped across as casually as if he were entering another room.

Ex-offender was exactly right.

He stopped at the front of the church, looked up at the blackened statue of Gladstone, at the defiant bronze figure of Bomber Harris . . .

Something began to suggest itself.

There were other statues around the front of the church. He didn't need to know whom they honoured. Even from behind, the bearing of these men told Thorne *what* they were. He turned and walked back towards the entrance of the church, remembering it even as he saw the three letters, spelled out horizontally on a pale blue cross, beneath the figure of a golden eagle. St Clement Danes was the RAF church . . .

Something blurred started to come sharply into focus.

He thought about the museum he'd walked past earlier with Russell Brigstocke. He remembered something Spike had said when he was talking about the differing backgrounds of people who were sleeping rough:

'*It's a right old mix, though. I fucking love it, like. You've got your immigrants, you've got . . .*'

And then Thorne knew *exactly* who might have their blood group as a tattoo.

*

It was funny, he thought, about old friends.

Sitting in the flat, he thought about the strange ways things could pan out if you came across them again. Funny how it happened as well. It might be that you just ran into someone from your past on a street somewhere, or on a train, or found yourself leaning against the same bar one night. It might be a phone call out of the blue.

Or it might all come about same as this had: it might all start with a letter . . .

It was weird, that was the other thing, how some that you'd never really been close to might turn out, a few years down the line, to be all right. To be the ones you got on OK with. While others – the blokes who you thought at the time would be your mates for ever; who you said stupid, soppy shit to after a few beers; who you felt really *connected*

196

to – ended up being the ones who caused all the fucking headaches later on. And, of course, sod's law, you could never tell first time round which were which.

Time could heal some wounds, *course* it could, but others were always going to fester.

He reckoned that basically there was always a good reason why people lost touch with one another. Sometimes it was an effort to keep a friendship going; when geography was against you or whatever. If the friendship was really worth it, though, you made the effort. Simple as that. If not, you let it go, and like as not the other person was thinking the same as you, and letting it go at exactly the same time.

If an effort was made later to get back in touch, there was a good chance that the party making the effort wanted something. It was certainly true in this case. Very bloody true all round, in fact. But, a decade and more down the road, you want different things, don't you? You want a quiet life and you'll do all sorts of things to keep it that way. You're willing – no, you're *happy* – to fight for what you've got; to keep hold of what you've worked so bloody hard to get.

They all needed each other back then. No shame in that. But life goes on, and people learn lessons, and you didn't need to be a rocket scientist, did you? When there isn't a real enemy around any more, you don't need friends quite so much.

197

1991

There are no longer any weapons trained upon the four men who have been tied up, and though those who have bound their wrists, and now their feet, are no more than fifty feet away, each allows his gaze, for at least some of the time, to drift towards the floor or to the face of the man nearest to him. The eyes of these men are no longer fixed and popping, as they would be faced with the muzzle of a gun or the blade of a knife.

The sand has become the colour of soil, and their olive shirts are black with the rain and pasted to their skins.

The four figures wearing goggles and helmets are also sitting now, or squatting, close together. Each still carries his gun, but it leans against a thigh or hangs loosely from a hand resting across a knee. Though their position might seem relaxed from a distance, they constantly eye the quartet across from them, and shift nervously. Heavily booted

198

feet are flexed, carving out miniature trenches in the sand, and those on their haunches bob and bend, their arms stretched and stiff against the ground to steady themselves.

Suddenly, one man lowers his *shamag* and spits, a thick trail of it which he pulls away from his chin before lifting the kerchief back into place. He shuffles forward and the others do likewise; they lean close together and talk.

They each have something to say, and though the exchange is heated at first, it settles quickly and the voices gradually lower. The words are getting harder to make out, but they are clearly given greater weight and seriousness, and now the men are close enough to touch one another. It starts with a slap that sounds like a bone breaking and a voice that has become little more than a low growl. Pleas give way to threats. Then promises. One man swears, pushes at a second, and finds himself clutched at like a lover. Heads are shaken quickly and nodded slowly until, finally, each man has a handful of another's jacket or an arm wrapped tight around his shoulder, and they bow their heads so that the helmets smack together. They look like football players in a huddle, desperate to pool their terror and their aggression and turn it into something they can use. Firing up for one last, big push.

And this is when it begins to look like a game.

They all rise to their feet, and after another half-minute, one – chosen or volunteered – steps away from the group. He examines his pistol. In the space that opens up between there is a bright smear on the horizon, fainter as it rises, like red ink creeping up a blotter.

The others watch as the man walks quickly towards the four figures on the ground, though two of those watching turn away at the last moment. They look like players gathered in the centre circle. Some unable to handle the tension of the penalty shoot-out; turning their backs, lowering their heads. Afraid to watch.

The men on the ground begin to move, quickly. They attempt to scramble to their feet, but it's hopeless. They fall on to their backs or faces, and struggle to reach one another. Now their eyes are popping again; wide, and shot with shattered vessels.

Time passes, though probably no more than half a minute, and the man who left the group is on his way back to them.

There's no way of knowing of course what any of them are thinking; those that stand waiting their turn, or the man who trudges slowly back. But though the goggles and *shamag*s give them all the same blank, robotic expression, it's easy to imagine that the faces beneath are equally expressionless.

He rejoins his friends in their centre circle.

Though three men have begun to scream, and weep, and pray, it's impossible to tell if he's scored or not.

FIFTEEN

The Media Operations Office of British Army HQ (London District) was housed in a building backing on to Horse Guards Parade. It had once been the barracks for hundreds of men, but these days the horses it stabled and the troops who paraded across its courtyards were engaged, for the most part, in ceremonial activities.

As Kitson and Holland had walked towards the reception area, they'd had to pass a pair of Household Cavalrymen on guard duty. The soldiers stood, unblinking in their scarlet tunics, with helmets polished to a mirrored finish, and Holland had only just fought off the childish urge to try to distract them, in the same way that giggling tourists and schoolchildren did all day long. Once inside the office, with a china cup of very strong tea, he confessed this to one of the Senior Public Information Officers sitting behind the desk opposite.

'Oh, they love all that carry-on,' the man said.

The second SPIO, seated behind a desk at a right-angle to the first, was eager to agree with his colleague. 'Especially if it's a couple of teenage girls doing the distracting. You'd be amazed how many saucy notes get stuck into those boys' boots.'

The office, which overlooked Whitehall, was large enough to have housed more than just the two SPIOs, but it was also somewhat dilapidated. Paint was peeling from the green door and eau-de-Nil walls, and though the brown colour hid it, the carpet was probably as thick with dust as the strip-lights above. Several large pinboards were covered with curling charts, sun-faded maps, and, on one, a colour photograph of the Queen in one of those oversized prams she was so fond of travelling around in.

Though many who worked in the building were civil servants, the two men who shared this office were actually retired army officers. This had been made clear early on, when each had introduced the other and had prefaced name with former rank. Ex-Lieutenant-Colonel Ken Rutherford was short and stocky, with silver hair that he'd oiled and swept back. Trevor Spiby, a former captain in the Scots Guards, was taller, and balding. A patch of red skin, which might have been a burn or a birthmark, ran from just below his jaw and disappeared under his collar. Each man wore a shirt and tie, but where Spiby had opted for braces, Rutherford sported a multi-coloured waistcoat. Their contrasting appearances gave them the look of an upmarket double act, and this image was furthered by the way that they bounced off each other verbally.

'Tea OK?'

'Be better with a biscuit ... '

'Are you sure we can't rustle you one up?'

Kitson thanked them and passed. Holland did likewise, the cut-glass accents of the ex-officers making him feel as though he belonged in *EastEnders*. He imagined his polite 'Thank you' sounding like he'd said, 'Get your lovely ripe bananas ... two bunches for a pahnd!'

'I don't quite understand why you've come to Media Ops,' Spiby said.

Rutherford nodded. 'The Met would normally liaise with the RMP.'

Russell Brigstocke had considered talking to the Royal Military Police, but all that was really needed at this stage was information. He was also wary of the 'can of worms' factor that so often came into play when one force of any kind attempted to make use of another. As far as the meeting itself went, it had been his decision to send Yvonne Kitson along. Most interviews were conducted by officers of DS rank and below, but on this occasion Brigstocke had thought it politic for an inspector to be present.

'It's a simple enquiry really,' Kitson said. 'I just need straightforward information and I don't need to waste a lot of anyone's time. To be frank, it was this office's contact details that were first on the website.'

'How can we help you?' Rutherford asked.

Holland gave a brief summary of the case, concentrating on the deaths of the two men with tattoos, whom they now believed to have been ex-army.

'It sounds more than likely,' Spiby said. 'The blood group is often tattooed, along with other things, of course.'

'Though not too much.' Rutherford was peering over his computer. 'Anyone with too many tattoos can be barred from joining the army in the first place.'

'I don't suppose you'd know what the rest of the tattoo might mean?' Holland handed a piece of paper across. Rutherford pulled on the half-moon specs that hung around his neck. He studied the letters for a few moments and passed it to Spiby.

'They're initials, clearly, but certainly nothing military springs to mind.'

'Do you have any records of the particular markings that certain soldiers may have had?' Holland asked. 'Scars, tattoos, what have you?'

'I'm afraid not.' Spiby looked to Rutherford, who shook his head emphatically. 'There are medical records, yes, but nothing that detailed.'

'DNA?'

'Oh, I doubt it.'

'Dental records, perhaps?'

'Yes, I think so. I'd need to check . . . '

Kitson leaned forward to place her empty cup on Spiby's desk. 'As we only have a name for one of these men, we're very much hoping we can use it to identify the other. Save for the different blood groups, these tattoos are identical, so we're assuming they had them done at the same time. That they served together.'

'It sounds a reasonable assumption,' Rutherford said.

'So if we give you this man's name, we thought you could give us a list of the other soldiers he served with.'

'Ah. *Not* such a reasonable assumption, I'm afraid. First, *we* can't give you anything; you'd need to contact the Records Office. Second, the records just don't work like that. They don't group the men together in that fashion. I'd be amazed if the Met's records worked a great deal differently.'

Kitson sat back in her chair.

'These men who were sleeping rough,' Spiby said, 'they had been out of the army for some time, correct?'

There was a pause. The silence was broken only by the sputtering of the ancient gas fire in the corner of the room. Holland cleared his throat. 'We think so, yes.'

'They were definitely not AWOL servicemen?'

'Not as far as we know ...'

'It *would* explain why they were sleeping rough. When a soldier is AWOL, they will go to extraordinary lengths to avoid being traced through official channels.'

Rutherford chipped in. 'I'm sure that Army Personnel could cross-check your name against a list of absent servicemen.'

'I don't think that's the case ...'

'So how far back are we talking?' Spiby asked.

Kitson looked across to Holland. He looked back at her, gave a small shake of the head. 'We're not sure at this stage,' Kitson said.

'When a soldier leaves the army, his records are sent to the Manning and Record Office at the Army Personnel Centre in Glasgow. Some time later . . . ' Spiby looked to Rutherford. 'Is it ten years, Ken?'

'Something like that.'

'Some time later, the records are moved to the Services Archive at Hayes. Glasgow would need to recall any file from there if you made an enquiry. You could try that to begin with, but in the first instance they tend to give out only name, date of birth and a confirmation of service.'

'There are constraints on the release of any other information,' Rutherford said.

Holland had started to feel very warm. He undid the top button of his shirt. 'This is a murder investigation, sir. I doubt those constraints would apply.'

Rutherford held up his hands in mock surrender. 'I'm sure you're right, Detective Sergeant, but with all the co-operation in the world I still don't think they'll be able to give you the information you're after. As far as the soldier whose name you *do* have goes, you may still need authorisation from his next of kin. You have that, correct?'

Now Holland was feeling hot. Thinking about who that next of kin might be . . .

'Which regiment did our man serve in?' Spiby asked. 'That might give us a start, at least.'

It was another question Holland couldn't answer. Kitson snapped her head round to stare at him. He could see that she was thinking about Susan Jago, too.

*

Kitson waited until she'd reached the end of the corridor and turned to walk down the stairs before she let rip. 'They looked at us like we were amateurs. Fuck it, we *are* amateurs. What the hell went on in there?'

Holland said nothing. He was still trying to put it together, trying to remember a sequence of events.

'I don't like passing the buck, Dave, but you were given the job of going into CRIS and writing up the notes for this interview.'

'I did, Guv . . . '

Kitson stopped. 'So why did we not know the answers to those questions?'

Holland had accessed the Crime Reporting Intelligence System first thing that morning. CRIS was a complete record of the case to date: every name, date and statement. There had been nothing relating to Christopher Jago's service in the army – the year of his discharge, the name of his regiment. Holland had presumed that the data had simply not yet been entered, but that Kitson and Brigstocke must already know the relevant facts. He knew now that he'd fucked up; that they'd all fucked up.

'Dave? Where's the information we got from Jago's sister?' The moment Kitson had finished asking the question, she knew the answer. 'Christ. There isn't any, is there?'

'That's the thing, Guv. I don't think Susan Jago has ever told us her brother was a soldier.'

'Hang on, let's think about this. I know she never bothered to tell us when she came down to ID the body. If the silly cow had mentioned it, we'd have put the whole thing together a bit quicker, wouldn't we? But we've spoken to her *since* then.'

'DC Stone called with the death message.' It was this phone call Holland had been trying to place in a pattern of what had been known, and when.

'Right. So, she'd have talked about it then, surely. Why the hell *wouldn't* she?'

Holland had no idea at all.

Yvonne Kitson was trying to stay calm. It was her team and she was ultimately responsible. She should have made sure. She should have *known* about this. Then it occurred to her that perhaps Susan Jago *had* told them about her brother and that they'd simply failed to process the information. 'Is it possible that DC Stone did not update the CRIS after he'd spoken to Susan Jago?'

Holland knew it was more than possible. There was no record of the conversation on the system. Stone might well have decided that as Susan Jago was no longer important to the investigation, he could get away without doing the update. But that still didn't explain it: Stone had spoken to Jago three days earlier, on the Saturday afternoon; that was hours before Thorne had figured out the army connection.

'It doesn't make sense. When DC Stone spoke to her, we still didn't know about the army thing. So if she *had* said anything, he'd have known it was important and would have passed it on verbally.'

They walked the rest of the way down the narrow

staircase, both thinking the same thing: *Why the hell wouldn't Susan Jago have told them?*

'Call Stone and double check . . . '

Holland took out his mobile, dialled Stone's number and got a message. He looked at his watch. 'It's lunchtime, Guv. He'll be in a caff somewhere with his phone switched off.' The lie had come easily, despite the anger he felt. Holland knew very well that whatever Andy Stone was eating, it wasn't lunch.

They emerged into a covered courtyard to find themselves part of a small crowd gathered for the daily mounting of the guard. A row of red-coated Life Guards on horseback stood facing their opposite numbers from the Blues and Royals, identical save for the dark coats.

Kitson and Holland stood with the hushed tourists for a few minutes and watched the ceremony. Cameras clicked furiously as the troops who had ridden down from Hyde Park Corner arrived; the huge horses walking two abreast beneath the arch to Horse Guards.

Holland leaned his head close to Kitson's. 'How come *we* never get saucy notes stuck in our boots?'

But Kitson was in no mood to laugh.

The place smelled of piss and hospital food.

As soon as Thorne had walked through the door he'd remembered what Spike had told him when they'd been talking about the facilities at the Lift; how most places were a lot different. He'd been putting it mildly.

The Aquarius day centre in Covent Garden catered

purely for those over twenty-five, but they could easily have upped the lower limit by fifteen years. Thorne hadn't seen a single person younger than himself since he'd got there, and, looking around, it was hardly surprising. The few people he had encountered were old – before their time or otherwise – and he couldn't imagine a twenty-five or thirty-year-old feeling anything other than deeply uncomfortable in the poky, dismal rooms and bare-brick corridors. Where the London Lift was light and well cared-for, everything about the Aquarius reeked of neglect, and a lack of the funding necessary to get rid of the stench.

In the closest thing he could find to a lounge, Thorne sat and tried not to breathe too deeply.

It felt like a doctor's waiting room. A windowless box with a dozen chairs pushed back against its flaking walls, and a table in the centre with old magazines and overflowing ashtrays scattered across it like litter.

Ever since he'd worked out how Jago and the other man might have been connected, Thorne had been absorbed in considering why someone who'd served and possibly fought for their country might return to Civvy Street only to wind up sleeping on it. Might end up spending their days in a place like this. The figures were alarming. Some sources claimed that one in every four rough sleepers was ex-armed forces, with the figure even higher for those who had been on the streets long term. Ironically, squaddies were given the skills that might help sustain them out-doors. They were *trained* to sleep rough. But what led so many of them to end up doing just that?

There would be the same risk factors that applied to anyone else, of course; the same triggers. And it wasn't hard to work out that there would be others, too, unique to a history in the armed forces: post-traumatic stress; difficulties with readjustment; drug and alcohol dependency arising from either of those two things. But these were just chapter headings from a case-worker's textbook. Thorne knew that if he wanted to understand, he would have to find some of these people, and talk to them ...

A man poked his head around the door, stared at Thorne for a few seconds and backed out again. The room's only other occupant had not even looked up. He sat opposite Thorne in a ratty green armchair, the floor around his feet littered with bits of foam stuffing that had leaked from its cushion. He gripped the wooden arms as though they were keeping him from rising up into the air, and stared at the front of a *Daily Star* that had sat unthumbed on his knees for the past fifteen minutes.

Neither Thorne nor anyone else knew whether Jago and the other victim had been killed because of their army background, or because they were homeless, or because of whatever events had led them from one to the other. Brigstocke had contacted the Ex-Service Action Group in hope of guidance. Meanwhile, Thorne knew that his role gave him an opportunity to talk to those who found themselves where Chris Jago and the other victim had once been.

That said, if Thorne had learned anything over the last few weeks, it was that reaching out to someone was never straightforward.

'This place is a shit-hole,' Thorne said. 'Isn't it? They should just lob a fucking grenade in and be done with it ...'

The man sitting opposite rose from his chair – letting the newspaper slide on to the floor among the foam debris – and walked out of the room.

Thorne got up and retrieved the paper. He turned to the sports pages and saw that, despite the draw they had scraped with Liverpool the previous Saturday, Spurs were still flirting dangerously with the bottom three.

Then he followed the man out.

Walking fast towards the exit, he thought about his father's war stories. Jim Thorne had been no more than nine or ten when the Second World War had broken out, and his army experience had taken him no further than Salisbury Plain. But he'd been happy to pass on the fact that he hadn't seen a pineapple until he was eighteen, and recalled nights spent below ground while the bombs fell on north London with a clarity that remained undimmed even at the end. Thorne knew this sort of thing was not uncommon, but still he marvelled at how his dad could describe every inch of an air-raid shelter, then forget to put on any underwear.

'For pity's sake, Dad ...'

'I forgot. I fucking forgot the bastard things!'

Thorne's father had told him, often, that he'd enjoyed his time as a soldier; that he'd needed the discipline and the routine. Thorne wondered if the problems of many of those who left the army each year stemmed from an

212

inability to deal with the chaos, with the lack of any pattern to their lives in the real world. It would certainly explain why so many regained the order they craved in another way, by moving quickly from army to prison.

He wondered if Jago or the other man might ever have done time . . .

Approaching the exit, he saw the man from the lounge, and something in the stance reminded Thorne of his father's friend Victor. He had a few years on Jim Thorne, had seen active service, and Thorne wondered what a soldier of Victor's generation would make of all this. He knew about how men with shellshock had been mistreated after the Great War, but did that compare with the fate that awaited so many who'd returned from Sarajevo, Belfast, Goose Green?

Thorne remembered reading somewhere that more British soldiers had committed suicide since returning from the Falklands than had been killed during the entire conflict.

The man from the lounge was standing at the door, arguing with someone who looked like a case-worker. Thorne hovered, pretending to study the row of tatty paperbacks on a shelf, not wanting to push past the men in the doorway.

'We were supposed to fill those forms in together,' the case-worker said. 'It's important, Gerry. You promised me you'd bring them in today.'

Gerry was clearly agitated. 'I forgot. I fucking forgot the bastard things . . .'

*

Back at Becke House, Holland made sure he got to Andy Stone first.

'Guess how many ways you're in the shit?'

The smile slid off Stone's face.

'I've tried to call you half a dozen times since midday.'

'The phone was off for an hour at the most, I swear,' Stone said.

'That's only one of the ways. Why didn't you update the CRIS after you spoke to Susan Jago?'

'When?'

'After you rang with the death message. Last Saturday afternoon.'

Stone opened and closed his mouth, looked at the ceiling.

'You're a fucking idiot,' Holland said. And he knew that *he* was too, and that Kitson felt much the same way. She was already in with Russell Brigstocke, and Holland wasn't so sure that the DCI would be quite so ready to blame himself. 'I walked into a meeting this morning, unable to answer the simplest question, because we hadn't got any of the information about Chris Jago that we should have been given by his sister.'

'I'm not with you . . .'

'When you spoke to Susan Jago last Saturday, did she tell you that her brother had been in the army?'

'No.'

Holland toyed with being pissy just for once and demanding a 'sir', but he decided against it. 'She said nothing about his service history at all?'

'Fuck, don't you think I'd have told you if she had?'

214

'I *thought* you'd have updated the CRIS,' Holland said. 'Looks like I can't take anything for granted.'

The implications of what Holland was telling him were starting to dawn on Stone. 'So she never said anything to *anybody*?'

Holland answered with his eyes. 'I thought Kitson had the information and *she* thought *I'd* got it off the system. It was never on the system in the first place.'

'Bloody hell.' Stone leaned back against a desk, folded his arms. 'After Thorne came up with the idea that the tattoo was an army thing, I did think it was strange that she hadn't mentioned it. I just thought someone would have checked with her. I thought someone would be getting in touch to ask her about it, you know?'

'Well, nobody did.'

'Hang about. Has it not occurred to you that she didn't say anything about him being ex-army because he *wasn't*. It's only a theory, isn't it . . . ?'

Holland shook his head, adamant. 'He was ex-army. That's an army tattoo.' Even as he said it, Holland was aware that this was still conjecture, but he knew instinctively that it was true. And, equally, instinct told him that Susan Jago had been deliberately keeping the information back from them. Yes, they *should* have checked, but they'd been so fired up by Thorne's theory that they'd neglected to get the simplest piece of procedure right. But the fact remained that Susan Jago had volunteered nothing. Holland had already called Phil Hendricks, asked about his and Jago's conversation in the car on the way to Euston, and she'd evidently said nothing to him either.

'So, how pissed off is Kitson about this CRIS thing?'

Holland had already taken a step towards Brigstocke's office. He needed to tell them that he'd spoken to Stone and confirmed their suspicions. That they needed to talk to Susan Jago urgently.

Stone shouted after him. 'I just presumed someone had called her . . . '

Thorne had sat through many tedious hours on stakeouts; in strategically chosen attic rooms or in the backs of unmarked vans. He had felt time drag as slowly as he'd ever imagined it could, and that was with the benefit of company, and coffee. With the prospect of a beer and a warm bed when it was all over.

Time spent on the streets passed like something that was spread over you; marked out in footsteps that could only grow heavier. And heavier still. There were moments when it felt like *no* time could have passed; when you found yourself staring into a familiar window or treading the same stretch of pavement yet again. It was only the blisters and the burning through the joints at the end of each day that made you certain it had passed at all.

Thorne settled back against the door of the theatre and thought about a couple of boys he'd seen in a narrow side street when he'd left the day centre: their skinny fingers cradled around the smoking rock; a flattened and gouged-out Coke can used as a crack-pipe.

He had come to understand just why so many of those with drink and drug problems had turned in desperation to such comforts *after* they'd begun sleeping rough. If anything – bottled or burned – could numb the pain of hours that spread like tumours, or speed up the ticking steps, then Thorne saw clearly that it was something to be clutched at and cherished.

He reached behind him, felt for the can in his rucksack. At least he still had the prospect of beer . . .

Deep inside his pocket, the tiny mobile phone was still cradled in his hand. When he'd spoken to Holland earlier, when he'd been told that they would be bringing Susan Jago down from Stoke for an interview, he'd told him to check whether her brother had ever been in prison. It couldn't hurt to ask.

From the sound of it, it wouldn't hurt to ask the woman a great many things. There had to be a very good reason why she was being secretive, and now they had to hope they would find it. Thus far, luck and guesswork had allowed them to take a few, faltering steps – in who knew what direction – but Susan Jago might provide the hand shoved firmly in the back. The push that would give them the impetus to catch up with a killer.

As Thorne took out the phone and dialled, he wondered whether Chris Jago had been a good soldier. He also wondered if he'd known the driver of the car that had killed him.

The man who answered the phone recited his number slowly, then asked who was speaking.

'It's Tom. I'm sorry for calling so late ...'

'It's not late, son. Don't worry.'

It had gone midnight, but Thorne's apology had been no more than a courtesy. If anyone had spent longer than he had on the phone to his father in the small hours, it had been Victor. Thorne had been fairly certain that he'd be awake.

'So, what's up?' Victor asked.

'Nothing, really. Just calling for a natter ...'

Even as he spoke, Thorne thought that, in truth, there was nothing very much worth talking about; nothing that would have any bearing on the case at any rate.

'That's fine, son. It's good to talk. Let me just go and turn the radio off ...'

Thorne watched as a pair of young women on fuck-me heels clattered past on the pavement opposite. It was far too cold for belly-tops and bare midriffs ...

'That's better.'

If anyone had ever told him where Victor had origi-nally come from, Thorne had forgotten, but he spoke with the faintest of accents. Somewhere Eastern Euro-pean, by the sound of it. It struck Thorne that he had no idea *which* army Victor had fought for. He realised that actually, there were a great many things he didn't know about his father's best friend. Things that he wanted to know. Like whether Victor had any family. What he had done before he retired. Where he had met his father, and how long they had known each other, and why he was the only one of his dad's mates who hadn't suddenly developed a busy life when the old man started going loopy.

'Tom?'

'What?'

'You're not doing a lot of nattering, son.'

'Sorry. So, how've you been? Keeping yourself busy?'

'Oh, yes, I'm always busy,' Victor said. 'What about yourself? How's the job?'

'You know . . . '

'When the phone went I thought it was him, you know? Just for a few seconds. Calling up with some quiz question, or one of his jokes, or trying to find out the word for something he'd forgotten. Remember how he used to do that?'

Thorne closed his eyes. He'd seen some film or read a book in which memory could be wiped out with a pill. Right now, even though good memories would be erased along with the bad, he'd take it.

'It's OK,' Victor said. 'I miss the silly old bugger as well, you know?'

Thorne felt suddenly as though he were only seconds away from sleep. 'I'm fine, honestly, Victor. I really didn't ring to talk about him.'

Then a low, amused hum. 'Course you didn't . . . '

SIXTEEN

Becke House was not a fully functioning police station. There were no cells – other than those the detectives were required to work in – and no formal interview suite. As with anyone else who had to be questioned, or held, Susan Jago was taken to Colindale. It had the necessary facilities in abundance, and the added advantage of being just five minutes up the road.

'How long d'you think this is going to take?' Jago said.

Holland opened the door and showed her inside. 'I'd say that was very much up to you, Susan . . . '

It was a narrow room and windowless, but cleaner than most. Jago dropped her handbag down by a chair and nudged it under the table. She looked up at the digital clock on the wall. Though she'd caught an early train from Stoke and been collected by uniformed officers from the station, it was already a few minutes after eleven o'clock. 'I was hoping I could get back to pick the kids up from school.'

'I'm not sure that's very likely,' Holland said. He reached across for her jacket and hung it on a coat-rack behind the door.

When Kitson entered the room, Holland took her coat, too. She nodded at Jago. 'Thanks for coming down so quickly.'

Susan Jago looked different from the last time they'd seen her. Her dark hair had been dragged back into a ponytail and there was no make-up to get ruined by tears. She looked more confident, certainly, but also harder. Holland had already gone through the Judges' Rules with her outside. He'd explained that she was not under arrest, that she was free to leave at any time, and that she was entitled to legal representation. She'd laughed at him as if he were being silly. Now, he went over the same ground for the benefit of the tape. The date was stated and the names of those present given for the record.

Jago glanced up at the camera high in the corner. The hardware had been recently upgraded. Now, as well as being recorded on two audio cassettes, the interview was being simultaneously filmed and burned on to a CD ROM. She looked back to the racks of shiny, wall-mounted equipment. 'I bet that lot cost a fair bit,' she said.

Kitson didn't want to hang around any longer than anybody else did. 'Miss Jago, did your brother, Christopher David Jago, ever serve in the British Army?'

If there was hesitation, it was only fractional. She

answered slowly and surely and with pride in her voice. 'Yes, Chris was a soldier.'

'So why did you choose not to tell us that?'

'When?'

'Let's start with when you came to London to identify a body that you believed to be that of your brother.'

'This is going to sound stupid, but nobody asked me.'

'You're right,' Kitson said. 'It does sound *very* stupid . . .'

'Well, I can't help that. I didn't think it was relevant.'

Holland spoke up. 'Surely, if you were looking for your brother, any information about him, about his past, would have been relevant, wouldn't it?'

'Look, I just wanted to know if it was him, and when it wasn't, I just wanted to get the hell out of there and go home. Nothing else seemed very important.'

Holland stretched out his legs, then withdrew them quickly when his feet made contact with Jago's. 'You had a long chat with Dr Hendricks on the way to the train station, didn't you? You were perfectly happy at that time to talk about your brother's history with drugs, about his mental problems, but, again, you never saw fit to mention his past in the army.'

She reached towards her handbag. 'Can I smoke in here?'

'I'm afraid not.' Kitson raised a finger casually towards the smoke alarm on the ceiling, neglecting to mention that it never contained any batteries. The no-smoking rule was her own. She hated cigarettes anyway, but also believed

222

that keeping an interviewee on edge would deliver better results more often than not.

Jago smiled weakly. 'What happened to the good cop sliding the fag packet across the table when the bad cop goes out of the room?'

'We're both bad cops,' Kitson said.

'Miss Jago.' Holland tapped a finger on the tabletop. He wanted an answer. 'You never mentioned your brother's army history during the conversation with Dr Hendricks. Is that correct?'

She nodded.

'For the tape, please . . .'

'Yes, correct. I never mentioned it, but I don't see why one's got anything to do with the other.'

'Don't you?' Kitson asked. 'How many ex-soldiers do you suppose end up sleeping on the streets, Susan? As opposed to ex-footballers, say? Or ex-bank managers?'

Jago shrugged.

'Let's move on a bit,' Holland said. 'A couple of days after that first trip to London, you were contacted by Detective Constable Stone, who told you that we had information about your brother's death.'

She shifted suddenly on her chair, as though there were something uncomfortable on the seat beneath her. 'Right, like it was good news. A fucking phone call from some smarmy, low-rank moron who'd obviously drawn the short straw, telling me Chris is dead. And now you're going to sit there and ask me why I didn't say anything about him being in the army again, aren't you? Well, I'm sorry if I had other things to worry about, like what I was going to tell my mother. Like how I was going to find out where the council had buried my brother . . . '

Holland could see by the look on Kitson's face that she was in no mood to be messed around. 'Let's not waste any more time with this, all right? I'm going to stop saying "forgot to mention" and "neglected to inform" and I'm going to call it what it is: lying. You lied to us, and you withheld information that might have been important to a murder investigation.'

Jago slapped her palms against her jeans and raised her voice. 'They're not the same thing. They're fucking not. You tell me when I lied . . . '

'What about the tattoos?'

The skin around her mouth slackened suddenly, as if the ponytail had been keeping it taut and had suddenly been removed.

'I haven't done anything wrong.' She held Kitson's stare, but her voice had lost all of its stridency.

'You were asked on a number of occasions, by myself, by DS Holland, and by DC Stone during your telephone conversation on 17 September, if you knew what the significance of the tattoos was. On each of those occasions you said that you did not.'

'*On each of those occasions* I was hardly thinking straight, was I?'

'You lied.'

'No.'

'You knew very well they were army tattoos.'

'I never lied. I've already explained that the first time I was messed up. I'd just seen a dead body, for crying out loud, I'd been looking at some poor sod with most of his face kicked to shit. Then, later on, when he asked me about the tattoos on the phone, I was in a complete state, wasn't I? Because I'd just found out that Chris had been murdered as well. How was I expected to think straight?' She shook her head, kept shaking it, but both Holland and Kitson could see immediately that she knew what she'd just said.

'That's a strange way of putting it, don't you think, Susan? Your brother was the victim of a hit-and-run driver, wasn't he? You'd been given no other information than that. You were told it was an accident. Yet you just said, "Chris had been murdered as well". Like the first victim had been murdered . . .'

Outside on the street a car was being revved up, and somewhere along the corridor a telephone was going unanswered.

Kitson leaned forward. 'Why did you lie to us?'

It hadn't taken very long. Susan Jago had been prepared, certainly, had been gearing herself up to front it out, but no amount of hard-faced posturing could mask the agony she felt inside. Once she started talking, it came quickly, like poison from a boil that's been lanced.

'I didn't think it mattered, I swear I didn't. It's like I told that pathologist bloke in the car, I just thought Chris had gone walkabout – you know? – and that he'd come waltzing back when he was ready. So why would knowing what he'd done before matter to anyone except me and him? I just wanted to forget all of it. I managed to convince myself that I didn't know much about his past and that it wasn't hurting anybody to leave it like that.' She looked from Holland to Kitson and back again. 'Then I found out he was dead, and I knew there were two of them. When I knew they'd both been murdered, I wanted to come clean about it all. I wanted to tell, honestly I did, but it was like I'd got so caught up in the lie that I couldn't figure out a way to make it right again . . . '

'Did you recognise the man you saw in the mortuary?' Kitson asked.

She raised her eyes, every trace of bravado long gone. 'I could really murder that fag now.'

'Did you recognise him, Susan?'

'Yes. He was in the crew with Chris. But on my children's lives, I never knew his name. I just saw a photo of the four of them together once, that's all.'

'What crew?' Holland said.

'Chris was a Tanky. He was in the 12th King's Hussars. That's a cavalry regiment—'

Kitson raised a hand, needing to slow things down a little. 'Four of them, you said. Why four?'

'There's four in a Challenger crew. That's the tank Chris and his mates were on. It was the four of them that went out and got those tattoos done just before they were flown out. The blood groups and those letters, which is just a piss-take, by the way, because they all hated the Royal Tank Regiment. There was some stupid rivalry, because they thought the

Royals were posh, and the Royals' motto is "Fear Nought", right? So Chris and the others got their own mottos done, as a joke: S.O.F.A. – Scared Of Fuck All . . . '

Holland was struggling to take all of it in, but he could sense its importance. The room seemed to constrict suddenly and grow warmer. It felt as though his ears were popping. 'We've got plenty of time to get all this down, Susan. Can you just tell us why you wanted to keep it a secret?'

Jago reached down and lifted her handbag on to her lap.

'You can have that fag in a minute, Susan,' Kitson said.

But it wasn't a cigarette packet Jago took out. It was a videotape. She placed a hand flat on top of it; then, after a few seconds, she pushed it across the table.

'I'll tell you anything you want to know,' she said. 'Anything I can. But I won't watch it . . . '

1991

There are two groups of men, four in each ...

Now all of them are gathered together. Those who were previously tied up are sitting much closer together, with the others squashed in around them, squatting or stooping. Though only four of these eight men are dead, the entire group is momentarily still.

Posed and posing.

Behind this bizarre tableau, for the first time the hulking figure of the tank is visible. Its side and its muddy track, streaked with petrol-rain, provide the perfect backdrop. It also offers something to lean the dead men back against.

After a few seconds we hear the voice from close by. Shouted this time. The words are just discernible above the relentless pop and spatter of the rain: 'Put your arms around them ... Give the fuckers a cuddle.'

Two of the soldiers do as they've been told. They lean

forward and each throws an arm around the shoulder of a corpse. The other two soldiers remain still, with their heads lowered.

'I can't see faces ... *Lift their heads up.*'

One of the soldiers is down on his haunches between two bodies, an arm now around each one. He looks across to one of those who has not moved. 'A bit late to pussy out now.'

After a few moments, the soldier who has been challenged stoops to grab the hair of the dead man and pull back his head. Close-up we see that the corpse's eyes are half closed and the jaw is hanging slack. Rain pours into the open mouth, spills from the side.

'Uh-oh ... losing one ... '

The body on the far right starts to tip to one side and slowly fall. The soldier behind, who has still not joined in, half reaches out a hand, then pulls it away at the last moment and allows the dead man to drop to the ground.

'For fuck's sake ... '

It isn't clear at first. The rain and the shadows, the dark sand and hair make it hard to distinguish. Then, on the body of the fallen man we see the patch that is wetter, blacker; high on the side of the head, and just starting to spread an inch or two across the sand.

'Watch ... '

A soldier has pressed his face against that of a dead man. He raises a hand and wraps it around the neck. He swivels the head around, one way and then another.

'Gottle of geer, gottle ... geer ... '

His friend laughs, pulling off a glove. He leans across and presses a finger to the back of the corpse's head. He looks at the stained fingertip, rubs it against his thumb for a second or two, then dabs it against the dead man's forehead.

A small red spot that starts to run.

'That's better. Want to make sure they let him in to Heaven.'

The soldier who'd let the body drop stands suddenly and reaches over. He grabs the soldier who is still putting his glove back on and drags him to his feet. Screams into his face.

'That's Hindus, you ignorant prick. Not Muslims.'

'All right . . . '

'Not fucking Muslims!' He pushes him away and the two soldiers stand and look at each other. The horizon is a glowing strip behind them.

Then, the camera drifts away, and down.

And white noise . . .

SEVENTEEN

Holland jabbed at the remote and stopped the tape.

After something close to half a minute, during which nobody spoke, Holland got up and moved across to the television. He crouched down by the VCR and ejected the cassette.

Brigstocke turned to the man sitting next to him. 'What d'you reckon?'

'I reckon it's something worth killing for,' Thorne said. 'Worth killing to keep hidden.'

'It's fucking horrible.' Holland stuffed the cassette back into a large Jiffy bag and sat down again. 'That's the fourth time I've seen it and I'm still glad I haven't eaten anything today.'

The three of them were sitting in beige armchairs, gathered around a coffee-table in the TV room at the London Lift. Though he'd moaned initially, complaining that he'd be in the shit if Lawrence Healey ever found out, Brendan Maxwell had eventually agreed to open the place up for them out of hours. It was just after seven on a Thursday night. Nearly thirty-six hours since Susan Jago had handed over the videotape.

'What about the sound?' Thorne asked. 'You can't make out a lot of what's being said. One voice is completely distorted early on, when they're doing that shit with the bacon.'

Holland grimaced. 'That's really hideous . . . '

'We're sending it to the lab at Newlands Park,' Brigstocke said. 'Having heard some of the things they've done with 999 recordings, I reckon they can enhance the dialogue for us. We might find out what everyone was saying.'

'So what *do* we know?' Thorne asked.

Holland took out a notebook, though he didn't really need it. 'It's the first Gulf War. Chris Jago was posted there from Bremenhaven in northern Germany in October 1990. The date on the tape tells us that what we saw took place on February 26th, 1991. As to exactly where . . . '

'I'm not sure it really matters,' Brigstocke said.

Thorne scratched at what had become a pretty decent beard. 'What does Susan Jago say?'

'She says her brother didn't want to go along with any of it,' Holland said. 'She says that he was the one at the end doing the shouting.'

'Of course she does.'

'It's impossible to tell who's who, so I doubt we'll ever know.'

232

'Like I said before, I'm not sure it really matters,' Brigstocke said.

Thorne shook his head, let it drop back against his chair. 'Nobody tried very hard to stop it. They were all involved on some level.'

'We *do* know one of the others is our mystery man in Westminster Morgue.' Holland picked up his briefcase and took out a grainy 10 × 8 photograph: a still from the video showing the four British soldiers; the moment before one of them moved forward from the group and checked his gun; just before the killing began. Holland laid the photo on the table, tapped at it with a fingernail. 'With a bit of luck, we'll have names for all of them by this time tomorrow.'

Brigstocke looked at Thorne. 'Holland and Kitson are going to pay the twelfth King's Hussars a visit tomorrow.'

'You're going to *Germany*?' Thorne asked.

Holland's expression soured. 'Bloody regiment got shifted back here five years ago, didn't it? They're based near Taunton now, so I get to go to Somerset instead. Shame. I could have done with a new overcoat.' Officers were given allowances of a few hundred pounds, usually in Marks & Spencer vouchers, if they were travelling to countries that would be warmer, or in this case cooler than they might be used to . . .

'Nice to see you've still got your priorities sorted, Dave,' Thorne said.

Holland stood and walked towards a varnished-pine bookcase in the corner. He laid a hand on top of the Jiffy bag as he passed the table. 'God knows what they're going to make of *that* mind you.' He sank down to his haunches in front of the bookcase and peered through the locked glass doors at the rows of videotapes and DVDs inside.

'It's going to be interesting, all right,' Thorne said.

'That's one word for it.'

'How are you going to play it?' Thorne looked across at Brigstocke and received a small shake of the head in return.

'You've got some good stuff in here,' Holland said. 'All the *Scream* movies. A lot of Jim Carrey stuff . . . '

Thorne pointed to the Jiffy bag. 'I think I'd rather watch *that* again.'

They all laughed, but nobody's heart was really in it. Least of all Thorne's.

'Why don't you find us a caff, Dave?' Brigstocke said. 'Bring us some teas back.'

Thorne had eaten no more than Holland, but for different reasons. Now he wanted a variety of cakes and sandwiches with his tea, and in the end Holland had to write it all down. When he'd gone, Thorne turned to Brigstocke. 'What was all *that* about?' He mimicked the strange shaking of the head that had gone on just before.

'I need to get this rubber-stamped by Jesmond first thing in the morning,' he said. 'He's gone higher up, but for what it's worth I've told him I don't think we should tell the army about the video just yet.'

Thorne considered this for a moment or two. 'It makes sense.'

Brigstocke looked relieved that Thorne was agreeing with him, but explained himself anyway. 'What's on this tape is a bloody big deal, and once the army gets hold of it they might well think they've got better things to worry about than a few murders.'

'You're worried they'll try and find some way to cover it up?'

Brigstocke looked worried about *something*, certainly. 'I don't know. Look, when our case is put to bed they can do what they want with it and I'll be happy to co-operate in any way I can. Right now, though, that tape's just evidence in my murder investigation, and I need their help.' He looked down at the photograph on the table. 'I need the names of those men, and if the army knows about this tape I'm not sure we'll get given them very quickly. See what I'm saying?'

'Like I said, it makes sense.'

'It does, doesn't it?'

It was obvious that Brigstocke was still nervous about having made such a potentially dangerous decision. He needed reassurance, and Thorne could understand why he'd sent Holland out before he'd gone looking for it. Thorne wanted to tell him that he was handling the situation well, that he was making a good job of a miserable case. He wanted to tell him that he wasn't the only one in the room who needed reassurance. The moment came and went . . .

'Jesmond might well bottle it,' Brigstocke said. 'If he orders us to hand the tape over, we'll hand it over and see what happens. The Met's worked well enough with the RMP when we've had to. It'll probably be fine ...'

'Or it'll be like we never had the tape in the first place.'

'We'll see ...'

'What about the sister?' Thorne asked.

'She's back home but we got pretty heavy with her. She thinks she's going to get done for perverting the course of justice.'

'Is she?'

'We'll let the CPS decide. It'll be a difficult one to call, because she never actually *did* anything. She was lying to protect a dead man.'

Thorne had never met Susan Jago. He imagined her as hard-faced and cunning. He pictured thin lips and dead eyes; features she'd have shared with one of the men behind goggles and a coloured kerchief. A man who'd tied up prisoners and executed them. 'She didn't know he was dead when she lied, though, did she?'

The two of them sat back in their chairs, waiting for Holland to return with the food and hot drinks.

'It's just such a fucking relief,' Brigstocke said. 'To have a motive. It's got to be blackmail, agreed?'

Thorne nodded. 'It's the only thing that explains why it's happening now.' It was the obvious conclusion. Someone was willing to kill to prevent this tape getting out. A threat had been made to expose what had happened fifteen

236

years before, and whoever had been threatened had reacted violently. Thorne looked at the picture of the four soldiers. Whoever was doing the blackmailing, the killer had decided to take no chances . . .

Brigstocke sat up, leaned down to study the photograph alongside Thorne. The conditions when the picture was taken, alongside that of the broken down image itself, had combined to give it the strange quality of a double exposure. The figures, dark green against grey, seemed incomplete, almost spectral. Brigstocke traced a finger along the row of soldiers. 'We know two of those four are dead, right? If the other two are still alive, we need to find them.'

'Especially if one of them's the killer,' Thorne said.

'I don't think it's very likely.' Brigstocke sat forward. 'A blackmailer's going to target someone with money. Someone who's done pretty well for himself. Right? Based on what we know so far, that doesn't sound like your average ex-squaddie . . . '

Thorne had to agree that it made good sense. He thought about the voice on the tape, distorted on occasion, and too close to the mike. The voice that had seemed to be giving the orders. 'Well that only leaves one option,' he said, nodding towards the blank screen. 'We're looking for whoever was behind the camera.'

By the time they'd finished at the Lift and Thorne had gone on his way, Holland and Brigstocke were off duty for the night. Brigstocke had gone straight home, and Holland knew that he should really do the same. Instead, he'd called the office to see who might still be around, and, finding that Yvonne Kitson had not yet left, had arranged to meet her for a drink. He'd jumped on the tube and headed all the way back north to Colindale, to meet the DI in the Royal Oak.

Inside half an hour they'd put away a couple each and begun to loosen up a little.

'Where are the kids tonight . . . ?' As Holland was asking the question he realised he was unsure what he should call Kitson. He couldn't remember having a drink with her on her own before, and something about it – and perhaps about the fact that they were drinking so fast – seemed to alter the dynamic between them.

'Tony's got them. He picks them up from the child-minder if I'm on a late one.'

'Right.' Holland hadn't heard Kitson mention her new bloke's name before.

'And "Yvonne"'s fine, by the way,' she said. 'I think we're off the clock in here.'

They took sips of white wine and lager-top and looked around at the pub's brightly lit and unwelcoming interior. The place had no frills, but was still very busy. As it happened, being very much the local for the Peel Centre, there were usually just as many coppers in the place as were to be found up the road in Becke House.

'What about you, Dave? You were somewhere near Leicester Square, weren't you?'

'That's right.' Kitson still had no idea that Thorne had

gone undercover, and so obviously had not been informed that Holland and Brigstocke had gone into the West End to meet up with him and show him the tape. 'Some old boy told one of the local lads he'd seen something on the night of the last murder. Waste of bloody time . . .'

'That's only a few stops from Elephant and Castle, isn't it? You could have been home in quarter of an hour.'

A copper, whose face he'd seen before in the pub and at various times around Becke House, came to the table and asked Holland if the empty chair opposite him was taken. Holland shook his head, watched the man take the chair across and join a group who looked like they were settling down to make a night of it. He turned back to Kitson. 'It's not fair on Sophie. I'm bringing such a lot of shit home with me at the moment, you know? Like I'm walking it through the flat and getting it everywhere. Dirtying everything . . .'

'Is this about the tape?'

'It's mad, I know. We see loads of horrible stuff, right? It's just seeing it happen like that. Watching them do it.'

'It's how you're *meant* to feel, Dave. You should be worried if you didn't.'

'This is going to sound stupid, but I don't want to pass any of it on to Chloe. *I* have to deal with it, but there's no reason why she should, is there? It's like passive smoking or something. I don't want her anywhere near anything that might affect her, and right now it's like I'm choking on

239

it. I feel like I'm carrying it around on my clothes and in my hair. Passive evil ...'

Kitson smiled as she raised her glass to her lips.

'Told you it was stupid,' Holland said.

Kitson shook her head. 'It's not that,' she said. 'I curse my three sometimes, but perhaps I should be grateful I've got so much chasing round to do. I'm too busy sorting out football kit, and nagging them about homework, and running a taxi service, to worry about bringing work home with me.'

'Maybe me and Sophie should have a few more kids,' Holland said.

Kitson drained her wineglass. 'My shout ...'

While Kitson was at the bar, Holland thought about the way Susan Jago had fought to protect her brother; to defend him, even in the face of the sickening evidence. He wondered what Jago's mother would think about what her son had done. He'd confronted the parents of those who had committed the most shocking acts and knew that in most cases they never stopped loving their children. They couldn't, any more than he could conceive of not feeling as he did now about his daughter, no matter what she did. For the families – especially the parents – of those who killed or abused, faith could be destroyed. But love, he knew now, was unconditional. When your children did such things, you did not stop loving them. You simply began hating yourself.

Kitson was coming back to the table with the drinks and she smiled as he caught her eye. Holland thought suddenly that she looked quite sexy. Asked himself what the hell he was thinking . . .

'What were you doing,' Kitson asked some time later, 'in 1991?'

Holland did the maths. 'I was sixteen, so I suppose I was going out a lot. I can remember coming back late from parties or clubs a couple of times and sitting up watching the bombing on TV. What about you?'

'I was just finishing college,' Kitson said. 'We were all dead against it, obviously. Not as much as with the last one, but there were still plenty of protests. We thought it was all about oil.'

A cheer went up as someone hit the jackpot on the fruit machine in the corner. Holland leaned forward, spoke up to make himself heard above the rhythmic chink and clatter of the payout. 'It doesn't matter whether you're a copper or a killer, does it?' He swallowed a mouthful of beer. 'How well do we really know anybody?'

Kitson raised her eyebrows. 'Bloody hell . . . '

Holland reddened slightly. He hadn't meant it to sound so stupidly portentous. 'I never had you down as a lefty, that's all,' he said.

'Watford Polytechnic was hardly Kent State.'

Holland laughed, though he didn't understand the reference. 'Even so . . . '

'And I never had *you* down as someone who takes such a lot of the job home with him.' She smiled, nodding towards Holland's glass. 'Speaking of which . . . '

'What?'

241

'If you *do* want to have any more kids, you'd best finish that, go home and get down to it . . . '

'You look wankered, mate,' Spike said.

Thorne grinned and swayed to one side, waving a young woman past as if he were a bullfighter. 'I *feel* wankered,' he said. 'Bladdered, fucked, off my tits . . . '

'How many of those have you had?'

Thorne had just about got used to the taste of Carlsberg Special Brew, but he hadn't been prepared for the kick. It was somewhere past chucking-out time and he'd been drinking steadily since he'd left the London Lift. Since he'd said goodbye to Holland and Brigstocke and begun trying to walk off the memory of what he'd seen on that videotape.

'Not enough.' Thorne could feel the weight of the cans in his rucksack. 'Plenty more, though . . . '

Walking hadn't done the trick, so he'd gone straight into the nearest Tesco Metro and handed over a quarter of his weekly money in exchange for eight cans.

'You should save a couple,' Caroline said.

He'd met up with Spike and Caroline on Bedford Street and they'd walked aimlessly around Covent Garden ever since. Thorne had announced that he wanted to go to sleep an hour before, that he had to get back to his theatre, but somehow he never quite kept going in any one direction and it seemed stupid to doss down anywhere while there was still a can open.

'Have one!' Thorne tried to reach behind into the rucksack, his arm flailing.

'I keep telling you, I don't want one,' Spike said. 'I'll take one off you to sell, mind you ...'

'You can piss off,' Thorne said.

Caroline pulled a face. 'That stuff tastes fucking horrible ...'

'I don't understand why you two don't drink.' Thorne held up the gold and red can and read the writing; the *By Royal Appointment*. 'If it's good enough for the Danish court ...'

'Prefer to save our money, like,' Spike said. 'Spend it on the good stuff.'

Caroline took Thorne's arm and hooked her own around it as they walked. 'I'll have a vodka, mind you, if there's one on offer.'

'I bet fuck all gets done in Denmark,' Thorne said.

Spike cackled.

'Be nice to get dressed up one night, wouldn't it?' Caroline reached out her other arm and drew Spike towards her. 'Go out somewhere and dance, and drink vodka and tonic or a few cocktails ...'

Spike leaned over to kiss her and Thorne pulled away from them.

He whistled. 'Give her a snog, for Christ's sake, and tell her you love her.' He was aware of how he sounded: the words not slurred exactly, but slow and singsong; emphasised oddly, like he was speaking through a machine. 'Go on, put your arms round her ...'

'*Put your arms round them ... Give the fuckers a cuddle.*'

Thorne stopped dead and shut his eyes. The can slipped out of his hand on to the pavement. 'Fuck . . . '

Caroline and Spike walked over.

'We need to get you bedded down,' Caroline said.

Thorne looked down at the thick, golden liquid running away across the kerb. He pushed the toe of his boot into it. His stomach lurched as he watched it spread and darken, leaking from the wound and staining the sand.

'I want to go to sleep,' he said.

Spike pushed him forward. 'I thought you boozers were supposed to have some kind of tolerance . . . '

Sleep hung around, but refused to settle. Instead, thoughts collided inside his thick head like oversized dodgems moving at half speed . . .

Atrocious was a meaningless, fucked-up word. A crappy meal could be atrocious, yes, or a shit football team or a bad movie. *Atrocious* didn't come close to describing the thing itself: the atrocity. That's what they were calling it. Brigstocke and the rest of them. Not murder. An *atrocity*. All about the context, apparently . . .

There were rats in the skip around the corner. He could hear them digging into the bin-bags. Chewing through styrofoam for crusts, and wrappers slick with kebab fat.

He'd probably seen things as bad in Surbiton semis and Hackney tower-blocks, or at least the aftermath of such things. He'd certainly *known* of worse – of acts that had left a greater number dead – happening in that war and in others. He'd watched them on the news. Weren't those things *atrocities*, too?

He belched up Special Brew, tasting it a second time. Moaning. Biting down into each sour–sweet bubble.

Why was what he'd seen on that piece-of-shit tape any worse than when a bomb fell through the red cross daubed on a hospital roof? These were not civilians, were they? This was soldiers killing soldiers. Yet, somehow it *was* worse. You knew perfectly well that things went wrong, that machines went wrong, and that people fucked up. But this wasn't fucking up; this was basic bloody horror. This was inhuman behaviour from those who'd been there – who were *supposed* to have been there – in defence of humanity.

He shifted, driving an elbow into the rucksack behind him and pulling at the frayed edge of the sleeping bag. He could smell himself on the warm air that rose up from inside.

If anything, what he'd seen on that tape, what had happened at the end, was more terrible than the executions themselves. But whoever was behind the camera hadn't filmed the actual shootings. There was no way, from seeing the tape, of knowing if each of the four soldiers had done his bit.

If each one of *ours* had killed one of *theirs* ...

He hoped it hadn't been the case; hoped that one soldier, or at worst two, had done all the killing. He pictured one of the soldiers lining up the prisoners and trying to kill as many as he could with one shot. If those heavy heads were close enough together, if all those ducks were in a row, would the bullet pass straight through one and into the next? Through two or three maybe ...?

Now the soldiers themselves were being hunted down and killed. It was hard to feel too sorry for them though, kicked to death or not. They weren't shitting themselves, were they? Sitting there, watching it happen, and waiting their turn.

He lay down flat and turned his head. The stone felt wonderfully cool against his face.

It had to be the man who'd shot the video, didn't it? Surely. That's what he felt in his guts, swilling around with the beer and the tea and the sandwiches. They'd know soon enough; they'd know what was happening when they found the other two soldiers. If they were alive, they could identify whoever had been pointing that camera.

Somebody shot soldiers shooting.

Fucking tongue-twister ...

Thorne smelled something familiar and opened his eyes.

He had no idea how many hours it had been since Spike and Caroline had dropped him at his doorway and left. He was equally clueless as to how long Spike had been back, sitting there on the steps with a skinny joint in his hand. Without a watch, Thorne relied on his mobile phone to tell him the time. Even if he could have dug it out now in front of Spike, he wouldn't have bothered ...

'When d'you come back?'

'Just.' Without turning, he offered Thorne the joint. 'Want some?'

Thorne groaned a negative. 'Where's Caroline?'

From the back, Thorne could see the shrug, and shake of the head, but not Spike's expression. 'Busy . . .'

Thorne's eyes had closed for what seemed like no more than a second when he heard something smack against the wall above him and felt something hit his face.

''Fuck's that?'

He sat up, wiping his mouth, and saw the messy remains of a burger scattered on the floor and across his sleeping bag. He saw Spike standing and moving towards two men in the middle of the street.

'What d'you think you're fucking doing?' Spike asked.

The man who answered was wearing a green parka and a blank expression. He slurred, mock-apologetic. 'Sorry, mate, I thought this was a rubbish tip . . .'

The second man was bald and thin-faced. He laughed and casually lobbed something else, whistling as if he'd launched a grenade. Spike stepped aside and watched the cup explode, sending ice cubes and whatever drink was inside spilling across the pavement.

'You arsehole.' Spike came forward, and the first man – taller and heavier than he was – moved to meet him.

Thorne was on his feet now, sobering up very quickly and struggling to free his feet from the sleeping bag. He watched as the man in the parka spread his legs and lowered his face into Spike's.

'You fancy it, you junkie cunt?'

Then things got very out of hand very quickly.

As the pushes are exchanged, and quickly become blows, Thorne begins moving down the steps. At the same time, the bald man charges towards him. Still tangled in his sleeping bag, Thorne all but falls into him, raising his fore-arms to meet the man's face as they collide.

As they struggle, Thorne is aware of Spike and the other man going at it a few feet away. He hears leather soles scraping against the road to gain purchase, then bodies hit-ting it as they both go down. Spike's attacker is taunting him as they struggle: calling Spike filthy; a disease; a dirty, AIDS-ridden fucker. Between these words he grunts with the effort of every punch.

Thorne knows that he's being hit and kicked, but he hears rather than feels the impact. The man is lashing out wildly, screaming at Thorne that he's dead as he swings fists and feet. Thorne grabs an arm, fastens one of his own around the man's neck and moves his hands quickly. He can feel the stubble on the man's head as he takes a firm grip of it and brings a knee up hard into his face.

The man slumps ...

His hands claw at Thorne's coat, pulling off a button as he goes to his knees.

Thorne spins away and in a couple of staggered steps he is on top of the man with the parka. Spike is flat on his back beneath them, his hands raised to protect his head. Thorne tries to grab hold of the arms that are pummelling Spike, to pin them back, but it's hard to get a grip of the shiny material.

A voice shouts something close to him and Thorne feels

a hand taking hold of his shoulder. He wheels round fast, pulling back a fist.

'I said that's *enough* . . .'

Thorne paused for half a second, panting and scarlet-faced, the fist still poised to accelerate forward. He was pissed, *very* pissed no question, but still he recognised Sergeant Dan Britton. The officer was wearing the same hooded top and combats he'd been wearing in the tube station. Thorne, fizzing with adrenaline and strong lager, was nevertheless 100 per cent certain that the man who'd taken hold of him was a copper.

He took a breath . . .

Then punched him anyway.

EIGHTEEN

'I was pissed,' Thorne said. 'I didn't know what I was doing.'

'You broke my sergeant's nose is what you did . . .'

The man opposite Thorne wore a blue suit over a white shirt and a tie with golf balls on it. He'd walked into the Interview Room, told Thorne in very blunt language that he was an idiot, and put two coffees down on the table. He'd identified himself as Inspector John McCabe and then sat back, waiting for Thorne to explain himself.

'How's he doing?' Thorne asked.

'Britton? His face is about the same as yours.' McCabe slid the coffee across the table. 'You look like shit warmed up.'

Thorne felt much worse.

He was starting to realise exactly what had happened. The lack of formality, McCabe's attitude, the mugs of coffee. It was becoming obvious what he'd done; and even as McCabe spelled it out, moments from the night before zipped through Thorne's semi-functioning consciousness like a dream sequence in an arty movie. Being pinned against the wall while others scattered; shouting the odds in the van; bleeding on to the smooth counter in the Custody Suite; making it clear that he could find his own way to the cells, thank you very fucking much. Telling anyone who'd listen that they had to ring this phone number . . .

Christ, he really *hadn't* known what he was doing.

'This is the stuff of legend,' McCabe said. He was somewhere in his late forties, but there was very little grey in the helmet of straight black hair. He was clean-shaven and ruddy, with a smile – much in evidence as he spoke – that was slightly lopsided. 'In years to come, the boys at SO10 might well be using this on courses.'

'All right . . .'

'It's the perfect example of how not to do things . . .'

Thorne picked up his coffee and leaned back in his chair. It was probably best to let McCabe get on with it.

'What you do is, you get yourself arrested for something. Something nice and trivial, you know, like *assaulting a police officer*. Then, when things get a bit tasty, because you're a total fuck-up or maybe because you're a bit frightened of spending a night in the cells all on your own, you start announcing that you're actually working undercover and giving out the number of your squad to all and bloody sundry.' A slurp of coffee and the lopsided smile. 'Done *much* undercover work, have you?'

251

'Are you finished?'

'Only you don't really seem to have grasped the basic concept.'

'I'll take that as a "no" then . . . '

They stared at each other for a few moments.

Thorne was finding it hard to dislike McCabe, much as he thought it would be the appropriate thing to do. Maybe he'd start disliking him later, when the hangover had worn off a little. 'Let me try and guess why you're so tetchy,' he said. 'You clearly *are*, smiling or not . . . '

McCabe said nothing.

'It might be piles, or money worries, or maybe it's because your wife has discovered that you're really a woman trapped in a man's body. If I *had* to choose, though, I'd say it was because you haven't been kept *informed*. Not about the undercover operation, obviously. That's need-to-know . . . '

'Not last night, it wasn't . . . '

Thorne nodded, allowing McCabe the point, then carried on. 'I'm talking about the rough-sleeper murders generally. Maybe as senior officer on a specialist unit that deals with the homeless, you feel that you should have had some involvement. That you should have been consulted more.'

McCabe's smile had disappeared.

'I know fuck all about it,' Thorne said. Decisions about who should be talking to who had been taken before he was ever involved, but he knew how these things worked. It wasn't just computers that had problems talking to each other, and much as Brigstocke had been loath to take this case on, once he *had*, his Major Investigation Team was as territorial as any other. When it came to expertise and information, the idea was to avoid sharing wherever possible. 'You know the game. Everyone takes what they can and tries to give sweet FA in return.'

'Like oral sex,' McCabe said. 'Right?'

'I'm not sure I can remember back that far ...'

McCabe leaned back, ran a finger and thumb up and down the golf-ball tie. 'I've not been here long, but I've made it my business to get to know this area. To forge some kind of relationship with most of the people who bed down around here every night. Your lot were complaining that no one was telling them anything, that they weren't being trusted, but the dossers *know* the lads on my team. They might have talked to them. *If* we'd been invited to the party.'

'You must have been consulted at some point, though?'

'We were *liaised* with.' He said the word with huge distaste. Like it meant *interfered* ...

'You're right,' Thorne said. 'It's stupid. Maybe they should have put the two of us together before I went on to the streets.'

McCabe nodded, like he thought that would have been an excellent idea, turning up his palms in weary resignation at other people's idiocy. 'So how's it going, anyway?' he asked. 'It's all gone a bit quiet since Radio Bob was killed.'

Thorne took a mouthful of coffee. Gave himself a few

seconds to formulate a response. As far as his own part in things was concerned, the cat was out of the bag and happily spraying piss anywhere it wasn't wanted. Nevertheless, he thought it might be best to keep quiet about other matters. He thought that McCabe had every right to feel aggrieved at being marginalised, and that if he were brought up to speed on the case, he might even prove to be of some use.

Still, something told Thorne to say nothing.

McCabe saw the silence for what it was. 'And it's *staying* quiet, is it?'

'Like I said, you know the game ...'

The crooked smile appeared again, but Thorne could see that it contained no warmth. 'So you're happy to suck up a bit when it's in your interests. When I'm sitting here deciding whether or not to put the complaints paperwork through on your assault.'

'Listen—'

'But when it comes to talking about your case, you've suddenly got nothing to say. Shame you weren't so fucking tight-lipped last night.'

'Don't I know it.'

McCabe pushed his chair away from the table and stood up. 'Whatever else happens, I hope Dan Britton presses charges. You can take your chances with the DPS ...'

The Directorate of Professional Standards. The people that investigated corruption, racism, blue-on-blue violence. They'd made headlines a few months earlier after prosecuting a pair of budding entrepreneurs from the Flying Squad who'd been caught trying to sell footage of car and helicopter chases to TV companies. Thorne had been subjected to DPS attention a few times before. He'd made his fair share of work for those who handed out smacked wrists. But the way things stood now, in his career – in his *life* – there were plenty of things he was more afraid of.

'I was in enough shit before I took this job,' Thorne said. 'A bit extra isn't really here or there . . .'

McCabe picked up his mug, and took Thorne's half-drunk cup as well. 'We'll see.'

'Listen, I was taken off the world's most tedious desk job to do this, for fuck's sake, so it's not like I'm committing career suicide, is it?' Thorne turned, spoke at McCabe as the inspector walked across the room. 'You can do what you like, but I've got to tell you, I could have ripped your sergeant's head off and things wouldn't be much worse than they were already . . .'

McCabe paused at the door. 'Things can always get worse, mate.'

'What happens now?' Thorne asked.

'You sit there and wait. Your guvnor's on his way over.'

Thorne turned back to the table as the door slammed shut. He leaned down to the tabletop and lowered his head on to his arms. He felt wiped out by the exchange with McCabe and hoped he might be able to get a bit of sleep before Brigstocke arrived. Even ten minutes would be fucking great . . .

He closed his eyes. He could hazard a pretty good guess at what sort of mood Russell Brigstocke would be in when he arrived. Thorne was fairly certain he wouldn't be bringing coffee.

From what Kitson and Holland had seen on the cab ride from the station, the army had built on, or fenced off, vast tracts of land in and around the lush river valley a few miles from Taunton that was now home to the 12th King's Hussars.

Standing at the main gate, as they'd waited to be escorted to the admin block, they'd been able to hear the boom of guns from ranges a long way distant and see sheep and cows grazing, unconcerned, on the hills that swept away on either side. Such incongruities were everywhere: a fully outfitted soldier in face paint and camouflage coming towards the barrier on a rickety bicycle; a car park full of Lagunas, Volvos and Passats, while fifty yards away, on a rutted patch of tarmac as wide as a football pitch, rows of tanks and other armoured vehicles stood in lines, some grumbling and belching out plumes of black smoke as they were repaired.

Major Stuart Poulter's office was small, but predictably neat and organised: a series of drawings illustrating the development of the modern tank was arranged along one wall; wooden 'in', 'out' and 'pending' trays were lined up along the front of his desk; and kit-bags of various sizes were laid out in one corner, as if he were expecting to be called away at any moment. Poulter was in his early-forties, a little under average height and with a thick head of dark hair worn relatively long. A full mouth and ruddy cheeks gave him an oddly girlish expression, but his body looked hard and compact under his uniform. He was immaculate in gleaming, brown Oxfords, light trousers, and a green sweater with leather epaulettes over regulation shirt, and khaki tie.

As they waited for their tea to be delivered, Holland explained just how confused he'd already become by the terminology; by the unfathomable series of initials and numbers on the signs that hung outside every office on the corridor. He wondered why an RSM was a WO1 while a CSM was a WO2, and even when he'd been told what OC and CO stood for, he wasn't certain what made commanding officer any different from officer commanding. Poulter, who chain-smoked, and smiled rather too much, explained patiently that anyone unfamiliar with the military was bound to find it all terribly bewildering at first.

Then, even though they knew that Poulter had been comprehensively briefed, Holland and Kitson were obliged to spend five minutes or so going over their reasons for being there.

'Just so we're singing from the same hymn sheet,' the major said.

The visit had, of course, been agreed between the army and the Met well in advance; the details hashed out in a series of telephone conversations between officers far senior to both Detective Inspector Yvonne Kitson and Major Stuart Poulter.

Poulter used a brass Zippo to fire up his second cigarette since the interview had begun and leaned back in his chair. 'I still think it would make more sense for the Met to liaise with the RMP on this.' He had a soft, comforting voice, like someone who might read out a weather forecast on the radio. 'But, ours is not to reason why. Correct?'

Once tea had been delivered and they'd got down to business, it became apparent that the system of tracking regimental personnel was every bit as complicated, every bit as arcane, as the command structure itself.

'We only keep any sort of record on soldiers who are still serving,' Poulter said. 'That's the first thing, and it's purely practical. Once they leave here, they're no longer my concern, and I can't really care any more. You should really talk to the AP Centre at Glasgow ...'

Kitson told him that they knew all about the AP Centre. She explained that they simply needed the *names* of those who had served alongside Christopher Jago. She gave a brief and relatively vague outline of exactly why those names were so important. The existence of the videotape was not so much as hinted at.

'It's basically about tracing the other three on the crew,' Holland said. 'We just need to know how we can get that information.'

'Which crew are we talking about, though?' Poulter asked.

'Like we said, it's the Gulf, 1991 ...'

'I'm clear about *that*, but this Jago might have been part

of any number of crews. Do you understand? Just in that single campaign.'

'Right . . . ' Kitson was starting to sense that this wouldn't be straightforward. That even though, this time, they'd come armed with all the relevant information, they were as far out of their depth as they had been when they'd interviewed Rutherford and Spiby at the Media Ops Office.

'I've been all over the UK,' Poulter said, 'and to most parts of Europe, right? I've been to Malaysia and Hong Kong and Belize; to Bosnia, the USA and Australia. And I've been to the Gulf. All in just the last ten years. Do you see what I'm driving at? Soldiers move around, *all the time*. Not only do they change location, but they also get shifted from troop to troop and from squadron to squadron.'

'What gets done with their records if that happens?' Kitson asked,

'It's fairly standard . . . unless, of course, the soldier in question has served at any time with one of the intelligence-based units. The SAS, the Special Boat Service, 14 Int, or what have you . . . '

'What happens then?'

'Well, those records *can* have a habit of disappearing, or at the very least a few chunks go missing. Normally, though, each man has a P-File, which is confidential and contains all the basic info: the courses he's been on, names and dates, his disciplinary record, that kind of thing. That file goes with him if he switches squadrons. There's also his Troop Bible, which gives admin details – passport number and so forth – but, again, that travels with the soldier.'

'So the paperwork is as mobile as they are,' Holland said.

Poulter turned, blew smoke out of the window he'd opened behind him. 'That's about right. And again, it's purely practical. We'd be swamped with the stuff otherwise. I guess you lot have got much the same problem, right? Filling every bloody form in three times.'

Kitson smiled politely, acknowledging the moment of levity. 'Why might a soldier move?'

'Any number of reasons. Troops go where they're *needed*, basically. You might be going to assist another regiment, right? To back-fill wherever it's necessary. On a tank crew, say, you might have trained as a driver, and if a driver on another crew falls ill or whatever, you get shunted across and someone else is moved into your crew and trained up. You work as crew and you also work as engineering support for crew, and if that expertise is required elsewhere, you go to plug that hole. Some commanders like to move their crews around as a matter of course and some don't, but either way it's all change once the ORBAT comes through.' Poulter saw the confusion on Holland's and Kitson's faces and explained: 'Order of Battle. That's any troop movement order, peacetime or wartime, right? Once that comes through, you go. Simple as that.'

Holland had begun by taking notes, but had realised fairly quickly that there was little point. Even so, he drew a line on his notepad, as if underscoring something of great importance. 'I understand all that, but surely when there's a conflict, like there was in the Gulf, it's a good idea to have some . . . continuity.'

'It's certainly a good *idea*,' Poulter said. He looked vaguely pleased, as if Holland had asked the predictably stupid civilian's question. 'When the regiment's deployed, that's when people really start to get switched around. Troops are reorganised all over again in accordance with battle regs.' He stuck the cigarette into his mouth and began to count off these regulations on his fingers: 'You can't go if there are any medical issues, any at all; you'll get left behind if you've got so much as a toothache, right? You can't go if you're underage . . .'

'I'm not with you,' Kitson said. 'How can you be under-age?'

'You can join up when you're sixteen and a half, right? After basic training and what have you, we get them at around seventeen, but you cannot be sent to war unless you're eighteen years of age. You're a gunner on a tank crew and the regiment gets deployed to a combat zone, right? If you're a week short of your eighteenth birthday, somebody else is going to get brought in to do your job.'

Kitson nodded. She couldn't help but wonder if the Iraqi Army had been subject to the same regulations . . .

'Then, once you're actually out there, everything can change again. People get injured; that's the most obvious thing. And I don't just mean as a result of enemy action.' He pointed out of the window towards the line of tanks that Kitson and Holland had seen earlier. 'You take a tumble off the back of one of those wagons and you're going to know about it. These things have a knock-on effect as well. One tanky breaks his arm, half a dozen crews can get shifted around.'

In his notebook, Holland circled the full stop beneath a large and elaborately shaded question mark. 'What about soldiers who were in the Gulf and are still with the regiment?' he said. 'Could we perhaps just talk to them? From what you said before, there should be a list of those people somewhere.'

'Yeah, I think that would be very useful,' Kitson added.

Poulter thought for a moment, before rolling his chair back and tossing his cigarette butt out of the open window. 'I'll go and have a quick word with someone about what you're suggesting,' he said. 'If you'd like to wait there, I'm sure I can rustle up some more tea ...'

Holland closed his notebook before Poulter walked past him on his way to the door.

NINETEEN

Spike had found him within half an hour of Thorne's release from custody.

'Fat Paul, who sells the *Issue* outside Charing Cross, saw you coming out. How was it?'

'Bailed for a fortnight,' Thorne said. 'Gives 'em time to decide if they want to go ahead and charge me.'

Spike looked surprised, as Thorne knew he had every right to be. 'I don't know how you managed to wangle that. Can't see there's much to decide, seeing as how you decked a copper.'

'They're waiting for medical reports or something.'

'Right ...'

'Plus, if they do me for assault, they know they might have to do one or two of their own.'

Now Spike thought he understood. 'Good thinking, mate. We'll get one of them disposable cameras, make sure we get some photos of your face. It's a right mess, like.'

Thorne had finally got a good look at himself in the Gents' back at the station after Brigstocke had finished with him. He looked every bit as worked over as he felt. One eye was completely filled with blood, while the other was half-closed above a bruise that was plum-coloured and blackening at its edges. There were scratches down one side of his neck, and a graze, livid against his forehead, from where he'd been pressed against the wall.

'Yeah, well.' Thorne could feel the air, cold on his wounds, and the pain that still sang along his shoulder blades where his arms had been driven up hard behind his back. 'There were quite a few of them in the end.'

'What d'you expect? You smack a copper in the face and a lot of his mates want to give you something to remember them by. Sounds like they did you a right favour, though . . .'

Thorne looked at the cut along Spike's cheekbone and the side of his lip that had split and swelled. 'I thought *you*'d be a damn sight worse,' he said.

Spike shook his head, looking smug. 'I kept my head covered most of the time, like. Bastard ribs are black and blue, mind you. Just sorry I never got a chance to stick the fucker.'

'You carry a knife?'

With half his lip as swollen as it was, the smile was as lopsided as McCabe's had been. 'I've always got a weapon,' Spike said.

They were heading north through Soho. The overcast streets were busy with lunchtime shoppers and workers hurrying to grab a bite to eat, or a quick drink to take the

264

edge off the rest of the day. Thorne and Spike walked slowly along in the centre of the pavement. The state of their faces allowed them to cut a swathe through pedestrians a little thicker than might normally have been the case.

'You're lucky they didn't pick you up with it,' Thorne said. He was thinking that, despite what he'd said to McCabe, things *could* have been a lot worse. If he'd been party to an assault with a deadly weapon, there'd have been bugger all Russell Brigstocke could have done about it . . .

'Sorry I scarpered, by the way,' Spike said. 'I had stuff on me. You know how it is, right?'

Thorne knew how it was.

'Otherwise . . . you know?'

'Don't worry about it.'

Spike sniffed and spat. He shoved his hands into the pockets of a scarred vinyl bomber jacket. 'I wanted to say thanks for wading in, you know? For trying to pull the tosser off me. Not that I was in any trouble . . .'

Thorne nodded solemnly, sharing the joke. 'Course not.'

'So,' Spike grinned as a young couple swerved into the street to avoid him, 'as a small token of my appreciation, I've got us both a job . . .'

Half an hour later and Thorne was hard at work. The sign he was holding had a bright yellow arrow drawn on it and bore the legend: MR JERK. CHICKEN 'N' RIBS. The restaurant was situated halfway along Argyll Street, and Thorne and Spike, with their gaudy advertising boards, constituted a cheap and cheerful pincer movement. Spike was at the Oxford Circus end of the street, his sign pointing hungry people one way, with Thorne doing his bit to encourage them in the other direction from a pitch down near Liberty's. Every half an hour or so the two of them would swap positions; pausing for five minutes' chat outside the Palladium.

At a couple of quid an hour, Mr Jerk was happy, and by the end of the day they would have made enough for Thorne to get a decent dinner and for Spike to get himself fixed up.

Thorne stood, propping up his sign; letting it prop *him* up. The features of those who moved past him were anonymous, in sharp contrast to his own, which had been punched into distinction ...

What he'd told Spike had been at least partly true. Brigstocke had done his bit to placate McCabe and the officer whose face Thorne had rearranged, but nothing had really been decided. There might well be charges to answer, either sooner as a rough sleeper or later, when the operation was all over, as one officer assaulting another. Unlikely as it was that he'd be allowed to walk away from the incident, Thorne was far more concerned with how his stupidity may have compromised the job he was trying to do. McCabe had given assurances that, as far as Thorne's undercover status was concerned, confidentiality would be maintained. But they were worthless: he could not possibly vouch for the discretion of every one of his own officers, never mind those hundreds of others – the beat officers, the Drugs Squad, the Pickpocket Teams, the Clubs and Vice boys – who moved through Charing Cross Station every day. The Met was no different from any other large organisation. There was talk and rumour. There were drunken exchanges and gossipy emails. Thorne thought about the man they were trying to catch; the man who might be a police officer. If word *did* get out, would the killer himself be able to hear those jungle drums?

He remembered something Brigstocke had said: '*The mouse doesn't know there's cheese on the trap, but we still call it bait* . . .'

When he'd stormed into the Interview Room at Charing Cross a few hours earlier, Russell Brigstocke was one police officer who certainly *had* looked like he wanted to kill him. The language of each *I told you so* had been predictably industrial, and he hadn't spared himself. He'd also aimed a good deal of invective at his own stupidity for trusting Thorne in the first place . . .

'I must have been fucking mental,' he'd said.

'Maybe it was that diet you were on . . .'

That hadn't helped, and it wasn't until Brigstocke was about to leave that he'd seemed to soften even a little. He'd turned at the doorway, exactly as McCabe had done, and let out a long breath before he spoke. 'At least you look the part now . . .'

Walking up now towards Oxford Street, Thorne could see Spike on his way towards him, spinning the sign in his hand as he bounced along. He looked twitchy, like his blood was jumping. He'd need paying pretty soon.

Thorne remembered the look on Brigstocke's face when

he'd spoken; it was somewhere between pity and relief. He'd always been confident that he could look the part. He just hadn't banked on *feeling* it.

The soldier standing at the side of Major Poulter's desk wore regulation combats over a green T-shirt, and Holland could not help but be struck by how good the uniform looked on her. As part of the Royal Armoured Corps, the 12th King's Hussars was an all-male regiment. Neither Holland nor Kitson had expected to see any women . . .

'This is Lieutenant Sarah Cheshire, our assistant adjutant,' Poulter said. 'She's the administrative wizard round here, maintains all the databases and so on. If you'd like to tell her exactly what it is you're looking for, I'm sure she'll do her best to sort you out.'

Kitson explained that they needed a list of all those soldiers currently serving in the regiment who'd also fought in the first Gulf War.

'Shouldn't be a problem,' Cheshire said.

Holland's charm was not quite as boyish as it had once been, but he turned it on nevertheless. 'That'd be great, thanks . . .'

Cheshire nodded and turned to Poulter. 'I'll get on it then, sir.' She was no more than twenty-two or three, with ash-blonde hair clipped back above a slender neck, and a Home Counties accent that Holland found a damn sight sexier than the major's.

'That's good of you, Sarah, many thanks. I can't see it taking you too long, to be honest.'

'Sir?'

Poulter looked across his desk at Kitson and Holland. 'Aside from myself, I don't think we're talking about more than, say, half a dozen men left in the regiment.' He smiled at Cheshire; drew deeply on his cigarette as he watched her leave the room.

'Why so few?' Kitson asked.

Holland shook his head. 'I thought there'd be a lot more than half a dozen.'

'Soldiers leave,' Poulter said. 'For many reasons. We lose a lot of men after a major conflict. A lot of them. It's all about pressure, at the end of the day. Pressure from others and pressure inside your own head. If you're lucky enough to have a family, then nine times out of ten they'll want you out. You've been and done your bit, you've been out there and risked your neck, so why the hell go back and do it again? If you were lucky enough to make it back in one piece, the attitude of your nearest and dearest is, "Why push your luck? Get out while the going's good."'

'Understandable,' Kitson said.

'Of course it is, but that's the easy pressure. And having that kind of support system makes it easy to readjust afterwards. For those without that system, and even for many who do have loving families, it's not quite so cut and dried. You come back, your head's still buzzing, you're in constant turmoil, and I'm not necessarily talking about men who've fought hand to hand or anything like that. Any length of time spent in a combat situation, or spent *in*

269

constant readiness for such a situation, is going to leave a good number of men in a fragile mental state.'

'Like post-traumatic stress disorder?'

'In some cases yes, but for many others it takes a different form. Some just crave the adrenaline high they experienced during combat. Back here, they just can't get it, can they? You can see the signs. Silly buggers signing up for parachute jumps and what have you. Anything to get the rush. These guys have got ten, maybe fifteen years of skills and drills, then they come back from combat and they've got sod all to do with them. That's why so many go wild, land themselves in trouble, and end up in prison. It's why they end up on the street, like with this case of yours ...'

The office door was held open by a tank shell. Kitson watched the smoke from Poulter's cigarette drift upwards, and then out into the corridor. 'You must have to do a lot of recruiting after a war, then,' she said.

Poulter barked out a smoky laugh. 'Quite the opposite. The numbers go through the bloody roof for some reason. Good job as well.'

'Why didn't *you* leave?' Holland asked. 'If you don't mind me asking ...'

Major Poulter took a moment, then leaned forward to grind out his cigarette into a tarnished metal ashtray. '"Mind" is putting it a tad strongly. But I can't see that it's strictly relevant.' He was trying to smile, but his eyes seemed to have grown smaller suddenly. 'I'm more than happy to answer what I understand to be the important question, which is whether I remember your man Jago, or any of the men in his tank crew. I'm afraid I don't.'

'Fine,' Holland said. 'Thank you.'

'I've already explained how things worked out there.'

'You made it very clear.'

'I may not have come within fifty miles of that crew, and even if I did, it *was* rather a long time ago ...'

Holland grimaced and saw Kitson do the same as an engine was cranked up to a deafening roar just outside the window. Poulter said something Holland couldn't hear but he nodded anyway. The noise explained why so many of the soldiers he'd seen had been carrying ear protectors, which they kept tucked into the belts of their blue coveralls.

It had become obvious that there was little to do but wait for the list of men who'd been in the Gulf, however small that turned out to be. They weren't likely to get any more useful information out of Poulter, but Holland decided to ask a question or two anyway, just for himself. They had time to kill, after all ...

'It strikes me that the army does precious little to help these men after they leave.' Holland cleared his throat, spoke up over the noise that was dying as the vehicle moved away. 'It's like they fight for their country, then you wash your hands of them, just when they need the most help.'

'There's a comprehensive army pension system.'

The major had spoken as if it were the end of the conversation, but Holland saw no reason to let it lie. Besides, he'd been doing a little reading up. 'Not if you leave too early, there isn't,' he said. 'Unless you've been wounded, you only get a pension if you do twelve years. That's right, isn't it?'

Poulter reached for another Silk Cut. 'Look, I can't say I completely disagree with you, but I do think the army does its level best in difficult circumstances. No, at the end of the day, pastoral care is probably *not* top priority, but you have to understand that the army has been doing things the same way for an awfully long time.' He summoned up a smile again as he leaned across the desk for something, then waved it around for them to look at. 'I still carry a bloody riding crop around, you see? We wear black ties at dinner and we still get issued with mess kits.' He lit his cigarette. 'Basically, we're still Victorian . . . '

Holland returned the smile. 'Well, the system for keeping records certainly is.'

The lid of the Zippo was snapped shut. 'Some would say that we've got rather more important things to do.'

The slightly awkward pause might well have gone on much longer if Sarah Cheshire had not appeared in the doorway brandishing a piece of paper.

'Come on in, Sarah,' Poulter said.

She walked over to the desk. 'It's not a long list, I'm afraid. There are seven men who served in Gulf War One who are still with the regiment.'

Poulter looked pleased with himself. 'I was more or less spot on, then . . . '

'Three of these are presently away on attachment elsewhere, leaving four, including Major Poulter, on site at this moment.'

Cheshire handed the list to Poulter, who looked at it, then passed it across the desk to Kitson.

'Thanks for that,' Holland said. He was pleased when Lieutenant Cheshire held his gaze a little longer than was necessary; then embarrassed when he felt himself start to redden.

'You already know that *I* can't help you,' Poulter said, 'but you're more than welcome to talk to the others on the list. You might be able to cross-reference any useful memories, but I have to say I think you'll be very lucky ...'

'We haven't had a lot of luck so far,' Kitson said.

'As I explained earlier, these men might not have served together, and even if they *did*, it was a fair while ago.' He turned to Holland. 'How long have you been with the Met, Detective Sergeant?'

For some reason, Holland felt his blush deepen. 'Just over ten years.'

'Right, ten years. And how many of your fellow cadets can you remember?'

Holland could do little but shrug. Poulter had a very good point.

Cheshire took half a step forward. 'I did have one idea,' she said. She directed her suggestion towards Poulter. 'I was wondering about the war diaries ...'

'That's good thinking,' the major said. He turned to explain to Holland and Kitson. 'The squadron adjutant would have routinely kept log-sheets, which would then have been collated into a digest of service. They're usually archived somewhere at HQ, aren't they?'

Cheshire nodded.

'They *might* mention Jago and his crew, but only if any of them were commended or listed as casualties.'

'Right, thanks.' Kitson felt fairly sure that neither of those things would apply.

'Thinking about it, old documentation might prove to be your best bet.' Poulter was warming to his theme. 'A lot of soldiers do hang on to stuff. You'd be surprised . . . '

'What about letters home?' Cheshire asked. 'If the men on this list are still with the same wives or girlfriends, they might still have the letters they wrote to them from the Gulf.'

'Right, that's another good thought. Soldiers often talk about their mates, or moan about the ones in the troop they can't stand, or whatever. If it's just the names you're after, that might be worth a try.'

Kitson agreed, of course, that anything was worth a try, but suddenly *everything* was starting to feel like a straw to be clutched at.

Once again, she thanked them for their suggestions. It was polite and it was politic, but with the mood she was in – as dark as the shadow that was moving rapidly across the whole investigation – it was hard to tell if they were genuinely trying to help.

Or simply trying to look as if they were.

They boarded the train back to London early; made sure they got themselves a table. Each of them had bought something to eat and drink on the concourse, and, as they waited to leave, both seemed happy to sit in silence, to concentrate on taking sandwiches from wrappings and stirring sugar into coffee. It wasn't until the train was pulling out of the station that Yvonne Kitson passed what would prove to be the journey's most pertinent reflection on their day.

'Nothing's ever fucking easy,' she said.

While Kitson tried to sleep, Holland leafed through a magazine, but nothing could stop him thinking about Thorne for too long. Late the night before, Holland had taken the call from the custody sergeant at Charing Cross. He'd passed on the news – along with the irritation at being woken up and the alarm at what Thorne had done – to Brigstocke, who had, presumably, passed it on in turn to Trevor Jesmond. It was a chain of conversations into the early hours that might well be used later to string up Tom Thorne . . .

Holland thought back to when he'd last seen him, walking away from the London Lift after they'd sat and watched the Gulf War tape. Thorne had seemed right enough at the time. Then Holland remembered how badly he himself had needed a drink; how much he'd appreciated the chance to sit in the pub with Yvonne Kitson and pour some of it out. He doubted if Thorne had anyone he could have shared a drink with and discussed what he'd seen. Anyone who could have told him that he'd drunk enough.

Against all prevailing wisdom, Thorne had been someone he'd looked up to since he'd first begun working with him, but even Holland had to admit that the DI's future was looking far from rosy. He might well be taken off this case straight away, and even if he was allowed to carry on, what would he come back to when it was all over? He'd been shunted off to the Yard when it became obvious that he hadn't recovered from the death of his father; that he wasn't himself. This latest misadventure wasn't going to help his case for returning to the Murder Squad, which, as anyone with any sense could see, was always going to be an uphill struggle. There were plenty for whom Thorne's presence on the MIT was even more unwelcome when he *was* himself.

Stupid, stupid bastard . . .

Holland stared out of the train window and realised that they'd stopped moving; that the train had been stationary for several minutes. He looked at his watch. He'd rung home to say he would be back late, and now it was getting later all the time. Sophie wouldn't be overly bothered, he knew that. He increasingly felt that she was happier when he wasn't around. But he'd be annoyed if he missed out on seeing Chloe before she went to bed.

The train began moving with a jolt. Kitson opened her eyes for a second, then closed them again. Rain was streaking the window, and some tosser in the seat behind was talking far too loudly on his mobile phone.

Later, Holland would call and tell Thorne how things had gone at the regiment. Find out how things had gone for him, too. How the daft sod was doing . . .

He flicked through the pages of *Loaded*, staring at pictures of scantily clad soap stars until he started to feel something other than irritation. He picked up the magazine, slid out from behind the table and walked towards the toilet.

TWENTY

Over the years, Thorne had felt more than his fair share of rage and regret, of lust and loathing, but he'd never been overburdened with guilt. He guessed it was because he spent his working life trying to catch those who should have been eaten up with enough of it for everyone. Many who had done the very worst things felt nothing, of course, but most people, even those without a shred of religious conviction, at least accepted that they *should*. For Thorne, it used to be that clear cut.

It wasn't that he never felt guilt at all; it was just that it was usually of the vaguely delicious variety that followed over-indulgence of one sort or another. Its more corrosive strain was one that never burned within him for very long. It could be neutralised by making the call he'd forgotten to make; by stepping forward; by having that awkward conversation he'd been putting off. The pain was short-lived and easily dealt with.

These days, though, Thorne could feel little else ...

He'd spent most of the afternoon mooching around the Strand; begging for a couple of hours, chatting to a pair of old boys who drank near the Adelphi and hanging around at a lunchtime soup run. Now, as the day turned from grey to charcoal, he moved quietly among the few tourists still left in the courtyard at Somerset House. This eighteenth-century riverside palace had, at one time or another, been home to the Inland Revenue, the Register of Births, Deaths and Marriages, and Oliver Cromwell's New Model Army. Now it was just another of the city's attractions: a place for visitors to take snapshots of history, or for families to gather in winter, when the water fountains were replaced with a skating rink. Thorne remembered that they'd filmed an ice-skating sequence here for that stupid film with Hugh Grant as the Prime Minister. Yeah, right. Another one of those picture-postcard movies where London looked dreamy in beat-bobby blue and Routemaster red. Where the snow never turned to slush, and the ethnic communities were mysteriously absent. Where, if there was no one sleeping rough, it wasn't because they'd been swept off the streets or were being kicked to death.

When Holland had rung the night before, Thorne had put on a good enough display of frustration and annoyance: at the way things had gone down in Somerset; at the polite enquiries about how they'd panned out for him at Charing Cross nick. In reality, he'd been feeling guilty as hell. He was screwing things up, and not just for himself.

He'd heard it in Holland's concern every bit as much as it had been there, loud and clear, in Brigstocke's curses. In that final comment from the doorway of the Interview Room when he'd talked about Thorne looking the part.

Thorne accepted that he wasn't always completely honest with himself. But why had he ever thought that his going undercover would be a good idea? Had he only convinced himself as a reaction to those who made it clear what a *terrible* idea they thought it was? Maybe everything that had happened in the last year – what he'd done and what had been done to him in return – had skewed his judgement permanently; made it no more reliable than if he were the one now suffering from dementia.

When he was eleven or twelve, his father had taken him skating a couple of times. Thorne had hated it. The Silver Blades at Finsbury Park was nobody's idea of a romantic location, with the frequent stabbings as much a feature of the place as the ice itself. Thorne remembered struggling around the outside of the rink, cultivating blisters, and getting knocked on his arse by older boys with earrings and feather cuts. He remembered getting to his knees, pulling in his hands quickly as the blades flashed by, then looking across to see his dad rushing on to the rink. He'd been embarrassed because his father had broken the rules by coming on to the ice in his shoes. He remembered the look on his father's face, the blush that had spread across his own, as Jim Thorne had skidded towards the boy who'd knocked him down and shoulder-charged him into the barrier. He remembered his dad pulling him off his knees, and brushing away the slivers of ice. Taking him over to hand in his skates. Across to where they could buy hot dogs and limeade ...

Thorne knew very well that guilt caused such memories to bubble up and burst, the air inside permanently fouled. Guilt poisoned a well that should have been sweet to drink from.

'I'm fine, honestly, Victor. I really didn't ring to talk about him.'

'Course you didn't ...'

It took Thorne a few seconds to work out that the vibration in his pocket was his phone ringing. He moved to a corner and stole a glance at the handset; saw that the missed call was from Phil Hendricks. More concern from a friend, and more false assurances. Another small measure of poison.

Thorne needed to find somewhere secluded from where he could return the call. He walked back out on to the Strand and turned east towards Fleet Street. The City would be emptying rapidly now, as the rush hour took its grip of the streets. A hundred yards along, he stopped at a stall selling the late edition of the *Standard*. Stunned, he read what was on the hoarding, then stepped closer to look down at a front page.

After no more than a few seconds, the man behind the stack of papers leaned across. 'Buy one or piss off ... '

Thorne just stared at the headline.

*

He woke up, cold and clammy, and certain that he'd been crying in his sleep.

The copy of the *Standard* that Thorne had shelled out for was flapping, two steps down from his doorway, the headline partially revealed as the page caught the wind: ROUGH SLEEPER KILLINGS, MET GOES UNDERCOVER.

A few steps further down, Spike was sitting, much as he'd been two nights previously, just before the trouble had started. He looked high and happy, and he stared at Thorne for a full ten seconds before seeming to notice that he was awake. He pointed towards Thorne's sleeping bag. 'New . . . '

'Yeah. Not *new* new, but . . . '

'S'nice, like. Brown . . . '

By the time Thorne had got back to his pitch after being released from Charing Cross, his sleeping bag – which had been left in the street during the mêlée – was nowhere to be found. He'd picked up this newer second-hand one from the Salvation Army centre on Oxford Street.

Spike stretched out an arm for the newspaper and dragged it towards him. Thorne watched, wondering what his response should be if Spike were to say anything about the headline. As it was, he turned straight to the back and began to flick very slowly through the sports pages.

'You follow a team?' Spike said, eventually.

'Spurs, because I'm stupid. What about you?'

'Southampton. Not properly for a few years, like.'

'Is that where you're from?'

Spike lowered the *Standard*, then folded it. 'Not far

away. Just some shitty little seaside town.' He ran his hand slowly back and forth along the crease he'd made in the paper. Stared at a spot approximate to where Thorne was sitting. 'Couldn't wait to get the hell out of it, tell you the truth. And they couldn't wait to get rid of me . . .'

It sounded like Spike had got himself into trouble before he'd come to London. It was the same story to one degree or another in most provincial towns. Kids reached a certain age, ran out of things to do and looked around for something to combat the boredom. It was usually drink, drugs, crime or a combination of all three. Some got out and got lucky. Others were drawn to those places where their blighted lives might flourish among like-minded souls. Many were destined to fare no better in London, Manchester and Edinburgh than they had at home, but they would not be short of company; equally doomed perhaps, but not quite as freakish.

'They let you out on police bail, right?' Spike asked.

'Right . . .'

'But what if you *needed* to be bailed out? If you needed someone to come and get you, to pay to get you out? Would you have anybody?'

Thorne said nothing. Thinking it would probably be Hendricks; Holland at a push. But beyond them . . .

'It'd be my sister, I think,' Spike said. 'It'd have to be. She bailed me out a year or so back, when I got caught with my stuff as well as Caroline's and this other bloke's, and they done me for dealing. So my sister stumped up the bail *and* gave me some extra cash on top of that.' His head dropped, and when he raised it again a smile was smeared across his face. His eyeballs were starting to roll upwards, creamy under the streetlight and cracked with red. 'She wanted to set me up for a bit, you know? To tide me over. I told her I was going to try and get myself clean, but I went straight out and used the money she gave me to score. Surprise, surprise, right? I think deep down she knew I would, 'cause she knows well enough what I'm like. She knows me better than anyone.' He stared at Thorne for half a minute, blinking slowly. 'She knows, right?'

Thorne nodded. From a club somewhere near by came the deep thump of a bass line. It was not 2 a.m. yet.

'I'd really have to be in the shit before I'd ask her for help again. Really deep in it. D'you know what I mean? Because I know bloody well I'd only let her down, and life's hard enough without feeling guilty all the time, right? It's not like she can't afford it, mind you. She's done brilliantly. She's got a really posh job, got herself a flash car and a swanky flat in Docklands and all that. It's just like it's become dead important for me *not* to ask my sister for anything. I'm fucked, right? I know I am. We're all completely fucked. But whatever happens, I'm not going to disappoint her again ... '

Spike unfolded the paper and turned it over. He stared down at the front page, mouthing the first few words of the headline. Thorne was looking down at him from six feet away, but even if he'd been eyeball to eyeball, there would have been no way to tell if Spike was really taking in what was in front of his face.

If he *was*, something in the story made him suddenly laugh out loud. He cackled and hissed, chortled to himself for the next minute or more.

Thorne could only wish he found it that funny.

TWENTY-ONE

'Dan Britton's not here,' McCabe said. 'In case you've come to apologise.'

Nothing could have been further from Tom Thorne's mind. 'Still pissed off, is he? Maybe he decided to get his own back by opening his mouth ...'

They were standing on the corner of Agar Street, on the north side of the Strand, a hundred yards or so from Charing Cross Station. Thorne had asked the desk sergeant to pass on a message: he needed to meet Inspector McCabe outside, *urgently*.

'I'll tell him,' the desk sergeant had said. 'He's most likely up to his neck.'

Thorne had leaned on to the counter. 'Tell him I've got information that could help prevent a serious assault ...'

Outside, the wind whipped the litter in front of passing

cars. 'I saw the paper.' The lopsided smile appeared. 'It's unfortunate.'

'It'll be a lot more unfortunate when I break his nose all over again.'

'Don't even *think* about accusing anyone on my team.'

'Well, *someone's* got a big mouth.' Thorne realised what he'd said straight away, and the mileage that the man would enjoy getting from it.

'Talk about pots and fucking kettles,' McCabe said. 'I don't know how long you've been mixing with smackheads and winos, mate, but you're starting to make about as much sense ...'

McCabe began to walk. He turned right along Chandos Place towards Covent Garden. Thorne watched him, then followed, a hundred yards or so behind. At a corner of the piazza McCabe stopped and Thorne caught him up. They stood on the edge of the Saturday morning crowd that had gathered in front of a heavily tattooed juggler.

'This bloke's good,' McCabe said.

Thorne grunted. There were a lot of people watching, and if one in five of them chucked a bit of money his way, the juggler would do all right for himself. Maybe he'd tell Spike to start practising ...

'Better than those arseholes who paint themselves silver and stand around pretending to be statues. I think I'd rather have junkies and dossers on the streets than out-of-work actors.'

'Shame our killer doesn't agree with you,' Thorne said.

McCabe turned slightly to look at him, as if he wasn't

sure whether Thorne was joking. As if he wasn't sure about Thorne, full stop. 'Seriously,' he said, 'I tried to make certain everyone got the message. I did as much as I could to keep the lid on.'

'Fair enough ...'

Thorne was starting to calm down a little. It didn't matter whether McCabe was telling the truth or not. There was nothing anyone could do about the leak now. But still, Thorne couldn't help but wonder why anyone would bother going to the paper with the story. 'It's not like it's a royal sex scandal, is it?' he said. 'It doesn't make sense.'

'Not giving Princess Anne one, are you?'

'Come on, they don't pay big money for this kind of tip, do they? So what's the bloody point?'

'Not big money, no,' McCabe said. 'But if it was one of your rough-sleeper mates, they'd settle for a few quid, or a bottle of Scotch. They'd take anything they could get.'

'Nobody I've met on the street has a clue ...' Then Thorne remembered the drunk outside St Clement Danes: the one who'd known he was a copper, who'd shouted about it until Spike had come along and shut him up. Could he have told the *Standard*? Could Moony have said something to somebody? Either was a possibility, of course, but Thorne was far from convinced.

'You wouldn't know if they did,' McCabe said. 'The Drugs Squad sent a UCO in a year or two back; before my time. He was sussed within five minutes. Silly beggar was buying everyone beer and sneaking off to hotels every night.'

'I've not been that stupid,' Thorne said. He continued quickly before McCabe could say anything. 'Not *quite* that stupid.'

McCabe turned back to the show, his interest waning suddenly. 'If it isn't about money, I haven't got a clue.'

'That's why I was only half joking when I suggested Britton. He's got a motive. I could understand him wanting to make me look like a mug.'

'It wasn't Britton.'

The juggler was tossing meat cleavers into the air. He deliberately let one clatter to the cobbles, making the stunt look that bit more dangerous. The crowd didn't seem overly impressed.

'Whoever opened their mouth did so for a reason,' Thorne said. 'They must be getting something out of it.'

There was one major change to the layout on the whiteboard at the far end of the Incident Room: the list of victims had been divided into two. The names of Mannion, Hayes and Asker now constituted a column of their own. Next to it, in black felt tip, was written: 'Unknown Vic 1' and 'Jago', with a line in red leading from those names to '12th King's Hussars' and another to 'Tank Crew'.

Beneath that were two question marks.

Of the large number of calls and emails that Brigstocke had fielded so far that day, he'd hoped that one or two might have gone some way towards replacing those question marks. He'd hoped that, despite everything Kitson and Holland had been told in Somerset, the army would have found some way to dig up the names of the other soldiers who had served on the tank crew with Christopher Jago in 1991.

One already dead. Two who might be, or might *soon* be ...

As it was, far too many of those calls and emails had been about Tom Thorne.

'It's a pain in the arse,' Brigstocke said. He and Holland were sitting in his office, having polished off a lunch of ham rolls and cheese-and-onion crisps brought across from the Oak. 'I've had that tosser from the Press Office on half a dozen times at least. Norman? He reckons he's got papers and TV all over him.'

Holland grimaced. He remembered Steve Norman from a case a couple of years before, when the MIT had been forced to work more closely than they'd have liked with the media. 'Slimy sod deserves something a lot worse all over him.'

Brigstocke didn't think it was funny or he wasn't listening. 'I said as little as I could get away with, but I think they're happy enough to let the story run for a while. Nobody seems desperate to squash it, anyway.'

'It's a bit late, I'd've thought ... '

'Norman's not an easy bloke to read, but he's sharp enough. We were going round the houses a bit, you know, discussing the story, talking about the UCO.' He raised his fingers, used them to put the initials in inverted commas. 'But I got the distinct impression that he knew we were talking about Thorne.'

There was a knock at the door.

Holland lowered his voice. 'Should he know?'

'He *shouldn't*, but if it was a copper who leaked the story, then it's hardly a major surprise.'

Holland remembered a little more about the case during which he'd first come across the senior press officer; about the way Norman had clashed with one officer in particular. 'Him and Thorne have got a bit of history ...'

Brigstocke barked out a humourless laugh. 'Is there anyone Tom Thorne *hasn't* got history with?'

Another knock, and, on being invited in, Yvonne Kitson put her head round the door. Holland saw something pass across her face on seeing that he and Brigstocke were ensconced, on guessing that they'd just stopped talking. But whatever she was feeling – curiosity, envy, suspicion – its expression was only momentary. He hoped that when the investigation was over, Kitson wouldn't be too pissed off that he'd been privy to the workings of the undercover operation while she had not. Holland thought he knew her well enough. He was pretty confident that she wouldn't feel slighted; that she'd put it down to the close working relationship he had with Tom Thorne.

'Am I interrupting, sir?'

'No, you're fine, Yvonne. Everyone OK after the briefing this morning?'

'I think so ...'

Once the story had appeared in the previous day's *Standard*, Brigstocke had been forced to say something to his team. He'd been forced to lie, told them that, yes, there was a UCO working as part of the investigation, but that the officer had been recruited, as might have been expected, from SO10. There was nothing else they needed to know.

There was no reason for anyone to doubt that this was the unvarnished truth. Even if they did, they certainly wouldn't have imagined that the officer at the centre of it all was Tom Thorne.

'You OK, Dave?' Kitson asked.

'Yeah, I'm good . . . '

Thinking about it, Holland might have preferred it if Kitson *had* been the one dealing with Thorne. To be honest, he could have done without the stress.

Kitson and Brigstocke spent a few minutes talking about another case. While the rough-sleeper killings was far and away the most high profile and demanding of the team's cases, there were, at least theoretically, another forty-seven unsolved murders on their books: dozens of men and women stabbed, shot and battered. Murders that were horrific and humdrum. Predictable and perverse. Gangland executions, domestic batteries, hate crimes. From sexual predation to pub punch-ups. Killings of every known variety, as well as a few that seemed to have been created just for the occasion. Some had come in since the rough-sleeper murders had started, but some dated back to long before. Thankfully, a healthy number were in the pre-trial stage, but there were still many that showed no sign of progress, and these were the ones that had been shoved on to the backburner. It always struck Holland as a ridiculous mixture of metaphors: some cases had gone so cold that no amount of time on any sort of burner would do them any good. The top brass had their own way of describing such things: they were fond of words like 'de-prioritising'.

He could almost hear Thorne's voice:

'*De-prioritised in terms of fucking manpower, maybe. In terms of money. Try telling the victim's family that they've been de-prioritised . . .*'

Holland knew that catching the man who was killing the ex-servicemen was the only acceptable outcome; that was *their* priority. He understood the decision not to reveal the videotape at this time. Still, he hoped when the time came, though some or all of those responsible would already be dead, that as much effort would go into investigating the murders of four Iraqi soldiers.

Kitson stopped on her way out. 'I'll let you get back to it.'

'Boy's stuff,' Holland said.

Brigstocke pursed his lips and nodded, mock-serious; masking the bullshit with silliness. 'Right. You wouldn't be interested . . .'

As she walked back towards the Incident Room, Yvonne Kitson tried to keep the irritation in check. She'd had enough of this crap the year before. When her private life had become the stuff of pub chat and water-cooler gossip.

She'd been as rattled as anybody else by Brigstocke's briefing that morning. Everyone had been talking since they'd seen it in the paper, of course, but hearing it from the DCI was something else. She knew very well that undercover operations could succeed only through secrecy, but still, she'd felt as a DI that she could have been taken into confidence. Brought within the inner circle.

She hadn't let Brigstocke or anyone else see how she was feeling, though. That was something else she'd learned the previous year. When Brigstocke had asked how everyone had taken it, she'd lied.

But hopefully she'd done so just a little better than he and Holland just had.

She walked back into a crowded and bustling Incident Room, wondering why it was that people whose job it was to find the truth lied like such rank amateurs.

*

He only came into the West End for work. At other times he couldn't see any point in it. In terms of shopping or entertainment, you could get everything you needed locally, and he preferred not to venture too far from where he was staying. It wasn't that he was a long way away; it wasn't too much of a slog to get into town or anything like that. Central London just wore him out. Once he'd returned home, and the buzz of the job he'd been doing had worn off, he was left ragged and wrung out, with a dull ache, as if a muscle he'd been working on was complaining at the effort.

The West End was greedy.

Everywhere your eyes fell, the place had its scabby hand out in one way or another, from sandwich boards to neon signs and a hundred foreign students with a thousand pointless leaflets. Everyone wanted something, and not just those poor, useless buggers with nowhere else to go. All of them: the people working in shops and behind fast-food counters and the ones in cars and those walking fast along the pavement, tutting and growling, looking like they were ready to kill someone if their progress was halted for even one second. They all wanted something – your money, or your time or your fucking attention – and if you wanted to make absolutely sure they got nothing, that no part of you was touched, it was crucial to stay on top of your game.

He wandered through the streets around Soho and Covent Garden, moving quickly between those places he needed to visit. There was a list of them in his pocket, and he'd worked through most of it already. He turned from Dean Street on to Old Compton Street, heading towards Piccadilly. Past the cruisers and the coked-up media wankers. Past a wild-haired wino, breathing heavily and scowling at the world from the doorway of a fetish-wear boutique.

As he walked, he realised where that dull ache came from. It was the effort of staying self-contained that drained you; of keeping yourself impervious to the offers and the pleas; to the promises of pleasure of one sort or another. It was as though he'd been forced to spend the day permanently clenched, and he knew that when he got home he'd need to spend long hours flicking through the channels or working at the controls of the PlayStation. Sleep wouldn't come until the knots had fallen out.

He wasn't complaining. You went where the job demanded, but still, he was pleased that he'd been able to define what it was that was niggling him. He'd write it down somewhere when he got back. All that stuff about greed . . .

At least it was an appropriate place to be, he thought. Considering why he was there in the first place. After all, if one idiot hadn't got greedy, none of it would ever have been necessary. They would all still be alive. The Driver and the Gunner and . . .

He waited until the man who was walking straight towards him had stepped aside before pulling the list from his pocket and checking the next address.

By the time it was dark he'd be well away, and he'd made an early start so as to be sure of it. He'd been around the West End late on a Saturday night before and it wasn't something he was desperate to repeat unless he had to. That was when the fights broke out and the gutter seemed as good a place to lie down as any; when *all* the alleyways ran with piss and every hidey-hole contained some moron throwing up or sleeping off the excesses.

On Saturday night you couldn't tell who was homeless and who wasn't.

*

The young blonde-haired woman was still unhappy with the background. She waved her hand, urging her subject to move just a little further to the right . . .

There was no shortage of photo opportunities in London. The gasometers of King's Cross were perfect for the seriously arty, as were the estates of Tower Hamlets and Tottenham for a certain sort of documentary-maker. Snap-happy tourists, of course, were spoiled for choice. The Americans and the Japanese on their European tours, the Geordies and the Jocks down for the weekend; they could all point their cameras just about anywhere, and few landmarks were more popular than Eros. Visitors to Piccadilly Circus clicked away oblivious, thinking that the figure atop the memorial fountain was the God of Love, and equally misguided about many of those who gathered around the steps of the monument. The statue was actually meant to be the Angel of Christian Charity, and a number of those within range of his bow were among the city's lost: runaways, junkies and rent boys for whom a little Christian charity was long overdue.

'No ... further ... keep moving ...'

The blonde spoke with a thick Scandinavian accent and kept waving from behind the camera, eager to keep the trio of scarred and scruffy-looking wasters out of her shot. Her boyfriend was growing increasingly impatient, unaware of the three figures on the steps directly behind him.

Spike and Caroline were tucking hungrily into greasy pizza slices, while Thorne sat engrossed in what was happening on the far side of the circus. He watched as a big man in an unfamiliar blue uniform leaned down to talk to a beggar outside Burger King. There was some head-shaking before the man on the ground snatched up his blanket and stalked away.

'Who's that?' Thorne nodded towards the man in the uniform.

Spike stood up and peered across the traffic. 'PCP,' he said.

'Piccadilly Circus Partnership.' Caroline shoved the last bit of pizza into her mouth and wiped her fingers on the back of her jeans. 'A bunch of local businesses pay for a few little fucking Hitlers to keep the streets clean. Someone told me they're in radio contact with the police and there's a huge control room full of CCTV screens in the Trocadero.' She pointed towards the huge entertainment complex on Coventry Street. 'They're *supposed* to be on the lookout for all sorts of stuff. Cracked paving stones, blocked drains or whatever ...'

'Yeah, right.' Spike was lighting a roll-up. 'These fuckers think some things smell a damn sight worse than that, like.'

Thorne watched the man in the blue uniform walking slowly across the zebra crossing towards Virgin Megastore. There were plenty of these cut-price coppers to be seen around the West End, differentiated – to any but the trained eye – only by the coloured fluorescent strips across their uniforms and peaked caps. Aside from the PCP goons, there were council-appointed city wardens patrolling the streets in pairs. Then there were the Met's own community support officers. The CSOs had the power to detain rather than arrest, and despite the publicity that had surrounded their introduction a few years previously, they were seen – not least by real police officers – as something of a joke.

'Look at that cocky sod,' Caroline said. 'I bet he goes home and gets his wife to piss on him ...'

In general terms at least, Thorne shared Caroline's suspicions. He thought that those who wanted to be full-time police officers were dodgy enough. Anyone who couldn't manage that, but still had some overwhelming desire to pull on a uniform and strut around trying to keep the streets clean, almost certainly needed watching.

Spike tried to blow smoke rings, but the breeze pulled them apart. 'Or he makes her dress up as a beggar and handcuffs her to the bed.'

Caroline laughed. 'With a sign saying "Homeless and horny" ...'

'Dirty bastard ...'

Thorne thought about the 'policeman' that Mannion and others had mentioned. The one who was supposed to have been seen asking questions prior to the first killing. Was it possible that this man had been one of these ancillary officers? With a few drinks inside you, wouldn't one uniform look much the same as another on a dark night? He thought it was unlikely. They didn't know for sure that the officer described had even *been* uniformed, but if he had, Thorne guessed that most of those sleeping rough around the West End, many of them living on the fringes of one law or another, would know a genuine copper when they saw one.

He turned, and watched a real enough police officer

marshalling the queue that was moving slowly into a matinee at the Criterion. He decided that thinking out loud could do no harm. 'Do you reckon this killer might be a copper?'

Spike sat down again. The smoke from his cigarette moved quickly across Thorne's face. 'Fuck knows. It's what a lot of people think.' He turned to Caroline. 'Caz thinks he's a copper, don't you?'

'Got every chance,' she said. 'That's why they've sent this undercover copper in to catch him. It's like in films, when they talk to convicted killers to find out what the one they're after is thinking. It takes one to know one kind of thing . . . '

Thorne nodded, thinking that he didn't understand what went on in his own head, let alone anybody else's.

'I wouldn't fancy doing it,' Spike said. 'Sleeping on the street if you didn't have to, with a killer knocking around.'

Caroline leaned across and touched Thorne's face. The graze on his forehead had scabbed over and the bruises were yellowing nicely, their edges indistinct. 'This undercover bloke'll be all right,' she said. 'If he's as handy with his fists as the coppers that did this, I don't think he's got much to worry about.'

TWENTY-TWO

'Where've you been?' Holland asked. He stepped into a shop doorway to escape the noise of the traffic.

'Sorry. I only just got your message. I fancied a lie-in ...'

'Where are you?'

'Hang on ... I can't see a street sign. I'm somewhere round the back of the National Gallery.'

'I was looking for you at the theatre.'

'That's where I normally am.'

'I know. I went in to the London Lift when you didn't return the call and that's where Brendan said you'd be.'

'I moved,' Thorne said.

Holland grunted, relieved that Thorne was OK but pissed off that he'd spent all morning running around like a blue-arsed fly, trying to find him. 'We've had a bit of luck,' he said.

'What?'

'Where can we meet?'

The three of them had walked the length of Oxford Street before Spike and Caroline had gone down into the subways beneath Marble Arch to catch up on some sleep. Thorne had crossed the road into Hyde Park and sat down on a bench near one of the cafés at Speaker's Corner. This triangle at the north-east corner of the park should have been a pleasant enough place to sit at this time of year. Even if the verge adjoining the bridle path had been freshly churned into mud, elsewhere the autumn crocuses were in full bloom, bright and lively. The railed in lawns were still lush, and, despite the plastic bags that danced from many of the branches, the leaves provided plenty more colour a little higher up – green and bronze and butter yellow on the ash trees.

Thorne knew that twenty-four hours earlier, as on every Sunday morning, the political pundits, the zealots and the nutcases would have been out in force. They'd have been up on their soapboxes, shouting about freedom and enlightenment, and aliens sending messages through their toasters, each one honouring the tradition of free speech which had been guaranteed on this spot by Act of Parliament a hundred and twenty-five years before. Halfway through this bleak Monday, freezing his tits off and with a headache just starting to kick in, Thorne found it far easier to picture the gallows at Tyburn, which had stood on the same spot for centuries before that. It took less effort to imagine the creak of a body swinging – of twenty-four at one time from the Triple Tree – and the bloodthirsty cries of the crowd than to conjure the voices of debate and discussion.

Holland dropped down on to the bench next to him and nodded towards the corner. A semicircle of pin oaks had been planted on its farthest boundary, fiery red against the off-white brickwork on the far side of Park Lane. 'What would you want to get off your chest, then?'

'Eh?'

'If you had a crowd, and you could talk about anything you liked . . .'

It was one of the main reasons why Thorne enjoyed having Holland around; why Thorne had made himself unpopular with anyone who'd stepped, however briefly, into the former DC's shoes. Holland had the pleasing knack of being able to punch through the hard shell of a black mood with one glib comment or seemingly innocent enquiry; with a stupid question in too cheery a voice. There were occasions, if Thorne was feeling particularly arsey, when he put this down to insensitivity on Holland's part, but more frequently he saw it to be the exact opposite.

'God knows,' Thorne said. 'The way things are going, I think I'll end up as one of the toasters-and-aliens brigade.'

'Sorry?'

Thorne shook his head. It didn't matter. 'What about you?'

'Where d'you want to start? I'd try to win the crowd

302

over to the idea that all children should be taken into care between the ages of one and sixteen. I'd ask them to support my campaign for police paternity leave to be extended to, say, five years, and to include free alcohol and Caribbean holidays. I'd ask if any of them wanted to sleep with me ...'

'Things a bit sticky at home?'

'How much room is there in your doorway?'

Thorne did his best to smile, and leaned back on the bench. He watched a pair of squirrels chase each other around a litter bin; saw a fat magpie hop lazily away as one of them ran at it.

Holland took off his gloves as he reached down to pull something from his briefcase. 'I'm only joking,' he said.

It was a magazine. Glossy, with a picture of a grim-faced soldier on the front: sand all around and sandbags at his feet; sheets of dust rising black behind him. In bold red lettering across the top: 'GLORIOUS'.

'It's the regimental magazine,' Holland said. 'That's their nickname: the "Glory Boys" or the "Glorious Twelfth". A woman from their HQ sent it. She's the assistant adjutant ...'

'She sent it to you?'

'Just arrived out of the blue. It's the spring 1991 issue.'

Thorne threw him a sideways look as he began to flick through the magazine.

'I'm sure she was genuinely trying to help.' Holland tried to summon a cocky grin, but blushed despite himself. 'But I think she *did* take a shine to me ...'

303

'It's bloody typical,' Thorne said. 'The finest detectives on the force applying themselves twenty-four hours a day, and we get a break because some woman, who's clearly mad or desperate, thinks you've got a nice arse.'

The magazine was a mixture of regimental news and notices. There were letters, quizzes and book reviews; advertisements for modelling kits, financial services and shooting weekends. There were obituaries for those who had long since left the regiment and for some who had died more recently, while on active service.

About half the magazine was taken up by articles and photographs. All these were the work of serving soldiers, and the majority of them concerned what had, in spring 1991, been the very recent conflict in the Gulf: '*Christmas in Kuwait*'; '*Desert Shield – A Trooper's Perspective*'; '*Into the Storm*'.

'That's the one,' Holland said. He leaned across and pointed to where a page had been marked by a piece of paper. 'That's the page she wanted us to see.'

Thorne unfolded the bookmark. It was headed with the regimental crest and Latin motto. The message was hand-written in blue ink: '*Thought this would be a shot in the dark, but I think we struck lucky. The photograph is what you'll probably be most interested in. Lt Sarah Cheshire.*'

'No kiss?' Thorne asked.

'I'm not listening,' Holland said. He pointed to a black-and-white photo that took up half a page of the magazine. 'Our four men are somewhere among that lot . . .'

Two dozen or so soldiers had posed for the camera,

arranged in front of, around and in many cases on top of three battle tanks. They all wore desert camouflage and berets. Each carried a rifle and no more than a few of them were smiling. There was a caption to the right of the picture: '*D Troop, 2nd Sabre Squadron. Bremenhaven. October 1990*'.

'Just before they were posted to the Gulf,' Holland said. He reached over again and jabbed a finger towards one of the soldiers. The faces were small in shot, the features indistinct. 'That's Jago ... '

Thorne looked at the list of names beneath the photograph. Jago's was certainly there, but the list was not structured in any way. It was impossible to tell how the names corresponded to the men in the picture, gathered as arbitrarily as they were.

'How do you know?' Thorne asked.

'We scanned the photo and emailed it to Susan Jago. She picked her brother out for us.'

'She pick out anybody else?'

'She told us before that she'd only seen one photo of the crew together ... and that was years ago.'

Thorne studied the photograph. He thought he could read fear – apprehension, at least – on one or two of the faces, but decided in the end that he was simply projecting. He couldn't see what was in the heads and hearts of these soldiers any better than he'd been able to see what was in the eyes of the four he'd watched committing murder on a grainy videotape. Those men were in front of him at that moment; he was looking at their faces.

And now, if any were still alive, there was a way to trace them.

'How did they get away with it, Dave? How did no one find out what they'd done?'

'Maybe someone did,' Holland said. 'The army might have known and hushed it up ...'

Thorne wasn't convinced. 'Or maybe they just buried the bodies.' He ran that through his mind for a moment; thought about holes being dug in wet sand once the camera had been switched off. Thinking about the tape reminded him of something else. 'Any word back from the lab yet? They were going to try and sort out the sound on the video ...'

Holland rolled his eyes. 'Believe it or not, we've now sent it to a special unit at the University of California ...'

'What? They can't do it here?'

'Not if you want a result this side of Christmas.'

'Jesus.' Thorne handed the magazine back to Holland. 'I presume we're going back to the army with these names.'

'Yeah, and this *should* make things piss-easy for them. We know none of them are still serving with the 12th King's Hussars, but we should be able to find out if any have moved anywhere else within the service. And now we've got the names, we can finally get on to the Army Personnel Centre.'

'I think we should start trying to locate them ourselves at the same time, though.' Thorne got to his feet. 'We might find them faster than the army can.'

'That's the plan,' Holland said. 'We just need to get hold

of someone with a decent memory. Someone who can remember the other three who were in Jago's tank crew.'

'Start with the rarest names, right? Leave the Smiths and Joneses 'til last . . . '

'Really?' Holland looked across at Thorne like he was telling him how to tie his shoelaces.

Thorne returned the look with knobs on. 'OK . . . Sorry, *Sergeant.*'

'We're shit out of luck as far as that goes, anyway.' Holland pulled on his gloves and stood up. 'Nothing too outlandish, I'm afraid. Not a single Private Parts or Corporal Clutterbuck among them . . . '

They walked south towards the Serpentine.

It had started to drizzle, and Holland reached instinctively for the umbrella in his case, then stopped when he saw Thorne moving through the rain as if he were unaware of it.

'So why did you move?' Holland asked. 'Are you trying to lower the tone in as many places as possible?'

'No choice. The bloke whose pitch I took is coming back. Today or maybe tomorrow. These things tend not to be very specific . . . '

When Thorne had seen him the day before, Spike had been insistent that Terry T was on his way back to London. He'd heard a definite rumour, at any rate, and seeing as how Terry would want his pitch back, it was a good idea for Thorne to look around for somewhere else to bed down. Terry T was a big bloke, after all, Spike had said, and with a seriously vicious temper. Thorne had taken the bait, pretending to fall for the same gag he hadn't fallen for on the first night he and Spike had met ...

'How's the face feel?' Holland asked. This was the first day he'd laid eyes on Thorne since his arrest, and the first time he'd mentioned Thorne's souvenirs of the occasion.

'What, have you only just noticed it?'

'I didn't think you'd want people banging on about it ...'

'Because I got my face smashed in?' Thorne's tone was suddenly edgy, and snide. 'Or because of *why*?'

They walked on in silence for a few minutes.

'Obviously, it looks pretty bad,' Holland said. 'The face, I mean. I just wondered if it hurt much, that's all. Thought maybe you could get Phil Hendricks to bung you a few painkillers or something.'

Thorne felt bad that he'd been snappy. 'Don't worry about the face, Holland. It looks like shit, but beneath the bruises my looks remain undamaged.'

'That's a shame,' Holland said.

They came out on to Carriage Drive opposite Hyde Park Corner. Thorne had decided to take the long way back and walk into the West End along Piccadilly. Holland was planning to catch the tube back up to Colindale.

'Do you want to know the worst thing about you being promoted?' Thorne asked. 'I can no longer enjoy the simple pleasure of calling you "Constable" as if it's spelled with a "u" and an extra "t" ...'

*

Saturday had been a bit hectic, but he'd got what he needed, and the rest of the weekend had actually been very pleasant. He'd taken a boat trip down to Greenwich and wandered around the Maritime Museum. Sitting in a nice pub by the river, he'd had a couple of pints and a Sunday lunch with all the trimmings. Later, he'd poked around a few of the little antiquey places and second-hand shops. He'd bought a computer game and a black suede jacket from the market.

If you could be bothered to look, there were *plenty* of places like that in London, north and south of the river; places with some charm and individuality; with a little bit of character. You couldn't help but wonder why those who ended up on the street chose to congregate like rats around the West End. Were they drawn to the bright lights or something? Did they think it was *glamorous*? He didn't understand it. Surely they could have gone wherever they fancied, slept wherever they liked. Wasn't that one of the few *good* things about being homeless?

For all that he'd learned about the lives of these people – and he'd made it his business to learn a great deal – he couldn't help but think that, for some of them, it was a lifestyle choice. There were a few, of course – the ones who were soft in the head or whatever – who would never be able to cope and were always going to end up on the margins of society, but for others it seemed to be about preference. From what he could see, those people didn't want to help themselves and scorned any offer of assistance from others. It was hard to have any real sympathy with that sort . . .

Bearing in mind what he'd been doing, he knew full well that he could hardly have been expected to think any other way, but that was genuinely his opinion on the subject. He firmly believed that he could do what he'd done and still be, you know, *objective* about what went on in the world. The people who had died had done so for no other reason than simple necessity. What had been done – what he'd *had* to do – was about no more than self-preservation. Well, that and the money, of course.

But nothing else.

He could honestly say that he hadn't borne any ill-will towards anyone he'd ever killed.

Today, with more work to do, he wasn't quite as relaxed as he had been when ambling about in Greenwich. It should all have been done and dusted by now, but when it came to protecting yourself, being safe rather than sorry was the only sensible approach.

He was spending a dreary Monday mastering his new computer game; sharpening up his reflexes and concentrating his mind. He'd get back to the matter in hand tomorrow.

TWENTY-THREE

As a trainee detective constable, Jason Mackillop was desperate for any chance to make an impression. It was easy to get lost on a major investigation such as this one. But it was also possible, if you were in the right place at the right time, with the right people at the end of the phone, to go from donkey to hero in a few minutes. They hadn't talked much about luck on the five-week Detective Training Course at Hendon, but all the trainees knew it was every bit as important as the stuff they had been taught: forensics; crime scene management; handling exhibits; disclosure of evidence; performance in the witness box.

At twenty-three, he was relatively young for a TDC. He was perhaps no more than six months away from being assigned as a full DC, but after the probation, the year on relief, and the two more as a dogsbody on the Crime

Squad, he was more than ready to step up. He'd already proved he could handle himself in most formal areas of the job, and catching a break like this one certainly couldn't hurt ...

Mackillop put down the phone, took a deep breath, and snatched up the piece of paper on which he'd been scribbling. He needed to pass on the information quickly, but for a second or two he wasn't completely certain as to whom. Should he observe the chain of command or just go straight to the most senior officer he could find? If he did, would he risk putting noses out of joint? It was fantastic to impress, but it might be a very bad move to alienate those just a step or two further up the ladder than he was.

He glanced around the Incident Room, feeling the paper warm against his sweaty fingers. They were a good bunch, by and large, with no more tossers than you'd expect on any team of this size: Andy Stone was the sort of bloke you'd like as a mate, but Mackillop was unsure how good a copper he was; Kitson seemed well liked, but she sometimes had that look, like you wouldn't want to get on the wrong side of her; Holland could be a bit distant, though he'd only just been promoted, and was bound to have a lot on his plate. Mackillop had never met Tom Thorne, the team's absent DI, but he'd certainly heard enough about him ...

Looking around, trying to make his mind up, he saw that Kitson was watching him from a spot by the coffee machine. Her eye flicked from his face to the piece of paper he was now wafting nervously from the end of his outstretched arm.

'All right, Jason?'

'Guv ...'

Mackillop walked across, decision made, and within a minute he knew it had been the right one. Once he'd finished telling her about the phone call and shown her what he'd written down, Kitson had done exactly as he'd hoped she'd do: she'd congratulated him on a job well done, then pointed him straight towards the DCI's office.

He couldn't see Spike or One-Day Caroline, and guessed they'd be in later, but there were plenty of faces Thorne *did* recognise as he looked around. He saw Holy Joe, and the drunk who'd shouted at him outside St Clement Danes, and others he'd exchanged a story or two with at the soup runs around the Strand.

He asked if any of the unfamiliar faces belonged to Terry T.

Brendan Maxwell craned his head, panned quickly around the café, then went back to his breakfast. 'No, I can't see him. Why?'

'That's his spot I've been bedding down in most nights and Spike reckons he's coming back. So I've got to find somewhere else.'

'Doesn't hurt to move around a bit,' Maxwell said.

Thorne rammed the last of an egg and bacon roll into his mouth and answered with his mouth full. 'S'pose not ...'

'A lot of my clients have been moving around a bit more lately.' They had been talking quietly anyway, but now Maxwell lowered his voice until it was barely above a whisper. 'Some of them have taken to sleeping in a different place every night, or getting themselves indoors. For obvious reasons.'

'I don't want to go into a hostel,' Thorne said.

He had purposely gone into the Lift early. The battery on his mobile was very low and he was borrowing a charger in Maxwell's office. They'd gone down to the café for breakfast while they waited.

Maxwell took a slurp of tea, then grunted and swallowed quickly as he remembered something. 'Did that copper find you, by the way? He was going to look for you at the theatre, I think . . . '

Thorne nodded. 'He tracked me down eventually.' He remembered Holland telling him on the phone that he'd come here; that Maxwell had pointed him towards the theatre doorway.

Since they'd met the day before in the park and Holland had shown him the magazine, Thorne had been anxiously waiting for news. It could only be a matter of time until they had names. It felt like they were turning a corner and picking up speed. Of course, he'd had the same feeling plenty of times before. Often, it just meant that you hit the brick wall that much faster.

'What's Phil up to?' Thorne hadn't seen Hendricks for nearly a fortnight.

The Irishman pointed a fork towards Thorne's face.

'He told me to make sure you took some painkillers if that was hurting . . . '

'They're fucking ganging up on me,' Thorne said.

Maxwell looked confused for a moment, shrugged when Thorne shook his head. On the far side of the café, a plate crashed to the floor. Maxwell joined in with the cheer as loudly as anyone else. 'You seeing a fair bit of the city, then?' he asked.

'I'm seeing a lot of it, yeah. But I don't know that "fair" is the right word.'

'Not the stuff you see in the guide books, is it?'

'It's like being on *Panorama*,' Thorne said. 'Only with more killing.'

In the queue at the counter behind them, voices were suddenly raised. Maxwell pushed back his chair and stood, ready to step in, but the man doing most of the shouting was already striding towards the door, telling anyone who'd listen that they could go fuck themselves.

Maxwell sat back down. 'You like all that nasty stuff, though, right? Phil was telling me. All that blood and guts and Black Museum shit.'

Thorne felt slightly irritated. He didn't know if Maxwell was being deliberately obtuse or if Hendricks had just put it across to him badly. Knowing how Hendricks had once tried to explain Thorne's love of country music by telling Maxwell that he liked songs about death and lost dogs, this was certainly possible. 'I like history,' he said. 'In London, a lot of it's just . . . dark.'

315

Maxwell pushed what was left of his breakfast around the plate. 'Getting darker all the time,' he said.

Thorne sensed a figure looming behind him and twisted his neck round to see Lawrence Healey standing there, clutching a tray.

'May I join you?' Healey asked.

Maxwell put his fork down and threw back what was left of his tea. 'I'm just on my way to a meeting. Tom?'

'Free country . . .' Thorne said.

Maxwell looked across the table before he turned to leave, something Thorne couldn't read in his eyes. 'Let me know if there's anything else you need . . .'

Healey tucked into a bowl of what looked suspiciously like bran. There was a carton of yoghurt on his tray and a cup of foul-smelling herbal tea. After a minute or two of silence and an exchange of awkward smiles, Healey cleared his throat. 'I was going to ask how you were getting on, but, looking at you, I'm not sure there's any real need.'

'You should have seen the other bloke,' Thorne said.

'I saw him yesterday, as a matter of fact . . .'

Thorne didn't know what to say.

Healey's voice, even posher than Thorne remembered, suited a tone of wry amusement very well. 'We have a weekly meeting with some of the officers from the Homeless Unit. Just a chat about anything that's come up.' He stared across at Thorne for a few moments, nudged his glasses a little higher, then went back to his cereal.

Thorne watched Healey eat. He looked fit and tanned under a brushed-denim button-down shirt. That said, most people would have looked well compared to Thorne himself. Or to any of the blotchy or the blasted, the washed-out or pasty-faced characters that moved around them. 'Thanks for the concern,' Thorne said. 'But I really wouldn't bother.'

'You might need some legal advice . . .'

'I'll be fine.'

'We can help you with that.'

Thorne said nothing. He turned and looked at the noticeboard for a while, decided he'd probably give the poetry workshop a miss.

'Things going OK, though?' Healey asked. 'Generally, I mean?'

'I've been better . . .'

'I know.'

'Really?'

'I do understand how hard it is.' Healey's voice was lower suddenly. He reminded Thorne of an over-earnest vicar. Or of Tony Blair. 'It's the adjustment that's particularly difficult . . .'

Thorne had actually found adjusting to other people the trickiest thing of all; to the way other people *saw* him. It was usually one of two reactions: he was avoided or ignored. In the first instance, pedestrians would steer clear, the more sensitive doing their best to make that feint to one side as unobtrusive as possible. In the second, he seemed to become completely invisible, as passers-by simply pretended that they hadn't seen him at all. Both reactions were gloriously British in their sly dishonesty, but no more so, Thorne decided, than some people's when confronted by people whom they actually *knew*. When greeting those they perhaps hadn't seen for a while. There was one phrase that Thorne particularly hated; it could cover a multitude of sins and was trotted out no matter how sick or sad the person on the receiving end appeared. No matter how frightful their clothes or hair, or how much weight they'd put on since the last time you'd seen them:

'*You look well . . .*'

Suddenly a hand fell on to Thorne's shoulder and a rheumy-eyed whippet of a man he'd talked to once or twice leaned down close to him. 'Great days, eh?' The man breathed sweet sherry into Thorne's face. 'Great days . . .'

Thorne had no idea what the man was talking about. He watched him walk away and accost someone at the next table, then turned back to Healey. 'I've met some fascinating people, though,' he said.

'What's it been now? A month or so?'

'Something like that. You lose track.' Thorne wasn't sure exactly how many rough sleepers came within the Lift's remit, but he couldn't help wondering if Healey knew as much about all his clients. 'What about you?'

'Sorry?'

Thorne was thinking about what Healey had said when they'd met in the corridor a couple of weeks before. 'We're both "new boys", remember? How are you settling in?'

'Oh . . . settled now, most definitely. Thank you for asking.'

'Just talking,' Thorne said.

'People can be suspicious of a new broom, you know? You just need to get your head down and get on with it, whatever anyone else thinks. A certain amount of tunnel vision definitely helps.'

The concern in Healey's voice had gone and been replaced by something a little more abrasive. Thorne saw that there was a resolve behind the nice-but-dim accent and the do-gooder appearance. He also understood exactly what Healey was saying. Tunnel vision was something he'd been accused of himself, though it was usually described somewhat less politely.

'It could help get you off the street,' Healey said.

'Maybe it's what put me *on* it.'

'You want to talk about that?'

'Not hugely . . . '

When Healey began removing the foil from his yoghurt carton, Thorne stood up and took his coat from the back of the chair.

'I enjoyed the chat,' Healey said.

Thorne bent to pile his empty plate and cup on to the tray. 'You need to get out more,' he said.

He slid his tray on to a trolley near the food counter, then looked back to make sure that Healey hadn't gone anywhere. He wanted to check to see if there'd been any messages, and as long as Healey was still eating, it was the perfect time to nip up to the office and get his phone back.

*

Looks played a major part in it; that's how Russell Brigstocke felt anyway. It was like being a hard man; like being feared. Yes, it was about what was inside your head, about having the will to dish out pain, and to take it, but once you had it going on up there, then what you looked like was the next most important thing. The set of your mouth, and the way your eyes absorbed the light – the way they sucked it in and smothered it – counted far more than your size, or how much weight your punch packed.

It seemed to Brigstocke that Jason Mackillop *looked* like a copper. He had short hair and skin that was pitted with acne scars. He was heavyset beneath a blue M&S suit, and he stood awkwardly, as though he were designed to be permanently leaning on something: the roof of an unmarked vehicle; the window sill in an airless interview room; a bar. What Mackillop looked like of course was a casting director's *idea* of a copper, but as most of those who did the job for real looked like financial advisers – Brigstocke himself included, if he were being honest – that was probably no bad thing. At that moment, with the TDC standing in front of his desk and brightening the day *right* up, he decided that Jason Mackillop was the sort of copper he could do with a damn sight more of.

'Right, let's have those names . . . ' Brigstocke said.

The list of soldiers in the *Glorious* photograph had been divided up and Mackillop had been the one who had struck lucky. Among those in his allocation had been the writer of the original article, and not only had First

Lieutenant Stephen Brereton been fairly easy to trace, but he'd had no great trouble providing the relevant information. Mackillop had already explained to Brigstocke how Brereton – now a major in the Corporate Communications Department of the MOD – had remembered Chris Jago pretty well. He'd talked about their time in Bremenhaven; about Jago's fondness for German beer and German girls. He'd told Mackillop how each crew in the troop had been tight with each other; how a friendly rivalry between the different crews had been actively encouraged. Brereton hadn't seemed to mind too much that he could not be told why the police were so interested, and had said he'd be happy to have a look through some of his old Gulf War journals and diaries. After no more than ten minutes, he'd called back with the names of the other three men who'd manned a Challenger tank alongside Chris Jago in the early part of 1991.

'That major down in Somerset . . . Poulter? He said that these crews got moved about all the time, that they were sometimes shifted around in battle situations. How can Brereton be certain these are the men who were in that tank on February 26th, 1991?'

'He isn't,' Mackillop said. 'Not absolutely, one hundred per cent, I mean. I gave him the exact date and he told me that his memory wasn't *that* good, but that he thought he'd remember if there'd been any injuries or last-minute transfers, you know? He wouldn't stake his life on it, but he couldn't recall any particular reason why that crew should have been split up.'

'Right . . . ' Brigstocke was holding out a hand, waiting to take the piece of paper.

Instead, Mackillop looked at his list, read the names to the DCI: 'Trooper Christopher Jago, he was the Gunner; Lance Corporal Ryan Eales, the Loader/Operator; Trooper Alec Bonser was the Driver, and the tank Commander was Corporal Ian Hadingham. I reckon this was our crew, Guv.' Then he stepped forward and passed the paper across the desk.

Jago. Eales. Bonser. Hadingham.

Brigstocke stared down at the names of four men who surely held the key to solving a series of murders. Four men who themselves had committed murder and who now appeared to be paying for it with their own lives.

'Obviously, we're still in the dark about which one of them is our first victim,' Mackillop said. 'It could be Eales, Bonser or Hadingham.'

Brigstocke nodded. 'Now we've ID'd the crew, we can put a bit more pressure on the Army Personnel Centre—'

'I'm already on it, Guv.'

'I can't actually promote you until you've made DC, you know, Jason.'

Mackillop reddened. 'Well, I'm not on it exactly, but Major Brereton said he'd talk to them and try to get at least the basic stuff to us a.s.a.p.'

'*Basic stuff?*'

'Individual pictures of the soldiers, and maybe some of the details that are in their records: height, weight, colour of hair, blood group with a bit of luck. Hopefully, we should be able to figure out which one our mystery corpse is.'

'Hopefully.' Brigstocke was thinking that they'd need more than a photo. The killer hadn't left any of the victims in a state that was particularly recognisable. 'He reckons he can do that, does he, this Major Brereton?'

'He sounded like there was every chance, yeah. I think they respond better when requests for information come from other soldiers.'

Brigstocke picked up the phone. 'Not like the way most people on the Job respond to each other, then?'

'Guv . . . ?'

'You'll know what I'm on about soon enough.' Brigstocke dialled a number, pointed towards the piece of paper. 'Well done on this, Jason. Your luck was in, no question . . . '

'Oh, it was pure bloody jam, Guv, I know that.'

'Luck's no use to anybody unless they use it. It sounds like you dealt with this Brereton bloke very well.'

Mackillop handled the praise like someone with far greater experience. Just a small nod. But Brigstocke caught the spasm of delight on his face, like a stifled sneeze, in the second or two before the TDC turned to walk towards the door.

Brigstocke leaned back in his chair and listened to the phone ringing on the other end of the line. He was as absurdly excited as Mackillop had been by the prospect of giving Detective Chief Superintendent Trevor Jesmond the first piece of genuinely good news in a while.

*

The four of them – Thorne, Spike, Caroline and Terry T – sat around a table in a grotty café behind the Charing Cross Road. Terry had returned from his travels with a few extra quid in his pocket and had insisted on shelling out on tea and doughnuts for everyone. This, and the fact that he was able to make the word 'cunt' sound like a term of endearment, made Thorne take to him straight away.

'You the cunt who's been sleeping in my pitch?' Terry had said on being introduced. The voice was high and hoarse, ripening a thick London accent.

Thorne had thought about it for a few seconds. 'Yeah, I think that'll be me. Just keeping it warm for you, obviously.'

'Fair play, mate . . . '

Terry T was every bit as tall as Spike had described, but he was also spookily thin. He was, Thorne guessed, somewhere in his late thirties, but he looked a damn sight older, with sunken cheeks, very few teeth and what appeared to be no hair at all beneath a floppy green hat. Like a cross between Nosferatu and the King of the Gypsies. A feather dangled from one ear and he'd taken off his scarf to reveal a heavy-looking, tarnished padlock on a chain around his neck, which had turned the skin beneath it distinctly green.

Terry had seen Thorne staring and reached up to finger the chain. 'Lost the fuckin' key, didn't I?'

'So where you been then, Tel? What you been doing . . . ?'

Spike was buzzing, and for more than just the usual reason. He was excited to have his friend back. Thorne felt a peculiar twinge of something that might have been jealousy, though it was probably no more than a sugar rush from the doughnuts.

'Been all over,' Terry said. 'Up north to Birmingham and Liverpool, then even further, mate. Up with the chilly Jockos.'

Spike dipped a doughnut into a glass of Coke, let the drips fall off. 'I thought most of them were here in London.'

'Plenty more where they came from,' Terry said.

Spike rolled his eyes, put on a cod-Scottish accent, and mumbled something incomprehensible. 'It's fucking disgusting,' he said. 'They come down here, they beg on our street corners, they drink our Special Brew ...'

Terry and Caroline laughed.

'How d'you get around?' Thorne asked.

'Hitching, mostly. Got a couple of free trains by keeping an eye out for the ticket collector and spending a lot of time in the bog.'

'I bet it's a bit colder on the streets up there.'

'I was indoors, mate. Sofa-surfing ...'

Instinctively, Thorne looked to Spike for an explanation.

Spike held out his arms as if riding a surfboard, repeated the phrase in a silly American accent. 'Sofa-surfing. Moving around, like. Dossing down on people's floors, sofas, whatever ...'

'Loads of people do it,' Caroline said. She'd poured a small mound of sugar on to the tabletop and had been absently toying with it: drawing patterns in the grains with her finger. All at once she chopped the edge of her hand on to the table and swept the sugar on to the floor. 'You think there's a lot of people sleeping on the street and in the hostels, you can multiply that by tens of thousands . . .'

More of those who, conveniently, could never be counted when the official figures were being produced; more of the so-called 'hidden homeless'. Thorne suddenly wondered if Terry T knew what had been going on while he was travelling. What had happened to some of those who had been unable to hide.

'So how long have you been away, Terry?'

Caroline flashed Thorne a look. He could see that she knew what was going through his mind, but he couldn't be sure what she was trying to tell him.

'Christ . . . it was a few days after that poor bastard got his head kicked in round Golden Square. When was that?'

'A couple of months ago,' Spike said.

'Did they ever catch the bloke who did it?'

Terry couldn't remember the last time he'd seen a paper or watched the news; he knew nothing of those who had died after that first victim. Caroline brought him up to date: she told him about the murders of Ray Mannion and Paddy Hayes; she leaned across to grab one of Terry T's long, bony hands and told him what had happened to Radio Bob.

Spike edged towards Thorne. 'Terry and Bob were mates,' he said. Like it wasn't obvious enough . . .

'Do they know why?' Terry asked eventually.

Spike snorted. 'Not got a clue, if you ask me, like.'

'There's supposedly an undercover copper sleeping rough,' Caroline said. 'To try and catch him.'

'They reckon the killer might *be* a copper,' Thorne said.

There was a small bowl on the table filled with sachets and sealed tubes: sugar, vinegar, mustard, mayonnaise. Caroline grabbed a handful and dropped them into her bag. She closed her eyes and leaned her head against Spike. He drummed his fingers on the tabletop, whistling something between his teeth.

Terry took out a plastic wallet and shook some money on to the table to settle the bill. 'He'll be a dead copper if I get hold of him ....'

They walked up to Centre Point, then stopped and stood about for a quarter of an hour. For a few, strange, minutes, Thorne felt like a teenager again; content to hang around with friends, not doing anything in particular. Just talking bollocks and winding each other up. Happy enough to say nothing at all if the mood wasn't right.

The feeling passed quickly enough. This was not about relishing space and free time and the absence of responsibility. It was about being lost.

They moved off again, crossing Oxford Street and heading north. 'I can't fucking believe I wasn't here,' Terry said. 'I can't believe I missed Bob's funeral.'

Caroline caught up with him. 'Listen, I'm sure you and some of the other lads can get together later and have a few drinks for him, eh?'

'More than a few,' Terry said.

Caroline looked at Thorne. 'You up for that?'

'Better watch him though, Tel.' Spike pointed at Thorne and began to shadow-box. 'After a couple of cans he thinks he's Lennox Lewis ... '

'I don't really know what I'm doing later,' Thorne said. 'I've got to find a decent place to get some kip.'

Terry turned to him. 'I was only joking about my pitch, mate. Plenty of room in there for two, if you want to stick around for a bit.'

Spike whistled. 'You on the turn, Tel?'

'I'll see ... ' Thorne said.

Caroline punched him on the shoulder. 'Tonight's sorted, so don't bother arguing. It's going to piss down later, so you're coming underground with us ... '

Major Stephen Brereton had been as good as his word. By mid-afternoon, photos and descriptions of the four men in the tank crew were being faxed through to the Incident Room. Holland and Kitson had stood over the machine as the information came through, inch by inch. They cleared a desk, laid it all out and looked for the answer that they hoped would be somewhere in front of them. Brigstocke had been right in guessing that the photos would not do the job on their own. They were simple head-and-shoulder shots of the four men in uniform, taken shortly after each had enlisted, but enough was likely to have happened since then to change the way each of the men looked.

They studied the information sheets on Hadingham, Bonser and Eales: dates of birth and of enlistment; potted service histories; basic physical details.

'Blood group doesn't help us,' Kitson said, reading. 'Eales and Hadingham are both O positive ...'

Holland was the one who spotted it. 'Found him ...'

'Show me.'

Kitson looked over Holland's shoulder and Holland pointed to the description of Trooper Alec Bonser. The Driver.

'He was five feet nine look, same as our John Doe. Eales and Hadingham were both six-footers. The body in Westminster Morgue has got to be Alec Bonser.'

Kitson carried on staring at the sheet of paper.

'It's got to be,' Holland said. 'I don't see any other—'

'You're right, I know.' Kitson pointed to another line of type. 'I was looking for something else. This is good news for *us*, maybe ...'

Holland saw that Kitson was pointing to the entry under *Next of Kin: Barbara Bonser (Mother)*.

Holland let out a long, slow breath and looked around. He could see that Andy Stone, Jason Mackillop and others had been earwigging; that they were hanging on every word. 'What about the death message?' Holland asked.

'I'll sort it.' Kitson gathered up the sheets of paper. 'I'll go and fill the DCI in and get the say-so ...'

'So we should start looking for Eales and Hadingham, then?'

'Looks like it.' She pulled out one of the sheets, glanced at it and thrust it back at Holland. 'You can make a start on our tank commander while I'm gone.'

As he watched Kitson walk towards Brigstocke's office, Holland wondered what *he* would say to Barbara Bonser if he were in the same position. What his own mother would say if it were *his* death message that was being delivered. He started to sweat, and to feel like he needed to sit down, when he began to wonder how he would react – how he would *really* react – were he ever to be told that anything had happened to Chloe . . .

An hour later the whiteboard had been updated. Blown-up pictures of Jago, Hadingham, Bonser and Eales had been added. The question marks had been removed. They had the names of the two soldiers who might still be alive and finally they had the names of *both* of those who were dead. Now, well into the locate/trace on Ian Hadingham, Holland had come up with nothing. The usual calls and searches to DSS and the National Voters' Register had failed to turn his man up, and though he hadn't expected it to be simple, he was wondering where to go next.

'*This is good news for* us, *maybe . . .*'

It suddenly struck him that he hadn't once put Sophie into any of those painful next-of-kin scenarios that had occupied his thoughts earlier. The realisation came like a fist in the gut; it winded him, and he knew he would be feeling its effects for a while. But at the same time it gave him an idea. A change of direction.

He looked again at Ian Hadingham's information sheet and turned back to his computer.

Brigstocke should have known better. All his years of experience should have told him there were only two chances the day would finish up as well as it had started.

Slim and none.

When he answered the phone and the caller introduced himself by stating his rank, Brigstocke presumed it was the Army Personnel Centre, or perhaps someone from the regimental HQ in Somerset. He was about to pass on his gratitude for their sterling work in getting the details sent across so quickly.

But he was not speaking to an ordinary soldier.

The Special Investigations Branch of the Royal Military Police was the army's equivalent of the CID. It was their job to investigate the more serious offences committed against army personnel and their families. An elite force of fewer than two hundred plainclothes detectives selected from RMP ranks, they had teams in constant readiness to be deployed anywhere in the world. But they were also there to investigate serious crimes committed *by* soldiers; policing their own, in much the same way as the bunch who might well be hauling Tom Thorne across the coals when all this was over. In Brigstocke's mind, this made them spooks; 'rubber-heelers', because you could never hear the buggers coming. If the ordinary squaddie felt the same way about them as the ordinary copper felt about the DPS, Brigstocke guessed they were as popular as turds in a sandpit.

331

Brigstocke was rarely quick to judge – and was certainly not in Tom Thorne's league – but the SIB man got up his nose from the off. He was a major, which, as far as Brigstocke knew, may well have equated in army terms with his own rank, but there was no reference to it. And certainly no bloody *deference*. He spoke to Brigstocke as if they were colleagues, which, considering he'd never so much as heard of the bloke before, was hugely irritating.

As they were talking – or rather as Brigstocke was listening – he kept wondering if he was on the phone to a copper or a soldier; or some bizarre hybrid of the two. The man certainly had twice the arrogance of either.

And to begin with, at least, he insisted on trying to be jokey.

'It's sod all like they make out on *Red Cap*,' he said. 'The women aren't nearly so attractive, for a start ... '

'I've never watched it,' Brigstocke said.

The major then went round the houses for a while, chatting about this, that and every other thing: asking Brigstocke how busy he was and comparing caseloads; no rest for the wicked, no thanks for a job well done and you didn't have to be mad to work here but ...

It took maybe ten minutes before he got to the point: 'So, this business with the tank crew ... '

Brigstocke repeated what Kitson and Holland had said that first time to Rutherford and Spiby at Media Ops; what they'd said a few days after that when they'd been down to the regiment's HQ in Somerset. He talked about a complex and consuming murder case: two vagrants who, it transpired, had been ex-servicemen, and two others whom they'd been trying to trace. They were trying to catch a killer; there was no more to it than that.

'So, how's it going?'

'We're getting there, slowly. You know how it is ... '

'You've traced the crew, though. You've got all four names now, yes?'

He'd have got that from the AP Centre. Maybe from Stephen Brereton. It didn't much matter.

'Yes, they came through this afternoon.' *Thinking: you fuckers don't hang about, do you?* 'The army's been very helpful ... '

'Well, of course, why wouldn't we be?'

Brigstocke manufactured a laugh. 'No reason,' he said. 'But if it's anything like the Met, sometimes it's got sod all to do with a desire to help and everything to do with red tape, you know ... ?'

There was a pause then. Brigstocke thought he could hear, through the faint hiss on the line, the sound of pages being turned.

'So, nothing you think we should know about?'

If Brigstocke were the paranoid kind, he might have heard that as *nothing you're not telling us?* If he were really going to town, it might even have been *nothing you're not telling us that we might know already?*

'If I think of anything, I'll get back to you ... '

Of course, Brigstocke had said nothing at all about the video. He'd been delighted, if a little surprised, that Jesmond, who was normally circumspect about such things, had backed his judgement and authorised him to keep quiet about it.

'I'm sure we'll speak again,' the major said, before hanging up.

They *would* be told about the videotape at some point. Once it ceased being active evidence, it would be handed quietly over, and then it would be up to the Redcaps what they did about it. Then, Brigstocke felt sure, the man he'd just spoken to would be back on the phone. Only this time, he wouldn't be quite as matey . . .

He was still thinking about these conversations, past and future, while Holland was speaking. He'd come into Brigstocke's office and begun to talk about the locate/trace he'd set up on Ian Hadingham.

Brigstocke pushed thoughts of the SIB Major to the back of his mind and concentrated on what Dave Holland was telling him.

' . . . so I went after his *wife* instead,' Holland said. 'Shireen Hadingham was listed as his next of kin. Not much more bloody luck with *her* until I started using her maiden name. She's gone back to calling herself "Shireen Collins" . . . '

'Her and Hadingham split up?'

'Not long after he came out of the army.'

'Did you find her?'

'Yeah. Five minutes. I spoke to her.'

'She confirm the tattoo?' Brigstocke asked.

Holland nodded. 'He was very proud of it, by all accounts.'

On the ceiling, a strip-light that was on its way out buzzed and flickered. Brigstocke could feel the day grinding towards its arse-end. He was aching to get out of the building; to get home and collapse on to a sofa. He wanted nothing more than to open a bottle and let a few children clamber over him for a while. 'Does she know where her ex-old man is?' he asked.

'Oh yes, and she's pretty sure he isn't going anywhere.'

'Get on with it, Dave ... '

'He's in Denstone Cemetery, just outside Salford.'

Brigstocke stared at Holland. He guessed he wouldn't be opening that bottle for a while yet.

'That's the thing,' Holland said. 'Ian Hadingham killed himself just under a year ago.'

TWENTY-FOUR

Thorne had parted company from Spike, Caroline and Terry T a few hours earlier. Caroline had insisted that they'd see him later – 'back at our place' – before she and Spike had disappeared, and Terry had wandered off in search of strong drink. On the pretence of doing the same thing, Thorne had gone his own way, grateful for the chance to spend some time alone; to get on the phone to Dave Holland and catch up with developments.

Things had been moving bloody quickly . . .

He'd never been one to write a lot of stuff down; certainly no more than he'd had to, and that was quite enough. He'd grown accustomed to carrying around a lot of information in his head, both mundane and monstrous, and to the fact that some of the grislier details had a habit of lodging there, unwanted, like the melody to some anodyne pop song. Working as he was, though there were a few bits and pieces scribbled on scraps of paper in his rucksack, he was having to remember much more than he normally would.

Now there were four more names he was not likely to forget in a hurry. Hadingham, Eales, Bonser and Jago. A quartet of soldiers, of killers. Perhaps of dead men . . .

Thorne had been less than gobsmacked to learn that ex-Corporal Ian Hadingham was already dead. There were no details as yet, but he'd have put money on the fact that this 'suicide' was about as kosher as the 'accidental' hit and run that had killed Trooper Chris Jago. And there was no doubt whatsoever as to how Alec Bonser, the driver of the tank, had died.

That was three out of four . . .

It was by no means clear cut, of course, but it certainly added credence to the theory that the crew was being targeted by the man who had shot the video; that whoever had been behind the camera on that ugly day in 1991 was doing the killing.

The warren of pedestrian subways that ran beneath Marble Arch had probably looked like a good idea on paper; in much the same way that sixties tower-blocks had seemed to make perfect sense until those unlucky enough had actually started to live in them. The tunnels honeycombed from Oxford Street to Edgware Road; from the tube station into Hyde Park, in a maze of long, intersecting corridors from which there were no fewer than fourteen different entrances and exits. By day, these subways were eerie enough. Once darkness had fallen, though the subways themselves were well lit for the most part, anyone with any sense would risk sprinting across four lanes of traffic rather than venturing underground.

When Thorne had been here a few days before, the morning he'd met Holland at Speaker's Corner, an old woman had been sitting on a bench outside Exit 6, feeding the pigeons. It had taken Thorne a few moments to notice her, to make her out clearly behind the curtain of wings, the shifting mass of greys and browns and slick-wet blues that surrounded her. The birds had engulfed the tiny figure, walking across her lap and sitting on her head and shoulders. They swarmed in a grubby mass around her feet and perched on every spare inch of the bench and on the handle of the shopping cart by her side. It had been a disturbing image, as though she might be consumed, but as Thorne had walked past he could see that the woman looked perfectly content. She'd sat there smiling, a cigarette dangling from her lips, talking happily to the pigeons as they flocked to devour only the crumbs from her hand. Thorne had slowed to listen, but whatever the old woman had been saying was lost beneath the noise of the feeding-frenzy.

Now, as he walked towards the subway entrance, there was only a mottled carpet of pigeon-shit around the bench as evidence of the woman's presence. If she were ever to disappear, the Council's Cleaning Department would have to be considered prime suspects . . .

Even halfway down the stairs, the sound changed. The noise of the traffic above became a hum; a low drone broken only by the bleat of a car horn or the distorted wail of an emergency siren. By the time Thorne was in the subway itself, though the noises from the street had receded, those from closer around him had become amplified. The ordinary sound of a cough, of an empty can blown or kicked along, of his own footsteps, was suddenly spookier; a full second passing between the sound itself and its echo, carried back on the wind that didn't so much whistle as growl along the concrete corridors.

The tunnels were about eight feet wide and more or less the same high. Once they might have seemed futuristic, these straight tubes with lights mounted every few feet along the walls, but now they were simply unnerving. Stinking of urine and danger and something sickly-sweet that Thorne couldn't quite place.

The tiles that ran along some walls, and the complex mosaics that were crumbling from others, contrasted with the graffiti-covered metal doors. Thorne guessed they concealed pipework. Small metal speakers were mounted along the ceiling. They were presumably there to carry Underground announcements, but something about the place made it easy to imagine a robotic voice conveying information to the survivors of a nuclear blast.

As Thorne walked deeper into the maze of tunnels, one or two people began to move past him. They all wore rucksacks or carried sleeping bags, and some had large sheets of cardboard folded under their arms. In each corridor there were already a number of people sleeping. At least, Thorne presumed there were; it was difficult to tell, as some of the boxes – the cardboard coffins, eight or ten feet long – could have been empty, but Thorne was fairly sure that most were inhabited. He wondered if the pigeon woman was down here somewhere. He briefly imagined her, boxed up beneath a blanket of dirty feathers, waiting for daylight; for the sound of claw-skitter and wing-beat.

When she might feel what it was to be needed again . . .

Thorne came to a T-junction and looked both ways. At the far end of the right-hand tunnel he saw two figures sitting against a wall. Spike and Caroline. He watched as Spike stood and whistled to him. He waved and began walking towards them.

Halfway along the tunnel, Thorne walked past a complex arrangement of boxes: two fastened together, one on top of the other, with a third coming off them at a right angle. A middle-aged black man sat near by, proprietorial outside his unique sleeping quarters. He wore a baggy grey hat that perfectly matched his beard, and the colour of his skin. He looked up from a paperback as Thorne passed and gave him a hard stare. Thorne held the look just long enough to make it clear he knew what he was doing and kept on going.

When he reached Spike and Caroline, Thorne sat down. He pointed back over his shoulder towards the man who, he guessed, was still staring at him. 'Neighbourhood watch?'

'Ollie's a cool bloke,' Spike said. 'He keeps an eye out, you know?'

Caroline moistened a Rizla and completed a skinny roll-up. 'He's also got the only two-storey bedroom down here. It's like one of those hamster houses.'

Thorne looked at the two huge cardboard boxes end-to-end against the wall next to them. 'Where do you get these things?'

'Round the back of Dixons,' Spike said. 'They're for fridge-freezers, you know? Those big, fuck-off American ones, right, Caz?'

'We fold 'em up, stash 'em during the day and then put 'em back together last thing.'

'It's flat-pack, like.' Spike had taken the tobacco and papers, was busily rolling a fag of his own. 'Same as you get from Ikea, only cheaper ... '

Caroline lit her cigarette, inhaled deeply, then pointed to the smaller of the two boxes, letting the smoke go as she spoke. 'That one's yours ... '

Thorne looked, and realised that Spike and Caroline would be sharing the bigger box. That they'd made the other one up for him.

'We got you some scoff an' all,' Spike said. 'We've already had ours ... sorry.' He produced a brown KFC bag and handed it to Thorne.

Thorne felt oddly touched. As he reached across for the bag, he was thinking that, in relative terms, there weren't many people he could think of who'd have done as much for him. There were plenty, with far more to their names than these two, who'd have baulked at equivalent acts of generosity.

'Be stone cold by now, like,' Spike said.

Thorne opened the beer he'd brought with him. While he tucked hungrily into the food, the three of them talked. And they laughed a lot. Spike was a natural storyteller and Caroline was the perfect foil; she happily fed him cues and helped him recount tales of life on the street, some of them horrific, despite the humour that Spike was able to wring from their telling. It was no different, Thorne thought, to a copper's war stories; to the gags that flew thick and fast across a room where the walls were smeared with blood and in which one occupant would fail to laugh only because they were dead.

There hadn't been a single night since Thorne had come on to the street when he hadn't sat or lain, desperate for sleep to take away the ache of cold or hunger, and thought that he would give nearly anything for the comfort of his own bed. That he'd have plumbed the depths of depravity for a curry from the Bengal Lancer and a Cash album on the stereo. But, sitting in a stinking subway with two junkies, watching water run down the wall behind them, and with cold KFC settling heavy in his gut, Thorne felt as good as he had in a long while.

'I want to get the stuff for our flat from Ikea,' Caroline said, suddenly. 'And I want a big American fridge.'

Such was the nature of their conversation: tangential; fragmented; comments that referred to conversations long since dead-ended . . .

'Got to get the flat first, like,' Spike said. He pushed his legs out straight, then raised his knees, then repeated the action. 'Yeah? See what I'm saying? Got to get the fucking flat.'

'It'll happen,' Thorne said.

Caroline sniffed once, twice and let her head drop back. She banged it against the wall, over and over again, though never quite hard enough to hurt. She spoke like a child, desperate to cling on to a fantasy; to be convinced that it isn't really the lie she knows it to be. 'When ... when ... when ...?'

'I'm not a fortune-teller,' Spike said.

'Tell me.'

'When we get enough money. You'll have to start nicking stuff from a better class of shop ...'

'I know how to get the money.'

'Fuck *that*!' Spike was clenching and unclenching his fists; quickly, like he was shaking away a cramp; like he was warming up for something. '*Fuck* that!'

Thorne could see that, all in a rush, things were starting to unravel. Their words were not overtly aggressive, but an agitation, an impatience, a *pain*, was colouring everything they said.

'You talked once about just needing a bit of luck,' Thorne said. 'Remember? You never know when that's going to happen.'

'Right, he's right,' Spike said.

Caroline snapped her head up and stared at Thorne. 'I know it's going to happen, because it *always* happens, and it's always *bad*.'

343

Spike shook his head, kept on shaking it. 'No ... no way, no way ...'

'I don't know anyone who has the good sort,' she said. 'We only have the shit kind. We get luck that's fatal ...'

They were starting to talk over each other. 'When it comes, we'll have enough money to get everything we want. Everything.' Spike was grinning from ear to ear, jabbering, high and fast. 'We'll get a place with room for loads of fucking fridges and the best sound system and all great stuff in the kitchen and whatever ...'

'You're dreaming ...'

'We can have massive parties, and when we feel like it we can check in to one of them posh places in the country and get straight, and then when we're well and truly sorted we can get Robbie back ...'

Caroline flinched and dragged her eyelids down. When she opened them again, though she made no sound, her eyes were wide behind a film of tears. She cast them down to the floor, her fingers spinning the thin leather bracelets around her wrist.

'He's here,' Spike said suddenly.

As fast as Thorne could turn to see the man walking towards them down the tunnel, Caroline was on her feet and on her way to meet him. It didn't take very long. There were not much more than half a dozen grunted words of exchange before the more important commodities were handed over.

Thorne looked back to see Spike unrolling a bar-towel on the floor, revealing three or four thin syringes, a plastic craft knife and a black-bottomed spoon with a bent handle. He then produced a small bottle of Evian from behind one of the boxes, looked across at Caroline, who was on her way back. Thorne could see the goose pimples clearly, the sheen that he'd thought was grease from the fried chicken.

'Get a move on, Caz, I'm sick ...'

Caroline sat back down and passed over a matchbook-sized wrap of folded white paper.

Spike snatched up the cigarette lighter, talking ten to the dozen as he opened the wrap, smoothed it out on the floor. 'Great to see Terry again, though, yeah? Told you he was a good bloke, like. He'll be fucking bladdered by now, off his fucking head somewhere with a few of Radio Bob's old cronies. Bunch of nutters, most of 'em, but Terry's not proud who he drinks with, like ...'

Using a supermarket reward card, Spike flattened out the heroin, shaped it carefully until he was satisfied. He thrust the card at Caroline. 'You cut, I'll choose.'

Caroline moved away from the wall, shuffled towards Spike, and towards the heroin. Now Thorne could see that she was every bit as strung-out as Spike was. Her tongue came out to take the sweat from around her lips. The translucent covers on the subway lights cast an odd glow across everything, but it wasn't this which gave her skin the colour of the old newspapers that blew down the tunnels. 'Don't fuck about,' she said. 'Cook it all ...'

Spike funnelled the wrap and carefully poured every grain of brown powder on to the spoon. 'You do me first, yeah?'

'Piss off. I'll do myself, *then* I'll do you.'

345

'No way. You won't be in any fit state to do fuck all then.'

'Just get a move on, tosser . . . '

Spike drew water up into the syringe, then let some out until he had just the right amount. He leaned down, concentrating hard as he released the water into the bowl of the spoon, then used the end of the syringe to mix the heroin into it.

And Thorne watched . . .

He wasn't shocked, but he'd never worked on a drugs unit; he'd never been this close to it before. He sat and stared, gripped by the process. Fascinated by the ritual of it all.

'You got vinegar?'

Caroline reached into her pocket, pulled out tissues, a plastic Jif lemon, the pile of sachets she'd grabbed earlier in the café. She handed a sachet to Spike. He bit off the end, squeezed some vinegar into the mixture and continued to stir.

'What's that for?' Thorne asked.

'This lot was only twenty quid,' Caroline said. 'It's not pure, so it don't mix very easy. The vinegar helps it dissolve a bit better . . . '

Thorne reached across for the plastic lemon on the floor. 'Making pancakes later?'

Spike put down the syringe and picked up the lighter. 'Taste well strange if we did, mate.' He held the flame beneath the spoon, nodded towards the lemon in Thorne's hand. 'It's not fucking lemon juice in there.'

'Anyone tries it on, they get a face full,' Caroline said.

Thorne took the cap off, sniffed, then drew his face sharply away from the pungent kick of the ammonia.

Spike laughed. 'I've got my weapon, she's got hers, like . . .'

Then Thorne became aware of another smell: the syrupy kick of the heroin as it began to bubble on the spoon; the vinegar slight, but noticeably sharp, beneath. He realised that this was the smell he'd noticed earlier. He held his breath . . .

Caroline reached over for the needle. She tore it from the plastic sleeve, and, after pulling off the orange cap, she attached it to the syringe.

'Come on, we're there,' Spike said.

There were a number of cigarette butts, of varying sizes, scattered across the bar-towel. Caroline took one from the bobbly, maroon material and used the knife to cut a thin slice from the filter, then dropped it into the liquid. Thorne thought it looked like those inedible slivers of something or other you got in spicy Thai soup . . .

While Spike held the spoon steady, Caroline placed the tip of the needle flat against the section of filter and drew the liquid through it, up into the syringe. Again, she expunged some of it back into the spoon to be sure she had exactly half.

'For fuck's sake, Caz, get a shift on . . .'

'This is for your benefit, mate, to make sure you get your share.' She lifted the spoon and placed it on the floor, out of harm's way. The handle had been bent in such a way that the bowl rested flat on the concrete.

Spike had already rolled up the sleeve of his faded, red hoody. As Caroline put the needle to his skin, he twisted the material that was gathered above his elbow and made a fist.

Caroline grunted as she dug around for a vein . . .

Spike moaned as she found one; as she drew blood back into the syringe; as the red billowed into the brown, like wax in a lava lamp; as she pushed the plunger.

'Flush it . . . flush the fucker . . . '

Twice, three times, she drew the blood back into the syringe and pressed it back into the vein. By the third time, Spike was nodding; each bounce of his head taking it lower. He raised it slowly, one last time to smile at Thorne, to beam like a baby at Caroline. 'Time for bed, said Zebedee . . . '

Caroline had already begun to clean out the syringe, drawing water in from the bottle and squirting it away on to the floor. She leaned across to kiss Spike, then gave him a push. 'Into your box, you silly bastard . . . '

Spike half fell, half crawled into the cardboard box, until all Thorne could see were the soles of his trainers. After only a few seconds, they stopped moving. Then Thorne watched as Caroline flushed the syringe again. She cursed, announced that the thing was 'juddery', and rooted among her collection of sachets for a pat of butter to smear around the plunger. Her movements were practised and precise, and she bit off the ends of her words as she talked, like they were bitter on her lips.

'Aren't you worried about sharing needles?' Thorne asked.

She shrugged. 'It's only him and me ...'

'But they're easy enough to get.' He pointed at the bar-towel. 'You've got new ones.'

'Everyone thinks we've got AIDS anyway, don't they?'

Thorne stretched out his legs and opened his mouth, but before he could speak she was shouting at him to be careful, and moving quickly to avert any risk of the spoon being knocked over; of losing the precious liquid pooled in its bowl.

'Who's Robbie?' Thorne asked.

She dipped the syringe back into the spoon, put the needle to the filter and drew up the remainder of the heroin. 'My kid. From before I met Spike. He'll be ten now.' She held the syringe up to the light. 'I lost him.'

Thorne watched as she pushed down a sock and flexed her foot. 'I'm sorry ...'

She looked up briefly from what she was doing. 'See what I mean about luck, though?' A smile that seemed to hurt appeared for just a moment. 'Mind you, my luck might have been shit, but at least Robbie's hasn't been too bad. It was his good luck to get taken away from me, right?'

Thorne couldn't think of anything to say. He could only imagine how badly she needed what the needle she was holding could give her.

For another few seconds she tried to get the needle into the right position, but it was tricky. She was right-handed and the vein she was after was above her left ankle. She looked up at Thorne, sweat falling off her. 'Could you give me a hand with this?'

'I'm a bit shit with needles ...'

'Please ...?'

Thorne had known there might be such moments; he hadn't signed on to go undercover thinking it would be easy. That he would never need to make tough choices. It took him only a second or two to realise that, as choices went, this was actually one of the easier ones.

It was the least he could do ...

He could feel something shift – in himself as well as in Caroline – as he pushed the drug into her. He swung round when it was finished, so that he was sitting next to her against the wall. He let her head fall on to him as she began to nod. 'I was thinking about this money thing,' he said. 'I know Spike doesn't like to ask, but couldn't his sister help? Just to get you two started, maybe?'

'Sister ...'

'I know he's funny about it, but it sounds like she wants to help him.'

Now the words dribbled from her, falling in thick, sloppy threads without emphasis or cadence. 'His sister's dead; died fucking ages ago. Years. When he was still at home ...'

'Caroline ...?'

It was maybe half a minute before she continued. 'When he was still at home, his dad used to mess with 'em, you know? With both of 'em. Used to hurt him and his sister and he couldn't stand it, so he got out.

'Got the fuck out ...

'He was older than she was, you see? A couple of years.

350

Older. So he left her there, and then a bit later on ... six months or something, you'd have to ask him, was when she took a load of pills. Chucked 'em down like Smarties ...

'Spike was ... you know? He was very fucked up. There was a nasty scene when they buried her ... That was the last time he saw anyone in the family. That was it for good then.'

'He knows it wasn't his fault, doesn't he?' Thorne asked.

'Like Smarties ... '

Thorne could hear someone singing in one of the adjoining subways. He was stroking Caroline's hair. 'I don't think it's hurting anyone that Spike pretends ... '

Caroline groaned.

'Everybody does it to some extent or other,' Thorne said. 'When they lose someone. People bang on and on about *letting go*, like it's the healthy thing to do, like we don't all need a bit of fucking comfort. We all keep our loved ones alive somewhere ... '

But she couldn't hear him any more.

At some point during the night, Thorne was woken by something. He reached out to touch the cardboard on every side of him. He was hot and stinking inside his sleeping bag.

From a few feet away, he could hear Spike and Caroline making love. The noises they made, their cries and the movement of their bodies inside the box seemed urgent and desperate. His hand moved to his groin, but did not stay there for very long. He was touched rather than excited by what he could hear: there was a reassurance in their passion, in the simple desire of each to please the other.

Thorne eventually drifted back to sleep, soothed by the rhythm of it and comforted by the affirmation of need. By an honest moment of human contact; by an act of love that had more meaning on cardboard than it might have had on silk.

The next time Thorne woke, he knew the cause straight-away; he could feel the mobile phone vibrating in his coat pocket. He groped for it, getting hold of the thing just as the shaking stopped. The glow from the illuminated screen lit up lines of grime on the heel of his hand; it was 6.18 a.m. and it had been Holland calling . . .

It rang again almost immediately.

Thorne pushed his way out of the box and took a few steps away from where Spike and Caroline were still sleeping. He squatted down, answered the phone with a whisper.

'Dave?'

'Thank fuck for that . . . '

During the short pause that followed, Thorne stood and waited for his head to clear a little. A plastic bag flapped along the tunnel and he shuddered as the draught whipped into him; icy against clammy skin.

'I just wanted to make sure you were alive,' Holland said.

'That's thoughtful, but it's a bit bloody early—'

'They've found another body. We haven't got anyone down there as yet.'

Thorne could smell piss and sugar, vinegar and grease. He glanced up and down the corridor, checking that there was no movement from any of the boxes. He wondered if the body might be that of Ryan Eales; if the killer had finally completed the set.

'Sir . . . ?'

'I'm listening,' Thorne whispered.

'A rough sleeper, looks like the usual method, in the doorway of a theatre behind Piccadilly Circus. D'you see what I'm getting at?'

Thorne saw exactly.

'Just keeping it warm for you, obviously.'

Now his head was clear, but the rest of him was suddenly leaden. He could feel a prickly heat rising . . .

There was a grunted laugh of relief before Holland spoke again. 'I just wanted to be sure,' he said. 'I thought it might be you . . .'

Thorne leaned back against the wall, breathing heavily. He stared down at the discarded chicken bones and scattered flakes of leprous-looking batter.

And was violently sick.

PART THREE

LUCK OF THE DRAW

TWENTY-FIVE

Holland and Stone stood on the platform at Stockport station, waiting for their connection to Salford. Both had hands thrust deep into pockets, and as they gazed along the track in the hope of seeing the train's approach, they could see the rain coming down in skewed, billowing sheets.

'Fucking hell,' Stone said, miserable. 'I'm still wet from the other night ...'

Holland nodded, remembering the downpour as they'd gathered at the crime scene, waiting for the sun to struggle up. The rain had hissed off the arc lights, and the only dry body there was curled up and stiffening in the theatre doorway. As with the other victims, there hadn't been a great deal that was recognisable about Terence Turner. He'd finally been identified by a friend thanks to the chain and padlock around his neck. Later, this had been removed with a hacksaw by a mortuary assistant, just prior to Phil Hendricks getting to work and doing some cutting of his own ...

'I'm going to see if I can grab some coffee,' Stone said. 'D'you want some?'

Holland eagerly accepted the offer and Stone walked towards the station concourse in search of what would be their third cup of the day. It was a little over twenty-four hours since they'd found the body, and Holland had slept for perhaps three of them.

It was accepted that the first twenty-four hours were 'golden'; that this was when they had the best chance of picking up a decent lead. As far as Holland was aware, at that moment they still had nothing, and he'd be surprised if anything changed. It wasn't always just a killer they were up against. Care and caution could get thrown to the wind in the name of urgency, and adrenaline was easily swamped by fatigue and protocol.

After they'd wrapped things up at the murder scene, a DS from the Intelligence Team had conducted the 'hot debrief' at Charing Cross police station. Every officer who'd been present had run through the notes in their incident report book and made a statement. These would need to be collated and added to the duty officer's report and the log that would later be completed by the DCI. This was all part of the procedure instituted in the wake of the Lawrence Report. There were those who thought it would mean fewer mistakes. Others, including Tom Thorne, were more sceptical. They thought that it was less about doing the right thing than being seen to do it.

Thorne ...

This was what, for some of them at least, had given the latest murder an unsettling significance, had brought it far closer to home. Those on the team who knew of Thorne's role in the investigation had come to an obvious, and disturbing, conclusion. Holland, Brigstocke and Hendricks had stared at the battered body of a man in a doorway; had watched it being bagged up and loaded into a wagon; had seen the progress of the pathologist's blade through its flesh, and known, as they looked on, that it should have been the body of Tom Thorne that was suffering such indignities.

Holland looked up, watched Stone walking back towards him with the drinks and thought about the phone conversation two nights before ...

'*That's thoughtful, but it's a bit bloody early.*'

He'd rung from home as soon as he'd been contacted about the discovery of the body. Sophie had been woken by the initial call, and he'd gone into the living room so she wouldn't hear him talking to Thorne. He'd felt a little embarrassed at how relieved he'd been to hear the miserable git's voice.

It was strange: Thorne had taken longer than anyone else to grasp the significance of just where Turner's body had been found. Maybe Holland had caught him at a bad time ...

'Train's coming in,' Stone said, still a few feet away.

Holland looked back and saw the train rounding a bend, moving towards them through rain that was getting heavier. The huge wipers were moving fast across the locomotive's windscreen.

Stone seemed to have cheered up a little. He put on a coarse, Hovis accent: 'It's grim up north,' he said.

Holland smiled and took his coffee, thinking that it wasn't exactly a bed of roses back where they'd come from.

'Do you want me to tell you how many of those kicks could have killed Terry Turner on their own? How many different bones were broken? How many of his teeth were actually smashed up into his nose?'

'Only if you want to put me off my lunch,' said Thorne.

They were sitting in a dimly lit pub, south of the river near the Oval. A television was mounted high on one wall. *Through the Keyhole* served only to highlight the lack of atmosphere in the place. Aside from a couple in their thirties who scowled at each other across scampi and chips, Brigstocke and Thorne were the only customers.

Brigstocke knew that, with Thorne looking the way he did, they'd have had a fair amount of privacy even if the place had been much busier. Though the bruises had faded to the colour of nicotine stains, Thorne was still far from a pretty sight. That said, though, he had never been a *GQ* kind of man, and many had given him a wide berth even when he *hadn't* looked like a battered sack of shit. Brigstocke had said as much to him as they'd collected drinks and cheese rolls from the bar.

Thorne held up his Guinness and smiled. 'Cheers, mate.'

'Those clothes are actually starting to smell . . .'

'I think *you're* the one they're worried about,' Thorne had said. He'd nodded towards the couple who'd given the two of them a long, blatantly curious look when they'd walked in. 'They think I'm some sort of over-the-hill rent boy and you're a *very* pervy businessman on a limited budget.'

The jokey tone hadn't lasted long . . .

'You said that going undercover would just be about gathering information,' Brigstocke said. 'We've got that information now. We know who the victims are, and we know why it's happening, so give me one good reason for you to carry on.'

'Because the killer hasn't gone anywhere.'

'We talked about this when you came to me with your stupid idea in the first place . . .'

'Things are much different now,' Thorne said.

'Fucking right they're different.' Brigstocke glanced towards the couple, then across at the woman who stood smoking behind the bar. He lowered his voice. 'The night before last it was *you* he tried to kill . . .'

Thorne put the half-eaten cheese roll back on to his plate. He wasn't hugely hungry. He'd gone to the Lift early and put away a full breakfast while he waited in vain for Spike or Caroline to turn up. Thorne hadn't seen either of them since the previous morning. He'd left the subway when Holland had called with news of the murder, then returned a few hours later to wake them; to tell them that he'd been into the West End and seen the police gathered outside the theatre.

To tell them that Terry was dead . . .

'You're not willing to consider the possibility that Terry Turner being kicked to death in that doorway was a bizarre coincidence, are you?' Thorne looked at Brigstocke. 'I thought not . . .'

'The killer knows who you are,' Brigstocke said.

'Thanks to one too many cans of Special Brew, the world and his fucking wife know there's an undercover copper on the streets.'

'Right, but this bloke knows it's *you.*'

'I'm well aware of that . . .'

'Do you think he knows you personally? Is it someone you've met?'

Thorne stared into his beer. 'He mistook Terry Turner for me, so I doubt it.'

'It was dark. It was pissing with rain. Turner might well have been out of it, asleep, with his back to the killer . . .'

'Terry was a foot taller than I am,' Thorne said. 'I can't see it.'

The door opened and a man walked in leading a greyhound. He climbed on to a stool at the bar and the dog dropped flat at his feet. The man exchanged a word or two with the barmaid, ordered a pint and turned to stare at the TV.

'We can skirt around the obvious question all bloody day . . .' Brigstocke said.

Over by the bar, the greyhound raised his head for a moment, yawned and let it drop again. The dog looked like he couldn't give a fuck, and so did his owner. The man seemed far more at ease than Thorne imagined him to be behind his own four walls: he looked at home; he looked like himself.

'Tom?'

'I'm listening . . .'

'Why? That's what we need to address. Why on earth does he come after you?'

Thorne took a second to collect his thoughts. 'OK, this is the best I can come up with, and you're not going to like it. I reckon he's shitting himself.'

'*He's* shitting himself?'

'I think he's panicking. I think he knows we're getting close. Maybe not to him, not as yet, but he doesn't feel safe because he knows we've put the nuts and bolts of it together. Like you said, we've got the names and we've got a motive. If Eales is still alive, and we can find him, the killer knows he can be identified.'

'So why not just kill Eales?'

'Maybe he already has,' Thorne said. 'Look, all I'm really saying is that I don't think this bloke's that bloody clever. He's felt cornered, he's started to panic and he's reacted, and I don't think there's a lot more to it than that. Who knows? Maybe he thinks I'm such a brilliant detective that he needs to get me out of the way.'

'Now it's getting really far fetched.'

'Whichever way you look at it, it wasn't a very clever

thing to do, but I think we're talking about someone who works on instinct, you know? If we're right about the blackmail angle, this whole thing is about him feeling threatened and trying to protect himself . . . '

The pub's business rocketed as a pair of lads came through the door. The dog barked half-heartedly and was silenced by a nudge from his master's boot. The barmaid lit another fag from the butt of the last one, and on TV, a blonde with a smile as overcooked as her tan was promising to find an elderly couple their dream home in the sun.

Brigstocke tore open a bag of crisps and leaned across the table. 'All this stuff he knows. How exactly does he know it?'

'That's the bit you're not going to like,' Thorne said.

'We're back to him being on the Job, are we?'

'I'm starting to think it's likely. If I'm right about why I was targeted, I can't see how else he'd know what was going on, unless he was a copper.'

'*If* you're right . . . '

'He knew more than who I was, Russell. He knew where I'd be.' Thorne pictured Terry T, fingering the padlock at his throat, offering to share the doorway that even now they were still trying to scrub the blood out of. 'Where I was *supposed* to be.'

Brigstocke said nothing for several moments. His face, distorted as it was through his glass of water, made it clear he was finding Thorne's point a hard one to argue against. 'So who are we talking about? How many people knew where you were sleeping?'

364

'You, Holland, Hendricks. Brendan Maxwell at the Lift. McCabe and maybe one or two others at Charing Cross.'

'Was McCabe's name last for any particular reason?'

'I just think he's worth looking at. Him and a few of his team.'

'Looking at?'

'Maybe we could get a couple of Intel lads on it. Keep an eye on him ... ?'

Brigstocke looked drawn suddenly, like another weight had been added to a load that was already unbearable. 'This kind of thing's easy to suggest. It's a piece of piss in a pub, but actually getting it done is a fucking nightmare. You don't really grasp any of that, do you, Tom? Christ, putting a DI under surveillance on the strength of something like this, on the strength of very little, is asking for trouble.'

Thorne remembered something he'd said to McCabe that still held true. 'I can't speak for you,' he said, 'but some of us are in plenty of trouble already. I don't think a bit more's going to make a lot of difference.'

Thorne stared and Brigstocke stared back at him; a grim expression that stayed frozen on the DCI's face for several seconds, until he stuffed a handful of crisps into his mouth.

Shireen Collins – Ian Hadingham's ex-wife – was a petite, attractive black woman who Holland guessed, once he'd seen her up close, to be somewhere just the right side of forty. She presented a fair bit younger – her hair in corn rows and her clothes suitably sporty – though with half a dozen kids under five running about, a tracksuit and trainers were probably the most practical choices.

She worked as a childminder, and Holland and Stone had arrived to find that she was looking after four children that day. 'Plus two of my own,' she told them, pointing out a boy and a girl. 'Those are mine. The really evil ones ...'

'They're nice-looking kids,' Stone said.

'The older two, *Ian's* two, are both at school.'

The flat, on the southern side of Salford, was on the ground floor; one of three in a Victorian conversion. 'The people upstairs work all day,' Collins said as she showed them in. 'So we can make as much noise as we like, which is great. Four- and five-year-olds make a *lot* of noise.'

From what Holland and Stone could make out, there were a couple of bedrooms and a large living room that ran off a kitchen–diner. They sat at a long kitchen table, from which Collins had been clearing the remains of lunch when they'd arrived. 'There's a bit left if you fancy chicken nuggets and potato faces,' she said. Having missed breakfast, Holland was seriously tempted, but the offer was declined. In the next room, visible through a serving hatch, the kids were gathered in front of a widescreen TV. Collins leaned through the hatch and issued gentle but firm instructions until there was something approaching quiet.

'They get half an hour with a video after lunch,' she said. 'So that's about as long as *we've* got.'

Holland threw his overcoat across a kitchen chair. 'That'll be plenty, Shireen.'

The conversation was not without interruption – punctuated by high-pitched chatter, cartoonish music and the occasional bout of tears from the next room – but Shireen Collins spoke openly enough. It was obvious that at some point she'd felt a great deal for Ian Hadingham. But it was equally clear that she'd moved on. From their marriage, and from his death . . .

'Ian was always a waste of space unless he was in a uniform,' she said. 'When he'd come home on leave or whatever, he'd just sit about feeling sorry for himself. He'd ignore me and he'd ignore the kids most of the time and to be honest, after a couple of weeks, I couldn't wait for him to get back to his bloody regiment. God, that sounds awful, doesn't it?'

'Have you been talking to my girlfriend?' Holland said.

Collins laughed. She tried to explain how it had felt; how she'd once felt jealous of the bond he'd so clearly shared with his pals in the regiment. How she'd resented it, and fought for her husband's attention, and then, in the end, how she'd simply given up competing.

'What happened after Ian came back from the Gulf?' Holland asked.

Collins laughed again, but rather more sadly this time. 'I'm not sure how much of him *did* come back,' she said. 'It was like he was somewhere else in his head and it wasn't a place where I was welcome. Actually, I'm not sure it was a place I'd've liked very much. I know they all went through a lot out there.'

Holland stared straight at Collins. He did not want to

catch Stone's eye; he knew Stone would be thinking the same thing he was: *You have no bloody idea . . .*

'He left the army pretty soon after he came home,' Collins said. 'It was all right for a while, for a year or so, and we even talked about having more kids, but something told me not to. That we'd've been doing it for the wrong reasons.'

'What did Ian do,' Holland asked, 'after he left the army?'

'All sorts of things, but none of them for very long, you know? He worked in warehouses, did some security work, tried to retrain as an electrical engineer, but he couldn't hold down a job. Had a bit of a problem with authority. It'd be fine for a few months, then he'd blow it. He was fired more than once for threatening people.' She opened her mouth to say something else, then changed her mind. 'His head was basically messed up afterwards.'

Stone nodded his understanding. 'So he moved out, right?'

'Right. We decided to separate a few years on from that. He moved out and eventually I got this place. He never went far away, like – he wanted to stay close to the kids and that – but he moved around.'

'He got a flat?'

'Lots of different flats. He didn't seem to like staying put too long; plus, he kept falling behind with his rent and getting chucked out of places.'

'How did he react when you met somebody else?' Holland asked. 'It can't have been very easy . . .'

There was a yell from next door. Collins stood to look in

on the children, but sat down again quickly enough. 'Ian wasn't exactly thrilled and he had a bit of a problem with Owen.' She pointed towards her young children. 'Owen's their dad. Things got a bit ugly and Ian was a big bloke. He was handy, you know? So we got the police involved and we decided against actually getting married, and it was fine after that. It was fine for me and Owen, I mean, but things went downhill for Ian pretty quickly.'

'Downhill?' Stone said.

'He started dossing down all over the place. Sleeping on people's floors and in shitty bedsits or whatever. Like he'd stopped caring, basically. He was drinking a lot and pissing off all his mates. Not that he had many left by then ...'

'Did he see any of his old mates from the army?'

'I don't think so.'

'Any of the lads on his tank crew, maybe?'

'He never talked about it,' she said. 'I wouldn't know if he had, but to be honest I'd stopped really listening to him, you know? He went funny the last few years. He talked a lot of rubbish. Before he died he came round to tell me that he was going to turn it all round. Banging on about how he was going to look after me and the kids, how he was going to see us all right. I never told Owen any of that, by the way. He'd've gone mental.'

Holland couldn't resist a glance at Stone this time. 'Did he say how he was going to turn it round? Was he talking about money?'

'Yeah, I think so, but he always had some stupid scheme

or other on the go. He was always on about getting himself sorted again. Silly bastard . . . '

'Tell us about when Ian died, Shireen?'

A boy came to the hatch and asked for a drink.

Shireen smiled; told Holland and Stone about her ex-husband's death as she mixed orange squash. 'It was booze and pills,' she said. 'He emptied a couple of bottles of both in some pissy little room just round the corner from here. They didn't find him for a week because the poor sod had nobody to miss him by then.'

'They never found a note, did they?'

'No . . . '

'You never thought it was odd that Ian killed himself?' Stone said. 'Bearing in mind what he'd said about turning his life around and all that.'

She looked at them, unblinking, and Holland thought he could see the unasked question in her confused expression. He thought it said a lot about how Shireen Collins was getting on with her life that she hadn't really asked them why, a year after her ex-husband had died, they wanted to talk to her about him. He also thought that if Hadingham was as big, as *handy*, as she'd said he was, then it couldn't have been easy for whoever had killed him to have forced those tablets down his throat. Mind you, if Hadingham had been pissed before it happened . . .

Suddenly, there were other children demanding drinks and attention and it was clear that half an hour had been a generous estimate.

'I'm sorry,' she said. 'Maybe you could come back . . . '

They'd taken a cab from the station. Stone asked if there was a number they could call or somewhere they could pick up a taxi. She gave them directions to a minicab office five minutes' walk away.

Holland started pulling on his coat. 'Do you mind me asking what you did with all Ian's things?'

'All the stuff he'd left here had gone long before he died,' she said. 'I gave the clothes and a few of his old CDs to a charity shop. A lot of it just went in the rubbish, to be honest.'

'Were there any videotapes?' Stone asked.

She seemed slightly thrown by the question. 'We had ... blank tapes for recording stuff on. We still use them, I think, for taping the football or *Corrie* or whatever ...'

'What about the things Ian took with him when he left?'

'No, they gave me everything that was in the room where they found him; all his personal belongings.'

'You don't remember a videotape?'

She suddenly looked embarrassed. She lowered her voice, and tried to look Stone in the eye, but couldn't quite manage it. 'D'you mean like porno?'

Handing Stone his jacket, Holland turned to her. 'It doesn't matter, really. It's nothing ...'

It was dry outside, but from the look of the sky it was no more than a lull, so they did their best to make the five-minute walk in much faster time.

'She's going to find out what he did eventually,' Stone said.

Holland shook his head. 'It's not up to us.'

'I don't think she'll be that devastated somehow . . . '

'Maybe she will. On her kids' behalf.'

'Right. I suppose it's going to piss on their old man's memory somewhat. Blow the whole war-hero thing.'

'Just a bit . . . '

'We're bang on about the fucking blackmail, though. That's for definite. Hadingham as good as told her he was coming into money.'

'Yeah. I just wish we had something more than what she says he told her.'

'You've become a damn sight harder to please since you became a sergeant, do you know that?'

'You're always hoping there'll be like . . . I don't know, a photocopy of the blackmail demand he made to whoever topped him or something. You know, by some miracle . . . '

'Her testimony's a confirmation though, isn't it?'

'It's just circumstantial, at the end of the day. I mean, it all helps, I'm not saying it doesn't. It's another piece of it. It's a *big* piece. But it's way too late to get any physical evidence, any forensics or whatever, so I can't see us actually pinning it on the bloke when we get him.'

'What about the tape?'

'Maybe he had it with him, which makes sense if he thinks he's going to make some major money out of it, and the killer took it. Or he never had one, which doesn't really pan out if we're sticking with the blackmail idea. Or it's lost . . . '

'Or he left it at home when he moved out and the bloke his wife was shagging taped *Match of the Day* over it.'

'You know, this is one of the many reasons why I'm a sergeant and you're not.'

'Bollocks!'

The rain came then, suddenly, blowing into them from behind and quickly soaking the backs of their legs. Stone carried on swearing, and though they couldn't have been too far from the minicab office, he started to run.

Holland just kept walking and watching Stone disappear into the distance. He couldn't be arsed to try and catch up.

TWENTY-SIX

Thorne tried and failed to make himself comfortable in the doorway of a tatty souvenir shop on Carnaby Street. There were half a dozen of these places knocking out multi-coloured Doc Martens and overpriced T-shirts on a street that hadn't been fashionable in donkey's years.

He could remember when London *had* been the centre of everything. When the city could still get away with it, and swing without looking like someone's dad at a school disco. Once or twice around that time, when he'd have been six or seven, his parents had brought him into town to do some shopping, and though they'd tended to avoid the likes of Carnaby Street and had made straight for the department stores, Thorne could still recall seeing young women in floaty dresses and men wearing bright military jackets. Or perhaps he only *thought* he could. He knew that memory tended to work like that. Maybe he was just filling in the gaps with pictures of Terence Stamp and Julie Christie ...

Either way, because he had at least been there in the sixties, Thorne had viewed the whole 'Cool Britannia' movement of a few years before with a certain degree of cynicism. With Union Jacks on frocks and cars and album covers, what started as a trend had quickly become little more than a marketing bandwagon to be hijacked by everyone from Marks & Spencer to New Labour. Still, Thorne had to admit that bands had at least rediscovered guitars, that tourist numbers had picked up, and that it had given a creative spark to many kids of Spike and Caroline's age.

It remained to be seen if tourists would be flocking to the West End for very much longer. Beneath a headline that read, THE LATEST VICTIM, a photo of a younger and altogether healthier-looking Terry Turner dominated the front page of the day's *Standard*. The news was well and truly out that Theatreland had become a killing ground.

Thorne wondered if the killer had seen the newspaper. Did he know yet that he'd killed the wrong man?

Before settling down for the night, he'd been along to Marble Arch, had gone down into the subway to see if he could find Spike or Caroline. He'd got little change out of Ollie, who, if anything, had eyed him with even more suspicion and hostility than when they'd first encountered each other.

'I'm looking for my mates,' Thorne had said. He'd pointed along the corridor, to the corner that was now deserted, but where he'd slept alongside Spike and Caroline a couple of nights earlier.

The old man had glanced up from his book. Narrowed his eyes. 'Look somewhere else ...'

It wasn't as though Thorne had been expecting to find them. He was well aware that Spike and Caroline kept strange hours. He knew what woke them and what put them to sleep.

In his doorway, Thorne pulled himself upright and moved his arms to the outside of his sleeping bag. He stared at the lit window displays across the street and listened to the dance music that was coming from one of the flats above.

He thought again about where the leak might have come from. He *had* to consider McCabe, whatever Brigstocke thought of the idea. Who else knew exactly where he would be sleeping? It was inconceivable that the information could have come from anyone closer to him. What ate away at Thorne was that, somewhere, he knew that he already had the answer. It couldn't be too hard to figure out who had been responsible; it was a basic two-piece jigsaw. Of course, other rough sleepers knew *where* he was, but they didn't have the other piece of it. None of them knew that he was an undercover police officer. At least, he *presumed* none of them knew. Certainty, of any sort, was a luxury he'd given up along with the rest of them, when he'd taken the decision to sleep on the street.

'*Do you want me to tell you how many of those kicks could*

have killed Terry Turner on their own? How many different bones were broken . . . ?'

Earlier, with Brigstocke, he'd played it down. He'd had to. But now there was no point pretending that what jumped in his guts and sucked away at his breath was anything other than fear. He'd felt it from that first moment underground, when he'd heard about Terry T's death, and it had settled, content inside him. It had quickly made itself at home, coating the walls; clingy and seeping . . .

Thorne had felt afraid a lot more lately. In the recent weeks and months there had been a general apprehension that he could not name, as well as a perplexing, irrational fear of specific things. He'd become jumpy in crowds; he was suddenly scared of escalators and of heights; he'd started feeling increasingly wary in cars. Thorne knew that some people became more nervous about flying the more frequently they walked onboard a plane, and he wondered if he was moving along the same lines.

Or perhaps this susceptibility to fear in all its forms was simply a part of getting older. His father had been afraid of all sorts of bizarre things. Thorne wondered if he was simply turning into his old man. He'd known it would happen eventually, it happened to just about everyone, but the process seemed to have put on a burst of speed with his father's death. It was as though he were part of some twisted, cosmic equation. He felt like he was changing to fill the hole left by his father's passing.

And there was the other thing: the trick that was played on you after the death of a parent. After the death of your last parent, when you became an orphan. The switch that was thrown ...

For the first time in his life, Thorne was starting to comprehend the pain of being childless; not to *feel* it, not quite yet, but to understand it. He now knew why those desperate for children spoke of it as a hole that needed to be filled. He had started to feel as though that hole might be inside himself somewhere; growing, but still hidden, waiting only for what covered it to drop away. He'd wondered if having children simply to stop the pain of not having them was a good enough reason. Was it the reason why most people became parents? Certainly, he could now begin to guess at the agony that Caroline must feel at being both childless and a mother at the same time.

Losing parents, and losing children ...

Thorne's mind shifted to the man behind that video camera. The man who had filmed the deaths of four men: four sons; quite possibly four fathers.

How were they ever going to find him if they didn't trace Ryan Eales? The most obvious place to start would have been the army, of course. They might at least have been able to shed some light on what sort of person was out there. What manner of individual might have stood on the black sand, soaked in shadow and petrol rain alongside that tank crew. It would be very difficult to make advances to the army now of course; not after certain ... important facts material to the case had been withheld. Brigstocke had confessed to Thorne in the pub that keeping the

378

existence of the videotape secret was a decision he was starting to regret.

Thorne had done his best to be sympathetic. 'We're *all* Sherlock Holmes with hindsight, mate. Don't give yourself a hard time about it.'

'If we don't get a result,' Brigstocke had said, 'there'll be plenty ahead of me in the queue . . . '

The music from the flat above the shop opposite had stopped. It was replaced by the tuneless singing of a trio of football fans who came down the street from the side of the Shakespeare's Head and began to move in Thorne's direction. He shrank a little further back into the doorway and watched them pass.

They didn't see him. Or, if they did, they didn't give a toss . . .

In those few, brief moments of clarity that come before sleep, Thorne thought of someone he could perhaps speak to, a person who might at least provide some insight into what had happened on 26 February, nearly fifteen years before. Thorne would have to be careful how he handled it of course, but nobody had come up with anything better.

He drifted off to sleep, deciding that he'd had worse ideas; thinking that he still had the business card stuffed inside his wallet back at the Lift. Hoping that he'd remember all this in the morning.

TWENTY-SEVEN

DS Sam Karim, who took responsibility for such things, had almost finished rejigging the layout of the whiteboard for the umpteenth time.

Still arranged at its centre were the photographs recently provided by the Army Personnel Centre: Chris Jago, Ian Hadingham, Ryan Eales and Alec Bonser. Portraits of four young men, all taken when they'd first been posted to the 12th King's Hussars.

Holland stood and watched while the shape of the case as it stood that day was laid out. It was hard to equate the quartet of fresh faces – scrubbed and set square, a hint of a smile on one or two – with those whom he knew had been hidden behind rain-streaked goggles and muddy kerchiefs; sweating, contorted; the eyes tight shut at the moment when the trigger was pulled.

Elsewhere on the board . . .

The list of those victims who had been murdered simply to disguise the true nature of the crime: Hayes, Mannion, Asker.

Terry Turner, murdered, it would seem, in error; sharing nothing but initials with the man for whom he'd been been mistaken.

The names of those on the fringes of the investigation: Susan Jago, Shireen Collins.

Those who had provided information, statemented or otherwise: Spiby and Rutherford at Media Ops; Brendan Maxwell; Major Stephen Brereton; Poulter and Cheshire at the 12th King's. One name had now been removed from this list, and from the contact sheet circulated to all officers: Paul Cochrane. The services of the National Crime Faculty profiler had been dispensed with, now that the motive for the killings had become apparent even to those without letters after their names.

'Last but not least . . .'

Karim drew a thick, black line down to a crudely drawn square that contained the only remaining question mark on the board. It was largely symbolic: a simple representation of their prime suspect; the man behind the video camera whom they now thought to be the reason why they were all there in the first place.

Karim stepped back and examined his work. It was far from the whole story, of course . . .

There was a side to the investigation that could not be encapsulated in crude capital letters or delineated by magnets and felt-tip pens. Thorne's contribution to the case was missing: information that had originated from him, or from sources close to him, would remain absent. This was also the case with details of the secondary intelligence operation, the small-scale surveillance that had just been mounted on DI John McCabe and several other officers from the Homeless Unit based at Charing Cross. The authorisation for such surveillance was need-to-know information that Brigstocke had passed on to none but his core team. As with any blue-on-blue operation, there was very good reason.

Somebody always knew somebody . . .

Karim walked away, and Holland approached the board. 'You're an artist, Sam.'

Stone was on his way back from the Gents'. '*Piss*-artist,' he said.

Jason Mackillop looked up from his computer and grinned. Stone moved across to join him, laughing at his own joke.

The whiteboard should have been replaced long ago. Countless murders had been mapped out across its surface over many years. As Holland looked, he could see, in what few white spaces were left, the faintest outline of old markings; the swoops and stabs of the pen just visible beneath the scratched and pitted metal. Death, terrible and tawdry; fury, loss, *grief* reduced to scribbled lines and letters; to names and numbers now long since wiped away and replaced. Holland licked the tip of a finger and reached over to rub at one of the ghost names. A name that had refused to fade completely . . .

'Dave?'

Holland started slightly and drew his finger quickly away. He hadn't been aware of Yvonne Kitson moving alongside him. He turned to acknowledge her, then shifted his gaze back to the board.

They both stared at it for a while.

They looked at the sweep of it; the way that so many were ensnared by the tendrils that snaked from its poisonous root. The names of all those it had touched: the innocent and the guilty and the dead. But one name was now prominent.

'How the hell are we going to find Eales?' Kitson asked.

Holland considered the question. 'Do the Home Office have any psychics?'

If they'd been lucky in tracing Ian Hadingham quickly, it had been more than balanced out by the complete lack of anything even resembling progress in the hunt for Ryan Eales.

The team had run 'full research'. Both the CRIS and CRIMINT systems had been scanned a number of times but had yielded nothing. Traces had been run via the National Voters' Register, the DSS, the DVLC and every local housing authority in the country. All major store-card and mobile-phone companies had been contacted, while the Equifax system – a software package giving access to a huge number of financial databases – was being run repeatedly without success. Thus far, save for a driving licence, a National Insurance number and a last known address that were all equally moribund, full research had come up empty.

The first conclusion, based on the fact that the recently deceased are often fairly easy to locate, was that Ryan Eales was probably still alive. The second conclusion was not quite so comforting.

'He doesn't *want* to be found,' Kitson said.

Holland knew she was right. He also knew that if Eales was lying low, he had very good reason for doing so. 'He's hiding from the killer.'

Kitson wasn't arguing. 'There's every chance. If he reads the papers, if he's been in any sort of contact in recent years with the rest of them, or their families, it's odds on he knows at least a couple of the other three are already dead. If so, he'd be justified in thinking he might be next.'

'And he might well have worked out that we know why . . . '

If Eales knew that the police were looking for him, he could guess that they had seen the videotape, so he would not be in any great hurry to step forward; to face the music for what had happened in 1991.

'It's another thing they're going to be good at,' Holland said.

'Who?'

'They're ex-soldiers. The training means that they're better equipped to survive life on the streets, like Bonser and Jago, but it also means they're good at making themselves invisible, if they need to.'

'Like being behind enemy lines,' Kitson said.

Holland thought of something. He walked to the board

and pointed to the name '*Poulter*'. 'Remember what he was saying when we went down to Taunton? If Eales ever served with the SAS, or one of those other intelligence units, he'd be even better at all that undercover stuff. And it would explain why we can't find any half-decent records on him . . . '

They looked again at the photograph of Lance Corporal Ryan Eales.

His was one of those faces whose expression had been softened by a smile. He was square-jawed, with wide, blue eyes and a sprinkling of freckles across a flattish nose. Sandy hair dropped into precisely trimmed sideburns; perfect rectangles below the maroon beret.

'He doesn't look all there to me,' Kitson said.

'They *all* look a bit weird,' Holland said. 'But maybe that's because we're looking at it after the fact. Because we know what happened later on.'

'I think you've got to be slightly odd to join up in the first place.'

'Not a lot of choice for some people,' Holland said.

Kitson shrugged, conceding the point. 'No stranger than wanting to become a copper, I suppose.'

'At least they get to travel . . . '

'Why did you join up, Dave?'

Behind them, Stone finished telling Mackillop the same, vaguely offensive joke he'd been telling everyone for days. The TDC laughed on cue.

'The mental stimulation, I think,' Holland said.

*

'Don't tell me. It's the Spurs–Arsenal game.'

'Well, as you mention it . . . '

'You want tickets for the match next weekend.' Alan Ward sounded amused rather than pissed off at the imagined imposition. 'I seem to remember I told you I could get them.'

'It's not the tickets,' Thorne said. 'Actually, I just wanted to pick your brains about something. Have you got a minute?'

'Glad to get out of this bloody edit, tell you the truth. Hang on . . . '

Thorne could hear Ward's own voice being broadcast in the background. Then he heard the man himself talking to someone: telling them he wouldn't be long, that he'd be outside if there was any problem.

Thorne had walked east to Holborn and then kept going towards the City. Past Smithfield Meat Market and into the ossified heart of the Barbican. This was the only residential estate in the City. Almost as free from pedestrians as it was from traffic, its looming tower-blocks were connected by a series of elevated walkways. Despite the arts centre, the museums and the smattering of trendy shops and restaurants, there was a strangely hostile feel to the place; something humming in the endless walls of concrete that rose up at every turn.

'Right, I'm all yours,' Ward said.

Thorne stepped into shadow, pooled with water beneath an overhang. Pressed the phone to his ear. The small talk was about as small, and over about as quickly, as it could be. Both said they were very busy without going into any detail. Ward said he'd seen Steve Norman quite recently and asked if Thorne had. Thorne told him that he hadn't, and they chatted about football for another minute or two.

'I wanted to ask you about the Gulf,' Thorne said. 'Did you go over? The first time ...'

'Yeah, I was there. I was a baby reporter back in '91.'

'Right, good.'

'I wasn't a baby by the time I came back, mind you ...'

'No, I bet.'

'It was fairly heavy,' Ward said. 'You know? I'd not been involved in anything remotely like that until then. Not that I was doing a great deal other than poncing around in front of the camera. But you still *see* stuff ...'

'That's what I wanted to talk to you about, really. Not about things you might have seen necessarily, but things you might have heard about.'

There was a pause. 'Is this connected to the rough-sleeper murders?'

Thorne had been right when he'd thought this would need careful handling. Ward was sharp; worse, he was a journalist. It hadn't taken much to pique his professional interest. Thorne guessed that Ward had got a sniff of something straight away; the minute he'd answered his phone, and a copper he'd met once, for five minutes, had reintroduced himself.

'What makes you say that?' Thorne asked.

'Nothing particularly. It's the case I'd presumed you

were working on, bearing in mind that we met after the press conference.'

It was Thorne's turn to be professional: 'I'm sure you understand that I can't comment on an active investigation.'

'Of course. But I'm *seriously* intrigued ...'

Ward laughed then, and so did Thorne.

'While you were out in the Gulf, did you ever hear anything about war crimes or atrocities?'

'*Atrocities?*'

'On *our* side ...'

Another pause.

'There was some stuff that came out a few years ago,' Ward said. 'In an American magazine – the *New Yorker*, I think. There was an incident, an *alleged* incident, on the road from Kuwait to Basra a few days after the ceasefire, when retreating Iraqi columns were attacked by Apaches and tanks. They called it the Battle of Rumailah, but it was just a massacre, by all accounts. A "turkey shoot" the magazine said. There were civilians in trucks, there was supposedly a bus filled with school kids ...'

'Jesus ...'

'There was another one just before the ceasefire, when four hundred Iraqi troops surrendered to a US scout platoon. Some of them were wounded, bandaged up, in clearly marked hospital trucks. They were gathered together, fed and what have you, then, according to reports, another unit turned up in Bradley armoured vehicles and just shot the lot of them. Opened up with machine-guns.

This is supposedly based on evidence given by soldiers who were there at the time, but, having said all that, I don't think anybody's ever been prosecuted.'

Thorne moved into sunlight again. He looked up as a jet roared overhead. From where he was standing, the plane appeared and disappeared between the tower-blocks before emerging into a muddy sky and banking towards City Airport.

'What about UK troops?' Thorne asked.

'In terms of war crimes, you mean?'

'Did you ever hear anything?'

'Stuff goes on,' Ward said. 'It always does. Some of the troops were based in Dubai for a lot of the time. I was there myself later on. You could buy sets of photos in corner shops, you know? Soldiers posing with bodies; with arms and legs. Trophies . . .'

'But you were never aware of any specific incidents?'

Ward suddenly sounded a little wary. There was an amused caution in his voice, as if Thorne had changed the steps to the dance that they were performing. 'I think you're going to have to be a *bit* more specific yourself . . .'

Thorne had known he might have to venture into this kind of territory, and he wondered for a second or two if it was worth plunging into the murk. He hardly knew Alan Ward, and couldn't be certain that anything valuable would be gained from talking to him.

But he was equally unsure there was a great deal to lose . . .

'Did you ever hear of anything involving a British tank

crew?' Thorne said. While he waited, Thorne watched a couple on a walkway ahead of him. They seemed to be arguing.

When Ward finally answered, his voice was close to a whisper, and Thorne could hear the excitement in it. 'What have you found?'

'Like I said before, I can't—'

'OK, I get it. Look, there were one or two rumours about something. No more than that, as far as I can remember.'

'About a tank crew?'

'Yeah ... I think so.'

'So, here's the thing,' Thorne said. 'If someone else was involved, someone apart from the four men in a tank crew, who might it be?' He glanced up again. The couple on the walkway were now embracing.

'I'm not with you,' Ward said. 'It could be virtually anybody. You're not really giving me a great deal to go on.'

'Another individual. A fifth man, present when this incident took place.'

'A fifth soldier, you mean?'

'I suppose so ...'

'Where precisely are we talking about?'

'I don't really know. We have to presume it's somewhere off the beaten track.'

'*Everywhere* was off the beaten track, mate,' Ward said. 'You just mean that geographically, the incident happened in isolation, right?'

That much, Thorne could be fairly certain of. 'Yes.'

'So we're talking about someone with access to a vehicle, then. An officer, perhaps?'

Perhaps, thought Thorne. They were certainly talking about someone who'd had no problem telling the four crewmen what to do. Someone whose orders had been followed.

Perhaps...

It was as positive as they were going to get.

'I have to make a small professional plea at this point,' Ward said. 'Can you make sure I'm first in line if this ever comes out?'

Thorne was slightly nonplussed. Ward was clearly every bit as ambitious as he was sharp. Still, bearing in mind that Thorne had called *him*, it was a reasonable enough request. 'I'm not sure I'll have a lot of say in it, to be honest...'

'This is what I do, Tom. Seriously, if there does come a time when whatever this is can be made public, I hope to hell you'll come to me. Like I said before, I'm seriously bloody intrigued.'

'Right...'

'Whenever you like, Tom. And it goes without saying that my sources always remain confidential. No names, no pack drill.'

'I've got it.'

'And there *are* perks, of course.'

'Are there?'

'Do you want to see the game next week or not?'

Thorne could think of nothing he'd like more. Cursing

bad luck and worse timing, he explained to Ward that, much as he'd love the tickets, he'd be far too busy to use them.

Russell Brigstocke viewed the prospect of a conversation with Steve Norman in much the same way as a trip to the dentist: it was something necessary but usually unpleasant. You could put it off and put it off, but you always had to go through with the bloody thing in the end.

And you had to wash your mouth out afterwards . . .

The nature of the investigation meant Brigstocke had been forced to endure a good deal more contact with the Press Office than would normally have been the case. The media had been all over them since Jesmond's first press conference, and Norman – whatever anyone thought of him personally – had proved extremely adept at his job. He'd kept the media's appetite for information sated, and had called in favours from reporters when they were needed. And one was very definitely needed now.

Using the press had brought them, circuitously, to Chris Jago. Now, as the hunt for Ryan Eales ran out of steam, using it again might be the team's last hope of a result. They had already run a fifteen-year-old picture of Eales in the *Standard* – inside the issue with the photo of Terry Turner on the front – describing the soldier as someone whom '*the police would very much like to talk to in connection with . . .* '

The calls were coming in, but they needed more, and they needed them faster.

'I think I can swing *Crimewatch* again,' Norman had said. 'Tonight?'

Over the phone, the senior press officer's voice had sounded even more nasal, more irritating than it did face to face. 'This is still a major inquiry, Russell, so I think it should be doable. They'll bump something else off until next week ...'

They'd broadcast a reconstruction of Paddy Hayes' killing on the show – which BBC1 put out live on a Friday evening – a month before, and there had been a further appeal for information after Robert Asker's murder. In itself, this had gone down as something of a coup. The programme-makers were notoriously squeamish, with a distaste for anything overtly graphic. The sensitivities of the viewers had to be their primary concern. Murder was acceptable, but only if it was tastefully done, and not too scary.

Taking the case on to such a show was usually a last resort, but most senior officers still considered it worth doing. It was television, so when they were asked for help, people reacted in much the same way as they would to a phone-in question on a quiz show: the answer might not be the right one, but there was always a healthy response.

'So what do we think?'

'That's great, Steve,' Brigstocke had said. 'Thanks.' The platitude had screamed inside his skull like the squeal of a dentist's drill.

'Just a quick update, yes? Something in the "urgently need to trace" round-up towards the end of the show.'

'That's all we need.'

'We'll get Eales' picture in vision for as long as possible. Wait for the phone lines to light up.'

'Let's hope so . . . '

'Well, even if nothing concrete comes of it, it's as much about being *seen* to do something a lot of the time, right?'

Brigstocke had been desperate to hang up by this point. To rinse and spit. 'I'd better go and talk to the chief superintendent,' he'd said. 'We probably need to put our heads together . . . '

'How clean is your suit?' Norman had asked.

Brigstocke had spoken to Trevor Jesmond after that, talked about tone and message and budget. Then he'd phoned home and asked his wife to set the video. Now, he stepped into the Incident Room and called for hush. The TV appeal would generate a lot of calls. A fair few nutters would come crawling out of the woodwork, but they would all have to be listened to, their information transcribed as if it were the Word of God, and every lead, no matter how iffy it sounded, would need chasing up.

'Usual good news–bad news routine,' he said. 'Most of you can forget about your weekend. Fishing, football, feet up, trip to B&Q with the missus. Not going to happen . . . '

A voice from the back of the room: 'Is this the good news or the bad news?'

Brigstocke shouted above the laughter. 'But the overtime's been approved . . . '

*

394

Thorne felt happier, more sure of himself and his surroundings, as the noise of traffic began to grow louder; as people moved around him in all directions and he could taste the fumes. Moving away from the Barbican's eerie sprawl, he walked up what had once been Grub Street, and thought about his conversation with a man whose profession, in its worst excesses, had come to be associated with the name.

There'd been no thunderbolts of insight, of course; nothing to quicken the pulse overmuch. But there was enough to think about. Thorne had already considered the possibility that the man behind the video camera had been an officer. It was a reasonable enough supposition, but it was still interesting to hear it from Ward; to have the notion validated by someone who'd actually been there. There was no room for more than four men in a Challenger tank. The fifth man had to have got there under his own steam. If Brigstocke could eke any more information out of the army, it might be worth asking which ranks would have routinely had access to vehicles back then.

And there was something else to interest the DCI: *'There were one or two rumours about something ...'*

If rumours of an atrocity had reached the press at the time, then it was safe to assume that the army would have been fully aware of them. Thorne felt pretty sure that they were every bit as aware fifteen years on. If the army knew at least *something* of what might have gone on on 26th February 1991, that would certainly explain the call from the Special Investigation Branch of the Royal Military Police.

He would enjoy telling Russell Brigstocke that he wasn't *completely* paranoid ...

The light changed on the pavement ahead of him, and Thorne looked up to see the sky darkening rapidly. He watched a ragged finger of cloud point its way behind a glass high-rise on Farringdon Road, and he followed it back towards the West End.

TWENTY-EIGHT

'Good of you to have made an effort,' Thorne said.

'Eh?'

Thorne looked over at Hendricks, straight-faced. 'The dosser's outfit ... '

'Cheeky fucker.'

'Honestly, it's nice of you to try and blend in. Maybe you should knock all this medical stuff on the head and try working undercover yourself. You've obviously got a gift.'

'I'm glad one of us has,' Hendricks said.

Save for the metallic aftertaste of bargain burgers, they might have been relaxing over a takeaway from the Bengal Lancer. Were it not for the rain, and the view of huddled bin-bags, they might have been watching TV in Thorne's front room; arguing about the football like a grossly unfit Gary Lineker and a shaven-headed, multiply pierced Alan Hansen.

As it was, they were leaning against a wall on Great Queen Street, beneath a covered walkway that ran alongside the Freemasons' Hall. They traded digs and shared silences, and drank the beer Hendricks had brought with him.

Hendricks tapped his beer can against the building, the frontage of which was decorated with Masonic symbols. 'Probably a fair few coppers hang about in there, don't you reckon? Pissing about with goatskin aprons and rolling up their trousers . . . '

'Talking of which, did you see Brigstocke on the box?'

'Is he a Mason?'

Thorne shrugged. 'Wouldn't surprise me. I know Jesmond is.'

'Brigstocke came across very well, I thought,' Hendricks said. 'Relaxed, you know? He's obviously in charge, but he looks friendly. You want to do whatever you can to help him.'

'He's good at all that stuff. He's been on courses.'

'I don't know what the response has been like.'

'Pretty good, I think,' Thorne said.

Holland had called Thorne within an hour of the broadcast. The programme had shown the original photo of Ryan Eales, together with a digitally aged image of the soldier's face, to give *Crimewatch* viewers an idea of what he might look twenty years on. Calls had begun coming in immediately.

'I wonder if the killer was watching,' Hendricks said. 'Maybe by showing that picture of how Eales might look now we're helping him find him.'

'I shouldn't worry. He hasn't needed anybody's help so far.'

Hendricks grunted his agreement and took a drink. 'I was thinking about the tape ... Do you reckon Hadingham had it with him when he was killed?'

'Definitely,' Thorne said. 'That tape was Hadingham's leverage. He wouldn't have let it out of his sight. The killer took it after he'd forced pills down the poor bastard's throat; and I think he took Bonser's too, after he'd kicked him to death. It certainly never showed up in any of his belongings or with any of his family after we'd identified him.'

'And the only reason he never got Jago's was that he'd left it with his sister.'

'Meaning?'

'Meaning that maybe Chris Jago wanted to leave that part of his life behind, you know?' Hendricks pressed on, though Thorne was already starting to shake his head. 'Perhaps Susan Jago wasn't bullshitting. Perhaps her brother *was* the one who wanted nothing to do with what happened; the one who was arguing with the others.'

It may or may not have been true, but Thorne wasn't sure it made any difference.

'They each took a copy of that tape, Phil, *each of them*, because no matter who did the shooting, they were all part of it. The fact that they all had the tape was the insurance. It's what kept all of them quiet.'

'Until Hadingham broke rank, and it got all of them killed.'

'Right.' Thorne held up his can, swilled the last of the beer around in the bottom as though it were fine brandy in a crystal snifter. 'And we can only presume that Ryan Eales has got the last copy . . . '

Nothing but the occasional car or pedestrian passed them in either direction. Those on foot moved quicker than normal, while the cars drifted, sluggish as hearses, through the rain. The two of them were sitting close enough to hear the rumble and hiss of the traffic on Kingsway, still heavy in the early hours of Saturday morning; vehicles moving south towards Aldwych and the river, or north towards Holborn, Bloomsbury and beyond.

'So, what are you going to do about Spike and his girl-friend?' Hendricks asked.

Thorne had already told Hendricks that he was worried about them; that he still hadn't seen either of them since Terry T had been killed. He'd asked around and had found out nothing that he hadn't known already. Spike and One-Day Caroline had both been very upset by Terry's death. It had hit them hard, Holy Joe had said. A strange and morbid thought had crossed Thorne's mind then. Would it have hit them as hard if it *had* been him that had been killed?

'I'll just have to wait for them to turn up,' Thorne said. 'I'm sure they will.'

Thorne knew that they would, but he also knew just how addicts could react when bad things happened, things that disturbed their routine or threw them off kilter. He could only hope that when Spike and Caroline did show up, it wasn't as two more names on a long list of drug fatalities.

You do me first, yeah? Piss off, I'll do myself, then I'll do you.

Vinegar and plastic lemons and one dose too many, in a box that looked enough like a coffin to begin with . . .

'Tom?'

'I'm listening.'

'I said, "I'm sure they will".'

Thorne looked up and smiled. 'I know.'

'It's . . . impressive that people in their situation can be so affected by losing someone, you know?' The beer was starting to make itself heard in Hendricks' voice. 'That these relationships can run so deep, I mean. Brendan's always on about this, but I could never really see it until these murders started. How the homeless are a community.'

'Brendan's right,' Thorne said. 'A small and very fucking weird one, that's for sure, but a community same as any other.'

'Will it survive this, d'you think? I mean, I know that people are supposed to bond during times of adversity . . . '

'It's the adversity that glues everyone together in the first place.'

'I suppose so.'

'They'll get through this.' As he spoke, Thorne felt a certainty that would not have been there a few weeks before. He pictured the faces of those he'd met since he'd been on the streets. He'd seen shame sometimes, and anger, in those faces. He'd seen disease and despair and a hunger for any number of things that could be dangerous to be around. But he'd also seen resilience, or at least the strength that can come through resignation. 'A lot of these people are being killed every day,' he said. 'Little by little . . .'

Hendricks reached into his plastic bag, rummaged for two more cans.

'Shit like this just makes you stronger,' Thorne said. 'You move a little closer together. We look out for each other.' He looked over at Hendricks. 'What?'

Hendricks held out the beer, unable to keep a slightly nervous smile at bay. 'You said, "we" . . .'

Thorne reached across and took the can. He'd already drunk three but was feeling unusually clear-headed. He wondered if all that Special Brew – a beer he'd sworn by everything he held sacred never to touch again – had somehow increased his tolerance to the weaker stuff. He popped the ring-pull. 'This stuff must be stronger than it tastes,' he said.

*

If you screwed up on a computer game, nobody minded. You could always have another bash. It was easy enough to go back and start that level again.

He wasn't screwing up; he rarely did because he got plenty of practice. But people – real life, flesh and blood, human fuck-ups – weren't quite as predictable as those he was happily blowing away on screen. The real ones moved around; they weren't where they were supposed to be. And they had an irritating habit of looking much the bloody same in a darkened doorway at three in the morning . . .

He'd planned to be long gone by now. Somewhere sunny and expensive, where people smelled good and the only ones dossing down outdoors were sleeping on the beach because they couldn't find their way back to the hotel. That had been the idea, anyway. Taking Thorne out of the picture was meant to be something of a last hurrah, but it hadn't turned out that way.

When he'd completed the level, he turned off the PlayStation and ejected the game. He sauntered through to the tiny kitchen to make himself some tea. It was important to wind down a little; you had to let the adrenaline level drop and level out if you wanted to get any sleep at all. He sat in his underwear, watched the kettle and waited. Trying to picture the sea. To imagine it like glass, lapping gently at the sand; to look down at himself, lying golden and satisfied, like a pig in shit with all his worries far away. This was something he'd become good at over the years: he'd developed the ability to lose himself, and to watch as he reappeared elsewhere; somewhere safe and still. But as the kettle boiled, the salt water began to seethe and the sea quickly grew rough. The waves became larger and crashed on to his beach, forcing him to move. Soaking the sand . . .

It wasn't time to relax quite yet.

He carried his tea back to the bedroom and lay down.

As soon as he'd seen that newspaper – the photo of a young man called Terry Turner below its lurid headline –

he'd realised that he'd made a mess of it. He'd known deep down that he wouldn't be going anywhere for a while. It was a pain in the arse, having to rethink, but to have left would have felt wrong. He knew that if he had done so, he could *never* have relaxed.

He didn't set a great deal of store by much any more, but he still believed in the virtue of a job well done.

TWENTY-NINE

There were no more cans in the bag.

Though Thorne – as far as he could work out – had drunk as many as Hendricks, he felt none the worse for it. He was still worn out and frightened; he was still lost. But for that moment at least he wasn't alone, and he welcomed the clear understanding of his place in the world that chance, or cheap lager, had lent him. It wasn't exactly a pleasant place to be; not where he was in the life he was pretending to have, and certainly not in the life that was truly his to live with. The life which sooner or later he would have to go back to. Face up to.

His place in two worlds …

'I think I should make a move,' Hendricks said.

Thorne grunted, waited, but it looked as though thinking about it was as far as his friend was going to get for a while. The rain had stopped, but water was running off the roof of the covered walkway, falling on three sides of him as he sat back against the wall.

He saw something else clearly, something which most people – even if they knew the truth of it – were happier to ignore. He saw the dreadful ease with which the line separating two worlds could be breached. He had chosen to take that step and could retrace it, but he knew that for those with no choice at all, it was usually a one-way crossing.

'We're only two pay cheques from the street,' he said.

Hendricks turned his head. 'Right . . . '

'Two pay cheques. A couple of months. That's all that separates a lot of us from sleeping in a doorway.'

Thorne had heard Brendan talking about this, so he knew it was likely that Hendricks had heard it many times. But he wasn't talking for Hendricks' benefit, and besides, the man who was now lying next to him seemed perfectly content to listen.

'I mean, obviously it depends on circumstances,' Thorne said. 'On having the right sort of family, or more likely the *wrong* sort of family. It comes down to not having the support when you need it most. You see what I'm saying? You're earning enough to pay the rent, or make the mortgage repayments, right? You make enough money to eat and have a social life. But you've got no capital of any sort, you've got decent lumps owing on your Visa, and on a few store cards, and you're paying for a car on tick or whatever. You get two months' notice and you're fucked. Really, it sounds unbelievable, but you could easily be comprehensively fucked. You might not realise that straight away, but your whole life can go down the toilet in those eight weeks.

'And this is not a fantasy, Phil. This is how a lot of people live And I'm not talking about poor people either, or drug addicts or piss-heads. These are not people on Channel Four documentaries. These are *average* people. These are average *families* a lot of the time, who can find themselves homeless very bloody quickly. Living in hostels and care homes before you can say P45.

'You've got two months. Normal notice period. Now, the council might pay your rent, but by the time those payments come through, your landlord's thrown you out on your ear because he can't be arsed waiting for his money, right? They might pay the interest on your mortgage, but there's a limit on that depending on how generous your local council is, and banks get stroppy pretty bloody quickly when the cheques start bouncing.

'Two months . . .

'You still owe money on your cut-up credit cards, and you lose the car sharpish because you can't make the payments on that, and it's weeks before the DSS gives you anything. So, bit by bit, you lose everything: job, car, house, credit rating. Wife and kids, if it all goes really tits up. It all just slips away; or it's taken away by force. If you've got good friends or close family who are there for you when this happens, then fine. Likely as not, you'll be all right. You might not fall too far or too hard. But if you haven't . . .

'I've met people, Phil . . . Most of them haven't finished falling yet.

'You'd be amazed how quickly good friends can become distant acquaintances. How fast close family just become people with the same surname. If you're unlucky, you find that blood means fuck all when you're in the shit. When you stink of failure.'

Hearing footsteps, Thorne looked up and saw a young man walking past on the far side of the street, swinging an orange-striped traffic cone at his side. He watched as the man leaned against a shopfront, heaved the cone up to his mouth and made his own Friday night entertainment by blowing trumpet noises through it.

Thorne looked to his right and saw that Hendricks' eyes were closed. 'Are you tired or am I boring?' he asked.

A smile spread slowly across Hendricks' face, then, with one of those sudden bursts of energy unique to men under the influence, he climbed rapidly to his feet and slapped his hands together. 'Right. I'm away . . .'

'How you getting back?' Thorne asked.

'I'll pick up a cab.' Hendricks squinted across the street at the cone trumpeter.

'He's great, isn't he?'

Hendricks turned back to Thorne. 'We must do this again. Well, not *this*, but when you're back, you know, let's have a proper night out. The four of us maybe. You, me, Brendan and Dave. Brendan likes Dave. Actually, I think he fancies him a bit, but he always denies it.'

'That would be good,' Thorne said.

Hendricks was ready to go. He looked from one end of the street to the other.

Thorne pointed to the right. 'Kingsway.'

'Kingsway,' Hendricks repeated. He turned and pointed himself towards the main road. Walking quickly, like someone trying too hard to look sober.

Thorne shouted after him. 'Cheers, Phil . . . '

Hendricks raised a thumb, without turning round.

The drunk with the traffic cone was now playing something vaguely recognisable, though Thorne couldn't put a name to it. Wondering if the man did requests, Thorne toyed with shouting across; asking if he knew the horn part to 'Ring of Fire'.

He took out his sleeping bag and tried to get settled for the night. Opposite, the man with the cone grew in confidence and technique. He played 'Mack the Knife' and 'When the Saints Go Marching In'.

After five minutes, Thorne stood up and shouted at him to piss off.

His eyes snapped open and he stared at the figure standing above him: a shape stooping out of shadow. Thorne cried out and kicked his legs forward, pushing himself away from danger, driving himself back against the wall.

'What's the matter with you, you daft fucker?' the man said.

Thorne gulped up his heart. Felt it thump against his teeth.

'For fuck's sake, you silly twat!'

The breath he'd been holding exploded from Thorne's mouth. 'Oh, Christ, it's you.'

Jim Thorne chuckled. 'You thought I was the killer, didn't you?'

'What am I supposed to think?' Thorne gestured angrily at his father. 'Standing there in the dark ... '

'Standing in the dark and pissing myself laughing, watching you scuttle away like a fucking girl.'

Thorne was still breathing heavily. He shuffled forward and moved to one side. His father stepped forward and sat beside him, groaning with the effort as he lowered himself on to the concrete.

'Anyway, son, I'm the one person you can be pretty sure *isn't* the killer, right? You've not sussed much of anything out so far, but I should hope you've worked that much out at least. Yes?'

Feeling like a kid, answering the question quietly, the sarcasm sounding childish and petulant as he spoke. 'Yes. *I know that much* ... '

'You know *all* sorts of things. All sorts. You know who the killer really is, for a kick-off.'

Thorne stared. His father's face was expressionless. 'You've got worse since you died.'

'You know his name, son.'

'Tell me ... '

'Hold your horses. Let's have some fun with it.'

Thorne saw where it was going. 'Oh, please God, no. Not a fucking quiz.'

'Don't be so boring. Right, list all the people who it

might be.' He leaned over and tapped at the side of his son's head. 'You've got all the names up there.'

'I'm tired,' Thorne said.

'Come on, I'll give you the first couple to start ...'

Thorne listened as his father gave him the first name, paused and then gave him a second. Thorne was impatient. He couldn't help asking, though he knew his father would say nothing until he was good and ready. 'Is either of those the man behind the camera? Is one of them the killer, Dad?'

The old man smiled, enjoying his secret. He began to list more names, and with each one Thorne felt himself drifting further towards sleep ...

Then back towards consciousness. And by the time he'd woken up, thick-headed and shivering, Thorne couldn't remember a single name.

THIRTY

There was nothing like a grisly death or two for putting things into perspective.

Holland sat at his computer, logged on and cast an eye across the daily bulletin. Each morning he did the same thing: scanning the reports on serious crimes that had come in overnight. It was useful to see what other teams were doing of course; to get a sneak preview at what might be coming his own team's way. And to get a graphic reminder – good and early in the day – that, all things considered, life could be a hell of a lot worse ...

Sometimes, if it had been a slow night, there was little to get excited about. But usually there was something: a body, more often than not, or a missing person who would soon become a body. Something to take Dave Holland's mind off the fact that he was putting on a bit of weight, or to push some imagined slight to the back of his mind, or to

412

make him forget about the row he'd had with Sophie the night before.

Saturday morning's bulletin was usually the best, or worst of the week. Depending on whether you wanted to be seriously distracted or were just interested in keeping your breakfast down.

It had been a vintage Friday night . . .

A man, age and ethnicity impossible to determine: hog-tied and barbecued in the back of a burned-out Nissan Micra in Waltham Forest.

Two teenage boys, one white, one Asian: the first killed, the second fighting for his life in hospital after a stabbing outside a club in Wood Green.

A woman, thirty-four: found at home by her boyfriend after gaffer-taping a twelve-inch Sabatier carving-knife to the edge of a table and pushing her neck against it.

Two murders, perhaps three; possibly even four. The Homicide Assessment Team would already have signed the Waltham Forest killing over to an MIT. They would be waiting to see if the boy carved up in Wood Green recovered. They would certainly be taking a good, long look at the man whose girlfriend had supposedly killed herself so inventively . . .

DS Samir Karim walked past Holland's desk and held up a coffee. 'Ready to get going as soon as I've got this down me . . .'

Holland nodded. He went back to the computer, pulled up the list of visits he'd been allocated to make later that morning and printed them out. While he waited for hard copy to appear, he looked at the details. He studied the names, addresses and comments attached; aware all the time of those other details, still there in the bulletin window, inactive and partially hidden on the screen.

While some had spent their Friday night busy with gaffer-tape, washing blood from their hands or disposing of petrol cans, others had been safe at home in front of the television, disgusted and entertained by *Crimewatch*'s crime-lite version of such events, before picking up the phone – four hundred and twelve of them – to do their bit . . .

'How come *we* never get any of the overnighters?' Andy Stone was pulling on his jacket and moving towards him.

Holland thought that Stone had good reason to be pissed off. Obviously, a great many of the calls that had come in after the programme had been made from outside London, so while those in the office liaised with the relevant local forces, members of the team had been dispatched bright and early. Officers were already on their way to Exeter, Aberdeen, Birmingham and half a dozen other cities. Such interviews were coveted, and with good reason. Holland was one of those who would not have said no to a night away from home; getting a little time to himself and giving his expenses a hammering in the restaurant of a decent hotel.

'Luck of the draw, mate,' he said.

'Couldn't you have swung something with the DCI?'

Holland thought that he probably could have. He wondered why, in spite of fancying the time away, he hadn't even bothered to try. Chances are, Sophie would have offered to pack for him . . .

'So who are you heading out with?'

'I've got Mackillop,' Stone said. He brandished a piece of paper with his own list of names and addresses. 'Me and Wonderbollocks are off to waste our time in Hounslow, Lewisham, Finchley. All the glamour locations.'

'We've got to check out every possible sighting, Andy.'

'I know,' Stone said. 'I'm kidding. Yourself?'

Holland pointed across to Karim, who waved back and dropped what was left of his coffee into a wastepaper bin. 'Me and Sam are going slightly more upmarket.'

'Eales hiding out in Mayfair, is he?'

'Well, we've got a woman reckons she's seen him walking a dog on Hampstead High Street.'

'Why are so many of these calls always from women?' Stone asked before wandering away.

Holland thought it was likely to be something to do with women being more observant, and more likely to respond to appeals for help. More inclined, when it came down to it, to get off their arses and make an effort. They wouldn't even have Eales' name if it hadn't been for that female assistant adjutant going the extra yard.

Seeing Karim heading over, looking ready for the off, Holland began gathering his things together. He guessed that he would be spending much of his day thinking about Lieutenant Sarah Cheshire, and nights away in posh hotels.

*

'I've put him in one of the rooms upstairs,' Maxwell said.

Thorne nodded. 'I'll follow you . . . '

Maxwell had collared Thorne in the café, explained that Lawrence Healey had found Spike passed out on the steps when he'd arrived to open up. 'Not that unusual,' Maxwell said, as he led Thorne towards the offices. 'Their sense of time gets totally screwed. Sometimes they turn up in the middle of the night expecting to get breakfast and just nod off.'

They walked up the winding stone staircase. Thorne stared at the face of the boy on a drug-awareness poster; the blackness of the mouth inside the smile. He could see that the resilience he'd described to Hendricks was only as temporary as the high.

'Healey actually thought Spike had OD'd,' Maxwell continued. 'He spent twenty minutes walking him round, slapping some life into him.' Maxwell grinned. 'Got a decent slap back for his trouble.'

'Sounds like Spike.'

'Looking at the state of him, though, I'm guessing it's only a matter of time . . . '

They arrived at a door marked 'PRIVATE. COUNSELLING IN SESSION'. Maxwell knocked and pushed it open. 'I'll leave you to it. Give me a shout when you're done.'

'Thanks, Bren.'

Maxwell took a step away then turned, smiling. 'Oh, I couldn't get much sense out of Phil this morning. He had a bit of a headache for some strange reason. But he did manage to tell me about the two of us going out on a double date with you and Dave. Sounds like fun ...'

Spike's head was drooping, and the smoke from a cigarette rose straight up into his face. He was sitting on a dirty cream sofa, similar to the one Thorne remembered from the room where he and the others had watched the videotape. Looking around, Thorne realised that this room was virtually identical to that one, save for the absence of a VCR, and the fact that there were AIDS information leaflets on the coffee-table, rather than the *Radio Times* and *TV Quick*.

'Thought I'd got rid of you,' Thorne said. He flopped into an armchair, leaned forward and began to drum his fingers on the edge of the table.

Spike raised his head, grinned and spread out his arms; croaked a cheer that quickly ran out of steam. He was wearing cammys and his cracked, vinyl bomber jacket. The T-shirt underneath was stained, dark at the neck, and when he let his head fall back, Thorne could see the small, square wad of bandage and the plaster.

Thorne stroked the side of his own neck. 'What happened here?'

'Abscess burst,' Spike said. 'Stunk the fucking place out ...'

The worst detective in the world could have seen that Spike was a long way gone. Thorne could only presume that he was carrying his works with him; that he'd managed to fix up somewhere since Healey had found him outside the Lift and brought him indoors. Thorne guessed that Spike had spent every waking hour since he'd last seen him as fucked up as he was now.

'Where've you been?' Thorne asked.

Spike raised his hands to the hair which lay, damp-looking, against his head. He gathered it between his fingers and tried in vain to push it up into the trademark spikes. 'Around. Where have *you* been?'

'I knew you were upset about what happened.'

'What happened?'

'What happened to Terry,' Thorne said. 'I knew the pair of you were upset.'

'I went to see my sister.'

'It doesn't matter where you were. I'm happy you're still in one piece.'

'She gave me some cash money . . . '

It was like talking to someone who was underwater, suspended beneath the surface of a liquid that thickened as they tried to speak. That was *setting* above them.

'Actually, in a way, Terry helped out a bit,' Spike said.

'How's that?'

'I needed gear, course I did, *loads* of it. Both of us did. Most of these cocksuckers are hard as nails, like; wouldn't matter what you said to 'em. But there's a couple of dealers who've sussed that it's always going to be good for business in the long run. They do me a favour one time, they know damn well I'll be back tomorrow . . .

'So I lay it on a bit thick, right? I tell 'em that my mate's been killed, for Christ's sake, and I need to get more stuff.

I tell 'em I *really* need a bit extra, you know, because of how horribly fucking upset I am. See? Simple ...'

Thorne just listened, unable to fill the pauses that grew longer between sentences. He watched as Spike raised an arm up and pointed a finger. Spun it around, making a small circle in the air.

'So, Terry dies, and I need the stuff ... and I get the stuff because I tell everyone how upset I am ... Then I work out what a sick bastard I am for doing that to get the stuff ... And I hate myself.' He screwed up his face, put inverted commas round 'hate' with his fingers. 'So then I need even more stuff ... and round and fucking round ...'

Thorne waited until he was fairly sure there was nothing else. He had no way of knowing if Spike was aware of the tears, any more than he was of the cigarette that was no more than ash and filter between his fingers. 'Where's Caroline?' he asked.

'Will that bloke call the police 'cause I clocked him?'

'Healey, you mean?'

'She's in Camden ...'

Thorne laughed. 'I feel like the quizmaster on that *Two Ronnies* sketch.'

Spike looked blank. It had been Thorne's father's favourite: Ronnie Barker as the man on a quiz show whose specialist subject was answering the previous question.

'*What is the last letter on the top line of a typewriter keyboard?*'

'*The Battle of Hastings.*'

'*Hosting a dance or enjoying yourself might be described as having a . . . ?*'

'*P.*'

'What's in Camden?' Thorne asked.

Spike began pulling at a loose thread on the cushion next to him. 'Dealer's place.'

'How long's she been there?'

'A couple of days.' He pulled the cushion to him, folded his arms tight across it. 'I took her round . . . '

Round and fucking round . . .

Thorne understood that Spike and Caroline had both been desperate. That each had found their own way of getting as much as they needed. 'Let's go and see her,' he said.

Spike moaned and shook his head.

Thorne stood and stepped across to him. He raised Spike's hand, lifted it until it was over the table, and squeezed until the burned-out nub-end dropped into an ashtray.

'Where exactly are you from?' Stone asked.

The barman turned from restocking an optic. 'Wellington.'

'Have you got some identification on you?'

The barman sighed, started rooting around for his wallet. 'I've got credit cards . . . '

Stone took another glance at the photo he was carrying with him, a composite of the original Ryan Eales photo and the digitally aged version. He looked back at the man behind the bar. 'Forget it, mate. It's OK . . . '

He walked back to where Mackillop was sitting. The woman next to him, who'd called to say that the man behind the bar of her local pub might well be the one they were after, looked up eagerly.

'He's fifteen years too young and he's from New Zealand,' Stone said. 'He's got a bloody accent.'

The woman, fifteen years older than she wanted to be, and from Hounslow, was less than delighted. 'I never said I'd spoken to him, did I?' She sat there for a few seconds more, then snatched up her handbag. 'I suppose I'm buying *myself* a drink, then ...'

Mackillop and Stone watched her at the bar. 'We could get something to eat ourselves while we're in here,' Mackillop said. 'It's near enough lunchtime.'

Stone looked at his watch and stood up. 'Actually, I'm meeting someone for lunch, so I think we're better off splitting up for an hour or so.'

Mackillop looked thrown. 'Right ...'

'If we do Finchley next, you can drop me off in Willesden on the way and I'll meet you there.'

'Fair enough.' He followed Stone towards the door. Lewisham, the other location on their list, would have been closer, but Mackillop wasn't going to argue. Especially when it dawned on him exactly how Stone was planning to spend his lunch-hour.

They grabbed cold drinks and a paper from a newsagent's, then walked across the road to a small pay-and-display behind a branch of *Budgens*. 'Fucking New Zealand,' Stone said.

He hung up his jacket in the back of the car, then turned on Capital Gold while Mackillop waited for his chance to nose the Volvo into traffic. 'So, you spend an hour or so in a caff or something, right?'

'I might just grab a sandwich,' Mackillop said.

'Whatever. I'll meet you outside the Finchley address, two o'clock-ish. Maybe just after.'

'How are you going to get there from Willesden?'

'I'll call a cab,' Stone said.

'Straight up the North Circular, I would have thought. Piece of piss this time of day.'

They drove along the London road through Brentford and turned north along the edge of Gunnersbury Park.

Stone sang along to an Eric Clapton track, put finger and thumb together as if holding a plectrum during the guitar break. 'If you get there before me, just park up and wait,' Stone said. 'I'll call to find out where you are.'

Mackillop tried his best to keep a straight face. 'Wouldn't it be simpler if I just tagged along to your lunch meeting?'

'You can fuck right off,' Stone said. 'Mind you, she'd probably be up for it.'

THIRTY-ONE

Thorne sprung for a couple of tube tickets and he and
Spike travelled the half a dozen stops to Camden Town.
Spike was asleep, or as good as, most of the way, while
Thorne was stared at by a young mother who hissed at her
two kids and made sure they stayed close by her. When
they stood to get off, the woman smiled at him, but
Thorne saw her arms tighten around her children's waists.

Spike dragged his feet and was easily distracted as they
walked along Camden Road towards the overground station. He stopped to peer into the windows of shops or talk
to strangers, few of whom seemed fazed at being drawn
into conversations with a junkie and a tramp. As places in
the capital went, Camden was pretty much a one-off.

Despite Thorne's efforts to urge him forward, Spike sat
down next to someone he actually knew, who was begging
outside the huge Sainsbury's. Thorne stepped away from

them and stared at his reflection in the glass of the automatic doors. His hair and beard were surely growing at a much faster rate than they normally did. He wondered if it was anything to do with exposure to air, fresh or otherwise. Though the bruises had faded, so had the rest of his face. The marks were still visible against the skin, like ancient tea-stains that stubbornly refused to shift from a pale, cotton tablecloth. He inched across until he was right in the middle of the doors; until he could enjoy himself being split down the middle whenever anyone walked in or out.

A security guard was eyeing him with intent, so Thorne decided to save him the trouble. He moved away and yanked Spike up by the collar of his jacket. Spike's friend moved to get to his feet, caught Thorne's eye and lowered himself to the pavement again.

Thorne wrapped an arm around Spike's skinny shoulders. 'Time to go and see Caroline,' he said.

They walked further away from the high street and the market, minutes from Thorne's own flat in Kentish Town. Halfway between the million-pound houses of Camden Square and the more modest accommodation of Holloway Prison, they stopped. Spike shook his head, like he was about to have teeth removed, and pointed towards an ugly, three-storey block set back from the main road.

'Up there,' he said.

They stared across at the green front doors for a minute or two; at the brown balconies and multi-coloured washing strung from their railings. 'Do you want me to wait here?' Thorne asked.

'Wait here for what?'

Thorne was starting to run out of patience with Spike's sulky attitude; with the drug and with the hunger for it. He wanted to grab him and tell him to get up to his dealer's flat and *do* something. To pull Caroline out of there, or smash the place up, or get down on his knees and thank the poxy shitbag who was fucking his girlfriend so they could get a bit higher for that much longer. Anything . . .

'I don't know,' he said.

Spike leaned against a parking meter. His breathing was noisy; cracked and wheezy. 'You could maybe come up, stand at the end of the corridor or something.'

'Come on then . . . '

They moved across the road like old men, with Spike talking to himself, then spitting at an Astra whose driver had leaned on his horn, furious at being forced to brake. At the base of the low-rise, on a small square of dogshit-and-dandelion paving, a kid on a skateboard looked at Spike as if he'd seen him before and Spike looked back.

As they entered the pungent cool of the stairwell, Thorne looked round, watched the boy pull out a mobile phone as he kicked his board away.

'It's always handy to know when someone's coming,' Spike said. 'The little fucker gets enough cash to keep him in football stickers.' He smacked his palms slowly against the blistered handrail as he led Thorne up to the top floor. 'Everyone's got some sort of habit, like . . . '

Climbing, Thorne watched Spike trying, in cack-handed slow-motion, to smarten himself up. He messed

with his hair and stopped to tighten the laces in his trainers. He straightened his jacket and tucked in his T-shirt,
and as they emerged on to a concrete walkway, Thorne
was still wondering who the effort was being made for.

A door opened, two or three from the end of the corridor, sixty feet away. A man stepped out: thirty or so, short,
with dark hair and stubble. He was wearing sandals, and
creased grey trousers below a polo shirt.

Spike stopped and waved. The man in the doorway
raised up his chin.

'That's Mickey,' Spike said. 'He's from Malta, so he's
got brown balls ...'

Thorne watched the man take a step forward so that he
could look down over the balcony.

Spike leaned in with a grin, spelled out the joke loud
enough for the man by the door to hear. 'He's a Malteser,
like, so he's got brown balls.' He looked round, gave the
man another wave.

Mickey smiled. 'Fucking *huge* brown balls ...'

Spike moved away from Thorne suddenly, and began
edging slowly backwards towards Mickey. He nodded at
Thorne, once, twice. 'It's OK, mate, I'm good from here.'

'Does your friend want something?' Mickey said.

'No, he's cool,' Spike shouted.

Thorne wasn't sure whether the dealer was talking
about drugs or trouble. The man certainly seemed happy
enough to provide whatever was required.

'Really, it's fine now,' Spike said.

He was spinning around slowly as he went. He walked

backwards then forwards between Thorne and the dealer, partially blocking the view as Thorne caught sight of a second figure emerging through the green door. Thorne stepped to one side to get a better look. To catch Caroline's eye.

She looked as pleased to see him as dead eyes would allow. She tugged on Mickey's shirt and pointed. 'He likes to beat up coppers,' she said.

The dealer smiled. Let the backs of his fingers move down the girl's arm. 'I like it. He gets a freebie if he wants one.'

'Honest, you can go now,' Spike said. He was starting to sound desperate, to look embarrassed that Thorne was there at all. 'We're sorted. Both of us. Right, Caz?'

Caroline pulled fingernails through her hair and walked back into the flat as if she'd forgotten something. Thorne watched Spike drift over to Mickey. Watched the dealer press his fist against Spike's and step back through the doorway.

'See you at the Lift later, then?' Thorne said.

Spike picked at the plaster, tore the stained wad of bandage from his neck and lobbed it over the balcony. As he followed Mickey inside, he stuck up a thumb without turning round, just as Hendricks had done the night before.

Thorne waited half a minute after the door had closed before walking up to it. A curtain was drawn across the only window and he could hear no sounds from inside, so he turned and walked back towards the stairs.

On the way down he took out his phone. He'd felt the

vibration of a message coming through as he and Spike had walked from the tube station. It was a text from Phil Hendricks, another gag based around the possible 'double date' with Brendan and Dave Holland ...

Thorne stopped and stared at the screen.

He'd felt it up to now as something annoying yet unimportant; like something caught in your teeth that you couldn't get at. That you pushed at until your tongue got tired and then gave up on. Suddenly, Thorne knew exactly what had been nagging at him. And he knew why.

'*You know all sorts of things ...*'

He remembered the voice from a dream and he remembered other voices, too. He remembered what Hendricks had said:

'*Brendan likes Dave. Actually, I think he fancies him a bit ...*'

And what Maxwell had said back at the Lift only an hour before. And, most important of all, what he'd said to Thorne a week or so before that ...

He dialled Brendan Maxwell's mobile number, the excitement building in him like nausea. 'Bren, listen, it's Tom. Remember you told me that a police officer was looking for me. A week ago?'

'I'm right in the middle of something ...'

'It wasn't Dave Holland, was it.' It was more statement than question.

There was a pause. Thorne could hear others talking in the background. Maxwell lowered his voice. 'Sorry, Tom, I'm not with you.'

'This was a couple of days before Terry Turner was killed. You said that a police officer was asking where I was, and you'd pointed him towards the theatre, yes?'

'Yes ...'

'I know that Holland *had* been in, because he couldn't get hold of me, so I presumed ...'

'Dave came in the day after, I think. If I'd been talking about Dave, I'd've said so, wouldn't I, because I know him. I'd never seen this other bloke before.'

'Right. And because I'm a fucking idiot, I've only just worked that out.'

'Is this important?' Maxwell asked.

Thorne began to move again. 'How did you know he was a copper?'

'Can I call you back?'

'I just need a minute, Bren ...'

Maxwell sighed. 'He introduced himself, then he showed me ID. I'm not a complete moron.'

'Do you remember the name?'

Another pause. 'No. Far too many names to remember.'

Thorne swung round fast on to another flight of stairs, began to swear with each step he took.

'Sorry,' Maxwell said.

'How did he get in to see you?'

'Same as anybody else, I think. They called me down from reception and buzzed him through.'

'So he would have signed in?'

'He certainly should have done. They're usually pretty

hot on health and safety. Do you want me to go and have a look?'

'I'll be with you in about twenty minutes . . . '

Thorne took the remaining stairs two at a time, feeling each step jar and burn in far too many places. He was aware of the skateboarder's eyes on him as he came out of the covered stairwell a whole lot faster than he'd gone in.

Rosedene Way was a quiet road, five minutes from the tube station and no more than a pitching wedge from Finchley golf course. The Volvo was not out of place among the Saabs and Audis; well-tended hanging baskets far outnumbered satellite dishes on the tidy thirties houses.

Mackillop had driven round for twenty minutes looking for somewhere decent to eat, and had eventually given up. He'd grabbed a sandwich from the M&S at Tally Ho corner and eaten it in the car. Now, he was stupidly early for the rendezvous with Andy Stone, but he was as happy where he was – with the car radio and a newspaper – as he would have been anywhere else.

He looked up at the top floor of the house they would be visiting; it looked like an attic conversion. He dropped his eyes down to the ground floor, where their interviewee lived, then left to where a woman was watching him while her dog relieved itself in the gutter. Saturday afternoon and there were plenty of people around. He smiled at the woman, who bent down smartly, plastic bag at the ready to clear up the mess.

430

Mackillop thought about what Andy Stone was doing. How long it had been since he'd done the same thing. He'd split up with his girlfriend four months before, and one pissed-up fumble with a Colindale WPC after a lock-in at the Oak was the closest to sex he'd managed since. Mind you, he'd probably get fairly close, at least by association, when Stone showed up, gagging as always to go over the highlights of his performance.

The woman with the dog gave him a good look as she walked past the car; her face like she could still smell the turd in her plastic bag.

He realised that he'd forgotten it was Saturday when he'd been talking to Stone about the best route to take. Traffic could very easily be snarled up on the North Circ. There wasn't a lot of choice mind you; it was a pig of a journey by tube, with at least a couple of changes between Willesden Green and West Finchley ...

He hoped he wouldn't have too much longer to wait.

When they started playing cheesy country rubbish, Mackillop quickly retuned the radio. Then he opened the *Express* to the crossword, folded it across the steering wheel and dug around in his pocket for a pen.

THIRTY-TWO

Maxwell found the page he was looking for and passed the centre's registration book across. He pointed at the date and entry that Thorne would be most interested in.

The name was scribbled rather than printed, but it was legible enough. 'DS Morley,' Thorne said, reading. 'Detective Sergeant T. Morley.'

'Like I said on the phone, he had a warrant card . . . '

They were alone in a small storage room next door to the laundry; the Saturday lunch rush was at its height and there were plenty of people in the building, both clients and staff. Thorne was fired up, but in spite of all that had happened it was still important, especially *here*, to maintain the integrity of the undercover operation.

Or, at least, as much integrity as he had left . . .

'What exactly did he say?' Thorne asked.

Maxwell sat down on a cardboard box marked

'Domestos'. The room smelled of polish and cleaning fluid. 'Fuck ... I'm not sure I can tell you *exactly* ...'

'Did he mention me by name?'

'I suppose he must have done. It was definitely you we were talking about.'

'Me specifically?'

'Yeah, as far as I can remember ...'

'First name? Second name?'

'I think he knew your first name. I think so ...'

'It's about whether he was looking for me, or just looking for "the undercover copper". D'you see the difference? It's about how much he *knew*.' Thorne stared at the name on the page, reached for his phone and dialled Scotland Yard.

'He knew enough,' Maxwell said.

As soon as he got through to the Information Room, Thorne gave his name and warrant number. He told the WPC that he needed a check run on an officer. 'The name is Morley,' he said, 'first initial "T". A sergeant ...'

The woman took down details of Thorne's request, said that she'd call him straight back.

'Any idea how long it's going to take?'

'You know how it works,' she said. 'I've got to check *you* out before I can do anything else.'

Andy Stone thought he'd got this one figured out; that they had an understanding, but she'd really surprised him. He'd thought it was all about sex; that she just wanted a quick session of an afternoon, same as usual. So he'd arranged to pop round for 'lunch'. He'd worked out that he'd have enough time to get there, give her what she wanted and get back in good time to meet up with Mackillop for the next interview. That was the theory, but it hadn't quite worked out that way. The woman had only gone and cooked him a meal. She'd actually wanted to have *lunch*. Not that she hadn't wanted to go to bed as well; she'd left him in no doubt that spaghetti Bolognese wasn't the only thing on the menu. But he couldn't just get straight down to it, could he? Not after packing all that pasta away. So, twenty minutes for lunch, fifteen to chat while they let it go down, then a decent half-hour bout between the sheets. Now there was no way he could make it across to Finchley in time.

He sat on the edge of the bed, pulling on his socks as quickly as he could, and making small talk; sneaking glances at his watch so as not to hurt her feelings. He thought she was starting to like him a bit too much. Maybe the whole cooking lunch thing meant that she wanted to move things on a bit between them. He'd have to give that some serious thought.

Shit: he hadn't even ordered a cab yet. He asked her if she had a number she used, and stood as she moved towards him, naked, to fetch the card from her purse. She lowered a hand to cup his balls through his underpants as she passed, and he stepped back, telling her that he really was going to be fucking late and reaching into the corner for his trousers.

She retrieved the card from her handbag and shouted out the number. Stone dropped back on to the bed, dialled as he watched her walk into the en-suite and bend to run the bath . . .

Fifteen, maybe twenty, minutes behind schedule . . . if he was lucky. He ordered the cab and looked around for his shoes, deciding that he'd call Mackillop once he was on his way.

The rhythmic drone became a high-pitched whine as one of the machines moved on to its spin cycle in the laundry-room next door.

'We're talking about the killer here, aren't we?' Maxwell said. 'Tom?'

'There's every chance.'

'So how did he know to come here and start talking to me as if he knew you?'

Thorne could still not be certain that the killer *didn't* know him. He looked up from the phone that was res-olutely refusing to ring. 'That's what I'm trying to make sense of,' he said.

Not that any of it made a great deal of sense. The killer may or may not have known the name of the undercover police officer he was looking for; following Thorne's indis-cretions in the aftermath of his arrest, that information was certainly out there. But even if the leak had come from McCabe or one of his team – even if DS T. Morley was one of that team – Thorne couldn't see how the killer had connected him to the Lift.

'It's freaky to think that I talked to the fucker,' Maxwell said.

'You get used to it.'

'Will I have to go to court if you find him?'

'Maybe. Phil can give you some tips . . .'

Maxwell smiled, but he looked uncomfortable. 'Thing is, I don't know if the image I've got in my mind is accurate or not? I don't know whether I'm remembering this bloke or if I'm imagining him. Now that I know what he did, you know?'

'We need to get you to a station as soon as we can,' Thorne said. 'Start trying to put an e-fit together.'

'If I hadn't talked to him, Terry Turner would still be alive, wouldn't he?'

Thorne looked away. '*I* should have put all this together a lot quicker, Bren.'

'If I hadn't told him where you were supposed to be sleeping . . .'

The phone buzzed in Thorne's hand.

The Information Room WPC told him that there were two T. Morleys serving in the Met. 'So I got on to both borough personnel offices.'

'Thank you,' Thorne said.

'Standard procedure. One's on a Murder Squad in Wimbledon. The other's a relief sergeant in Barnet. He's the one that's got a crime report attached to his records. Trevor Morley—'

'Crime report?'

'He's not actually been back at work that long. He was mugged in a pub car park three months ago. Nasty attack, fractured his skull . . .'

Thorne didn't need her to tell him that the mugger had never been caught. Or that, among other things, Sergeant Trevor Morley's warrant card had been stolen during the attack. He didn't need to tell her that the warrant card would have been the reason Morley had been attacked in the first place.

He thanked the WPC for her help. She told him she'd pass a report on to the Information Room's chief inspector, who might well need to get in touch with him. Thorne said that would be fine before he hung up.

'Not a real copper,' Thorne said. 'He was using stolen ID.'

The information didn't seem to make Brendan Maxwell feel any better. 'It had his photo in it.'

'Easy enough to paste in. How closely did you look?'

Maxwell shook his head. About as closely as anybody looked at anything.

'Whether you're remembering his face or imagining it, we still need to get you somewhere and get it down. I'll call someone and get it sorted.'

'I don't know how much detail I can give anyone.'

Thorne started pressing buttons on his phone, searching for Brigstocke's number on the memory. 'Just start with the general stuff,' he said. 'Height, build, colouring ...'

'He was big. Six foot two or three, and well built. He looked pretty fit.'

'Hair?'

'Medium, I suppose, fairly neat. And he had a beard.

437

Not ginger, but sandy-ish. He was that kind of colouring. Light-skinned … blue eyes, I think … and maybe a bit freckly, you know?'

Thorne knew.

He felt that rare, yet familiar, tickle of excitement. The shuddery spider-crawl of it at the nape of his neck, moving beneath the hair and the collar of his dirty grey coat. 'Do you recycle?' he asked.

Maxwell looked and sounded confused. 'Yes …'

'Where?'

'Out by the wheely-bins.'

Maxwell opened his mouth to say something else, but Thorne was already on his feet and moving towards the door.

THIRTY-THREE

Fucked-up weather and busybodies. Jason Mackillop reckoned they were both about as British as you could get.

It was one of those bizarre, early-autumn afternoons that
couldn't make up its mind: sunshine, wind and rain in a
random sequence every half an hour or so. Now, it was
spitting gently, and Mackillop stared through the streaked
windscreen at the man with the plastic carrier bags, who
was walking towards the car and staring back with undis-
guised curiosity.

Stone had called a few minutes earlier to say that he was
running late. Mackillop had heard the grin in Stone's voice;
the implication that it was all due to his phenomenal staying
power. Now Mackillop would be sitting there like a lemon
for another twenty minutes or more ...

The man carrying the plastic bags walked a few yards
past the target address, then stopped and came back.
He stared until he caught Mackillop's eye. He adjusted

the grip on each bag and took slow steps towards the car.

Mackillop leaned on the switch. He let the window slide down as far as possible without letting in the drizzle.

'Can I help you?' the man said.

Mackillop had been about to ask much the same question. He reached into his jacket, produced his warrant card. 'No, I'm fine, thank you.'

The man gave a small nod, hummed a reaction, but showed little inclination to move.

'Do you live there?' Mackillop asked.

'Yes, I do.' He turned and stared back at the house, then spun back around to Mackillop. 'It's four flats, actually.'

'I know.'

'I think they made a nice job of the conversion.'

'Right . . .'

The man looked round at the house again. 'I've not lived there for very long, mind you.'

Mackillop decided that it couldn't hurt to get a bit of background information while he was waiting for Stone to show up. The man seemed keen enough to help. 'Do you know a Mr Mahmoud?'

'I'm not sure.'

Mackillop fished under the newspaper on the passenger seat, pulled out his page of notes. 'Asif Mahmoud . . .'

'What does he look like?'

'He's the tenant on the ground floor.'

The man leaned down a little closer to Mackillop's window. The spatterings of rain darkened the material of his knee-length raincoat and baseball cap. 'The one with

440

the dope, right? You can smell it when you come in late sometimes.'

'Right, thanks,' Mackillop said. If the man was right, the likelihood of their visit being a complete waste of time had just rocketed. 'Mr Mahmoud's helping us with something, that's all.'

The man smiled to himself, looked both ways along the street.

'Can I ask which flat is yours?' Mackillop asked.

'Flat D. Up with the gods. All those stairs keep you fit, I tell you that ...'

'Top floor?'

When the man saw Mackillop looking, *really* looking, at him for the first time, he smiled again, and swallowed. Then his expression became suddenly serious, and he asked Mackillop exactly who he was, which branch of the police he was with and where he was based. Mackillop calmly gave him all the information he asked for.

'Trainee?' the man said. 'Like a junior doctor kind of thing?'

'That's right.'

'Sort of like doing your basic training.'

'Listen ...'

The man took a couple of paces backwards, to allow Mackillop room to open the car door. 'I'm Ryan Eales,' he said. He held up his plastic bags. 'I need to go and put this shopping away ...'

Thorne and Maxwell pushed through an emergency exit into a covered service yard at the rear of the building. The recycling bins – half a dozen of them, each filled with clear glass, green glass, plastic or newspapers – were lined up next to three huge wheelies. The place smelled of cat-piss and damp wool, and every available inch of brickwork was covered in graffiti, elaborate and largely illegible. Thorne knelt down, threw the lids off the bins until he found the one he was after, and began pulling out piles of old newspapers.

Maxwell walked to the edge of the covered area, put his hand out into the rain. 'I suppose you'll tell me what you're doing when you're good and ready.'

'I'm hoping we won't need to bother with that e-fit.'

'And last week's copies of the *Sun* are going to help, are they?'

'This might be utter bollocks, of course. I could be way off the mark.'

'From what I've heard, that would be my bet,' Maxwell said.

With a wide range of staff and clientele, the Lift catered for a variety of tastes when it came to reading matter. Thorne dug through back-copies of most of the daily tabloids and broadsheets. He picked up and threw away dozens of freebies aimed at Australians and New Zealanders, music papers, TV magazines and issues of *Loot* until he found something he was interested in.

He seized on a crumpled edition of the *Standard*. The headline disturbed him no less than when he'd first seen it: ROUGH-SLEEPER KILLINGS. MET GOES UNDERCOVER.

Maxwell looked over Thorne's shoulder. 'That's when the cat came out of the bag, right?'

Thorne opened the paper and began to read. 'This is how he knew ...'

'Knew what?'

'You asked me back in there. How did he know to come here and start asking questions? I don't think he knew to come *here* specifically, but he knew it would be a good idea to visit places like this one, because they fucking told him. Listen ...'

He read from the newspaper story: '"It's understood that the Metropolitan Police has liaised closely with an organisation working with rough sleepers, in order that the undercover officer concerned can integrate with the homeless community as smoothly as possible".'

Maxwell walked back towards the building, taking it in. He turned and leaned back against the door. 'Bloody hell ...'

Thorne read on, growing angrier by the second. Not only had the story announced his presence, it had also, unwittingly or not, given a killer the means to find him.

'So he reads that and he works out that somebody must know something.'

'It wasn't rocket science, was it?' Thorne said. 'Somebody at one of the hostels, one of the shelters, one of the day centres. At Crisis, or Aquarius, or here. He just made a list. He visited all of them, flashed his nicked card and asked a few vague questions in the hope of getting lucky and coming across someone who'd been "liaised with". You might have been the first person he talked to or the fortieth. Doesn't really matter ...'

'So, even though he knew your name, chances are he didn't know *you*?'

'God knows . . . probably not. We can be fairly sure he was getting his information from the newspaper, as opposed to anywhere . . . closer to home.'

There were still many things Thorne couldn't be sure about, like how the killer had known his name. But it was starting to look as though a stolen warrant card was as near as it came to police involvement in the killings themselves. It might therefore be safe enough to take surveillance off McCabe and the others at Charing Cross.

Thorne held up the paper. 'I still don't know who leaked *this*, though.' He tossed the *Standard* towards the mass that had already been discarded and went back to searching through the main pile. He still hadn't found the newspaper he was actually looking for.

Eales' flat was small, but smart and extremely tidy. Once inside, a tightly winding flight of stairs covered in coir matting rose straight into a bed-sitting room, with an arch at one end leading through to a tiny kitchen, and a door at the other, which Mackillop presumed opened into the bathroom.

Eales was putting his shopping into cupboards, while Mackillop sat on a stiff-backed chair in the bed-sitting room, still unable to believe how jammy he'd been.

'I know it's not huge,' Eales shouted through from the kitchen. 'But I don't have a lot of stuff . . . '

Mackillop was buzzing. He felt like he'd been in the Job for years. He couldn't wait to clock the look on Stone's face

444

when he finally turned up; when the DC saw which of them had *really* got lucky that lunchtime.

'You still wouldn't believe what the rent is, mind you ...'

'It's nice,' Mackillop said, meaning it. His own flat in a modern block was bigger, but strictly functional. He liked the polished floor in this place, the stripped beams in the ceiling and the stained-glass panels in the bathroom door.

'It'll do,' Eales said.

'It'd do for me ...'

'Good job I've just done a shop.' Eales was walking in from the kitchen brandishing an unopened packet of Digestives. 'Coffee won't be a sec.' He handed the biscuits across and turned back towards the kitchen. 'If your partner's going to be a while, you might as well put your feet up ...'

While he waited for his coffee, Mackillop continued to look around. Eales had said that he didn't have much, but Mackillop thought he could be fairly positive about at least one of the ex-trooper's possessions; the one which, without any doubt, would be the most valuable. There was a VCR beneath the small TV at the end of the bed, and a number of unmarked videotapes piled on top of it. Mackillop couldn't help but wonder ...

'Why have you not contacted us, Mr Eales?' he asked.

Eales walked back through, handed a mug to Mackillop, and sat down on the edge of his bed. 'I haven't done anything wrong,' he said.

'You did know we were trying to trace you, though? You didn't seem very surprised to find a policeman on your doorstep.'

'A little, maybe.'

'It was obvious you knew who I was looking for.'

'I didn't know *anything* until I saw it on the TV the other night. I've not seen a newspaper in a while. I've barely been out of the house.'

Mackillop took out a biscuit from the packet on the floor, held it up. 'Except to go shopping.'

'Once every couple of days,' Eales said. 'You've got to get supplies in. And when I go, I don't hang about.'

'You've been keeping your head down?'

'Something like that.'

Mackillop knew why, of course. Even with his life under threat, Eales would hardly have been mustard-keen to go to the police; to explain the reason why he was next on a killer's list. Mackillop also knew that, by questioning him, he was almost certainly moving well beyond his remit. So far, he hadn't been short of luck, but the sensible part of him was wondering just how far he could push it. 'I'm guessing it's not your name on the rent book . . . '

'It's a name I use sometimes.' Eales slurped his coffee. 'I pay the rent, and that's all anyone seems bothered about.'

'You've not used your real name for a while, have you?'

Eales walked over, leaned down to grab a few biscuits, then sat again. 'Have I not?'

'I know that because we've looked. *Everywhere* . . . '

'I didn't think you were here to nick me for not filling in forms correctly.'

'I'm not,' Mackillop said. 'But it's natural to wonder why you might be so keen to stay anonymous.' He watched as

Eales downed the rest of his coffee in three or four swift gulps; amazed, as his own mug was still hot to the touch.

Eales stood, gestured with his empty mug. 'I'm going to get some more.'

Mackillop followed him towards the kitchen. 'Mr Eales . . . '

'I've moved around a lot in the last few years.' Eales spoke with his back to Mackillop, taking coffee and sugar from the cupboard, moving across to the fridge for milk. 'I've done a few strange jobs, you know? Worked for one or two dodgy characters . . . '

'Dodgy how?'

'Dodgy, as in secret. I do what they pay me for, I fuck off and I keep my mouth shut. This isn't the sort of work you pick up at the Job Centre, you know?'

Mackillop thought about it, guessed that Eales was talking about working as a mercenary. He watched the man's shoulders moving beneath his sweatshirt. Eales certainly looked as though he kept himself useful. 'We're not really interested in what you've been doing,' he said. 'We're actually here for your own good. But I think you know that, don't you?'

Eales turned, looked at him.

Mackillop was starting to grow impatient with the caginess; tired of going round the houses. Here was someone who'd taken part in a brutal war crime; their only hope of catching a man who'd perpetrated an atrocity of his own fifteen years down the line.

'Do you know *why* we've been trying to find you, Mr Eales?'

447

Eales began to look a little nervous. He reached for his mug and dropped his head to sip from it. Mackillop waited a few seconds, then pulled out his phone, deciding that maybe it was a good time to see how far away Stone was ...

Eales moved forward, suddenly enough to slop hot coffee across the floor. To make Mackillop step back. 'Show me your warrant card again. Straight away, please.'

Mackillop did as Eales asked. Watched as he took a few moments to regain control and recover his composure.

'I'm sorry for ... sorry about *that*,' Eales said. 'You know damn well that I've got every right to be a bit jumpy, so let's not kid each other.' He snatched a tea-towel from the work-top, tossed it on to the spill and pushed it around with his foot as he spoke. 'I knew Ian Hadingham had topped himself last year, all right? *Supposedly* topped himself. And I knew Chris Jago was missing because I'd tried to get in touch with him. So that, on top of Hadingham, was enough to make me nervous. Then I open a paper three weeks ago and see a picture of a dead man who looks very much like Alec Bonser. I see his picture, and I see a picture like *this* ...' He rolled up the sleeve of his sweatshirt. There were several tattoos: a row of Chinese symbols, two Celtic bands, a lion's head – but the important one was high up, just below the shoulder.

Letters faded to the blue of his eyes:

O+
S.O.F.A.

'I've no idea if he killed Chris Jago or not, but I'm the fourth member of that crew, and I want to stay alive as long as possible, thank you very much. I'm not claiming to be Brain of Britain, I was just a pig-thick squaddie, but it seemed like a good idea to keep a fairly low profile. Like you said, I kept my head down, and I've got away with it. Until now, at any rate.' Eales shrugged, blew on his coffee. 'You lot might want to talk to me, but last time I checked, that wasn't fatal.'

Mackillop felt like straps were being fastened tight across his chest. Dry-mouthed in a second, he sucked in the words and tried to arrange them into the question that was begging to be asked: You've no idea if *who* killed Chris Jago?

But he said nothing. The suspicion that he was out of his depth had suddenly become a horrible certainty. He felt like he was back on the course, that this was part of some elaborate training exercise. It was as if Eales were one of his tutors playing a role and this was the crucial point in the assessment process. The part where he could fuck up everything if he wasn't very careful. Mackillop knew that he was being given the chance to put the big question, but he also knew that the moment belonged by right, and by seniority, to others ...

Eales nodded towards the mug in Mackillop's hand. 'Do you want another one of those?'

The clever thing to do, the *correct* thing, was to back off a little. To sit tight, and wait for Andy Stone to arrive. Mackillop handed the mug across and turned back towards the bed-sitting room.

449

THIRTY-FOUR

THE LATEST VICTIM. THE FIRST PICTURE . . .

The newspaper felt a little spongy. It was stained in places by whatever liquid had pooled, brown and viscous, in the bottom of the bin. But the headline remained stark enough; the expression on the face of the young Terry Turner still hopeful, and heartbreaking.

'Weird to see him looking so young,' Maxwell said. 'Without the bloody padlock . . . '

Thorne tore through the pages until he found the one he was after: the photo of another young man, this one in uniform, staring into the camera; wide eyed and half smiling, like it didn't much matter what was coming.

Thorne got up off his knees. 'Look at this.' He folded the newspaper over and handed it across.

Maxwell stared at the picture for a few seconds, at the appeal for information beneath it, then turned back to

Thorne. The expression on his face made it clear that he wasn't sure what he was supposed to be looking at; what he was meant to be seeing.

'Could that be him?' Thorne asked.

Maxwell went back to the photo. '*This* bloke?'

'Could he be our Detective Sergeant Trevor Morley?'

'How old's this picture?'

'Just look, Bren ...'

Maxwell did as he was told. Let out a long, slow breath ...

Thorne moved quickly across to stand alongside him, nodded down at the photograph. 'That was taken when he joined up in the late eighties.' He suddenly remembered the digitally aged version that had been broadcast the night before; that Hendricks had talked about watching. 'Did you not see this on *Crimewatch* last night?'

'I was out,' Maxwell said.

'Shit ...'

'I was out on the streets, *doing my fucking job*. Fair enough?'

'Just stick twenty years on his face, all right? He'd be late-thirties now, somewhere round there. Hair longer, obviously. A beard. From what you said, the colouring's the same, right?'

'Sandy, but with some grey. And the freckles are darker, but I suppose that would have happened ...'

'Look at the mouth,' Thorne said. 'The smile would almost certainly be the same.'

'Maybe. Yeah ... this could be him.'

451

'*Could be*, or *is*?'

'Jesus. I should have looked at this properly when I saw it the first time. I read about what had happened to Terry; that's all. I never really took this in.'

'Well, now's your chance. Come on, Brendan.'

Maxwell stabbed at the page. 'The face has filled out a bit and it's lined. Not wrinkles exactly; hard lines, like creases, you know? Like it's weathered.'

It was good enough . . .

Thorne knew that they'd made a huge mistake; that they should at least have *considered* the possibility of this for longer and not dismissed it as quickly as they had. Though the evidence had certainly pointed towards the man behind the camera, they'd got it the wrong way round.

'It's me . . .'

'What?' Maxwell turned, thinking that Thorne was talking to him, but he saw that Thorne had his phone pressed hard to his ear.

'We've been idiots, Russell,' Thorne said. 'Ryan Eales isn't the next one on the list. He's the one who's been working his way *through* it . . .'

Ryan Eales turned side on, leaned against the wall in the archway between kitchen and bed-sitting room. 'Bit of luck that I came back when I did. That you were sitting outside in your car like that.'

'We'd have knocked on your door eventually,' Mackillop said.

'I might not have answered it.'

Which would, Mackillop thought, have been understandable. All in all, things had turned out pretty well. It was equally likely that, if there had been no reply, and the man in the ground-floor flat turned out to have been the pothead Eales said he was, that nobody would have bothered coming back. Mackillop laughed. 'I suppose we should be grateful that you'd run out of biscuits,' he said.

'Right . . .'

The weather had changed suddenly yet again. Sunshine was screaming in through the big bay window and a smaller skylight towards the bathroom, flashing where it kissed the white walls and the varnish on the honey-coloured floorboards. From where he was standing, near the top of the stairs, Mackillop saw the gleam from two pairs of boots, highly polished and placed side by side between bed and wardrobe. He saw magazines neatly piled beneath the bedside table and freshly ironed shirts folded symmetrically on a chair next to the bathroom door. 'You can tell the person who lives here's ex-army,' he said.

Eales seemed to find this funny. 'How come?'

'The boots.' Mackillop pointed across to them. 'The way they're arranged; the way everything's laid out. Neat, you know, and well organised.'

'It's just the way we're taught to do things.'

'It must take a lot of effort, though.'

'Not really,' Eales said. 'You do things a particular way because it makes sense. Being organised and tidy makes things simpler.'

Mackillop considered this. 'I thought about the army myself before I joined the Met. For a short while, anyway.'

'You'd've been good.'

'You reckon?'

'Chances are, if you're a good copper.'

'Getting there,' Mackillop said. He felt himself redden slightly. Looked around the room once again. 'Yeah, definitely a soldier's place ...'

Eales smiled. 'Look underneath the bed.'

Mackillop glanced across, then started to move when Eales nodded his encouragement. As he bent down, he could see that the base of the bed was actually a drawer. He pulled it out and found himself staring at a collection of military memorabilia: a dress uniform, pressed and folded; a gas mask; badges and medals displayed in open cases; bundles of photographs. And weapons: grenades, guns, knives, a highly polished bayonet ...

'Bloody hell!'

'Don't worry, the guns have been decommissioned,' Eales said. 'Firing pins removed and barrels drilled.'

Mackillop reached towards one of the pistols. 'May I?'

'Help yourself. That smaller one's a Browning nine millimetre. It's Iraqi.'

Mackillop's hand hovered above the gun. He wondered if it had once belonged to one of those soldiers he'd seen kneeling in the desert. Taken from him before another was put to the back of his head. He picked up the bayonet instead.

'That's seriously sharp, by the way.'

'I bet.' Mackillop stood and held the bayonet up in front of himself. In the skinny mirror of its blade he could see the reflection of the bathroom door, the TV and VCR, the black wire that snaked across the floor from the PlayStation to the controller.

'Nice, isn't it?' Eales said.

'This might sound morbid, and a bit ... geeky or whatever.' Mackillop turned the hilt, throwing a sliver of reflected sunlight across Eales' face. 'Has this thing ever ... killed anyone?'

Eales walked across and took the bayonet from Mackillop's hand. 'This?' he said He examined the blade as if he were seeing it for the first time, leaned forward and slid it into Mackillop's belly. 'Not until now ...'

The policeman's hands flew to the hilt, wrapped themselves tight around the soldier's; hands that were bigger and stronger and drier. He tried to push, and when he opened his mouth he produced only the gentle pop of a bubble bursting.

'You ready?' Eales asked. 'Here we go.' He nodded, counting quietly to three, before twisting the bayonet and dragging it up hard, through muscle, towards the sternum.

Mackillop sighed, then sucked the air quickly back in, as if he'd just dipped a foot into a hot bath or touched a sensitive filling.

There was only the sound of breathing for a while after that, laboured and bubbly, and the low moan of boards beneath shifting feet, as both sets of fingers grew slippery against the hilt.

'Luck always runs out in the end,' Eales said.

And he never broke eye contact, not for a moment. Holding fast to what was bright in Jason Mackillop's eyes, which seemed to blaze, just for that final second or two, before it went out. Like the last dot of life as a TV screen fades to black, shrinking quickly from a world to a pinprick.

And then nothing.

PART FOUR

FINISHED FALLING

THIRTY-FIVE

At first, he told everyone later, he thought that Mackillop had simply got tired of waiting for him and buggered off . . .

By the time Andy Stone's taxi had finally worked its way through the Saturday afternoon traffic and reached the house where Asif Mahmoud lived, the Volvo was nowhere to be seen and Jason Mackillop wasn't answering his phone. Stone had visited the ground floor flat. He'd been told by Mr Mahmoud that though he hadn't seen any police officers, he had heard comings and goings. Someone had come into the house a short time earlier, then left again fairly soon afterwards. Stone had immediately knocked at the other three flats in the building – including, of course, the one on the top floor – but had received no reply.

Confused and pissed off, he had decided to head back

to Becke House, so had made his way to the tube station. It wasn't until thirty minutes later, when he got above ground at Colindale, that the message had come through about Ryan Eales ...

'How long d'you think Stone missed him by?' Thorne asked.

Holland was pulling sheets of paper from his case. He looked up. 'Impossible to say for sure. It must have been pretty close, though. Hendricks has the time of death at somewhere between one-thirty and two-thirty ...'

'I was calling Brigstocke just after two,' Thorne said. 'We should have moved faster. *I* should have moved faster.'

When, after an hour, TDC Mackillop could still not be contacted, a team had been dispatched back to West Finchley. While the car – which was found in a side street behind Finchley Central Station – was being towed away, witnesses described seeing it parked outside the house on Rosedene Way. A woman who'd been walking her dog gave an accurate description of Mackillop, and a man who lived opposite gave a statement saying that he'd seen the driver of the car talking to someone on the street.

More officers had gathered, serious and uneasy, as the Saturday began to dim. An armed unit was called into position. Residents were evacuated and the road was sealed off, before finally – five hours after he'd driven into Rosedene Way – the door to the top flat at number forty-eight was smashed open, and Jason Mackillop was found ...

Thorne had never met the murdered trainee. He wasn't

sure whether that made it easier or not to deal with his death, but it certainly made it easier to idealise him as a victim. Thorne didn't know if Mackillop had bad breath or a foul temper; if he fancied himself or was close to his family. He'd never seen him at work, or fallen out with him, or heard him talk about anything important. Thorne knew only that he was naive, and keen, and almost ridiculously young. This *not knowing* made Jason Mackillop less real than many victims. But it didn't mean that the dirty great slab of guilt that had been laid down on top of the others, had any less weight.

'He shouldn't have gone in there on his own,' Holland said.

Thorne looked wrung out by exhaustion and anger. 'That doesn't help.'

'It's all Andy Stone's got to hold on to . . .'

It was Monday afternoon; two days since Ryan Eales had murdered Jason Mackillop and fled. Police, continuing to investigate the killings of homeless men in and around the West End, had taken a room at the London Lift to conduct interviews, including one with a rough sleeper known only as Tom.

Thorne and Holland were catching up.

'He must have got out of there in one hell of a hurry,' Holland said. 'No money in the place, but he seems to have left more or less everything else behind.'

They were in a poky, self-contained office in one corner of the bigger, open-plan admin area: a small sofa and a chair; a desk with a grimy computer and several heaps of cardboard files. The day was grey outside the frosted glass of a thin window. Thorne took the sheets as they were handed to him. 'He knew that after what he'd done it wouldn't much matter if we got hold of this stuff. And it's not like any of it gives us a *name*, is it?'

Holland passed yet more paper across: photocopies of documentation found during the search of Eales' flat. All indicated that, although Eales had killed the other three men in his tank crew, as well as Radio Bob and Terry T and the others, he'd actually been working with somebody else. Or rather, *for* somebody else . . .

The man behind the camera.

Thorne had been made aware of all this within hours of the entry into Eales' flat, but this was his first look at the material evidence. He flicked through the bank statements and credit-card slips as Holland talked.

'Half a dozen different accounts, in four different names, and he managed to empty all but one of them before he did his vanishing act. Major payments into one or other of his accounts within a few days of Jago's death, and Hadingham's "suicide". Money paid in after each killing.'

'All in cash?'

'All in cash, and completely untraceable to anybody. He was well paid for what he did.'

'He was very good at it,' Thorne said.

Holland dug out another piece of paper from his case and held it out. 'And very good at not being caught . . .'

Thorne took the sheet and began to read.

462

'I meant to tell you about this,' Holland said. 'Then, when everything kicked off on Saturday afternoon, you know, I thought it could wait.' He pointed. '*That*'s how they got away with it. Remember, we were talking about what they did with the bodies of the Iraqi soldiers? When we went to Taunton they told us about these war diaries, and at the time I didn't think it was worth chasing up, because our boys would only have been mentioned if they'd been wounded or commended . . .'

Thorne saw where it was going. 'You're shitting me . . .'

'I just double checked.'

Thorne read the words aloud. '"Callsign 40 from B-Troop, under the command of Corporal Ian Hadingham, engaged with and destroyed an enemy tank, killing all four on board . . ."'

'The Iraqi tank surrendered,' Holland said, 'or was captured or whatever. Then, after they'd shot them, Eales and the others just put the bodies back in the tank and blew the thing to shit. Whether anybody ever found out or not . . .'

'They got *commended*?' Thorne looked as though he might be close to tears of one sort or another. 'Christ on a bike . . .'

Holland was rummaging in his briefcase again. 'Something else that just came through. We finally got the transcript back from that lab in California: the techics who enhanced the sound on the video.' He passed across the sheaf of papers, and closed his case.

Thorne took what was handed to him without really looking at it and placed it on the desk with the rest of the paperwork. He groped for the swivel chair behind him and slid clumsily on to it. 'Another couple of loose ends tied up. It's all good, I suppose . . . '

'None of it gets us anywhere, though. Right?'

The silence that hung between them for the next few seconds was answer enough.

'So what's happening indoors?'

'Everyone's busy,' Holland said. 'Fired up, like you'd expect, you know, but . . . '

'Aimless,' Thorne said.

'The Intel unit's digging around. Hoping that the paper trail might throw up an address or something. Somewhere Eales might hole up.'

Thorne was dismissive. 'He's long gone.'

And Holland didn't argue. He suspected that the brass had already taken the decision to scale down surveillance at all ports and airports.

The fact was that Mackillop's death and Eales' flight had torn the guts out of the investigation, and everyone knew it. It might, in other circumstances, have been what united the team and drove it on with renewed vigour, but this was more coffin-nail than spur. Though they wanted Eales more badly than ever, they had to accept that, for the time being at least, they weren't likely to find him. And, despite what they now knew, there was little chance, without Eales, of ever catching the man who'd bankrolled at least half a dozen killings over a year or more. Overstretched budgets were always important factors, as were limited resources and time constraints, but once a team lost the *appetite* for it, everything else became secondary.

'What did Brigstocke say?' Holland asked. He had a pretty good idea, of course, and wondered if he was over-stepping the mark by asking. But he guessed correctly that Thorne had long since forgotten, or stopped caring, where such marks were.

'He was "officially" telling me that the undercover operation was to be wound down. That I should go home and have a bath . . . '

Thorne was obviously making light of it, but Holland wasn't sure whether to smile or not. 'When?'

'I'll stay out another night, I think.'

'OK . . . '

'There's a few people I need to say goodbye to.'

'Then what?'

'Then a decent curry, a good night's sleep, probably a very pissed-off cat . . . '

'That's not what I meant,' Holland said.

Thorne smiled. 'I know it isn't.'

Brigstocke had called the evening before, when the dust kicked up by Mackillop's murder had begun to settle. He'd made it clear that he was brooking no argument as far as pulling Thorne off the street was concerned, so Thorne didn't waste any time by initiating one. Eales had gone. There would be no more killings. There was no longer any point. When it came to exactly what Thorne would be returning to, Brigstocke was a little less dogmatic. It may just have been that the decision

465

had yet to be taken, but it was equally likely that Brigstocke had simply fought shy of delivering one blow on top of another.

As things stood, if it *was* to be a continuance of his gardening leave, Thorne would give in to it without much of a fuss. The thought of going back to the team, back to how things had been before, unnerved him. He felt as though he'd lost his way during some long-distance endurance event; as if he were staggering, miles off the pace, in the wrong direction. He couldn't do anything else until he'd completed the course, however laughable his finishing time was. He knew he couldn't really compete, but he needed to cross the line . . .

'"I don't know" is the simple answer,' Thorne said. 'I don't know what *they* want. I don't really know what *I* want.'

Holland filled the pause that followed by reaching for his coat. 'Do you think Eales spoke to whoever's paying him before he left? Warned him?'

'Maybe, but I don't think he had a great deal to warn him about.' Thorne gestured towards the papers on the desk. 'There's nothing there that incriminates anybody. I think Eales knows how to keep his mouth shut. How to keep secrets.'

'Probably a good idea. Considering how many people died because one greedy fucker couldn't.'

Thorne eased his chair round slowly, one way and then the other. 'We set so much store in trying to get hold of Eales, thinking that he'd tell us the name of the man behind the camera. I'm not actually sure it would have done us any good.'

'You don't think he'd have given him up?'

'Eales is still a soldier,' Thorne said. 'Name, rank and serial number, right?'

Holland picked up his case and crossed to the door. 'Are you sticking around here for a bit? I need to get back ...'

Thorne grunted; he didn't look like he was ready to go anywhere.

Holland recalled walking through the café on his way up and seeing the addict Thorne had been spending so much time with. The boy had been sitting with his girlfriend, whose name Holland had never learned. Holland thought about what Thorne had said earlier; wondered how difficult he might find it to say some of those goodbyes. 'Your mate Spike's downstairs ...'

Thorne nodded, like he already knew. 'We're supposed to be playing pool.'

'We can have a game some time, if you want,' Holland said. He hovered at the doorway. 'Later in the week, maybe. That pub round the corner from your place has got a table, hasn't it?'

'I'll give you a call, Dave,' Thorne said. 'When I've got myself sorted.'

He sat for a few minutes after Holland had left and let his mind drift. Sadly, however hard he tried, it wouldn't drift quite far enough.

For want of anything else to do, he reached for the

467

documents scattered across the desk and began to thumb through them. It always came down to paper in the end. Filed and boxed up in the General Registry. And it felt as though this case was heading that way pretty bloody quickly; not cold exactly, but as good as. The case, such as it was, would be handed over to the Homicide Task Force, or perhaps the brand-new, FBI-style Serious and Organised Crime Association. These were the pro-active units responsible for tracking down and charging prime suspects who had gone missing. Thorne felt fairly sure that Eales was already abroad; that he would not make himself easy to find. The world was becoming smaller all the time, but it was still plenty big enough.

He stared down at the bank statements; at the payments, each one representing a man Ryan Eales had killed. He looked at the amounts and was unable to stop a part of his brain making the perverse calculations: fifteen hundred pounds per kick delivered; something like that ...

He thought back to the case he'd been working on the previous spring: to the hunt for another man who'd chosen murder as his profession; book-ended by two fires, twenty years apart. A young girl dead, and an old man. Now, here was Thorne, sitting in the old man's coat and gnawing at the decisions he'd taken. At the series of judge-ments, considered and otherwise; from one burning to another.

He pulled the Gulf War transcript to the front and glanced down at it. The printed dialogue and descriptions were horribly effective prompts. His mind called up the associated images from the videotape in an instant as he read: the groupings of the men, and the rain striking the sand like black candle-wax, and luminous horror like a cat's-eye in the darkness.

A soldier waving papers taken from the Iraqi prisoners. No sign of what was to come. *'We are keeping these.'* (LOUDER) *'Do you understand?'*

While decisions – including that which would determine his own future – were being made, Thorne wondered if the Met had taken one to hand the tape over to the army. He wondered too, in spite of all the bickering between the Met and the RMP that would surely follow, if the army themselves would be very surprised. Had Eales and his fellow-crewmen effectively covered their tracks in 1991?

'Where d'you get it?'

'Say again?'

(LOUDER) *'Where d'you get it?'*

'This?' (SOLDIER HOLDS UP BACON STRIPS). *'I brought it with me.'*

Or was that commendation in the war diary little more than an exercise in sweeping shit under the carpet?

'That reminds me, I could kill a fry-up ...'

'That stuff fucking stinks, Ian ...'

Thorne read the next line ...

And stared, breathless, at the page. At five words, spoken out of vision. A phrase that told him everything.

He knew who the man behind the camera was.

Thorne shut his eyes and pressed himself back in the chair, thrown by the excitement and the terror of being suddenly and completely without doubt. It was a sensation he'd almost forgotten: the sickness and the surge of *knowing*.

Then, quick and painful as a low punch, Thorne knew something else: that the man who had paid Ryan Eales to commit murder would walk away from it as surely as Eales himself had so far managed to do. Certain as he was of the man's identity, and of what he had done, Thorne knew that there was no way on God's earth that he could prove it.

Five minutes, perhaps ten, passed as Thorne weighed it up.

He stared into the thought, into the white-hot heart of it, until at last he began to make a few decisions. Each would be dependent on the decisions of others, but as Thorne stood and gathered his things together, he felt as energised as he had in a long while. He might yet fail to cross it, but now at least he had a bloody good idea where the finishing line was.

He came out of the office and descended quickly towards the lower-ground floor. If Spike was still there, the two of them could chat while they played pool. They would have plenty to talk about.

Thorne had decided that if he was going to get off the streets, he needed to come clean ... in every possible sense. He was going to tell Spike everything.

THIRTY-SIX

He heard the man coming long before he saw him.

The footsteps sounded hesitant; he could recognise the tread of someone unfamiliar within the network of the tunnels from a mile away. He'd heard such echoes many times before: the click-clack of heels slowing, then speeding up again as confidence comes and goes; the scrape of a leather sole against the concrete as the wearer turns to get their bearings, or decides in which direction to proceed. Or whether to proceed at all ...

When he finally saw the man rounding the corner, Spike stood. He leaned back against the wall and waited; tried to look unconcerned as the distance between the two of them shortened, as the man moved towards him through puddles of water and deeper pools of shadow.

'Am I in the right place?' the man said. Still twenty feet or more away.

The fear would have killed any strength in his voice anyway, but with the sound moving effortlessly, as it did through the air underground, Spike had no need to speak much above a whisper. 'Depends,' he said, 'on if you've got shitloads of cash in one of those pockets ... '

When the man stopped, it was three or four arms' lengths away from Spike. He looked around quickly. Took in his immediate surroundings. 'This is nice,' he said.

Spike said nothing.

The man nodded towards the large cardboard box behind, and to Spike's right, against the wall. 'That where you sleep?'

'It's a lot better than some places,' Spike said.

The corners of the man's mouth turned up, but it could hardly have been called a smile. 'Tell me how you got the tape.' It seemed that the small talk was at an end.

'I told you when I called ... '

'You told me fuck all,' the man said. 'You talked a lot of crap and I've had a few days to think about it since then.'

'What's the matter? Don't you want it? That's fine with me, like. Only you seemed keen enough on the phone ... '

'Tell me.'

It was never really silent down in the subways. There was always the muffled roar of the traffic overhead, the buzz of the striplights, the eerie beat of dripping water. These were the only sounds for several seconds.

Spike rubbed his hands across his face. Through his hair. 'What d'you want me to say?' His voice was hoarse;

cracked with nerves and desire. 'You want me to tell you I'm a fucked-up junkie? Do anything to score? Desperate enough for money to shit on a mate?'

'Now you're starting to persuade me,' the man said.

'Thorne told me he was a copper, like. That he'd been working undercover because of these murders. He told me about the case, about why everyone had been killed.'

The man didn't blink.

'He talked about everything,' Spike said. 'What happened all them years ago in the fucking desert. He told me who you were and he told me about the tape.'

'Why?'

Spike shrugged. 'Fuck knows. Because it was his last night, I suppose, and the stupid bastard thought it didn't matter. He said that the bloke who did the actual killing had legged it and there wasn't anything else anyone could do ...'

The man thrust his hands into the pocket of a long leather coat and pressed his arms close to his body. It was getting very cold in the early hours. 'So, you just sat there, took all that in, and saw an easy way to make a few quid?'

'More than a few, mate ...'

'Don't try to be clever.' It was a simple directive. Spoken quietly, and with the cold confidence that comes from being used to having such instructions followed.

'Look ... I was fucked off with him,' Spike said. 'For bullshitting me all that time. For making me and my girlfriend and all the rest of us look like idiots. It was a good way to get my own back.'

473

The man looked unconvinced. 'It was a good way to make some money.'

'Yeah, all right. Course it was. Obviously, after what he told me, I knew that the tape was valuable. That you'd probably pay a fair bit to get it back. When he said he had the tape *on* him, I started to think about it, you know? I was thinking about a shedload of smack and that. And a flat for me and my girlfriend.' Spike grinned, bounced a fist against his leg, as he thought about those things again. 'She wants us to get a place together, you know?'

'You just took it?'

'When he was asleep, I grabbed his stuff and fucked off. I know he's looking for me, but I'm pretty good at keeping out of people's way, you know?'

'He said this was the only copy?'

Spike widened his eyes. 'Thorne's fucking mental. I told you. I reckon being on the street has made him go funny, made him see things a bit twisted, like. He more or less nicked it, from what he was saying. Got some other copper he knew to hand it over to him on the quiet.'

'Why would he do that?'

'Don't ask me. He was ranting about showing it to somebody. About using it for something.'

The man seemed to think about this.

'Listen,' Spike said. 'I don't really want to know about any of it, all right? Like you said, I'm just doing this for the money.'

'Now, that I *do* understand,' the man said. 'It's what started all this in the first place.'

Spike lifted a sleeve and rubbed the sweat away. 'Starts everything, mate. Only some of us need it a bit more than others ...'

The man peered at Spike with curiosity and disgust, as though the wreckage of an accident had been taken away and he was staring at a bloodstain on the road. 'My good fortune in this case,' he said.

Spike reached into the inside pocket of his jacket, pulled out a plastic carrier bag and wrapped it around whatever was inside. 'Tape's in here,' he said.

The man made no move to take it. 'You know that if you're fucking me about I'll find you,' he said. 'However good you think you are at keeping out of people's way. I'll *pay* someone to find you.'

'Thorne told me what's on here.' Spike shook the package. The tape rattled inside. 'I haven't watched it, but I know what you did. I know what happened back then, and what happened later on with cars and tablets and with army boots, so I know what you're capable of.' He looked across at the man and held his stare. 'I'm a junkie, and a liar, and a fucking thief. But I'm not stupid ...'

The man seemed impressed by this. When his hand came out of his pocket it was holding a bulging, brown A3 envelope.

'How do we do this, then?' Spike held out the plastic bag at arm's length. It shook in his hand. He dropped the arm and took a breath; tried to sound casual. 'You want me to chuck it over or what?'

The man stepped forward suddenly, and kept coming

as Spike moved backwards, away from him. When Spike was against the wall, the man gently lifted the package from his hand. Six inches taller than Spike, he looked down and pressed the envelope against the boy's chest. 'Quite a bit in here,' he said. 'Quite a lot of shit to put in your arm ... '

The man's eyes swivelled in an instant to the cardboard box and at the same moment he took a step back. At the sudden noise; at the movement ...

A week before, back at the Lift, when they'd been playing pool and talking about how it might work, this had been the moment that had caused Spike to laugh out loud. Back before Thorne had gone to Brigstocke or Brigstocke to Jesmond. Before Jesmond had gone higher to wherever the buck stopped. This had been what they'd called the 'rat' moment.

'He'll probably think it's a rat,' Spike had said. 'A fucking big one, like. He'll probably shit himself ... '

The man's reaction when Thorne appeared from inside the box – sitting and then standing up in one smooth movement – was less dramatic than Spike had predicted, but Thorne could certainly see that he'd sprung a powerful surprise. 'I'm guessing those football tickets are out of the question now,' he said.

THIRTY-SEVEN

Alan Ward nudged his glasses, then reached to grab a handful of hair at the back of his head, as if that might be the only way to stop himself shaking it. He'd carried on moving backwards as the sides and lid of the box had burst outwards and upwards, and now he stared at Thorne and Spike across the eight or so feet that separated one wall of the tunnel from the other.

Thorne glanced to his left. 'All right?'

Spike nodded, without taking his eyes off Ward.

'This is ... interesting,' Ward said, finally. He looked both ways along the length of the tunnel.

'No point in going anywhere,' Thorne said.

'Because ... ?'

'Because there are police officers at every exit. Why did you think it was so quiet down here tonight?'

'Stupid bastard,' Spike said.

The slow shake of Ward's head became a nod of acceptance, and, as Thorne watched, an excitement of sorts came into the journalist's eyes. Though he was clearly anxious – the muscles in his face and neck singing with it – there was also a calmness in his voice and in his manner, as though he were somehow relaxed by the tension.

He glared at Spike. 'That little fucker wired up, is he?'

Spike just smiled.

'Or have you got something set up in the box?'

Thorne nodded up at the roof of the tunnel, towards one of the small, metal PA speakers that was now more or less directly above Ward's head. 'The mike's in there,' he said. 'And the camera. Seemed appropriate to get it all on film as well.'

'You haven't got *anything*.'

'You know we've got plenty . . . '

Ward cocked his head as if he were weighing it up. Then he casually dropped the package he was carrying to the ground and began to stamp on it. The noise, as the tape's plastic housing first cracked and then shattered, echoed back along the tunnel from left and right.

Thorne waited for a couple of seconds. 'Well done,' he said. 'You've just stomped the shit out of a Jim Carrey movie.'

'I don't believe you . . . '

'Not that we couldn't have tied you to these latest killings without the tape anyway, but did you really think we'd only have *one copy*?'

Ward turned angrily to Spike.

'Since when do junkies tell the truth?' Spike asked.

Ward's unsettling calmness had all but vanished now. Thorne was aware only of the adrenaline, of a *readiness*, in the man opposite him. And something else at the furthest edge of the rush: Ward's barely concealed fury at the hopelessness of his situation.

There was nothing practical to be gained by it, but still there were many reasons why Thorne felt the need to push and to bait. To glory, and to let Ward *see him* glory at his impotence.

'So, lucky or unlucky, then?' Thorne said. 'The day you came across that tank crew. What d'you reckon, Alan?'

Ward seemed to find the question funny. Asked one in return: 'For me or those Iraqis?'

Thorne answered with a look.

'Lucky for me, definitely,' Ward said. 'Very lucky. And you can make your own luck up to a point, but it's what you do with it that makes the difference.'

'What were you doing there?' Thorne asked.

'I was driving around, monitoring radio transmissions, and I heard Callsign 40 radio through that they'd thrown a track.' Ward leaned back against the wall and looked hard at Thorne. This wasn't reminiscence. It was education. 'I heard REME telling them that the engineers couldn't get out there for a couple of hours, and I was near by, so I thought I'd head across and see what was happening. By the time I'd got there the men in the Iraqi tank had just driven up and surrendered. Popped their lids waving fucking white flags . . .'

'Very stupid of them.'

'See, I had my nice bit of luck right there, and ordinarily that's all it would have been. If all I'd wanted was to point my little camera and watch a few of our boys capturing a few of theirs, that would have been handy. But it was much more than that. Because I wanted *much more* than some boring bit of footage that might or might not have given me a bit of clout next time I was negotiating a pay rise.'

'So you ... *encouraged* them.'

Ward was still, and focused, his eyes unblinking in the artificial light. When he spoke, it was clear to Thorne that what he said was deeply felt. The frigidity and scorn for life that Thorne knew to be at the core of this man were belied by the twisted passion of the words.

'Have you ever thought you were about to die?' Ward asked. 'Or even that you were about to be the one to take a life? Have you ever really experienced that sort of excitement?'

Thorne had little intention of answering, and Ward had even less of giving him the opportunity.

'I suppose, because of what you do, that you've felt it more keenly than most, and let me say straight away that I admire what you do. Really. Perhaps you *have* been in the sort of situation I describe, but can you even begin to imagine feeling those things for days, for weeks, on end? Constantly. Can you imagine it becoming something that you *live with*?' He flicked his eyes to Spike, spat the words out at him. 'That ... *heightened* feeling in the body becomes something that's more powerful than any drug. And when you come down from it, you fall a very long way and you fall very hard.'

'What the fuck do you know about it?' Spike said.

Ward just smiled and turned his attention back to Thorne. 'Those boys were trained for it ... And they *were* boys, emotionally at any rate. They were taught to expect it, whipped up into a state every day until, eventually, not seeing combat became far worse than seeing it. They needed the high, can you understand that? They were sent over there to do a job and then some of them didn't get a chance to do it. There were lads out there turning on each other. Shooting fucking camels. Anything to get *close* to that buzz.'

'You wanted it too, though, didn't you?'

Ward's eyes widened. 'I was ... frustrated, yes,' he said. 'And me and that situation were just fucking perfect for each other. They thought it was about to happen, Hadingham and Eales and the others. They'd been told that the enemy was close, that there was every chance of engaging at any fucking moment. Then the machine lets them down and they can do nothing but watch their mates disappear into the distance. Feel that buzz disappear with them.'

'What did you do?'

'I hardly had to *do* anything,' Ward said. 'I was the catalyst, if you like; that's all. They just needed someone to give them a nudge in the right direction, to tell them that what they were thinking about doing, what they *wanted* to do, was absolutely understandable. That it was all right.' His voice had become quieter, more intense, and when he paused there was a rattle in his breath. He nodded towards the plastic bag at Thorne's feet, to the remains of the video inside. 'I don't know what you think you've seen on the tape, but I promise you that even the ones that weren't so keen to begin with, the ones that needed a bit of persuading, they got the biggest thrill of their lives that day. Ryan Eales, for one, spent the rest of his life trying to recapture it.'

'By killing for you?'

'For me, among others. He was a professional.'

'Usually . . . '

Ward nodded his agreement. 'Yes, you're quite right, of course. Usually.'

Thorne could sense Spike bristling next to him.

'He did rather fuck things up,' Ward said. 'When it came to getting *you* out of the picture . . . '

Now this *was* practical. This was not about poking at the corpse of the case for personal gratification. This was something Thorne very much wanted to know.

'How did you get my name?' he asked.

Ward stared back at him.

'Like that then, is it?' Thorne said. 'No names, no pack drill. Right?'

Thorne watched, enjoying it, as realisation passed like a shadow across the face of the man opposite him.

No names, no pack drill.

The five words that Thorne had read on the transcript

of the videotape. The same phrase that Ward had used when they'd spoken on the phone.

That had told Thorne all he needed to know.

'How did you get my name?' Thorne asked again.

Ward said nothing, but in the smirk that transformed his features, Thorne suddenly saw *exactly* where the man standing opposite him had got his name. The source of the leak became obvious. Thorne filed the information away. He would deal with it when he had the chance.

Spike's reaction to Ward's knowing smile was altogether different, and more dramatic. He pushed himself away from the wall, the growled mutterings turning to something almost feral as he launched himself across the width of the tunnel.

It all happened before Thorne had the chance to do much more than cry out: '*Spike* . . .'

Spike was off-balance and throwing punches before he'd even reached his target, and by the time his hands, and Ward's, had stopped moving, the two were locked clumsily together, side on to the tunnel-wall.

And there was a knife at Spike's throat.

Now Thorne could see real desperation, real danger in Ward's eyes. His situation was hopeless, so there was little else for Ward to lose. Thorne knew that moments such as these were when lives were most easily, and most pointlessly, lost.

'You know you have to put that down,' Thorne said. His eyes never left the blade.

He watched it pressing against Spike's neck and

wondered if Ward was thinking about what lay ahead; about slaughtering a boy who meant less than nothing and seizing this one last chance to feel that buzz.

'I can't see that I have to do anything.'

'Let me just get some officers in right now and they can take you out of here without any more fuss or any fucking about. Fair enough? Alan?' Thorne took a tentative half-step towards them. 'You know that's the clever thing to do, right?'

But Ward was not the next one to speak . . .

As Spike began to talk, Thorne became aware of the one element in the bizarre tableau facing him that he had not taken in. The most crucial detail. Down at his side, poised delicately in his right hand, Spike was holding a blood-filled syringe.

'*I've always got a weapon!*' Thorne had presumed Spike had been talking about a knife . . .

Spike eased the flap of the long, leather coat aside and brushed the tip of the needle against Ward's thigh. Scraped it across the material of the trousers. 'This'll go deep into your muscle every bit as quick as you can move that knife, like.' Spike's mouth was pressed close to Ward's cheek as he spoke. 'I don't give a fuck, really. It's completely up to you, mate. Do you want dirty, junkie blood running around in there? Mucking you up inside? How much of a fucking *buzz* would that be?'

With Ward's focus now down to where he could feel the needle, Thorne inched closer. 'Get rid of the knife and we can sort this out.'

'Do you want AIDS?' Spike whispered.

'For Christ's sake, take it easy,' Thorne said. 'Both of you.'

'How d'you fancy that?'

'Shut up, Spike ...'

Without moving the knife, Ward leaned his head as far away as he was able from Spike's. 'Please. Keep still ...'

'I think that should be exciting enough for you,' Spike said. 'And it'll certainly be something you'll live with every day. Though not for very long, like.'

'Don't ...'

'What? Don't 'cause you'll kill me if I do? Or don't 'cause you're shitting yourself?'

'Drop the knife and let me bring officers in here,' Thorne shouted.

'Bring 'em in now. You can bring 'em in right now and he'll do fuck all.' Spike was gabbling, loud and high pitched; his eyes fixed on Ward, rattling out the words on fractured breaths. 'He'll do jack shit, I swear, whatever happens, because he's fucking terrified. Because he's a coward. He's a fucking coward who lets someone else clear up his mess, who pays somebody to kick men to death when they're asleep. He'll do nothing because he's all talk. Because he wants the high, but he hasn't got the bottle to do what it takes to get it. I've met his sort loads of times, like. They love to be around it, they fucking love the idea of it, but when it comes to shooting up, they're afraid of the needle. They're shit scared of it. Like he's afraid of *this* one. So bring the others in. He'll do nothing.'

Spike leaned in to Ward, yelled up into his face. '*Bring them in!*'

Within a few moments of the echo dying, Thorne had made his decision. He knew that they'd be hanging on every word. That, were it not for the layout of the tunnels, which made it impossible to get close without being seen, they would have been all over Ward already. He knew that there'd be armed officers standing by. That nobody would need asking twice ...

He looked up at the speaker and gave the order, not needing to raise his voice very much. 'Get down here ...'

Immediately there were distant voices raised, then footsteps, and Thorne turned to see Holland, Stone and half a dozen other officers tearing along the tunnel towards them. They shouted as they ran. Making sure Ward knew they were there, telling him to drop the knife and lie down on the floor.

Ward did exactly as he was told, as Spike had predicted he would. He dropped the knife and threw himself to the floor the instant that Spike stepped away from him. But almost as soon as his face hit the concrete, Spike was on him again, flipping him over, kneeling across his chest and holding the tip of the needle an inch from his eye.

Thorne shouted Spike's name.

Holland bellowed a warning.

The rest of the team were no more than thirty feet away, and approaching fast ...

It was a toss up as to whether Thorne or one of the others would get there first, but before any of them had a chance, Spike had fired a fine jet of blood into Ward's eyes, and, with the smallest movement of his wrist, directed it down, across Ward's lips and into the mouth that had opened to scream.

'That's for Terry,' he said. 'For Bob and all the rest . . . '

The second Spike had tossed the syringe and begun to move, Ward was seized and turned back on to his belly. An officer ran around and made a grab for Spike, but Thorne stepped quickly across and ushered the boy away. Led him down the tunnel and pressed him hard into the wall. 'Jesus . . . What d'you think you're doing?'

Spike said nothing. Regaining his breath, looking back down the tunnel to where Ward was being pulled to his feet. His hands cuffed behind him. Unable to wipe away the blood that was running down his face and chin.

Thorne was looking, too. He nodded towards Ward. 'What you threatened him with . . . Are you—?'

'Course I'm fucking not,' Spike said. 'We get tested every month, me *and* Caroline. But *he* doesn't know that, does he?'

Thorne watched, listened as Ward begged the officers around him for a tissue, a rag, a scrap of paper. *Anything*. 'Not unless somebody tells him,' he said.

Spike was calm again.

That grin.

'We've been scared to death for weeks. Now it's his turn to see what that's like. Let the bastard sweat for a while . . . '

THIRTY-EIGHT

If the sea down below him wasn't quite as smooth as glass, it was still blue. It sounded good, like a *hush*, and the sun was hot and Ryan Eales was happy enough. He lay and soaked it all in. Feeling, for the third or fourth day on the trot, that he was finally starting to get his breath back. It was a fortnight since he'd been forced to cut and run, which was longer than it would normally have taken him to recover and relax, but then it had been a kick-bollock-scramble.

Cut and run . . .

He'd had to think *so* fast when he'd come strolling up and seen the car outside the house, and right until the moment when he'd pictured the bayonet under the bed and had the idea, he hadn't been sure if admitting who he was and bringing him inside had been the cleverest decision of his life or the most stupid. Even when it was done, when the copper had slid back off the blade, he'd known that the other one was on his way. That he had to move double bloody quick.

It had taken him only minutes to get packed up and out of there, and he was proud of the way he'd done it: moving through the place at speed, but taking everything in; taking a mental inventory as he'd walked around the bedroom, gathering up only what was essential. Passports and papers; a few clothes and all the cash. As long as he had money, he was always able to pick up the pieces.

It hadn't been the first thing he'd done, of course. He'd realised straight away that he needed to get the car out of sight; how important it would be in buying him a little time. He'd dug around in the copper's pocket for the keys; dropped the Volvo off in a side street and walked back to the flat. He'd still been in there getting his things together when the second copper had come knocking. He'd frozen then; crept to the front door and stood there until he'd heard the footsteps going back down the stairs.

'Be careful with that . . . '

A family with small children was arranged on the other side of the pool. He heard a ball bouncing towards him and the feet of one of the kids slapping on the tiles as he ran to retrieve it. Eales raised his head, reached for the ball and threw it back. The boy smiled at him. Said, 'Thank you,' when prompted by his mother.

'You're very welcome,' Eales said.

Definitely starting to relax . . .

He felt a tickle, and looked to see sweat rolling across the indigo letters on his shoulder. He thought, as he did often – as he did long before Ward had contacted him with the offer of a job – of the other three men whose bodies bore the same design. They could not have known, on the drunken evening they'd all stumbled into that tattoo parlour and gone under the needle, anaesthetised by strong German lager, how bound to one another they were destined to become.

They would live and die as a crew.

All those years before in the desert, there'd been a couple who hadn't wanted things to go as far as they ultimately had. But it never mattered. It was ironic really, he reckoned, and maybe even a bit sad, because the ones who didn't fire a shot that day ended up paying the same price anyway, thanks to one person being stupid and greedy.

It just proved, he thought, how some decisions were best taken for you by others ...

Ryan Eales lay back down and tried to sleep.

A white spot – the retinal memory of the sun, high above him – darted behind his lids like a tracer bullet; like the point of light he'd seen two weeks earlier in the police officer's eyes, bright before shrinking.

He rolled his eyeballs, and watched as the pinprick danced across the black.

The lift carried him up towards the top floor of Colindale police station. The CID and the Burglary Squad were on the first floor, the Criminal Justice Unit and CPS offices on the second, but Thorne was heading for none of these.

He let the empty cardboard box he was carrying bounce off his knee; pictured Spike slapping out a rhythm against his legs or drumming his fingers on a tabletop in McDonald's ...

Though it was far from official policy of any sort, Thorne had persuaded Brigstocke to dig up some money for Spike. There was a fund to pay informants, to cover the expenses of those who gave their time to help police operations, so it seemed reasonable to reward Spike for his efforts. He'd certainly earned it in that subway.

There had, of course, been the business with the blood, and once the scene in the tunnel had been cleared, it had required a major effort to keep Spike from being arrested. Thorne had worked hard to convince the team that Spike had been provoked, while at the same time admitting that the boy *had* exceeded the boundaries that had been laid down ...

'I can't think where he gets *that* from,' Brigstocke had said.

It was hardly a fortune, but the money Thorne had wangled might pay for the deposit and first month's rent on a flat. He wasn't naive enough to believe that it would stop Spike feeling guilty about his sister's death, or help get Caroline's son back, and he was even less starry-eyed after a lesson from someone who knew how it worked far better than he did.

'It's a big step,' Maxwell had said. 'People can go from sleeping rough to getting their own flat and fuck it up straight away. They invite all their mates round for parties, let junkies and boozers trash the place, find themselves chucked back out on the street within a few weeks.'

Thorne could do no more than hope that Spike and One-Day Caroline got their big American fridge, and held on to it for a little while longer than that.

The lift doors opened and a man in a sharp grey suit stood aside to let Thorne and his cardboard box out.

The office was near the end of the carpeted corridor, and Thorne didn't bother to knock.

'Thorne . . . '

Though this was Steve Norman's only word on looking up from his desk, his face said an awful lot more: expletives mostly; the sort people blurted out when they were particularly worried.

Thorne walked towards the desk, tossing the empty cardboard box at Norman from several feet away.

Norman stood up, fumbling clumsily for the box as it knocked a photo-frame and pen set flying. 'What the hell d'you think you're doing?'

'That should be big enough,' Thorne said. 'And it's strictly for personal items only. I don't want to see any Metropolitan Police Press Office staplers going in there, all right?'

'I don't know what it is you want, but—'

'I want you to hurry up. You can write your resignation letter later on.'

Norman shook his head, squeezed out half a very thin smile. 'I'd heard rumours,' he said. 'People were saying you'd lost it.'

Thorne moved towards him quickly enough to make Norman take a step back and find himself against the wall.

'Alan Ward hasn't really started talking,' Thorne said. 'Not about *some* things, anyway. I reckon it's probably just because he hasn't been asked the right questions yet. What do you think?'

Norman looked like he was thinking about a lot of things, but he said nothing.

'I mean, obviously, they want to put the murder investigation to bed first.' Thorne leaned against the wall, his face a foot or so away and level with Norman's. 'That's fair enough, wouldn't you say? It's understandable if inquiries as to where Ward may have got certain bits of information from aren't exactly top of the list. There's even a chance that they might *never* come up . . .'

'Are you trying to threaten me?'

'*Trying?*'

'I wish you'd get on with it . . .'

Thorne's eyes flicked to the cardboard box and then back to Norman. 'Empty your fucking desk . . .'

Norman looked over to where a pattern of coloured rings was snaking its way across his computer screen, then down at his highly polished brogues for a few seconds. He sighed, irritated, as though the whole affair were some trifling inconvenience, then stepped forward and began throwing open drawers.

Thorne walked across to the window and took in the view across the RAF Museum to the M1 beyond. He spoke to Norman without turning round. 'If I thought you'd done it for money, you'd be the one going in a box, do you understand? But I think you were just trying to impress him.' He pointed out of the window. 'I could see that when I met the pair of you in the car park down there. You were like a kid who doesn't have many friends, making sure everybody knows you've got a new best mate. I'm guessing that after you'd leaked the story about there being an undercover copper out there, Ward came to you sniffing around for more information. Trying to find out exactly how much you knew. So you thought you'd show off a little ...'

'I thought he was after a story,' Norman said. 'That's all. I thought he was angling for an exclusive. I couldn't have known what he really wanted, for Christ's sake ...'

'He probably flattered you, right? Told you what a valuable source you were; said that the two of you worked well together. Made you think you were important. Gave you a hard-on, right?'

'He said he'd do nothing with it until after it had all come out ...'

'So you gave him my *name*?'

Thorne saw the movement in the glass: a small nod.

'It was only to be used as part of a bigger story, once the investigation had been completed. Look, I fucked up, fair enough? Thorne ...?'

Thorne turned, pointed to the files that Norman had taken from the drawers and dropped on to the desk. 'Into the box. You've got five minutes.'

Norman did as he was told.

'I suppose I should be grateful that you fucking up didn't get me killed. It was my good luck that it wasn't me who got kicked to death. Very bad luck for you though, because now I'm still here to make sure you answer for the man who *was* killed.'

'Terry Turner.'

'Knowing his name won't convince me that you give a shit ...'

Norman started to move faster, his face for the first time betraying the fear that Thorne might actually do something physical. He used the edge of his hand to drag pens and paper-clips from the desktop into the box, then paused to look up. 'You were wrong about one thing,' he said. 'It wasn't me who went to the papers with the under-cover story in the first place. I can't make those decisions; you know that. It came from higher up, from an officer on your side of things ...'

Thorne knew Norman was telling the truth. It made sense. There would have been those who believed, once Thorne himself had been arrested and shot his mouth off, that the operation had been fatally compromised. That one more leak couldn't hurt.

'There was a lot of criticism,' Norman said. 'A hell of a lot of pressure. The body count was going up and it looked like we were getting nowhere. Someone decided it would be a good idea to let people know that the Met was actually *doing* something.'

Someone decided.

Jesmond ...

Thorne turned back to the window, saw the mid-October afternoon turn a little brighter, and decided after a minute or two that he wanted to get out and enjoy some of it. At the door he turned and watched as Norman dropped the photo-frame and pen set into the box and sat down heavily in his chair.

'This might well be it,' Thorne said. 'I haven't really made my mind up. I might leave things as they are. Then again, I might go official with it if I wake up tomorrow in a pissy mood. We'll have to see how I feel, Steve. There's always a chance that I might decide to wait a while, a few weeks or a couple of months say, then turn up unannounced one night. Just pop by, somewhere you aren't expecting me, with a lump hammer or a cricket bat. See how you're getting on . . .'

He didn't wait around for Norman's reaction. He walked back down the corridor, thinking about what Spike had said in the tunnel.

'Let the bastard sweat for a while . . .'

Thorne stared at himself, blurry and distorted in the dull metal of the lift doors. The beard was gone. Not just the extra growth from his days on the streets, but the whole thing, revealing the straight, white scar that ran across his chin. His hair was shorter than it had been in a long time. He'd lost a little weight, too, he thought.

He'd had his old man's overcoat dry-cleaned, which had got rid of the smells he'd *wanted* rid of. And though he'd normally have preferred something a little shorter, and perhaps not as heavy, he thought it looked pretty good. They reckoned there was a cold snap on the way, so he guessed he might have to wear it a good deal from now on, and probably right through the winter. He'd need it most days, like as not.

It would go back in the wardrobe after that, as soon as the weather picked up. He'd hang it up, then maybe look at it again next time the temperature dropped; think about bringing it out next year. It wasn't really his style, after all. But he'd wait and see how he felt.

He'd wait and see how he felt about a lot of things ...

The lift stopped at the first floor and an officer Thorne recognised got in. They'd worked together five, maybe seven, years before, on a case he could barely remember.

The man looked pleased to see him. Nodded as he reached for the button, then turned with a smile as the doors closed.

'Tom. You look well ...'

ACKNOWLEDGEMENTS

I began work on this book in September 2003, eight months before the publication of certain photographs, the sacking of a Fleet Street editor and the scandal surrounding the treatment of Iraqi prisoners by US soldiers. Truth is not always stranger than fiction, but sometimes it's pretty bloody close ...

Current research by organisations such as Crisis and the Ex-Services Action Group suggests that between one in three and one in five homeless people have spent some time in the Armed Forces. The most recent study revealed that up to 30% of those in hostels, day-centres and soup runs and 22% of homeless people surveyed in London on a single night, were ex-services. Despite the best efforts of those working on behalf of the homeless community and the increased awareness and activity of the services themselves, there is little to suggest that these figures are much different today.

499

There are, of course, many people without whom this book could never have been written. Without whose time, trouble, expertise and good advice it would have been *lifeless* ...

Terry Walker, Gulf War veteran and author of *The Mother Of All Battles* – ISBN 190416610–5; Rick Brunwen of the Ex-Service Action Group (ESAG); Sinead Hanks and Scott Ballantyne, co-authors of *Lest We Forget*, the Crisis report into ex-servicemen and homelessness. Above all, I want to thank Neil and Anna and the young people on the street who were willing to speak to me.

From the British Army I am hugely grateful to: Simon Saunders and Lt Col Peter Dick-Peter at G3 Media Operations, London; Major Alex Leslie (RTR); Major Ian Clooney (RTR); Major Tim David (Directorate of Corporate Communications) and all at the 1st Royal Tank Regiment in Warminster.

The support group: Sarah, Susannah, Alice, Paul, Wendy, Peter, Mike, Hilary.

And Claire. Above and beyond as always.

Now read on for the beginning
of the next Tom Thorne thriller,

Buried

You think about the kids.

First and last, in this sort of situation, in this sort of *state*; when you can't decide if it's anger or agony that's all but doubling you up, and making it so hard for you to spit the words across the room. First and last, you think about them . . .

'Why the hell, why the *fuck*, didn't you tell me this earlier?'

'It wasn't the right time. It seemed best to wait.'

'*Best?*' She takes a step towards the man standing on the far side of her living room.

He moves back instinctively until his calves are squashed against the edge of the sofa and he almost topples back on to the carefully plumped cushions. 'I think you should try to calm down,' he says.

The room smells of pot pourri. There are lines on the carpet showing that it has recently been vacuumed, and the carriage clock that can be heard ticking loudly when the shouting stops sits on a highly polished pine mantelpiece.

'What do you expect me to do?' she says. 'I'd really be interested to know.'

'I can't tell you what to do. It's your decision.'

'You think I've got a *choice*?'

'We need to sit down and talk about the best way forward—'

'Christ Almighty. You just march in here and tell me this. Casually, like it's just something you forgot to mention. You walk in here and tell me all this ... shit!' She's begun to cry again, but this time she does not lift a hand to her face. She shuts her eyes and waits for the moment to pass. For the fury to return, undiluted.

'Sarah—'

'I don't know you. I don't even fucking *know* you!'

For a few seconds there's just the ticking, and the distant traffic, and the noise bleeding in from a radio in the kitchen, turned down low when she'd heard the doorbell. Inside, the central heating's working overtime, but there's still plenty of sun streaming into the room through the net at the windows.

'I'm sorry.'

'You're *what?*' But she's heard him well enough. She smiles, then laughs. She gathers the material of her dress between her fingers as her fists clench at her sides. There's something starting to twitch in her belly now; a spasm takes hold at the top of her leg. 'I need to get to the school.'

'The kids'll be fine. Honestly, love. Absolutely fine.'

She repeats his last word; and then again, in a whisper. There's no stopping the tears this time or the scream that comes from deep inside; or the swell and the surge that take her fast across the room, her hands clawed and flying at the man's face.

The man raises his arms to protect himself. He grabs the fingers that stab at his eyes, and, once he has them, as soon as he is in control of her, he tries to keep her still; to guide her firmly away. 'You've got to stay calm.'

'You. Rotten. Fucker.' She snaps back her head.

'Please listen—' The spit hits him just above the lip and starts to run into his mouth. He swears at her; a word he rarely uses.

And he pushes her . . .

And suddenly she's dead weight, falling back, opening her mouth to cry out, and smashing down through the glass of the coffee table.

A few seconds' ticking. And traffic. And the buzz from the kitchen.

The man takes a step towards her, then stops dead. He can see what's happened straight away.

Her back hurts, and her ankle, where she's caught them on the edge of the table as she's fallen. She tries to sit up, but her head is suddenly as heavy as a wrecking ball. The moan rattles from her chest, and her shoulders grind glass into the carpet beneath her. She lies, breathless, across the ragged jewels and slivers, recognising a song from the distant radio at the same moment that she feels the warmth and the wetness at the back of her head. Spreading at her throat, and creeping down inside the neck of her sweater.

by Kathryn Croft please

The

527

D0247122

This book should be returned/renewed by the latest date shown above. Overdue items incur charges which prevent self-service renewals. Please contact the library.

Wandsworth Libraries
24 hour Renewal Hotline
01159 293388
www.wandsworth.gov.uk

For more information about nov...
visit www.kathrync...

The Mother's Secret

KATHRYN CROFT

Ⅰℂ CANELO

First published in the United Kingdom in 2022 by

Canelo
Unit 9, 5th Floor
Cargo Works, 1–2 Hatfields
London, SE1 9PG
United Kingdom

A CIP catalogue record for this book is available from the British Library.

Print ISBN 978 1 80032 521 0
Ebook ISBN 978 1 80032 520 3

Look for more great books at www.canelo.co

Printed and bound in Great Britain by Clays Ltd, Elcograf S.p.A.

For Marti

PROLOGUE

We all make mistakes. Do things that can't be undone, no matter how much we wish we could retrace our steps, pause for a single moment to consider the consequences of our actions.

This, though, was not a mistake. I have never undertaken any action with such alacrity.

And I have no regrets.

You made your own mistakes, didn't you? Yet up until your very last moment you didn't doubt your judgement. Perhaps that was your biggest mistake, because maybe if you'd at least shown some remorse then I might not have struck that blow.

I had to do something to stop you.

And I was willing to do anything.

PART ONE

ONE

Now

I know you lied.

That's all the email says.

I check the sender's address: theliesthatbind@gmail-.com. It should be illegal to hide behind an anonymous email address. Why should a person be able to obscure their identity online? I stare at the message again. Deliberately brief – designed to incite fear. What does this person know about me?

Next to me, Jamie sleeps, his elbow too close to my body. This is a double bed, yet whenever he spends the night it feels as though we're stuck together in a space as claustrophobic as a coffin. With a sigh, I nudge him further away. I'm not being cruel; sometimes I just cannot bear the hot sticky feel of anyone's flesh against mine. And now, I know I have something else to worry about.

Jamie mumbles something, and with his eyes still closed he edges back to me, so quickly I sit up and throw the duvet off my clammy legs. It's not even six a.m., yet sunlight streams through the window, making it feel as though it's already ninety degrees. It's only May and it's being reported that we're already having a heatwave

5

not witnessed since the seventies, and while the whole country rejoices, I silently count the days and hours until the nights are shorter, and I can once again feel an ice-cold chill on my skin.

'Where are you going?' Jamie asks, his eyes still shut. I should have known he'd wake up the second I tried to grab some time for myself. He places his hand on my back, and I feel the excessive heat through the oversized T-shirt I've slept in. One of Aiden's, I think, and I wonder, yet again, why I haven't thrown it away like I have everything else. And why I even have it in the first place.

'I've got a load of work to do,' I tell Jamie, stretching my arms upwards. It's not a natural gesture; I just need something to distract me because I'm starting to feel the walls closing in on me. *Because it's time.* Perhaps I've known this was coming, but the message pinging into my inbox this morning has cemented it in my mind. I have to do this now.

The excuses I offer Jamie come hard and fast: I'm behind with my marking, there are sessions to plan and students coming who will expect me to be prepared. I can't let them down.

'Eve,' Jamie says, his voice a croaky half-whisper, 'a bit longer in bed won't hurt, will it? Let me persuade you to stay.' His warm hand reaches for mine.

I flinch and pull away. 'Sorry, I can't.' He has no idea how important this day is to me; he's unaware of the nausea bubbling in the pit of my stomach.

He admits defeat too easily. 'Okay, spoilsport. How about I come over this evening after work? We can get a takeaway. Bottle of wine.' Lose ourselves in oblivion, he means. That's what we always do when we're together. I know what I'm hiding from but what about Jamie? I've only known him for four months, but everything I've learned about him could fit on a Post-it note: thirty-three – two years younger than me; a freelance website designer; twin sisters he doesn't get along with; and he lives nearby in Enfield. That's it. The extent of my knowledge. It's not that he doesn't share information, more that I don't let it seep into my brain. I can't let myself know more about him. Familiarity terrifies me. And if I asked questions of him, he would do the same, and then sooner or later I would slip up.

'I need a shower,' I tell him. 'Do you mind seeing yourself out?'

My small dining table is set up as it usually is for my tutoring sessions. The textbooks I'll need are in a neat pile, my pencil case parallel to them, and a stack of loose paper sits in the middle, where either of us can easily reach it. I've laid out a plate of biscuits, leaving off the custard creams. It's Maya who'll be coming, and I've never once seen her eat one, although the chocolate Bourbons always disappear.

Today, more than any other day, I welcome the distraction the next hour will bring; I don't want to think about what this morning's email means. Maya will appear promptly at ten a.m., if not a few minutes before, her large bag of textbooks and revision guides weighing her down. Tardiness is her enemy. 'I hate being late, miss,' she'd told me at our first session. 'It makes me anxious and then I can't concentrate for the rest of the time.' I admire this punctuality in someone so young, and have told her so, even though I've never shared that I am exactly the same way.

Right on time, she rings the buzzer at 09:59, and I promptly let her in. 'Oh, miss, I'm so hot,' she gasps, pulling off her thin cardigan. 'How can it be so hot? This is London, we're not in Ibiza!'

I try not to shudder at being called *miss*; the title haunts me, reminds me of someone I no longer am, but I've long ago given up trying to get Maya to call me by my first name. 'It feels weird, miss,' she'd claimed when I first suggested it. 'Kind of disrespectful.' I don't point out that as she's eighteen, I wouldn't have any problem with her calling me Eve.

'It probably doesn't help wearing those,' I say now, gesturing to her skinny jeans, which have huge rips down the legs. 'Shorts might have been a better option today.'

She fans herself with her Oyster card and lets out a huge puff of breath. 'Or a bikini?' she offers, and we both chuckle.

It's only when Maya sits down that I realise something seems different about her today, aside from the sweat glistening on her skin, and the fact that her thick black hair is scraped back into a long ponytail. It's not her clothes – she's wearing one of her usual close-fitting tops, which always make me feel old. I long ago lost touch with fashion trends and now I select dark-coloured outfits that help me blend in. Clothes that make me look neither glamorous nor frumpy, just average and bland. No, it's something else about Maya. She doesn't seem herself.

'So, only two more weeks, Maya,' I say, pulling out two copies of an old exam paper. I slide one towards her. 'I thought we'd work on a practice question together. How does that sound?'

She offers a small nod and stares at the sheet, making no move to open her bag and take anything out. This is not like her. Something is definitely wrong. Immediately I assume the worst: she knows about me. It's caught up with me before I've even made the attempt to put things right. Nausea once again floods through me. Could it be Maya who sent me that email?

'Is everything okay?' I ask, forcing the words out. Even though I don't want to hear her tell me she knows what I did, I need to make sure she's all right. And she is still here after all, so maybe she wants to give me a chance to explain.

'Yeah,' she says, her eyes fixed on her hands, which she fans out in front of her. I'm surprised to notice her nail polish is chipped; she's usually so careful about her appearance.

'I know I'm just tutoring you for your A-levels, but I'm not a bad listener if there's anything troubling you.' *Please don't let this be about me.*

Still without looking up, she opens her mouth but doesn't speak.

'Maya?'

I can't see her eyes, so it's only when tears splatter onto the table that I know she's crying. Ignoring the discomfort I feel, I leave my seat and crouch down beside her, tentatively putting my arm across her back. She needs me, so I won't shy away from soothing her.

'Please talk to me, Maya. It's possible I might be able to help. I'll definitely try my best, even if it's got nothing to do with your studies.'

She looks up, her dark brown eyes glistening. 'It's not schoolwork,' she says. 'Nothing like that.'

It must be family, then. All sorts of terrible scenarios cross my mind, and I try to recall what I know about her home life. As far as I'm aware, she gets on well with both her parents, and she's close to her older sister who's away at university. Nothing Maya's said has ever set off any alarm bells, and I've been trained to look out for warning signs. I prepare myself to explain that if she's in any danger then I will have to report it.

'Then what is it? What's happened?'

'I'm pregnant,' she blurts out, her eyes wide.

Aside from the fact that she's only eighteen, this isn't a catastrophe. Her words shouldn't make my body feel as if it's folding in on itself, as though I'm being crushed from the inside.

And all I can think is that I am the last person she should have told.

TWO

Before

I walk across the car park far too quickly, the ice beneath my feet threatening to topple me onto my back. My hand rests on my stomach but still I don't slow my pace.

Usually I enjoy the drive home, pleased to have that gap between work and domestic life, but right now I curse myself for wanting to settle in a different part of London than the school I teach in, just because I was worried about bumping into students at weekends. It will be at least forty-five minutes until I get back, and with every passing second I bleed more heavily.

Somehow, though, I still have that morsel of hope in me, and I pray that it will suddenly stop, that this time it's just one of those inexplicable bleeds which can happen sometimes. That this time my baby is still alive.

'Miss Conway?'

I don't turn around, even though I immediately recognise the voice. Justin Foley's father. The annoying parent who feels the need to try to meet me on an almost weekly basis, despite the fact that his son's doing well in school and is never in any kind of trouble. In fact, Justin is likely to achieve top grades in all his GCSEs.

If I keep walking, maybe the man will let this one go. After all, he hasn't made an appointment, so he could just be picking up Justin and it's just a huge coincidence that he's right behind me in the staff car park.

'Miss Conway?' Louder this time. Closer. I want to yell at him and point out yet again that my title is Mrs, not Miss, as he always insists on calling me. The school should be able to do something about nuisance parents. The scream is right there in my throat, waiting to erupt. I should shout the words at him, let out all my pain, make sure he knows that right now I'm losing another baby and he needs to leave me alone. For a second I almost do; the words are at the edge of my tongue, ready to fire out, but I quickly reconsider. There is no way I will share my personal business with this annoying man.

I ignore him once more and speed up. I'm nearly at my car and I fumble in my bag for my keys, longing to get home to Aiden and let out all the grief I've been bottling up today.

But then he's caught up with me and there is no way to pretend I haven't heard him.

'Sorry,' he says, 'I was calling but it's noisy out here, isn't it?' He gestures to the air.

I've never been grateful for the heavy roar of traffic until now. 'Mr Foley. How can I help you?' It's the most professional voice I can muster and it takes everything I've got to produce it. All day I've had to plaster a smile on my face, carry on as if my whole body, and my world, isn't crumbling.

'I was wondering if you've had a chance to speak to Justin's maths teacher yet. About him attending those extra evening sessions.'

This isn't the first time I've wondered why I wanted the head of year role. It's teaching I love: being in the classroom and witnessing those light-bulb moments when a student suddenly grasps what you've been trying to teach them. Not this. Especially not now.

It was only yesterday he was in my office requesting that I put his son's name forward. Yesterday. When I still had my baby inside me.

'I'm sorry, Mr Foley—'

'Alex, please.'

'Um, I'm sorry but as I explained yesterday, those classes have been set up specifically for students who are behind and need extra help. Justin clearly doesn't—'

'Right, okay. I understand. But I'd really like him to have some tuition. It's a crucial time, isn't it? We can't gamble with his future.'

I refrain from pointing out how overdramatic he's being. 'Then you have the right to organise that outside of school, Mr Foley, but it's not something we can provide for students who aren't—'

'I've got it!' He throws his hands up and smiles. 'Could you perhaps organise sessions for those students who are... more capable?'

This is the first time I've heard him admit that his son is actually very bright. While I want to wipe the smug smile off his face, he does have a good point. 'I'll look into that,' I offer, 'but I can't promise anything. It will all come down to funding.' *Please leave me alone now. I just need to get home.*

'I've sent you an email,' he continues, ignoring the fact that I'm turning around, oblivious to my silent pain.

'Oh, have you?' I feign ignorance though I noticed it this afternoon, and it remains unread in my inbox; it won't be important.

'Yes, just wanted an update really. I seem to spend so much time asking you about his other subjects and I forget that you're actually his English teacher as well as his head of year.' His eyes flicker to my stomach, which, once again, hasn't even had a chance to protrude. Feeling like I'm wearing a sign across me, advertising it to the world, I wrap my jacket tighter around me.

Get rid of him. Say anything you can to make this stupid man leave you alone.

'He's doing extremely well in English, as he is in all his other subjects. You must be very proud of him, Mr Foley.'

He smiles. That's worked. Perhaps he's one of those parents who just wants to constantly hear how amazing their kid is.

'Thank you. That's great. Well, I'll let you get on.' He starts to turn away but spins around to face me again. 'Um, are you okay? Forgive me for saying this but you look a bit pale.'

Hearing his concern makes it harder to keep my tears at bay. They are right there, ready to flood out, and I can't let that happen in front of a parent. Or anyone at school, other than Sophie.

'I'm fine, it's just been a very long day.'

'Okay. Keep me posted, won't you?'

'Posted?' I can't even remember what I've agreed to.

'On the extra classes for Justin? His mum and I are a bit worried he's not as focused as he could be. I'm sure you understand.'

What is wrong with this man? His son is one of the most conscientious students I'm teaching this year. Is there no communication in their house?

'Will you be taking the English classes?' he continues, even though I haven't answered.

There are no extra classes. Probably never will be. Just leave me alone.

'Because I know Justin thinks you're a great teacher, and you've already got a rapport. It might set him back a bit if he had a different teacher.'

This man really is something else. I have no more of a rapport with Justin than I do any of my students.

'Well, that's nice of you to say, but—'

'Anyway, you seem like you're in a rush. How about I make an appointment instead? For next week? It would have to be after school, of course, as it's impossible to leave work too early.'

No! I want to scream, but I don't want to give him any excuse to complain about me. He's just the type of parent who would do that, who would never see how aggravating he is and that he's brought it on himself. 'Yes, of course. Anyway, I'd better get going.'

I feel his eyes on me as I walk away and make a mental note to give Justin even more praise than usual when I next see him, just for having to put up with this man as his father.

—

Aiden's in the kitchen when I get home, rooting through the fridge, pulling vegetables out and sniffing them before throwing them back in.

How can I tell him? This will be the fourth time I've had to break the news that there won't be a baby after all. It might not be his body it's happening to but each time we lose a pregnancy, part of him rips wide open, too.

15

'You're home early,' I say, pulling off my coat and draping it over the back of a chair. I don't have the energy to put it in the cupboard under the stairs. I don't care where it goes.

'I wanted to give you a break and cook dinner for a change. You need to rest and take it easy.' He smiles and resumes his rummaging. 'Not sure what on earth I can make, though. Might be looking at a trip to Sainsbury's.'

'I don't need to rest or take it easy,' I say. 'Not any more.' And the flood of tears bursts out, splattering across my cheeks, dripping down my sleeve as I try to wipe them away. It feels as though they will never stop.

'Oh no!' Aiden rushes over to me. His arms wrap around me, pull me in as tightly as they can. 'I'm so sorry, I'm so sorry. When? Why didn't you tell me?'

Pulling back slightly, somehow I find the strength to explain. 'This afternoon when I was in the middle of a lesson. I felt the gush but couldn't check until the lesson ended. I kept hoping… I was wrong.'

'And you carried on teaching? You should have come home.'

'I couldn't let my Year 11s down. We were doing exam practice.'

'Oh, God, Eve.' He pulls me in again.

My body starts to heave and guttural noises that barely sound human escape from between my lips.

Aiden holds me like that, not saying a word, just offering me his unspoken support. He strokes my hair until finally I'm ready to breathe again.

'Are *you* okay?' I ask, because this isn't just happening to me.

'Gutted.' He shakes his head. 'I really thought it would be okay this time. You were a lot further along. I was so sure.'

I warned him not to think like that, not to ever be sure until we were holding a baby in our arms. 'I need a shower,' I say, turning away because seeing him in pain is worse than feeling my own.

'Let's get more tests done, Eve. It's happened too many times now. There must be a reason and they just haven't found it yet. We need to know, don't we?'

'Okay,' I say, already knowing we've had every test imaginable. Sometimes things are just unexplained, the answers hiding, mocking us. But I will keep that flicker of hope alive, for both our sakes.

THREE

Now

She's beautiful. Her hair, already shoulder length, is thick and shiny, not dark like mine, but almost identical to her father's dirty blonde tone. There is no doubt in my mind that this is Kayla.

I think of Claire, of all the hours I spent sitting across from her while she let me talk and say whatever I wanted or needed to, how she helped me see that I can be the mother Kayla deserves. And now I'm here, seeing my daughter for the first time since I had to walk away.

The woman she's with is holding her hand as they cross the road, and Kayla gazes up at her, smiling as they walk together. They are clearly both comfortable with each other.

It stands to reason that Aiden will have needed child-care. He's an architect and runs his own small business, so there is no way he could have left his job to be a stay-at-home father. The last I knew, his parents lived in Edinburgh, and were years away from retirement, so I doubt they would have moved back here, even though I'm sure they will have wanted to help out.

I have had just over two years to build myself up to this moment, but I'm still not prepared for the surge of grief that overwhelms me. Today was just meant to be about seeing her, even just catching the briefest sight of her, and I wasn't prepared to feel so bereft. Helpless. Guilty.

Then there is the email. It's all about to catch up with me and I can't let that happen.

Kayla is nearly two and a half now, and I know nothing about her, except what she was like in those early newborn weeks. What's her favourite colour? I like to imagine she likes royal blue, as I do, but looking at her now it's clear she loves pink. My absence will have shaped her, turned her into a child she might not have been had I not left.

Even though there's no chance either of them will know who I am, I keep my distance. I almost feel as if there is an invisible barrier stopping me getting too close. As if we live in two different worlds and will never be capable of connecting to each other's.

Being here, watching her like this, makes me feel like a criminal. Yet here I stay because there's no way I'm turning back.

Aiden won't have shown Kayla any photos of me, I'm sure of that. Once he'd come to terms with what I did, although probably never able to accept it, he would have tried to bury all thoughts of me and the life we had together. That's the kind of person he was; he dealt with things by pushing them aside, pretending they didn't exist and, instead, focusing on the here and now. Perhaps he had it right. Maybe things would be different if I hadn't been so terrified of the future and I'd instead learned to live in the moment.

The woman and my daughter reach the other side of the road – heading to the park, I'm sure – and just as they step onto the pavement, Kayla stumbles and falls to the ground. The woman struggles to maintain the grip on her tiny hand. Instinctively I rush forward, but quickly stop myself. She is fine, and the woman is lifting her up and hugging her tightly, opening her mouth to utter words of reassurance. Sharp pains shoot through my abdomen, threatening to bring me to my knees. That should be me comforting her. I fight the urge to run to her and grab her.

After a few moments, Kayla begins to laugh. I can't hear it, but the joy on my daughter's face is too painful to witness. Turning away, I head back to East Putney Tube station.

Now I know more than ever what I have to do. It might cost me everything, but I'm doing this for my daughter.

–

'She's not having a good day today,' Jo, one of the carers, tells me.

Most evenings I come here, sitting with Mum for hours until she wants to go to bed, and every time I wait for them to tell me that today she's been happy, that they actually saw her laugh, or even produced a hint of a smile. It's probably too much to hope that she will have taken part in one of the activities the staff arrange on a daily basis.

This is a decent place. I wanted Mum to be somewhere close to my flat in Southgate, and it was a brand-new building that even now, two years after being opened, still somehow looks clean and fresh. There's no denying the unmistakable smell here that speaks of illness and loss of bodily functions, mingled with lavender and all the other fragrances that are used to mask everything else, but I'm so used to it that I no longer notice. All the staff I've come across are friendly, and I know Mum's well looked after here. No, it's more than that – the staff actually really like her, I can tell. But still, I never wanted this for her.

'She had an argument with Matilda and accused her of stealing from her,' Jo is telling me as she puts some towels away in the store cupboard.

I raise my eyebrows, wondering if it's possible that Matilda might have actually taken something. That this time Mum isn't mistaken and knows what she's talking about. I mention this to Jo.

She shakes her head. 'I wish that were true but Matilda's been in bed all day with a cold.'

Jo knows me well now; she's been here from the beginning, and I'm here three times a week, four if I can manage it around tutoring. I'm grateful that sometimes she'll sit with Mum and me, keeping us both company until she's needed elsewhere.

'Okay, thanks for telling me. I'll go and make sure she's okay.'

I rush along the corridor to Mum's room but hesitate outside her door because I never know what to expect. Usually she's happy to see me but not always. There have been occasions when she's screamed at me to leave her alone, as if I'm a stranger, right before begging me to unlock the door of the hotel so she can get the bus home. *It's right across the road*, she always insists, even though Pine View is nowhere near a bus stop.

'Hi Mum, it's Eve,' I say, pushing through the door. The smell of her perfume wafts across to me, mingled with the smell of cleaning products. Chanel N°5. Mum might often forget who people are, or what things do, but she never forgets to put on her perfume every morning.

I try to leave everything behind when I come here – all the baggage that weighs me down – and focus only on her. As hard as it is being here, seeing her like this, in some ways it's also an escape for me.

She's sitting by the window today, staring out of it with an open book on her lap. At first I'm surprised – she gave up reading long ago – until I realise it's her photo album.

'Eve, I'm so glad you're here. They've… they've locked me in again and I can't get out. I keep telling them I'll miss the bus if they don't open the doors, but they won't listen! Just what kind of hotel is this?' She turns back to the window. 'And it's raining, have you seen my umbrella? The red one with the yellow stripes?'

I head over and put my arm around her. She's describing the umbrella she had when I was a little girl, one I don't remember seeing as I got older.

'Don't worry, Mum, I'm here now and everything will be okay.'

Her shoulders are scrawny, as though there's barely a millimetre of flesh separating her skin from the bones underneath.

'You'll help me get to the bus stop?' Her eyes are large circles, pleading with me, and I can barely keep my tears from falling. I need to be strong for her. I'm the only security she has in this unfamiliar world. 'It's just across the road, you know. I really need to get home. I'll need my umbrella, though. Now, where could it be?'

'Yes, Mum. I'll help you get to the bus stop, and we'll look for your umbrella, but why don't we have a cup of tea first? I can tell you all about my day.'

She loves to hear my stories, even though she won't remember a thing I've said once I walk out of here. There is never anything exciting to tell her, so maybe it's just the lull of my voice she likes to hear.

There's no kettle to make hot drinks in Mum's room – it wouldn't be safe – so I head to the communal small lounge to make us both a tea, focusing on each step of the process so that anxiety doesn't cripple me. I've read all about mindfulness, how good it is for healing, but it's easier said than done actually practising it. Making tea for Mum anywhere other than her own house will always feel strange. She's been here for just over a year now, and every day I'm riddled with guilt that I couldn't continue to look after her myself. It was the third time a stranger found her wandering around by the busy main road that forced me to realise I had to do this.

When I get back and hand her a cup of tea, she thanks me and places it on the side table. She'll forget it's there now unless I keep reminding her to drink.

'You've been looking at the photo album.'

She nods. 'Yes, would you like to see it?'

I tell her I would, and don't mention that I could describe every photo in there and the order they follow, including the clothes everyone is wearing.

'Here, look!' she says, flipping the pages until she spots one.

I glance at the photo she's pointing to. It's the one of her holding me as a baby, where I'm wearing what looks like a christening gown, even though Mum insists it was just one of my usual outfits.

'Beautiful. Look at that face,' she continues.

And as I've expected, I feel the inevitable stab through my heart, because it's not me I see but Kayla. We were almost identical as babies. Quickly I turn the page because I don't want to think of it now, or picture her in the park with her nanny. Most of all, I don't want to remember my lie.

Thankfully, Mum doesn't seem to mind, and she's happy for me to flip through the rest of the album. All the other photos are harmless. My dad. Grandparents. Me as a young girl, much older than Kayla.

When we've finished, I read to her and then it's time to leave so Mum can have dinner with the other residents. There are only five of them on this level, which I'm thankful for. Mum has not enjoyed the few occasions when they've had all the residents eating together in the large dining room downstairs.

I stand and pick up our mugs of tea; both have been barely touched today.

'Where is she?' Mum suddenly asks while I'm pouring the tea down the bathroom sink.

'Who, Mum?' I'm used to this kind of question and wonder to whom she's referring this time. An old friend or colleague? It will be someone she has only just remembered, a memory that's formed suddenly.

'Your baby,' she says. 'Where's your baby? What have you done with her?'

And the mug I'm holding drops to the floor, smashing to pieces.

—

Jamie is waiting outside my flat when I get home, and my heart sinks. It shouldn't, but of course it does given the day I've had. My instinct always tells me that he's a decent man, but company is the last thing I need right now. And sometimes – a lot of the time – I can't bear to be touched.

'Maybe it's time I had a key?' he asks with a smile. 'Your neighbours will think I'm a stalker or something!'

I live on the top floor of a converted Victorian property on a fairly busy road, but no one pays any attention to anyone in London. There are faded Neighbourhood Watch stickers on lampposts, but I've lived here for two years and nobody has ever held a meeting or introduced themselves as running the scheme. 'I don't even know them,' I tell him.

Jamie's smile disappears. 'I was only joking, Eve.'

I try to offer him some reassurance, but my attempt falls short. I can't stop thinking about Kayla, and my pregnant student, and how badly I handled Mum's mention of my baby. She hasn't brought Kayla up for months now, and I thought I was safe from further questions. In the beginning when she'd ask, I'd simply tell her that Kayla was with Aiden, that I'd bring her next time, and soon enough Mum stopped asking.

'Do you mean me when I was a baby?' I'd asked when I'd recovered from the shock of her question. Despicable. Haven't I done enough harm to people without adding more lies?

'No. No! The baby,' she'd insisted. 'My baby. *Your* baby.' And she'd begun to get agitated, standing up and cradling her bony arms.

'Where's the baby?' she'd repeated, ignoring my attempts to comfort her.

And then I'd sat there and told her that I'd had no choice but to walk out on my baby and husband – that staying would have been the worst thing I could have done – because I couldn't bear keeping it from her any more. Or was it because I knew she wouldn't remember what I'd said the next time I saw her? I really hope it's the former.

She'd stared at me for agonising minutes, and I prepared myself for an attack. When she finally did speak, it was to ask me if I had the latest bus timetable.

'Are you okay?' Jamie forces me back to the present. I still haven't opened the front door.

'Just exhausted.' I offer a smile.

'Well, we could get a takeaway – save either of us cooking?' He doesn't give me a chance to answer. 'Look, I know we hadn't made plans to see each other tonight, and you've probably got a ton of work to do, but… well, I missed you. Ah, look, I've said it now. I missed you. And I bloody like you. A lot. What's the point in playing games and pretending I don't?'

I stare at him for a few seconds, unable to form a response. And he returns my stare, searching my face for a sign of anything positive, I'm sure.

'Okay, then. I see I've made a mistake,' he says when I can't speak, and he turns away, brushing past me as he walks off.

I should go after him; he doesn't deserve this. All he wants is a nice evening with me, so why can't I just give that to him?

Because you need to go now. Go and get your daughter back before it's too late.

FOUR

Before

When I first met Sophie, I didn't take to her at all. I've never told her this, even though she wouldn't be offended. In fact, it wouldn't surprise me if she hadn't been particularly keen on me either.

I'd already been at the school for a year before she started – a fresh and confident newly qualified teacher – and was happy to show her around the department and help her settle in. I quickly realised that she was aloof, unfriendly, and didn't seem interested in forming any kind of friendship with any of her colleagues. I'd just met Aiden and our relationship was developing, so I didn't give anything other than work, and him, much time or thought. I kept my distance from Sophie, until she needed my help one day with a difficult student we both taught.

Sophie was already known as one of the strictest teachers in the school, but it didn't make any difference because for some reason Ryan Hart had taken a dislike to her and was constantly antagonistic in class. I, too, had initially had difficulty with him, yet, in time, we'd somehow managed to develop a mutual respect. I could never manage to explain to Sophie quite how that had happened.

'He's driving me crazy with his disruption,' she told me. 'I've tried everything other than killing him so what am I supposed to do?'

We'd both laughed, as inappropriate as her comment was, and that was the beginning of a friendship I can't imagine being without.

And now, seven years later, I sit on Sophie's sofa, marvelling at how clean and tidy her house is when she is a new mum of twins. Next to me, she effortlessly breastfeeds one of the babies, the other one sitting in his bouncer, kicking his legs out as if he's doing a fitness workout.

'Please don't look at me like that,' I say, forcing a smile.

'Like what?'

'With pity. Or guilt. I don't know… something.'

Sophie shakes her head. 'Oh, Eve, I'm so sorry. I was really rooting for you to be okay this time. I can't believe it's happened again.' Her eyes flick to Jasper in the bouncer – or is it Jensen? They're nearly five months old and I still can't tell them apart.

'It's not your fault,' I assure her. 'Please don't feel bad.' Phrases like this have become programmed into my brain, an automatic response to stop people feeling uncomfortable around me. Do I mean them? I want to but most days I'm not convinced I do.

'I know,' she says, wiping some milk from Jasper or Jensen's chin. 'But it makes me feel awful that I wasn't excited when I found out I was pregnant.'

That's an understatement. The memory of that lunchtime is still ingrained in my head: me walking into the English office and finding Sophie in tears, something I'd never witnessed before, even when she was struggling with Ryan Hart. She hadn't planned it, she'd admitted through her fountain of tears. Damien and she had so many plans, so many things they wanted to do before they were plunged into parenthood. They were that kind of people: a couple who couldn't sit still and spent every school holiday abroad. The Inca Trail in Peru was next on their list.

'I'm too young,' she'd insisted, but then quickly admitted that, of course, thirty-two was not too young at all. 'You know what I mean, though. I'm not *ready*.' Then she hugged me, repeatedly telling me how sorry she was, that it was so unfair after everything I was going through in my desperate attempt to be a mum.

Despite the rocky start to her pregnancy, Sophie has embraced motherhood and makes it seem effortless, even with twins. 'Look at you now, though,' I say. 'You're an amazing mum and you love them to pieces.'

There it is: that guilt mixed with pity on her face that I don't want her to feel.

'It was the worst timing, though, wasn't it?' She bites her lip, chews it.

I'd just had my second miscarriage, so it was difficult to digest her news, yet still I clung to hope. I seemed to be able to fall pregnant fairly easily; it was keeping a baby inside me that was the problem. Back then I had no idea that I'd still be struggling now.

'What's happening to me is not your fault,' I tell her. I glance at Jensen or Jasper playing in his bouncer. I need to change the subject because this isn't good for me, or for Sophie. 'Will it be strange coming back to school?'

She immediately understands my need to change the conversation. 'I really thought I'd be dying to get back to work, but actually I'm not. Does that surprise you? Who'd have imagined I'd be happy to be at home watching Baby TV? But I've kind of got into a groove here. It's actually quite nice not having to bother doing my make-up every morning. Or scrambling around making resources for my lessons. I never thought I'd say this but having twins is actually easier than dealing with thirty teenagers all at once.'

The room falls silent as we both realise that when we're together now, there is no getting away from baby talk, no matter how hard we try. This is Sophie's entire world now.

'So how are things at school?' Sophie finally asks.

'Nothing's changed,' I say, although perhaps everything has. She's been away from work now for so long that I can't even remember what I've filled her in on. 'Apart from that new maths teacher, Owen. Did I tell you about him?'

'Yes, you did,' she says, smiling. 'And are all the single teachers still after him?'

We both laugh, and for a fraction of a second it feels like it did before. Before my first miscarriage. When I was able to laugh without that underlying heaviness that cuts short any joy I feel.

'Come on, let's have some lunch,' Sophie says, jumping up with one twin then scooping down to lift the other out of his bouncer. 'These two could do with a nap and then I'll be right down to make us something. Omelette and salad okay? I don't think I've got much else in.'

Before she leaves the room I call her back. 'I feel awful for not knowing this but how do you tell the twins apart?'

Sophie chuckles. 'That's easy, Jensen has a bit more hair.' She gestures to the twin she's just been feeding. 'Don't feel bad, though – Damien still gets them mixed up.' She's about to walk off again but then she stops. 'Oh, I'm sorry, I should have asked you if you want to have a cuddle? I don't want you to think I won't let you hold them. Just, you know, trying to be respectful of your feelings.'

'I'd love to,' I say automatically, and before I can think further, Sophie is placing one of the twins into my arms. The weight of him feels strange for a second, but then as I grow accustomed to him and he snuggles into me, it begins to feel right. And if I close my eyes, just for a second I can pretend he is mine.

FIVE

Now

It wasn't hard to find out where Aiden lives now. He still runs his business from the same place in Ealing, and all I needed to do was make sure I got there before he left and follow him home from work. It felt wrong, intruding on his life in that way, and I had no idea what I'd do if he turned around and spotted me, but my desire to find Kayla was far greater than dealing with the consequences of discovery.

I wasn't expecting him to still live in Putney, assuming it would hold too many painful memories. For me, I had to get as far away as possible.

From across the street, I take in every detail of the house. It's nothing like the Edwardian property we rented together. It was always our plan to buy once we started a family, and I wonder if Aiden owns the one I'm standing before. It's a small semi-detached new build, and I'm sure he'd be able to afford it on his own.

There are lights on, so I know he's home, although I can't see anything through the blinds.

Kayla will be in there, and I want to picture her, but somehow the image of her from earlier has vanished from my memory. All I can see is a three-month-old baby, staring at me, expecting me to know what to do, to make everything better.

It's past nine p.m. now, heading nearer to ten, so she'll definitely be in bed – I know with certainty that Aiden will be strict about her bedtime routine. The reality is, though, I actually have no idea what their lives are like now, how they spend their time together or what kind of relationship they have. They are both strangers to me, where once I knew every inch of my baby, and thought I knew my husband.

It is strange to give him that label; he will have long ago stopped thinking of me as his wife, even though neither of us has tracked the other down to file for divorce.

Do I really think I'm going to knock on the door? No time of day would make it easier, but so late at night? It's not as if I briefly walked away from my life. It's been two years and three months, give or take a few days. Two years which feel like seconds as much as they are a lifetime. But that email means the clock is ticking, so I must act now.

My feet move forward, taking me in a direction I'm desperate to go in, yet terrified of. Towards Kayla. I can do this – I just have to keep moving.

The front door opens, and I freeze. I'm not ready to be seen yet; it won't be on the terms I've prepared myself for. I want to be at the front door, not standing here across the road, purposeless. I need to have rung the doorbell, to ensure that I am the one who has found them, not the other way around. Even though it's already clear that I've been found.

There's no hiding place here. I am out in the open, illuminated by the street lights. There is nothing I can do. So I stop where I am   perhaps I'm not able to move even if I want to – and wait for fate to determine what happens. The loss of control is my worst nightmare.

It's her. The woman who was looking after Kayla this afternoon. She looks older than I assumed she was: nearer to thirty than twenty. Strange that she's still here when Kayla would have gone to bed hours ago. Then, just as my mind starts piecing together this scenario, Aiden appears behind her and pulls her towards him, wrapping his arms around her and kissing her on the forehead. She nestles into him, and I want to turn away but I can't. Once again I'm frozen. Mentally and physically.

Seeing Aiden with someone else shouldn't send excruciating spasms of pain through my body and weaken my legs. No. He stopped being mine the second I walked away.

But this changes everything. I am already far too late.

–

When I get home an idea takes shape in my mind and I can't let it go. I need to know everything about my daughter, including who the woman is. Although I don't know her name, I can look on Aiden's Facebook account and see if there are any details of her on there. He's never used social media that much but it's worth a try.

I deleted my own Facebook account years ago, when I was pregnant with Kayla, because suddenly it felt too intrusive to have my life out there. Even though I'd never been one to share personal things on it, it felt good to have no record of me on the Internet. Yet when I wanted to find Aiden, I set up an account with a fake name so that I could see his. The irony of this strikes me now as my mind flits to the message I received that morning as I log on with

34

my new email address, using my middle name, Farrah. I go straight to Aiden Conway's profile. My husband. His profile picture is an old one, one I took of him while we were on holiday in Portugal, and I'm shocked that he still hasn't changed it, especially given that he has clearly moved on.

My stomach churns as I scroll down the page. Surprisingly, Aiden's account isn't private. Possibly because he doesn't use the account much, but Aiden hasn't been strict with his security settings and I can see a few photos from the past year or two. There aren't many, just some of Aiden with work colleagues at a Christmas party, but the most recent one is one he's been tagged in.

Nicole Richardson has tagged Aiden Conway in a post.

And now I'm staring at the woman I saw earlier at his house, and at the park with Kayla on the first day I went there. Nicole Richardson has her arm around Aiden, their faces so close together that it's hard to tell where one begins and the other ends, as if they are one person.

I can't breathe. They look so in love, so *right* together that it's hard to see how Aiden and I ever fitted each other. That photo makes it look like no one else in the world exists except the two of them. And Kayla, of course.

Desperate to see a photo of my daughter, I keep scrolling through Aiden's timeline, not surprised when I find no trace of Kayla. Aiden would never plaster our daughter all over social media; he was too protective of her, too private, even when she was a newborn baby.

I click on Nicole Richardson's name, but her account has the highest security settings, so I can't see anything aside from her name and profile picture. Closing Facebook, I shut my laptop and try to control my breathing.

Nicole Richardson, who are you?

—

Jamie opens the door and stares at me. I thought he'd be happy that I'm here, that I was doing something good, putting something positive into the universe to make up for what I've done. I could have stayed at home, agonising over my next steps, but I've come here now to show Jamie that I do care about him. Instead of being pleased, though, he seems disappointed. Almost on edge.

'I'm sorry,' I say. 'I shouldn't have just turned up here. I know it's late.' I turn to walk away but he steps out and reaches for my arm.

'Don't go. I'm the one who should be sorry for just leaving like that earlier. What can I say — I'm an arse sometimes.' He chuckles. 'Want to come in?'

I glance up at the window of his flat. It's usually Jamie coming to my place, so it feels odd being here. Out of my comfort zone. 'I just came here to apologise,' I tell him, making no move to go anywhere.

'Well, can you come in and do it? I know it's not cold out but I don't really want to be standing barefoot on my doorstep. Excuse the mess, though — I didn't think I'd have company this evening.'

Inside, Jamie tidies away the remains of his dinner, which he's left on the coffee table, while I sit on the sofa and wonder what I'm doing here, despite my earlier determination to do this for him. I can't get the image of Nicole Richardson out of my head and nothing feels right any more. There's nowhere I want to be except with my little girl. And even though I have no right to want this – I don't want her around a woman I don't know.

'Shall we watch something on Netflix?' I suggest, because that way I don't have to talk. Even though I've come here with the intention of proving to Jamie that I do want to be with him, I can't seem to offer anything of myself right now.

'Okay,' Jamie agrees. 'Netflix it is, then.'

Jamie convinces me to stay the night, and I lie in his bed, listening to the soft sounds of his breathing. I can't tell if he is asleep as he's facing away from me. I've been refreshing the inbox on my phone, wondering if another email will come, but so far there have been no more messages. I'm sure it's just a matter of time.

I'm distracted, even more so than usual, but I keep reminding myself that there's nothing more I can do tonight. Kayla will be asleep, and there is no way I can go back round there at this hour and demand to see her. Finding out that Aiden is with someone else has thrown me off course, making it more urgent that I get to Kayla.

Does Nicole Richardson live with them? Does Kayla think she's her mother? I only have myself to blame but these questions burn inside me, fuelling my anxiety, along with the fear that's been there since I read those words. *I know you lied.*

'Who are you?' Jamie says, turning and resting his hand on my stomach. He traces the line of my thin C-section scar with his finger. Surgery to remove fibroids, I've told him, and he's never pushed for more details.

'What do you mean?' I ask.

'We've been together, what? Four months? And I feel like we barely know each other. Maybe it's because we met in such a random way.'

An accidental meeting in a coffee shop. Something that could so easily not have happened if I hadn't left my phone on the table. Jamie had come running after me, shouting at me to stop. I didn't turn around to start with because I thought he was just trying to talk to me – I'd seen him looking in my direction too often in the coffee shop and, although he was attractive, I didn't want to get to know anyone. Or for anyone to get to know me.

'No, I don't think that's it,' I say. 'Sometimes it's just better to stick with the idea we have of people,' I tell him. 'Safer. Don't they say ignorance is bliss?' This is definitely true; before the email came, and before I found out about Nicole, I at least felt I was on stable ground. Now the earth feels as though I could crash through it at any moment.

Jamie frowns. 'And what does that mean?'

'Nothing.' But also everything. If he really knew me then he wouldn't want me here in his bed. I know that as a fact. 'Just that you probably like the *idea* of me,' I tell him.

'That's all there is to like until you get to know someone, though. But why won't you let me know you? And you don't seem to want to know me either.' He's not sulking as he says this, merely stating facts. 'I feel like you're not... invested in us.'

I don't speak. What can I say that won't be a lie? He deserves more than this, even if *I* don't.

'I'm sorry, Jamie.' Now I feel vulnerable. Exposed. Why can't he just leave things as they are? The walls begin to close in on me.

'Sorry for what? Not liking me enough?'

In a way he is so very wrong. He will never know the steps it's taken for me to share even this little of myself with him. 'Jamie, it's late and I'm tired. Can we please talk about this another time? Please.'

'Right, okay. Another time.'

He turns away and silence folds over us. I close my eyes, knowing there will be no sleep for me tonight.

And minutes later, maybe even seconds, Jamie speaks again. 'You need to like me enough or leave me alone, Eve.'

As I stare at his back, it hits me how easily Jamie's fondness would be able to turn to hatred.

SIX

Before

'You haven't been honest,' Aiden says.

We're walking along the canal, holding hands, yet both of us in separate worlds. Sometimes it's the things we do that tear relationships apart, and other times it's the things we can't have.

It's freezing outside, even for January, and I pull my scarf tighter around my neck. 'What do you mean?' I ask this, even though I already know.

'At the adoption meeting. You were so quiet. You don't want to do this, do you?'

We've spent the last couple of hours talking to a social worker called Casey, going through the entire process. The whole time we were talking I got so caught up in Aiden's happiness, in his desperation to be a father by any means, that I let myself get carried away.

Now, though, the doubts have set in.

'I do... I'm just...'

'I know it might feel strange for you – but look at my mum and dad. Do you ever feel that they're anything other than my parents just because they adopted me?'

'No, of course not.'

'It's too painful to carry on hoping, Eve. I feel like every time it happens it breaks you even more.'

Four miscarriages. Nothing since then. Not even a sniff of a pregnancy. But I'm not broken. I'm not ready to give up.

'Think about it, Eve. We're not eligible for IVF funding and, even if we were, there are no guarantees it would work.' Aiden squeezes my hand. 'I look at my own parents and it doesn't bother me that I don't share their genes. They've been the most amazing parents, and role models, that I could wish for. We just want to be parents, don't we? To hear a little voice calling us Mummy and Daddy.' This is something Aiden has repeated to me often, so I know he means every word.

Still, my mind searches for reasons to fight this. 'Casey said we're both young. I'm only thirty-one, Aiden, and you're thirty-five. What if we haven't given it enough time?'

'Then we could still keep trying. You know I come from a big family; it wouldn't be any problem if you got pregnant after we adopted. It would be... amazing!' His smile stretches across his face. 'And you've always said you were lonely being an only child, that you wanted to have at least two kids. You even said your mum wished she'd had more because your dad was always working away and you had to play by yourself while she was teaching her piano lessons.'

Aiden's mention of Mum reminds me that I have yet to share with him that I'm worried about her; I've noticed lately that she's forgetting things I've only just told her.

'So, what do you think? Shall we go for it?'

'Yes,' I say, 'let's do it.'

—

'Are you okay?' Aiden asks later that evening

I'm curled up on the sofa, cradling the mug of tea he's made me. 'You just don't seem yourself.'

'It's all a lot to take in, isn't it? I mean, are we really doing this?'

'Yes, of course. I'm so ready for this, Eve, aren't you? It just feels right, doesn't it?'

The truth is that since our adoption meeting, I've become more convinced that this is not the path for us. Do I tell Aiden the truth and crush him, or soldier on for his sake? He's given up hope of me giving birth to our child, and I'm not ready to do that. It's only now I can admit that to myself, after the reality of what adoption involves is starting to set in. It's easy to look at Aiden as an example of what can go right, but my mind keeps focusing on all the things that can go wrong.

'Do you really not care?' I ask. 'About having a child with no genetic link to you. I imagine that sometimes being adopted could make it even more important to someone to have biological children.'

His answer is immediate. 'No. I really don't care about that. Maybe that would bother a lot of people but it doesn't worry me, and believe me, I've given it a lot of thought. I'd still be a dad, wouldn't I? Still do all the things any parent does, so why does it matter if the child doesn't have my genes?'

He says he has given this a lot of thought; when did it first occur to him? How many miscarriages did it take for him to give up on what we've wanted so badly?

I'm about to ask him this when the house phone blares out. I stare at Aiden for a second. Someone calling at this time of night can never be good news. He answers it while I'm still registering what's going on.

'Hello? Oh, hi, Jackie. Everything okay?'

I freeze. It's Mum.

'Hang on a sec, here she is.' Aiden hands me the phone.

'Can you believe this? I've locked myself out,' she says before I've even greeted her. 'Do you think you could pop over with my spare key?'

Frustration overshadows my relief. Pop over. She's making it sound as if she lives around the corner, when Redhill is actually over an hour away from us. 'Of course. But it will take a while. What will you do until I get there?'

'The back gate's open – I'll just sit in the garden and wait.'

'Mum, it's freezing! Can't you go somewhere in the car?'

'Well, I could but the keys are inside with my house keys. They're all on the same key ring.'

This isn't like Mum. She's usually so organised, so together. 'Where had you been this evening, then?'

She hesitates, and I wonder if I've crossed a line, if I'm treating her like a child when she's sixty-two. 'To Rosemary's. I decided to walk as it was a nice evening.'

'Okay, well, I'll be there as soon as I can. But can't you call Rosemary? I'm sure she wouldn't mind picking you up and letting you wait at her place?'

'Oh, no, I won't do that. She's probably gone to bed. It's late, isn't it? Don't worry, I'm fine just waiting in the garden. I've got a book in my bag so that will keep me occupied until you get here.'

There's no point arguing with Mum – she's too stubborn. Whenever I point this out she just laughs and tells me it's where I get it from.

As soon as we end the call, I relay to Aiden what's happened then reach for my mobile and scroll through my contacts; I'm certain I have Rosemary's number here somewhere.

'I'll go,' Aiden says. 'It's late and you have to be up earlier than I do. It's a long drive.'

I assure him I'll be fine. Besides, I think Mum would be embarrassed if Aiden turned up. She didn't even tell him on the phone what had happened.

'What are you doing?' Aiden asks. 'Don't you need to get going? Otherwise it will be nearly midnight by the time you get there.'

I tell him I need to make a call and press the phone to my ear. I'm about to hang up when Rosemary finally answers, her voice groggy.

'Eve? Oh! Is everything okay? Is your mum okay?'

I apologise for calling so late and tell her about Mum locking herself out of the house.

'Oh, that's annoying,' she says. 'Why didn't she call me? She's welcome to stay here if she can get here by cab. I've been out with some old friends this evening and had a couple of drinks.'

'Wasn't Mum with you?' I know the answer before she even speaks.

'No, love. I actually haven't seen her for a couple of weeks. I've been meaning to catch up with her, though. Is she okay? Shall I call her and tell her to come here?'

Mum won't thank me for calling her friend, but there's no way I can leave her outside in the cold, especially this late at night. It's a pretty safe area, but I still can't bring myself to do it. 'Actually, I know it's a big ask but would you mind jumping in a taxi and going to pick her up?

Then I can come straight to your house to get her? I'll pay for it, of course.'

Rosemary doesn't hesitate. 'That's no problem at all. I'll just get dressed and go.'

'Thank you. Traffic should be okay at this time but I'd better get going. Sorry again for calling so late and asking such a huge favour.'

I put on a coat and check through my bag for Mum's spare key. 'I'm worried about her, Aiden. Don't you think this is all a bit weird?'

'What do you mean?'

'The fact that Mum forgot her keys for one. She never does stuff like that.'

'Eve, we *all* do things like that from time to time, even the most organised of us.' He smiles to show me he means me.

'I know, but there's other stuff too. I've been meaning to talk to you about it but, well, with everything that's been going on I just haven't brought it up. It will have to wait now.'

Aiden follows me downstairs. 'I think sometimes you read too much into things, Eve. You shouldn't always analyse things beyond their surface, you know. Sometimes there just isn't more than what we see.'

Now is not the time for this discussion; there are more urgent things to devote my headspace to. Perhaps he is right; I do tend to overthink things.

But what can explain why Mum lied to me tonight?

SEVEN

Now

It's been easy to ignore that email, erase it from my consciousness, because I don't want to accept it. But now, as I sit holding my phone and staring at new words, I know that I need to act faster.

Nowhere to hide

Deliberately vague, just like the first one. Yet I know exactly what it means. It means that I need to get Kayla back, and I need to do it now.

'Miss, did you hear me?' Maya's voice breaks into my thoughts.

'Sorry. Tell me that again.' There are still a few minutes left of our session, but Maya has already completed all the tasks I've set her today.

'I was asking you what you think I should do. About this.' She rubs her stomach. There's no bump there yet; her action must be purely instinctual. I haven't seen her since she revealed her unplanned pregnancy during our last session, and it's taken almost an hour for her to bring it up, so I'm a bit taken aback that she has.

'Oh. Um. Well, it's your decision of course. Only you know what's right for you.'

She raises her eyebrows. 'Please don't say that. I know you're right, but I want to know what *you* think I should do. What would *you* do?'

Part of me wishes I could tell her the truth: that I'm the last person she should be seeking advice from. 'I don't know if I can answer that,' I say. 'It's got to be your choice, Maya. I can't influence your decision; it wouldn't be right.'

She stares at the ceiling and her eyes start to glisten. 'My choice.'

'Yes, that's what I want to make clear. This is *your* choice – nobody else's. It's your body.' I pause, wondering whether to ask this next question, or if it's delving too deeply into her personal life. She's already told me about the pregnancy, though, so it's probably too late to worry about that. 'Does the father know?'

She nods. 'Yes. And he's a good guy. We've been together a few months, and he says he's happy with whatever decision I make.'

I'm relieved to hear this. 'Does he go to your school?'

'No. He's a bit older than me. Twenty-two. I know his cousin and we all just hang out sometimes. That's how we met. But he really is decent. He's just finished college.'

'You're both so young,' I say.

'I know, but we could make this work, couldn't we?'

Maya is desperate for me to give her an answer, to help her reach a decision, when I should have nothing to do with this. 'Yes, if that's what you really want. Plenty of people have children young. Do your parents know?'

'No, but I won't be able to hide it for much longer. I might start being sick or something soon.' She gently pats her stomach. 'I will tell them. I just need to get my head around it first. Once it's out there it becomes real.

47

No longer just about me and Connor.' She stares at the wall for a moment, frowning. 'I'm only eighteen. I've got university and then a career to think about. How would I be able to do anything?'

'People have overcome much harder situations, Maya. But it's important not to go through this alone. I'm sure your parents will support you if you open up to them.'

She reaches for her pen and repeatedly clicks the nib. 'I don't know. They're great and everything, but we've never discussed anything like this. I don't actually know how they'll react. I think they'll be disappointed. They just want the best for me. They'll see this as a huge mistake.'

I think of Mum, of how much I keep from her, and not just because of her illness.

'I'm sure they'll be there for you, no matter what. I really think you should talk to them. You'll feel much better for it.' My words feel hollow, as if there is no meaning behind them. I am the last person who should be giving Maya advice about her pregnancy.

'I do feel better just talking to you,' she says, taking me by surprise again, because I'm not sure how I'm able to talk to her about pregnancy.

'I can't tell you what to do, Maya, but I can listen if that's what you need.'

'Do you want children, miss?'

Her question shoots out so suddenly it floors me, takes away my breath. 'It's got to be the right time,' I manage to say.

'Yes, you're right,' she says. 'And this isn't for me, is it? How will I ever do anything? I've got at least another twenty years to think about having a baby. I must be crazy.' She starts gathering her things together.

'No, Maya, I didn't mean it like that. My situation is very different.' I should tell her about trying for so long to have a successful pregnancy, about how we can't just assume we will have a baby the minute we decide we're ready. I can't speak about any of that, though, because I fear once I start I won't be able to stop. And no one can know.

'It's not different, though, is it? And you're older than me, so how can I even think that I'm ready for this when you aren't yourself?'

Her tears come hard and fast now, and I instantly put my personal discomfort aside and rush forward to hug her. 'Look, just calm down and don't do anything hasty. This is a huge decision to make, and the pregnancy hormones could be playing havoc with you. I strongly recommend you take some time to think about it all. And please will you talk to your parents? And talk to Connor some more. Make sure you both see things the same way, that's so important, Maya. You're in this together, aren't you?'

She nods, but when she looks up at me her expression is blank. And when she walks out of the door, I realise I have made things worse.

—

There's no answer when I ring Sophie's doorbell, standing here as if two years haven't passed, as if I was only here yesterday. There is no telling how she'll react to seeing me, but I need to be with my daughter and, of all people, Sophie should understand that.

After a few more seconds of silence, I turn to walk away, resolving to come back tomorrow, and then I hear my name. I recognise the deep tone immediately. It's

Damien. I wonder if he's her husband now – they were always talking about getting married. He's standing by the open side gate, staring at me with a frown. How long has he been watching me?

'Eve, is that you? My God, it is.' He's still frowning, and staring at me as if I'm a hallucination, some trick of his mind. I can only imagine what's going through his head.

Taking a step forward, I assure myself I can do this. I've got to get used to the shock I will invoke in people when I reappear. 'I know this must be a bit of a surprise but is Sophie here? I really need to talk to her.'

He glances at the house and walks towards me. 'She's not home. She took the twins to the park.'

'The one around the corner?'

He nods and continues staring at me. I almost wish he would just ask me why I did it; it couldn't be any worse than facing his silent disapproval.

'I'll go and find her there, then,' I declare, and although he doesn't say anything, it feels as though his eyes are tracing my movements as I walk away.

–

The park is exactly as I remember it. It's Saturday, so it's busier than usual and this fuels my confidence. Somehow, it feels as though it will be easier to talk to Sophie while we're surrounded by people. I can't explain why; perhaps it's something to do with there being safety in numbers.

The twins will be around three and a half years old now, unrecognisable to me, just as Kayla was the other day. They, like my daughter, won't even know who I am, even though their mother was once my closest friend.

Nerves overwhelm me as I get closer to the bright yellow gate. I don't know if I'm ready for this, but if it brings me to Kayla then I have to see it through. *Whatever it takes*.

Sophie's standing in between two swings, easily pushing both of the twins at once. Nothing's changed then; Sophie, for all her initial reluctance, still makes motherhood look easy. She's wearing a grey hooded top and skinny jeans with white trainers; her hair is tied up in a messy bun on top of her head. A *mum bun* she always called it. A pair of oversized sunglasses are perched on her head, and she looks effortlessly glamorous, even dressed so casually. The boys, of course, are huge compared to my memory of them, and I would never have recognised them as hers.

As I watch the three of them, I wonder what kind of mother I would have been if things had been different. If I had been able to stay with my daughter. It's a question I'll never know the answer to.

Sophie spots me the second I'm through the gate, squinting at me through the sunlight. Stopping her rhythmic pushing of the swings, she stands shaking her head with her hands on her hips, waits for me to approach.

'I didn't believe it when Damien texted me just now,' she says. 'I told him he must be mistaken and he'd got you mixed up with someone else. I said there's no way, but it's really you.' She lifts the twins from their swings. 'Just play on your own for a second, boys. Mummy needs to speak to someone.'

Someone. That's all I am to her now.

'What the hell, Eve?' she says once the twins are out of earshot.

Where do I begin? There's so much I can't bring myself to explain to her, not before I've talked to Aiden first. I hope she'll understand that.

Sophie doesn't give me a chance to say anything. 'Does Aiden know you're back?'

'No. I know I've got a lot of explaining to do,' I tell her. I barely recognise my voice. I'm not used to speaking to people who know things about me. 'Can we go over there?' I point to the bench that a mother and her toddler have just vacated. 'You can still see the twins from there.'

'Fine,' she says. 'Boys, I'll just be over there.'

'Go on then,' she says as soon as we've sat down. With no sunglasses on, the sun glares at me and I can barely see her, so I stare straight ahead, watching her sons tear around the park. They are carefree in a way that Kayla will probably never be. I have scarred her for life with my actions.

'I'm sorry,' I say. 'I don't know how to begin trying to explain, but I just want you to know that I'm so sorry.'

'It's not me you need to apologise to,' she says. 'It's Aiden. And Kayla. Your daughter.' Sophie's not going to make this easy for me. 'How could you do it, Eve? Walking out on them like that. Kayla was three months old!' She shakes her head. 'I can't even look at you.'

I have to face her admonishment, but I will stand my ground. There are things Sophie can never begin to understand, things I will never let her. 'I'm here to put things right. With everyone, especially Kayla and Aiden. I needed to see you first, though.'

'Two years later you want to put things right?' She shakes her head again. 'Why now?'

This is a question with too many answers. *Because I've never stopped loving my daughter, never stopped thinking of her; because I need to put right what I did; because of that email.* I try to explain to Sophie that I'm here to do what's right for Kayla, but, understandably, she is struggling to get past her anger.

'Look at me, please. You were my best friend and I let you down, I know that. But if our friendship meant anything to you then can you please put your anger aside and help me?'

Her expression softens, offering me a glimmer of hope that we can get through this together. 'You've hurt people, Eve. The people who cared about you the most, and now you just want... what? Forgiveness? That's asking a lot.'

I fight the urge to hang my head, shrink into myself; I will stand my ground in spite of everything. Sophie has always had the ability to diminish people. I just never thought she could, or would, do it to me.

'You met someone else, didn't you?' she demands. 'Thought you could have a better life with him? After everything you went through with Aiden. My God.'

'No! That's not what happened – I swear to you.'

She turns away from me, focuses her attention on the twins. 'That's what we all assumed. Including Aiden. Why did you leave, then?'

'I... I just had to. Please look at me, Soph.'

She turns to me and her eyes narrow. I'm fighting a battle I can't win here.

'Can we meet up later and talk somewhere else?' I ask. 'When the twins are in bed? Around eight maybe? We can talk about it all then.'

She shakes her head. 'I don't think you coming to my house is a good idea. You shouldn't have even gone there just now. Haven't you heard of calling? Giving people a warning when you're about to reappear out of the blue?'

Her words sting, but I let it go. 'If you don't want me in your house then come to my flat.' I reach into my bag and scribble my address on a sheet of paper. It would be much easier to tell her it verbally so she could put it in her phone, but I don't want to give her any excuse to not take it.

'I don't know,' she says.

'Just think about it, please, Soph. I'll be home all evening.'

Even though I don't want to leave without any assurance that she'll come, I stand up and walk back through the park, ignoring the joyful squeals of laughter that fill the air. The sounds of family life that I will never have.

It's up to Sophie now. I just hope she's quick because the clock is ticking and it's only a matter of time before I get another email. Or worse.

EIGHT

Before

'Are you okay?' Helen asks, leaning across to my table. It's Year 11 parents' evening and, although I normally enjoy them, I could do without it tonight. This is the first time I haven't sat beside Sophie, and it feels strange that she's sitting at home with her babies, rather than here. Helen is friendly enough, but I've never felt comfortable enough to open up to her like I always have with Sophie.

'I'm just tired,' I tell Helen. 'It's been a long day.' I stare at my appointment list and see that Justin Foley is due next. No doubt it will be his annoying dad with him again, but at least his father always turns up; many parents don't bother.

They're not due for a few minutes, so I pull out my phone to text Aiden. Things between us have been strained since I admitted to him that I don't want to go ahead with adoption, that I'm not ready to take that step. My decision hit him hard. His dream of being a dad had been tangible, just for a short while, and now I've ripped it away. Now we are back to square one, with no idea when it will happen, or if it ever will.

I'm typing my message when Justin appears, still in his school uniform. 'Hi, miss.' He sits down, and when I look up I'm surprised to find he's alone.

'On your own?' I ask, wondering how I can have this session without any parent present.

'Oh, no, Dad's here. He'll be here in a second.'

And then the man himself appears. 'Miss Conway,' he says, holding out his hand for me to shake. 'How are you?'

'Fine, thank you. Let's get started.'

For the next few minutes I try not to think about anything other than Justin's progress, and after several moments, I even find myself warming, ever so slightly, to his dad.

'I forgot to ask if you can do extra tutoring sessions, miss?' Justin asks when we're just about finished. 'I'm getting a bit worried about exams now and don't feel I'm on top of all the revision.'

His father hasn't even mentioned this lately and hasn't sought to have a meeting for a while, so I'd given it no further thought. I'm surprised the request is coming from Justin when his father is standing right here. 'Um, I don't really—'

'We'd pay you, of course,' his dad interjects. 'Whatever the going rate is. I just want the best help for Justin.'

I'm about to repeat what I've already told him many times – that Justin is fine and really doesn't need the extra help – but I glance at my student and see his desperation. 'Please, miss.'

'I suppose I could help,' I say.

'Great,' says Mr Foley. 'We'll be in touch.'

They both stand to leave and before I have a chance to regret what I've just agreed to, my phone starts to vibrate on the table. It's Mum. Again. She knows I'm doing a parents' evening tonight, so this can only mean that she's in trouble. Scooping up my phone, I apologise to the student and parents waiting to be seen next and rush outside to the corridor, mentally preparing myself for the latest disaster. Because things are only going to get worse.

—

'Thank God you're okay,' I say to Mum, wrapping her in my arms.

She seems surprised by my concern. 'Of course I'm okay, it was just a little accident, I'm not hurt.'

The kitchen windows are open, yet the smell of the charred tea towel won't dissipate. I imagine it will be days before it does. 'What happened, Mum? Are you sure you didn't turn the gas on?'

'No, I didn't. I'd made a cup of tea and went upstairs to the bathroom but when I came back down that tea towel was on fire. Spread over the hob, which was on. I have no idea how it turned itself on, but I definitely didn't do it. I had a sandwich for lunch so wouldn't have needed to use the cooker.' She rushes to the sink and lifts out a plate. 'See. This was my sandwich plate. Cheese and tomato. I would have had ham but I've run out.'

'But what about dinner?' I check my watch and it's nearly seven p.m.

'That's what I meant. I had a sandwich for dinner.'

I'm too relieved that she isn't hurt to question her about her meal choices. 'Oh, Mum. Thank goodness you're okay. That's all that matters.'

She places the plate back in the sink, even though she has a dishwasher and never washes by hand. 'You don't believe me, do you? You think there's something wrong with me!' She raises her voice.

'No, please calm down. I believe you, okay?'

'Good. Because I'm still your mother. I'm not a child and don't need to be patronised.'

'Okay, Mum, you're right. Shall I make some coffee?'

'No, thanks – I've just had one.'

I glance around the kitchen and there is no sign of a mug anywhere. It could be in the dishwasher, though. I mustn't assume that everything she says is untrue.

'It's a lovely evening, shall we go and sit in the garden?' I suggest, mainly so we don't have to inhale these fumes any more.

'Yes, good idea. I'll just get the back door key.'

She fumbles in her bag and pulls out her key ring. It's odd that she keeps the back door key on there; I'm sure she used to keep it separately in a kitchen drawer. Now's not the time to question her about it, though.

I don't know what compels me to check, but I pull the handle and find the back door unlocked.

Mum looks up. 'Oh, how strange. I can't remember when I went out that way last. Must have been this morning.'

Outside, we sit at the garden table, and Mum asks me about my day. She's chatting so normally that I begin to believe I've been worrying for nothing. We all forget things and make mistakes. Maybe I'm suffering from anxiety and it's causing me to think the worst about every situation?

'When are you and Aiden going to come for dinner?' Mum asks. 'I haven't seen him for ages.'

This is true, and it would be good for him to be around Mum for a bit, just to reassure me either way. 'I'll speak to him tonight. He's going to Edinburgh soon to stay with his parents for a few days. They need some help redecorating the house, and he hasn't seen them for ages.'

'Oh, that's nice. Lovely people, aren't they?' Mum says, smiling. 'Aiden's such a wonderful young man and it just goes to show what having a loving family can do for a child.'

It's as if she knows, even though I haven't told her we were considering adopting, and I know Aiden wouldn't have spoken to her either. 'Yes,' I say. 'It is. But it's not for everyone.'

She sighs. 'I worry about you, Eve. Oh, I know right now you're the one worrying about me, but it's been giving me sleepless nights to think of what you're going through.'

'We're doing okay, Mum. And I'm only thirty-one. I've still got time, haven't I?'

'You always did have such a positive outlook,' she says. 'You got that from your dad, I think. Oh, I wish he was here to see what an amazing young woman you've turned into.' Her eyes glisten. It's not often that she talks about Dad, but when she does it always chokes her up. 'Even when he was diagnosed with lung cancer – he carried on smiling, carried on working. He said he wasn't going to let that beat him. And he never once moaned about working with asbestos for all those years, even though that's what ended his life. What strength of character.'

'I miss him,' I say. As young as I was when he died, his absence has left a chasm within me that should have been filled with his huge personality.

'We both do.' She leans closer to me, as if she's about to tell me something confidential. 'Eve, you need to stop worrying about me and start thinking of yourself. I'm absolutely fine. There's nothing wrong with me at all. Just focus on you and Aiden and having that family you're both desperate for. Nothing else matters.'

We sit in the garden long after the sun has set, and I lose myself in Mum's words and thoughts. They are so strong and clear that I convince myself I have got this all wrong, that I have been worrying for no reason. Mum is fine.

She has to be.

–

Aiden's in bed when I get home, and despite my best efforts not to make too much noise and wake him, he stirs and opens his eyes. 'Is everything okay with your mum?'

I tell him about my visit, and even though he's looking at me, responding to my words, it feels as though he's only half present. I've really hurt him by not wanting to proceed with adoption.

'At least she wasn't injured,' Aiden says, rolling onto his back. 'Jackie's a tough woman. She'll be fine. It's you I'm worried about.'

'I'm fine. I'm always fine,' I tell him, changing into my pyjamas.

Aiden watches me, lines creasing his forehead. 'Come here.' He lifts my side of the duvet and pulls me towards him. 'We need to stick together in this, Eve. Otherwise I'm scared of what might happen to us. Things like this rip relationships apart, don't they?'

I nod and cuddle into him. And when our bodies merge together I convince myself that this time will be it. That in this exact moment we are making our baby. The one who will stay with us.

NINE

Now

Someone has been in my flat. I can sense it. It smells different, a scent that doesn't belong to me and has no place in here.

It's other things too – subtle, barely perceptible. The TV remote control too close to the DVD player, the kettle too far from the wall. And in the bathroom, the hand soap is right next to the tap when I always leave it nearer the edge of the sink.

The email first, now this. What will be next?

Grabbing a knife from the kitchen drawer, I search the flat, and even though fear is coursing through me, I will not let it win.

But when the doorbell rings, I jump.

It will be Sophie, nobody else. I've invited her here and now she's come. I just need to focus on that. I quickly return the knife to the drawer then head to let her in.

The last thing I expect to see when I fling open the door is Jamie standing there, his hands in his pockets. I know disappointment must be carved into my face, but I'm powerless to suppress it. Jamie doesn't deserve this, but it's Sophie I need here. Everything depends on me getting through to her.

'Can we talk?' Jamie says, looking past me. If only this scrutiny was because he wants to make sure I'm not in the middle of a session, that there's no student here I need to get back to, but I know it's not that. Jamie might say he trusts me but he knows something is off; he just can't piece together what that is. He probably assumes I'm cheating on him.

I want to ask him if he's been in my flat today, but I know it won't have been him. 'It's really not a good time,' I say, scanning the street for any sign of Sophie. How would I explain to either of them who the other person is? This is complicated enough already. 'What if I come over later?' I tell Jamie. 'We can talk properly then. I can cook dinner or treat you to a takeaway?' I try to sound casual, as if I'm not desperate to hurry him off.

He hesitates, and these ticking seconds make me believe I might just get away with this.

'No. We need to talk now, Eve. I'm sick of being brushed off.' He folds his arms. 'Are you going to let me in, then?'

I've never seen Jamie like this before and it doesn't feel right. Again, I stare out at the street, where Sophie still hasn't made an appearance. Perhaps she won't come at all; she didn't actually agree to be here at eight and it's now twenty past. My hope dwindles and I reluctantly stand aside to let Jamie in.

As soon as we're in the kitchen he wrinkles his nose. 'It smells funny in here. Different.'

'Probably one of my students,' I say. So he's noticed it, too. Confirmation that it's not all in my mind – someone has been in my flat without me knowing. I turn my focus

62

back to Jamie. 'So how come you're here? I thought we'd talked about everything the other night?'

Jamie's eyes widen. 'Really? That was talking? And I thought women were the ones who were supposed to overanalyse everything.' He raises his hand. 'No offence.' When he sits down at my table he runs his fingers over the grooves in the wood, staring at them as if he finds them fascinating. He is nervous, his usual confidence missing in action.

'You're right, we do need to talk, Jamie, I just can't do it now. Later, though. I'll come over to you, I promise. We'll sit down and talk about everything, for as long as we need to.'

'Like I said—'

The doorbell rings, and we both freeze.

'Oh, you're expecting a student.' Jamie stands. 'Sorry, I'll go.'

'It's not a student, it's a friend.'

Before I can say another word he's striding to the door, and just as I'm about to grab his arm to keep him back he stops himself. 'Go on. Answer it, then. Don't let me stop you.'

Again, this aggression is out of character for Jamie, but I don't dwell on it because I'm too relieved that Sophie has come. I barely even care that I will now have to give both her and Jamie an explanation, because I am now one step closer to Kayla and ending this before it ends me.

Jamie's shoulders drop when I open the door and he sees Sophie standing there instead of the man he no doubt expected.

'Thank you so much for coming,' I say, leaning forward to hug her. It's an instinctual act, one I do without any thought, despite how things are between us now. Sophie's body tenses and she barely moves her arms to respond to my embrace. Turning back to Jamie, I notice he is frowning.

I introduce them both, and they tentatively shake hands. Perhaps they both sense that this is an unusual situation, that none of us is comfortable.

'Jamie was just leaving,' I say.

He hesitates before finally moving towards the door. 'See you this evening then, Eve?' It feels like more of a demand than a question.

I nod and usher him out. As soon as I close the door behind him and am alone with Sophie, I notice how different she looks to when I saw her earlier in the park. Her hair is fluffier, as if it's just been washed, and hangs in loose waves around her shoulders. She's wearing what look like the same jeans, only this time she has on heels and a silky vest top with a deep V-neck. She still looked good in the park, but there is something different about her now, standing here alone without the twins hanging off her, more like the woman she was when I first met her.

'So, you did meet someone else then?' she says. 'Jamie.'

'No, it's not like that. I've only known him for a few months. I didn't lie to you.'

She scans my hallway, and it's hard to read her expression; all I'm certain of is that she'll be trying to work out this new version of me. This is a small flat – definitely not suitable for more than one person – but it's in fairly decent condition and I try to make the best of the space.

'Do you own this place?' Sophie asks.

'No. It's rented. I left the house with Aiden, so there's no way I can buy my own place.'

'Well, leaving him the house is the least you could have done when you left him as the sole carer of your daughter.' She shakes her head. 'Sorry. On the way over here, I swore to myself I wouldn't give you a hard time like I did in the park. I came to hear your side of things.'

'Thank you,' I say. 'That means everything to me, Soph.'

In the kitchen, Sophie declines my offer of a drink, and I get myself a glass of water and sit with her at the table. Although she's promised she will hear me out, she leans forward, her shoulders hunched, and I know it's only a matter of time before she is on the attack again.

'You know I wanted Kayla more than anything, don't you? You remember everything Aiden and I went through before she came along?'

'Of course, and I was there with you every step of the way, wasn't I?'

'Please just let me finish. You have to understand that this has nothing to do with our friendship. I valued that more than anything.'

She looks at me, opening her mouth but quickly closing it again. She's ready to let me talk.

'When Kayla was finally here, I... I just couldn't handle everything.'

Her mouth opens again and she stares at me. 'What do you mean? What exactly couldn't you handle?'

The events that led me here flash through my head, and I shut them down. I can't speak the words, relive them, make it all real. 'I just couldn't deal with my life any more,

Sophie. I'm sorry I can't explain it any better than that.' There is no way I can tell her any more than this.

She shakes her head. 'This is unbelievable. Are you trying to say you just didn't want Kayla any more? That you had some kind of postnatal depression?'

Her words send me cold, but I have to confront this. 'I don't know what it was, Sophie. Maybe it was that.'

Again, she shakes her head. 'Do you realise you're not making this any better? If you want people to understand you then you have to explain more than that. Surely you can see that?'

'Of course I can. It's just… this is all I can give right now.'

'Was it Aiden? You didn't love him any more?'

'No. It was nothing like that. I loved them both with every fibre of my being.' That's exactly why I had to go. I wish I could help Sophie see this.

'Well, if you're not able to explain it, people will just think you couldn't be bothered with the hard work that comes with having a baby.'

Nobody matters except Kayla, Aiden, Mum and Sophie, though, so let people think what they will.

'I realise that. Look, I know how terrible it was walking out and now I need to put things right. That's all I care about.'

Sophie crosses her legs, and in this moment she looks just like she does when she's about to give a student a lecture. 'If you were struggling then why didn't you talk to me? Or Aiden? You could have got help. You didn't have to walk out. You were never a quitter before.'

The truth swims around my head, and I focus on that split second before it all could have been different. That's all it took for everything to change. A second. And then there was no going back.

'There is no excuse for what I did. None at all. I just need help to put it right.'

Sophie sighs. 'The time for me to have helped would have been back then. Anyway, what is it you think I can do?'

Here goes nothing. 'My plan is to talk to Aiden. On his own, just the two of us, but before I do I need you to tell me how things were after I left. I know this won't be easy – for either of us – but I need to approach him in the right way, and, well, the truth is he's a stranger to me now. I know nothing about his life, and I doubt he's even the same person. Anything you could tell me would help.'

She frowns. 'If you're looking for some insight into how he might react then nothing I say will give you that. It's impossible to know what Aiden will think or do. Only he knows that.'

'I do understand that. I just want to be a mother to my little girl. And in order to do that I need to know how they've both been over the last two years.' I move closer to Sophie and reach for her arm. She flinches but doesn't pull away. 'I'm so sorry to ask this of you, but there's no one else who can help me.'

There is a long pause before she responds. 'Aiden called me on the morning you disappeared. He thought that because you and I were so close I must know where you were, and it took a lot to convince him that I had no idea. He even accused me of lying, of covering up for you. Got quite confrontational and I've never known him to be like that.' She shakes her head. 'I understood, though. He was distraught and needed to lash out at someone I suppose.

He was a complete mess when you walked out. Not only was he coping with a tiny baby, but his marriage had fallen apart and he had no idea why. Damien and I both had to go round there on that first morning to help him as he was in such a state.'

It crushes me to hear of Aiden's suffering. I've been fully aware of the pain I would have caused him but hearing about it makes it more real. 'I should have talked to him first. I know that now. But I wasn't thinking clearly.' How could I have been when my mind was clouded with fog? When nothing was right.

'So where did you go?' Sophie asks.

My body gives an involuntary shudder as I'm forced to recall those early days. I had no purpose, no goal, I was just existing. It was as if I didn't belong in this world. 'I drove down to Cornwall and stayed in a B & B. I just needed to be away from everyone and everything. Believe me, I know how dreadful that sounds when I had a three-month-old baby at home, but I think I just blocked it all out.'

'Erased your life, you mean. Pretended your daughter didn't exist.'

'I know that's what it looks like,' I say, staring at the floor.

'Do you know how appalling that is?'

I nod. It's impossible to make Sophie see that I didn't have a choice, that I was protecting my family as best I could by leaving. There is no way she will understand that. 'There wasn't a single day that I didn't think about Kayla, though. I never forgot about her.' I stare at Sophie, and she's shaking her head, glaring at me as if I'm pure evil. I need to keep her talking about Aiden, rather than have her focus on me. I'm not ready for that. 'Did you stay in touch with Aiden after that?' I ask.

'Yes, a bit. His parents came down from Scotland for a few weeks. They couldn't stay much longer because of work commitments. It broke their hearts to have to leave him and Kayla, and they tried their best to convince him to move in with them for a while, but you know Aiden. He wanted to try to deal with it himself. There was no way he would leave London.'

I remember Aiden's parents' reaction when I had all the miscarriages. How his mum hugged me tighter than even my own mum, and that when we pulled away from each other her tears had soaked through my top, and I could feel them on my skin; she was feeling my pain as acutely as I was. 'Yes, they're lovely people,' I tell Sophie. Another bond I've managed to destroy. 'So what did Aiden do after that?'

'He coped, Eve. He sucked it up and dealt with the gaping hole you'd left. He might have fallen apart to begin with but he got used to it, and he's a great dad, despite what was thrown at him.'

'And you're still in contact now?'

'A little.'

'So you must know about Nicole Richardson then?'

Sophie stares at me. It's not often I ever witnessed her lost for words. 'How do you—'

'It doesn't matter. Do you know how long they've been together?'

Her forehead furrows. 'Around a year. Something like that. Look, sorry, Eve, but I'm getting a bit fed up of answering all these questions when you've barely said anything about why you left.'

It's only right that I should answer her questions, but I need to know one thing. 'Do they live together?'

Sophie rolls her eyes. 'What did you expect? You left him, Eve; he was bound to move on eventually.'

I haven't expected this. Finding out Aiden was with someone else, someone who would be in Kayla's life, was one thing; this feels like my insides are being torn apart because it might mean something worse. 'Does Kayla know about me? Does she know who I am, Sophie?'

Sophie takes so long to answer, and that in itself tells me all I need to know.

'I don't know. That's the truth, Eve. She was three months old. She wouldn't remember you, would she? You'd have to ask Aiden what he's told her.'

I believe Sophie. She's too much of a straight-talker to lie to me about this. Besides, it's not as if she'll be trying to protect my feelings.

She stands up and walks to my fridge. There's nothing stuck to it with magnets; no photos or pictures, or signs that anyone lives here. 'How about you actually answer some of my questions now?' she says. 'Where did you go after Cornwall? Did you get a teaching job?'

'I lived in Dorking in Surrey for a while, once I got my head together a bit. And I couldn't teach because I didn't want Aiden tracking me down.' I wait for her admonishment but it doesn't come. 'I did private tuition instead. Used my maiden name. Then I moved here over a year ago.'

'Why did you come back to London? It obviously wasn't to get Kayla back or you wouldn't have left it so long.'

'I couldn't get enough tutoring work, so I thought I'd have more students in London. I really had no choice, but it wasn't easy to do.'

'And you picked all the way on the other side of London. Nowhere near Kayla. What changed?'

So many things changed. *I* changed. 'I just couldn't be away from her any longer,' I tell Sophie.

She comes back to the table, slides into her chair. 'Aiden tried to find you. For months. You did a good job of disappearing. Your mum didn't even know where you were. Why would you do that to her?'

Mum. It was a few months before I went to see her, even though I'd been texting her to assure her I was okay. Explaining to her that I'd left my family was one of the hardest things I'd ever had to do. Then her illness got worse and everything with me faded into the background.

'I'm not proud of that, Sophie.'

'None of this makes sense. A lot of people struggle with having a baby but they don't run away.'

'I know. Look, I really can't talk about this now, please understand that. I need to talk to Aiden first.'

Sophie reluctantly agrees and drops her questioning. She glances around my flat again. It's not in a bad state, but she'd probably consider it soulless and uninviting. There's barely any colour in here and nothing about it feels permanent. 'So, you think you can bring Kayla up here?' she asks. 'Is that your plan? To take her away from Aiden, after he's done everything for the last two years, and pull her away from all she knows?'

This is all I've thought about for months, but I can't let Sophie know that. 'No, of course not. I know that can't happen and I'd never want to cause her any more pain, but I need to be in her life, Sophie. In whatever way that's possible.'

'Good. Because she's nearly two and a half, and she'll be aware of so much. And Aiden won't let you just come in and say, "Hey Kayla, I'm your mum, come and live with me".'

'I know all this, Sophie, which is why I came to you for help.'

She ignores me. 'The three of them seem to have a good life together, and you can't just come and disrupt it. Aiden won't let that happen. He's been through too much already.'

Her words, although true, slice into my flesh. 'I just want to see Kayla. To be in her life in any way I can.'

'There's Nicole to think about too. I'm sorry, but it's true. She's a decent woman and she's an integral part of Aiden's and Kayla's life now, so you need to get your head around that.'

There is nothing I can say to this, because once again everything Sophie says is the truth. I know she's not saying it to be unkind, that's not who she is. Or who she *was* at least. I don't know her any more; I've just been assuming she's the same person, but everyone around me has been changed by my betrayal.

'I assume Nicole looks after Kayla when Aiden's at work?'

'Yes,' Sophie replies. 'And why does this feel like a police interrogation? Aiden's not the one who did anything wrong.'

'I'm sorry. I just need information before I can speak to him. I need to know exactly what will be involved.'

'Like I said before, it's not something that can be planned like that, is it? There are people's lives and feelings involved, and there's no way to predict anything.' She shakes her head. 'I get it, Eve, you're like me and need to be in control, to organise things and assess every possible outcome. It comes with being a teacher, but I just don't think that will work in this case. If you're going to do this, you need to do it carefully, and see what happens. I don't think there's anything more I can tell you, and to be honest, I don't have a clue how Aiden will react. I really don't.'

I stand up and walk to the window. Outside, the pavement is lit up by the street lights and it hardly looks like night time. When I first rented this place, I couldn't get used to the kitchen overlooking the front of the building, when I'd been able to see the back garden from our family kitchen, but now I find it comforting. It eases my claustrophobia when I'm sitting at the table tutoring for hour after hour. It's nice to glance up and see that the world outside still exists. Even if it's a world in which nothing is right.

'Don't go to Aiden,' Sophie is saying.

'I have to. I need—'

'Wait, just hear me out. Let me talk to him first. I think the news of you being back will be better coming from me. Less of a shock.'

I'm surprised by her offer and need a moment for it to sink in. I hadn't considered this as an option and try now to visualise it. Half of me thinks that perhaps Sophie is right; the two of them have been in touch for these two years, so she might have a better chance of easing Aiden into this new situation than I would myself. But the other

73

part of me believes this is my mess to clear up, so I am the one who needs to face Aiden. I try to explain this to Sophie.

'Yes, all that's true, but I think if you just turn up on his doorstep it might cause him even more pain. At least I can warn him, give him a chance to talk it through and get his head around it. Then the two of you can meet up and discuss everything.' She sighs. 'I'm just trying to look out for him, Eve. And *you*, actually. I can't condone what you did, but I suppose you must have had your reasons, even if I don't know what they are and none of it makes any sense.'

'Thank you, Sophie.' In the past I would have hugged her at a moment like this, but she seemed ill at ease with my earlier embrace so I don't repeat that now.

'You'd better give me your phone number so I can let you know what happens with Aiden.'

We exchange numbers, and Sophie stands up to leave. She's been here such a short time that I want to ask her to stay, to promise her we can talk about anything, just like old times, but the words won't leave my mouth. No matter how much I long for her company, for that window to the past to be opened permanently, I just have to be grateful she's helping me at all. That will have to be enough for now. But something is telling me that Sophie's not the person I used to know.

When I'm alone, I remember that someone has been in my flat.

Next time, I will be ready for them.

TEN

Before

It's been thirteen weeks now, and still I can't let myself believe that there's a baby growing inside me. Thirteen. That's an unlucky number, isn't it? So I spend the week waiting for it to happen, for the smallest sign of blood or anything else to show that this baby is no more, just like all the others. Why should this time be any different?

But it is. I know it as surely as I know my own name. I just don't want to admit it.

This time I've waited to tell Aiden; I would only be getting his hopes up, bringing that joy I usually love seeing on his face for nothing. But he knows something is wrong; I'm barely eating and spend most of the time I'm not working in bed. I need to tell him.

I do it over dinner – beef chilli, which Aiden has gone to a lot of effort to make – and watch as the hugest smile erupts on his face.

'Wait, say that again!' His eyes are wide with delight.

I can barely look at him. 'I'm pregnant. Fourteen weeks tomorrow. I've got a dating scan in the afternoon.'

'I can't believe it! Why didn't you tell me before?' He rushes over to me and folds me into him. 'You wanted to wait this time in case...'

Slowly I nod.

'Oh, Eve, this is amazing news. I was beginning to think it would never happen. Especially as we haven't—'

'Now you understand why?' I force myself to look at him. 'I just wanted to be careful.'

Aiden stands and walks round to me, kneeling down and resting his head on my lap. 'I was so worried... I thought... you've been so distant lately, and after all the adoption business, I was starting to think we wouldn't be okay.'

I stroke his hair, focus on the smooth strands that are out of place, try to block out all the thoughts that are exploding in my head.

He looks up at me. 'I know it will be difficult but we need to try to be positive. This is the furthest you've ever got, isn't it, so this baby is here to stay.'

And that's exactly what I'm afraid of.

ELEVEN

Now

Three days have passed since Sophie suggested talking to Aiden for me. Seventy-two hours have never felt so long, and I plod along on autopilot, sick with anxiety, unable to focus on anything but my urgent need to be with my daughter. And the fact that I'm running out of time. There is a clock ticking; the emails are evidence of that. There's barely a moment when my eyes aren't glued to my phone, waiting for the next one, and now I'm also desperate for news from Sophie.

'I'm going up to the Lake District at the weekend,' Jamie is saying. 'To visit my parents. It's been so long since I've been to see them – life just seems to get in the way, doesn't it?'

'It's good that you're making time for them,' I say, staring out of the café window.

'Do you realise we've never actually done this before?' Jamie says.

I turn to him. 'What?'

'Met up for a coffee during the day. It's always evenings, isn't it?' He winks. 'This is nice, though. And it feels apt to be sitting in a coffee shop with you – together this time.'

Jamie's reference to how we met might make me return his smile, if I weren't so distracted. When I see how his face lights up with that smile, I realise that, despite everything, I want Jamie to be happy. That's what made me agree to meet up with him this afternoon, even though I'm about to crack open at any moment.

'Anyway, I was thinking,' he continues, 'maybe you could come with me?'

'To meet your parents?' I can't hide the horror on my face, and Jamie's happy expression quickly vanishes.

'Yeah. They're nice people, Eve, you'll love them. Have you ever been to the Lake District? It's amazing there. Especially if you're just used to this concrete jungle.' He gestures around us.

'I, um...'

'Just say yes. Don't overthink it. It'll be nice. I think you could do with a break. I don't know what's been going on in your life but you seem... a bit stressed or something.'

'I don't know, Jamie.'

'Look, I don't know what will happen with us, if there even can be an *us*, but it could just be a weekend away. A break for you. Don't think of it as meeting my parents; we'd just be staying with them. Or we could do a hotel if you don't want to stay at their house?'

I'm about to say it's probably not a good idea when I see a familiar figure across the road. Although I'm instantly aware that it's someone I know, it takes me a moment to work out that it's Maya, my pregnant student. It always takes me by surprise when I see a student outside of a tutoring session, or outside of school when I used to work in one, almost as though they don't exist in any other setting.

She's standing in the middle of the pavement, having what seems like an argument with a boy. He's gesticulating wildly, and Maya is shouting at him, her own face creased in anger. I've never witnessed her like this before and I wonder if I ought to go to check she is okay, but before I can move she is walking away, leaving the boy standing there shaking his head.

'So that's a yes, then?' Jamie is saying, oblivious to what's happening outside.

I nod, without remembering what I'm agreeing to, because right now all my focus is on Maya.

'Great! I'll let them know we're coming.'

As I turn back to Jamie, it sinks in that I've just agreed to spend the weekend at his parents' house. Miles away from Kayla. 'I, um—'

His phone rings, and with a quick apology he rushes to answer it.

I whisper that I'll be back in a minute and leave the café to see if there's any sign of Maya. She's long gone, though, and so is the boy she was arguing with. I check my appointments on my phone and see that she's not due a session until Friday. I text her and ask if she's okay, explaining that I've just seen her in the high street, and that I'm here if she needs to talk.

Back inside the café, Jamie has finished his call and is at the till paying for our drinks. 'I'm sorry,' he says when he spots me, 'emergency at work, I have to go.'

'Don't worry.'

He kisses my forehead. 'I'll call you later. So glad you're coming next weekend,' he says, and then he has gone, and I'm left wondering how I just agreed to this when Kayla is slipping further away from me.

—

'What are you doing here?' Sophie asks. Her tone isn't unkind, just fused with shock at the sight of me standing on her doorstep when she is the one who was meant to contact me.

'I'm sorry, but I've been going out of my mind. I know you, Sophie, and I know you will have spoken to him by now, so what aren't you telling me?' As I stare at her, I feel certain that I cannot trust her; how can I when I don't even know if I can trust myself?

'You'd better come in,' she says. 'The twins are in bed, and Damien's out with his work friends.'

Stepping into Sophie's house after all this time is like travelling back in time. Not much has changed; it's still got Sophie's stamp all over it, her way of matching colours, picking the decorative accessories that perfectly comple-ment each room. She always used to joke that if she ever got fed up of teaching she'd go into interior design.

'He won't see me, will he?' As soon as I've said it, I know it's the truth. I've spent so many hours imagining my first conversation with Aiden, planning to defend myself, that it never occurred to me that Aiden might refuse to see me.

'I'm sorry.' Sophie heads to the living room, and I follow her, surprised to find toys scattered all over the floor, even though the twins must have gone to bed a while ago.

'What did he say?'

She starts clearing away the mess, only stopping when I grab her arm.

'Please, Sophie, just talk to me.'

'I decided to ask him to meet me for a drink. I thought it might be better if I spoke to him in person. We used to meet for drinks sometimes after… you know.' She waits for my reaction, as if I might object.

'Okay. What happened?'

She sighs. 'Oh, I don't know if I handled it right at all. I mean, it's not a normal kind of situation, is it? There's no advice anywhere for how to deal with something like this.' She looks flustered, out of her comfort zone. I'd always thought that nothing could faze her. Unless there is another reason her usual confidence is absent.

'Aiden seemed on edge even before we started talking, so looking back, maybe it wasn't the right time. I began by asking if he ever thought about you.'

I don't want to hear the answer to this.

'He said that yes, he did. Even though he tried not to, every time he looked at Kayla he saw you in her. Those were his words, Eve.'

My breath catches in my throat. I haven't been expecting this. All signs pointed to Aiden having completely eradicated any sign or thought of me from his life. *But not our daughter. She is always there.*

'Then I just came straight out with it and told him that I'd seen you. He fell completely silent. I mean, for ages. He just didn't seem to know what to say. I really hated being the one to do that to him.' She stares at her feet. 'I care about him, Eve. He and I became close when you left. Good friends. I don't want to see him hurt, and I definitely don't want to be the one to hurt him.'

'It's not you who's done anything to him,' I offer. 'Only me.'

She shakes her head. 'I'm involved now, though, aren't I? Anyway, eventually he just said he didn't want to know.

He said you were in the past and he had a new life now. That was it.'

It is a shock to find out that Aiden didn't ask any questions, didn't need the huge gaps to be filled in. 'And what did you say?'

'I tried to defend you, Eve. I know that's hard to believe after how I reacted to seeing you, but I did my best. I told him everyone deserved a second chance. And do you know his response? He told me quite calmly that this isn't true – that murderers, for one, don't deserve a second chance, and neither do people who can be cruel enough to walk away from their babies.'

I try to push aside the hurt I feel at being compared to a murderer by the man I once loved. Who once loved me. 'Maybe Aiden's right,' I say. 'But this isn't just about giving me a chance. This is about giving Kayla a chance to know her mother.'

Sophie holds up her hands. 'A mother doesn't walk away from her child.' She turns from me and begins clearing the toys away, piling them into a basket in the corner of the room.

I ignore her comment, storing it away to analyse later. 'I just want to see Kayla. She's the only person who matters.'

Sophie sighs. 'Maybe Aiden just needs some time to get his head around it all. I did just spring it on him. Like I said, I think I handled it all wrong. So, what will you do now?'

'I'm not sure. But I'm not giving up, Sophie. I know this will sound strange, because I'm the one who left, but being away from her for these years has almost killed me.'

Sophie frowns at me, trying to work out the enigma that I am, that this whole situation is.

She must see that I will do whatever it takes to have my daughter in my life, and neither she nor Aiden are going to stop me. And now, this is more important than ever.

TWELVE

Before

'We've done it,' Aiden says.

I turn to him. 'Don't say that. She's not out yet.' Inside me, the baby wriggles, showing her defiance. Despite everything I'm saying to Aiden, I believe she is determined to be here, that nothing will stop her coming into the world.

'Well, they're taking us down in a few minutes and the C-section won't take too long, so I reckon we could be meeting her in less than an hour.' His mouth spreads into a grin. He's so excited, and I desperately want his enthusiasm to infect me, to seep into my body and fill me up, but all I feel is numb.

This baby is overdue; they've tried everything to encourage her out, including inducing me, and nothing has worked. So now they're going to slice me open and pull her out. I shudder at the thought, even though I know I won't feel anything, and that in some ways this is the better option. Right now, I feel as though I'd never be able to push her out, that my whole body would shut down and refuse to do anything – and then what would happen to both of us?

'I know you're worried,' Aiden continues. 'And you will be until you're holding her in your arms, but I promise you, everything will be okay.'

He can't promise me this, though, can he? This is not something he can control. And now his words are making me feel even worse. Devoid. As if there is nothing left of me. *It's hormones, it must be. That's what's making me feel this way. Soon she will be here and everything will be okay. Nothing else will matter once I'm holding her in my arms.*

'Did I tell you that your mum's on her way?' Aiden says. 'I thought I'd better warn her that she wouldn't be allowed in yet. I told her to take her time and wait for visiting hours.'

I'd forgotten about that. All morning I've been looking forward to Mum being here, to see her holding her grand-daughter. Like a young child I'm praying that my mum being here will make everything okay. 'Was she all right with that? I know how desperate she is to meet this baby.'

'Yeah. Actually, she said she had some things to do first so it could be early evening before she gets here.'

She won't have told Aiden what it is she needs to do, so I don't bother asking. Mum seems to have become increasingly more secretive over the last few months, and I have to force even the most trivial bits of information from her. 'Oh, don't worry about me,' she insists. 'You're pregnant, you've got loads on your plate, just focus on you and Aiden.' Whenever she's said this, I've wanted to tell her that I need something else to focus on, more than anything.

The midwife comes to take us to the theatre. She's cheerful and bubbly and just about everything I don't need right now because her smiling and joking might just tip me over the edge. 'Are you ready to meet your baby?' She beams, and I force myself to appear happy, as if this is the most amazing day of my life.

Aiden clutches my hand, and I try to focus on the only thing that matters. We are about to become parents. Then everything will be okay. It has to be.

–

'Here she is.' The doctor holds her up over the blue curtain and, beside me, Aiden gasps. Her arms and legs are crossed, and she looks like a little Buddha, silently praying. It's a few seconds before she cries, and in that time, I imagine that no sound will ever leave her tiny body, that she will remain silent forever.

Aiden strokes my arm and kisses me on the forehead. If I had the energy, I would push him away. 'You did it, Eve, you did it!'

But what did I do? I only lay here while on the other side of the curtain two doctors cut me open and pulled her out, all the time talking to each other so casually as though what they were doing was akin to cooking a meal. They are the ones who *did it*.

A voice in the room calls out the time. It's hard to know to whom it belongs because there are so many people in here. *Twelve minutes past three*. I think I'm supposed to always remember this time, to commit it to memory so that I can remind her on every birthday that this is the time she arrived in the world.

'Isn't she cute?' Aiden says while they place her on the scales to check her weight. 'I know I'm biased but she really is.'

'Seven pounds seven.' Another voice speaking, yet another thing I'm supposed to remember.

'Yes,' I tell Aiden. 'So cute.' Maybe I'm just saying this because I'm supposed to. The truth is, I don't actually know what she is or how I feel.

The bouncy midwife places her on my chest, delivering a speech about the importance of skin-to-skin contact. 'Does she have a name yet?' she asks. If she smiles any harder her face might crack open.

'Kayla,' I manage to say, forcing myself to smile, too, making myself look at my baby. That's it. That's all I have to do. Acknowledge the correct behaviour and force myself to do it.

'Kayla Rose Conway,' Aiden adds, squeezing my hand.

–

While I'm still in the hospital, I am protected. All I need to focus on is trying to establish feeding. I haven't even had to change a nappy yet; the midwives just float in and do it every hour or two – they don't even ask if I'd like to have a go. I should ask if I can try myself, insist on it even. That's what most mothers would do, and I need to prove that I'm okay. That I'm normal.

'It's not working,' I tell the new midwife who's taken over from the smiley one. She's not nearly as friendly and seems tired, even though she's only just come on shift.

'Don't worry, it takes time,' she assures me.

I've been trying to pump breast milk for over twenty minutes and haven't seen a single drop of anything, not even colostrum. They keep telling me how important it is to give this to the baby, and all that's doing is making me feel like a failure. Like I've let Kayla down already when she's only a few hours old. This is what it's going to be like; me constantly letting her down.

'We'll try again in a little while,' she says. 'In the meantime, she can have another bottle.' Without even asking me she opens the curtain and leaves to prepare some formula. Why are they doing everything for me? Don't they realise that they're just leaving me clueless?

I glance at the woman in the bed next to me and see her little baby snuggled into her chest, happily feeding. It's just me then. I'm the only one who can't get to grips with this.

'Here we go,' the midwife says as she returns. 'Would you like to have a go?' She's already handing me the bottle and picking Kayla out of her bassinet.

I can't. 'Could you please do it?'

She doesn't say anything but stares at me before finally picking up Kayla and effortlessly feeding her while standing up.

Aiden comes back from the coffee shop downstairs and hands me a large latte. Throughout this pregnancy I've avoided caffeine, done everything I'm supposed to do, but now I will enjoy it.

'No luck yet then?' Aiden asks.

'It takes time,' the midwife says before I can answer. Maybe she's nicer than I thought. She finishes feeding Kayla and silently places her on my chest. I stare at my baby and wonder why she doesn't feel like mine at all. How is that possible when I carried her for all this time, when I was so desperate to hold a baby in my arms? And now she's here all I want to do is pass her to Aiden, or the midwife. To anyone who will have her.

'I'll have to get going in a minute,' Aiden says when the midwife has left us to it. 'I've only got an hour to get to the airport to pick up Mum and Dad.'

I listen to Aiden tell me about the people who have passed on their best wishes, my mind completely empty. I'm scared of him leaving me alone with Kayla, but also relieved when he kisses me goodbye promising to be back soon. At least now I don't have to pretend.

–

When he's gone, I turn on my side and try to rest. Kayla is asleep in the bassinet next to me, and I watch her, waiting to feel something.

On the table by my bed, my phone vibrates. I consider ignoring it but it could be Mum, or Aiden. Reaching across, I look at the screen and see it's a text message from a number I don't recognise.

Even before I click on it, I already know who it's from, but still I check, just to be sure.

And then I press delete.

THIRTEEN

Now

Standing outside Aiden's office in Ealing makes me feel as though no time has passed. As if it could just be one of those evenings when I'd come to meet him after I left the school, and we'd both share our days with each other. When I was training to teach, my tutor told us that nobody understood the life of a teacher like another teacher, but he was wrong. Aiden always understood. He got it when I'd had a hard day and needed to offload, and he'd listen while I'd sometimes talk for hours about something I was struggling with. Yet now things couldn't be more different, and I am the last person he will want to see waiting for him.

With no idea what time he'll leave the building, I sit on a wall in the car park, hoping he still leaves at around six p.m., just as he used to. I'm prepared to wait all night if I have to.

'What the hell are you doing here?'

Aiden is marching towards me, his face red and his eyes slits of pure anger.

Quickly I stand. 'Can we just talk? That's all I'm asking.'

He stops when he reaches me. 'Over two years. You turn up after this long and think we can just talk? Leave me alone, Eve, I've got nothing to say to you.'

He's about to walk off but I grab his arm. The feel of him is alien to me now, even after all our years together; it could be a stranger I'm grabbing hold of. He swipes his arm away but I have to believe that somewhere, deep inside him, is the man who once loved me. Or at the very least, a man who will want some answers.

The scowl on his face distorts him, makes him a stranger. 'What do you want? You must want something after all this time, otherwise you wouldn't be here. So what is it?' I have never heard Aiden speak this aggressively.

'I just want to talk. Please. Just give me a few minutes of your time.'

'You know you don't deserve that, don't you?' His eyes bore into me.

'I'm Kayla's mother and I won't go away. Don't you think it's better if we can just talk?'

Aiden sighs and his skin reddens. He wasn't often stressed, but on the few occasions when I witnessed it, his face would do exactly this. Some things never change. 'How did you get here?' he asks.

'I got the Tube, why?'

'I need a bloody drink. There's a bar a short walk from here.' He stalks off, not once turning back to check whether or not I'm following.

–

While Aiden gets the drinks, I find a table and sink into a chair. Every inch of my body is pulsating with anxiety, but at least he's agreed to talk to me. This is progress.

He sits down, and it hits me that nothing I say will be good enough, no apology big enough, to make any amends for what I did. I try to explain this to him.

'Why?' he asks. 'That's what I've been asking myself all this time. Why would you do it? Especially after everything we went through before finally having her.' He lifts his drink and stares at it, swilling it around. 'All this time I thought there must be another man, even though I couldn't believe you'd ever do that to me. To anyone. Sophie assured me there wasn't. And at least *she* can be trusted. So that just leaves a big fat question mark.'

'I left because I couldn't handle it, Aiden. My life. Any of it.'

He stares at me, clearly disgusted. 'You wanted a baby more than anything. Four miscarriages, Eve. All that grief. I don't understand.'

And you never fully will. Because all I can do is give you just enough to hope that you will have a small inkling of an idea why I had to go. The rest is too monstrous, too toxic to share with anyone.

I look around and this place is full of people enjoying the company of others, engrossed in casual, light-hearted conversations. I'm willing to bet nobody is discussing anything as dark and twisted as Aiden and I are.

'I know it was awful, and I live with that knowledge every single day.' I wish I could add that it follows me around, hovers over me like a thick cloud about to burst and there's no shelter from it. Maybe it would help Aiden get inside my head, but I only say, 'I had to leave, Aiden. I just couldn't stay. Not then. I'm not here to make excuses, just to see if we can move forward somehow.'

He picks up his glass and takes another long swig of what looks like gin or vodka. 'That's not an answer. I have no words for you. If only you knew what a beautiful, amazing little girl Kayla is. You left her without a mother, and whatever your reasons, that's unforgivable. I'm just glad she doesn't remember you. She knows nothing about you.' He turns away from me, cannot bear to look me in the eye.

'I understand why—'

'You don't understand anything, Eve.' He raises his voice, and an elderly couple seated near us turn to stare. Oblivious to their frowns, Aiden continues. 'What do you want? To have Kayla back? Well, that's not going to happen. There's no way I'll let you do any more damage to her, just because you suddenly feel ready to be a mother. It's two years too late for that.' More people turn to stare at us.

'I know I hurt you,' I tell him, my own voice barely more than a whisper; I'm hoping if I speak quietly then he will do the same. 'Tell me what I can do to make things right. Please. I'll do anything.'

'There's only one thing that will make things better. Staying away from us. Will you do that?' Now he does look at me, fixing his eyes on me in a staring contest.

'I... I need to see her, Aiden. Please. There must be a way we can work this all out. I'm not trying to take her away from you, but can I just see her?' I have never begged for anything before but here I am, laying my soul on the line.

He shakes his head and downs the rest of his drink. 'I'm going to the toilet.'

I hope that while he's gone he'll see sense in agreeing to my request. I check my phone to pass the time. Maya has only just replied to the text I sent her earlier, assuring me she's fine. Then almost immediately she sends another message, asking if she can come for a session tomorrow afternoon. I reply yes to this and am about to follow up to ask if she's sure she's okay when Aiden returns.

'I need some fresh air,' he says. Once again, with no invitation for me to follow, he stalks off.

My heart sinks. He needs more time, and even though time is something I cannot afford to give him, for all our sakes, I know that pushing him might mean I lose Kayla for good. I've been fully prepared to go to extreme measures to get her back but having Aiden on my side is the much better option. Gathering my jacket and bag, I head after him. He walks so fast that by the time I've got outside he's already crossing the road.

'Aiden, wait!'

He turns around. 'I can't do this, Eve. I... don't know how to do this.'

And then he is gone, leaving me behind. 'Just let me see my daughter!' I scream into the night, but there is no reply.

FOURTEEN

Now

'Are you okay, miss?'

I turn to Maya, who is chewing the end of her pen and staring at me instead of working on her essay plan as she'd been doing before my thoughts pulled me away from here. I've been picturing myself last night, standing outside Aiden's house once again – only metres away from my daughter – so close to hammering on that door. In the end I couldn't go through with it. I don't know what I will do yet, all I know is that it's already taking too long, the situation getting more desperate.

I force a smile. 'I'm fine, Maya. How's that essay plan going?'

'You just look… pale? Yellow. Sick or something.'

She won't be used to seeing me without make-up on; every day I make some effort, even if nobody is going to see me. Today, though, I just couldn't face it. I assure Maya I'm fine, but she continues to stare at me, frowning, trying to work out what's going on.

'I think I've finished,' she says after a few minutes, sliding her paper across to me.

'Okay, good.' I stare at her neat round writing but the words just blur into each other. She hasn't written enough for the question to have been properly addressed, but I will deal with that later. 'We can go through it all next session.' I place it in my folder. 'You said you wanted to talk to me. Is this about what I saw yesterday?'

She hangs her head. 'That was Connor. I told him I can't keep this baby, and he kicked off, right in the street in front of everyone. It was awful!'

I knew Maya was unsure about her pregnancy, and yet hearing her say this with such conviction is a shock. I must respect her decision, though, and I, more than most people, know what she could face if she has this baby without being one hundred per cent sure. And even if she is sure, there are no guarantees about anything.

'Do you think I'm a terrible person? To not want it?'

'No, not at all. As I've said before, this decision has to be yours, nobody else can tell you what to do. You have to do what's right for you, Maya.' These words are flowing from my mouth, but my head is screaming at her to give this baby a chance, that one day she might regret her decision.

The relief on her face shows me just how much she doesn't want this baby, that nothing will sway her, and that she is desperate for someone to be in her corner. 'Connor just doesn't get it. He thinks we can do it and live happily ever after. He told me it's wrong to have a termination. That it's murder.'

'Well, people have different opinions about it, but it's your body. He is the father, though, Maya, so maybe you shouldn't be so hard on him?' *Like I was on Aiden, not giving him a choice in anything.*

'I tried to talk it through properly and tell him exactly how I felt, and he seemed okay to start with, but then he changed his mind and went bat-shit crazy.' She smacks her mouth. 'Oh, sorry for swearing.'

'Have you talked to your parents yet?'

'No. I'm not keeping the baby, so they don't need to know. That would just mean two more people trying to force me to keep it. I don't need that pressure, miss. I want to travel this summer. Visit places other than London. There's a huge world out there and so far I've seen none of it. How can I do that if I have this baby?'

'Like I said, you have to do what's right for you. I can't agree with you not telling your parents, though.'

'I'm eighteen, miss, I'm not a kid.'

'I know that, and it's up to you who you tell. Look, maybe you shouldn't be talking to me about this? I'm your tutor. I don't know if it's appropriate.' *It's too late to tell her this now – you are already involved.*

Her eyes widen, and for a second she looks like a young child, not someone who should be weighing up the choice about becoming a mother. 'You said you'd help me.'

'I know, Maya, and I meant it. I'll support you in any way I can,' I tell her.

'Then can you please just listen to me and let me talk?'

'Yes, of course,' I say, because what else can I do? 'So have you spoken to Connor since the argument?'

She shakes her head. 'He's been messaging me loads but I haven't replied. I just feel like I need to be left alone a bit. Like this is my problem to deal with.'

'Okay. You're not worried about what he'll do, are you?'

'No, he wouldn't try to hurt me or anything. He's not like that.'

I tell her I'm glad to hear that, and she begins clearing away her things. 'I've actually found a clinic and have an appointment next week. I just want this done before my exams.' Her words are so cold and clinical. Is that how I was when I decided to leave? Is that how I *had* to be?

The exams are looming. And after that Maya will no longer need tutoring.

'Please be sure,' I say to her as she leaves. 'That's all I ask.'

'If you think about it, miss — how can we ever be really sure about any huge decision we make? There's always that alternative road, isn't there? I've been thinking about this. It's like there are two of me. One is going off to university to study for her degree, while the other one is going to be a young mum. They're both valid choices, aren't they? I just have to make one decision and stick with it. That's all I can do.'

She waves goodbye and leaves me standing at my door, watching her head down the street. Although I admire her ability to think philosophically about this, I call her name, planning to tell her that she's wrong, that there is a third option, one where she gets to do both things. She doesn't hear me and disappears around the corner before I can call her name again.

There is no way I can let Maya make a mistake like my own. I quickly grab my trainers from the hallway, not bothering to tie the laces.

Rushing outside, I don't notice the woman walking towards me until I've rammed into her, almost sending her crashing to the ground. Her large handbag flies from her shoulder and lands on the pavement, scattering some of the contents.

'I'm so sorry, I—' My words stop short when I take in the familiar features of this woman.

Nicole Richardson.

And she's outside my flat, scooping down to gather up her belongings.

She looks up at me, her bright blue eyes huge and kind, showing no annoyance at the fact that I've nearly knocked her over. 'Please don't worry, I should have moved out of the way when I saw you rushing.' She smiles. 'You're Eve, aren't you?'

I only manage a nod; shock has rendered me speechless.

'I'm Nicole, Aiden's partner. I'm so sorry to turn up like this but do you think we could talk?' Standing up, she pulls her bag back onto her shoulder. 'I know this is a bit of a shock,' she says, 'and I really hope it's okay that Sophie gave me your address. Please don't be angry with her, she was just trying to help after the state Aiden was in last night when she came over.' She pauses and takes a deep breath. 'Basically, I'm here because all that matters is Kayla's well-being. We all need to do what's right for her, don't we? I've gone over this in my mind and I can't see how keeping you away from her will be good for her in the long run. Aiden doesn't agree, and I totally understand his feelings, but, well, Kayla has to come first here.'

I stare at this woman, convinced I must be mistaken. This can't be Nicole Richardson – Aiden's new partner and the woman who has been raising my daughter – standing here telling me that I shouldn't be prevented from seeing Kayla. I turn to look in the direction Maya left, of course she is long gone now, and half expect to be alone when I turn back.

But Nicole is still there, right in front of me. And even though I've already seen her from a distance, and her picture on Facebook, close up she is nothing like I've imagined. Her long hair is much lighter – almost a reddish blonde – and she's taller than I assumed she'd be, at least two inches taller than me. We are nothing alike. Clearly Aiden doesn't have a type. Either that or he's made a conscious effort to find someone who bears no resemblance to me.

It takes me a few moments to gather my thoughts, and now that I have, the main thing running through my head is that this woman is the key to bringing Kayla and me together.

I smile to show her my gratitude. 'Does Aiden know you've come?'

She shakes her head. 'No. And I really don't like lying to him, but there's too much at stake here – mainly Kayla's well-being – so I had to weigh up my choices.' She glances up at my building. 'Look, I'm a complete stranger so I'm sure you don't want me in your flat. Is there somewhere near here we could go and talk?'

'There's a park a few minutes away with an outdoor café area. It's not usually busy during the week. We could go there?'

'Perfect,' Nicole says. 'And thank you for talking to me.'

–

'No, it's me who should be thanking you,' I say as we walk. 'This situation is just... well, difficult is putting it too mildly, so I appreciate you talking to me. If you don't mind me asking, how did you meet Aiden?'

She hesitates, and I wonder if I've crossed a line. 'We met at his work,' she says. 'I was on a long-term temporary contract there as a PA to the managing director. It's a funny place there, people aren't too friendly, so I was always having lunch on my own. Until Aiden took pity on me and sat with me one afternoon.' She smiles, clearly recalling a positive memory. 'I suppose we just hit it off, and I was eternally grateful that he'd made working there a bit more bearable. I mean, it's fine if you're at the top like Aiden, but I was just a temp and clearly at the bottom of the heap, so wasn't worthy of anyone's time. Even my own boss made no effort to make me feel comfortable.'

That sounds just like Aiden. He never liked to see anyone lonely or unhappy. I almost say this to Nicole but don't want her to think I still have any residual feelings for him. She needs to know that all I'm interested in is seeing my daughter. And quickly.

'I'm glad he found you,' I say, meaning every word.

Her forehead creases. 'Thanks. Anyway, it was quite a long time before we got together. He just wasn't looking for a relationship, and neither was I.' She pauses. 'No, I definitely wasn't but that's another story. Well, eventually Aiden and I were just such good friends and it felt so natural for our relationship to progress.' She slows down and turns to me. 'Sorry, I'm sure you don't want to hear all this.'

'I'm just grateful we can talk. Aiden was not ready, or able, to hear anything I had to say. I do understand but I need him to give me a chance.'

She nods. 'Well, it's not going to be easy. None of this is. Is that the park? I could really do with a drink. It's so warm, isn't it? Funny, we moan all winter for a bit of sun and a decent summer, and then as soon as we get one we complain that it's too hot.'

As I listen to her talking, somehow, despite everything, I think I like this woman.

Nicole offers to buy us drinks, but I rush forward to the counter. 'No, I insist. This is the least I can do.'

She asks for an orange juice while I opt for a mineral water.

'Please don't think I let Kayla drink juice,' she says. 'It's strictly water at home and only juice as an occasional treat when we're out.'

'You really don't have to explain anything like that to me,' I tell her, but I'm pleased that she has. 'I can tell she's a healthy and happy little girl.'

Nicole frowns, and I immediately realise my error. I could try and cover it up but I won't lie to her, especially not after she's making this effort. 'I should explain. I saw you with her going to the park the other day. I was never going to approach her but I'd just gone to your house, just to see where she was living. It was purely coincidental that you were both heading to the park at that time. I really hope you believe that. I just... needed to see some part of her life, to feel close to her in some way. There's no way I would have introduced myself.'

Any minute now she will stand up to leave, tell me I need to get some help. Instead, though, Nicole turns to me. 'I do understand that, Eve. I may not have children of my own yet but I can imagine that bond you must have as a mother never goes away. No matter what. You'll get no judgement from me. I just want what's best for Kayla. And Aiden, of course.'

We make our way to an empty table and bench.

'Sophie explained a lot to me,' Nicole says as we sit down. 'And she really defended you when Aiden was refusing to hear anything, so I know you had your reasons for leaving. I respect Sophie a lot, and I've come to think of her as friend, so I know she wouldn't take your side without good reason. Not when we've become so close.'

I'm surprised to hear this. Sophie led me to believe that they weren't in a great deal of contact, but I can't hold it against her for playing their friendship down. 'I know how it looks to other people, and how it *is*. I did a terrible thing by walking out on my baby and nothing will justify that, but all I can do now is try to make up for it, and I'll do whatever I can to put things right. I'm fully aware that it's not something that can be easily fixed, but if we can all just communicate then maybe we'll find a way?' As I say this, I realise how many times I've had to repeat those words in the last few days.

She sighs. 'I can't make you any promises but I'll try to talk to Aiden.'

'Maybe he just needs some more time?' I suggest. 'This has all come out of the blue and must be a bit of a shock for him. You know him better than I do now. Do you think he'll come around?'

Nicole curls her lip. 'He's a reasonable man, so I would say, yes. Just give him a bit of time.'

'Thank you. I can't tell you how much it means to me that you're willing to help me for Kayla's sake. It's more than I could ever have expected.'

'My mum always used to say to me, "Be kind to other people – that's the most important thing in life, then everything else will just fall into place." Kind of like karma, I suppose. I try to put out into the universe what

I'd like to get back, and that's to be treated with kindness.' She stares into the distance. 'Unfortunately, sometimes it doesn't always work, but, hey, we can't control other people's actions, can we?'

As I study this woman, it's hard to believe that anyone would treat her with anything other than kindness. It might be understandable if I, in particular, felt something negative towards her, when she is a woman who knows my daughter inside and out, more than I ever will. Right now, though, all I feel towards her is warmth and gratitude. Being here shows that she must really love Kayla.

'You're taking a risk, Nicole. If Aiden finds out you've come to see me then he'd… well, I can only imagine being betrayed is not something he deals with well. I'm grateful you're trying to help but perhaps I should just try to get through to him on my own. I don't want this wrecking your relationship.'

Nicole smiles. 'Thanks, but I'm doing this because it's what I believe in, even though it's not going to be easy for Aiden, or me. Kayla needs to have you in her life, so I'll do my best to help Aiden see that. As I said before, I can't make you any promises but I'll try.'

'Thank you.'

She reaches into her bag and pulls out her mobile. 'Would you like to see some pictures of Kayla?'

My eyes widen. 'Really? Are you sure?'

She nods. 'The only thing is, I might be in a lot of them with her, but if you're okay with that? I do love a selfie!'

There's no space in my head to wonder how I feel about this – I can only focus on seeing my daughter.

Nicole begins tapping the screen. She stares at it for a few moments, swiping sideways before finally holding it up to me. 'Here she is. Isn't she beautiful?'

I stare at the picture and my body seems to fill with joy and pain simultaneously. In the photo I'm looking at, Kayla's dressed in a red pinafore dress and is throwing her head back and laughing at something. Looking at her, I am overwhelmed with the feeling that she is my baby, yet she also feels like a complete stranger. As though she could belong to anyone.

Nicole swipes the screen and a new photo appears – in this one she is there with Kayla, their faces pressed together, both of them pulling goofy expressions. This time I feel the physical pain as though I'm being stabbed through the chest. I lean forward, hoping Nicole won't notice anything is wrong. I can't let her think this is a problem for me, not when she's doing so much to help.

'She's such a happy child.' This is all I can manage to say.

Nicole puts her phone in her bag. 'I know this must be hard for you, and to be honest, it's a little weird for me too.'

'Yes, it must be. You've been bringing her up for around a year so she must feel like...'

'Like she's mine?' She pauses. 'I don't try and pretend she is or anything like that, but when you spend every day with someone and are responsible for their well-being, well, it's hard not to get attached.'

I nod, even though the weight of her words crushes me. Of course it would be like this; how could it be any other way?

'Also, I'm so sorry to say this but it's better if I just come out with it.'

Every part of me wants her to stop. To not say whatever it is she's about to. Ignorance is supposed to be bliss, isn't it?

'I'm really sorry but Kayla calls me mummy.'

FIFTEEN

Before

Aiden's gone to work – his paternity leave over in what felt like seconds rather than weeks. I'm sitting on the sofa, in my milk-stained pyjamas, holding Kayla on my shoulder in an attempt to get her comfortable. Nothing is working this morning and she's wriggling and moaning, unhappy with any position I hold her in.

There's a baby music class this afternoon. I should take her to that, try to get a grip on myself and whatever it is I'm experiencing. *But I won't because I can't. There is no way I will manage to bundle her into her pram and leave this house. I don't know what will happen out there; in here it is safe.*

Everything changes the second I'm alone with Kayla. *She* changes. She was grizzling before Aiden left but now she ramps it up. It's as if she knows that I'm terrified of her, terrified of everything.

I try feeding her but she refuses the bottle, and a quick check of her nappy shows me it doesn't need changing. Sleep then – it's got to be that. Even though I know what will happen, I cross the room and place her in her Moses basket, silently praying that this time she'll stay put and fall asleep, that she will be powerless to fight her exhaustion. But the second her back touches the mattress she howls, a deafening shriek that I'm sure the neighbours across the road will hear.

Before Kayla, even when I lost all those babies, when I felt more pain than I thought any human could face, I tried to be strong, to keep my sadness contained. Now, though, I have no control over my emotions, and tears flood out while I pace the living room desperate to comfort this baby who doesn't feel like she belongs to me at all, rather that I've been handed her by a mother and asked to watch her for a moment. Surely after three weeks I shouldn't still feel this way.

'What do you want?' I whisper my words even though there is nobody other than Kayla around to hear me. 'I don't know what you want!' Louder this time. I glance at her Moses basket and decide I will put her in again, and this time leave her to try to settle herself. Aiden and I have both said that we will never leave her to cry, but if she's crying when I'm holding her then surely it makes no difference if I leave her.

I make my way towards it, feeling as though I'm not in control of my footsteps. I will put her in – she will be safe – and then I will go and make myself a cup of tea. Despite having no appetite, I should eat, even though food will only make me sick. Still wearing my maternity clothes means that Aiden hasn't noticed I've already lost all my pregnancy weight and am now half a stone lighter than I was before I got pregnant. I can't have him worrying about me, not when he's the happiest he's ever been. Kayla has made him complete, just like I'm supposed to feel.

As I'm about to place Kayla in the Moses basket, the doorbell rings. I freeze. I'm not expecting any visitors, or any deliveries, and don't want anyone to see me like this, so I choose to ignore it. And then the WhatsApp message pings.

> Are you home?

I drop my phone on the floor and stare at it. Then I rush upstairs with Kayla, hoping her cries can't be heard from outside.

The doorbell keeps ringing, and Kayla keeps howling. I shut the bedroom door and sink to the floor, clutching the baby to my chest.

Waiting for all of it to stop.

SIXTEEN

Now

'Eve? What are you doing here?'

Once again Sophie is shocked to see me standing at her door but underlying that is something else. Guilt? How ironic it is that I'm the one who has betrayed everyone, yet I cannot seem to trust anyone. Sophie hasn't been honest with me, though, and I'm here to find out why.

'Can we talk? I left it until this late so that the twins would be asleep.'

'You've clearly never had children then if you think…' Her hand clamps to her mouth. 'Oh. I wasn't thinking. I was just trying to say that it's not always as easy as putting them down for the night and then getting on with things. They still often wake up needing something. Even at this age.'

I glance past her. In the hall there is no sign of anyone, and no noise.

'As it happens, they're actually sleeping well so far tonight. I think nursery tired them out. And Damien's working late tonight. Come in.'

Without asking if I want anything, Sophie boils the kettle and it feels like it did years before. Whenever we saw each other, the kettle would go on without either of us asking if the other wanted coffee. It was taken for granted, something that would always be, just like we assumed our friendship was.

'Nicole Richardson came to see me.' I let her name fill up the room.

Sophie stiffens and stares at the mugs she's just pulled from the cupboard.

'I gave her your address,' she says, quickly recovering. 'I thought it was the right way forward as she was so supportive of you when I spoke about you.' There is no apology for not checking whether it was okay with me first. Even in Sophie's mind — my closest friend — I have gone beyond deserving that courtesy. 'And not surprisingly, Aiden wasn't going to give you the time of day,' she continues.

'I'm not here to have a go at you, Sophie. I'm glad you did it. Nicole was…'

'Great, isn't she? She's a lovely person — I knew I was doing the right thing.' She smiles, but it's more to herself than to me, as if she is congratulating herself, vindicated in some way.

'Yes, she was kind. I'm just wondering why you made it seem that you weren't really in contact, when apparently you're good friends.'

Sophie abandons making the coffee and folds her arms, staring at the floor. 'Are you really asking me to explain myself to you?'

'I'm just saying there's no need to cover up anything that happened afterwards.'

'Maybe I was trying to spare your feelings,' she declares, raising her voice. But she's not looking at me; a clear sign that she's lying.

'I know that,' I tell her. But everything's changed, hasn't it? I don't know anyone around me any more. And they don't know me.

'The truth is my loyalty has to be with Aiden now. I'm sorry.'

Tears prick at my eyes, and I have to turn away from Sophie.

'And I care about Nicole too. When Aiden met her, I was so happy for him. She was just so *good* for him, Eve. And she's just so easy to get along with. I immediately bonded with her.'

Despite finding this hard to hear, I can see precisely what Sophie means. 'So, you know her well, then?'

'Very well. What you see is what you get with Nicole.'

'Kayla calls her mummy.' This is what I've come here to say, the lead weight that's been pressing on my chest since this afternoon.

Sophie nods. 'What did you expect? Kayla doesn't know any different. I know it happened organically – Nicole wouldn't have made her do it.'

But would Aiden have? Did he despise me so much that he needed to erase every part of me from Kayla's life? I want to ask Sophie this but I can't trust where her loyalties truly lie, not that I expect them to be with me.

'What's the plan anyway?' Sophie asks, and I'm grateful she has changed the subject.

'Nicole's going to try to convince Aiden to let me see Kayla. Until then it's just a waiting game.' One which crushes me for every second longer I'm away from my daughter.

'I know Nicole will do her best,' Sophie says. 'If anyone can get through to Aiden, she can.'

These words shouldn't hurt so much but they're bullets tearing into my flesh. *You left him. Remember that. You are the one who walked away, not Aiden. But I had no choice, did I? It was all taken out of my hands.*

My phone beeps in my pocket, and I pull it out, desperate for something to distract me from these thoughts. It's Jamie, asking if I want to come over later. I'm about to reply that I will when another text arrives, this time from Nicole.

> Not sure if this is a good idea but can you meet me and Kayla in the park opposite our house tomorrow morning at ten? Aiden doesn't know, and I hate keeping it from him, but I'm doing this for Kayla.

I read the words again, just to ensure I'm not mistaken. Kayla. Tomorrow. I'm going to see her properly, close enough to take in every inch of her face.

'Is everything okay?' Sophie asks.

'Um, I think so. That was Nicole.' I hand her my phone so she can read the message for herself, to verify that my mind isn't messing with me.

Sophie nods, as if she's been expecting this. Have the two of them already discussed this plan to meet in the park? 'I knew she'd come through for you,' she says. 'How do you feel?'

'Terrified. Excited. A mixture of both.'

She hands me a mug of coffee. 'You won't tell Kayla who you are, though, will you? I think that would be the totally wrong thing to do.'

'Of course not. I would never just blurt it out.'

Sophie's eyes narrow. 'Because she thinks of Nicole as her mum, so it would be damaging for her to suddenly be confronted with this.'

I try to hide my annoyance; Sophie has helped me after all. 'I know. I would never do that.'

'Nicole thinks—'

'You've spoken to her about this already? You knew she was going to ask me to meet them in the park tomorrow?'

'No. I mean, not really, I only know that she cares about Kayla, and that she thinks keeping you from her could ultimately do more harm than good. I didn't know what exactly she was planning.'

It was only this afternoon that Nicole turned up at my flat, so that means they have communicated in the last few hours. This shouldn't surprise me when Sophie has already admitted that the two of them are close. I try to ignore the unfair and irrational feeling that Nicole has replaced me in three ways: as Aiden's partner, Kayla's mother and Sophie's friend.

I don't say anything, taking a sip of coffee to stall for time before I have to speak again. I came here with a million things I needed to say, to ask her advice on, but now I'm in the house of a stranger, one I need to be wary around.

'I just want to see Kayla,' I say eventually. 'I can't think past that at the moment.' The words in those emails invade my head. Seeing my daughter can't come quickly enough. I almost offer to let Sophie know how it goes afterwards, but she doesn't need me to fill her in; Nicole will probably do that for me.

'I'd better go,' I tell her. I don't know what's happened since I got here but these walls feel unfriendly. Sophie's not doing anything to make me feel unwelcome, yet I no longer want to be here. I have to trust my instinct.

It's raining when I step outside, and darkness has fallen fast. The air is so cool now that it would be easy to believe that autumn is approaching, even though summer has barely begun.

Remembering Jamie's text, I reply to him as I walk towards the Tube, letting him know that I'm on my way to his place. I won't be able to sleep tonight and it will be nice to have his company. I need to try to focus on him tonight.

He replies with a smiley face and a kiss, and this assures me that I'm doing the right thing.

—

'What are you hiding?'

My naked body freezes. All I can hear are my deep breaths, echoing through the room. 'What do you mean?'

Jamie strokes my stomach, and I can't help but flinch. It's funny how only moments ago his hands were all over me and I could lose myself in him, yet now I cannot bear to be too close to him. It's always this way.

'I don't know, I just feel like when we, you know, do what we just did then, I get all of you – the whole Eve, and I feel like in those moments I really *know* you.' He smiles. 'But then, like now, I feel like you're not all here.'

In any other circumstances, if I had never met Aiden, then I would have really warmed to Jamie. I can see that we would have worked together. But how can I explain to him that it can never be this way? That I can never be who – or what – he needs?

And he can never be what I need. He is not someone who will just want me for company, someone who won't ask any questions or expect anything. Someone who will just let me be.

'We always seem to end up back here, don't we?' I say, pulling the duvet over me, shifting away from him. 'Maybe I should go.'

'Every time I arrange to see you, I tell myself I'm not going to put pressure on you, and that we can just have a nice time together. Then I see you and… it just goes out of the window. I don't know how to be like that with you, Eve. I don't know how to be *casual* with you. I want more than that. And the crazy thing is – I've never been like this with other women. I usually just go with the flow, that's the kind of person I am, but you… you just…'

I pull my knees up, hug them to my chest. 'And I have the opposite problem. I don't know how to be more than casual with you. Please don't take that the wrong way – it's nothing about you, it's just who I am.'

'I know. I've realised that. But you're under my skin and I don't know how to get you out. I don't think I even *want* to get you out.'

I pull him towards me and stroke his back, trying to lose myself in the feel of his warm, smooth skin. He needs this comfort, and it's the least I can do. Yet instead of being in the moment with Jamie, all I can do is picture Kayla. Running around the park, her long hair flying wildly behind her. And then she is calling, 'Mummy', but it's not me she's speaking to, of course it isn't. It's Nicole.

And then an email pings into my inbox.

Tick tock, tick tock.

SEVENTEEN

Now

I'm early. It's not even half past nine yet but I couldn't wait any longer. I would have come here at five a.m. if I'd thought the park would be open at that hour. There are already a handful of people here – mothers with toddlers, most of them glued to their phones, pausing for air while their children run around freely. These women would never have left their babies. None of them would have done such a despicable thing.

The only entrance to the park is a small red gate, and I keep my gaze fixed on it, desperate to see my daughter appear.

What will my first words be? As I sit there, I imagine all kinds of scenarios, even though it's impossible to predict what might actually happen. I know nothing about young children – she is a toddler now – so there is no way to foresee the conversation we will have.

It's nearly half past ten by the time they arrive. I see Nicole first, opening the gate as she clutches Kayla's hand. She spots me and gives a small wave, but Kayla doesn't notice the gesture and tries to pull Nicole over to the swings. Nicole bends down to her and points in my direction, explaining something to Kayla that I have no way of hearing. It is a bizarre scene to experience: my daughter with the woman who has been her mother for over a year. And here I am – an outsider.

Standing up, I head across to them, forcing a confidence I don't feel in any part of my body. *Kayla is my daughter. Kayla is my daughter. No matter what happens, no one can change that. Not ever.* The mantra plays through my head, fuelling me with the power to see this through.

'Hi.'

Nicole looks up, confusion on her face. 'Eve, hi! This is a nice surprise.' She raises her eyebrows, and I immediately know what she's silently telling me: *Play along with it. I've got it all worked out.*

'Yeah, I, um, I just thought I'd have a walk and enjoy the sun.'

She leans down and wraps her arms around me. 'Well, it's nice to see you.' She leans down to my daughter. 'Kayla, honey, this is my friend, Eve.'

Kayla squints up at me and then slowly brings her hand up in a half wave. She doesn't smile but eyes me suspiciously. Her eyes are dark now, just like mine. They were still blue when I left, the colour undecided as with all newborn babies.

It takes all my willpower not to grab her in my arms and tell her how much I love her. 'Hi, Kayla, it's nice to meet you.' As soon as I've said this, I curse myself; I'm sure this isn't the way to talk to a toddler. I knew it wouldn't be easy, but this is far harder than I imagined.

'Swing, Mummy,' Kayla says, ignoring me and pointing across the playground.

Despite Nicole warning me that Kayla addresses her this way, the pain of hearing it for myself, straight from my daughter's mouth, cripples me.

'Okay,' Nicole is saying. 'Can you play on the small climbing frame for a second, and I'll be right over?'

Kayla nods and heads off, seemingly happy to play independently. She must be a confident child, and that's all thanks to Aiden and Nicole.

'Sorry,' Nicole says as soon as Kayla's out of earshot. 'I just thought it would be easier to let it seem that we just bumped into each other, otherwise Kayla will go home and tell Aiden everything. She might only be two and a half but she's a little chatterbox, that one.' She pauses. 'I have to admit this has been really difficult, and it's hard for me to know exactly what to do. I did try talking to Aiden again last night but he really wouldn't listen. In fact, he's completely shut down. He won't even entertain having a conversation about this, even though it's so important.' She stares at Kayla. 'I can only think that this is bringing up all kinds of unresolved feelings for him, and he's just not able to see what's best for Kayla.'

Even though I'm trying to take in these words, I can't tear my eyes from Kayla. I'm confused by what Nicole's saying; does she mean that Aiden still has feelings for me? I can't let her think that I'm any kind of threat. 'I'm sure the only feeling Aiden has towards me is anger about me leaving. Please don't think that there's anything else. Things move on. I doubt either of us are the same people we were two years ago.'

'Oh, I'm so sorry,' Nicole says, 'I didn't mean to make you uncomfortable. You're right, things change and I'm completely secure in our relationship.' Her face lights up as she turns to Kayla again. 'All that matters is this one. She's such a beautiful little girl. And I don't just mean on the outside. She's also the kindest, most gentle child you could meet. We're so proud of her.' Nicole's eyes widen. 'Oh, sorry – this is weird, isn't it? I'm going on and on about Kayla and she's *your* daughter.'

'It's okay,' I tell her. As much as it hurts, I have to be rational about this, and not let my emotions control me.

Nicole pats my hand. 'It's just so hard because… well, not being genetically related to Kayla doesn't stop her being a huge part of my life. And I really do love her to pieces.' She continues watching Kayla before turning back to me. 'Take Aiden, for example. He was adopted yet Pete and Marie are his parents, pure and simple.'

'I know. He couldn't have asked for a more loving mother and father. Nicole, can I confide in you?' The words are out before I'm sure of what I'm doing.

She moves closer to me and places her hand on my arm. 'Yes, of course. I know that might sound weird given our situation – and because you don't really know me – but ultimately we're all here for Kayla, aren't we?'

I stare at her, the woman who it should be easy to dislike, and all I can sense from her is genuine warmth. It's true that I don't know her, but my instinct is telling me that she's okay. That I can trust her. 'The truth is,' I begin, 'that I've been longing for this moment and, now that it's here, I really don't know what to say to Kayla. I don't know how to be around her.' I turn to watch Kayla, who is now busy moving giant counting balls from one side of a bar to the other. 'I thought it would all come naturally, that maybe she'd sense something about me, but there's nothing, is there? There's no bond, nothing to make me stand out to her in any way. I had no idea how hard this would be.'

Nicole nods, as if she completely understands what I'm explaining. 'Is that what you wanted to happen? For her to know you're her mum without anyone having to say anything?'

I consider her question. 'Not exactly. I wasn't expecting the impossible, just for... I don't know, for her to smile at me or something.'

Nicole reaches for my hand. 'Look, I totally get how difficult this must be for you. Actually, difficult is not the word, is it? It's an impossible situation. Just try to remember that she's two and a half. We've tried to bring her up to be careful around strangers, so that's probably why she wasn't over-friendly with you. Please don't think it means anything.'

'You're right. I need to accept that this will take a lot of time and nothing's going to come easily. That's okay. After what I did, I don't expect anything else. I suppose it just shocked me, that's all.'

'Kids take a while to get used to people, and this is the first time she's seen you. The more you see Kayla, the more you'll have a chance to bond.'

'Yes. That's what I want more than anything.'

Nicole turns back to check on Kayla, but she doesn't need to. I have been watching her the whole time. She is safe. 'We'll just have to understand how Aiden feels. Today I just wanted you to have the chance to see her properly, but I can't keep lying to him or keeping things from him. You'll have to give this time. I will try to talk to him again, though.'

'Thanks, Nicole. I don't want anything to come between you two, so don't push it too much. I'm happy to keep trying to get through to him myself.'

She bites her lip. 'You could. I don't know, though. Is that a good idea? Maybe it's best if you leave it to me?'

I tell her she's probably right just as Kayla runs over to us.

'Mummy, the swing!'

Even though Kayla is speaking to Nicole, I crouch down to her level. 'How about *I* push you?' I offer.

Kayla stares at me for what seems like minutes before shaking her head. 'No. I want Mummy.' She rushes forward to Nicole and throws her arms around her.

Her words tear me to pieces, and it's all I can do to pull myself to standing again. Over Kayla's head, Nicole mouths *I'm sorry*. I shake my head and hope she knows I'm trying to tell her that it's not her fault.

'Come on, then,' Nicole says to Kayla, and I watch as they head off to the swings, hand in hand. Mother and daughter.

Even though I feel like an intruder spying on someone else's life, I won't give up. I can't. Not when there's so much at stake. I've come this far, and nothing will make me run from my daughter now.

–

'What the hell?'

His voice echoes through the park, and I know immediately who it is.

I turn, and Aiden is striding over to me. Even from this distance I can tell his cheeks are flushed. A pang of familiarity stings me, a blurring of the past and present as I recall how easily his skin reddens.

'Get away from her,' he shouts again.

Standing up, I glance over at Nicole and Kayla, neither of whom have noticed Aiden appear. It's busy and noisy enough here to mask his shouts too, and I'm grateful that Kayla hasn't heard him.

'Keep your voice down,' I say. 'Please.'

'Why should I? What the hell are you doing here, Eve?'

Before I can answer, Kayla rushes over to us, wrapping her arms around Aiden's legs. 'Daddy!'

'Hey, bunny,' he says, scooping her up. He turns to Nicole, his voice softer now. 'What's going on?'

Nicole reaches for his arm. 'I, um—'

'I just turned up here, hoping to see you all.' The lie comes easily; I can't cause trouble for Nicole after what she's done for me.

Aiden stares at me; there will be a multitude of things he wants to say to me, most of them probably accusations, but he is mindful of Kayla hearing what must be kept between adults.

'Why don't we go home?' Nicole says before Aiden can speak. 'I'll tell you what, Kayla – let's get the Play-Doh out and we can make some cupcakes.'

'Yay!' Kayla says, reaching out her arms for Nicole. Aiden passes her over and hangs back while Nicole and Kayla head off.

'You can't do this,' he hisses now that he has free rein to let me know what he thinks. 'You have no right.'

'I just wanted to see her, Aiden. I swear to you I haven't said anything.'

'Did you think Nicole wouldn't know who you are? She's seen photos of you, Eve. If she'd noticed you here she would have taken Kayla away immediately.'

'Why are you acting as if I'm a danger to her, Aiden?'

'But that's the problem, isn't it, Eve? That's exactly what you are and we both know it.'

EIGHTEEN

Before

'Shall I pop over after school?'

It's lunchtime, and I can tell from the chatter in the background that Sophie is calling me from the staffroom. Her voice is full of enthusiasm; Kayla is eight weeks old now, and Sophie's only laid eyes on her once. I've become a master at making up excuses to avoid leaving the house, to avoid other people. 'Kayla's a bit poorly,' I tell her. 'I think she's picked up a cold from somewhere. She's been sleeping a lot today, probably just needs to rest.' It sounds ridiculous: what else can an eight-week-old baby do?

'Oh, no – poor little poppet. You won't want visitors then. Maybe next week? It will be great to see you both again. I feel like it's been a very long time, Eve.'

I force myself to believe that by next week I will feel okay, that I will want to be around people, to lose myself in chatter, to feel normal again. It will take a lot more than just hope, though. 'Definitely,' I say, filling my voice with forced confidence.

'Well, I'd better go, I really need some food and I still have to set up the classroom for my rowdy Year 8s. Lord help me!'

I promise that I'll call her, and when I hang up relief floods over me; keeping up the pretence gets harder with each day. How much longer will I be able to fool people?

Kayla's asleep on our bed – the only place she would settle this afternoon. I'm still not dressed and desperately need to shower and wash my hair, but I can't leave her here alone. She's showing no signs of rolling over yet, but the second I rush to the bathroom could be the exact moment she decides to attempt it for the first time. Our bed is too far from the floor, too, so there is no way she would be okay if she fell. I'm sure at this age her skull isn't even fused together yet.

Picking her up to transfer her to the cot is not an option either; her eyes are bound to pop open the second I try to lift her. No, I'll have to wait for my shower, like I always do, until Aiden gets home. He thinks I prefer to have them in the evening when I've got more time, even though for as long as he's known me I've had my showers in the morning. It was a ritual I never deviated from until Kayla was born.

Kneeling beside the bed, I watch the rise and fall of Kayla's tiny chest, take in the calming sound of each breath she takes. With her eyes closed she looks so peaceful that it's impossible to believe what a monster she can be at times. I know none of it's her fault; she didn't ask to be here. I made that decision for her, and now I don't know what I've done. Even though I'm the one who carried her inside me, it is Aiden she has bonded with. The second he picks her up she is calm and soothed, until he hands her to me. It's as if she despises me. My rational brain tells me that this is impossible, that there is no way for her to understand this emotion, yet that is exactly what it feels like. A cruel and deliberate hoax.

I lie down on the bed next to Kayla and continue to stare at her, trying to force myself to feel love – or anything positive – for this tiny helpless being, but the truth is I just want her to keep sleeping. I don't want her to wake up; I want to live in this moment forever. A permanent pause.

The next thing I'm aware of is being woken by deafening shrieks, close to my ear. Kayla's still in the middle of the bed, exactly where I placed her, and I'm right up against her. My heart thuds and I struggle to breathe. I could have crushed her. She could have suffocated under my weight.

Quickly I scoop her up and take her downstairs for a feed, trying to push aside my fear and guilt over what could have happened. For a few hours, I am extra caring towards her, ignoring her constant squirming, as if she is desperate to be out of my arms. Grateful that she's not crying at least, I place her on her play mat and sing to her. Kayla seems to like this and stops groaning to listen to me. Finally, I have found something that calms her.

–

'How was your day?' Aiden asks.

We're sitting at the table eating a meal I managed to throw together once Aiden came home and took over with Kayla. He offered to cook, but the thought of even just another half hour of holding the baby or singing to her felt like something I couldn't manage. At least while I was preparing beef chilli, I was free, a different person somehow, albeit temporarily.

And now Kayla is fast asleep in Aiden's arms while he eats, peaceful and content, as if she is right where she belongs and she has everything she needs right there with him.

'It was good,' I tell him. 'I got some cleaning done too.' There is no need for me to have added this untruth, and I also should tell him about the dangerous situation I put Kayla in. I have become a deceitful liar, while Aiden was always the person I could tell anything. What am I afraid of? He would never judge me. For anything. He would only try to help.

And he would also realise that I'm not the woman he thought I was. That he doesn't know me. I don't even know myself. All I know is that everything is wrong and sooner or later something terrible will happen. The walls will close in on me.

Aiden puts down his knife and fork and smiles. 'D'you know what? I don't think I knew what true happiness was until this little one came along. I just feel so... content.'

A switch flicks inside my head, and I picture myself screaming at him. *You're not the one who has her all day. You come home in the evening and see the best of her. You don't have to deal with the relentless slog, the isolation and monotony. The crushing fear.*

But in a moment of clarity which comes immediately after this thought, I understand why I'm silently attacking him. It is my guilt. Because I can't change what happened.

Aiden watches me, waiting for me to agree. This is another opportunity for me to explain how much I'm struggling, but I let it die. There is no way I can start talking about it. Not now. Not ever.

Later, I stand under the shower with the too-hot water burning my skin. Even though it hurts, the pain is somehow comforting. In here, I am in a bubble, separate from all that exists outside of this door. I close my eyes and pretend I'm no longer here, or anywhere. It is a comforting thought.

And then, without any warning, I am wondering what it would be like if Kayla was the one who didn't exist.

NINETEEN

Now

Maya hasn't turned up for her tutoring session. I've called her mobile several times, and it just rings until her voicemail kicks in. She's never done this before, and I can't help but worry, especially after witnessing her argument with Connor the other day. And considering the things she said last time I saw her, there is every chance that she is no longer pregnant, that something has forced her to take action sooner rather than later. I will always have space in my head to worry about her, even though I have enough to fear. For me. For Kayla. The walls are closing in.

For over an hour I've been standing by my window, watching out for Maya, my mind torn between worry over her and the next steps to take with my daughter. Aiden will not let me near Kayla, so now I have to fight back in a way I didn't think I'd ever have to consider.

On my phone, I research local solicitors dealing with family law. It won't be cheap, but I will take on more work to cover it; Aiden has left me no choice.

Once I've narrowed it down to three firms, I make a note of their numbers before texting Nicole. After thanking her for bringing Kayla to the park, it's only right that I let her know what I'm considering doing if Aiden isn't reasonable about this.

Her reply is immediate: she understands but hopes I will give her a chance to speak to Aiden before I do anything. As much as I want to get things moving, this is the least I can do for her.

Outside, Jamie's car pulls up, and I see him tapping something into his phone. I turn around and stare at my weekend bag, dumped by the living room door. It's packed and ready, all I need to do is grab it and lock up my flat, head off with Jamie to the Lake District for a couple of nights. I owe it to him. I've got Maya's address, so I will ask him if we can make a quick detour on the way.

The second I answer the door and see Jamie's face, I know something is wrong.

'We can't go,' he says. 'I'm sorry, my dad's just called and Mum's been taken to hospital. They think it's a stroke or something. I'd literally just pulled up outside when my phone rang. I'll have to cancel our trip.'

'Oh, Jamie, of course. I'm so sorry. How is she doing?'

'Dad didn't say too much, he's too choked up. I'm going straight up there now so I'll let you know more later. Sorry to do this to you, Eve.'

'Please don't apologise, just get going. And let me know how she is.'

He leans forward and kisses my forehead. 'I will.'

Shutting the door behind him, it occurs to me that fate has taken this out of my hands. I'm not meant to spend the weekend in the Lake District with Jamie.

Perhaps fate has something else in store for me.

–

Everything about this is wrong. I'm standing outside Maya's house and I have no right to pry into her life like this; whatever she does outside of our tutoring sessions is none of my business. She is also eighteen. A young adult.

I feel like an intruder walking along the path to her front door. I haven't been given her permission to be here, and I only know where she lives from the admin forms my students fill in. I'm crossing an ethical line to be here, but I need to make sure she's okay.

The woman who answers the door is a carbon copy of Maya and looks barely a few years older. I assume it's her sister until she speaks – her voice is deep and filled with the knowingness that comes with age. 'Hello,' she says, raising her eyebrows.

'I'm so sorry to turn up like this. I'm Maya's tutor – Eve Martin.'

The woman smiles. 'Oh, yes. Maya talks about you all the time. Thank you so much for helping her with her English. I'm Maya's mum, Bal.'

I nod. 'Um, I just came because we had a session booked for this morning but Maya didn't turn up. I'm a bit worried about her. If it were any other student I'd probably just think they couldn't be bothered, but that's just not Maya. She's never missed a session before.'

Bal frowns. 'She's not here. She stayed at a friend's house last night and hasn't come home yet, but please come in.'

My body won't let me move. I'm comfortable out here, where the space isn't too personal, and have no desire to enter the home of a stranger, even though I know Maya, and her mother seems kind. 'Um, that's okay, I don't want to keep you from—'

'No, no, you must come in.'

Despite my reservations, I give in. I'm doing this for Maya.

The house is small and, although it's clean, it's cluttered with ornaments, all crammed so tightly together that it's impossible to distinguish one from another. I try not to stare at the chaos while Bal leads me through to the kitchen.

'Can I get you anything? Tea or coffee?'

'No, thank you. I really just wanted to quickly check on Maya.'

Bal seems disappointed. 'Are you sure she had a session today? There's nothing in the calendar, and Maya's always so careful about writing everything down.'

Now I'm confused. Could I have got the dates wrong? I don't usually make mistakes with appointments but it's possible given everything that's been going on. 'That's strange. Perhaps I've made a mistake, then. I did try to call Maya but got no answer — have you heard from her at all today?'

A frown appears on Bal's face, and for the first time since she opened the door to me, I sense she is wary of me now, that perhaps she finds it odd that I am here just because Maya didn't turn up for a session.

'She said she didn't feel well during our last session, so when she didn't turn up this morning I just wanted to check there's nothing wrong. Her exams are soon and this was one of our last sessions.'

'I haven't had a text from her, no.' Bal stares at me for a moment. 'I know you only see her a couple of times a week but have you… noticed anything different about Maya lately?'

I have to be careful here; Maya has confided in me and I can't be the one to expose her secret to her family, no matter how much I wish she would talk to her parents. 'I'm not sure what you mean?'

'Oh, it's probably just me being an overprotective mum, but she just seems to have become a bit distant lately. Her dad's noticed it, too. We've always been a close family but Maya never seems to be here. It's as if she's deliberately avoiding us.'

'Please don't worry – I think she's just growing up. She's a young woman now and is just starting to live her own life.'

'Oh, I know you're right. But… oh, never mind. I'm sure I'm just overreacting.' She smiles. 'Do you have children?'

For the first time in two years my answer comes immediately, with no forethought. 'Yes. I have a daughter called Kayla.' As soon as the words are out I realise my error. This is not a stranger I'm talking to – I am linked to this woman through my student. A student who thinks I have no children. My cheeks flush and sweat oozes from my palms. Perhaps there's a chance I will be lucky and Bal won't think to mention this to Maya.

'How lovely! How old is she?'

Or perhaps it is the first thing she will mention to Maya when she gets home. 'Two and a half.'

She smiles and nods. 'That's such a lovely age, isn't it? I do miss the girls being so young. The house felt so alive when they were little, and now it's just like a lobby where we pass each other in the mornings and at night, saying hellos or goodbyes, never stopping long enough for a decent chat. Maya's sister is away at uni in Manchester, so we only see her during the holidays.' Her mouth becomes a thin smile. 'Just make the most of every second. It's gone before you know it, and then you're worrying about where they are and what boys they're involved with.'

I need to get out of this house, to breathe in some fresh air and loosen this rope around my neck. But I need to endure this; I've got to make sure Maya is okay. 'Maya's got a decent boyfriend, though, hasn't she?'

'Oh, Connor's a nice boy. It still feels as though Maya's too young for all that, though. I know she's not, of course, but, well, you'll see when your little girl reaches eighteen. It doesn't get any easier.'

I will make sure this happens; that I am always there to help her through difficult teenage years. That I keep her safe.

'Do you expect Maya back this morning?' I need to change the subject before Bal realises something is wrong, that I am not all I claim to be.

The frown returns to her face. 'I don't know actually. I'll text her now. See where she is.' She crosses to the worktop and reaches for her phone, her long manicured nails clicking on the screen as she types in a message. 'She's normally good at replying. Let's just give it a minute.'

Immediately Bal's phone beeps, and she smiles as she reads the text. 'She's fine, nothing to worry about. Says she's just woken up and didn't realise she had a session today. I'm so sorry she's made you waste your time coming here. Not many teachers would have bothered.'

'I'm just glad Maya's okay.' We both fall silent; there is nothing more to say. 'Well, I've taken up enough of your time. It was lovely to meet you. And don't worry about the session today. I can see Maya tomorrow or Monday, just tell her to text me.'

'That's so kind of you,' Bal says. 'Maya's so lucky to have you as a tutor.'

I study her face – she barely looks older than me, so she must have been extremely young when she had children. Clearly she could handle whatever motherhood threw at her.

Guilt clamps hold of me as I walk out of the house. I have let Maya and her whole family down. I should have told Maya about Kayla when she first revealed that she didn't want to keep her baby; that way at least she might have considered that she could end up regretting her decision. I could have told her all the things I wish I'd known before I walked out. It probably wouldn't have changed her mind but at least I could have tried. *Do anything to protect the people you care about, even if it's at your own cost.*

Inside the car, I buckle my seatbelt and reach for my phone.

> Maya, it's Eve again. Please text me so I know you're okay.

Filled with hope that she'll reply this time, I sit for a few minutes staring at a phone that remains silent. It's only when I drive off that it pings, the familiar sound of an email landing in my inbox. I will ignore it until I get home; at least that way I have the drive home to pretend it's junk or spam. Something from a mailing list I'm subscribed to.

For the rest of the day my phone has been silent, and I haven't even heard from Jamie. It's as if I'm in a vacuum, separate from the rest of the world, unable to communicate with anyone. Except the person intent on reminding me that time is running out.

Giving up on today, I climb into bed and pull the duvet up to my chin, despite the heat. Just as I'm drifting to sleep, my mobile rings and Nicole's name lights up the screen.

'Sorry it's so late,' she begins, 'but I just had to call and tell you. Aiden's agreed for us all to have lunch together. Can you believe it? I guess all my nagging has paid off!'

Her words force me awake, and I sit up. 'That's... great. Thank you, Nicole.'

'I think there'll be a long road ahead of us all, but this is the first step, isn't it? Anyway, can you do tomorrow for lunch? At ours?'

'I'll be there.'

'For Kayla we'll just stick to the story about you being a friend of mine for now. Aiden's insisting on that. I guess further down the line we'll work out what to tell her about everything.'

I agree and thank her again. 'How did you convince him?'

'It wasn't easy,' Nicole explains. 'But I think he realises you're not going to let this go. And I did mention that you could take legal action. In fact, I told him that I would do exactly the same in your position. You are her mum after all, aren't you?'

I was hoping Aiden would have agreed without fear of my threat, but it doesn't matter. I'm going to see my daughter tomorrow and this time it's with Aiden's blessing. And once I am back in her life, they will never get me out.

TWENTY

Before

How is it possible to feel so alone when this shopping centre is full of people? I glance at Kayla, lying on her back in her pram, and know with certainty that this is worse than loneliness. Being here alone would allow me to browse the shops. Or have a coffee and read a book. I wouldn't feel lonely; I'd feel at peace. But I'm not alone and I have a baby who needs me for every single thing, who relies on me.

Kayla didn't ask to be here; she is innocent in all of this. It's my fault, all down to my choices. She stares back at me and produces a vague smile, but this loving gesture does nothing to penetrate the numbness. Perfunctorily taking care of her physical needs is all I can give her.

As desperate for a coffee as I am, for a kick of caffeine to help me feel at least something, there is no way I can stop pushing this pram for long enough to sit down. I've seen other mums relaxing in coffee shops while their babies sit happily on their knees, or in their prams – but not Kayla. No, I have to keep her moving.

I only ventured out today because she wouldn't sleep anywhere, even in my arms. But now I'm here, and for the last hour I've been pacing up and down the shopping centre, and Kayla still won't sleep.

Please, I silently beg. *Please just close your eyes and fall asleep, and then maybe — just maybe — I will dare to nip into Costa and order a latte. Extra strong.*

Of course she doesn't, and as I wander up and down, shedding tears for myself, and for Kayla, it strikes me that I am the only person here on my own.

The lift opens as I walk past it and I stop and stare through the glass door. Just for a second — a fraction of a second — I picture myself pushing Kayla into it and sending it up while I stay down here and walk away. She would be safe. Someone would find her.

I am a monster.

I turn around to see if anyone is watching me, if anyone could tell what I've just imagined doing — but nobody is looking. Everyone is minding their own business.

And that's when I see him. He's walking away from me, and I only have a view of his back, but it's definitely him.

Quickly, I turn and push the buggy in the other direction.

—

'You can't avoid me forever!' Sophie says, making her way into the house. 'I've been desperate to see this little one. Come here, give her to me.' She eases Kayla from my arms and holds her out in front of her to have a good look. 'She's beautiful, Eve. She looks just like Aiden. And you, of course. She's definitely got his mouth, hasn't she?'

'Do you think so?'

'Oh, yeah. Now, you get the kettle on while I entertain this one.'

It's only five o'clock and I'm already in my pyjamas, but Sophie doesn't seem to have noticed. She's too smitten with Kayla to pay attention to how I'm dressed.

'So, where's that husband of yours?' she asks, following me into the kitchen.

'Working late. Not back until around nine tonight.'

'Why didn't you say? I could have stayed and cooked you dinner. Only I told Damien I'd just be popping out for an hour, so he decided last minute to meet up with his friends tonight.'

I tell Sophie not to worry, that actually I'm quite tired. 'Think I'm coming down with something.' I never thought I'd be able to lie to Sophie, but now it happens with ease. 'That's why I'm wearing these.' I tug at my pyjama bottoms, and Sophie laughs.

'I didn't notice!' she says. 'That's not like me. Anyway, you take this little one back, and I'll make the drinks. You do look a bit pale actually.'

'I'll be okay. Why don't I make the coffee and you can cuddle Kayla? You have just been complaining that you never get to see her.'

'True. I'm happy with that.' She strokes Kayla's cheek. 'I really miss these early days, when they're just so... cuddly. Strange, isn't it? Before I had the twins I was never a baby person. Now I'd love to go back and have those newborn days again.'

This couldn't be further from my own feelings. I would give anything to be out of this fog, and Sophie would happily relive it with her twins. This woman is my best friend, yet I'm now struggling to find any common ground with her. *Of course it would be this way, everything's changed. Your life is no longer anything like hers, even though you are both mothers.*

'How are things at school?' I ask. It's a lifetime ago since I was there, and when I go back I will walk through those doors a different person.

Sophie raises her eyes. 'Oh, nothing ever changes, does it? I love being in the classroom but the planning and marking is still a grind. And it's hard being away from the boys so much of the time.' She looks around. 'Got to keep paying the mortgage, though.'

Another glaring difference between us. I would give anything to be working again, to be able to leave this house for a few hours every day. To focus on my students instead of my own pain. I haven't told Sophie my plan yet; perhaps I hadn't even confirmed it in my own mind until now. 'I'm thinking of giving up teaching,' I say.

Her mouth hangs open. 'No! Really? But you love it!'

It takes me a moment to compose my answer. 'It's like you said – now I'm a mum everything's changed. I can't imagine coming home and spending all evening marking when all I'll want to do is play with Kayla.'

Sophie stares at me for a long time. 'Really?' she asks again.

She knows I'm lying – she can see straight to my core.

'I might just do tutoring or something. Fit my hours in around the baby.'

'That does make sense. But wouldn't you be lost without teaching? It's... who we are, isn't it?'

Who I *was*. That person no longer exists. 'Maybe you're right,' I say to pacify Sophie because the way she's looking at me is making me feel exposed. 'We'll see what happens.'

Finally she smiles, and I'm off the hook. 'We never know what the future has in store for us. That's what I love about life,' she says.

And that's exactly what terrifies me.

TWENTY-ONE

Now

Aiden opens the door with no hint of a smile, no warmth whatsoever on his face. He stares at me for a moment before finally speaking. 'You'd better come in, then.' His words are mechanical and forced, as if he has promised Nicole he will be on his best behaviour for her sake. *It's me*, I want to say. *The woman you once loved.*

Stepping inside, I'm not prepared for the feeling that overwhelms me: I am out of my depth here, somewhere I don't belong and have no right to be. Then I hear Kayla's giggles coming from upstairs; a reminder that I need to see this through.

The house smells of citrus, and I notice patches of water on the hallway floor where someone must have recently mopped. 'Shall I take my shoes off?' I ask Aiden, and he gives a slight nod. Some things never change.

Aiden gestures for me to head into the first room off the hall – a small but light and airy living room. Some of Kayla's toys are scattered across the floor, yet somehow the room doesn't look messy, just full of life. It's funny how much warmer a home can feel with children living in it.

'Nicole's just changing Kayla's clothes,' Aiden mumbles. 'She managed to pour water all over herself.'

'What was she doing?' I ask, praying we can keep this small talk going, and that he won't retreat.

'Drinking from her cup. She's generally fine holding it but she dropped it. Anyway, does it matter?'

I hold up my hand. 'No, I was just showing an interest, nothing more. I'm not here to analyse how you parent.'

'No, you lost the right to do that a long time ago. Anyway, it's how Nicole and I parent. We're in this together, whether you like it or not.' His voice is barely more than a whisper.

Aiden's hostility saddens me. This is not the man I remember, no matter what's happened. He was always a fair and kind person, someone willing to try and see all sides of a situation. Not for the first time, it hits me that what I did has changed so many people's lives.

'I'm not here to argue. I just want what's best for Kayla.'

'Just because Nicole—'

'Hi, Eve, thanks for coming. I didn't hear the doorbell.' Nicole stands in the living room doorway, clutching Kayla's hand. She turns to her. 'Kayla, do you remember my friend who we saw in the park the other day? Eve.'

Kayla nods shyly, then grabs onto Nicole's leg. In her other hand she's holding a cream-coloured bunny. 'Can I play, Mummy?'

Hearing Kayla address Nicole this way makes me feel sick, but I force a smile.

'Of course you can. It's lunchtime soon, though, okay?' Nicole gently ruffles Kayla's hair, and a deep pang of envy runs through my body.

I watch as Kayla sits on the floor and rummages through her toys, oblivious to me. I was stupid to think there might be some sort of invisible link between us that would show her who I am without anyone even telling her. She still has no idea. I could be anyone. I thought just being in her presence would be enough, but as each second passes it's clear that it won't be.

'Has Aiden offered you something to drink?' Nicole asks, walking over to him and patting his arm.

'I'm sure he was just about to,' I say, and Nicole laughs. How ironic that this stranger is making me feel more comfortable than the man I used to know every inch of? 'Just water, thanks.'

'It's buffet food for lunch. Bits and pieces like sausage rolls, sandwiches, that kind of thing. I thought I could do a roast but Kayla's been a bit clingy the last couple of days, so I haven't had a chance to get organised. Plus, I'm not feeling too great. Nothing serious, just exhausted I think.'

'That's because you're doing so much,' Aiden says. 'Kayla and I really appreciate it, though.'

He's said this for my benefit, but I brush it off. Aiden doesn't have to like me; I'm here now in his house and this is the first step, no matter how awkward it feels.

'Right,' Nicole says, 'Aiden, can you come and help me get the food ready and Eve can play with Kayla for a minute?'

My heart races. Are they really going to leave me alone with Kayla?

Aiden stares at Nicole and doesn't say anything. He's trying to communicate silently with her, to tell her he doesn't want this. But before he can protest, she grabs his arm and leads him off to the kitchen, telling Kayla that I will play with her while she gets lunch ready.

As much as I want this, as soon as they leave the room, I am far out of my comfort zone. This should come naturally to me, yet I have no idea how to talk to Kayla, how to be around her.

I move across to her, where she is engrossed in playing with her doll's house, and sit on the floor beside her. 'That's a lovely house,' I begin.

She doesn't look at me but nods. 'Mummy got it for me. For my birthday.'

Although I have nothing to compare it to, it strikes me that she speaks remarkably well for a two-and-a-half-year-old.

'Well, it's very special. I bet your little dolls love living in it. I'd love to live in a house like that.'

Again she nods, picking up one of her figures and handing it to me. 'That's Lucy.' She holds the doll out. 'You can have her.'

'Oh, can I? Thank you very much!'

'You're welcome!'

Pride for this little girl fills me up. In those first three months of her life, I could feel nothing, yet now I am flooded with emotions – with love – for *my* little girl.

We play quietly for a few minutes. My conversational skills have escaped me as my mind tries to absorb that I'm finally with my girl, doing something normal, that any mum would do.

'Mummy!' Kayla suddenly says, and for the briefest of moments I actually believe she is speaking to me. Then she is standing up and running to Nicole who is framed in the doorway, watching us.

'Lunch is ready!' she says, scooping Kayla into her arms.

It's clear that none of us really knows what to say as we sit around the table picking at our food. Thankfully,

Kayla provides us with distraction and fills the room with her toddler chatter. Before now I have never been an envious person, but witnessing the interaction between my daughter and Nicole consumes me with grief.

Aiden pushes his food around his plate, hardly touching it. Several times I notice Nicole glaring at him, but he cannot bring himself to look at me, or make any attempt to speak to me.

'I just need to help Kayla on the toilet,' Nicole announces suddenly. 'Aiden, you can come and help.' It's not hard to guess what she's doing; she is planning to instruct Aiden to be more civil to me. Nicole promises they won't be long, and then the three of them head upstairs.

Left alone, my head begins to pound, so I reach into my bag for some paracetamol. I take two, but I doubt they will do anything to relieve the painful throbbing.

Minutes tick by and if it wasn't for the dull rumbling of voices floating downstairs, it would feel as though I am alone in this strange house. A home that isn't mine but should be. The lunch on the table is still yet to be finished, and I stare at the dark pink lipstick mark on Nicole's glass of water.

'Sorry about that,' Nicole says a few minutes later, taking me by surprise. Aiden and Kayla follow behind, and we resume eating as though there's been no interruption.

If Nicole has indeed spoken to Aiden about going easier on me then it's made no difference and the next hour passes painfully slowly. I try to focus on Kayla, but the whole time she's either clambering onto Nicole's nap or begging Aiden to swing her up in the air.

'It's time for your nap now, young lady,' Nicole says once we've finished our food. She turns to me 'And then the three of us can talk.'

Aiden grunts something, and again Nicole serves him with another scowl before whisking Kayla upstairs.

'I know this must make you feel very uncomfortable,' I say to Aiden. 'But I'm not going away. I want to be in her life and nothing's going to stop that.'

Aiden stares at me. 'And have you stopped – just for one second – to consider how this is going to work? Do you think we can just suddenly say, "Hey, Kayla, Eve is actually your mum. Surprise!"'

'No, of course not!'

'What then? You tell me how this can possibly work!'

'I… don't know exactly. Maybe we can get a counsellor involved or something? To help us work out the best way forward?'

'There is no way any of this can be good for Kayla. No way!' He's raising his voice now, forgetting to keep it low so that we're not overheard.

'Neither is denying I'm her mother, keeping the truth about who she is from her. That's not—'

A scream from upstairs cuts me off. It's Kayla – something's happened. Jumping from my seat, I rush into the hallway, heading for the stairs, not caring that it's Aiden's house. He follows behind me, trying his best to get past me.

Nicole is sitting at the top of the stairs, doubled over, clutching her stomach. Not Kayla then. Kayla is okay at least. But Nicole needs help.

Aiden finally gets past me and flies up the stairs, kneeling in front of Nicole. 'Are you okay? What's happened?'

She looks up at him, her eyes wide and frightened, and even from further down the stairs I can see the tears sliding down her cheeks. 'Something's wrong... my stomach... it hurts so much.'

'Let me help you downstairs.' Aiden gently guides her down to the living room, and Nicole collapses on the floor, clutching her stomach.

'You need to get her to the hospital,' I say.

Flustered, Aiden reaches for his mobile. 'I'll call an ambulance.'

'No,' Nicole manages to say, 'I don't need an ambulance.'

I lean down beside her. 'Nicole, has this happened before? Do you know what it could be?'

She shakes her head.

'I think you really need to get to A&E. I would take you but I didn't drive here today.'

Nicole lifts her head and turns to Aiden. 'Can you take me?'

'Of course, but what about Kayla? I'll go and wake her up.'

'No, Aiden.' Nicole turns to me. 'Can you stay here with her?'

Even though she's talking to me now, it takes me a moment to register what she's asking, what it means.

'Yes, I... of course I can.'

'No way,' Aiden chimes in. 'We can't leave Kayla here with Eve. That's insane!'

Nicole gasps. 'We're not waking her up to drag her to the hospital. I could be there for hours! Eve will be okay looking after her.'

Aiden stares at me before turning his attention back to Nicole, writhing around on the floor. 'No. I'll call your mum,' he says. 'She'll come.'

Nicole's skin turns paler by the second, and she lets out a groan. 'It will take her too long to get here. And I think she's out today. Please, Aiden, can we just go? Now!'

'Kayla will be fine,' I say. 'When she wakes up, I'll just tell her you'll be back soon and we're going to have some fun and play some games. She'll be fine, Aiden.'

'She doesn't even know you! You're a stranger to her!'

'Aiden, please.' Nicole's voice is strained. 'I need to go now!'

Helping Nicole up, Aiden finally acquiesces. 'You'll need to keep checking on her as the baby monitor's broken.' He's talking to me but refuses to look in my direction. 'Her room's the first on the right at the top of the stairs. I'll call from the hospital and tell you where everything is. She'll need a snack when she wakes up.' He shakes his head. 'I don't bloody like this.'

'Aiden, please!' Nicole pleads. 'We need to go now, it's getting worse.'

When they've gone, leaving me alone with Kayla in their house, despite hoping that Nicole will be okay, I can't help but marvel at how fate has once again conspired to bring me closer to my daughter.

—

I leave it half an hour before I check on Kayla, and in that time I don't move from the sofa. It feels like a violation to walk around their house, to take in their belongings and form a picture of how they live, especially when Nicole is in hospital. And she is the reason I'm here, after all. She is the one who has helped me. I pray that she'll be okay.

Standing by her door, I listen to the sounds of Kayla's steady breathing. The blinds are down in her room, so I can only make out her outline, but being here with her fills me with warmth. It is so different from the last time I would have watched her sleeping. *I didn't think I could love you then, Kayla, but now I know that there is no way I can't. No way in hell will I let you go again.*

Instead of going back downstairs, I close her door again and sit at the top of the stairs, close enough that I will hear when she awakes.

It's another hour before she does, and when I go in to get her up, explaining where Aiden and Nicole are, she bursts into tears.

'Mummy!' she screams. 'I want my mummy!'

TWENTY-TWO

Now

Aiden arrives home by himself, walking into the living room to find Kayla cuddled up to me, fast asleep. He stares at us, taking in the unusual scene, and I wait for him to rush over and grab her away.

'How's Nicole doing?' I ask, checking the time. He's been gone for five hours. That can't be good.

He doesn't try to take Kayla but flops onto the sofa, a different man from the one who left this house earlier. 'Not very well. They can't work out what's going on. It's not her appendix, and they couldn't scan her today so they're hoping they can do it tomorrow. She told me to come home.'

I gesture to Kayla. 'She was so upset that you both weren't here, but I managed to calm her down eventually. It took a long time but I was able to distract her and then we played for ages. I didn't know what to do for her dinner, so I made her boiled egg and toasted soldiers. It's what Mum always told me I used to like as a toddler.'

He raises his eyebrows. 'And she actually ate it? She never eats eggs.'

'Not all of it but she did okay. Sorry she's not in bed. I didn't want to wake her by transferring her upstairs.'

'It's okay. I'll carry her up in a minute.' He buries his head in his hands. 'What if it's something they can't cure?'

'Don't think like that, Aiden. They'll get to the bottom of it and whatever it is, they'll give her the treatment she needs.'

He stares at me, his expression unreadable, and I prepare myself for an attack.

'You're right.' Standing up he leans down to extract Kayla from my arms.

As he carries her off, it occurs to me that Aiden is being civil to me. All the anger seems to have dissipated like air from a burst balloon. I wouldn't go so far as to say there is warmth there, but something has definitely changed.

'Can I do anything?' I ask when he comes back downstairs.

'No. I'm used to being on my own. Kayla and I will manage until Nicole's back home and feeling well again.' He glances at me, then stares at the floor. 'Thanks for helping, though.'

'You don't have to thank me, she's—' I stop myself before I say something that will remind Aiden that he doesn't want me around.

'It's late and I'm tired,' he says, 'and it feels a bit weird you being here. It did earlier too, but now it's even... stranger.'

Standing up, I tell him I understand. I'm desperate to ask him when I can see Kayla again, but now is not the time. This is progress, I tell myself. Don't push it.

'How's Jackie?' Aiden asks, his question coming from nowhere. Aiden always liked Mum, so I shouldn't be too surprised that he's asking after her.

'She's... doing as well as it's possible given her dementia.'

His eyes widen. 'Oh, I had no idea. After you left, I tried to talk to her, to see if she knew where you were, but she wouldn't answer. And she never returned my calls. And then suddenly her house was up for sale.'

Despite the awkwardness of our situation, I find myself telling Aiden all about Mum. How there was a final incident where she nearly set her house on fire and wasn't safe to live on her own any more. How the doctors were quite surprised because she was only in her mid-sixties, and because it escalated so quickly. 'She was in hospital for a while and then she lived with me for around a year until I had to... well, she went into a home just for respite care but they recommended that she stay there.'

'You mean you gave up on her, just like you did on your daughter.'

His anger has resurfaced; I should have known it would.

'No, it wasn't like that. I had to work and I was struggling to look after her. I—'

'And she didn't ask about Kayla? About your husband?'

'She was in hospital for so long, and I just made excuses, and then she just... seemed to forget about you. Forget that I had a family. I'm not proud of this, Aiden, and I tried to talk to her at times but then she'd forget again.'

He doesn't say anything, once more becoming impossible to read. It used to be that I could tell what he was feeling; now he seems just as numb as I am, except when Kayla and Nicole are around. It's time for me to go home; I'm just going to make things worse by staying here any longer.

Aiden sees me to the door, and I step out into the night.

'I won't let you take my daughter away from me,' he says, pulling the door closed.

–

Someone is sitting on my doorstep when I get home. A small genderless figure covered up by a hooded top and loose jogging bottoms. Assuming it's someone waiting for my downstairs neighbour, I give a small nod and fumble in my bag for my keys.

'Miss, it's me.'

I instantly recognise Maya's voice and do a double take. 'Maya! Are you okay?'

She stands up. 'Sorry, I've been waiting here. You told me once you don't really go out that much, so I assumed you'd be home eventually.'

'You shouldn't be out here alone at night.'

'I had nowhere else to go. Everything's just… a big mess.'

'Come inside,' I tell her. 'We can talk properly in there.'

'Thanks, miss.'

'Maya, don't you think it's time you started calling me Eve?'

She laughs, but the sound dies abruptly in her mouth the second it's uttered.

'I'm sorry I missed my session yesterday,' Maya says as soon as we're inside my flat. 'And for not returning your calls.'

'I was really worried about you. It's just not like you.' I cross to the kitchen and fetch her a glass of water.

'Thanks. I can't believe you came to my house to see if I was okay. Teachers don't normally do stuff like that, do they?'

'Probably not, but this is a bit of a different situation. You're *pregnant*, Maya, I'm just looking out for you.'

Her unblinking eyes stare at me, and it feels as if she's reading far too much of me, seeing too deeply into my mind, even though I know that's impossible. *Paranoia. That's what this is.*

'What did you say to my mum?' she asks, staring at the floor.

Her aggressive tone is one I don't recognise coming from her. My stomach lurches, forcing me to get ready for an attack. 'I only said you hadn't been feeling well during our last session, so I was worried about you.'

'Really? That's it? You didn't say anything else?'

'Maya, what's going on?'

'My parents know,' she says, standing up and walking towards the window. I haven't yet had a chance to pull the blinds down and the street light casts an orange glow onto her skin.

'I'm sorry to hear that. I promise you it didn't come from me, though. I'd never do that, Maya, it's not my business to discuss with anyone.'

'Well, somehow they know. And it seems a coincidence that it was straight after your visit.' She turns to face me.

'Did they say it was me who told them?'

She shrugs, turning away once more. 'No, but only because they were too angry to care about where the info came from. Too busy having a go at me.'

I recall the conversation I had with Maya's mother yesterday; nothing she said suggested she would be the type of parent who would turn against her daughter for getting pregnant at eighteen. She only came across as kind and loving, someone who would never let her children down. Have I misread the situation? It wouldn't be the first time my instinct has let me down.

I head over to the window and ask her to look at me. 'I'm so sorry that's happened. Who else knew and could have told them? Could it have been Connor?' The argument they had in the street plays through my mind; clearly something isn't right between the two of them.

'He would never do that,' she says, still staring out of the window.

I shrug; this time I have truth on my side. 'Then I don't know what to suggest. It's possible your mum just worked it out. Mothers often have an intuition about their children.'

'You'd know all about that, wouldn't you?'

The floor shifts beneath me and I feel my knees buckle, fear threading through my veins. 'What does that mean?'

'Who the hell are you?' she says. 'Are you even a real teacher?'

'Of course I am. Maya, what are you talking about?' But I know exactly what she means.

'You told my mum you have a daughter.' She gestures around the flat. 'Where is she then? Where's this daughter? You don't have one, do you?'

For over two years I've known this moment would come; a time when I'd be caught out and someone would confront me with the lie that I am. Yet despite this, I am unprepared, speechless and struggling to breathe.

I cross to the sofa and sink into it, closing my eyes for a moment. It would be easier to pile another lie on top of the one I'm already living and tell Maya it was a niece I was talking about, not a daughter, but I'm not going to deny Kayla any longer. 'Sit down, please,' I tell Maya, my voice firm and resolute. I have to take back control of this situation.

She must sense something has shifted because she does as I ask and joins me on the sofa.

'I *do* have a daughter. Her name is Kayla and she's two and a half.'

Maya's mouth drops. I don't think she expected me to open up so easily. 'I don't understand,' she says. 'Where is she?'

And that's when I tell her. Everything except the part that I will never speak aloud to anyone. There are tears sliding down Maya's cheeks by the time I've finished; a reaction I haven't anticipated.

'I never even thought about that happening,' she says. 'It must have been horrible. I can't even…' She swipes at her eyes and shakes her head. 'I'm sorry I made you… talk about this.'

'I hadn't meant to blurt it out to your mum,' I explain. 'I think it just came out because Kayla's right here in my head all the time, and I know I've got a fight ahead of me.'

'I hope you get her back,' she says, and for a few minutes the two of us sit in silence.

I have no idea what thoughts are coursing through her head, but she's still here, she's not leaving, so I comfort myself with that.

'Talking to you has really helped,' she says after a while. 'Thank you.'

'Maya, my life isn't yours. I had problems after having my baby, but that doesn't mean you will.'

She nods. 'I know you're right. I think I just needed to weigh everything up from all angles. It's good to do that, right? Before making such an important decision.'

'Of course.'

'I can't believe this is happening. I had my life all figured out. Uni, travelling, career. What's happened to me?'

I grab her hand. 'I wish I had an answer for you. I'm sorry you're going through all this, but you will work it out and do what's right for you. Things always turn out okay in the end, even though it might not feel as though they will.'

'Do they?' She stares at me with her wide, dark eyes. 'Isn't that only in books? I don't think I believe in happy endings any more, miss. My parents hate me and I'm constantly fighting with my boyfriend. I don't even feel connected to my friends any more. They're not pregnant. They're living their lives while I'm throwing up every day. I can't do this any more!'

I tell her that she doesn't have to do anything she doesn't want to do and let her cry onto my shoulder. Is this what it's like having a daughter, I think as I try to stop her shaking. And soon enough, I will do this for Kayla whenever she needs me.

Eventually Maya's sobbing subsides and she begins to calm down. I ask her if she's ready to go back home, and she shakes her head.

'No way. I can't face them. And I can't go to Connor's either.'

My offer comes without any internal debate, because I know what it's like to feel so isolated, for there to be no one you can turn to. 'You can stay here tonight. I'll make my bed up for you with fresh sheets, and I'll sleep on the sofa.'

'Thank you. You don't have to do that,' she says.

'Have a break from everything tonight. You'll be able to face things in the morning and nothing will seem as bad as it does now.'

Maya nods, and I leave to go and sort my bedroom out for her.

—

In the morning, I knock on my bedroom door and ask Maya if she'd like some breakfast.

There's no answer, and when I gently push open the door, I see that she's gone, the bed neatly made.

And no sign that she was ever here.

TWENTY-THREE

Before

Mum was meant to be here twenty minutes ago. She's never late for anything. I've called her three times but there's been no answer.

Beside me, Kayla sits in her bouncer; she looks far too small for it and it seems as though her head is hunched forward. I try to straighten her up, to make her more comfortable, but she lets out a moan and starts crying.

I try Mum's phone again and leave a message. 'Mum, it's me again. Is everything okay? Are you on your way? I've got my appointment in half an hour and it will take me at least that long to get there. I hope you're okay? I'm really worried about you.'

What if something's happened to her and it's all because I've lied to her, called her over here under false pretences? She thinks I've got a hospital appointment, when the truth is that I've got an interview with a recruitment agency. Neither she nor Aiden know that I'm planning on leaving the school – I can't deal with the questions my revelation will raise. They will think I've lost my mind.

The rational side of me – if there is still one left – tries to remain calm. There are a hundred reasons why Mum could be late. Traffic might be awful or she's had some sort of emergency she's had to deal with. I shouldn't assume the worst. But it's hard to ignore the anxiety I'm riddled with.

'You won't sleep, will you?' I say to Kayla, keeping my voice gentle even though I feel like screaming. I read that even though babies this age can't understand the words you're saying, they understand tone of voice.

Gathering Kayla's things together and shoving them in her changing bag, I check her nappy and transfer her to the car seat. I'm sick with nerves about leaving the house with Kayla, but I need to check that Mum is okay.

—

She answers the door immediately. 'Eve! This is a nice surprise. What are you doing here?'

For a moment I wonder whether I've made a mistake. Perhaps I never asked Mum to babysit after all. It's not as though I can think straight lately. Then I remember speaking to Aiden about it, giving him the same excuse I'd given Mum about a hospital appointment. Just a routine postnatal check-up, I'd said, knowing he wouldn't probe any further. I'd only mentioned it to cover myself, just in case Mum happened to say anything to him. That's the trouble with lies; even the small ones pile on top of each other, ensnaring everyone around you until it all comes crashing down.

'I came to check you're okay,' I tell Mum. 'You were meant to be coming over to babysit at ten?'

She clamps her hand to her mouth. 'Oh, yes, oh dear. I'm so sorry. What was it you had to do?'

'A hospital appointment. I've missed it now.'

'I'm so sorry. Can you call them and explain you're running late? I can watch Kayla here for you.' She peers past me to the car, where I have left Kayla dozing in her car seat.

My instinct tells me that I shouldn't agree to this. With her forgetfulness, Mum is probably not safe to watch Kayla, and it's not as if I actually have a hospital appointment. *But it's still an emergency. I cannot go back to the past and having my interview is an important first step.*

'Okay. I won't be too long. Everything's in her bag. I'll just get her.'

'Oh, it will be lovely having her here.'

Driving away, my mind plays over all the dreadful things that could happen to Kayla if Mum isn't up to watching her. But still I keep my foot on the accelerator, bursting each scenario in my head as if I'm popping a balloon. I need to do this; I have no choice. And then I will feel better. Then, maybe, I will be able to feel love.

–

The recruitment agency woman I spoke to on the phone – Leonie – is nothing like I imagined. She sounded young on the phone, yet she must be in her fifties at least.

'Sorry I'm so late,' I say, holding out my hand. 'Awful traffic.' I don't mention Kayla, or that I'm still on maternity leave.

Leonie flashes a smile. 'Don't I know it. I've been late to work every day this week and that never usually happens. I don't know what's going on. Now let's see…' From a file, she pulls out the CV I emailed her yesterday. 'As I said on the phone, this is very interesting. We don't normally get many teachers looking for admin work.

That's quite a change.' In other words, she thinks I'm out of my mind. Teaching is supposed to be a career for life, not something you change your mind about after a few years.

'I feel it's time for something else,' I explain. 'And I do have admin experience. Before I was a teacher I worked in an office for a couple of years.'

She nods and shifts her glasses further down her nose. 'That's great but the problem is it might be quite hard to place you somewhere. You've been teaching for a few years, so employers might find it hard to accept you do actually have a broad skill set. I'll be the first to say that teaching is definitely a profession with transferable skills, but it might not be easy for me to convince people of that.'

I try not to show my frustration. 'I know I can do admin work. I can take on any challenge. I'm a hard worker – I just need someone to give me a chance.'

'Well, leave it with me and I'll see what I can do.' She pushes up her glasses and scans my CV again. 'I have to be honest with you, though. It's a bit unfair for me to place you in an admin role when you've got your teacher training and qualifications. You see, there are people out there who only have experience in admin work, so it's almost like taking a job from them, isn't it?'

I stare at this woman in disbelief. Despite her enthusiasm on the phone, she has no intention of helping to find me a job. She's wasted my time, and Mum's time.

'Thank you,' I say, standing up. 'I'll wait to hear from you then.'

'Yes, I'll be in touch.'

It's not sadness I feel as I make my way back to my car – it's anger. Strong and intense, I'm a volcano about to erupt.

And then, when my phone rings, a number I can recall from memory appearing, I throw my phone to the ground and watch as the screen shatters.

TWENTY-FOUR

Now

With no tutoring sessions booked in, I'm free to replay the events of yesterday; how distraught Kayla was when it dawned on her that Aiden and Nicole weren't there. 'I want Mummy!' she'd cried repeatedly. Followed by, 'Where's Daddy?' Her sadness almost broke me, and all I wanted to do was hold her tightly and comfort her. I kept my distance, though, instead distracting her with silly faces and funny games. But in Kayla's mind, and in her heart, Nicole is her mother. It was just through sheer tiredness that she happened to fall asleep on me.

This is what I think about as I clear away paperwork and make a half-hearted attempt at tidying the flat. As I strip the sheets off the bed, I wonder why Maya left without saying anything.

I send Nicole a text message to see how she is, but even after an hour there is no reply.

Jamie FaceTimes as I sit down to eat breakfast, his unshaven face filling the screen so I can't help but notice the large dark circles under his eyes.

'How's your mum?' I ask.

He shakes his head. 'Not too good. She's not speaking very well, slurring her words and stuttering, but the doctors have said that's to be expected after a stroke.'

'I'm so sorry, Jamie. That's definitely what it was, then?'

'Yeah, looks like it.' He flicks his eyes to the ceiling. 'It's so weird. I mean, you know your parents are getting older and things could happen but when it actually does it's still a shock. It's bloody awful.'

Now is the time to tell him I understand this, that I live with it every day. Perhaps explaining about Mum will bring us closer together. Maybe that is what I want. *But then how do I tell him about Kayla? About who I really am. It's such a huge thing to withhold. And where will it lead?*

'My mum's in a care home,' I say. This is safe ground, this is all I have to tell him for the moment, and maybe sharing my story will help him in some way. 'She lived with me for a while until I just couldn't manage any more. I couldn't keep her safe no matter what I did. She kept disappearing and putting herself in danger. It broke me to do it but it was the safest thing.'

On my phone screen, Jamie's eyes widen. 'I'm sorry,' he says. 'I had no idea.' There is no accusation there, no *why didn't you mention this before?* and I'm grateful for this.

'It makes you realise, doesn't it?' he continues, 'that we never know what's about to happen to us in the next minute. I need to start living my life more. What's it they say? Carpe diem. Seize the day or something like that.'

'Actually, I think it means *pluck* the day, but that doesn't sound as good, does it?'

Jamie laughs. 'Trust you to know that. I can tell you're an English teacher.'

Maybe he does understand me a tiny bit. For these last three months he must have been paying attention, even while I deliberately wasn't.

'*Seize* does sound better,' he says. 'And that's what I'm going to do. When I get back let's do something different. Go somewhere we've never been. Have a real experience. Together.'

I don't hesitate this time. 'I'd like that.'

'Let me think of something we can do, then,' Jamie says. He's clearly perked up in the last couple of minutes, and even the dark circles underlining his eyes appear to have shrunk. 'Anyway, I'd better go. Dad wants to go for a walk while Mum's sleeping. I'll probably drive back home tomorrow, or the day after. One of my sisters is on her way from France, and she can stay for as long as necessary. God help Mum! Amy's a complete nightmare and will be more trouble than she is help.' He lets out a deep breath which turns into a whistle. 'I wish I could stay up here longer, but there's nobody to cover at work this week. I'll text you later, okay?'

Once he's gone, I call Aiden. Even though he won't like it, I have to check how Nicole is. And it worries me that she hasn't replied to my message. He answers just as I'm about to give up.

'Eve,' he says, 'I can't talk now.'

'I was just calling to see how Nicole is?'

In the background a scream erupts, and Aiden muffles the phone.

'Is that Kayla? What's going on?'

'I said I can't talk right now,' he hisses.

'Is Kayla okay?'

'She's fine. She's just upset. She wants Nicole and doesn't understand why she's not here.'

'So she's still in hospital?'

'Yes, and I was supposed to be at work over an hour ago.'

'I'll come over and help,' I say, already standing up to gather my things. 'Traffic shouldn't be too bad now, so I can be there in about forty minutes.'

'No. No way. We'll manage.'

'How? Nicole's mum is away and your parents are in Scotland. Sophie's at work, so who else is there?'

'I do have other friends, Eve.'

'Can they come right now?'

Silence.

'Right, I'm leaving now.' I hang up before he can say another word; I'm not going to miss this opportunity.

–

Aiden scowls as he opens the door. Thankfully, Kayla is clinging to his leg so he stays quiet and lets me in. In her other hand she clutches her bunny.

'Hi, Kayla, I'm here to look after you for a little bit while your daddy goes to work.'

She stares at me and nods. 'My mummy's in *hop-sit-al*,' she says, and I can't help but smile at her pronunciation.

Crouching down to her level, I take her hand. 'Yes, she is. And the doctors are making her all better so she can come home very soon to be with you.'

I stand up again and face Aiden. 'Is there any news?'

'Her scan's in an hour, so hopefully they'll know more then.' He ruffles Kayla's hair. 'We need to brush this, don't we?'

'I can do that,' I say, but Aiden has already turned away, leading Kayla into the kitchen.

Following them inside and closing the front door behind me, I notice the mess and clutter that has spread through the house since Nicole hasn't been here; a sure sign that he needs her around.

In the kitchen, Aiden brushes Kayla's hair. She's still got hold of her bunny and she strokes its ears. 'This is Flopsy,' she says, holding it up to me. 'Mummy got her for me.'

I lean forward and take a close look. 'She's lovely, I wonder if she wants some breakfast?'

Kayla's eyes light up. 'Yippee! Let's make it.' She points to a small toy kitchen in the corner of the room. I didn't notice it the last time I was here, although that's hardly surprising when I felt so overwhelmed in this house. Somehow today it feels different, as if I might actually fit in here. It's too early to assume I can just slot into Kayla's life, though, but for now I will live in this moment.

'Kayla,' Aiden says, 'can you find Flopsy's hat? I think it's in your room.' He puts down her hairbrush, and she rushes off.

'Just so you know,' he continues, turning to me, 'I'm not happy about this at all. But all I can think about right now is Nicole so…'

'Kayla will be fine with me, Aiden. Just like she was the other night.'

'This doesn't change anything,' he says, gathering his wallet and keys and stuffing them into his pocket.

'You don't have to be so angry with me all the time, Aiden. Can't we just try to move forward?' I whisper this because I can hear Kayla thundering down the stairs.

He ignores me. 'This won't be for long. Nicole will be fine and then—'

'Daddy! Got it!' Kayla flies into the room, waving a small yellow hat above her head. She fumbles around trying to place it on the bunny, but it continually slides off.

'Let me help,' I say, and Kayla nods.

'Bye, sweetheart,' Aiden says, kissing her forehead.

And then he is gone, and I am alone with my daughter. Nobody watching over us.

—

It feels like only minutes have passed before Aiden is opening the front door and calling Kayla's name. His face drops when I appear in the hallway alone.

'We're playing hide and seek,' I explain. 'Kayla's hiding in the kitchen.'

He nods and peels off his jacket, dumping it on the shoe cabinet instead of hanging it on a hook. In his haste to get to the kitchen he doesn't notice it drop to the floor.

'She's fine, Aiden. Everything's been fine,' I say to his back. I don't tell him that I also found time to tidy the house. As distraught as he is, perhaps he will never notice.

Kayla squeals when she realises Aiden is home, and I loiter in the hallway to give them a moment together. I'm grateful that the two of them have such a strong bond, that he has given her a good life in spite of me.

I stay where I am and close my eyes, allowing the sound of laughter to wrap around me, to lift me up. I know this serenity will only last a moment.

Kayla rushes into the hallway, snapping me back to the present. 'Eve, Eve, Daddy's home!'

'Yes, that's good, isn't it?'

She nods and grabs my hand, shocking me with how tiny and soft her own hand feels. I'm not used to this. The only children I have anything to do with are my students, all of whom are years older than Kayla. 'Come and see my daddy!'

In the kitchen, Aiden is rooting through the fridge, while Kayla runs through the open back door into the garden. 'I visited Nicole in my lunch break so I could come straight home to Kayla.'

'How's she doing?'

'Tired and in a lot of pain. We have to wait for her results, but she's going to be all right, I know it.'

I nod. 'I'm happy to hear that. Look, I'll get going now and leave you to it. Unless you need me for anything?'

He shrugs and doesn't look up. 'I suppose you can stay for some food. If you're hungry.'

I try to contain my surprise. 'Are you sure? I don't want to get in the way.'

'Stay or don't stay. Whichever.'

This is as good as I'm going to get from him. 'I will, then. Thanks.'

He frowns. 'Judging by the contents of this fridge, it will have to be spag bol.'

I tell him this sounds good, and he snorts.

'Really? You never used to like it. You always said that any kind of pasta is dull.'

'Well, maybe I'm a different person now.' I wish I could make him see that.

He raises his eyes. 'I'll just put Kayla to bed first.'

'Can I do it?' The second I ask I know it's a mistake, that I'm pushing him too far, too soon.

'I don't think that's a good idea. What will Kayla think if I let some stranger put her to bed when her dad's right here?'

I stare at him, smarting from his cruelty, even though I understand it. 'I'm not a stranger, Aiden.' My voice is a whisper, despite Kayla being at the back of the garden, too far away to hear us.

Watching our daughter from the window, he ignores me again. 'I really don't need this,' he mutters to himself.

'What about if I just came upstairs with you? I'd love to see her proper bedtime routine.' My heart thuds in my chest; I'm desperate for him to agree, to let me in just a fraction.

Seconds fly by without any response from Aiden, until eventually he heads to the door and calls out. 'Come on, Kayla, it's bedtime now and Eve's going to help us.'

Kayla runs to the door and jumps into Aiden's arms. 'Can she read me a story? I want *The Gruffalo*.'

Aiden raises his eyebrows, clearly as surprised as I am. 'Yes, of course,' he says, heading out of the kitchen with our daughter in his arms.

–

Later, once Kayla's asleep, we sit down to eat. To start with, Aiden's frosty silence makes it a bizarre experience: we are two people who can't speak to each other sharing a meal together. But by the time we've finished, it feels as though Aiden has warmed to me – even if only a fraction – and we find ourselves discussing friends we used to know. Laughing even. As if time has erased itself.

'Hi.'

I turn and Nicole is standing in the doorway.

Aiden's cheeks redden, and he quickly stands, stumbling over his words. 'Nic, are you okay? What's happened? You're supposed to be in the hospital.' He rushes over to her and gently hugs her.

'I discharged myself. I couldn't stand to be in that place for another second.' She turns from Aiden to me. 'I'm guessing Aiden needed you to babysit? Thank you so much for helping, Eve. I really appreciate it.'

Aiden frowns. 'But you need to wait for your results. I can't believe they let you leave.'

Nicole explains that she had to sign a form to state that she was leaving against the doctor's recommendation. 'It's just to cover themselves. I'll be fine.' She turns to me. 'Is someone going to get me some food, then?' She tries to laugh but it obviously hurts her stomach.

'You need to sit down,' Aiden says. 'There's no spaghetti left but I'll get you something else.'

'I was only joking, I'm not actually hungry. Stop fussing.'

I need to explain my presence here to Nicole, even though nothing about her suggests she is jumping to any wrong conclusions. 'I came over this morning to watch Kayla so Aiden could go to work. He didn't want me to but he was desperate.'

Aiden takes Nicole's hand. 'She's right. I didn't have much choice.'

'I'm glad you could come,' Nicole says. 'It's the right thing for Kayla.'

'She's missed you so much,' Aiden says, kissing Nicole's forehead.

Nicole nods. 'I'll have to spoil her tomorrow. Take her somewhere nice.'

'You're not going anywhere until we find out what's wrong,' Aiden says. 'I'm taking the day off work so I can look after both of you.'

'Let's just see how I feel in the morning.'

I tell them both I need to get back to my flat. 'I'm glad you're feeling well enough to come home, Nicole. Please let me know if I can help with anything.'

'Thank you so much, Eve.'

Neither of them sees me to the door, and as I walk away I can't help but feel disappointed that Nicole came home early.

TWENTY-FIVE

Before

'She's beautiful. Such a doll. She looks just like you, Eve.'

Aiden's mother is standing over Kayla's cot, gazing down at her with a smile that's ready to burst from her face. This is the first time she's met Kayla and all she's done since she arrived is gawp at her, repeatedly telling me how much she is my doppelganger. It's bizarre how much people love to comment on who a baby looks like, as if it is a huge shock that they could actually resemble their parents. Still, I'm grateful that Marie and Pete are here.

'And she definitely has Aiden's ears, don't you think? His were exactly the same when he was little. Sticking out just ever so slightly! So cute!' She guffaws and reaches down to stroke Kayla's cheek.

Don't wake her up! I need her to keep sleeping.

Marie's attachment to her granddaughter was immediate – an unbreakable bond – yet here I am still waiting for love to overwhelm me.

At least for the next week I will have company, and perhaps that will help me to feel normal again. Maybe Marie will be able to comfort Kayla where I can't.

Marie finally turns away from Kayla and looks me up and down. 'Are you okay, Eve? You look exhausted.

You know, you must rest while Pete and I are here. We may have only brought Aiden home when he was seven months old, but I can imagine how hard these early days are. Anyway, we're here to help and do whatever you need us to do.' She reaches out her arms, and I turn away, pretending I haven't noticed. I can't bear to be hugged by anyone.

'Thank you, Marie. We're so grateful for your help.' I need Marie to think I have everything under control, that everything is normal. Thankfully, I managed to clean the house before they arrived, even though it meant leaving Kayla to scream in her bouncer. Keeping her close to me, where she could see me, made no difference. It never does.

'Where's my little angel, then?' Pete's voice booms into the room, and in her cot Kayla stirs.

'Shhh, keep your voice down, she's asleep!' Marie tuts.

'Oops, sorry. I'm just excited to see her.' Pete steps into the room. 'Ah, there she is – sleeping beauty. So angelic, isn't she?'

Yes, because she's asleep. Wait until she wakes up and then you will see a different baby.

Pete embraces me. 'Lovely to see you, Eve. Sorry we couldn't come sooner. Marie's been champing at the bit to get here. Driving me crazy!'

Marie slaps him gently on the arm. 'Of course I've been desperate to see Kayla. She's my first grandchild.'

And last from us, I almost say. *Definitely the last.*

Pete winks at me. 'Don't expect to see your baby for the next week, love!'

His words lift me up, release me. What's wrong with me? Most new mothers would be terrified of their newborn baby being whisked off by their mother-in-law, yet I am already desperate for Marie to take over with Kayla.

'Although you do look like you could do with some rest,' Pete adds.

Marie nods. 'She does. Tell you what, how about when Aiden gets home from work the two of you go out for dinner by yourselves? We'll watch Kayla and put her to bed. Oh, I know you don't want to leave her but it will do you the world of good, so I won't take no for an answer.' She smiles, satisfied that she's got everything all planned out.

I pretend to mull this over, to be struggling with saying yes. 'Well, okay, I guess it couldn't hurt for an hour or two. If you're sure?'

'Take as long as you need. All you have to do is show us where everything is and we'll be fine. Stay out all night if you want to.'

—

'This feels weird, doesn't it?' Aiden says, lifting his glass of wine and staring at it as if he's unsure what to do with it. 'I keep turning to see where Kayla is.' He takes a sip. 'It's nice to be out for a change, though, isn't it?'

He has no idea just how true that is for me. I feel like I can breathe again as the tension drains from my body. Now, for a couple of hours at least, only Aiden and I exist. 'How's work?' I ask. I have to steer him off the subject of Kayla. 'Sorry I never have a chance to ask you properly.'

'It's a bit stressful at the moment. The restructuring means everything's up in the air and it's creating a lot of uncertainty. I know I'll be okay, but I feel bad for everyone who won't be.'

This is news to me. How can I not be aware of something so important going on with Aiden? My anxiety has overwhelmed me so much that I haven't paused for even a second to listen to what Aiden has been telling me.

'I'm sorry, I know you told me, I just—'

'Hey, it's fine. You've been busy with Kayla, and I know it's all-consuming at the moment.'

Yes, but it's not the endless cycle of changing nappies, feeding and winding – it's the fact that I can't seem to love my daughter. I wish I could tell Aiden this, put it out there once and for all and share my truth. But I can't do that to him; he is happy and I won't strip that from him. 'It's no excuse for not listening to you,' I say.

He takes my hand. 'Listen, you've given me Kayla, the most amazing gift I could ask for, so I'm not going to moan about you not listening when I drone on about work.'

Our food comes, and I savour every mouthful of my risotto, relishing the fact that I can eat without being interrupted, without having to hurry. I don't want this evening to end. I want us to be the people we were before we wanted to be parents.

Then my phone rings, shattering the peace in my mind. I leave it in my bag, try to buy myself a few moments to think of an excuse for not answering.

Opposite me, Aiden is frowning. 'Aren't you going to get that?'

'No, this is our special night.'

'It could be your mum, though.'

He's right. I at least need to check to see. I reach into my bag, but thankfully the phone stops ringing. I check it, the broken screen still clear enough to read. My stomach plummets when I see that number again. 'It's not Mum,' I say. 'Just one of those nuisance numbers.'

'So annoying,' Aiden says, focusing on his food once again.

And now I need to do the same, as difficult as it is. 'I've had an idea,' I say, leaning forward. 'Why don't we go away, just for a couple of nights? It doesn't have to be anywhere too far. It would be nice to get out of London for a change, wouldn't it?'

Aiden's eyes widen. 'I don't know… Kayla's a bit young, don't you think? And she's still not a great sleeper. It might be a bit difficult doing all the night feeds away from home.'

'Actually, I meant just the two of us. Your mum and dad could babysit – they'd love that. I mean, Marie practically forced us out tonight, didn't she? I think she would love any chance she could get to have Kayla on her own.'

I wait for Aiden to smile, but it doesn't come. Instead, a frown appears on his forehead. He's supposed to look happy, relieved that I've suggested this. He's not meant to be staring at me as if I'm trying to convince him to give Kayla away to the people at the next table.

'I don't know, Eve. Leaving her for a couple of hours when she's asleep at night is a bit different from going away for a few days. We can't – she's too young. What if she freaks out and thinks we've abandoned her?'

And with his words I plummet to the ground. How stupid I've been to hope that just for a short space of time I could escape. 'You're right,' I say, fighting back not tears but rage. 'We can't leave her. I don't know what I was thinking.'

Before Aiden says anything else, I excuse myself to go to the toilets, rushing into a cubicle where I slam my fists against the wall. I stare at the toilet and imagine smashing my head against it until there is nothing left of me and no more pain left to feel.

'Are you okay?' Aiden asks when I get back to the table. 'I was about to send out a search party.'

'I just felt a bit nauseous,' I explain. 'Better now, though.'

'Good. Maybe your food was a bit off? Ha, if I didn't know any better I'd wonder if it was morning sickness, but, well...'

I'm grateful that he doesn't finish this thought. I don't need him to remind me that for so long now I've been too exhausted for any kind of intimacy.

'Shall we get dessert?' I'm not hungry but neither am I ready to go home yet. I need this moment to last as long as possible.

'Never say no to dessert,' Aiden says, grinning. How quickly he's able to move on from anything negative in our lives. How does he not see that everything is falling apart?

I've bought us some more time here in this restaurant, but the minutes tick by loudly in my head; a constant reminder that this time will soon be over.

On the way home, while Aiden drives the short distance to our house, I close my eyes and pray that I never have to wake up.

TWENTY-SIX

Now

When my phone rings the next morning – Nicole's name flashing on my screen – my first reaction is panic that something's happened to Kayla. Guilt and anxiety merge into one to immediately make me assume the worst. That I am too late.

'Hi, it's Nicole.'

'Is something wrong?' I ask.

'No, course not. Everything's fine. But I do have a favour to ask. Aiden's working today, and I've got something urgent I need to do. Would you be free for just a few hours to look after Kayla this afternoon? I'll pick her up later.'

I'm stunned by her request. Even though Aiden was civil towards me yesterday, I assumed that was only because he was worried about Nicole. I had fully expected to have a fight on my hands again just to get to see her. I had prepared myself for a war.

'Of course I will. Does Aiden know?'

'Oh, hang on. Kayla, no, sweetheart, you can't have Mummy's iPad. Sorry, Eve. No, Aiden doesn't know. He seems to have already forgotten just how much you've helped us. I'm sorry. We'll get through to him, though.

Look, I'll have to go, but could you pick her up in an hour?'

–

'We're just going to visit someone, Kayla. Someone very important to me.'

I don't know when the idea to take Kayla to visit Mum occurred to me but now we're on our way – with me driving as fast as I safely can so as not to waste any time – it feels like the only thing that makes sense. I have only a few hours, and with Aiden still reluctant to let me into Kayla's life, there's no telling when I'll get another opportunity like this.

'Who?' Kayla asks, and in the rear-view mirror I see her shuffling around in her car seat.

'My mummy. She's not feeling very well, and I thought we could both cheer her up.'

'I've got a mummy too!' she exclaims. 'I love my mummy!'

'Yes, you have, and she loves you, too.' I force myself to smile. Nicole has been so nice to me, and I loathe myself for resenting her, for believing that if it was just Aiden and Kayla then I would have got through to him by now.

When we arrive, despite my earlier determination to bring Kayla to Mum, I begin to have doubts. There's no predicting how Mum will react to anything, and I fear this won't be the reunion my heart wants it to be. There's every chance Mum will freak out, or Kayla will get scared; anything's possible with Mum's disease.

For Kayla's sake, I push aside the doubts and take her inside the building, my heart soaring when she reaches to grab my hand.

'Who's this little beauty, then?' Silvia, one of the carers, asks. She's standing by the reception desk, gathering some papers together.

'This is Kayla, my friend's daughter,' I explain. 'I'm babysitting and thought it would be nice for Mum to have some company other than just mine.'

Silvia crouches down to Kayla's level and tells her it's lovely to meet her. 'Jackie will be so happy to see you. She loves seeing the little ones whenever they come to visit someone; this will make her day.'

I'm not sure how true this is – especially when Mum rarely leaves her room, but I'm grateful that Silvia is helping to make Kayla feel comfortable.

Outside Mum's door, I take a deep breath. It's impossible to know how this will go, but I'm here now so there's no way out of it.

'Eve, is that you?'

I'm about to greet her until I realise it's not me Mum's addressing, but Kayla. She reaches out and strokes her cheek.

Kayla giggles. 'I'm not Eve. I'm Kayla!'

This information is unimportant to Mum, and she continues staring at her granddaughter, taking in every inch of her. 'Oh, you're such a beautiful little girl, aren't you? Now, why haven't you come to see me for so long?'

Another giggle, and then Kayla trots into the room, throwing herself on the bed. She reaches into her bag of toys and pulls out a small hairbrush and her doll.

'How are you doing, Mum?' I ask. I long to hug her, but since dementia took control of her brain, she recoils at most physical contact.

'Oh, I'm still waiting for that bus,' she replies, raising her eyebrows and drawing closer to me. 'Do you know, I think they're just trying to keep me here! I can't understand why. Nobody needs any piano lessons.'

It is particularly poignant to hear Mum say this. She'd been a piano teacher for many years, right up to her early sixties. Despite there being a piano in the residents' lounge downstairs, Mum hasn't touched even a key for at least two years.

'It's okay, Mum. The bus will be here later – you won't miss it.'

She studies my face, wrinkling her own as if working out whether she believes me. 'Oh, that's good.' She turns to Kayla, who, thankfully, is too engrossed in her doll to pay attention to our conversation. 'Now, young lady, who's this dolly, then?'

While I get Kayla a snack, I watch the two of them with equal measures of pain and delight circling through me. They both speak so animatedly together that it's hard to believe they are strangers. *Not strangers, though, not really. They are family, bonded by blood, no matter the circumstances. I want to be able to come here all the time with Kayla, to see the joy on Mum's face again. Only Aiden and Nicole are standing in my way, even though Nicole doesn't realise that she is.*

With Mum and Kayla so engrossed in their chat, I'm the only one who notices when there's a knock on the door and Silvia pokes her head around it. 'Hi, sorry to interrupt but could I have a quick word in private, please?'

I stand up and head to the door.

'It's just to go through a query with your direct debit,' she says, keeping her voice low, even though it's unlikely Mum would understand what she's talking about. 'Not your fault, of course, our system crashed, so we're having to get everyone to submit another form.'

I glance at Mum and Kayla, and even though both of them are clearly at ease with one another, there's no way I can leave them here alone, not even for a minute.

'That's fine, but do you think someone could come in and stay with Mum and Kayla for a minute?'

She nods. 'Of course. Let me just grab Ryan.'

Once I've sorted out the direct debit form, I rush back to the room to find Mum and Kayla still enjoying each other's company. Somehow Kayla has put the hugest smile on Mum's face, something I haven't seen for a long time. *This is meant to be – the pieces of my family put back together again. Whatever I have to do to keep it this way doesn't matter.*

–

'Eve, can we talk? I'm outside your flat.'

I've just put on my pyjamas, so the last thing I'm expecting is company. Especially Nicole's. And there is no good reason I can think of for her turning up like this. She must have found out I took Kayla to see Mum without checking with them first. 'I, um. Okay. Come in.' I press the buzzer and hear the front door open, having just enough time to throw on my dressing gown before she's standing in front of me. I prepare to defend myself.

'I'm sorry it's late,' Nicole says, smiling apologetically. Her eyes fix on my dressing gown. 'Oh no, I didn't think you'd be in bed.'

'I wasn't. I just like to get comfortable in the evening.' She still isn't confronting me, so I offer her something to drink.

'No, thanks. I can't stay long. Aiden will be wondering where I am.' She steps into my flat and glances around. 'I just wanted to thank you for today. It was really kind of you to step in at such short notice.'

She could have said this on the phone. There's something else going on here.

'Kayla's been so distraught about me being ill, and you really helped take her mind off everything. With your mum's help of course.'

There it is. This is what she has come here for. 'Nicole, I'm really sorry. I didn't plan to take Kayla there, it's just that I always visit Mum. I didn't have a chance to ask you on the phone, or when I picked her up.'

She holds up her hand. 'Oh, please don't apologise. I actually think it's lovely that your mum got to see her. I'm assuming you didn't mention who she is, though?'

I shake my head. 'No, of course not. And even if I did, Mum's not in a good state to remember anyway.'

Nicole reaches for my arm. 'Aiden told me. I'm so sorry. I'm really close to my mum so I can only imagine how hard it is for you both.'

'Will you come and sit down? You've only just been in hospital.' I head to the sofa, and Nicole follows. 'Does Aiden know?'

'No. I didn't tell him, but...' And then tears are trickling down her cheeks, which she vigorously tries to swipe away.

Instinctively I move closer to her and place my arm across her shoulders. 'Nicole, what is it? What's happened?'

'This feels so strange, I'm not sure I should even be talking about it. Aiden would feel so... betrayed.'

'Please trust me, Nicole – nothing you say here will ever get back to Aiden, I promise you that.' The irony is that I'm expecting her to trust me when I don't even know if I can trust myself. If I had to break my promise to Nicole in order to get my daughter back then I would do it like a shot.

Nicole takes her time but eventually she begins to talk. 'Things have been a bit… strained between Aiden and me lately. We used to always be a team, especially when it came to parenting, but now it feels as though we can't agree on anything. There's this horrible tension between us all the time and… it's just hard to deal with.'

This is my fault. I have done this to them. 'I'm so sorry. I never wanted to cause problems for you both. When I came back, I didn't even know Aiden was with anyone –'

'Please don't think I'm blaming you, Eve. This is not your fault. All you've done is come back to try and be in Kayla's life – I could never blame you for that. I would have done exactly the same thing.' She turns away. 'The problem is that Aiden just doesn't see this. And I've been pushing and pushing him, and now I feel like he's turning away from me.'

'Oh, Nicole, I'm so sorry.'

'Aiden's a good man. You know that – you were married to him. He goes out of his way for people and is the most amazing father to Kayla.'

There is something surreal about talking to my ex-husband's new partner about the man I was married to. Still am, technically. Nicole might be with Aiden now but there is a whole side to him that she can never know. She will never see the man he was when we were together. I believe that she's tried to get through to him, but I'm convinced I would stand a better chance if I could just reach the person he was, the person he still must be somewhere inside him. Nicole, as nice as she is, is the one who is preventing that.

'I know all this,' I tell her. 'I just need him to understand *me*.'

Nicole grabs my hand. 'Please, Eve – I'm begging you, please can you just give us some space for a while? Time for Aiden to get used to everything without me putting pressure on him. I just don't know what damage it will do to our relationship if things carry on as they are. I'm still totally on your side with this – I want Kayla to have you in her life – but I'm just asking you to be patient.'

Seconds tick by, Nicole's words – and what they mean for me – crashing around my head. 'How long?' I ask. 'You're asking me to stay away but for how long?'

She shakes her head. 'I don't know. For however long Aiden needs.'

'Okay,' I say. 'I see I have no choice.'

'And there's one more thing. Don't you think it's time, maybe, that you got a divorce?'

Even though she's right, I'm stunned that she's bringing this up now. 'What does Aiden say about it?'

'It's what he wants. And I'm sure it's what you want too?'

I nod. 'Then all he has to do is ask. I would never keep him tied to me.'

'Good. Thank you,' she says, leaning forward to embrace me. 'Thank you so much, Eve.'

I see her to the front door and watch as she gets in her car. There are always casualties in a war, I think.

That's not going to stop me.

TWENTY-SEVEN

Before

They say babies can pick up on how their mothers are feeling and it somehow affects their behaviour. Before having Kayla I was sceptical about this. It's not as though babies are born with some kind of sixth sense, are they? Yet now I know there's truth to this.

Nothing I do soothes Kayla, yet the second she's in Aiden's arms all the tension in her tiny body releases itself and she's suddenly at peace. The second she feels herself in his arms. I don't resent her or Aiden for this; it's just one thing to add to the long list of reasons why I shouldn't be a mother.

'It's because you're always with her, and I'm a novelty,' Aiden says, and I wonder how he can't see what's staring him directly in the face.

Today she's been whining all morning, so I decide I'll take her to the park. It's on a main road, meaning the roar of the traffic might drown out her cries. Anything is better than sitting in this house waiting for the walls to crush me.

Miraculously, Kayla falls asleep before we arrive at the park, so I grab a takeaway cup of tea from the coffee shop and sit on a bench, pushing Kayla's pram backwards and forwards in the hopes of keeping her asleep.

An elderly lady walks over and joins me, smiling down at my sleeping baby.

'Just beautiful,' she says.

Out of politeness I nod, keeping inside the words I really want to say; words that would shock anyone listening and prove once and for all that she should be taken away from me.

The lady turns to me. 'You look exhausted, dear. I hope you're taking care of yourself too. It's all well and good people fussing over new babies but who takes the time to ask the mothers how they're doing?'

'Yes,' I say. 'Yes, you're right. That's exactly how I feel.'

She smiles. 'You do everything for that little one, don't you, with barely any acknowledgement? Hardest job in the world, I say. Well, you're doing a grand job. Just look at her. Not a care in the world.'

I want to reach for this lady – this stranger – and wrap my arms around her. Since giving birth to Kayla she might be the first person who's actually considered *me*. Aiden, of course, is doing his best, but he's so consumed with Kayla that I don't think he's had any room in his mind to fit me in, just as I haven't with him.

'So how many children do you have?' I ask, wondering whether someone who understands so much could ever face having a second child.

'Me? Oh, no, dear. I made the decision long ago not to have any, and to this day it's been the best choice I've ever made.' She smiles.

I'm so stunned by her declaration, and the force with which she delivers it, that I can't find any words to offer a reply.

'Anyway, I'll be going now. I only sat down to rest my legs for a minute before I get to the supermarket. You take care now.'

Watching her walk away, I feel even worse than I did before I spoke to her. But why? She didn't say anything to insult me, and even if she didn't want children, she still understood that a mother needs care too.

Screams of joy erupt from the playground, and I turn to watch a young mum with her two children. They're probably around two and four, and she seems to be managing both of them with ease, negotiating both of their different needs while remaining calm. She's another Sophie: strong and capable. I try to tell myself this will get easier – and maybe one day I'll be like Sophie and the mum I'm watching now – but then I look down at my tiny baby and she seems a lifetime away from the children in the playground.

It shouldn't surprise me when I glance at Kayla and find her staring at me. 'Well, that nap was all of five minutes,' I say.

On the bench next to me, I notice a chocolate wrapper. 'I need to put this in the bin over there,' I tell Kayla. 'Just stay here for a minute.'

The bin is near the entrance to the park, and I head over to it.

And then I keep walking past it, not once glancing back.

TWENTY-EIGHT

Now

It's just gone seven a.m. when Jamie calls the next morning. 'Can we see each other?' he asks.

The memory of Nicole being in my flat last night, and everything she said to me, is still pounding in my head. I can't blame her; Aiden is the one who has made this difficult – he is the one I have to deal with.

'Eve? Can you hear me?' I turn my attention to Jamie. He is the one I need to focus on now, along with Kayla of course. And now it is time to tell him about my daughter. Maybe he can help me find a way to get her back.

'What's happened? Is your mum okay?' I ask.

'Yeah, she's all right. My sister's there now, so at least Dad's got some help.' He pauses. 'Can we meet this morning?'

'Of course. Do you want to come over here?'

'Can we make it somewhere central? I've got a lunch meeting with a client in Leicester Square. Can you be there by ten?'

I tell him I'll see him there, and hang up, my curiosity piqued by his request to meet this morning when it's a full working day for him.

He's there before me, standing outside the station, engrossed in something on his phone. It surprises me that he made it here before me – I'm usually the one who arrives first.

'Hi,' I say, reaching to hug him.

He pulls away from me, his body tense. 'Let's walk.'

I know Jamie isn't big on public displays of affection – and neither am I – but I know instantly there's something else going on here. Nothing about his manner or body language is right. 'Okay. We can grab a coffee and find somewhere to sit.'

'I don't have time for a coffee,' he says. 'This won't take long.' He's barely looking at me as he says this.

'I thought your meeting was at lunchtime?'

Jamie stares ahead. 'It is. But this won't take long.'

I stop walking and tug at his sleeve. 'What's going on?'

He scans the area then points. 'There's a bench over there. Come on.' He walks off, and I follow, unease rapidly spreading through my body. This is out of character for Jamie. I expect this frostiness from Aiden – but Jamie?

As soon as we're sitting, he turns to me, his eyes hard and cold. He has become a different person. 'Did you ever want things to work with us?' he asks, almost spitting his words at me.

'Yes, of course I did. Where's this coming from?'

Jamie stares at the ground, his white trainers kicking at dust on the pavement. He still doesn't look at me. 'I find that hard to believe.'

'What's this about, Jamie? I know I've been distant but I thought we were past that. We were going away together to see your parents before your mum got ill. I don't do things like that lightly. You mean a lot to me and I'm sorry about how I've been before.'

Nothing changes in his expression, even though he must know how difficult it is for me to bare my soul like this.

'You might be many things, Eve, but I never had you down as a liar.' He stares right at me now, his eyes burning into me so intensely that I feel my face flushing, even though I'm not sure what he's talking about. That's the trouble with being guilty – it never leaves you, even if the current situation has nothing to do with what you've done.

'What are you talking about? I know I've—'

'Cut the bullshit, Eve. Just tell me the truth.'

'About what?' But suddenly I know without Jamie having to explain. He knows who I am, what I've done. About Kayla. *There's no way he can know the rest, though. No way anyone can.*

'At first I was angry with you because you'd lied to me. Then the more I thought about it the more I realised I could never be with a person who could walk away from their own baby. It just doesn't bear thinking about.' He shakes his head. 'I want to have my own kids one day so this is just… awful. The whole thing makes me sick to my stomach. I don't know who the hell you are.' He turns away.

So many thoughts flash through my mind as we sit here in this tableau, frozen, while all around us the world carries on. To anyone passing we will look like a normal couple, sharing some time together. Nobody would be able to tell that both our worlds have just shattered.

There are several things I could say to Jamie right now, one of them being an apology, yet somehow I can't manage it. 'There are two sides to every story, Jamie.'

He shakes his head. 'Not when it comes to abandoning a *baby*. There's nothing you can say that will make that okay. What the hell, Eve? I knew you were separated, but Jesus, this has well and truly winded me. I can't even look at you.'

One thing I've learned in life is that sometimes it shows strength to admit when you're defeated. To protest and try to force someone round to your way of thinking only hurts both people. I won't do that to Jamie, especially when, ultimately, he is right. I did a terrible thing and losing him is just another price I will have to pay. How ironic that it comes at a time when I'd just begun to let him in, when I was actually ready to tell him everything myself.

'I'm not going to try and change your mind,' I say, fighting back tears I refuse to let out. I won't make him feel guilty. 'I'm sorry I didn't tell you.'

He doesn't accept my apology. 'You let me get invested in *us* and all the time you were holding back something so... I can't even describe it. I thought I loved you, Eve. Ha, that's a joke, isn't it? Because you were never the person I fell for.'

Instinctually, I reach for his arm, but he yanks it away, moving further from me on the bench. 'You're right. I wasn't. I'm sorry.'

'Save it, Eve. I'm not even the one you need to say sorry to, am I?' He shakes his head again, the disgust he's feeling almost palpable.

'Will you at least let me tell my side of the story?'

'No. I've heard enough about it. The only thing that might excuse it is if your husband was abusive, but he wasn't, was he? In fact, I hear he's a decent guy who's raised your daughter without you.'

I can't argue with this; everything Jamie's said is true. 'Who told you?' I ask.

He ignores me and stands up 'It's over, not that anything ever got started. Let's just go our separate ways now. Don't call me. Ever. In fact, delete my number from your phone.'

Before I can say anything else, Jamie walks away, and I'm left watching him as he disappears into the crowd of people floating around Leicester Square.

–

I have never been a drinker, not even on social occasions, but Jamie finding out about me has left me desolate, and I find myself sitting alone in a bar in Covent Garden, already on my third wine. I'm aware of people watching me. I'm not dressed to be meeting anyone for a business lunch, or even a date, so it's obvious what I'm doing. I may as well have a sign plastered across my head.

Focus on Kayla, I keep telling myself. *You've got to find a way to get her back, even if it's not with Aiden's blessing.* But the truth is, even though I couldn't see it, Jamie mattered too. And now there's also the unanswered question of who told him, and what it means for me.

Even though I know it's wrong, I pick up my phone and text Jamie, telling him that I will leave him alone but begging him to tell me who told him about me.

He probably won't reply but I have to try. Surprisingly, though, after twenty minutes and another drink, a reply comes.

> Leave me alone, Eve.

There has to be a way to find out, yet nothing comes to me, and this only deepens my anxiety.

The irony is that I was ready to tell Jamie about Kayla – and maybe there would have been a chance he might have understood if he'd heard it from me – yet it was taken out of my hands. This is not the first time fate has opened the ground beneath me, leaving me to free fall into whatever abyss lies beneath.

'What a loser,' I think I hear someone at another table say, but I don't look up for confirmation that they're talking about me.

They couldn't be more wrong about me.

–

It's dark when I step off the Tube at Southgate, teetering for just a moment because I'm unaccustomed to so much alcohol surging through me, almost paralysing me.

Yet, somehow, I make it to my road, relieved to reach my cobalt blue front door. I don't know who decided to paint it that colour, or when they did, but it's the only house on the street with such a brightly coloured door. I laugh to myself, even though nothing at all is funny.

I don't know what makes me stop at my car, leaning against it even though it's parked right outside the house and I could be inside within seconds. Something feels strange and even though I turn and am staring right at the problem, my brain takes a while to register what I'm looking at.

The driver's side window and the front windscreen have been smashed, as if someone has battered them with a hammer. Shards of glass lie scattered by my feet – which I failed to notice before – the pavement decorated with glistening fragments.

'What the hell?' I say into the still night. There isn't a single person around to hear me.

Glancing at my ground floor neighbour's window, everything is dark and there's no sign that she's home. But the lights are on in the house next door, so I rush up the steps to the front door, pounding on it until a woman in her mid-fifties answers. Although I've seen her before, we've never spoken, barely even acknowledged each other.

'Can I help you?'

'I'm… I live next door—'

'I know that. But why are you trying to break my door down?'

'Sorry. I…' I turn to the road and point. 'That's my car there. Did you see anyone outside this evening?'

She peers into the night. 'Oh. Someone's done a job on it, haven't they? You must have really upset someone.' She shakes her head. 'Sorry, I didn't mean to make light of it.'

'Did you see anything?'

'Nope. I've been in the back room all evening and didn't hear anything either. Have you called the police?'

It hadn't even crossed my mind. It's not as if they would have a chance of finding out who did this, and there's no

CCTV around here. I look up at the other houses but no one else seems to be home.

'Thanks for your time,' I manage to say, carefully negotiating the steps back down because a trip to A&E is the last thing I need right now.

Back in my flat, I double lock the door. I've never been a paranoid person, but the chances of my car being targeted at random are slim.

Even though I live in London and crime isn't uncommon, there was no reason for this attack — my car is a five-year-old Peugeot, with nothing of value inside.

My hands are clammy with sweat, and I rush to the kitchen for some water, the glass slipping from my hand before I've had a sip. Crouching down, I clean up the glass, trying to shut out all thoughts and focus only on the task at hand. It's almost a relief to have these tiny shards to turn my attention to, and I spend longer than necessary clearing up the mess in order to still my mind.

I can't escape this though, and my mind races. This was deliberate. An escalation after ignoring those messages, and my conviction that someone was in my flat.

It is happening. It is all finally catching up with me.

TWENTY-NINE

Before

'What the hell are you doing? That's your baby!'

The young girl grabs me and spins me around, her grasp surprisingly strong for someone so thin. 'I just saw you with it and now you've left it in the park!'

I snap to my senses and shrug her off, still feeling the hard pressure of her grip even though she's no longer got hold of me. 'My baby is a *she*. And no, of course I wasn't leaving her. I just thought I'd lost something on the path. I was having a quick look for it without disturbing her. She'll wake up if I start pushing her pram.'

The girl turns to her friend. I'm lucky enough that they're both probably too young to realise that babies often need motion to keep them asleep. 'She's lying, Nisha. She was dumping her baby.'

Thankfully, her friend is sceptical. 'I dunno, Ella, she looks all right to me.'

Keep believing that. Assure your friend that nobody in their right mind would leave a baby in the middle of the morning, in a park which lies next to a busy road.

Without another word, I head back to Kayla, leaving the two of them to debate this situation by themselves. As I walk away, I hear Ella attempt to convince Nisha that they should call the police.

A short walk has never seemed so long, and Kayla is shrieking when I reach her. Luckily the constant hum of traffic has stopped the two girls noticing she's never actually been asleep. 'Let's go home,' I whisper, as if nothing has happened, as though this is just an ordinary morning.

The problem is that the two girls are standing right by the park exit, leaving me no way to avoid them. I've become adept at subterfuge, though, and I stroll towards them, my head held high because they need to think I've got nothing to hide. I'm just an ordinary mum.

'Hey, wait!' the one called Ella shouts. 'We're calling the police – you can't just *go*.'

Keep calm; you can do this. 'Honestly, this is all a big misunderstanding. Why would I leave my baby in this park? That's just ridiculous. I only live a couple of minutes away.' My legs are weakening by the second – I don't know how much longer I can keep this up.

Nisha grabs her friend's arm. 'Come on, let's just go. This is nothing to do with us.'

'But it's a *baby*! What if she's crazy or something, and then we hear about it on the news tonight?'

Silence consumes us all as we're each left to create our own versions of this scenario in our minds. Something changes in Nisha's expression; I can almost see the doubts cross her face, like clouds overlapping the sun. 'Yeah, maybe you're right, we should call—'

'Look,' I interject, desperate to get control of this situation. 'How about this? I'll call my mother right now, and she can be here in less than half an hour. She'll assure you that everything's okay.'

The girls glance at each other. 'What about the baby's dad, then? Where's he?'

'My husband's at work.' *Leave him out of it; there is no way Aiden can hear about this.* 'He's in really important meetings all morning, so there's no chance of me getting hold of him. Please, I'll call my mum right now then we can all get on with our days.'

Seconds tick by feeling like minutes. Then finally Ella acquiesces. 'Go on then, call your mum. But she better be here in half an hour or we're definitely calling the police.'

I turn to walk away, wondering how I've managed to get away with this, knowing that I don't deserve to.

'Hang on a minute.'

I spin around, and Ella is pointing her phone at me, snapping my picture before I can register what's going on.

'It's evidence,' she declares. 'In case you don't come back.'

And as I walk away, terrified, I know that this is what I deserve.

–

At Mum's house, we transfer Kayla into the spare Moses basket. She fell asleep in the car on the way here, and Mum managed to carry her in without disturbing her.

While Mum makes us both a sandwich, I sink into the sofa and prepare to tell her my story. Or *a* story at least.

'What on earth is going on?' Mum asks. Her tone isn't unkind; I think she's more annoyed with those two girls interfering in our family business. 'Why would they think you were leaving Kayla in the park?'

I'm at a crossroads here – with choices to make that could either change my life for the better, or for the worse. I could be honest with Mum, tell her how much I've been struggling since Kayla was born, and ask for her help. She would offer it, of course she would, and there would be no judgement. Then she would swiftly take control of the situation, and I wouldn't have to tell her the whole truth, only that I'm struggling with the baby blues or something like it. Mum is a rock and if I asked her to keep it to herself, she would help without dragging Aiden into my mess.

I put down my uneaten sandwich. 'Oh, Mum, I—'

Her phone rings, a deafening tone blaring into the room. 'Sorry,' she says, 'I'd better quickly take this.'

I watch her as she speaks, at first concentrating more on her facial expressions as she talks than what she's saying. Until I realise something is wrong.

'Oh dear. I can't believe this. I don't know how this could have happened,' she's saying, grabbing her diary from the coffee table. 'I never forget an appointment. Please apologise for me, won't you?' She frantically flicks through the pages. 'I can't understand why it's not written here.'

Although I've got the gist of it, Mum explains what's happened as soon as she's finished on the phone. 'Can you believe I had a lesson booked in and completely forgot about it? I can't believe this. And the poor girl has her piano exam next week.'

'Oh, no. But don't worry, maybe you wrote it somewhere else and forgot to copy it in there?'

Mum stares at me, a frown etched on her forehead. 'That's the strange thing, Eve. I *did* write it in my diary. Look, it's right here.' She jabs her finger at today's page. 'See. And the terrible thing is, I checked this page first thing in the morning, just like I always do.'

And while I'm in the midst of assuring Mum that these things happen, I know with certainty that I can never burden her with the truth about me. Any of it.

THIRTY

Now

It takes me all morning to sort out getting my car window fixed. I could dip into my sparse savings to stop my insurance skyrocketing next year, but I need to keep as much as possible saved. Things are coming to a head, and I can't shake the feeling that I might need this money soon.

On my phone, I check my inbox and read the first email again. *I know you lied.*

And then I click *reply* and begin typing, my hands shaking.

> I know it was you who damaged my car. Just so you know, I'm not scared of you.

Even as I press *send*, doubts creep through my head. Perhaps I have got this wrong. And what then? All I can know for sure is that someone deliberately targeted me, but I have no firm evidence of anything. Or anyone. What if it was Aiden? He doesn't want me back in Kayla's life, so maybe this is a warning sign to keep away. Even though an act like this is completely at odds with his character, I long ago realised you never know what people are capable of.

Without a plan for what I will say, I call Nicole's mobile. She's asked me to give them some space but there's something I need to know.

'Eve?' Her voice is a whisper, and I hear her shutting a door. 'Are you okay? Is something wrong?'

'I'm sorry I'm calling after you asked for space, but I need to ask you something.'

'Okay. Of course. Aiden's in the shower so I'll have to be quick, otherwise he'll know I'm talking to you.'

I explain what happened to my car and hope that she realises what I want to ask before I have to say it. She doesn't, though, instead asking if I need some help to get it fixed.

'No, thank you but that's not why I'm calling. I just… look, I'm sorry to ask this but I need to know if I've been targeted or whether it was random. Kids trying to steal it or something.'

Finally realisation dawns. 'Hang on, you think it might have been *Aiden*?'

'No. I don't know. I just don't know what to think.'

'Aiden's actually feeling a lot better now. I told him you'd agreed to leave us alone to decide what to do in our own time, and it was like a lead weight was lifted from him. I swear, I could actually see his shoulders loosen. Sorry, I know that's not what you want to hear right now, but it just wouldn't make sense that he'd smash your car up.'

Nicole has a point. Then who?

'Also,' she continues, 'I can put your mind at rest. He worked from home yesterday and we were together the whole day. Night too.'

'Okay.' This narrows things down. 'I had to check, though, I hope you understand that?'

'I know. Things are difficult right now but that doesn't mean it will always be this way. Thank you again, Eve, for giving us this time. Actually, while we're on the phone, I just wanted to let you know that we might be taking Kayla to visit Aiden's parents in Edinburgh on Sunday. It's just for a few days.'

We end the call, and I throw my phone onto the couch, letting out a frustrated growl. There is no way I'm letting Kayla go again.

—

I haven't contacted Sophie since I turned up at her house last week, yet here I am again with so many things I need to say to her. She may once have been my closest friend, but I can't ignore my gut instinct. The feeling that she's hiding something runs through my blood, and I can't shake it.

Damien opens the door, the twins hovering behind him, and he seems surprised to see me standing on his doorstep once again. 'Eve. Um, Sophie's not here. She went to her mum's this morning and isn't back yet.'

I don't let this deter me. 'Would you mind if I came in and waited for her?' It's not fair of me to put him on the spot like this but I'm running out of options.

'I don't know if—'

'I wouldn't ask if it wasn't important,' I assure him.

'Okay. I suppose.' He stands aside to let me past, and once I'm inside I relax a little. The twins are here. It will be okay. And now I'm inside, he won't get me out easily.

'Do you have a day off today?' I ask, remembering that Damien is a project manager for a large chain of department stores. John Lewis, I think it was. At least that's what he used to do.

'Nope,' Damien says. 'Working from home. Supposed to be at least.'

'Please don't let me stop you. I'll just sit down and wait; you really don't have to keep me entertained.' I flash him a smile, try my best to appear confident when my stomach is performing somersaults. Even though I spent a lot of time with Sophie those years ago, Damien was usually at work, so I haven't been around him much.

He considers my words, but just when I think he'll agree, he shakes his head. 'No, it's fine. I was due a break anyway. I'll sit with you.' He glances at his watch, and I know he's hoping Sophie will be back soon.

At least five long minutes pass while we sit in awkward silence, with me scrolling aimlessly through my phone just so that neither of us feels obliged to talk. The twins have drifted off to the kitchen, quietly watching something on an iPad, so it's a surprise when Damien speaks.

'I have to say, it took a lot of guts for you to come back.'

I stare at him, wondering if he's being genuine or whether he's leading up to something I won't like. 'You're the only person who's said that.'

He nods. 'I can imagine. We humans aren't always good at compassion, are we? We like to think we are, but when it really comes to it we're too quick to judge others.'

Damien is right; other than from Nicole, all I've faced since I came back is anger and judgement. 'Thanks for saying that.'

He stares at me and smiles, and just for a moment I feel as though he can see right through me, as though he knows everything. It's impossible, yet there is something about the way he's watching me. My alert level rises.

'I have to say, though, I was as shocked as everyone else when you left. From everything Sophie used to tell me it seemed that you and Aiden were as close as it's possible for two people to be.'

'We were. It wasn't about him.'

'I'm guessing Sophie told you about the aftermath? How much Aiden needed our support?'

'Yes, a bit. It couldn't have been easy for any of you. I can only apologise for that.'

'Oh, please, no need. It was mostly Sophie who was there for him. I was working such long hours back then – you might remember – so I wasn't here to help much.'

Damien is going somewhere with this, leading the conversation, trying to broach something. I could ask him outright so that he doesn't have to take this long road and waste his and my time, but I need to hear everything he has to say.

'I regret it,' Damien says.

'What?'

'Not being around more to help Sophie. She had the twins, work, and Aiden and Kayla round here most of the time.'

This is a surprise to me; as long as I'd known him Aiden had never wanted to be a burden to anyone. He was fiercely private too, and it would have been hard for him to ask for help. I mention this to Damien.

'You're right,' he says. 'It wasn't Aiden inflicting himself on us, no, he'd never have done that. It was Sophie who was always taking the twins round to him. Or getting our parents to babysit so she could go and cook for him or sort the house out. Whatever he needed.'

Sophie never mentioned this. 'That's Sophie, isn't it?' I say. 'She'll do anything for anyone.'

Damien looks at me for a second before answering. 'Yes, that's Sophie all over.' He should be smiling as he says this, yet he isn't.

'What is it, Damien? What are you trying to say?'

He seems stunned by my question, and I wonder if I've got it wrong, that my inability to trust anyone is making me paranoid.

'Things had settled down before you came back. Everything was how it should be, and now... he was round here the other night when he should have been at home with his family.'

'Who? What are you talking about?'

'Aiden, of course. After you left, they were always together and... I'm not the jealous type, but even I started questioning everything. It happens, doesn't it? People who spend a lot of time together become closer and then...'

Sophie and Aiden? It's not possible.

'Damien, are you saying you think the two of them had an affair or something?'

'I don't know. It's possible, though, isn't it? She was always putting him and Kayla first, maybe even before the twins.'

'That's because Kayla was a newborn baby.' I say this but do I really believe it? If Sophie had developed feelings for Aiden then it would explain how cold she's been towards me.

'I just felt something was wrong about it back then. It was only when Aiden met Nicole that the two of them seemed to back off from each other. But now you coming back has come between the two of them, and he's back here needing Sophie again.'

I tell Damien that he's reading too much into this.

'I hope I am,' he says. 'But I know this much at least: your little girl became like a daughter to Sophie. As important to her as the twins. There's nothing she wouldn't do for her, and maybe that's why they—' His phone pings, and he fishes it from his pocket to check. 'That's Soph. She says she's going to stay for dinner at her mum's. Sorry, Eve.'

'It's okay. What were you about to say, though?'

He looks at me, and I see from his expression that something has shifted. 'Nothing. Shall I tell her to call you?'

'Tell me what you were about to say. I know it was something.'

He stares at me, then shakes his head. 'Just drop it, will you?'

One of the twins shouts to him, something about the iPad not working, and Damien abruptly stands. I'm not going to get any more out of him.

'Please tell Sophie to call me. It's urgent.'

He looks at me as if I'm asking him for the world.

'I'll sort all this out, Damien, I promise you that. Whatever it is.'

He nods, and I stand up and tell him there's no need to see me to the door. The walls are closing in on me, and I need to get out of here.

Outside, with the fresh air enveloping me, I try to focus my thoughts. Every word Damien said just now spins around my head.

It's now more important than ever that I speak to Sophie.

THIRTY-ONE

Now

Sophie doesn't call that night, and the next morning there is nothing but silence from my phone. Right now it feels like I'm in a maze, with everyone knowing the right direction to the exit except me. I'm missing something huge here, but I have no idea what it is.

When she still hasn't called by eleven a.m., I grab my phone and call her instead, fully prepared to leave a voicemail.

'Hello?'

'Sophie, it's Eve.'

'I know.' Yet she answered the phone as though she didn't know who was calling.

'Did Damien mention that I stopped by yesterday?'

'Stopped by? That makes it sound so casual, as though you were just popping in for a coffee. That's not what you were doing though, is it?'

I ignore her jibe. 'We need to talk, Sophie.'

'I helped you, didn't I? I don't know what more there is to talk about. I know we were close once, but things have changed, haven't they? Surely you can see that?'

Yes, I can. If only she knew what else I can see so clearly now. 'I don't want to fight with you, Sophie, I just need to talk. And then if you never want to see me again, I'll respect your decision.' I can't let her know that I might be the one who ends up making this choice.

Her answer is to remain silent, but I'll wait as long as I have to.

'Fine,' she says. 'Tonight.'

'Let's meet for dinner,' I suggest.

'I'm not sure about—'

'Come on, Sophie. For old time's sake?'

After a long pause, she agrees. And now it's just a waiting game.

–

She's twenty minutes late, and I sit alone in Café Rouge, feeling like I've been stood up by a date. I know that's what the staff here must be thinking. It's not important, though; I long ago stopped caring what other people think of me.

I'll give it ten more minutes and if she hasn't shown by then I will track her down. Just as I'm about to check my phone again, Sophie appears.

'Well, this feels weird,' she says, slipping into the chair opposite. 'I can't remember the last time we went for a meal somewhere.'

'Before the twins were born,' I say. 'Pizza at the Italian place that closed down. It was after a parents' evening.'

She frowns. 'How do you remember that? I don't at all.'

'Well, a lot's happened since then.'

'What's this all about?' Sophie asks. 'Why did you need to see me so urgently?'

I haven't planned how I'll approach this; perhaps I thought in my mind that meeting for dinner would

216

rekindle something in our friendship, encourage her to be straight with me, but as Sophie said – everything's changed. 'I'm not going to pretend this conversation is anything other than what it is. I just want honesty from you, Sophie.'

'Well, that's rich coming from you, but I'm not you, am I?'

'Someone smashed my car windows the other day, and I don't think it was random.'

Her eyes widen. Is this a sign she knows nothing about it? 'I'm sorry. That's a shitty thing to happen.'

'It's not just the inconvenience of having to fix the windscreen, it's more a case of why someone would do it. What does it mean? I've been going over it and it can only be some sort of warning. A pathetic one, I have to say. Why can't people just come out and say what their problem is?'

'Look, I'm sorry for what happened, but what's this got to do with me?'

'Probably nothing, but I had to go through all the people in my life at the moment, and it's a short list. Aiden, Jamie and you.'

And the person who has been emailing me.

Sophie shrugs. 'What about your students? Maybe one of them is angry with you because they failed an exam or something? Maybe they think you didn't tutor them properly.'

'No. This is about Kayla, it has to be.'

Before Sophie can respond, the waitress comes over and asks what we'd like to eat. 'A croque monsieur for me, please,' I say, handing my menu back. It takes all my effort to keep my hand from shaking.

'Just a Prosecco for me, please,' Sophie says. 'Nothing to eat.'

'Are you sure?' I ask. 'It's my treat.'

'No appetite I'm afraid.'

The waitress heads off, and I stare at Sophie. In the past she was the one I always turned to whenever I needed to talk, at least until I could no longer talk to anyone. I trusted her with my life, yet now she is no more than a stranger.

'I don't understand what you're trying to say,' Sophie continues as soon as the waitress has gone.

There's no time to ease into this gently. 'Why did you tell me you didn't see much of Aiden and Kayla after I left?'

Looking at Sophie now, her eyes wide with shock, she looks as if she's just been caught stealing. I've never seen her caught off guard before now, and a wave of guilt washes over me. I'm not the one in the wrong this time, I have to keep that in mind.

'Damien told you.'

'The point is, why didn't *you* tell me?'

'It's my business, though, isn't it? You left, so I was there for Aiden. I did tell you that.'

'Not exactly. You made out that you were only in touch occasionally. You didn't mention that you had such a bond with Kayla.'

And with Aiden, although I'll save this information for later.

Sophie sits up straighter. 'Why does that matter? Yes, I helped Aiden a lot with Kayla in the early days, so she means a lot to me.' Her eyes narrow. 'Wait, are you suggesting that I don't want you around Kayla? And that I smashed your car windscreen to warn you off?'

Now that she's said it herself out loud, it doesn't seem to fit. So I can rule her out.

'Maybe it was that boyfriend of yours? He didn't seem happy when I met him the other day. Maybe he doesn't want you being around Aiden.'

Despite everything that's happening between Sophie and me right now, I find myself telling her that Jamie and I are no longer together.

'So you've left him too? Even more reason for him to be the one who smashed up your car.'

No. There's no way. 'He's... he was a decent guy,' I say. 'And I didn't leave him. It was the other way around.'

For a second, I expect Sophie to throw out a remark about me deserving it, but she doesn't. 'Even good people can be pushed to their limit,' she says.

I ignore this because there is no way it was Jamie. 'The trouble was, I have far too much baggage, even for someone as decent as Jamie to handle.'

'Hmmm. I imagine it's not easy telling people what you did.'

'I've actually never told anyone. Mum's illness meant I never really had to explain it to her properly, and I've kept away from people on a social level. I never went back to the school so...'

The waitress brings Sophie's Prosecco, and she lifts her glass and stares at it before taking a sip. 'How did you end up in a relationship then?'

Jamie flashes into my head. Kind, funny, talented Jamie. Not someone who would deliberately hurt me, surely? 'It was meant to be casual. I never thought he'd develop deeper feelings for me, or I would have stayed away from him.' But would I? It had been a huge shock to me when I'd started talking to him and actually began to feel something physically. For so long I hadn't wanted anyone to be anywhere near me, then inexplicably I couldn't stop wanting Jamie. Until he'd fall asleep – then I needed him as far away from me as possible. I don't tell Sophie any of this.

'Is it really over between you two? It doesn't seem like you're over him.'

'It's more a case of him being over me.' I would have Jamie back in an instant and give him the relationship he deserves this time. Again, I say none of this aloud.

'Well, I hope you leave him alone then,' Sophie says, and with her words she is right back to being a woman I can't trust. 'Speaking of which, I hope you're leaving Aiden and Nicole alone too now? Oh, don't look so surprised. Aiden and I do actually talk, Eve. There's no law against that.'

When I don't reply, Sophie begins her attack. 'Don't you think you've been selfish enough? They're a *family*, Eve. The three of them. Then suddenly you come along and shatter their lives, and it's like Aiden's right back to how he was when you left him.'

'I… that's not—'

'I can't listen to this any more, Eve. I feel like I'm betraying all of them just being here with you.' She stands up and hoists her bag onto her shoulder. 'You're never going to have Kayla back in your life. Just stay away from all of us.'

And then she's gone, a waft of her perfume lingering behind to mock me.

THIRTY-TWO

Before

Sometimes it feels as though I'm being watched. The rational part of my brain – yes, it's still there somewhere – tells me this is ridiculous, yet I often feel a presence with me when I'm alone with Kayla, a constant reminder of something I want to forget.

For days now I've expected Mum to mention the incident in the park to Aiden, but she hasn't. She hasn't even spoken of it to me; it's as if her memory has completely erased any record of it. She was more distressed about forgetting her student's piano lesson that day.

I should be thankful for this, but of course I'm not. It means that Mum is worse than I suspected. I've let my own troubles push her issue to the side, but I can no longer ignore it. Something is wrong with her and I need to help her. She won't listen to me, though, and insists she's fine, that she doesn't need to see the doctor. So for now all I can do is monitor her closely.

'How come I'm getting daily calls?' she'll ask.

'I'm a new mum,' I explain. 'I just need to hear an adult voice.'

She laughs, and then I do too, even though I'm crumbling inside. This is how our phone calls go more often than not.

Sophie is coming round with the twins today. Both of us being parents should have made us closer than ever, yet I couldn't be further away from her. Talking to her is like being with a virtual stranger, someone I might have just met at a baby group.

It's a ripple effect. One thing happening that disperses and eviscerates everything else in your life. Sinister and silent.

Kayla is sleeping well today; she's settled in her Moses basket and I'm sitting on the floor beside her, knowing I should make the most of this rare moment to myself, yet unable to summon the energy to move. Even when I'm having an easier time of it, there is no difference. I still can't feel a thing when I look at her peaceful tiny face.

'It's not your fault,' I whisper. 'You didn't ask to be here. None of this is your fault.' I say this over and over, hoping the repetition will seep into my brain and manifest love. But there's nothing but disconnection from the tiny being I brought into the world.

'Oh, you look awful!' Sophie says, bounding into the house with the twins clutching her hands. 'Are you sick?'

Sophie has just given me the perfect excuse. 'Yes, I am. I'm sorry, I should have told you not to come. I don't want to pass anything on to any of you.'

'Don't worry about us. The twins seem to have super-hero immunity, and I can't remember the last time I had even a cold.' She hesitates and frowns. 'Unless you're not up to company? The twins can be rowdy devils, so I'll totally understand if you'd rather we go.'

I look at Sophie and I'm torn. Company of any sort is the last thing I want, but she's made the effort to come and see me. How can I turn her away now? The me before

– that's how I've become accustomed to thinking of myself now: two different versions of Eve, *before* and *after* – would never entertain the idea of telling her to leave, even if I was genuinely ill. But I'm not that person. I will never again be that person. I'm the *after* Eve and I can't bear to be around Sophie, or anyone else, now.

'I'm so sorry,' I say, 'but I might just need to sleep while Kayla's napping.'

Sophie hugs me. 'No need to apologise. We'll catch up when you're feeling better. Come on, boys, we have to go home now.'

At least the twins are too young to understand why they've been here for less than two minutes.

From the upstairs window, I watch while Sophie bundles them into the car. I'm a terrible friend, a terrible mother, and no kind of wife to Aiden at the moment.

Lying down on the bed, I let myself believe I'm alone, that the house is silent because Aiden and I are yet to start a family. I'm not sure if I manage to sleep, but when Kayla's shriek penetrates my ears, I feel as though I haven't had a second of peace.

–

Later, when I'm carrying her downstairs after changing her nappy, I imagine myself tumbling down the stairs, crashing to the bottom. Would I be okay? Would Kayla survive such an awful fall?

And every time after this, it's impossible to carry her downstairs without this thought in my head.

THIRTY-THREE

Now

Walking home from the Tube, it strikes me how alone I am. Although the past couple of years have made me immune to this, it is different now. This is about Kayla, not me. And now I have no choice but to take things further.

Someone is right behind me, almost too close. I'm about to turn around, but then I feel the arm around my neck, the whispered breath in my ear. 'Don't bother screaming. We need to have a little chat. That's your place over there, keep walking and I'll be right behind you.' The arm eases off me, and I quickly assess my options. Running is not one of them. He'd catch up with me before I've even gone a metre. Nor will shouting for help do any good – there's nobody around, and hardly any lights on in any windows. My mobile phone is buried somewhere in my bag, and there's no way he'll give me a chance to grab it.

Stay calm. Don't panic. You can deal with this. He knows where I live, so clearly this is someone who knows me; I'm not being targeted at random.

But I don't recognise his voice.

My body becomes numb and I'm walking on auto-pilot. There will be a way out of this; there has to be.

We reach my door, and he's standing right behind me, too close, but not close enough that anyone passing by or watching from their window would suspect anything. Perhaps it only looks like I'm inviting him in, that I might be spending the night with him. I shudder at this thought.

'Get in,' he says. 'Quick.' He pushes me forward.

My hand shakes as I pull my keys from my pocket, despite my determination to get through this unharmed. I don't know what makes me do it, but before I turn the key I spin around and face him.

He's young, no more than nineteen or twenty, and as I stare at his face I realise that I've seen him before. I know exactly who he is.

'Does Maya know you're here, Connor?'

His eyes widen, and he steps back. He hasn't expected me to address him by his name. For now, at least, I have taken some control from him. I have to just hang on to that, and then I can get through this.

'How do you…? Ah, who cares, just let me in.'

'You didn't answer me. Does Maya know you're here?'

'We'll get to that in a minute, now just shut this bloody door.' He slams it behind us and shoves me forward. It's not a violent shove, and I won't let it unnerve me.

'What are you doing here, Connor?' I ask once we're inside, standing in my living room like two characters in a film who aren't sure where they should be.

'You're an evil bitch,' he says, taking a step towards me.

I flinch but quickly recover. Maya has told him about my lie, then. But it's none of his business; it doesn't make sense that he's here. 'It's got nothing to do with you.'

He leans into my face, hatred seeping from his pores. 'Nothing to do with me? You killed my baby and you think it's got nothing to do with me?'

Silence thunders down on me. 'Your baby? But...' And then I realise. This is not about Kayla at all; this is about Maya's baby. *Their* baby.

Still, I need clarification. 'What exactly are you talking about?'

'It's because of you that Maya got rid of our baby. It's all your fault.' He's spitting his words now, saliva spraying onto the carpet.

'Okay, just calm down a minute. Please, sit down and we can talk about this. I haven't seen Maya this week. She hasn't even texted me.'

Connor doesn't sit down; he stays too close to me, his eyes still wild with rage. I take a step back, try to hold my nerve.

'She told me all about your little chats during your tutoring sessions,' he hisses. 'I know you gave her advice about the pregnancy. Told her to get rid of it.' He raises his voice. 'Some shit about thinking about her future.'

I need to try and calm him down. 'Connor, listen, you've got it wrong. All I did was let her talk, and then I told her to speak to her parents.'

'And that did a bloody lot of good, didn't it!' He's yelling now, and strides to the window and back, his hands clenched by his sides. 'I never thought for one second they'd want her to get rid of it. I thought if they knew—'

'So it was you who told them? Maya blamed me to start with.'

He ignores me. 'This is a sick world when grandparents won't even fight for their unborn grandchild.' He's shaking now, either from rage or sadness, or more likely both.

'Connor, please sit down. I can see why you're so upset. It must feel as though you had no choice in any of this, that it was all taken out of your hands.' *We are the same. If only he knew.*

He stares at me, and it's hard to tell how he'll respond. For a moment I envisage him smashing his fist into my face, taking out his anger on the only person he can. 'And what the hell would you know about that?' he snarls.

I sit down myself, hoping he will mirror my action. 'Everything actually. More than I can ever say.'

His eyes narrow, and just for a second something replaces the anger. Curiosity, perhaps.

'I'm not sitting down in this bloody place,' he says, looking around. 'This is where you encouraged my girlfriend to get rid of our baby.' He spits on the floor, and I pretend I haven't noticed.

'You love Maya, am I right?'

'Yeah, I did. So?'

'And you probably know her better than anyone?'

He flicks his head, which I take as a sign of agreement.

'Then you will know that Maya is an extremely intelligent, savvy young woman with a mind of her own. She's so headstrong, even if I'd wanted to talk her into anything, there was no way I could have. You must know that, Connor.'

He thinks about this for a moment, and I dare to hope that finally I'm getting through to him. 'But she was undecided. Then suddenly she knew there was no way she could have it. How can you explain that sudden change? Eli?'

It's hard not to wonder if my story about Kayla had anything to do with Maya's decision. A wave of guilt washes over me. But everything I've said to Connor is true; Maya made her own decision, and I never tried to steer her in any direction. *Yet things can happen inadvertently. You know that better than most.*

'Look, Connor, you may not believe me but I'm here, looking you right in the eye and promising you that I did not encourage Maya to have a termination. I was her tutor and would never have offered any kind of advice in that way. All I told her to do was speak to her family. And talk to you about how conflicted she felt. That's it. If that somehow unwittingly led to her final decision then I'm sorry, I truly am, but I really don't believe that's what happened.'

Finally, he sits on the sofa and buries his head in his hands. 'That was my baby in her stomach. Gone. Just like that.'

'I know, and it's heartbreaking – I totally understand that. But, listen – how old are you?'

He looks up, frowning. 'Twenty-three next month. Why?'

'You're still so young. You've got a whole lifetime ahead of you. Loads of time to have children.'

'What the hell? Is that supposed to make me feel better?'

'No, nothing can right now. But in time the pain will ease, and you'll find a way to live with it. Believe me, I really do know what I'm talking about.'

He doesn't answer but at least the anger has dissipated. Now I will just leave him alone for a moment to process everything I've said.

'I came here to hurt you,' he says, eventually. 'To hurt you like I've been hurt. But now that I'm here I know I don't even need to do that. You've got enough enemies, haven't you? They can do the job for me.'

I freeze. 'What are you talking about?'

He ignores me and stands. 'I hope one day you know what it feels like to lose your kid,' he spits, marching out of the room without looking back.

As soon as the front door slams, I rush to the window and fling it open. 'Connor! Wait! It was you who smashed my car windows, wasn't it?'

He glances up, and it's hard to tell but it seems as though he might be smirking.

THIRTY-FOUR

Now

'Did you bring my little girl?' Mum asks as soon as I step into her room. Her face crumples when she sees I'm alone. 'Oh, I do look forward to seeing her.'

'Not today, Mum. I promise I'll try to bring her next time.' I won't make a promise to her that I cannot keep.

'What's wrong with you?' Mum asks. 'Why are you so... funny?'

'Funny?'

'You know. Not right. I don't know. You're just not right, not right at all!'

'Okay, Mum, please just calm down. I'm fine. Everything's okay.'

There is some truth in this. It's been days since Connor forced his way into my flat, yet I'm not afraid. Instead, his actions have spurred me on to take action of my own. And now there is a strange calmness flowing through me.

'Tell me what you've been doing today,' I say to Mum.

'I tried to go to the bus stop across the road. But the door was locked. Again! Can you believe that? I won't be staying in this place again, that's for sure.' She looks around at her clean, tidy room. 'And look at it, it's a mess. What kind of hotel is this? They don't even have room service. I think I want my money back!'

'Okay, Mum, let's see what we can do. But how about we have a coffee first?'

I spend the next couple of hours focusing all my attention on Mum. I wish I could tell her that everything's going to be okay, that soon enough she will be able to spend much more time with Kayla.

I feel guilty that I can't stay longer today, but there's something I have to do, and it can't wait any longer.

–

It's nearly five p.m. when I get home. Today has been a day of moving forward, making things happen, and I'm exhausted so, as soon as I'm inside, I check each room in my flat and then get ready for bed.

My buzzer goes just as I'm rummaging through the cupboards to find something to eat, and I rush to the door, hoping that it's Jamie. There can't be anyone else who would come here, and if it was Connor again then I'm sure he wouldn't be ringing the buzzer.

Aiden's is the last voice I'm expecting to hear. 'Eve? I know it's late but can we talk?'

Confused, I let him in and quickly change into jeans and a T-shirt before I open the door. 'What's happened? Is Kayla okay?'

'She's fine. I think we need to talk, though.'

He comes inside and makes his way to the living room. 'This isn't the kind of place I'd expect you to live,' he says, taking in his surroundings.

'I didn't have much choice. Besides, it's fine for just me.'

'Kayla could never stay here,' he says, more to himself than to me.

'Is that what you've come here to say? Bit of a waste of your time, isn't it? You and Nicole wanted me to stay away, which I've done, so why are you here now?'

'Can I sit?' he asks.

'Does Nicole know you're here?'

He shakes his head. 'No. Not yet. I came straight from work. Anyway, she's gone to her mum's for a couple of days. She's still not feeling well and needed to rest. Kayla's with Amy, the childminder.'

He walks to the window and stares at the street outside, saying nothing.

'What are you doing here, Aiden?'

Slowly he turns to face me. 'I'm not sure. I've just spent so much time hating you that I think I've... lost sight of things.'

'What things?'

'Well, what's best for Kayla I suppose. All this time I've felt that keeping you away from her is for the best but, well, now I'm not so sure.' He stares at the floor now, clearly finding this all difficult to admit.

My heart begins to race. 'Are you saying that I can see Kayla?'

'Yes. No. I don't know.' He crosses to the sofa and sinks into it. 'Nicole keeps telling me not to keep Kayla away from you. Maybe it's finally sinking in.' He looks up at me. 'Can you just sit down or something? You're making me uncomfortable hovering over me like that.'

I do as he asks, even though I don't want to sit. I'm too sick with anxiety about how this will all pan out.

'I know you took Kayla to see your mum,' he says. 'Oh, don't look so surprised – Kayla talks nonstop, there's no way she wouldn't mention it.'

So this is the real reason Aiden is here. 'I... I had to. It was my day to see Mum and I couldn't miss it, but Nicole needed me to babysit.'

'It's okay, Eve. I know all that and I'm not angry. Nicole explained it to me. The way Kayla was talking about Jackie, it just really hit me. It's not just you she's missed out on, it's your mum too.'

Even though I'm hearing these words, I can't quite believe them. Is it possible that Mum has unwittingly forced Aiden to be reasonable? 'I'm glad you see things this way now.'

He nods. 'I wasn't always there for you, though, was I? When we were together.'

Even though I don't know where his question has come from, I assure him this isn't true, that I never felt that way.

'Look what happened with Jackie. I remember that you often worried about her, and I'd dismiss it, tell you it was nothing, that we all forget things sometimes. I'm... well, I'm sorry I didn't listen. I was thinking about this earlier and imagining if it was my mum.'

'It would have made little difference even if she'd seen a doctor sooner.'

Aiden shakes his head. 'I shouldn't have just brushed it off, though. Once I even told you that maybe the stress of not being able to have a baby was getting to you.'

He needs to be convinced that this wasn't his fault. After all, it had been easy to tell myself that Aiden was right. Mum was fine. Of course she was. Because if she wasn't then what did that say about my world? She was my anchor, and I hoped I was hers. Ultimately, I was the one who didn't push hard enough for her to see the doctor.

'I suppose, looking back, it's clear there was something going on,' Aiden continues. 'I would have helped you both. I hope you know that.' Then he is shaking his head again before burying it in his hands. 'What did I do wrong, Eve?'

Still shocked at the turn our conversation has taken, I head over to him and kneel before him. 'Nothing at all. It was all me, none of this had anything to do with you.'

He doesn't seem to hear me. 'I thought I was an okay husband. Nobody's perfect, I know that, but I always tried to do what was right for you, and Kayla once she came along.'

Came along. It's a terrible and inaccurate term, making the whole process of bringing life into this world seem effortless, when for so many people that's not the case. In the end, though, I suppose Kayla did just *come along.*

Once again, I have to fight the pain in my body. *What's done can't be undone.*

'You did everything you could,' I say. Even though something has changed with Aiden, and he is offering me hope, I need to get him out of here. 'Shall we talk on the phone to arrange some visitation?' I say.

'Yeah, let's do that.' He takes my cue and stands up. A frown appears on his face. 'I have to say, you don't look happy. I thought you'd be overjoyed.'

'Of course I am, this is what I've wanted. Thank you, Aiden.'

But sometimes things come far too late.

–

It's an hour later when the phone call comes – Aiden shouting down the line, his words so indecipherable that

I have to ask him to slow down and tell me again what's happened.

'It's Kayla! Someone's taken her! She's gone!'

PART TWO

THIRTY-FIVE

Now

Nearly three months have passed since Kayla was taken. We don't speak of her as *missing*; that doesn't accurately describe what she is. All the evidence points to Nicole having taken her, especially as no one has seen her since.

At first questions were raised: how is it possible that a child can be taken from her childminder so easily in broad daylight? I feel sorry for Amy – a young woman who'd only just set up her own business – because I know she blames herself. It wasn't her fault, though. Kayla saw someone she knew and ran to her. We know it was a woman, and that she had on a denim jacket like the one Nicole had been wearing all summer – and by the time Amy knew what was going on it was too late. They were gone.

Aiden and I are convinced it was Nicole, even though the police can't track her down. How can people just disappear from the face of the earth? Especially in a world with such advanced technology. Yet that seems to be what's happened. At least it gives us hope that Kayla is safe. Neither of us can bring ourselves to believe that Nicole would harm her, although the possibility constantly hangs in the air – a huge question mark, a darkness that has become our constant companion.

The emails haven't stopped, and now there are also silent phone calls, so I know that Kayla's disappearance is unrelated. This at least brings a minuscule amount of relief.

In the beginning I threw questions at Aiden: why would Nicole take her when she was living with you anyway? What was going on in your relationship that she would do this?

It took him a while to open up to me, but then he finally admitted that Nicole had been acting strangely since I showed up. She'd become cold towards him, as if there was something weighing her down. He was too consumed with keeping Kayla from me to pay enough attention to it, though, and now it's too late. I told him that she'd said something similar about him, that time when she came to my flat and confided in me that she and Aiden weren't getting along.

'There's something else,' he told me. 'Nicole was the one who smashed your car up. I'm so sorry, but I didn't tell you because I wanted to protect her. I should have known she was on the edge.' At least that puzzle has been answered.

Even though it's been so many weeks since Kayla was taken, Aiden is only now beginning to trust me again. Slowly. He barely spoke to me to start with, but then he must have come to realise that I am the only person who shares the same love for Kayla that he does, in spite of my time away from her. It probably helped that he was with me when she was taken, so he'll know it's not possible that I was involved. I try not to think about that. Instead, I have gradually started allowing myself to enjoy being close to him again, despite the constant anxiety and sadness of our missing girl.

'Are you sure you're okay with Sophie coming over?' Aiden asks me now. 'I know things aren't good between you.'

That's an understatement. Even in Kayla's absence, Sophie still can't bring herself to forgive me for anything. This has just given her more ammunition, and she's tried to convince Aiden that I am the one who took Kayla.

'Think about it,' she'd said to him, 'you and Nicole had told her to stay away from you all and then suddenly Kayla's missing. Look what she's done before. I wouldn't put anything past her.'

I forgive Sophie for this, though. 'She's done so much to try and help find Kayla,' I tell Aiden now. 'It's only right that we both thank her.'

He joins me where I stand, staring through the kitchen doors at the garden Kayla loves to play in, and places his arm across my shoulder. The feel of him is strange: not quite right but not wrong either, a no man's land.

'You have every right to be in this house. You're Kayla's mother. And it was never really Nicole's place. She might have chosen furniture and decided where to put things, but I always paid the mortgage by myself. I never asked her for a penny.'

'Well, she was looking after Kayla, wasn't she? She couldn't work.' Even after what she's done, I try not to automatically attack Nicole and assume the worst of her. After all, there are always reasons we do what we do, even if others can't understand them.

The doorbell rings, and my stomach lurches. I stay where I am while Aiden goes to answer, preparing myself to face a firing squad.

Aiden's voice drifts from the hall. 'Thanks for coming, Soph.'

Then Sophie's. 'You don't have to thank me. I'm just so sorry this is happening to you.' There's a pause and the sound of rustling, as if they are hugging. 'After everything you've already been through.' Another pause. 'Is she here then?'

She. I'm not someone who deserves to be called by name.

'I hope you know what you're doing, Aiden. I can't say I like it, but I guess I understand.'

'We're just Kayla's parents, sticking together to try to get our girl back. There's no need to read any more into it. Anyway, Eve's in the kitchen, come through.'

Here we go. I put on a smile and wait to face, yet again, the woman who was my closest friend.

It's more of a shock seeing Sophie now, after only three months, than it was after those two years. She's still dressed smartly, with full hair and make-up, yet there's something different about her. I stare at her, trying to work out what it is, but I can't place it. 'Hi, Sophie.' Do I hug her? Shake her hand? In the end I keep my arms by my side and do neither, because she's staying by the door, as far away from me as possible.

'Eve. You look well. I don't know how when it's your daughter who's missing. I mean, look at Aiden, he's a mess – no offence – but then I suppose you're used to not having her around.' No-nonsense Sophie. Straight to the point.

Aiden jumps to my defence. 'Sophie, that's not necessary. Eve's suffering just as much as I am. She's just holding it together better. Don't have a go at her.'

I have to hold it together for your sake, Aiden, because I owe that to you. I won't let you see me fall apart when you need me to be strong.

Sophie holds up her hands. 'Okay, okay, I'm sorry. The past doesn't matter anyway now, does it? We just need to focus on finding Kayla.' She steps forward into the kitchen. 'What's the latest?'

While Aiden fills her in, I put the food together. It's only a buffet lunch, just like Nicole provided that first time I was invited here. It seemed pointless cooking a big meal; neither Aiden nor I have much of an appetite.

'I still keep leaving messages on her voicemail every few days, and on Facebook, but she never responds,' Sophie says while we sit down to force ourselves to eat.

'No, she's too clever for that,' Aiden says. 'She won't use her phone or social media because then the police would be able to trace her.'

Sophie nods. 'Well, the only good thing in all of this is that Nicole loves that little girl. She'd never hurt her.' She reaches for Aiden's hand and takes hold of it. I try to ignore the gesture and focus on what she's just said. She is right, and this is exactly what's kept me from losing my mind.

'But she has hurt her, hasn't she?' Aiden says. 'She's taken her away from me.' He stares at his plate of food. 'If Nicole thinks that's not hurting Kayla, then she's deluding herself.'

'I know,' Sophie agrees. 'And clearly she's not in her right state of mind to do something like this, but what do you think tipped her over the edge?'

Aiden's eyes are on me; I know it even without looking. 'I don't know,' he says, 'maybe she just... felt threatened.'

Sophie glances at me. 'By Eve? What do you mean?'

'If you're suggesting she thought I was trying to get Aiden back then that's ridiculous,' I protest. 'He hated the sight of me, and Nicole knew that.'

Sophie rolls her eyes. 'Well, what if she comes back? Changes her mind and realises she's done something wrong by taking Kayla. This is what she'd come back to.' She flaps her arms around.

'There's nothing going on with us. There wasn't then and there still isn't now,' I insist.

'But you're here. And when was the last time you went back to your flat?' Sophie says.

I ignore her. There are many reasons I don't want to go back to my flat. In absence of a response, Sophie turns to Aiden. 'I think you're making a mistake.'

I try to remain calm. 'Sophie, I sleep in the spare room. Every night.'

She ignores me. 'Aiden, I told you this was a bad idea. Maybe you do sleep in different rooms, but only the two of you know that. To the outside world it looks like you've shacked up together.'

I stand up. I'm not going to take this abuse from anyone, even Sophie. 'I'll be here for as long as Aiden needs me to be. Kayla is our daughter and, like it or not, Sophie, we're in this together. I walked out on them once, I'm not doing it again. They need me – more than ever.'

Without giving her a chance to respond, I leave the room and rush upstairs to the spare room, closing the door behind me so I can't hear what they're saying. I don't want to know what words Sophie uses when she urges Aiden to cut me out of his life. The fact that my friendship with Sophie is over is already cemented in my head; I don't need any more proof.

–

Later, when we're alone, Aiden tells me that I didn't have to leave. We've just eaten dinner, both of us pushing food around our plates before giving up and leaving it untouched, and now we sit on the sofa with enough space for two people to fit between us.

'I wanted to give you time with Sophie,' I say. 'Besides, I was clearly distracting her and this was meant to be about Kayla. Not that anything does any good. Why haven't we found her yet, Aiden? I feel like I'm not doing anywhere near enough to get her back.' Tears splatter onto the velvet cushion I'm clutching.

Aiden nods. 'I know exactly what you mean. How can we just sit here while she's gone? It's not right, Eve. Nothing about this is right. I feel like for all these months we've been going full speed to find her and now it seems like there's nothing left to do. Like the momentum's been lost. Everything feels like it's just… stopped.'

I move closer to him, placing my hand on his arm. 'This is the worst pain imaginable, isn't it? But we have to keep it together and focus on the one positive thing. Kayla loves Nicole, so even though you're not there, it won't be as bad as it could have been if a stranger had taken her. Nicole will probably be telling her some story about you having to work loads or something, or that they're on a fun holiday. She won't want to see Kayla upset.'

He forces a smile. 'I want to believe that. I just can't say anything for sure any more. You think you know someone, and then...'

'I know.' I pause. There's something I've needed to know and now is the time to ask. 'Aiden, do you blame me for Nicole taking Kayla? If I'd never come back then she wouldn't have done this and you'd all still be together. Happy.'

Aiden is emphatic in his response. 'No, of course I don't because whatever Nicole's reasons, *she* made the choice to take Kayla. That's down to her alone. She could have talked to me, told me how she was feeling. There were so many different choices she could have made.'

Just like I could have done things differently, too. Only sometimes it's not that easy. 'Thank you. I needed to hear that.'

Aiden studies my face. 'You carry around enough guilt, don't you? Anyway, it's me who needs to thank you. I don't know what I would have done if you hadn't been here right now. Believe it or not, you're actually getting me through this.' There are tears in his eyes as he speaks, something I'd never seen until Nicole took Kayla.

When he reaches for my hand I let him, and we sit in silence as minutes tick by, taking us further away from Kayla but closer to each other. It feels as though something monumental is about to happen between us; I've slept here more often than not over the last few months but have never sensed anything like this.

Without any words, Aiden pulls me towards him, and I let him, even though I probably shouldn't. Our lives are already complicated enough – surely this won't help. Yet it doesn't feel wrong when he presses his lips to mine and we find each other for the first time since long before Kayla was born.

Afterwards, when Aiden's finally sleeping beside me, I stare at him and wonder how any good will come out of what we've just done.

THIRTY-SIX

Before

'Are you still attracted to me?' Aiden asks.

I'm half asleep, my mind frazzled from being up all night with Kayla's cluster feeding, so perhaps I've only imagined that he's asked me this. Perhaps I should have expected it; I haven't let him anywhere near me for so long now.

'Of course I am.' But am I? I no longer know, and even if I was, it would be impossible to let him anywhere near me. Not since I've become this other person; a hollow shell of myself. 'I'm sorry,' I say. 'I just don't… you know, before Kayla was born, I was worried something might happen to her if we did anything, and now I'm just so tired all the time.'

He grabs my hand. 'I know. You're doing such an amazing job, all day every day on your own. I should try to do more to help. Give you a break.'

'You're already doing everything you can. You have to work.'

Aiden leans over me and peers at Kayla, who, miraculously, is fast asleep in her crib. 'Look at her though. Look at the beautiful being we created.'

My throat dries up and no words come out. I need to agree with him, smile and tell him she's the most amazing thing that could have happened to us. But nothing comes.

Thankfully, Aiden's phone rings and I'm relieved to hear it's his work, calling him in for an emergency meeting.

'Sorry,' he says, 'I thought I'd be able to watch her while you have a shower.'

I muster the biggest smile I can manage. 'It's fine, I can pop her in the bouncer so she can see me. She'll be happy then.'

'See. Supermum. I told you that you're amazing.' Aiden jumps out of bed and throws on a jumper and jeans.

And when he leaves the house, I stand at the window in my pyjamas and watch him drive away, helpless to stop panic and anxiety flood through me.

The rest of the day is okay. I manage. Kayla sleeps a fair amount, and I even doze off myself while she's napping. The house is fairly clean and tidy, and, somehow, a kind of peace envelops me. Maybe this will be okay after all. I allow myself to hope, but then it happens.

The text comes right in the middle of this hope, shattering my world to a thousand pieces.

THIRTY-SEVEN

Now

'I'm sorry,' Aiden whispers in the morning. 'Are you okay?' Even though we were married – still are – in the harsh light of day it now feels awkward, as if last night we were drunken strangers who are now waking up to face the consequences of the night before.

All I can manage is a nod, which seems to help him.

'I didn't plan that. It just... felt so natural.' He stares at the ceiling. 'Since Kayla's been gone I didn't even think I'd ever want to do that again with anyone. But being with you makes me feel close to her. I'm sorry if I—'

'I knew what I was doing,' I say. Maybe the way Aiden has explained it is true for me too. If Kayla can't be here with us then reconnecting with each other might be a way for both of us to feel close to her.

If it didn't feel so wrong.

I don't ask Aiden what last night means for us now; I was happy with how things were, with being together yet not *together*. Now everything is messy and blurred. And it is a place I cannot go.

'Marianne's coming at ten,' Aiden reminds me. 'Are you still okay to be here for that? I just can't get out of this meeting I'm afraid.'

Before I met Marianne, I envisaged a police liaison officer to be someone whose role was to comfort people with cups of tea. I've since learned that she's so much more than that. For one, she's a detective, and secondly, nothing gets past her, not even the minutest detail. I have faith in her, and believe she wants Kayla back with us as much as we do. As well as this, I have not once felt any judgement emanating from her, and she knows what I did. *At least as much as anyone can ever know.* I've even come to think of her more as a friend than anything else, as strange as that may seem. That's how she makes me feel.

'I'll be here,' I tell Aiden. 'I was planning to go home after that, though.'

Aiden's face falls.

'I mean just to pick up a few things. Sort my flat out a bit.'

'Oh, okay. I thought you meant... never mind. I'm glad you're coming back.'

Of course I'm coming back. Kayla's my daughter and this is her home. She'll need me once we've found her; Nicole will have scarred her more than I ever did when I walked out. I'm going to be right here to help her through it.

Aiden kisses my forehead then climbs out of bed. While he's in the shower I pull on his dressing gown and head across the hall to Kayla's room.

Not long after she was taken, Aiden moved the furniture around in here, determined to erase every trace of Nicole. She had organised where everything went, and I think it helped him to change it all, to somehow make it just his and Kayla's space. 'It will be a nice surprise for her when she comes home,' he'd said.

I sit on the floor by her bed and bury my head in her duvet, wondering what she's doing at this moment. All I know for sure is that she will be different – a child Kayla's age will change significantly in three months. I don't think this has occurred to Aiden, and I never mention it; it will be too devastating for him to hear.

Just as always, I can't stay in here for too long; that's like admitting Kayla will never be back here. *She will. Even though it looks hopeless right now, I will not give up on her. I owe it to her to make sure she's back here with us. Her parents.*

When I hear Aiden turn off the shower, I slip back into the hall. I don't want him to see my vulnerability; I owe it to him to be strong for all of us.

–

'How are you holding up?' Marianne asks before she's even through the door.

'We're still trying to find a way to live with it,' I reply, blinking away tears. Why is it that you can soldier on, keeping it all together, then as soon as someone enquires how you are the floodgates open?

She puts her arm around me. 'I can't lie and say it gets easier, but you mustn't give up hope.' In the few months I've known her, it's clear that Marianne is sharp and intuitive; she must immediately notice that I need a distraction. 'Why don't you get the kettle on and then we can have a talk about everything?'

Marianne likes her coffee strong. Not black, but with only a tiny drop of milk. I asked her once why she bothers adding it at all, and she told me it's surprising what a huge difference even the smallest amount of milk makes. Now it's hard not to make her a drink without thinking of this.

'So how are you and Aiden getting along?' she asks once she's filled me in on the investigation. There's nothing new to report, no sightings of Nicole or Kayla; it's as if they never existed.

If this was Sophie I was talking to, the Sophie from before, I would tell her what had happened last night with Aiden, explain to her that I'm not sure how to feel about it and welcome her advice. She would hand it to me straight, no pussyfooting around. I have a feeling Marianne would too, but I'm not about to make her cross a professional line, no matter how comfortable I feel with her.

'It's nice spending time with him,' I offer. 'It feels like the right thing to do.'

She smiles. 'It's great that you're supporting each other. Especially when you have a complex history. I admire you both for that. Something like this can either tear a couple apart or bring them closer, and I see it's done the latter for you.' She holds up her hand. 'Not that I'm suggesting you're a couple.'

I sense that a question lurks beneath this statement. 'It does feel like we are,' I admit. 'I know that might sound weird, but I'm here often, and our whole lives have become about finding Kayla. Or waiting for her, because, to be honest, that's what it feels like we're doing more than anything else.' Like we're standing still, futile, while the world keeps moving forward around us, taking us further away from Kayla.

Marianne nods. 'I know it's frustrating, and you can't see everything that's being done, but we really are putting everything into searching for Kayla. So in a way you're right, but while you're both here in this house, seemingly just waiting, we're constantly moving for you.'

I want to take comfort from her words. Marianne is a person I can believe in, but can I say the same for anyone else involved in the investigation when I've barely had any dealings with them? Aiden has been the one who's been at the forefront of this because of our complex situation.

'Doesn't everyone assume that Kayla's not in danger because she's with the woman she thinks of as her mother? How can there be the same sense of urgency there would be if a stranger had abducted her?' I don't know why I'm bringing this up again when Marianne has heard me say it many times before. Same sentiment, different words. She always has an answer that seems to pacify me, at least for a while.

'Until we find Kayla and bring her back home, everyone will be working as hard as they possibly can to find her. I promised you that when I first met you and I'm still making that promise now. And take comfort from this: Kayla's with someone she knows. The childminder was convinced it was Nicole who she ran to.' Again, this is nothing we haven't been over before.

'I try every day, sometimes it just gets so hard to keep that hope alive.'

She nods. 'I imagine it's even harder after not having had her in your life all these years.'

'It's like a cruel joke the universe is playing. Karma or something. Just when I come back to try to make up for everything, she's snatched away from me.'

Marianne offers a sympathetic smile. 'Yes, I can understand that. Looking back, are you sure you can't think of anything at all about Nicole that set off any alarm bells? Was there anything she said or did? Even just an offhand remark.'

I've had plenty of time to think about precisely this, pull it apart in my mind, inspect every interaction I had with Nicole, but there's nothing other than her suddenly becoming cold towards me. I tell this to Marianne.

'And I know you've said before that Aiden hinted at her behaviour seeming out of character, but are you sure you can't think of why this might be?'

'No. He was very protective of Nicole; he didn't want to give anything about her away. I think he thought he'd be betraying her, and if there's one thing I know about Aiden it's that he's fiercely loyal.'

Marianne frowns. 'Unfortunately, some people don't deserve our loyalty. I hope Aiden's not beating himself up about it.'

'Yes and no. He's quite pragmatic about things. He believes that people are responsible for their own actions. I was worried he'd blame me for this because I came back and shook up their lives, maybe inadvertently pushing Nicole into taking such drastic action. But he told me he doesn't. He said Nicole did this herself and she's the only one at fault.'

'That sounds like a decent man to me,' Marianne says. 'And believe me, there aren't many of those around. I should know.' She pauses. 'Did I tell you I'm divorced?'

Marianne's openness is exactly why I sometimes forget I'm talking to a police officer rather than someone I've known for years. 'I didn't know. I'm sorry.'

'Don't be. He was an arsehole. The whole time we were married he was involved with another woman. Younger than me of course. What a cliché. I think he would have carried on lying to this day if he hadn't got her pregnant.' Marianne says all this with no hint of bitterness or jealousy, and I admire her even more for that. 'Still, at least he did the right thing and stood by her. Think they're married now. I wish her the best of luck.'

Images of Maya flash into my head. And Connor. He wanted to stand by her but wasn't given a chance. I've forgiven him for what he did when he threatened me because his actions came from his suffering. Since Kayla was taken neither of them have crossed my mind much, but Marianne has just reminded me there was something Connor mentioned that I initially dismissed. He'd said something about me having enemies. At the time I'd thought he might mean people who knew what I'd done, like Sophie and Aiden. Jamie even. But could he have been talking about Nicole? Is it possible he saw her at my flat? Maybe he even spoke to her. I'd been meaning to check on Maya after he confronted me that night, but Kayla's disappearance erased everything else from my mind. Until now.

Marianne is still talking, something about humans having a remarkable ability to deal with anything life throws at them. 'We're quite astounding really, aren't we?' she says, and I nod my agreement, my mind distracted with thoughts of talking to Maya.

–

It's another hour before Marianne says she has to go, and as soon as I've closed the door I text Maya, practically begging her to meet up with me. I'm clearly crossing some teacher/student boundary, but right now I don't even know if I'll ever be able to teach again. Nicole could have taken Kayla to a different country, and if that's what she's done then how will we ever get her back?

In the back of my mind the niggling thought stays with me for the rest of the day: *Maya's boyfriend knows something, and I need to know what that is.*

THIRTY-EIGHT

Now

'How did it go with Marianne?' Aiden asks when he gets home. He plants a kiss on my cheek, reminding me of the time before. That's how I've come to think of my life before leaving. I have no idea how to label the present time, but it doesn't matter; all that's important is finding Kayla.

'It's always good to see her. There's just never any news, or anything new to focus on with the search.'

He sinks into the sofa and sighs. 'People keep asking me how I'm able to go to work,' he says, 'and it feels truly horrible. There I am, drawing up plans for people's houses, to help make their lives better, while our little girl is probably crying for me every day. Am I a bad person, Eve?'

I shake my head. 'No, of course not. It's how you're able to function and carry on.' We'd talked about this when Nicole first took Kayla, and I completely understood why Aiden needed to keep working, to cling on to some part of his life that was still normal. 'I also need to keep this roof over our heads,' he'd said. 'Nicole could come to her senses at any moment; and what would happen if they came back and I'd lost the house?' His anguish had been palpable, and I'd wanted to reach out and hold him right then, even though I kept my distance. It was many weeks until we were comfortable with each other, almost carrying on as though I'd never left them those years ago.

'Until it happens to you,' Aiden continues, 'you imagine you'd be out there every day, searching the streets every waking hour, but the truth of it is we're just helpless, aren't we? Waiting for Nicole to see sense and bring her back.'

Even though my thoughts about it mirror his, I wonder if there is actually more we could be doing. That might just mean going over the same things we've already done, but at least it's action. 'Can't we approach Nicole's parents again?' I suggest. 'And her sister? See if there's anything else they can tell us?'

'I already emailed them all again yesterday. They've been really supportive, Eve – I don't think they'd be holding anything back from me. They're just as angry with Nicole as I am. They still can't believe she's done this.'

'And her friends? What if we contacted them again?'

Aiden shakes his head. 'Nothing's changed. They're also on our side. Nobody's heard a thing from her. They'd be telling the police if they had. Damn it! I just want her back!' He stands up, and his eyes glisten. 'Sorry,' he says. 'I'll be back in a minute.'

When he leaves the room, I check my phone to see if Maya's replied, even though I would have heard the alert if she had. There's nothing. She probably won't ever respond to my message, and I can't just sit around and wait. I need to take some action. For Kayla. And for Aiden. For my family.

Aiden doesn't know where I've really gone. I'd told him I was going back to my flat to pick up some things, but I had another reason for wanting to head out. He would tell me I'm being crazy, if he knew the truth, and say that there's no way my ex-student can help us find Kayla. No way at all. Realistically, I know this, but I've had enough of standing still; I need to do *something*.

Even though it doesn't mean that Maya's home, I'm relieved to see there are lights on in her parents' house, meaning somebody at least should answer the door.

Unfortunately, it's Bal who does, and she stares at me, frowning and silent. Maya must have told her the truth about Kayla by now, and I have no doubt that she's the type of woman who is audacious enough to confront me about it. I exhale and prepare to defend myself.

'Hi, I'm sure you remember me? Maya's English tutor. I'm sorry to turn up like this but I really need to speak to her. I wouldn't have come if it wasn't so important.'

Bal leans forward, pulling the door with her. 'You knew, didn't you? That Maya was pregnant.'

'Yes. She confided in me during one of our sessions, and I couldn't betray her by telling you. I promise you, Bal, I tried my best to get her to talk to you. That was the only advice I gave her. I never advised her on what she should do about the baby, please believe that.'

Bal doesn't respond, her stony expression remaining in place. 'Why should I believe anything you say when you've proven yourself to be a liar? What are you doing here? What do you want from Maya?'

Although it hasn't been my plan, it's unlikely I'll get through the door if I don't tell Bal as much as I can. 'If you let me come in, I'll explain everything. Please, Bal. I can't talk out here on the doorstep.'

After some hesitation, she agrees, leading me into the lounge. It takes ten minutes to explain why I lied about not having a daughter, and even though I see flickers of judgement in her eyes while I'm speaking, at least she is listening, saving her opinion until she's heard all I have to say.

'You had postnatal depression,' she states. 'Maya didn't explain this clearly. She said you left because you'd made the wrong decision about having a child, and she didn't want to do the same.'

Chinese whispers, I think. Maya would never have taken everything I said and concluded that I simply regretted having a baby. Still, that's not important here. 'Bal, I promise you I had no intention of swaying Maya in either direction. I kept telling her it was her choice alone, nobody else's.' *Not even Connor's – not when it comes down to it.*

'That's not what bothers me,' Bal says. 'A termination was the right thing for her. She's not ready to have a baby. And I'm not ashamed to say I told her exactly how we felt about it. You spend so many years educating your daughters about contraception and then they go and... have an accident.' She shakes her head. 'It makes me sad. Maya's not the first and she won't be the last. I'm not heartless, I just want what's best for my daughters. I'm sure you're the same – now.'

Her dig doesn't go unnoticed. 'Yes, I just want Kayla to be confident to make her own choices. Good ones I hope. They may not always be, but I'll be there to support her, no matter what.' My turn to have a dig. I wonder how everything was resolved between Maya and her parents after that night she came to my flat, desperate to avoid going home.

'It's not always as easy as that,' Bal says, shaking her head. 'You'll find that out when your girl gets older.'

I catch my breath. Will I get to see Kayla growing older? Or is she Nicole's now – a punishment that the universe has dished out to me. *But it's not just you – it's Aiden too, and he did nothing to deserve this.*

'Please, Bal. Can I just talk to Maya quickly?'

'You still haven't explained why you need to speak to her. What's this all about?'

Here goes. I only hope it convinces Bal to help me. I tell her what's happened to Kayla and, as she listens, her face softens.

'Missing? That's awful. I'm sorry,' she says once I've explained. 'And you think her stepmother took her somewhere?'

'Technically Nicole isn't really her stepmother. They weren't married.'

She ignores this. 'I don't understand how Maya can help, though?'

It might be best to be totally honest and explain that Connor turned up to confront me, but once again I don't feel it's my business to talk about Maya's boyfriend to her mother. Experience has taught me that she wouldn't appreciate this. 'I just need to know if Maya ever saw anyone hanging around my flat when she came for tutoring sessions. We're assuming it's Nicole, but the police aren't ruling out any possibilities.'

'I'm sorry,' Bal says. 'Unfortunately, Maya's not here. She moved out weeks ago and is living with one of her friends.'

She's not going to make this easy for me. 'Do you think you could give me the address? I'd really appreciate it, and it might just help find my daughter.'

Bal ponders this for a moment. 'Well, I suppose. What kind of person would I be if I didn't help another mother who needed it?'

—

I may have jumped over one hurdle but getting Maya to help me won't be as easy. The fact that she hasn't replied to my text speaks volumes, especially as we didn't leave things on bad terms. *What is it, Maya? Why won't you talk to me?*

Her new home is only ten minutes from her parents', in a huge block of flats on an estate in Barking, which couldn't be more different from her family's leafy, tree-lined street. Things must have been bad for her to prefer living here, I think, before reminding myself that the young often value space and privacy away from their parents and would probably place this over luxury most times. Still, I can't help but shudder to know that this is where Maya has chosen to be.

There's no intercom system, so I walk straight up the stairs to Maya's flat. A young red-haired girl answers the door, holding it open for me without saying a word.

'Oh!' she says, 'I thought you were someone else. Can I help?'

'I've come to see Maya. Is she home?'

'Um, she's… who are you?'

'I'm her English tutor.'

The girl's eyes widen. 'Her tutor? But she's finished her—'

'It's okay,' a voice from the hallway says. Maya. Sounding different somehow, older maybe.

Then she appears beside her friend, and I can hardly believe she's the same girl. How is it possible to change so much in only a few months? Heavy make-up masks her face, making her look much older than eighteen. Her long wavy hair has gone, replaced with a straighter, shoulder-length bob.

'What are you doing here, miss?'

Some things never change, and I can't help but smile at the way she still addresses me. 'Can we talk?'

She turns to her friend as if needing confirmation, but the red-haired girl just smiles and watches both of us.

'I suppose.' She turns to her flatmate. 'Lara, is that okay? I won't be long and then we can get out of here.'

It's only then that I notice both girls are dressed for a night out: short skirts and sparkly tops, heels far too high for anyone to walk comfortably in.

'I won't keep you,' I promise them both.

Inside, the flat is as dingy as I'd expected it to be, although they've done their best to brighten it up with modern prints and artificial flowers. There's no avoiding the stained dark blue carpet, though, which doesn't match anything in the house. This is not Maya. At least not the girl I used to know. But judging from what I've seen so far – how do I know who that was? Standing here is surreal, and I can't quite make sense of it.

Lara announces that she's going to finish getting ready, and leaves Maya and me alone.

Maya speaks first. 'How did you find me?' She sits on the tatty sofa, crossing her legs and leaning forward.

There's no invitation for me to sit too, so I stay standing. 'Your mum gave me your address. I went there when you didn't reply to my text.'

'I've been busy,' she says with no hint of guilt or embarrassment.

'How did your exams go?'

'Is that what you wanted to see me for?'

'No, but I'm interested. I always like to know how my students get on after tutoring.'

She shrugs. 'They went fine.'

'Then you're at uni now? What degree did you decide on?'

'None. I'm taking a year out. To reassess my life.' I should have known this. Something about Maya alerted me to it.

'Well, deferring a year is often a good idea. What will you do?'

Maya holds her hand up. 'Miss, this feels like a police interrogation. Can you just stop being a teacher and tell me what you're doing here?'

I sit next to her. 'Okay. Remember I told you about my daughter Kayla? She's gone missing. It looks like my husband's girlfriend took her.'

Maya softens, just as her mother did earlier. 'I'm so sorry. That's really... awful.'

'Yes, it's been a very difficult time for me and her dad.'

She frowns. 'But didn't he hate you? After you left and everything.'

'Yes, he did. Something like this has a way of bringing people together, though, so we're putting aside everything else to focus on Kayla.'

She nods. 'I don't see how I can help.'

'I know this might be difficult for you to talk about, but it involves Connor.'

Her eyes widen, and she folds her arms across her body. A defensive gesture that suggests talking about him will cause her pain. But I need to do this. 'I don't understand,' she says. 'What's any of this got to do with Connor?'

I tell her about him paying me a visit, how threatening his behaviour was, how he left with the comment about me having enemies.

'What a bastard,' she says, then claps her hand over her mouth. 'Sorry.'

'Please don't apologise. He was just hurt, Maya. I'm sure he wouldn't have done anything to me.'

'Who knows? People are capable of anything, aren't they?' This is the old Maya back, the one I remember. 'Wait a minute. You don't think he took your daughter, do you? Or helped that woman take her?'

'No, I don't. I mean, it's possible, but I don't think Nicole needed any help. To the outside world, Kayla was her daughter. It wouldn't have been suspicious to anyone. That's how she's got away with this.'

'Then what's Connor got to do with it?'

'I think he was… watching me for a while. Waiting for the right moment to get to me. And I think he might have seen someone else hanging around my flat, otherwise why would he have mentioned enemies?'

She shrugs. 'I don't know.'

'So, you never got back together then?'

'No. No way. He scared me by how aggressive he became because I wanted a termination. He just wasn't the guy I thought he was.'

'I'm sorry he didn't support you,' I say.

She rolls her eyes. 'He'd say that I was the one who didn't support him. He had this thing about girls expecting the guy to always watch out for them, and he used to say why can't it work both ways? You know, we want equal rights and all that then we still want to be looked after. What a ridiculous stereotype. How did I ever find him attractive?'

'Sometimes we don't see who someone really is until extreme circumstances are thrown at us. Better to know now, though, than find out after years, or marriage or kids.'

Maya nods. 'Yeah. True.'

'So do you know where he lives now?'

'I heard he moved to east London to live with his cousin. Doing all right for himself.' She stares around the room. 'Not like me. No uni, just a part-time job in Starbucks.'

'Oh, Maya. What happened? How did you end up here?'

Tears fall from her eyes, sliding down her cheeks and dripping onto her top, blending in with the sparkles. My heart aches for her. 'I just... everything changed after the... termination. I just didn't feel like the same person. I wasn't expecting to feel guilty. I was so sure of my decision that it never occurred to me I might regret it.'

'And do you?'

She shakes her head. 'I don't know. Maybe. Sometimes. I see babies everywhere and wonder what mine would have looked like. I dream about babies, too. It's horrible. I thought I'd just get on with my life and never look back but…'

'I'm so sorry. Were you offered any counselling?'

'Yeah, I had some before and after but thought I was okay. That I didn't need it. I'm strong, right? I can handle anything.' She rolls her eyes. 'Then I got my A-level results, which were really good, and I should have been excited, but instead I felt numb, like it didn't matter any more. I met Lara, and she just works and parties and enjoys herself. I looked at her and thought: I need a bit of that.'

I want Maya to know that it's not too late for her. This is only the beginning of her life. She has her whole future ahead of her and this is just a temporary interruption. 'Maya, it's not bad to take some time out for yourself. At any age. But please don't give up on your dreams. Start afresh next September and, in the meantime, I don't think it's wrong to just live a bit, get it out of your system.'

She wipes her eyes and grabs her phone from the coffee table. 'Thanks, miss. Let me just find Connor's address. And I'm coming with you. I can't let you go to that arsehole's place on your own – who knows what he'll do?'

THIRTY-NINE

Before

Fight or flight mode. It's our body's way of protecting us against threats, an innate survival instinct kicking in. But I think there's also a third option. One where you do neither of these things, instead becoming frozen, almost accepting of your situation.

It feels as though I've done nothing so far, which is why today I've found the energy to take action. Maybe this will be it, a way to climb out of this hole, instead of letting the soil bury me deeper.

The doctor's waiting room is full today, and I sit in the corner, hoping to disappear into the wall. Perhaps when they call my name, I'll stay silent and pretend it's not me, and then when they've given up, baffled, I could get up and leave. This surgery is big and impersonal enough for me to do that.

'Eve Conway?'

The doctor's standing by the door, searching faces, and without wanting to I stand and make my way towards her, my legs taking control of my brain. Too late now. Too late for anything.

In her office, she introduces herself as Dr Humphreys, and I take a seat while she settles behind her desk, typing something onto her computer. 'Now,' she says, with a smile, 'what can I do for you today?'

Even though her tone is friendly, for a moment I consider making up some problem with my periods or something similar, because it feels as though I will never get the truth out. But I'm here now – I have to keep going.

'I, um, something… I've just had a baby and I think I'm really struggling.' There, it's done. Some of the truth, at least, is now out there and can't be taken back.

Dr Humphreys stops typing and gives me her full attention. 'I see. Okay, why don't you tell me exactly what's going on and then we can see how best to help you?'

Finally. Someone kind who can help me. So why does this fill me with dread? There are so many things I won't be able to tell her, so how can she really help me? 'I… can't seem to bond with my baby. I know it can take time, but she's nearly three months old now, and surely it should have happened by now?'

'Not at all. These things can take time. It's all perfectly understandable. Your hormones are still all over the place, and you're a new mum on top of that. Who wouldn't have a bit of a wobble?' She smiles, and more than anything I want to believe her, and have faith that I can get help.

Now is my chance to tell her it's more than this, so much more, to tell her the truth. All of it. Free myself from this prison I've created with my silence. But I can't even form the thoughts, let alone say the words.

I lean forward and try to smile. 'Yes, I know you're right. It just takes time to get back to normal, then?' I ask this even though for me there no longer is a *normal*.

She starts typing again, and I let myself get lost in the click of her nails on the keyboard. 'I'm just going to ask you a few questions,' she says.

Then she is asking me about suicidal thoughts and thoughts of harming my baby, forcing me to snap to attention. I can't have her making a record of these things about me, there for medical staff to see for the rest of my life.

Lie, lie, lie.

'No. Nothing at all like that. It's more just feeling low and… not really coping with the newborn stage.'

Tap tap tap.

By the end of her questions she is smiling, and I feel as though I've just passed an exam. Any minute now she will congratulate me and hand me a certificate.

'Well, judging from your responses, it looks like you could have the baby blues. It's very common. You have no previous episodes of depression, so I'm fairly confident that this will pass if you get the right support.' She opens her desk drawer and pulls out a card. 'This is a free online counselling service where trained counsellors offer cognitive behaviour therapy. It's all done on your computer or tablet whenever is convenient for you. I really recommend it. All sorts of issues can be addressed by CBT, and this online service is definitely the way forward. No long waiting lists or having to travel miles for sessions. Give it a go and see how you get on. But in the meantime, if you start to feel worse in any way, please do come back here straightaway.'

Nodding, I take the card and thank her, feeling even worse leaving her office than I did walking in. Because now it seems clear to me that there's nobody who can help me.

–

'Thanks for looking after her,' I say to Mum. She's rooting through her kitchen drawer while Kayla sleeps on a huge cushion on the floor. I should question Mum about whether she is safe lying there like that, but I don't have the energy. Kayla is breathing, and Mum is right here with her.

'What are you looking for?' I ask.

'A stamp. I know I bought some the other day and I always keep them in the drawer, so I don't know where they've got to.'

It's happening again. 'I thought you kept them in your purse. In case you need one when you're out.' This has been what Mum has always done, so it's strange that she's questioning it.

'No, I don't,' she protests. 'I keep them right here. I always have done.'

'Do me a favour, Mum – will you just have a quick look in your purse, just to humour me?'

She stares at me with wide angry eyes, as if I've just accused her of a crime. 'Fine,' she hisses, heading to the hall, where her bag sits on the phone table. 'But I'll expect an apology after, Eve.'

When she returns and delves into her purse, she frowns and pulls out a new book of stamps. 'How strange. I must have put them there by mistake.' She glances at me. 'I remember now – I was really distracted that day and wasn't concentrating. Well, at least I've got them now. How funny that I put them in my purse.'

There is no way I will point out that this is where she has kept them since I was a child.

Later, while we sit down with coffee and wait for Kayla to wake up, I ask Mum if she'll make a doctor's appointment. 'Just so they can put your mind at ease... about these little things you keep forgetting.'

She stares at me. 'What do you mean? What exactly are you saying, Eve? That I'm losing my mind or something?'

'No, of course not, I just—'

'I think you should go now,' she says, standing up and taking my unfinished mug of coffee from me.

'Mum, Kayla's still sleeping.'

'Just go!' she screams, her voice a high-pitched screech.

Kayla's eyes ping open, and she quickly begins to cry, the deafening sound mingling with Mum's shouts for me to get out.

And as I drive home, with Kayla sobbing in her car seat, Mum's behaviour, together with that text message, make my head feel like it will explode at any moment. And I drive far too fast, way too recklessly, my mind envisaging smashing at full speed into a lamppost.

FORTY

Now

Unlike Maya's flat, Connor's is surprisingly nice. It's more of a maisonette, on a road similar to mine.

'Bet you didn't expect him to live in a place like this,' Maya says, folding her arms and stopping outside the small gate.

'I try not to make assumptions,' I say.

Before tonight, I didn't know anything about Connor other than what I saw for myself the night he forced his way into my flat. On the drive over here, Maya told me that his cousin owns a car valeting business, and Connor works with him now. 'They're doing very well,' she'd pointed out. 'And he hasn't even been to uni.'

'You don't have to come in with me,' I tell her now. The minute we got in the car I regretted not insisting that she stay at her flat. She should be on her night out with Lara. I shouldn't be dragging her into this.

'Oh, I want to see him. We've got unfinished business.'

Maya sounds so adamant that I give up trying to talk her out of it. Yet despite the strength and determination she's exhibiting, surely underneath there must be some apprehension. 'Do you miss him?' I ask.

There is no hesitation in her answer. 'No. I hate him.' She turns to me. 'I know you're going to tell me that hating someone isn't good, but I can't help how I feel. It doesn't mean I lose sleep over him.'

The thing is, she probably does. Whatever's happened since, the two of them share something that can't be erased, no matter how much time passes. They will forever be linked by Maya's unplanned pregnancy.

'It doesn't look like anyone's in,' I say, focusing on the task at hand. I can't get distracted by the past – even Maya's – because Kayla's future is all that matters right now.

Maya tuts. 'No. He's probably out drinking with his stupid friends.'

It never occurred to me to think what I would do if Connor wasn't in. 'Let's check,' I say.

Halfway to the front door, Maya begins to giggle.

'Sorry,' she says when I ask her what she's laughing at. 'This is just weird, isn't it? You were my English tutor and now we're here on a hunt for your daughter. It's just…'

'Surreal? Yes, I know.'

She grabs my arm. 'Let's do this.'

Despite the lack of lights in the place, Connor is at home, opening the door and staring at us, his eyes wide with shock. 'What the hell?' he says. 'What is this?'

'You remember me, don't you, Connor? I just need a word with you. Can we come in?'

'Are you crazy? I'm not letting you in here.' Although he's talking to me, his eyes are fixed on Maya, a clear demonstration that his feelings for her still exist. Her presence here has floored him, which can only work to my advantage.

Stepping forward, Maya takes over. 'Let us in, Connor. Eve's daughter's been taken, and we need to help find her.'

He frowns. 'Taken by who?'

Maya steps forward. 'Let us in and we'll tell you everything.'

'But how am *I* supposed to help? It's got nothing to do with me.' Connor turns to me. 'You can't think that just cos I threatened you a bit I'd take your *daughter*. That's sick, man.'

'That's not what I think at all,' I assure him, even though it has indeed crossed my mind. 'And you're not in any trouble. She's been missing for three months now, so the police would have already knocked on your door if I'd mentioned you, wouldn't they?'

He digests my words then slowly nods. 'I s'ppose.'

Inside Connor's flat, the lights are dimmed, but I can see enough to know that this property is cared for. He doesn't invite us to sit down, but we do anyway, and even though he's scowling, he also sits, opposite Maya, his eyes fixed on her.

'What do you think I can do?' he asks, leaning forward with his elbows resting on his knees.

'That night you came to see me,' I begin, 'it wasn't the first time you'd been to my flat, was it?'

He glances at Maya but she looks away.

'It's okay,' I say. 'Maya knows everything. And we both understand why you were so angry with me.'

'She had nothing to do with my decision, Con,' Maya says. 'Nothing. I made it by myself. And I'm sorry it hurt you.'

Now it's Connor's turn to look away, his eyes glassing over. 'I don't want to talk about it. It's done, isn't it?'

Maya nods. 'Yes, it is. Please just help Eve.'

Even though I've been telling Maya for a long time that she can call me by my first name, it's funny to actually hear her doing it now when until tonight she hasn't been able to.

Connor lets out a huge sigh, stares at the floor. 'No, it wasn't the first time.'

'And when you were in my flat you told me I had a lot of enemies. Do you remember that? I called you back to explain what you meant, but you ignored me. Connor, I really need to know why you said that.'

He shrugs. 'It was nothing. I was just talking.'

Maya stands up. 'What the hell, Connor? Just tell miss what you meant! You don't say something like that for no reason.'

'All right, calm down, will you? No need to get hysterical.'

'There's every need, Connor, when a little girl is gone.'

Seconds tick by and nobody says anything. I could urge him, and try my best to persuade him, but I feel as though he will give in before long. He's not telling us to leave, which means there's every chance he will tell me what I need to know.

Finally, he speaks. 'I was watching your flat,' he says. 'I had to. Didn't know anything about you so I had to get a feel for your movements.'

'You need help, Connor!' Maya declares. 'That's just disgusting. That's stalking, that is.'

He glares at her. 'I thought you wanted my help?'

'Yes, we do,' I say before he and Maya get into something. 'Please carry on.'

'I was there one night, and I saw someone smash your windows. Made my day, that did. Showed me that you deserved everything you got, if I wasn't the only one wanting to mess you up.'

Maya throws up her arms. 'Will you—'

'Wait,' I say. 'Are you telling the truth? It really wasn't you who smashed my car?'

He looks pleased with himself. 'Nope. I didn't care about your car – it was *you* I wanted to smash up.'

Maya picks up a cushion and hurls it across the room at him. 'Jesus, Connor, you really are a piece of work.'

'It's okay, Maya.' I stand up and move closer to Connor. 'This woman who smashed my car windows. What did she look like?' Nicole's image floats around my head. How friendly and kind she looked when I first met her, definitely not the kind of woman who would smash car windows. Or take a child.

'What are you on about? It wasn't a she. It was a man.'

The ground shifts beneath me. Connor must have got this wrong. 'A man? That can't be right.'

'Listen, I was right there, hiding behind a car and got a good solid look at the guy. Believe me, it was definitely a man. And he was mad as hell.'

A man. A man who hates me enough to do something like that.

My mind searches for answers. Answers I don't want to believe. I wanted to believe that it was all over. I try to explore other options. It was the day Jamie ended our relationship, and I'd spent the day drinking in a bar. *Jamie.* He was so angry with me, so it would make sense. But my mind struggles to believe Jamie would have done that.

'If I showed you a picture, would you recognise him?'

'Course.'

Flicking through my phone I quickly search my photos for one of Jamie. There's only one – a selfie Jamie took of us on his phone and then sent to me. I hadn't wanted to take it; he spent a long time nagging me to until I gave in. How horrible that I never wanted pictures of us. No wonder he felt as though I didn't care.

I hand my phone to Connor and wait for him to confirm what I already know.

'Nope,' he says – handing it back – 'that's not the guy. He looked nothing like that.'

Then that only leaves one option. I flick through my phone again, typing into Google until the image I want comes up. 'Is this him?' I ask, showing Connor the image I've found.

This time, Connor frowns, studies the picture for too long. After what seems like minutes he looks away from the screen.

'Nah, that's not him either.'

Hearing Connor say this, all of a sudden everything becomes clear. I know exactly who smashed my car windows. And it's all I can do to stop my legs giving way beneath me.

FORTY-ONE

Before

I knew when I woke up this morning that I was heading towards something. Or hurtling. Spiralling. My head was fuzzy, unable to make sense of anything – and still is now, hours later. Perhaps this is my new normal, what's to be expected for someone like me.

Only one more hour until I can put Kayla to bed and say goodbye to another day where I don't even know what I've done or accomplished.

'Shall we have a bath?' I say to Kayla in the sing-song voice I've managed to perfect. Babies pick up on tone of voice apparently, so this is one way I keep her protected from the ugly truth about me.

I hold her while we watch the bubbles, and then I place her in the bath seat and gently wash her. She seems happy this evening and giggles as the soapsuds slide down her arms; baths usually have a calming effect on her, and I wish she could stay in here until bedtime. But her skin is new and sensitive, so it has to be a quick splash only, and then I will face her anger while I fight to get her dry and into a sleepsuit. I've almost become immune to this all now, accepting of it, even though I know I'm one bird step away from being tipped over the edge.

She's so helpless, lying there, unable to move and dependent on me for everything. Her life is in my hands – more responsibility than I could ever have imagined. This thought inflates and expands in my head until it's crushing my skull.

I glance at the tap. If I just turned it on, it would fill the whole bath up with water until it was over her tiny head, and she wouldn't be able to save herself. I shake my head. *No, no no.* But the thought is there, sticking to my skull, and I am unable to dislodge it. *Do it, do it, do it.*

And then I am screaming and lifting Kayla out of the bath, clutching her to me and wrapping her in a towel. Tears stream down my face as I whisper to her. *I'm sorry, I'm sorry.* Over and over.

But no apology will ever make up for the monster I am.

Later, I pretend to be asleep when Aiden comes home. He's been at a work leaving do tonight, so it's past midnight when he slips into bed. He wouldn't have recognised me if he'd come home at his usual time. He would have seen a woman shaken and lost, unrecognisable. Broken. There was no way tonight I would have been able to hide what I've managed to hide for these months. That, if given the chance, I am a woman capable of the worst atrocity.

I leave it until Aiden's breathing signals that he's in a deep sleep and then I grab some clothes and get dressed. The suitcase I packed earlier with essential items is already in my car; there is plenty I'm not taking and I don't care about leaving anything behind.

Sitting on the bed, I watch Aiden for a minute, taking in every detail of him, capturing a photo in my mind that I'll be able to retrieve at any time. And then I stand over Kayla's cot. *This is for the best, my darling girl. Mummy isn't safe to be around. You deserve so much better than this; so much better than the hand you were dealt. None of this is your fault; please don't ever believe that it is.*

My eyes are pools of tears as I silently say goodbye to my child. I desperately want to scoop her up and hold her to me, take in her baby scent just one last time.

Finally, I feel what I wanted to from the very beginning. Love.

But it is far too late now.

FORTY-TWO

Now

Aiden's in the kitchen on his laptop when I get home. It's funny how I've come to think of it as my home over the past three months, even though it isn't and never will be. He looks up and smiles. 'Did you get everything you needed?'

'Yes, I've got a bag in the hall.'

'Great, that means you won't have to go home for a while, then.'

'We need to talk,' I say, sitting down opposite him.

Aiden's skin pales. 'What's happened? Is this about Kayla? Has Marianne said something?'

'Do you remember when someone smashed my car windows? Months ago.'

He frowns. 'Yeah, I told you Nicole did it.'

'Did she? It wasn't you?'

There's a pause before he answers. 'No. Absolutely no. Why would I have done that?'

'To warn me off. You didn't want me in Kayla's life then, did you?'

There's a long pause before he answers. 'You're right – I didn't. But I'm telling you now, I didn't do it.'

'Okay,' I say. 'Maybe it was Nicole. That would make sense, wouldn't it?'

Aiden shrugs. 'Nothing would surprise me about her. Nothing at all.'

'Do you want coffee?' I ask. Aiden is lying to me and I need to find out why. There is no need now, we are in each other's lives, fighting to find Kayla, so what reason would he have to keep the truth from me?

But he is not the only one lying. There could be a reason he has to, just like I have mine.

And I need to know what it is.

'What are you doing this evening?' I ask. I need to know I can trust Aiden, because finding Kayla depends on it.

'I've just been checking in with Nicole's friends on Facebook,' Aiden replies. 'They're still so shocked by it all.'

'I'm sure they are,' I say. 'This isn't something the Nicole they knew would do.'

'I'll kill her when I get my hands on her,' he says.

As I boil the kettle I watch Aiden, his head buried back in his laptop. Confusion clouds my mind. One minute he is smashing my car windows, the next he is bringing Kayla to my flat, arranging for us to spend time together.

I shudder at this thought and fight every urge I have to flee this place. Is he the one who's been sending me emails? Breaking into my flat? I need answers, and the only way to get them is to be right here with Aiden.

'I've had an idea,' Aiden says. 'Shall we go and see your mum tomorrow? I've taken the day off, and it would be nice to see her again after all this time.'

I hand him his coffee. 'You know she won't recognise you, though? That can be quite hard to deal with.'

'Oh, I know. But maybe you can explain who I am? And she loves Kayla, doesn't she? Even if she doesn't remember who she is. Maybe she'll just like me as a person and not even need to know I'm your husband.'

The word sends me cold. 'She'll love you,' I say. 'She always did.'

He smiles. 'Jackie. What a character she was. It's so sad.'

'We'll go and see her,' I say. I raise my mug. 'Do you mind if I take this to bed? I don't know why but I'm absolutely shattered tonight.'

He taps something on his laptop. 'Go ahead. I'll just finish up here and won't be far behind you.'

As I turn and walk away, I wonder how I'm going to spend another minute, let alone nights or weeks here.

'Which room?'

I spin around. 'What's that?'

'Which room will you be sleeping in?' The look of hope in his eyes turns my stomach.

'Do you mind if I sleep in the spare room tonight? I'm just feeling a bit... I think I might have a cold coming.'

He frowns. 'Of course. Wherever you feel comfortable.'

'Just tonight,' I assure him, and as I head upstairs I pray that something will happen tomorrow to help me trust him.

—

In the morning Aiden brings me coffee and toast.

'What's this for?' I ask, sliding myself up in bed.

'You said you weren't feeling well last night, so I wanted to do this for you. It's not much, just some jam on toast. To be honest, I couldn't sleep so I just got up.

Keeping busy takes my mind off everything. Not that anything does really, but you know what I mean. I've already had three coffees.'

I have to remember this. Aiden is suffering too. I am not the only one who has lost Kayla. 'Thanks,' I say. 'It's kind of you.'

'How are you feeling today anyway?'

'Okay. I think the sleep helped. I'm all ready to visit Mum.' And to find out why Aiden lied. I'm itching to search through his things, although that will have to wait until I'm alone in the house.

—

'Who's this?' Mum asks when we arrive. I'd called ahead to ask the carers to let her know I'd be bringing someone, even though now it doesn't seem there was much point.

Aiden steps forward and shakes her hand. 'Hi Jackie, I'm Aiden.' He waits for signs of recognition, but Mum only stares at him blankly.

'That's a nice name,' she says. 'Come in and have tea.'

'A coffee would be lovely, thanks Jackie.'

Mum looks around the room. 'I, um, I think I don't—'

'We can make it, Mum,' I say, placing my hand on her shoulder. 'Aiden, would you mind getting coffee from the residents' lounge?'

Aiden agrees and when he's left the room, I feel as though I can breathe again, albeit temporarily.

'What a lovely man,' Mum declares. 'I knew you'd find someone special. You just need to settle down and start a family now. You're still young enough. You don't want to leave it too late though.'

'We're just friends,' I say, safe in the knowledge that Aiden can't hear. It's better that I get this out of the way now, even though there's every chance Mum will mention it again once he's back.

'Oh, that's a shame,' Mum says. 'I do wish you'd find someone nice.'

I wish I could tell her about Jamie – how I had someone decent and didn't value him. All I need is Kayla, though. Then Aiden's lie won't matter.

As if Mum can sense I'm thinking about my daughter, she asks about Kayla. 'What a lovely little girl. Why doesn't she come and see me any more?'

'I'm afraid we've got some sad news.' Aiden. Standing in the doorway, empty-handed. My heart almost stops; how long has he been standing there?

'Oh dear. What sad news? Where is she?'

'She's gone missing,' Aiden says. There are tears in his eyes, and I want to scream at him. *If you love our daughter then why are you lying to me?* This wasn't the man I married. The man it tore my heart to shreds to walk away from.

Mum clamps her hand to her mouth. 'That's terrible! What happened?'

'Well, my ex-girlfriend has taken her, and the police can't find either of them. She could be... on the other side of the world by now.'

'But I only saw her yesterday. We were right here doing a jigsaw.'

Aiden freezes. He's not used to dealing with Mum's dementia; he is wondering how it's possible that Kayla was here yesterday.

'She disappeared after you saw her,' I say to Mum.

Aiden visibly relaxes, and I spend the next hour planning my next move while Aiden charms Mum. He should realise that it's pointless; there's little likelihood of Mum even remembering Aiden if we ever visit together again, let alone remembering anything he says.

—

On the drive home, Aiden announces that he has to pop into work for a while.

'I thought you had the day off,' I say.

'I had an email when we were with Jackie, and there's something I need to sort out. A client wants to change something in the plans I've already finalised. Typical! It won't take long, though, to go through it with him. Will you be okay?'

'Of course. I'll just work on updating the missing posters and the website. I'm not giving up hope, Aiden. Ever. We're going to find our little girl.'

With his eyes still fixed on the road, he reaches over and grabs my hand. 'This is why I still love you.'

His words are almost a whisper, barely audible above the hum of the engine, but I hear them clearly enough and they shoot spasms of pain through my body. I should say something in reply, but nothing comes out.

'Sorry, I shouldn't have said that. I don't want to put any pressure on you, but I really do mean it. I thought I was over you, Eve, but I never really was.'

'Neither was I,' I say. 'I just… blocked it all out. Kayla being taken made me realise, though, that it's just me and you and our little girl. That's all that's important to me.'

'So, this Jamie – it really is over then?'

'Yes,' I say, squeezing Aiden's hand, while outside rain begins to splatter against the windscreen.

'Are you sure you'll be okay?' Aiden asks. 'I could try to get out of going to work. You just seem a bit… down.'

Maybe I haven't been doing a good enough job of hiding my suspicion. 'No, I'm fine, honestly. I just want Kayla back, that's all.'

When we pull up at the house, I have to hold myself back from rushing inside. If I can just act normally then everything will be okay.

As I wave goodbye to him and step inside, sadness fills my heart. How can the man I once loved have become someone I cannot trust?

—

Inside, I watch Aiden drive off and I lock the front door. If he comes back for any reason I will say that I heard noises and got worried. Now I can search the house with no fear of him catching me.

There's no need to check the kitchen; over the last three months I've come to know every inch of space in there, and there's nothing that isn't meant to be in a kitchen. There isn't even a drawer for junk or papers, so Aiden must keep everything in the bedroom or the desk in the spare room. Although I've been sleeping in the spare room – other than the night before last – I don't think Aiden would leave anything he didn't want me to find under my nose. Come to think of it, he's too smart to have anything in the house at all, especially as he has no problem leaving me here alone, so my search is probably futile.

In the bedroom, I open the wardrobe and find no evidence Nicole even lived here. None of her clothes hang from the rails, and all I can find that might be hers is a pink and grey checked wool scarf. Strange, given that I'd heard Aiden telling the police Nicole had hardly taken anything to her sister's, therefore he'd expected her to come back and collect everything else.

I wasn't always here when Kayla first went missing; Aiden preferred to deal with the police alone and it's only now that it seems significant. Was it deliberate? If so, why?

By the time I've checked every room upstairs, including the bathroom, I'm certain that this house doesn't hold any answers.

My phone vibrates in my pocket, and I pull it out, expecting it to be Aiden. It's not though, it's Maya.

> Are you okay? Have the police heard anything? Did you confront your ex?

Yesterday at Connor's flat, when I showed him Aiden's Facebook profile, I didn't let on that he was my daughter's father, the man I married, and neither Connor nor Maya would have realised. Maya only knows me as Eve Martin – my maiden name – so the surname Conway wouldn't have meant anything to her. When they asked who he was, the lie slipped easily from my tongue – just a disgruntled ex. Nobody I had anything to do with any more. I don't know if they believed me but they didn't ask any questions. After determining who had smashed my car, they were too busy discussing Maya's decision.

I send a reply immediately.

> Not yet. Thanks for your help anyway. Both of you. I hope you two can be okay with each other.

Within seconds, Maya has replied.

> Actually, funny story, but after you left we talked for hours and we're kind of sorting things. Doesn't feel good to be on bad terms with him.

Reading this brings a smile to my face. They might both be young but it's clear that they care deeply for one another. I send back three smiley faces and then it hits me.

There is someone who can help me. If they can only find a way to forgive me.

FORTY-THREE

Now

I'm not prepared for how I'll feel when I see him standing in front of me, the questioning look on his face which only makes him more attractive. For a few seconds we both stare at each other until he breaks the silence. 'What are you doing here?'

'I'm so sorry, Jamie, but I had to come. I know you probably don't want me inside your flat, so could we go somewhere to talk? It won't take long, I promise.'

He shakes his head. 'I said everything I had to say to you months ago, please don't do this.'

'No, you've got it all wrong. This isn't about our relationship.'

Now the frown appears once more. 'But there's nothing else we've got to say to each other.'

Jamie's leaving me no choice now – I'm going to have to tell him right here on his doorstep. 'My daughter is missing. And I really think you could help me if you could just spare me five minutes?'

It takes a moment for what I've said to sink in. 'Missing? That's awful. What happened?'

'Please, I'll tell you everything but can we just go somewhere and talk.'

Jamie's already patting his pockets and closing his door. 'The pub round the corner shouldn't be too busy. Come on.'

He won't let me buy the drinks and insists on getting them himself. I've only ordered an orange juice, and it feels wrong to let him spend even that amount on me with the way things were left between us, and the way I was during our relationship.

He sits opposite me and sips his beer while he waits for me to tell him what happened to Kayla three months ago. I hold back nothing, including the part about practically moving in with Aiden, because he needs to know this.

Jamie listens silently until I've finished, and when he opens his mouth to speak I half expect him to tell me he wants nothing to do with this.

'So wait, one minute he's telling you he wants you to spend time with your daughter and the next he's smashing your car windows. That doesn't make sense.'

I nod. 'I know. And then he denied that he'd done it. I don't know what to think.'

'This doesn't feel right, Eve.'

'That morning in Leicester Square, you never told me how you found out about me leaving Kayla those years ago. I need to know who told you. I need to know whether or not it was Aiden.'

Jamie's answer comes without hesitation. 'It wasn't him.'

'Then who?'

'It was Nicole Richardson.'

Shock momentarily paralyses me. 'You know Nicole?'

293

'Yes... I mean no, not really – she just came to my flat one night and said she knew you and needed to talk to me about you. She said she had some information that I'd want to hear.'

'You didn't know her then? And you let her into your flat?' This doesn't sound like something Jamie would do. He's too cautious, too sensible.

'She had a photo on her phone – of you and a little girl – and said it was really important that she talked to me. Then she started crying and begging so I just... let her in.' He stops and waits for me to say something.

I can't be annoyed with him; I know how Nicole comes across. There's nothing disturbing about her, so it's understandable that Jamie wouldn't have been nervous about letting her into his home. 'Then what happened?'

He puts down his beer, and as he talks his eyes glance to the left. I remember reading somewhere that this is a sign of someone recalling a memory, a signal that they're telling the truth. After everything that's happened lately it feels as though I'll never trust anyone again, but at least I can still believe in Jamie. 'I got her some water,' he is saying. 'She just seemed so distraught. And then when she calmed down, she told me how you were married to her partner. Aiden. I knew she was telling the truth because you'd mentioned him before. She went on to tell me about Kayla, and as you can imagine, it was like a punch to my gut. I mean, I knew you were a bit of a closed book, but I had no idea your past was so...'

I look away. 'I know, you don't need to say it.'

'She said you were trying to get Kayla back, and she convinced me that you wanted Aiden back as well. That you wanted to be a family again. She made out that you'd stop at nothing to make this happen.'

It's all starting to make sense now. Jamie is a reasonable man; he would have heard me out and listened to my reasons for leaving, unless he believed I wanted to be with someone else, that our relationship really was dead. Sadness overwhelms me – Jamie should never have been hurt like this. 'That wasn't true at all,' I tell him. 'I promise you.'

He doesn't respond. 'I'm so sorry, Eve. If I'd have just told you when you asked me then maybe she wouldn't have had a chance to take your daughter.'

'It's not your fault,' I say. 'She would have found a way.'

Jamie's eyes widen. 'I've just thought of something. If Aiden smashed up your car and then the next minute turned up at your place telling you he wanted to let you see your daughter, doesn't that suggest he had something planned?'

'What do you mean?' But even as I ask this, I think I already know the answer.

'Your daughter. What if he had no intention of letting you see her? What if he and Nicole arranged this whole thing?'

Hearing this, I am frozen. 'No… it can't be that.'

'How can you be sure?'

'I can't. But I need evidence.'

'Then get it,' Jamie tells me. 'I hope I'm wrong, but you need to at least find out for sure.'

'I'm just going to keep an eye on him,' I say. 'If, by any chance, he knows where Kayla is then he'll slip up. He's bound to. If I keep pushing him and getting him to do things he'll find hard when he knows Kayla isn't really missing, then he's bound to weaken. Lies can't be sustained forever.' This thought turns me cold. Sooner or later I will have to face my own.

'But you need to be careful. If you have any feelings for him—'

'I don't! I never wanted him back. I only ever wanted my daughter back in my life.'

Jamie doesn't look convinced. 'You ended up practically living with him – can you understand how that looks?'

'Yes, I can, but there's nothing there. I did love him once, but we were over long before I walked out.' Saying that out loud feels like I've been cleansed. I can finally admit what I've been unable to: that Aiden and I never stood a chance. 'What reason would I have to lie to you about that now? Like I said, I'm not here to try and worm my way back into your life. I only want to find my daughter. Please, trust me, Jamie, like I have to trust you. There's nobody else I can talk to about this.'

'What about that friend who came to your flat that time?' he asks. 'The time you couldn't wait to get me out the door.'

'I'm sorry for that. Sophie was my closest friend before I left Kayla and Aiden. We taught at the same school.'

'Did she know you were leaving?'

'No. I didn't tell a single person. I couldn't. It was like I was sleepwalking through my life.'

'Hmm. That would explain why she seemed so angry with you.'

I'm surprised that Jamie noticed this in the few minutes he was in Sophie's presence. I haven't given him enough credit for the perceptive and intelligent man that he is.

Again, I'm filled with sadness that I couldn't be enough for him.

'I got back in touch with her to see if she could help me get in contact with Kayla. Understandably she wasn't happy. I betrayed our friendship by leaving, and she also saw Aiden at his lowest. She and her partner Damien helped to pick up the pieces. I lost more than just my family when I left.'

'Can you talk to her now?' Jamie suggests. 'If you were so close once, surely she'd believe you about what Aiden's doing. Maybe she can help somehow?'

'I don't want to drag Sophie into this, it's not fair on her. When this is over and Kayla is found, I hope Sophie and I will be able to have some sort of friendship. For now, though, I have to leave her alone.' I won't hold out too much hope of this friendship, though – maybe sometimes it's just too late to go back.

In the midst of thinking about this, something occurs to me. 'Hold on, I've had a thought. The one thing I know for sure about Aiden is that he loves Kayla. There's no way, if you're right about everything, that he wouldn't have seen her these last three months. No way. Even if she's with Nicole. It would devastate her to be away from him, and he wouldn't put her though that. I know that for a fact.'

Jamie frowns. 'Are you sure? It sounds like he can't be trusted. He wouldn't want the police finding out, so he probably wouldn't risk seeing her. What he's doing is a crime, and he won't want to end up in prison.'

'That's just it – the police aren't looking at him, or me. In the beginning they had to make sure we weren't involved, but I know they don't suspect either of us now.

This gives Aiden free rein to do whatever he wants and go wherever he likes.' I think about all the late meetings he's had lately, all the urgent times he's been called into work, even though he was meant to take time off. Could Jamie be right?

'That's how I'm going to find her. Aiden will lead me right to her.'

'I don't know about this, Eve. You need to be careful. I don't like the sound of it.'

'All I need to do is get a photo or video of him meeting up with Kayla or Nicole. He'll never even know I'm there. That should be enough to convince the police he's been lying to them. They'll do the rest.'

'Okay,' Jamie says. 'I can see I'm not going to talk you out of this, am I?'

'Not when this involves getting my daughter back.'

He stares at me for a long time. 'It's so hard to work you out,' he says eventually. 'Part of me thinks I should still hate you for lying to me, but then part of me believes you must have had good reason because you just don't deliberately hurt people. That's not who you are.'

I should tell Jamie everything, even though we are no longer together, and finally rid myself of what's been burning inside me all this time, eating away at me and destroying me piece by tiny piece. If anyone would understand, it's him. As always though, just thinking about talking causes me to shut down.

'Thanks for saying that,' I say. 'It means a lot to me.' Even though we're no longer together, I somehow feel comfortable with Jamie, right now in this moment, more than I ever did before. It's the lies which form the barrier.

'Will you let me do it?' Jamie asks as I stand up to leave.

'Do what?'

'Keep an eye on Aiden. Maybe I can follow him? He doesn't know me, does he? It might be safer.'

It takes less than a second for me to consider this. 'Thanks, but I need to do this by myself. I'm the one who set this in motion when I left those years ago, so I'm the one who needs to put this right. For my daughter.' And I won't drag Jamie into my mess.

'At least keep me updated then. Every day.'

I promise to do this and, just as we say goodbye and I step outside the pub, my phone beeps. It's a text from Aiden.

> Where are you? I just got home and you're not here. Worried about you.

His words should fill me with fear, but all they do is fuel my determination.

I'm going to find out the truth.

And get my daughter back.

FORTY-FOUR

Now

For three days Aiden doesn't leave the house. It's as if he knows that I'm suspicious of him – even though my rational brain tells me this is impossible. Even if he somehow found out I'd gone to Jamie's a few days ago, he could only assume that I might still have feelings for him, not that we were piecing together what might have happened to Kayla.

'I can't face work,' Aiden tells me. 'I think it's all finally caught up with me and I need a break. I want to spend time with you. You don't have to go back to your flat for a while, do you? Being with you makes me feel closer to Kayla.'

As I listen to him – these words that would ordinarily melt my heart – I wonder if it's possible that he became such an accomplished liar. I tell him I don't need to go home. This is exactly where I need to be.

With each passing hour I begin to feel claustrophobic, a prisoner who can't escape even though the door is wide open. Does Aiden want it this way? Is he enjoying it? If he does know where Kayla is then inflicting emotional pain on me must be his endgame, to get me back for leaving him. Despite how heinous this makes him, I can't believe that he would hurt me physically, even though the more I think about it, the more I wonder if he wants me out of the way somehow. There can be no other reason he's doing this. He could have just disappeared with Nicole and Kayla, so why else would he stay to put on this sinister show? I am a threat to his life with Nicole and Kayla; he knows that if I took this to court, I would have every right to see my daughter. He had every chance for us to work together, yet ultimately he didn't want me to spend even a second with Kayla.

Paranoia sets in. What if having me out of the way is his only option?

In the harsh light of day, it's easy to convince myself this is nonsense – that of course Aiden would never hurt anyone. I try to cling on to this thought. He is just a father desperate for his daughter back, a man who still loves the mother of his child.

On the fourth day, I grow increasingly uncomfortable, until respite finally comes. The police need Aiden to come down to the station to check some CCTV footage, to rule out a possible sighting of Nicole. Since Kayla's disappearance was on the local news, there have been plenty of false alarms, and I have no doubt that this is yet another one. It will get Aiden out of the house for a couple of hours, though, and that's exactly what I need.

–

Renting a car was Jamie's idea. He would have lent me his, but we can't take the chance that Nicole saw it outside his flat when she turned up on his doorstep. This is the safest way for me to follow Aiden, and as soon as he announces that he's going somewhere, I will be right behind him.

At the rental place, I pick a black Ford Focus, a popular car that shouldn't attract attention. It's very different to drive than my Peugeot, so I drive around for a while, making sure I'm completely comfortable with it, and that Aiden is still at work, before I park it on our road.

–

'How did it go?' I ask when Aiden gets home around half an hour after me.

He peels off his coat. 'It wasn't her,' he says. 'I really had my hopes up this time, but no – the woman on camera definitely wasn't Nicole. Too tall. I suppose I can see why they thought it was her. She looked about the same build, but it definitely wasn't.'

I hand him a glass of wine and tell him not to be disheartened. 'We'll find her. I have no doubt in my mind about that.'

Oblivious to what I really mean, Aiden pulls me towards him and buries his head in my hair, breathing in my scent. I force myself to hold him when what I really want to do is shove him away, demand the truth.

'Will you stay with us once we find her?' he whispers. 'That's what you want, isn't it? For us all to be together?'

'That's what I want.' I have no trouble getting the words out because I'm determined to win this battle.

But when he pulls back, his mouth searching for mine, it's a struggle to react. Do this for Kayla, I tell myself, but after only a couple of seconds I pull away, faking a cough. 'Sorry,' I say. 'Think I need some water.'

He stares at me, and for a moment I feel as though he can see into my mind. 'Thanks for the wine but I'll have to have it later. Work called when I was at the police station. They need me to go in for a couple of hours.'

Is he telling the truth? I can't help but question him. 'I thought you were having a break?'

'I am. I will. This is important though. Nobody else can do it.'

'Okay,' I say.

Here we go. This is it.

—

Following Aiden as he drives, I start to believe that he *is* actually going to work. He's heading in the direction of Chiswick, and I envisage myself turning back around, admonishing myself for thinking the worst of him. Then everything changes when he makes a right turn and heads in the opposite direction from his office.

I continue at a safe distance, even though he won't know this car. I've got my hair tied up and sunglasses on, just in case he does notice someone trailing him.

It's over half an hour before he pulls into a road and begins to slow down. My heart hammers in my chest. Is Kayla only metres away from me? Something occurs to me, erasing any hope: unless he takes Kayla out somewhere, it will be impossible to get a photo of the two of them together. And I will need evidence. It's the middle of the day, so there's no way I can sneak up to any windows without being seen.

Aiden stops outside one of the houses and reverses into a parking space out front. There's no off-street parking on this road, so I need to keep driving past, otherwise he'll notice me, yet if I carry on, I'll lose sight of where he's going. There's no guarantee he's heading into the house he's parked outside.

Fate is with me today, and by the time I've doubled back, he is knocking on the dark red door of the house I assumed it would be. I've driven past before I can see who lets him in, or if he has his own keys, but this is progress. Proof that I'm not just being paranoid.

Parking across the road, further down but close enough to see when Aiden leaves, I slide down in my seat and call Jamie.

'I followed him,' I say. 'Right now I'm parked outside a house in Hayes, and Aiden's just gone inside. He told me he was going to work.'

'That was quick,' Jamie says. 'I was thinking this could go on for weeks. Months even.'

These last few days have felt anything but quick for me. 'What if Kayla's in there, Jamie?'

He must sense the adrenalin coursing through me. 'Okay, just slow down, though. Let's think. Are you sure there's nothing else he could be doing? Visiting friends or something?'

'He would have said. If this was all innocent then he wouldn't have told me he was going to work.'

'True. It doesn't look good.'

'I need evidence that I can take to the police. A photo of him with Nicole or Kayla.'

'How are you going to do that without being seen? It's the middle of the day.'

'I know. And Aiden or Nicole might not walk out with Kayla.'

'Just call the police,' Jamie says. 'If Kayla is in there then they'll soon find her.'

'I need to be sure before I go to them. Just in case we're wrong. What if he's seeing some woman and doesn't want me to know? I can't mess this up, Jamie. I've got one chance to get this right.'

'Hmm. Have you thought about what will happen after? With Kayla, I mean. You can't just announce that you're her mum and expect she'll be allowed to live with you.'

His words sting, but he's speaking the truth. 'I haven't worked it all out. I know it won't be easy, but there'll be a way. There's no way Aiden and Nicole are fit to be her carers after this.'

'True, but you'll have a lot of bureaucracy to deal with. Just don't get your hopes up.'

Jamie doesn't need to tell me this; I know that if Aiden has any part in Kayla's disappearance then it doesn't just erase my past, or guarantee that my future with Kayla will be without extreme challenges. 'I won't. I just want her back, Jamie. Even if I'm not the one she'll live with for now.'

'It's funny,' Jamie says. 'I feel like I've learned more about you in the last few days than I did the whole time we were together. All it takes is honesty, right?'

I fight back a tear that tries to break free.

It's over two hours before Aiden emerges. Alone. From this distance it's impossible to read his expression. As I've assumed, there will be no chance to get a photo – not even one from this distance.

He's walking briskly to his car, and I need to get out of here and beat him home before he asks questions about where I've been. Rush hour traffic will make this a tough game to win, especially as Aiden will know these roads and any shortcuts better than I do, but I stick to the same route Aiden used to get here, assuming that is the quickest way.

–

Once again, fate is rooting for me today and I make it home before Aiden. I hunt through the fridge to see if there's anything I can cobble together for dinner, anything to make it look like I've been busy at home. Lentils, chopped tomatoes and spaghetti are all I can find that can be thrown together; it will taste bland without anything to flavour it, but it's the best I can do. One thing for sure is that Aiden won't protest about it; he's still hardly eating at home under the pretence of worrying about Kayla. I imagine he fills himself up when he's away from the house.

When Aiden still isn't home by the time the food is nearly ready, I begin to think I left him too early. What if that house was nothing to do with Kayla, and he's gone straight to her afterwards? Another house, somewhere else. I'm about to throw the food in the bin and go back to Hayes when I hear the front door open, and Aiden calling to me.

'Hey,' he says, walking into the kitchen. 'That smells good. What is it?'

'A veggie spaghetti thing,' I say, trying to scrutinise his tone, analyse each word he speaks.

'How did you know I'd be back now?'

An oversight. I need to be more careful. 'I didn't. I was going to just have mine and keep yours warm.'

He eyes the food, and any second now he will tell me that spaghetti can't be kept warm or reheated, that you have to eat it straightaway.

'Thanks,' he says.

'How was work?'

'Tough day, actually. Too many meetings. I was stuck in the office all day and didn't even have time for a lunch break.'

He delivers his lie flawlessly, moving across to me and leaning in to kiss me. I turn my head so he catches no more than my cheek. 'I'm actually feeling quite hungry,' he continues. 'I'd forgotten what having an appetite feels like.'

'Don't beat yourself up,' I say. 'Marianne explained that it's completely normal to do everyday things, even to enjoy doing them. It doesn't mean we don't love and miss Kayla.'

'You always know what to say,' he says. 'I'd forgotten that about you. Forgotten how strong you are.'

I have no idea what he's playing at by saying this. Is it all just part of the game to make me feel secure with him? To have me believe that he loves me? 'Strong enough that I left?' I ask, baiting him. He will have no idea what it took for me to walk out of the door that night, and to set up my life of isolation.

'Let's not talk about the past,' he says. 'Focus on now, that's all that matters. They will find her, Eve, I'm convinced of it. There are only so many places Nicole will be able to hide.'

I have to hand it to Aiden, if I didn't know the truth I would fall for every word he says. Telling me that the past no longer matters would be all I'd have needed to hear. Validation. Except that it could never have been enough, not when the past is really *all* that matters. Especially now.

'Are you going into work tomorrow?' I ask Aiden as we eat dinner. The food hasn't turned out too badly after I added far too much salt and pepper.

'Yeah, I'll have to. There's only so much time I can take off. I know I said I needed a break, but being in the office today showed me how much I'll get behind if I don't go in. I'm sorry, we'll still have plenty of time together, though, won't we?'

All I can manage is a nod, a smile that dies as soon as he looks away.

I will follow you tomorrow. Make sure that really is where you're going, and then I've got somewhere of my own to visit.

'I think I'll get in touch with the counsellor Marianne recommended. Talk it all through. Are you planning to see her, too?'

Aiden smiles. 'They've arranged for me to see someone at work. It will be easier for me to do it in my lunch break.'

Of course you will. That way I will have no idea that you're not actually going to anyone.

'Good. We both need to stay strong for Kayla, don't we?'

'Like I said, Eve, that's what you are.' There's darkness in his tone when he says this, and I'm sure it's not just me reading too much into every word. That can't be the case when every word he produces must be a lie.

I offer to clear away after dinner, but Aiden tells me to leave it. 'Why don't we have an early night?' he says.

My body freezes; I know exactly what he means, and I'm running out of excuses for keeping my distance. 'My period's just started,' I blurt out, even though it's not due for another week. Even when we were married, Aiden had no clue about where I was in my cycle; it was always up to me to tell him when we needed to try each month. I only hope he remains oblivious now.

'Okay, no problem,' he says. 'It was just what you said earlier that got me thinking. About Marianne saying it's okay for us to still enjoy things. Don't worry, though, we've got plenty of time, haven't we?'

I nod and smile, try to contain my nausea.

Aiden starts clearing up while I head upstairs and get ready for bed. When I slide under the covers, I listen to the sounds of him clanging around downstairs.

The next thing I know is that the house is silent except for Aiden's light breathing somewhere close by. He's standing by the door watching me; I can feel it without opening my eyes.

FORTY-FIVE

Now

Morning can't come quickly enough, and I wait for Aiden to leave for work, listening to the sound of him showering and brushing his teeth. Domestic noises that hint at normality, the mundane even. But underlying that is the menacing sense of time running out. One thing last night has taught me is that I can't keep up this act for much longer, not without sacrificing the core of my being. And I will never do that.

I'd closed my eyes while he stood at the door, feigning sleep as I'd done before, but this time waiting to hear his footsteps coming towards me. That would have been it – I would have fought with every fibre within me, even though that would have signalled the end of whatever sick game this is he's playing.

If it had ended there and then, at least I would have come to know what he's planning to do, his hand forced unexpectedly. But here I am, ready to fight another day.

And now, once again, I pretend to be asleep when he pokes his head around the door to say goodbye. 'See you later,' he whispers, the thoughtful act making me shudder.

As soon as I hear the front door shut, I jump up, already fully dressed and ready to go. I can't lose sight of him; I need to know whether he really is going to work. When I knock on that door, it's Nicole I want to deal with, not Aiden, not yet.

Surprisingly, Aiden is telling the truth this time, but I park and wait until I see him walking into his office building, just to make sure.

–

Commuter traffic slows my journey considerably, so it takes almost an hour to get to the house in Hayes. Now that I don't have to worry about Aiden spotting me, I can pause to take in every detail of it. It's similar to Aiden's and looks like an innocuous family home, not the kind of place that harbours an abducted child.

As I'm about to get out of the car, Jamie texts to ask how it's going. I tell him that I'm prepared to face Nicole, but inside I wonder if this is true. I don't know how she's going to react to seeing me. Will she become violent? Surely not with Kayla in the house. All I have to do is keep her talking, though, and with my phone inside my pocket be ready to dial 999.

I repeat this plan in my mind as I head to the front door, my head held high. I'm not the one in the wrong this time; I have every right to hunt for my daughter.

Outside the house, the enormity of what I'm about to face hits me. I don't know what Nicole's capable of – or Aiden. Stifling my fear, I keep my focus on Kayla.

My heavy knock on the door seems to reverberate around the quiet street. Seconds tick by and nothing happens, until a shadow appears through the mottled glass panel. I draw in a deep breath.

'What are *you* doing here?'

My eyes take too long to tell my brain who I'm staring at; none of this makes sense.

'Well, say something! What are you doing here?'

Marie. Aiden's mother. Not Nicole. What is *she* doing here?

Somehow amidst the fug of scenarios my mind is conjuring up, I manage to speak. 'Where's Kayla? I want to see my daughter. Now.'

Marie frowns. 'What's going on? Why are you asking us about Kayla? How could we possibly know where she is? Are you…?' She turns around and shouts into the house. 'Pete? Eve's here and she's asking about Kayla. I think she might be having… an episode or something?'

Hearing her speak about me like this causes me to become alert. 'Marie, I'm completely fine, I just want to know where my daughter is.'

Pete hurries to the door and stands beside his wife. My parents-in-law. They still are, whether any of us likes it or not. 'Maybe you'd better come in,' he says, gently nudging Marie aside.

I don't hesitate to go inside, despite the fact that I already know Kayla isn't here. They wouldn't be letting me in if she was. Following Pete into the lounge, I'm struck by how similar this place feels to the home they had in Scotland. The layout of the furniture is identical, and I recognise many of the ornaments and paintings hanging on the walls.

'When did you move from Edinburgh?' There are so many questions I need answering and this seems like the best starting place. I don't know which one of them I'm addressing. Either. Both. It doesn't matter.

Pete glances at Marie before speaking. 'Around a year ago. We wanted to be closer to Aiden and Kayla. We would have come sooner but it took us a long time to sell our house.'

Aiden never mentioned this. Neither did Sophie, and she must have known they'd moved back here. I even remember her mentioning them. It's not surprising that Aiden has lied, but why would Sophie? I don't believe she knows anything about Kayla's disappearance; I've got to have faith that not everyone is rotten to the core.

'Maybe you should sit down, you look a bit pale,' Marie says, and again I catch a glance passing between the two of them. 'Pete, can you get her some water? She doesn't look good.'

I came here prepared to find my daughter, and now I'm confronted with this. I have no idea what to make of anything, no idea where to start.

When Pete hurries off to the kitchen, Marie turns back to me. 'You're shocked that Aiden didn't tell you about us moving back, aren't you? Well, you can't blame him. We told him we wanted nothing to do with you. Not after what you did to your little girl. To *our* Kayla.'

Nothing Marie says makes anything clearer. 'Did you know I was back?'

She nods. 'Aiden told us everything. We even know you've been spending a lot of time together since Kayla was taken, and I'm going to be blunt – I advised Aiden against it. It's obvious Nicole took Kayla and ran because she was scared of losing the little girl she's brought up since she was a baby. In a way, you forced her hand by turning up like that. She probably thought you were after Aiden too, and let's face it, that's exactly what it looks like now.' She finally pauses for breath.

Part of me understands Marie's resentment. Aiden was neglected by his birth mother, so it's no wonder she's trying to picture things from Nicole's perspective. Still, I must defend myself because I am nothing like the woman who Aiden was taken away from. 'That's not how it happened, Marie. And I was never trying to take Kayla away from either of them. I just wanted my daughter back in my life, however that was possible. Don't I have that right? I'm her *mother*.'

Marie shakes her head. 'And Aiden's her father. But now look what's happened. Even Aiden doesn't have her. This is all your fault, Eve. You should never have come back.' There are tears in her eyes now, convincing me that she doesn't know where Kayla is. Aiden must have kept it from them too, probably assuming they would never accept him doing this. No matter how much they despise me, it would go against everything they believe in morally.

'I'm sorry I hurt you all,' I say, handing Marie a tissue from the pack in my pocket.

She takes it and dabs her eyes. 'Do you know what this did to Aiden? You walking away from your baby, just like his birth mother did to him! Twice! How could you do that?'

'Wait, what do you mean twice?'

'You know what I mean. That heartless woman ripped our boy to shreds again. And the second time he was old enough to be totally scarred by it.'

Although I have no idea what Marie is talking about, I need her to believe I do, so that she'll keep talking. 'I know it was awful—'

'Eight years old! And he was so excited to meet her. We went through so much just to arrange it all, and that evil woman told him she didn't want anything to do with him, and that he should stop thinking of her as a mum because he meant nothing to her.' Marie shakes her head, her face now red with anger. 'I mean, she could have just ignored our requests for a meeting; she didn't have to say all that stuff to him. And that's not even all of it, is it? I can't even bring myself to repeat what else she said before the social worker dragged her away. It took years of counselling for Aiden to come to terms with it all.'

I'm stunned into silence. Aiden has never told me any of this, and he's never shown anything but a healthy attitude towards his adoption and what led up to it. He always said he'd been so young that he never knew any different.

'So how you could do that to your own daughter, which amounts to the same kind of thing, I don't know,' Marie is saying. She pauses. 'Aiden said you had postnatal depression?'

'Yes. I didn't really know it at the time but I... wasn't in my right mind.'

'You could have talked to us, Eve. To me. I understand how hard it is raising a baby. I know we weren't there for Aiden's newborn days but being a parent to a child of any age is a challenge. I could have helped you.'

For a brief moment I forget the man Aiden has become and remember how he was. 'You coming into his life was the best thing that ever happened to him,' I tell her.

Marie doesn't thank me for this compliment, perhaps she feels I'm not worthy of issuing one. 'It wasn't easy, though,' she says. 'Nothing worth having ever is.'

Pete returns and hands me a glass of water. Out of politeness I drink some of it, even though I'm not thirsty. He sits down next to me and shakes his head. 'Now why on earth would you think we know where Kayla is? Can you understand how strange that sounds?' His tone is gentle, reminding me how kind the two of them always were to me, how much they welcomed me into their family.

'I followed Aiden here yesterday. I was convinced he was lying to me, telling me he was going to work when he wasn't.'

Marie sighs. 'Yes, dear, he *was* lying to you. Because we insisted on having nothing to do with you. He thought it was easier this way. But why on earth would you think he knows where Kayla is? Did you think she was *here*? That we were actually hiding her?'

Hearing this spoken aloud makes me realise how improbable it sounds. Have I been so desperate to believe I will see Kayla again that my mind has concocted this story about Aiden? But the evidence was there: he smashed the windows of my car, and Nicole had insisted that he'd been at home that whole evening. *Circumstantial at best.*

'Aiden is devastated about Kayla,' Marie adds. 'He's even more broken than when you left, and believe me, that cut him to pieces. He's never been the same since. And now he has to deal with Nicole betraying him, too. He doesn't deserve all this, he's a good man. He's only ever wanted to do right by Kayla.'

'I don't know what to think right now,' I admit. 'It's been a bit of a shock finding out you both live here.'

'And seeing you has taken *us* by surprise too,' Marie says. 'Tell me something, Eve. Do you love our son?'

Not any more. It's impossible. 'I would never hurt Aiden again,' I say. 'I promise you that.'

They both turn to each other again, and I wish there was a way to know what they were thinking.

'Well, you and Aiden have a lot of talking to do,' Marie says. 'When Kayla comes back to us – and I do believe Nicole will do the right thing eventually – there's a lot you'll need to work out.'

'Yes, I know.' Then something occurs to me. 'Look, I have no right to ask this but could you just do something for me? Please don't tell Aiden I came here. I promise I'll talk to him myself, but I just need it to come from me.'

Marie turns to Pete and frowns. 'I don't know, Eve, so many lies have already been told.'

'I will talk to him as soon as he gets home from work. All I'm asking is that you don't call him in the meantime.'

'We can do that,' Pete says.

Marie shakes her head. 'But—'

'She's still Kayla's mum,' he says. 'And the two of them have a lot to sort out.'

We all fall silent, and it feels as though for now, at least, there's nothing left to say. I tell them I need to go, and neither of them object.

–

In the car I call Jamie and tell him what's just happened.

'Well, this is weird. What does it mean?' he asks.

'I don't know. It doesn't look like Aiden's hiding Kayla, though. But I can't be sure about anything any more. I honestly don't know what to think.'

Jamie falls silent. 'I don't like this, Eve. It's all a bit strange and I'm worried about you.'

'You don't need to be,' I assure him. 'I'm made of titanium you know!' I force this joke even though I'm sure neither of us is in the mood for humour.

'What will you do now then?' Jamie asks.

'Go back to Aiden's. Act like normal. I'd rather go to my flat but I can't rest until I'm one hundred per cent sure he's not guilty of anything. Maybe I'll follow him again tomorrow and see. That's the only way to know for sure, isn't it?'

'Yeah, I suppose you have no choice.' He sounds just as disappointed as I am.

'I really thought I'd find her today, Jamie. I feel crushed that I'm no closer.'

'Don't give up,' he says. 'Eve Martin doesn't quit, does she?'

–

When I get back to Aiden's there's no sign of his car. I let myself in with the key that he so readily gave me and dump my bag on the console table. I head to the kitchen, unable to think further than making myself a strong coffee, and when I reach the door my heart almost stops when I see Aiden sitting at the table, staring at me, his arms folded. There's no phone or laptop on the table; it's as if he's been doing nothing but wait for me to walk in.

FORTY-SIX

Now

'I got back early,' he says. 'Where have you been?'

'I went to Westfield.' I have no idea why this, of all places, shoots into my head. I've never been there, and it's unlikely Aiden will believe I've spent an afternoon shopping.

Aiden nods. 'Really? Did you get the Tube?'

'No, I drove, why?'

'Your car was outside when I got home.' He says this so calmly, and somehow that just makes it more sinister.

To my relief an excuse pops into my head, as if it's been there all along, just waiting for the moment to be extracted. 'My car's been playing up so I hired one. I need to be able to get around easily. Continue looking for Kayla.'

There's no way he'll believe this; all of a sudden it feels as though this game of cat and mouse has tipped heavily in his favour.

'You didn't mention it.'

'I know... I just—'

'Oh, I'm sorry,' he says. 'I didn't mean to sound like I don't trust you. I do, you know. Even after everything. It's not fair of me to do that to you, though. I'll really try to work on that, I promise.'

Relief. Everything might be okay. He just has trouble believing I won't leave again.

'What will you do tonight?' he asks.

Planning what I will do next, how I can find Kayla now that I'm not sure Aiden is responsible for her disappearance. 'Not much,' I say. 'A coffee. Bath. Try to read a book. Why?'

'Will you come somewhere with me? There's something I want to show you.'

'What is it?'

He smiles. 'I can't tell you yet. That would ruin the surprise, wouldn't it? Please, just trust me.'

Doesn't Aiden remember that I never liked surprises? I need to know what I'm in for, every step of the way. His face is full of excitement, though, like a child who can't wait to show you something they've made especially for you, that they're sure you will love. 'Okay. Do I need to get ready or anything?'

'No, you're fine as you are. Come on, we'd better go now before the traffic gets any worse.'

–

We crawl through London, most of the time at a standstill because, despite our best efforts to leave the house immediately, it took over half an hour to get in the car. Marianne had called Aiden just as we were leaving, and I watched him closely as he spoke, trying to analyse every twitch of his facial muscles, the cadence of his words, trying to find something to latch onto that would help me know.

But it was no longer there – that confidence I felt that I had it all worked out. Now I was just out to sea – adrift and unsure what to make of anything. Aiden had ended the call by telling Marianne he'd see her tomorrow. 'Another possible sighting,' he'd explained.

This is another reason to believe I'm wrong about Aiden; Marianne has spent enough time with him, surely she would suspect something if there was anything there at all. She would know if he was lying, wouldn't she?

'You're not going to tell me where we're going, are you?' I ask.

'I could,' he says. 'I really want it to be a surprise, though. Is that okay? I know you don't like surprises but can you just humour me?'

There's something different about Aiden's mood tonight; it's lighter, almost peaceful. All the tension seems to have slipped away. 'Something's changed,' I say, because I've never been one for keeping quiet about things that seem important. 'Did Marianne say something?'

'Actually, yes. She was really optimistic this time. Told me there's a good chance this eye witness really did see Nicole. I'm daring to believe it was her. Does that make me a fool?'

'No,' I say. 'But how come she didn't want to see us now? Surely we need to follow up on this lead as soon as possible?'

'She did want to see me tonight. But I told her we had to do something important first.'

There is no way Aiden wouldn't rush there immediately. Unless of course he already knows where Nicole and Kayla are. Have I made a terrible mistake by getting into this car? There's a chance I was right all along, and if so, now I've played right into Aiden's hands. I was blinded by Marie and Pete, unable to believe that they have any part in all of this, but what if they do? They could have told Aiden I'd been at the house.

I try to keep my voice steady. 'I didn't hear you saying that to her.'

'You went to the bathroom, remember? I must have said it then.'

'That's true,' I agree. I will play along with this, just as I did before, and let Aiden think I'm oblivious, at least until I can work out what to do.

Staring out of the car window, I try to control my shaking limbs. I turn up the radio, hoping the club music they've just started playing will somehow ease my nerves. We're on the North Circular now, moving faster, the road ahead clear because rush hour passed long ago. What am I heading towards? I consider quickly unbuckling my seat belt, throwing open the door and jumping out, but we're in the middle lane and there's no way I would come away without broken bones, or worse. Besides, this might be my chance to find out the truth, no matter what the cost to me.

'Do you remember when we first got married?' I ask, hoping that by bringing alive our shared story Aiden will think twice about whatever he's got planned. 'And we moved into our house in the same week? We sat on the floor with an Indian takeaway and couldn't believe we had our own place. We had barely any furniture. Paper plates and cups.' I chuckle. 'That night was one of the most special moments of my life.' This is no lie; it's one of the last times I remember feeling truly at peace with the world, that everything was as perfect as it was possible to be.

Aiden keeps his eyes fixed on the road but nods. 'Mine too. It feels like it was a calm before the storm, doesn't it? I mean with all the miscarriages.'

That seems like a lifetime ago, as if it's a story belonging to someone else, because ultimately Kayla came along far too easily. 'Yes,' I say, wondering where this is going. Every word Aiden speaks feels rigidly rehearsed, designed to evoke a specific reaction. Pain?

'Funny that you couldn't enjoy Kayla then. After going through all that heartache to finally hold her in your arms. You know, that's what I've never truly understood. It's not as if she was a mistake, was it? We'd tried for years to have her.'

It's coming now. Aiden's finally giving himself away. I haven't expected him to drop the pretence so quickly, especially when we're still driving. 'It's not as simple as that,' I say. 'Postnatal depression can affect any woman, regardless of their journey to motherhood.'

'You sound like a self-help book,' he says. 'Is that what you tell yourself to justify what you did?'

I hold my ground. 'No. I don't try to justify it. I try to make amends for it.'

He snorts. 'And is following people around, spying on them, how you do that?' He turns to me briefly. 'Oh, don't look so surprised. Did you think my parents wouldn't tell me you paid them a visit? For someone so intelligent, you really have shown some stupidity. Count-less times.'

'Finally, we can stop pretending,' I say. 'I'm actually relieved, Aiden, because I'm tired of your twisted mind games.'

He throws his head back. 'Games? This is no game, Eve. Unfortunately, this is real life, and you're just going to have to deal with it.'

I keep my eyes fixed on the road, my hands feeling for my seat belt. 'Tell me where you're taking me,' I demand, even though I already know he won't. This is part of the torture, letting my mind imagine all kinds of terrible scenarios.

'I'm actually doing you a favour,' he says, turning off the North Circular onto the M1. 'I'm going to give you the answer you've been looking for.'

Aiden falls silent after this, refusing to elaborate when I ask him what he means. Eventually I give up; all I can do now is wait for the right moment. I've tried to keep track of the route Aiden has taken so far, but all I can determine is that we're now far from London, far from anything familiar.

'I know you won't hurt me,' I say, even though I know nothing of the sort. 'Physically, I mean. Why would you risk going to prison when you've got a daughter to look after? That's your plan, isn't it? To scare me off so I leave you and Nicole alone to bring up Kayla.'

He snickers. 'You think you've got it all worked out, don't you?'

'I'm pretty sure I have now, yes.'

'Well, I have to warn you against assuming anything in life. It just doesn't get you anywhere. Look at me, I'm living proof of that. I assumed I had a loving wife, someone who cared for me and our daughter.'

Now's my chance; I've got to try. I reach into my pocket and feel for my phone, surprised to feel nothing but the fabric of my coat.

'Looking for this?' he says, reaching into the side of his door and pulling out my mobile. He winds his window down and tosses it out, as if he's discarding a piece of chewing gum.

People always talk about how vulnerable and lost they'd feel without their mobiles, but that's nothing compared to how I feel now, knowing that without my phone I have no way of getting help. Knowing that my life might depend on it. 'Do what you like to me, Aiden. All that matters is Kayla.'

'Oh, no, now you've ruined my surprise.'

'What are you talking about?'

'I'm taking you to Kayla, of course. But first it's your turn to answer some of my questions.'

FORTY-SEVEN

Now

We're in dense woodland, miles from the road we took off the motorway. And it's dark now, no street lights to guide us. Several times I shake my head in disbelief. This has got to be some sort of joke because it's too surreal to be anything else. I'm wearing the worst shoes for this type of environment: flat ballet pumps that are now crusted with mud. My feet have begun to blister. Aiden, I realise, is wearing hiking boots. How did I not notice this before? He's only ever in trainers when he's not working.

It sickens me that he's so sure of himself, so confident that I'll follow him that he doesn't even hang by my side, instead striding ahead and insisting I keep up. 'You want to see her, don't you?'

I won't though, I'm sure of that. Whatever we're doing out here, he's not bringing me to see Kayla. This should terrify me, but I feel only numb. I can handle whatever is coming. I will get out of this somehow.

Suddenly Aiden stops, and as I catch up with him he shoves me to the ground. My fall draws blood on my palms, and although I don't feel any pain his action has diminished me. 'This is as far as we go,' he says, hovering over me.

'So, what then? You're going to kill me? I think you've been watching too many Mafia films.'

He laughs then, his sinister chortle echoing around the trees. 'Why would I want to kill you? That wouldn't be a punishment, would it? No, you need to suffer much more than that. And there's only one thing I could think of that would hurt you above anything else.'

'What are you talking about?' But somehow, I already know. It's something I can't even begin to comprehend, but it all makes a hideous kind of sense now. Perhaps I even knew it the second he said he was bringing me to Kayla.

I just didn't want to believe it.

'Kayla!' I scream. 'You wouldn't! She's your daughter!' I try to jump up, but Aiden shoves me back down with his foot, the thud of pain winding me.

He points to a mound of fresh earth a few metres away, his mouth twisted into an evil snarl. 'But she's not, though, is she, Eve? And I think it's about time you told me the truth.'

FORTY-EIGHT

Before Kayla

It's taken me by surprise how much I've come to enjoy tutoring Justin Foley. I still stand by the fact that he doesn't need extra help, that he's one of those kids who could get the highest grades with no revision whatsoever. But if his father wants to splash out on these sessions, and Justin actually wants them, who am I to argue?

Besides, it's just another thing to take me away from having to face Aiden after I told him I didn't think I could go through with adoption. *At this time*, I'd said, because I didn't want to rule anything out for the future. After all, how do any of us know how we're going to feel about something given a bit of time? Things alter. People change.

Case in point: Alex Foley. Over the last few weeks, we've taken to chatting for a while after I tutor Justin, and he's gone up in my estimation. He somehow seems more human. Less frustrating. There's something about being in a person's home that can make you warm to them and see a side of them you can't glimpse from short interactions. In fact, I've learned things about him that shed light on his overbearing manner, almost make it understandable.

He's the head of a giant hedge fund company, and with that title comes huge responsibility for people's money, and for his employers. As well as this, he's a single father, bringing up Justin alone since his ex-wife moved to Paris for work. 'She does visit Justin whenever she can,' he explained, 'but it means all the day-to-day care is down to me. I won't get help, though. I'm determined to raise my son myself.' What's not to admire about that?

This evening, Justin seems distracted, his eyes darting to the huge Roman numeral clock on the kitchen wall every couple of minutes. I call it a kitchen but this room – which our whole house could fit inside – is more of an *everything* room. It has a sofa and TV, a dining table, and everything most people have spread throughout their homes. Considering Alex Foley's job, though, this place isn't too extravagant. 'You wouldn't believe this, but I don't really care about money,' he'd told me the first time I came here. 'They're so bloody right when they say it doesn't necessarily bring you happiness.'

'Justin, are you okay?' I ask. It's not like him to be so unfocused.

'Yeah, miss. It's just… well, I'm meeting this girl this evening. And I'm a bit nervous.'

I can't help but smile. 'What exactly is making you nervous?'

'Because she's beautiful, miss. Everyone's after her and I'm lucky she even looked at me. D'you know how many followers she's got on Instagram?'

Although I'm tempted, now is not the time to preach to him about the hazards of social media. Besides, for a sixteen-year-old, Justin seems to have his head firmly screwed on, something I believe is partly down to his dad.

'She's lucky too,' I say. 'Don't forget that.' And I mean it. It's easy to see that Justin is growing into a handsome young man, but he's also a decent human being. He's never in any trouble at school, and he's polite and friendly to everyone. A credit to his dad, even if I didn't want to acknowledge that in the beginning.

Justin beams, his cheeks turning puce. 'Thanks, miss.'

'I'll tell you what – how about we finish up now? You've worked hard for weeks, so I don't think losing ten minutes will make any difference. You can go and get ready.'

'Thanks, miss.' He gathers up his things and strides out of the room. It's then that I notice Alex hovering in the doorway. He pats Justin on the shoulder then heads over to me.

'We really appreciate all you're doing,' he says. 'You're really good with the students. You seem to care about them as people, not just as learners, if that makes any sense?'

'Teaching's not the easiest job in the world, so I wouldn't do it if I didn't genuinely care.'

'I'm guessing a lot of people do it for other reasons though. Maybe they just want the long holidays.'

'No one I've ever met went into it for that reason.'

Alex chuckles. 'That's what's refreshing about you, Eve. You're not afraid to disagree with me. To tell it like it is. Most people I'm around go along with whatever I say. I could be arguing that the earth is flat and they'll jump to agree.'

'Well, some people really do believe it *is* flat,' I say, packing up my pencil case.

Again, he laughs, and I'm surprised to find it pleases me that he finds me funny.

'Will you stay and have coffee?' he asks. 'Seeing as you've finished a bit early?'

Although I'm flattered by his invitation and pleased that he wants to spend time talking to me, I should get home to Aiden. I can't keep avoiding him; we need to address our future, and the fact that it will probably be a childless one.

'Maybe another time?' I offer. Weeks ago, I would have given a simple *no thank you*, and once again I'm caught off guard by the fact that I actually want to spend time talking to Alex.

'Please?' he asks. 'I find it very hard to de-stress after work, and it's nice to be able to chat with someone. I'll even stretch to some biscuits. How does that sound? Come on, surely I can tempt you with a Bourbon?'

Even though I should stand firm with my offer to postpone, I find myself saying yes. Another half hour can't hurt, and Aiden will still be at work for a few hours at least.

'Great,' Alex says. 'Let me get that coffee on.'

—

I'm far too relaxed here, sitting on the sofa with my legs tucked under me, as if I'm at Sophie's rather than the father of one of my students. Is it possible that I've come to think of Alex as a friend without realising it?

'So, who is Eve Conway?' he asks, looking at me intently.

'What do you mean?'

'Teachers always seem like people who give up their whole lives for their calling. I just wondered who you are beyond what you do. There's so much more to you, isn't there?'

Is there more to me? All I feel like is a woman who keeps losing babies. A woman who will end up childless. What more is there to me?

'I like your question,' I say. 'And I wish I had a good answer for it. I'm just not sure I even know who I am beyond being a teacher.'

'Oh, come on,' he says. 'You're a beautiful young woman – there's got to be so much more to you. In fact, I'm willing to bet there is, and you've probably worked out by now that I'm the type of man who only bets on things I can win.'

But I've stopped listening after he called me beautiful. It was thrown into the statement so casually, as if it was an indisputable fact, not just someone's opinion. Why does this warm my insides? I'm a married woman with a husband who loves her – a compliment from another man shouldn't make me feel this way. I need to fight back against these pointless and dangerous feelings. Show him I'm far from perfect.

'I'll tell you who I am,' I say. 'I'm a woman who can't have a baby. There you go, that's me.'

I've shocked him. He doesn't know what to say. 'Oh, I—'

'Even if I'm lucky enough to fall pregnant, I always miscarry, and there's no point in doing IVF because even if it works, I'll probably still lose the baby. I don't think I could put myself through that again. I think I'm done with it. I don't know, though. It's all up in the air.' The words spill from my mouth in a hurry, and I realise I've been desperate to say them out loud.

Alex grabs my hand. 'Okay. Well, firstly I think that's extremely brave of you to talk about. And secondly, I think you could do with a drink.'

—

The reason I keep talking is because Alex is listening. Really listening. We're alone in the house now; Justin has left to meet his girlfriend, and I'm sharing thoughts I've never before dared to give voice to.

'But you love your husband, and it sounds like he loves you. Why do you feel you can't be honest about adoption?' Alex asks.

'Because it's almost like a smack in the face for him. He was adopted, so what does it say when his own wife won't even consider it?'

'He'll understand.'

Alex can't know this, yet he speaks with such authority. I start to laugh.

'What's so funny?'

'Are you always so self-assured?'

'I have to be. I wouldn't be where I am today without having confidence. I'm not arrogant, though. Please don't think that.'

'I don't.' I laugh again. 'I did find you annoying to begin with, though.'

His eyes widen. 'Annoying? Not sure I've ever been called that before. But I can see why. I did harass you a bit about tutoring Justin, didn't I?'

'Just a bit.'

'I'm sorry. If you don't ask, you don't get, though.'

What must it be like to be Alex Foley? To assume that everything will always go your way. I ask him this.

'How else do you get what you want? Life's too short to sit by and wait for things to happen. You have to grab every opportunity you can. Grab it by the balls!'

I burst into laughter, and it feels so good. It's been a long time since I've been able to do this. 'Thanks for making me laugh,' I say.

Alex smiles. 'I aim to please,' he says. 'Admit it, I've taken your mind off everything, haven't I?'

'Yes. Somehow, weirdly, you have.'

He gets up from the chair he's sitting on and walks across to me, sitting beside me on the sofa. Then he is leaning forward, pushing my hair back from my face and whispering into my ear that I'm beautiful.

I jolt backwards. 'I have to go.' I try to stand but he gently pushes me backwards, leaning onto me, his weight against me, his mouth finding mine.

'No,' I say, but maybe it's not loud enough because he's not stopping. 'No!' Louder this time, but he's still not stopping, and instead he's lifting my skirt, pulling down my tights, his hands creeping up my legs. I freeze. Did I make him think I wanted this? What have I done?

'Get off me, Alex, just stop.' I lash out, thump his back, kick my legs as hard as I can, but he doesn't say a word as he treats my body as if it belongs to him, as if he can do what he likes, as if I want him to.

I scream, but it doesn't sound loud enough; it's not enough to stop him. I can feel him against me now, and then he's shoving himself inside me, ignoring my screams, perhaps even enjoying them.

Through a waterfall of tears, I bite down on his shoulder as hard as I can, taste his salty skin, try to inflict enough pain on him to make him stop, but it doesn't work. There is nothing I can do, no way to slip from under his weight. I am powerless.

My whole body freezes and I am forced to endure this for as long as Alex Foley wants it to last.

FORTY-NINE

Now

'No!' Aiden says, shaking his head. 'No, you're lying! You wanted to sleep with him... he didn't do that to you. You were going there for weeks, pretending to only be tutoring his son, when it was him you really wanted to see. He gave you attention and you enjoyed it! Well, now you'll get to know what it feels like to lose everything. You snatched my life from me, and the baby that was supposed to be mine. This is what you deserve.'

'I swear to you, Aiden – that man was a monster and he forced me. I'm sorry I didn't tell you. I'll regret that for the rest of my life,' I say, my voice catching on the final words.

'You took all choices away from me, and we were supposed to be in it together. Now I don't even have a daughter... how can Kayla mean anything to me now?'

I ignore him, glance at the mound of earth. The shallow grave he's brought me to. 'What have you done, Aiden? What did you do to Kayla? She's still your daughter. She's the little girl you brought up. What have you done to her?' I'm screaming now, unable to control my tears, my fear.

'Do you expect me to believe that you got pregnant after one time? One time that this man supposedly forced himself on you?'

But Aiden wavers now, and I can tell he doesn't believe his own words.

'Don't you think that's something I've asked myself over and over? How cruel fate was to make Kayla his and not yours? Do you think I *wanted* this? I would have done anything to change it.'

Aiden believes me, I know he does. He doesn't want to because of what it means, but he knows that I would never lie about this. 'I would never cheat on anyone,' I manage to say, even though I can't take my eyes off the place I believe Kayla is buried. 'Aiden, what the fuck have you done?'

He's slumped to the ground now, pulling at his hair. I rush over to the mound, tearing at the soil with my hands, my screams echoing through the woods. It feels like I'm getting nowhere, each small amount of earth I manage to fling aside hardly making a dent.

Then I hear voices, floating, far away. Or maybe close by. I can't tell. Shouts. And Aiden crying. I ignore it all; I need to get to Kayla.

Arms wrap themselves around me, pull me away. A gentle voice I recognise. A voice I can trust.

'Eve,' Jamie says. 'Eve, you have to stop. It's okay, the police are here. You're safe now.'

I stare at him and he seems ghost-like, blurred through my lens of tears. 'No, no, it's not okay. She's in there.' I point a trembling finger. 'My baby is in there! He's... he's...'

Then two police officers are helping Jamie move me, urging him to keep me away. I turn and see Aiden being escorted to a police car by two other officers, his arms behind his back and handcuffs on his wrists.

And then I am falling into Jamie, my heart shredding into a million pieces.

FIFTY

Now

'She's not there,' Jamie is saying. 'Eve, listen to me.' He grabs my shoulders. 'Kayla isn't in there!'

I stand up, wriggle out of Jamie's arms and run towards the scene of crime officers who have dug up the grave that Aiden brought me to. Then Marianne is beside me, confirming what Jamie has said. 'It's okay, Eve – Kayla's not here. There's nothing here. We know where she is. Aiden's told us everything.'

'Please take me to her,' I beg. 'I need to see her.'

Marianne nods. 'Okay, yes, of course we can do that. We've got officers going to the location she's at, but it's at least a three-hour drive from here, so it will be a while before we can get her back to London. Social services are going with them to pick her up. Come on, let's get you back. We need to get you checked out at the hospital. Did he hurt you?'

I shake my head. 'Not really. I'm okay. It was my mind he wanted to hurt.'

Marianne takes my arm and leads me away.

It takes hours to give my statement at the police station to two detectives I've never met before. I'm still shaken, even though in the end Kayla wasn't buried in that pile of earth. For those minutes, Aiden made me believe she was in there, and that I'd lost my daughter. That he had killed her. That will stay with me forever.

As well as this, I also had to tell Aiden the truth about what had happened to me, and how Kayla came to be, and I wasn't prepared for that either. I was never going to share my story with anyone, but he forced my hand. I'd spent enough time blocking it out, and then dealing with it through counselling, that I thought I'd never have to relive it.

One of the detectives leads me to a room where Marianne is waiting for me. She stands up when I walk in and hands me a cup of water. 'How are you holding up?'

I take the water, even though I've already had two coffees in the interview room. I've been hoping that caffeine is good for shock, but I've never heard that anywhere so most likely it's not true. 'Kayla's okay,' I say, because it doesn't matter right now how I am. My daughter is fine. 'Do you know anything more about where she's been?'

'Aiden's still being interviewed, but from what I can gather so far, he was visiting her in Henley once a week. He'd told her he had to be away for work, so she and Nicole were having a holiday so that they wouldn't miss him. How thoughtful of him, right?' She shakes her head.

'Can I see her?'

'Soon,' Marianne says. 'I'll sort something out, but it's a complicated situation, isn't it? Kayla knows Nicole as her mum. We need input from social services about how to proceed with it, and unfortunately that's not going to happen as quickly as you'll want it to.'

'She won't still live with Nicole and Aiden, though, will she?' I want to add that neither of them is her parent, but the reality is – whether I like it or not – they both have been and nothing can erase that.

'No. Very unlikely. They're facing serious charges. Of course, Aiden's paternity being under question is going to make this even more complex.'

My poor innocent daughter. She doesn't deserve things to be so complicated, such a mess. It would be too easy to blame Alex Foley for what he did to me that night, but Aiden and I have a part to play in this too. I could have been honest with him from the moment it happened, and given him some choices and decisions. We could have made them together.

'Can I ask you a question?' Marianne says. 'Did you know Aiden wasn't Kayla's father?'

I nod, shame creeping through me.

'But how could you be sure?'

'Because I knew my cycle inside and out. And Aiden and I had been a bit distant with each other that month it happened. I was actually relieved I would have a break from taking ovulation and pregnancy tests, from praying my period wouldn't arrive.' I pause to have a sip of water. 'How did Aiden know? I've been trying to work it out but I just can't. I didn't tell a soul. Not even my closest friend.'

'That we don't know yet. He hasn't said. We will ask him, though, because I'm guessing this was the starting point for his hate campaign against you.'

A hate campaign. Why does it feel as if it was so much more than that?

'Did Aiden say anything about sending me emails? Saying things like he knows I lied? They started months ago, right before I came back for Kayla.'

Marianne scratches her forehead. 'No. You never mentioned this.'

I explain about the emails. The sense that someone had been in my flat. All of it. 'If it wasn't Aiden then I know exactly how he found out about Kayla not being his. Alex Foley. He must have told him.'

'Did he know you'd got pregnant?'

'I don't think so. He used to call all the time and send me messages, but I always ignored him. I couldn't even bear to read most of them. He was acting like we'd had an affair or something. It was… as if I had to relive the attack again every time I got a message or my phone rang. He had no idea I'd got pregnant as a result of his… his…'

'Rape,' Marianne clarifies. 'That's exactly what it was, Eve. Even if you chose to be in his house, chose to have a drink with him, even if you'd enjoyed his company. And he will not get away with it.'

I nod.

'We'll question Aiden about this. I'll let you know what he says.' Marianne hugs me. 'I think you should go home now and get some rest. Someone will drive you home. Is there anything you need from Aiden's?'

So many of my clothes and toiletries are there but I shake my head. I don't want to go to that house, even with a police escort. 'There's nothing I can't do without,' I say.

She sees me out to reception, where she asks someone to take me home, but then I spot Jamie, sitting in the waiting area, his eyes fixed on his phone.

'I won't need a lift,' I tell Marianne.

She looks towards Jamie and smiles. 'Good,' she says. 'You'll probably need someone to talk to tonight. I'll call you in the morning and let you know where we are with everything.'

—

When he drops me off, Jamie insists on coming in. 'You haven't been at your flat for ages, what if he's been in there? Done something to your things?'

'Well, if he has, it can't be any worse than what he's already done. But, if you really want to, then it would be nice to have some company.'

Inside, I check each room, relieved to find nothing out of place. Then Jamie and I sit together, with only the street light shining through the windows lighting the room. I ask Jamie how he found us in the woods.

He raises his eyebrows. 'Don't you remember me telling you?' he says. 'When we were still there, you asked me what I was doing there and I told you.'

I shake my head. 'I was all over the place. I couldn't seem to focus on anything until they told me that Kayla wasn't there.'

'That's totally understandable. Anyway, after we spoke on the phone I couldn't stop worrying. I didn't trust Aiden, so I just wanted to make sure you were okay. I know you can handle yourself, but I'd texted you and you didn't reply, so I decided to drive past his house, just to make sure everything looked normal. It was pure luck that

I got there just as you were driving off with him. I thought you'd seen me because it seemed like you looked straight at me, but I guess you didn't. I followed you both. I know you'd told me you thought you'd got it wrong after all, but I just couldn't believe that. Good job I trusted my instinct.'

I laugh then, because what were the chances of Jamie turning up at that exact moment? A few seconds later and he would never have known where we'd gone. And then what? Only Aiden knows what he was really planning to do to me. And what if I hadn't told him the truth? He would have continued assuming I'd had an affair, his hatred eating him up, making him act in ways maybe he didn't even know he was capable of.

The laughter quickly dies. 'There are some things I need to tell you,' I say.

'Okay,' he says, and then he takes my hand while for the third time that night I recount the horror story that for years I kept locked away.

Jamie listens in silence, never letting go of my hand and when I've finished, I flop against his shoulder and my tears soak through his T-shirt.

'I'm so sorry you went through all that,' he says, eventually. 'That man is scum. Worse than scum. I can't even think of a word for him.'

'Do you know what made it even worse? He didn't even think he'd done anything wrong. He acted as if it was consensual, as if I hadn't told him to stop.'

Jamie's hand lets go of mine and clenches into a fist.

'He even used to try to call and message me, can you believe that? I used to ignore them all, delete them before I'd even read them, but when Kayla was three months old, just before I left, something made me read a message he'd sent. He said he'd been thinking about me and wondering whether I wanted to have a drink with him at his place. Looking back, I think it was that text that really tipped me over the edge. The fact that the words by themselves were so harmless, so polite even. I can't describe what that did to me. It was like he was doing it to me all over again with his silent denial. Reading that text made me want to die.'

Jamie grabs my hand again, and when I look at him I notice his eyes are glistening. 'Did you reply?'

'No. No way. I deleted it. I couldn't bear to have it on my phone. Why did he keep contacting me? Why would he do that?'

'More manipulation and controlling behaviour. I think I might know the answer to this, but why didn't you go to the police? When it first happened?'

There's no simple answer I can give to this. It was a culmination of lots of things. Firstly, I didn't think they'd believe me. I was there voluntarily having a drink with that man. We'd built up a kind of friendship and I even enjoyed his company, often staying for a chat after I'd finished tutoring. He might have even got Justin involved to try and say I'd spent a lot of time with his dad, and I couldn't let him drag that poor boy into it. I explain this to Jamie. 'You know, a lot of women would consider him an attractive man.'

Jamie shakes his head. 'None of that should matter. Even if you were attracted to him in any way, you still said *no*. You didn't want it to happen, and he knew that.'

'I know. It's just… as soon as I left his house I began to doubt myself. You know, maybe I didn't fight hard enough, maybe I wasn't being clear enough when I was telling him no. Maybe he thought me kicking and thrashing at him was part of some fantasy.'

'That's understandable.'

'And then I also didn't want life to change. I didn't want Aiden to know and feel guilty that he couldn't stop that happening to me. I didn't want to be a *victim*. For people to look at me with pity, like you are now.'

'It's not pity, Eve. It's admiration.'

'Thanks. Anyway, as time went on, I tried not to think about it. I buried it in a corner and made sure it was well and truly covered. I was convinced that if I ignored it then my life with Aiden could carry on as it was. Nothing would be different. But then I missed my period and had to take a test. I think I knew it would be positive before I even saw the line on the stick. After one horrendous act I was pregnant. I convinced myself I'd have another miscarriage; after all, I'd already had four so what were the chances of this pregnancy being okay? That's what got me through at first. But every week that went by with me still being pregnant, only made me sink even further into a hideous depression.'

I also tell Jamie the other reason I didn't report Alex Foley to the police was because I didn't want him having anything to do with Kayla. 'I didn't even want him to know of her existence, or question whether she might be his. I wanted so badly for her to be Aiden's, and I know that sounds so messed up, but it was easier to convince myself nothing had happened and just shut that man out of my thoughts and life.'

'Eve, I'm so sorry you had to go through all that,' Jamie says. 'So Aiden's definitely not—'

I shake my head and cut him off. 'No, and I never told him. I couldn't. All he wanted was a family, and I'd already told him I didn't want to adopt. I know this will seem weird but I didn't want to break his heart. I knew he would have loved a child who wasn't genetically his, so it felt like the only thing I could do.'

I continue with my story, revealing to Jamie – a man who only a few months ago knew so little about me – the most intimate details of my postnatal depression. How the second Kayla was born I struggled to bond with her because all I saw was Alex Foley and what he did to me. How, triggered by that final text message, it got so bad that in the end I had to leave because I was worried I was a danger to my own daughter, that I might harm her. How it took me two years, with the help of counselling, to heal, so I knew that Kayla would be safe with me.

'I'm so sorry I thought the worst of you,' Jamie says, shaking his head.

'That's only because I never gave you a chance to know me.'

'Everything makes sense now. The reason you couldn't let me in. I get it all now.'

We sit holding each other, talking everything over until the sun rises in the sky, shining through the blinds. And even though the future is far from certain – with Kayla, with Jamie, with Mum – all I know is that right now, I'm right where I need to be.

FIFTY-ONE

Four months later

Kayla rushes towards me, her long hair tied in a ponytail which swings from side to side as she runs. 'Eve, Eve!' She almost bowls me over in her excitement, even though she's a fraction of my size.

'How's my girl?' I say, lifting her up into the air and twirling her around.

She giggles, and there is no sound better than this, nothing more uplifting.

Sophie catches up, the twins running beside her, and she pulls me towards her; another thing that can't be beaten is one of Sophie's bear hugs. 'How are you doing?' she says. 'You okay?'

'I am right now,' I say, placing Kayla back down and watching her run off with Jasper and Jensen, all of them chasing after each other as if it's the most exciting thing in the world. I remember how much I used to struggle telling Sophie's boys apart, but now that they are four it's easy to see the subtle differences in their features.

'I'm so sorry,' Sophie begins. 'I—'

'Don't, Soph, please. You don't need to apologise for anything. Come on, let's sit.'

It's October now and, other than us, the park is empty. I lead Sophie to the same bench we sat on those months ago when I first came to see her. It's not just the weather that's different now; everything has changed.

'It makes me sick when I think about it all,' Sophie says once we're sitting. 'Alex Foley got away with it for all this time. I really hope he goes down for it.'

'They're trying to build a case, but it's his word against mine. I have no proof. And he's now trying to claim that I'm only saying he forced me because my husband found out I'd cheated on him.'

'That piece of shit.'

'I can't believe he went to Aiden months ago and told him we'd had an affair. That's what started Aiden off.' The worst of it is that now he wants access to Kayla, and I don't know what I can do to stop him. 'He's got money, Soph. That's what scares me. Money helps people to do anything, to get away with anything.'

'That's true. But don't ever stop fighting.'

We both know that I won't. If there's one thing I've learned about myself from all this it's that I never give up. Not ever.

Everything being out in the open was never going to be straightforward, and when the truth was finally out, I struggled with the issues that will affect Kayla for the rest of her life. A DNA test by the police has confirmed that Alex Foley is her biological father. There's nothing I can do about that and both the choices I'm faced with have far-reaching consequences for Kayla. If I keep it from her as she gets older, and then she finds out somehow, I can't bear to think about how that would make her feel. And finding out is highly likely given how easy it was for Aiden to prove he wasn't her father, after Alex Foley had planted the seed in his head. All it took was a DNA testing kit from Ancestry.com – a present Nicole had got him which she thought might help him fill in some gaps about his own biological family. Now Kayla's results are on there, easily accessible.

And if Kayla found out in this way, not only will she have to deal with what Alex Foley did, but also the fact that I kept it from her. It's already bad enough that I missed out on over two years of her life. On the other hand, if I tell her the truth then she will always have to live with the fact that her father is a rapist.

This, more than anything, is what has prevented me sleeping so many nights. Until I realised that, ultimately, there is only one choice. I will not lie to Kayla about who she is. And it will be my job to make sure she has enough confidence to handle the sadness, or anger, that she will inevitably feel at times.

'How are you finding having three kids to look after?' I ask Sophie, although I already know. She's thrown herself into it like she does everything else and is doing a damn good job.

'You know this is only temporary, don't you?' she says. 'They'll make a decision soon and Kayla will be living with you. Where she's meant to be.'

'I hope so,' I say, 'but in the meantime there's no one I'd rather her be with.'

'I'm so sorry about how I treated you,' Sophie says. 'I'll never forgive myself.' She has apologised to me every time I've seen her, even though I always assure her there's no need, that I understand completely. 'And I know what Damien thought about me and Aiden, but I promise you there was never anything more than friendship between us. I admit I probably got too involved in his life but being there to help him made me feel closer to you, and I missed our friendship.'

I take her hand, just like I always do when guilt overwhelms either of us.

Still running around the park, Kayla squeals as Jasper catches up with her and they tumble to the grass. A few months ago, I wondered if we'd ever see her smile again, but Cassie, the child psychologist, has done wonders for her, and with small steps is helping Kayla adjust to everything that's happened.

Sophie smiles. 'It's definitely helped her being around the twins. They're such comedians it's impossible not to feel happy around them. Not sure where they get that from as it certainly isn't Damien. He's not even forty, yet he seems to have turned into this grumpy old man. I never thought that was actually a real thing! I can assure you it bloody is!'

'I hope it's not too much for him having Kayla living with you?'

She laughs. 'Well, he does liken our house to a zoo, but he's only joking. He loves her to pieces and is thrilled to be helping. Everyone's on your side, Eve.'

This is a relief. It's amazed me how many people are rallying around me now that everyone knows the truth. I only wish I'd been able to speak out before, instead of isolating myself from the world.

'That's good to hear. How did it go yesterday, then?' I wasn't going to ask her, wasn't sure I wanted to know anything other than what the police tell me about the case, but now I'm here I have an overwhelming urge to know everything. The more information I have, the better prepared I will be to keep fighting for Kayla.

When Nicole first begged Sophie to see her, so that she could explain her part in it, Sophie refused. And she refused every time after that, until I told her she should do it. Perhaps I softened because I know what it's like to be desperate to explain yourself, only to keep hitting a brick wall with people. I can't take away the fact that Nicole raised Kayla for all that time, and ultimately did what she could to keep her. Would I have done any different?

Aiden, however, I find it harder to feel anything but anger towards. If he'd just tried to keep me from Kayla by taking her away himself, then I might have understood. But the chilling and calculated way he tried to mess with my mind is unforgiveable.

'Are you sure you want me to talk about Nicole?' Sophie says.

'Tell me.'

I listen intently while Sophie explains that she met Nicole in a bar, after the kids were in bed. 'There's no way I would have let her come to my house, not with Kayla there. And I didn't want to go to her sister's place either. A bar seemed like the best option.'

To Sophie, Nicole had looked like a ghost: pale and thin, nothing like the confident woman she'd been before. Sophie had almost walked past her, not realising it was her until Nicole grabbed her arm as she walked past her table.

The first thing she'd told Sophie was that she had no idea what Aiden was planning to do. She only knew that Aiden wanted Kayla far away from me, and that was of course what Nicole wanted too.

'Do you believe her?' I ask Sophie.

'I think so. Wait till you hear the rest. She said she had no idea that Kayla wasn't Aiden's, and it was a huge shock to her. She swore that she would never have helped him hide Kayla otherwise.'

'Isn't it all too convenient, though? Now that they're in trouble with the police, suddenly she didn't really know what was going on?'

'Perhaps. But I really believe Aiden was manipulating her too. Did you know she can't have children?'

This is a shock to me. 'What? No, I didn't. How did—'

'Remember when she had to go to hospital that time you were there?'

I recall it clearly; I can picture the way Nicole was doubled over in pain as if it's happening now in front of me. 'Yes. She said they were doing tests but she was really vague about it.'

'That's when she found out she had endometriosis which was so severe that there was no way she'd ever have her own baby. It had spread to her bowel even.'

'That's awful.'

'She told Aiden, and according to her, that made him even more desperate to get you away from Kayla. They'd always planned to have children – not quite yet as they felt Kayla was still so young and needed them, but in time. She said this was so devastating for them.'

Along with the sadness I feel for Nicole, a twinge of sympathy finds its way into my bones for Aiden. We'd had years of infertility and loss together and then it was happening all over again with Nicole. Worse, though, as she'd been given a definite answer. I, at least, had the label 'unexplained', which gave me a fraction of hope.

It was after Nicole had been in hospital that she became cold towards me, suddenly not wanting me to see Kayla when before she'd been my strongest advocate. I mention this to Sophie.

'Well, this explains why. I think she was worried that Aiden and you would reconnect because of Kayla, and she probably felt she couldn't compete, especially when she would never be the mother of his child. She had no idea that when she disappeared with Kayla, Aiden would practically move you into the house. She thought he would eventually join them and that you'd give up hope of ever finding Kayla.'

'And what? Stop looking? That would never have happened.' I stare at the ground. 'Does she know that Aiden and I slept together?'

Sophie shakes her head. 'I would never have told her, and I doubt he did.'

'It was only once. It felt so wrong. I think that cemented in my head that he and I were never going to have a future. Which is just as well I suppose, as that was never his intention anyway. He just wanted to hurt me, to make me love him again and then snatch it away from me.'

'His idea of payback,' Sophie says. 'Which shows how messed up he was.'

'Did she mention Aiden's parents?' I'm desperate to hear that they really didn't know anything about this.

'Yes, she did. She said Marie and Pete had no idea. Aiden let them believe that Kayla really was missing. Awful, isn't it? Hey, have you thought about whether they'll still be able to see Kayla?'

'She loves them,' I say. 'And they love her. I'll never stop them seeing each other. It's all just so complicated.'

I turn to watch Kayla and the twins. 'So what's Nicole going to do now? Please tell me they're not together.'

'No. She's adamant that she's moving on. She did say, though, that Aiden doesn't believe the truth.'

I know this already. The police have been telling me that he insists I'm lying. That I'm manipulating everyone. 'I know why,' I say. 'It helps him.'

'What do you mean?'

'If he let himself believe me, then what does that say about him? He did all of this because he thought I'd betrayed him in one of the worst possible ways, so he doesn't want to acknowledge that he did all this based on Alex Foley's lies.'

It occurs to me now that perhaps Aiden was just as much a victim of that man as I was. I refuse to think of myself in those terms now – I am a survivor, not a victim, a phoenix rising from the ashes.

'I'm going to see Aiden,' I say, only just determining to do this now.

Sophie's eyes widen. 'Really? Is that a good idea?'

'Yes, I think it is. I need him to understand. And I know that somewhere inside him is the decent man I used to know.'

—

Later, I meet Jamie for a drink in Leicester Square, at the same bar I spent the whole afternoon drinking in after he ended our relationship. Apparently, it's a day of coming full circle.

I'm there early, and when he walks in he waves as he spots me and makes his way towards the table I've managed to find us.

He leans in to kiss me and it feels right, as though I'm right where I'm meant to be. As though I am home.

'So,' he says, pulling out a chair. 'Big day tomorrow. I'm finally going to meet your mum.'

'Yep. Are you ready?' I've already told Mum all about Jamie, even though I'm sure she won't remember what I've said. 'She has very high standards,' I joke. 'It will take a lot to impress her.' I'm enjoying teasing him, the easy banter we now have with each other that only comes from intimacy.

'Is that right?' Jamie says. 'Well, she'd better get used to me, because I'm not going anywhere.'

And as we sit here while evening merges with night, and talk about Jamie's parents, and Kayla and Mum, for the first time in so many years, I actually know with certainty that everything's going to work out.

–

Jamie wakes me in the middle of the night, gently shaking me until I fully come around.

'Alex Foley is dead!'

I shoot up, suddenly wide awake, and see Jamie staring at his phone. 'What? How?'

'Apparently they think it was a burglary. Maybe he tried to fight them off and it got out of hand?'

I grab Jamie's phone and read the news article. 'Poor Justin,' I say when I've finished taking in all the details. I should be shocked, but somehow I'm not. And nor am I sad, because now Kayla is free of that monster.

Finally, this is a new chance for me and my little girl. No Aiden, no Nicole, and no Alex Foley. Just me and Kayla, as we should be, together.

EPILOGUE

What goes around comes around. Isn't that how it goes? Poetic justice, perhaps?

There was no way I was going to let a man like you into Kayla's life, and you would have got your own way by throwing around all that money. Well, money can't help you now that you've got what you deserve.

The same can be said for me, of course, because now I've lost everything – although that's to be expected after the things I was driven to do.

And now at least I've made up for my actions; Kayla will never have to know the truth about what you did to her mother, the woman I loved.

ACKNOWLEDGEMENTS

This was the hardest book I've written so far, and it really wouldn't have made it into anyone's hands without the insight and advice of so many talented people. Thank you to my agent, Madeleine Milburn, for your early feedback and encouragement, as well as everyone at the Madeleine Milburn Literary Agency who cast an eye over it. There were times I felt completely lost in this book, unable to step outside of it and see just what it could be.

I owe a huge debt of gratitude to Leodora Darlington for helping me to finally step outside.

A massive thank you to Louise Cullen for all the work you've done on this book – it's such a pleasure working with you and I appreciate all you are doing. Thanks also to the rest of the team at Canelo – I couldn't have found a better home for my books.

Thank you to agent Liv Maidment for everything you do, you're always there to listen, help and advise, and it's very much appreciated.

As always, thank you to my husband and children for being a reason to step away from the computer, and for reminding me to be mindful – I'm truly blessed to have you all.

I don't thank my parents enough for fostering my love of reading by making sure I was surrounded by books as a child and never ran out of things to read. Thank you, Grace and Phillip Mckee!

To all book bloggers and reviewers and everyone who has read or is reading this book, thank you for choosing one of my books. There are millions of others you could have picked to read at the time you were looking, so I really appreciate that you chose one of mine. Thanks for continuing to read books and for keeping them alive by doing so. So much in the world is changing but books are here to stay!

A Letter from Kathryn

Thank you so much for choosing to read *The Mother's Secret*. I hope you enjoyed it! Books should take us on a journey as well as entertaining us, and I really hope I've managed to achieve that with this book. I also hope it managed to take you by surprise!

If you'd like to keep up-to-date with news of my forthcoming releases, please do follow the link below to sign up for my newsletter. Your email will never be shared, and I promise I'll only contact you when I have news about a new release.

www.kathryncroft.com/mailing-list

Reviews are so important to authors, so if you liked the book, I'd be extremely grateful if you could spare a moment to leave me a short review on Amazon, Goodreads, or wherever you purchased it. I really do love hearing readers' thoughts, and your reviews help me to reach new readers. I'd also really appreciate any recommendations to friends or family who you think might enjoy the book.

Please also feel free to connect with me via my website, Facebook, Instagram, or Twitter. I'd love to hear from you!

Website: www.kathryncroft.com

Facebook: authorkathryncroft
Instagram: authorkathryncroft
Twitter: @katcroft

Thank you again for all your support – it is very much appreciated!

Kathryn xx